MISSISSIPPI BLOOD

Greg Iles is the author of fourteen *New York Times* bestselling novels, including the No.1 bestseller, *The Quiet Game*. His books have been made into films, translated into more than twenty languages and published in more than thirty-five countries. *Mississippi Blood* is the final volume in the ground-breaking *Natchez Burning* Trilogy, which has been published to critical acclaim and optioned for TV. The first novel in the saga, *Natchez Burning*, was heralded by *The Times* as 'the thriller of the year'.

Greg spent most of his youth in Natchez, Mississippi, and graduated from Ole Miss in 1983. He currently lives in Natchez with his wife, and has two children.

GregIlesAuthor
@GregIles
www.gregiles.com

ALSO BY GREG ILES

The Bone Tree

Natchez Burning

The Death Factory (e-novella)

The Devil's Punchbowl

Third Degree

True Evil

Turning Angel

Blood Memory

Dark Matter (US TITLE: *The Footprints of God*)

Sleep No More

Dead Sleep

24 Hours

The Quiet Game

Mortal Fear

Black Cross

Spandau Phoenix

GREG ILES

MISSISSIPPI BLOOD

HarperCollins*Publishers*
1 London Bridge Street
London SE1 9GF

www.harpercollins.co.uk

Published by HarperCollins*Publishers* 2017
1

A catalogue record for this book is available from the British Library

ISBN: 978-0-00-741134-4

This novel is entirely a work of fiction.
The names, characters and incidents portrayed in it are
the work of the author's imagination. Any resemblance to
actual persons, living or dead, events or localities is
entirely coincidental.

Printed and bound in Great Britain by Clays Ltd, St Ives plc

MIX
Paper from
responsible sources
FSC® C007454

For Betty and Jerry Iles,
who came out of tiny southern towns
and climbed books like stairs to rise.
Thank you for everything.

For the truth is a terrible thing. You dabble your foot in it and it is nothing. But you walk a little farther and you feel it pull you like an undertow or a whirlpool. First there is the slow pull so steady and gradual you scarcely notice it, then the acceleration, then the dizzy whirl and plunge into darkness. For there is a blackness of truth, too. They say it is a terrible thing to fall into the Grace of God. I am prepared to believe that.

—Robert Penn Warren, *All the King's Men*

MISSISSIPPI BLOOD

PROLOGUE

GRIEF IS THE most solitary emotion; it makes islands of us all.

I've spent a lot of time visiting graves over the past few weeks. Sometimes with Annie, but mostly alone. The people who see me there give me a wide berth. I'm not sure why. For thirty miles around, almost everyone knows me. Penn Cage, the mayor of Natchez, Mississippi. When they avoid me—waving from a distance, if at all, then hurrying on their way—I sometimes wonder if I have taken on the mantle of death. Jewel Washington, the county coroner and a true friend, pulled me aside in City Hall last week and told me I look like living proof that ghosts exist. Maybe they do. Since Caitlin died, I have felt like nothing more than the ghost of myself.

Perhaps that's why I spend so much time visiting graves.

HENRY SEXTON IS buried in a small churchyard in Ferriday, his tilted stone exposed to the cold wind that blasts over the Louisiana Delta fields. The simple marker displays the usual census information. Below this is his epitaph, six words chiseled by the black folks who attend this saltbox church, and who keep the grave of this white journalist trimmed to perfection.

Wasn't that a man?
—MUDDY WATERS

Enough said.

CAITLIN'S GRAVE STANDS in the Natchez City Cemetery, in the flat square below Jewish Hill, not far from the Turning Angel. Her stone is white Alabama marble, tall and thin and strong, just as she was. Her mother wanted her buried up north, but her father persuaded the family that since Caitlin had intended to marry and raise her family in Mississippi, then here she should remain.

I chose her epitaph, a line she often quoted and attributed to Ayn Rand.

The question isn't who's going to let me; it's who's going to stop me.

Rand never actually said that; the line seems to be a paraphrase from a conversation Howard Roark had in *The Fountainhead*. Nevertheless, it sums up Caitlin's approach to life and work about as well as anything could. A few people have asked me if that epitaph is appropriate, given that Caitlin was murdered as a consequence of her reckless pursuit of a gang of killers. I tell them I was never a fan of Ayn Rand, but the old hypocrite got that one right. And if there was a moral or lesson in Caitlin's death, I'm too thick to see it. If you want to make sense of this world, don't come to me for answers.

I'm fresh out.

I stand on the high bluff over the river most every day, trying and failing to piece my life back together as winter changes to spring and my father's murder trial approaches. Dad's being held in protective custody in Louisiana by the FBI. He wasn't allowed to cross into Mississippi to attend Caitlin's funeral. I'm told he beat his arthritic hands against the bars of his cell when he got word that Sheriff Billy Byrd would jail him in Natchez if he crossed the river—beat them until he broke some bones in his right wrist. I don't know for sure.

I haven't spoken to him since Caitlin died.

FORREST KNOX IS buried on family land, the former Valhalla hunting camp. Last week I parked my car on the shoulder of Highway 61 and hiked in alone, my pistol in my right hand, and searched among deep tire ruts and FBI evidence markers until I found the gravestone.

Forrest's marker bore a chiseled Confederate battle flag, which was a desecration of that banner, and also the words *Unflagging devotion.* I stood there a while, sick deep in my guts, only then realizing that I'd been hoping to cross paths with Forrest's uncle—Snake.

After a while I kicked over the stone, dropped to my knees, and used the butt of my gun to smash the chiseled flag as best I could. All I managed to do was chip a few stars off it. Heaving for breath, I got to my feet and fired five bullets against the granite slab, which did the job. Then I pissed on the grave—a good long piss that steamed in the cold and muddied the earth—and walked back out to the highway.

Yeah, well. If you don't want the whole truth, stop reading now.

If you go on, don't say I didn't warn you.

CHAPTER 1

FOR THE PAST few weeks I've been writing as a strategy for staying sane. Strange to admit, but there it is. Since Caitlin's death, I've been having trouble with some of the basic principles of existence, like time. Chronology. To be frank, I don't have it in me to describe the events that constitute the immediate fallout of her death, or of my father's arrest for murder. You should probably read a couple of articles from the *Natchez Examiner,* Caitlin's old newspaper. Caitlin's older sister, Miriam—a corporate financial officer from New York—has been running the paper since Caitlin died, and she has vowed to stay on until the last of the Knoxes has been jailed and the Double Eagles smashed for all time. I'm not sure Miriam Masters realizes how long that could be.

The two articles below were written by Keisha Harvin, a twenty-five-year-old black reporter from Alabama who's been hounding the Double Eagles like a Fury incarnate. Caitlin hired Keisha from another Masters paper only two days before she was killed. Fittingly, for the past eight weeks, Keisha has been living across the street from Annie and me, in Caitlin's old house. I don't think she sleeps much, nor does she pull any punches, no matter who she's writing about. My father has suffered in her stories—as he should—and through Keisha's writing the Knox family has become a national symbol of the most atavistic and depraved instincts in the American character.

More than once I've tried to persuade Keisha to pull back a little and think about her safety, but like Caitlin she believes that her work means more than her life. I'm not sure a twenty-five-year-old is qualified to make that decision, but I do know this: where good people stand against evil, sooner or later fate demands a reckoning. When that day comes, I hope I'm close enough to Keisha Harvin to do some good.

NATCHEZ EXAMINER

December 30, 2005

Trial Date Set for Dr. Tom Cage
by Keisha Harvin

Circuit Judge Joseph Elder has set a trial date of March 13 for local physician Thomas J. Cage in the murder of Viola Turner. In a case that has drawn national attention, Dr. Cage is accused of murdering his 65-year-old former nurse in the wake of a pact that would have required him to euthanize the terminally ill woman, who had been his employee thirty-eight years earlier. The fact that Dr. Cage is white and Nurse Turner was black has complicated the situation, since it has been revealed that Mrs. Turner had a child by Dr. Cage in 1968, when Cage was married. Mrs. Turner was a 28-year-old widow at the time, her husband having recently been killed in the Vietnam War.

District Attorney Shadrach Johnson stated: "I don't want anyone to be confused about this murder charge. This is not a case of euthanasia. If a doctor simply provides the drugs that a patient uses to end his or her life, that is a special class of crime in Mississippi: physician-assisted suicide. But if a physician administers those drugs himself, it's murder, plain and simple—even if it's done as a so-called mercy killing. But this is a case where the physician had a personal stake in keeping his patient silent about a fact that could destroy his reputation, and also his marriage. That is why Dr. Cage has been charged with first-degree murder."

Adams County sheriff Billy Byrd said that his department has been working around the clock to be sure that the DA's office is fully prepared to give Dr. Cage the speedy trial guaranteed by law. "Some Mississippi counties drag around for a year or more getting ready to prosecute," Byrd commented. "But this poor woman was dying from cancer when she was murdered, and her family deserves justice. I've met extensively with the relatives, and they are really broken up about what happened. I don't want to bias anybody, but I don't know if I've ever seen a case where the facts were so clear. But I'll leave that to DA Johnson to sort out with the jury."

Jury selection will begin ten weeks from today. At this time Dr. Cage is not confined at the Adams County jail, but at the Federal Correctional Institution at Pollock, Louisiana. Special Agent John Kaiser of the FBI explained: "Dr. Cage is being held in protective custody. He's a material witness in a major federal investigation, and his life is in danger." Asked if Dr. Cage would be in danger if held in the Adams County jail, Agent Kaiser declined to comment.

Dr. Cage will be defended at trial by noted African-American civil rights attorney Quentin Avery of Jefferson County, Mississippi, and Washington, D.C. To date Dr. Cage has made no statement in his own defense. But in a telephone interview yesterday, Mr. Avery said: "It should not be overlooked that Viola Turner's brother was murdered by the Double Eagle group in 1968. Events surrounding that crime could very well impact this case." Natchez mayor Penn Cage, the son of the defendant and a former Houston prosecutor, declined to comment on either the trial date or the statements by District Attorney Johnson, Sheriff Byrd, or Mr. Avery.

NATCHEZ EXAMINER

January 3, 2006

Knox Likely to Be Removed from FBI's Most Wanted
by Keisha Harvin

Last week's apparent suicide by a former member of the infamous Double Eagle group may lead the FBI to remove the name of Chester "Snake" Knox from the FBI's Ten Most Wanted list. Sources close to the investigation report that evidence found at the scene of former Ku Klux Klansman Silas Groom's death links him to several felonies, including the bombing of an FBI plane carrying evidence from the Vidalia airport to the FBI crime lab in Washington on December 17.

Groom was discovered in his home last Thursday, shot through the head, a revolver still in his hand. Sources say a suicide note and additional evidence discovered at the scene may link Groom to several murders, including those of *Natchez Examiner* publisher Caitlin Masters, who was killed on December 16, 2005, in Lusahatcha County, and also of Double Eagle founding member Sonny Thornfield, who supposedly committed suicide in the Concordia Parish jail eighteen days ago.

Local supervising FBI special agent John Kaiser declined to comment on this new evidence, but FBI spokesman Eric Templeton in Washington said: "While Snake Knox may be guilty of kidnapping and even other murders, it was the bombing of the Bureau jet that placed him on our most wanted list. We are generally satisfied that Groom was the culprit in that case, and the list will probably be altered accordingly." When asked how a seventy-eight-year-old man could have planted a complex explosive device on an FBI jet, Agent Templeton stated: "The Double Eagles were mostly military veterans with explosives experience. Silas Groom had more weapons expertise than your average Al Qaeda terrorist, and you don't have to be an Olympic athlete to sabotage a small plane."

At least one local law enforcement official, Concordia Parish sheriff Walker Dennis, has raised doubts as to whether Groom actually committed suicide. Sheriff Dennis said, "I'm going to wait for the medical examiner to release his findings, but anybody would have to concede that there's been an awful suspicious rash of suicides recently. And Groom's death could take a lot of heat off Snake Knox, which, if you ask me, is where the heat belongs. My department won't let up in our hunt for Knox, even though the FBI seems to think he's lit out for a nonextradition country."

The contents of Silas Groom's suicide note remain undisclosed. But in a macabre touch, the *Examiner* has learned that a rare twenty-dollar "Double Eagle" gold piece that served as the group's membership badge was found atop the bloody note that reportedly confessed some of Groom's crimes. Like all authentic Double Eagle badges, that gold piece was minted in the year of the holder's birth, in Groom's case 1933. According to the diary of journalist Henry Sexton, the only exceptions to this practice were that Double Eagle members born after the gold piece was no longer minted carried original JFK half-dollars minted in 1964. This is supposedly the badge still carried by Snake Knox.

Rumors linking the Double Eagle group to the 1963 assassination of John F. Kennedy remain unverified. All efforts to identify the evidence being carried from Vidalia to the Washington crime lab on the downed Bureau plane have been stymied by the FBI. The Bureau has said only that this evidence pertained to its recent investigation into the Double Eagle murders that occurred in the Natchez-Vidalia area in the 1960s. The aircraft involved was a Cessna Citation II, and it burned before fire and rescue personnel could reach it. The Bureau has not disclosed whether all or part of the evidence on board survived the crash.

Thirty-six years ago, a different small plane crashed at the Concordia Parish Airport after supposedly colliding with another aircraft flown by Snake Knox. Four people died in that incident, but Knox, an experienced crop duster, walked away unharmed. This alleged midair collision occurred while Concordia was still an unattended airfield and was witnessed only by the young nephew, now deceased, of Snake Knox. The diaries of Henry Sexton have cast doubt on the FAA report made at the time, but unless Knox is apprehended and alters his original story, this earlier crash will remain a closed investigation.

As for the downing of the FBI jet, a local Vidalia man who requested anonymity said: "Nobody in this area knows more about small planes than Snake Knox. Nobody knows more about bombs, either. But that's all I've got to say about that. Snake Knox ain't somebody you want to get on the wrong side of, even if he has run off to Costa Rica or wherever. Sooner or later, he'll be back. You watch and see."

CHAPTER 2

I'M BLASTING ACROSS the Louisiana Delta at eighty-five miles an hour, primeval darkness covering the land like a shroud. My xenon high beams bore a tunnel through the night, triggering a riot of eyeshine from startled deer, possums, foxes, raccoons, and the occasional cow resting close to a fence. Our bodyguard's armored Yukon tracks us from 150 yards back, far enough to spare me a migraine during the hundred-mile drive home from the prison that holds my father, but close enough for Tim Weathers to play Seventh Cavalry should that become necessary. Every now and then there's a juddering thump as I round a curve and smash over the broken armor of a dead armadillo, yet my daughter, Annie, sleeps on beside me, one hand resting lightly on my forearm, which I've left on the console to reassure her.

Another angelic face floats in the rearview mirror. Through the blur of fatigue I see it as Caitlin's, but it belongs to Mia Burke, Annie's twenty-year-old caretaker. Mia's eyes are closed, her mouth slightly open, and susurrant snores pass through her parted lips. Exhaustion keeps both girls sedated through potholes and roadkill, exhaustion plus the drone of the engine and whine of our tires, topped off by the voice of Levon Helm and the Band singing "The Weight," the live version from *The Last Waltz*.

As Pops and Mavis Staples begin singing harmony like dark angels floating down from heaven, some semblance of peace washes over me. How much soul and conviction must a white man have to sing lead in front of angels like that? Levon is an Arkansas country boy as rail-thin and tough as the bastards who killed Caitlin, yet he somehow sings with the wounded humanity of a man without a tribe, a man who has known both love and grief and understands that one is the price of the other.

I wish I believed in God, so that I could blame Him for Caitlin's murder. But as a man without faith, I'm left to blame my father. My mother believes Caitlin brought about her own death and would have done even had my father not turned all our lives upside down. I haven't the strength to argue the case. Mom simply wants me to forgive Dad enough to visit him in prison. But I can't bring myself to do that. So I sit outside in the car, or else down the street in a Wendy's restaurant, while Mom and Annie go through their ritual at the prison, Mia tending to Annie while Mom spends time alone with Dad.

More times than not, I set aside the perpetual pile of crap that comes with being a mayor and sit pondering the chain of events that brought me to this pass. It's true that Caitlin let her ambition drive her to a cursed place she should never have gone alone, and she died for it. But had my father not hidden the truth of what transpired on the night Viola Turner died, Caitlin would never have become obsessed with Henry Sexton's quest, or picked up his torch after he martyred himself to save us, or followed a bloody trail to the abomination called the Bone Tree.

She would be alive.

We would be living with Annie in Edelweiss, our dream house overlooking the river, and well on our way to giving Annie a brother. That thought haunts me, probably more than it should. The night before Caitlin was killed, we made love in that house for the first and last time: a desperate attempt on her part to calm me down after a standoff with a corrupt sheriff. I had no idea then that Caitlin was pregnant. Forrest Knox told me later, as a torment, and the autopsy confirmed his revelation. Had I foreseen the doom we were racing toward on that last night, I would have locked the door of Edelweiss and held her inside until . . . what? It's pointless to speculate. Somehow, I sense, no matter what I did that night, Caitlin would still have died, and Annie and I would still have wound up here. Which is . . . where?

Lost.

When someone you love is murdered, you learn things about yourself you'd give a great deal not to know. If you kill the person who robbed you of that life, you discover that vengeance can't begin to fill the fulminating void that murder leaves behind. Nothing can, except years of living, and then only if you're lucky. Annie and I learned that the first time, when cancer took her mother.

Caitlin was our luck.

Nine weeks ago, our luck ran out. Caitlin's murder hit us like an artillery shell from a clear blue sky. And the first thing blown apart by that kind of shell is time. Day and night lose their meaning. The passage of moments and hours wobbles out of kilter. Clock faces trigger confusion, even panic. In the demi-world of mourning, one's sense of selfhood begins to unravel. The strong find ways to re-orient themselves to the superimposed temporal structure observed by the rest of the world, but no matter how hard I've tried, I haven't been able to do that.

My work has suffered so badly that everyone at City Hall is engaged in a conspiracy to pretend I'm functional. That's hard to admit, but if I'm honest, something isn't quite right with me. My hold on reality is more tenuous than it should be. My sense of control has eroded to the point that I've questioned my sanity. But given all I've been through . . . perhaps that's a sane response. Perhaps the only one. Because my family has imploded.

My mother lives in a motel near the Federal Correctional Institution at Pollock, Louisiana, where my father is being held by the FBI (thirty miles behind us now, and thankfully fading farther every minute). I had to withdraw Annie from middle school, and only Mia Burke's altruistic intervention has prevented her from becoming paralyzed by grief and terror. Mia's done a lot to hold my head above water also, which isn't fair to her, but she volunteered, and frankly there's no one else to lean on.

My cell phone pings beneath the music. It's lying sideways beside the Audi's central handbrake. Pinning the steering wheel in position with my left knee, I reach across my lap with my left hand to check the phone without disturbing Annie.

The message reads: *U ok? Not getting sleepy, are u?*

It's from Tim Weathers, our bodyguard for the night, tailing us in his Yukon. Actually, the vehicle doesn't belong to Tim. It's the property of Vulcan Asset Management, the Dallas-based security firm that employs him.

I'm fine, I type. *Girls sleeping.*

They need it, he replies.

Apart from Caitlin's death, this may be the most difficult adaptation of all. We live surrounded by bodyguards. A necessity, of course, everyone agreed. Total security, twenty-four hours a day. And not the oversized guidos you see guarding pop divas and pro athletes, but retired Special Forces soldiers like my friend Daniel Kelly, who's been missing in Afghanistan for months now. Men who understand the job of protection and have the skills, restraint, and experience to do it right.

The financial burden of maintaining such protection is crushing. Over the past almost two and a half months, security firms have billed me more than a hundred thousand dollars. But I see no alternative. It's like hiring round-the-clock nurses for an ailing parent: until you have to do it, you have no idea what ceaseless attention really costs. To my relief, Caitlin's father has paid half the balance of every bill. He offered to pay every cent, but I still have some pride left. I can't afford this level of expenditure for long, but every time I wonder whether we might be able to relax our vigilance and stem the hemorrhage of cash, John Masters's words ring in my ears:

"Penn, if anything were to happen to you or Annie, Caitlin would never forgive me. I accept that my daughter is dead, but I don't accept that my obligations to her will ever end. So you hire the best and send me the bills. I don't give one goddamn how high it goes. You killed Snake Knox's nephew. Until that son of a bitch is pumped full of embalming fluid, I want you living like the president of the United States. I failed to protect my daughter, and I can barely stand to look in the mirror. Don't make the same mistake with yours."

I don't intend to.

Thus we have lived with at least one bodyguard—and sometimes three—within yards of us twenty-four hours a day. Today, during our weekly drive to and from the Pollock prison, we've had only Tim, an ex-SEAL from Tennessee. Tim has become like a favorite uncle to Annie, and a brother to Mia and to me. As usual, Annie saw her grandmother first today, and then her grandfather while Mia walked down the road and shared a cheeseburger with me at Wendy's.

Juvenile, maybe, but that's the way it is.

More eyeshine flashes out of the empty fields beyond the shoulders of the highway. This drive is like a night tour of some vast wildlife refuge, a southern safari inundated by the sulfurous, miles-long reek of a skunk's defensive spray. The bright orbs flashing in the darkness run the color spectrum: yellow for raccoons, green for deer, red for foxes and possums, blue for the occasional coyote. The land seems peopled by luminous ghosts, yet the explanation is simple enough. The *tapetum lucidum* layer of crystals behind all those retinas evolved to enhance night vision by reflecting light back through the eye, so that it can be used twice, not once. But like the TV lights that always blinded me when I arrived at the Walls Unit at Huntsville to witness executions, the blaze of my Audi's xenon headlamps renders that adaptation useless, blasting all those sensitive eyes sightless—

"Daddy?" Annie's hand lightly squeezes my right arm. "I need to pee."

My daughter is eleven years old, but when she speaks from half sleep, her voice sounds exactly as it did when she was three or four.

There are no lights ahead, only blackness. But my brain quickly riffles through its file of stopping points in this near desolate landscape. "I think there's a gas station about eight minutes ahead, Boo. Can you wait?"

"Uh-huh. Don't forget and pass it, though. I gotta go bad."

A voice from behind me says, "I second that sentiment."

Glancing up at the rearview mirror, I see Mia watching me, a wry smile on her face.

"I'm hungry, too," she adds. "I'm going to be huge by the time I go back to school."

Mia must be tired; otherwise she would never mention the prospect of leaving us—not within Annie's hearing—even though the eventual day of parting is inevitable. Mia's very presence is a miracle, one based on a generosity I can scarcely comprehend. Two years ago, when she was a superachieving high-school senior at my alma mater, Mia took care of Annie for one summer, then during the school year on afternoons when I was working. She was the perfect babysitter: a smart, vivacious, and motivated girl from a family of modest means, driven to work for the things her private school classmates took for granted. Her drive and practicality rubbed off on Annie every day, and I was thankful.

But late that year, a classmate of Mia's drowned in a nearby creek, and a childhood friend of mine was charged with killing her. Mia proved instrumental to solving that murder, and as a reward, my grateful friend—a physician—helped her attain something that had proved beyond her reach, no matter how hard she worked: tuition money for her first-choice college, Harvard.

By pure chance, Mia was on her way home for Christmas break when Caitlin was killed. As soon as she heard the news, she came over and did all she could to comfort Annie, who had already begun to regress to the paralyzing, hyper-anxious state she'd experienced after her mother died in Houston. Within a week, Annie developed a worrisome dependence on Mia. I didn't know how I was going to keep her from losing control when Mia had to return to Massachusetts. To my amazement, though, three days before Mia was scheduled to leave, she sat me down and said she'd decided to take a semester off in order to help Annie "get back to normal."

I argued, but not too hard or for too long. Mia told me she'd been scheduled to do a semester at an archaeological dig in the Yucatán, so it wasn't like ditching a real semester. By this time, my mother had already decided to relocate to be near Dad's prison, and that settled the issue.

"There's a light," Mia says. "Up on the left."

She's right. What I remember as a solitary service station stands on the edge of the flat fields about a mile ahead, like some radio relay station in the desert. Taking out my cell phone, I speed-dial Tim behind us.

"What's up?" he asks.

"We're pulling off at that gas station. Girls need a bathroom."

"Let me catch up before you turn."

"Copy that."

This kind of tactical conversation has become second nature over the past weeks. Sixty seconds' driving carries us to the turn, and Tim is behind us by the time I roll the wheel left and clunk onto a gravel-studded dirt lot near the concrete pad that supports the old gas station.

I park on oil-stained concrete under the sagging awning/canopy that covers the pumps, and Tim pulls in behind us. As soon as he exits the Yukon, Annie jumps out and runs into the station. Tim follows, and Mia and I trail them inside.

The temperature's dropped ten degrees since we left the prison. The interior of the station smells of scalded coffee, old grease, and disinfectant. A lone attendant is working the night shift, an elderly woman wearing a hairnet. She stands behind a greasy glass case holding the last of some fried chicken and potato logs. While Annie uses the restroom, I scan the meager offerings on the snack rack, then ask if the woman has fresh coffee. She says she'll make a new pot.

"Where's your men's room?"

"Outside. Turn right when you walk out."

Tim starts to follow me out, but I point at my left ankle and ask him to stay with the girls. He nods and tells me to keep my eyes open.

The darkness outside carries the faint sweet scent of airborne herbicide. I didn't notice it during my short walk into the station. It's too early for crop dusting; maybe a farmer is mixing chemicals somewhere nearby. That odor hurls me back to childhood. When I was a boy in my grandfather's fields, I'd run beneath the toylike biplane as it dropped billowing clouds of poison, joyfully waving my arms, never dreaming those clouds could seed cancer in my blood and bones.

The men's room also takes me back to childhood. A closet-size cubicle, cold as a deep freeze yet fetid with the stench of human waste and chemical cleaners, a heavy funk with an astringent tang that would burn your throat if you breathed it too long.

Sliding the flimsy bolt into a hole in the door frame, I square up to the tall old wall urinal, unzip my fly, and piss against the stained porcelain. How many times have I made this drive between Natchez and the federal prison? I wonder. Two and a half months, driving it once and sometimes twice a week. Nine times, I guess, and every time I waited alone while Mom and Annie met with Dad in the visiting room.

Zipping up, I reach out to flush, then decide not to touch the rust-pitted handle. As I turn to the door, a shoe crunches on the walk outside. It's probably Tim, but for some reason the sound makes me freeze.

Ten seconds pass . . . then twenty.

Did I imagine it? Female laughter penetrates the wall behind me. *The girls are still inside the station. And if they're still inside, then Tim is, too.*

So whose footstep did I hear?

Taking my cell phone from my inside coat pocket, I start to call Tim, then stop. I'm probably being paranoid, but I don't want to drive him into an ambush. Shifting my phone to my left hand, I crouch, pull up my left pant leg, and draw my Smith & Wesson Airweight .38 from the ankle holster I've worn since December. Then I back against the urinal.

The pistol's wooden grip is chipped from being hammered against Forrest Knox's gravestone. Using only my left thumb, I text Tim: *Heard something outside rr. Possible threat. Stay inside with girls. I'm locked in.*

As I press SEND, the bathroom door handle turns, then stops.

My hand tightens on my pistol.

Then the door presses against the bolt, testing its resistance.

"Just a minute!" I call, as any man would in a normal situation. "Almost done in here."

No reply.

Using my left thumb, I text Tim: *Call cops.*

Out of the pregnant silence comes a muffled voice, barely audible through the thin metal door: *"I've got a message for you, Mayor. Come out and get it."*

Jesus.

With a shaking hand I text: *Threat real!*

"A message from who?" I ask.

"You know. Now come out and hear what I got to say. If you keep fucking around in there, your daughter's gonna walk out of the station, and things are going to get bad real quick. So shake your dick and come on out."

There's no way that's Snake out there, I think, even as I wonder if it could be. John Kaiser is positive that the old Double Eagle has fled to a foreign country. But if it's not Snake . . . then who? And whoever it is, is he alone?

"Are you coming, Cage? Or do you want your little girl to take the message for you?"

All the saliva has evaporated from my mouth. A strange compulsion pushes me to open the door, but somewhere in my brain burns the certainty that I'll be shot the moment I expose myself.

My heart lurches when my phone pings in my hand.

Backup on way, reads Tim's reply. *I'm coming to you. Stay put unless you hear shooting. If you do, come out firing, just like I taught you.*

Don't leave the girls! I think, but before I can text those words, the man outside jiggles the handle, then rattles it hard. For a half second I consider firing through the door.

Who would I be killing? What if the guy isn't armed?

Either way, I can't stand here while Tim risks his life to protect my child.

Moving to the side of the door, I reach toward the bolt with my left hand, but before my fingers touch metal, the door crashes open, numbing my arm to the elbow.

I see no one.

Then an indistinct figure takes shape a few feet from the door, a white T-shirt cloaked in darkness. No one is more surprised than I when my right forefinger pulls the trigger on the .38. Thunderous concussions blast through the tiled cubicle, and the bald crown of a head appears as my target stares down at the holes stitching his belly and chest.

I'm suddenly, sickeningly sure that I've shot some hapless truck driver who was too deaf to hear me say the bathroom was occupied.

Then the figure falls onto his back.

One leg of his jeans rides up his calf as he falls, revealing the bone hilt of a Bowie knife protruding from a motorcycle boot. Then the glint of nickel flashes in his left hand—a pistol. Edging up to the bathroom door, my .38 still gripped tight, I peek outside, glancing left and right.

Nothing.

Darting forward, I kick the pistol from the downed man's hand, then jerk back like I would from a shot rattlesnake, half expecting it to strike in a death spasm. The pain etched in the downed man's face signifies life.

"Goddamn it!" shouts someone from my left.

As I whirl toward the voice, a stranger standing at the corner of the station levels a pistol at me, and before I can aim my own a shot rings out. I tense against an impact that never comes. The stranger teeters, then grabs for the wall to steady himself.

"Freeze!" shouts a voice with military authority.

The wounded man raises his gun again, but before it comes level with me, something snatches away part of his skull.

He drops to the cement with a thud that tells me he was dead when he hit.

"Sitrep, Penn!" Tim calls from around the corner.

"Two down. I don't know if there's anybody else."

"Assume there is! I'm coming to you."

Tim appears at the corner in a combat shooting posture, then turns in a fast but deliberate circle, reading the encircling darkness.

"Annie and Mia?" I ask.

"Locked in a cold storage inside. Your guy dead?"

"Not yet. I disarmed him."

"Let's get clear. We'll have to come back to talk to the sheriff and staties, but that's later."

"Just a second." I breathe, looking back at the man I shot. "Cover me."

Walking forward, I look down at the gasping man. A high whistle accompanies each breath, and a black circle the size of a dinner plate has soaked his shirt.

"He's gone," Tim says from behind me. "We need to get the girls into the Yukon, Penn."

"Go do it. This guy said he had a message for me."

"I can't leave you."

"You work for me, Tim. I'm ordering you to cover the girls. I can take care of myself."

The ex-SEAL's shoes scrape as he sprints around the corner of the service station.

Kneeling beside the wheezing man, I move so that he can see my face above his.

"You the mayor?" he rasps, his breath almost corrosive with decay.

Meth addict, I think. "That's right."

"You shot me, motherfucker."

"You asked for it."

He raises a leather-clad arm and tries to grab my throat, but I easily bat his weak limb out of the way.

"You said you had a message for me."

"Call the paramedics, man. I'm hurt bad."

"Give me the message first."

"Call the medics or I won't tell you!"

"Tell me the message, or I'll shoot you in the heart and tell the FBI you tried to stab me with that knife in your boot."

The man starts to speak, but his words disintegrate into a wracking cough that sprays a mist of blood between us. I jerk back instinctively.

"Tell me, damn it!"

"It's not for you. It's for your old man. The doc."

Something in me goes cold. "What?"

"Your daddy's nigger lawyer's gonna try to blame that old woman's death on Snake."

"What old woman? Viola Turner?"

He coughs again, but this time I manage to dodge the spray. "That's the one," he hacks. "The nigger nurse."

"How the hell would Snake know what Quentin Avery is planning to do?"

The man shakes his head. "I'm just passing the message, man. Snake says: 'Wives and children have no immunity.' Those exact words. You got that?"

"I heard you."

"If Avery tries to blame Snake, your daughter won't live to hear the verdict."

"You're paying a high price to be a delivery boy."

"Call the ambulance, man! You got the message."

"I don't like that message. I'll call you an ambulance from the road. But I'll be honest with you: I don't think you're gonna last till they get here. Better make your peace with whatever you believe in."

His eyes roll back, then lock onto me again. "You son of a bitch."

I rise to my feet and wipe my face on my sleeve.

"If I die," he croaks, "you're a dead man. And not just you . . . your whole family. That's VK law."

"VK? What the hell's that?"

"The Kindred, man. You let me die here, you'll find out more about it than you ever wanted to know."

"Guess I'll deal with that when the time comes. You shouldn't have threatened my little girl."

The roar of an eight-cylinder engine shakes the ground and buffets the air to my left. I look up and see Tim beckoning me from behind the Yukon's bulletproof glass. I can't see the girls, but after I climb in, I realize why. They're hunkered down in the well between the second- and third-row seats. *Safe as houses.* The Yukon's armor package will stop .308 Winchester FMJ rounds. After hugging both girls from above, I kneel on a second-row seat with my pistol out, ready to provide defensive fire if we're attacked.

As we pull onto the dark ribbon of Highway 65, bright metal glints in Tim's headlights. He brakes when the lights pick out the silhouettes of two big Harley-Davidson motorcycles parked on the shoulder only forty yards from the station.

"They must have been following me with their lights off," he says. "Did it feel like a simple robbery attempt?"

"No way. He had a message from Snake Knox."

"What was it?"

"He couldn't get it out."

Tim shakes his head. "Too bad. They must have followed us all the way from the prison. It's time to call the FBI."

"Daddy?" Annie whispers from the darkness behind me.

"Stay down, Boo. We're all okay."

"Are we going home?"

Scanning the dark road and shoulders, I reach back into the blackness and squeeze what feels like Annie's shoulder. "Not yet. We have to go back to the gas station and talk to the police. But we're not going back until it's safe. Maybe half an hour."

"We heard shooting. Is everything going to be all right?"

"Absolutely," I tell her, but it's a lie. Given what just happened, things are going to get worse before they get better.

The question is, *How much worse?*

CHAPTER 3

JOHN KAISER GOT three FBI agents to the service station within thirty minutes of the shooting. To my relief, the biker I shot had been dead for some while when they arrived. He hadn't even survived until the local deputies who first reached the scene found him. Kaiser himself showed up a half hour later. He was sorry I'd had to kill the guy, but after examining the corpses, he couldn't hide his excitement. Both dead men were wearing black leather jackets, and among the various insignia on those jackets, the letters *VK* were emblazoned on the right arm of each in a kind of neo-Gothic script.

"Most cops think VK stands for 'Viking Kindred,'" Kaiser tells me as he crouches in the dark with a flashlight aimed at the jacket patch. "Actually, the true gang name is *Varangian* Kindred. 'Varangians' is an old Slavic name for Vikings, and 'vikings,' of course, means 'raiders.' But *Varangian* Kindred is too hard to remember, so the name devolved into Viking Kindred, or in most conversations, just 'VK.'"

"Why the hell would these VK guys be following me to deliver a message from Snake Knox?"

Kaiser continues to study the various insignia on the jacket. "In the last couple of years, we've started to see a cross-pollination between white supremacist prison gangs and the one-percenter biker gangs. You know what those are?"

I had dealings with one-percenters like the Bandidos MC when I was an assistant district attorney in Houston. "The term comes from Heraclitus, right? '*In any battle, out of every one hundred men, ten shouldn't be there. Eighty are just targets. Nine are good soldiers, and we're lucky to have them. But one, that one is a warrior, and he will bring the others home.*'"

Kaiser's eyes stay on mine for a few seconds. "I actually found that to be true in Vietnam. The old Greeks knew a thing or two." The FBI man gets to his feet and walks to the restroom door, then turns, seeming to check the angle of the body.

"That was good shooting, Penn." He looks back at me. "Are you sure he didn't tell you what the message was?"

I lied to Kaiser because I didn't understand the meaning of the message. I mean, I understood it on a literal level, but I also sensed that there was more to it. And to find out if I'm right, I'm going to have to see my father.

"Positive. He could barely talk. All he did was cuss me. Threaten me."

"Okay."

"So—Snake Knox and the VK?"

Kaiser taps the palm of his left hand with the back of his right. "I think it's pretty simple. After Forrest died"—he gives me a quick look to let me know that he knows I killed Forrest Knox—"the Double Eagles began to disintegrate as a criminal organization. I think they relied on crooked cops for muscle, and with Forrest dead, that cadre evaporated. Snake must have had some kind of line into the VK and decided to use them to replace his old muscle. Probably a drug connection, since the biker gangs move a lot of guns and drugs."

"Where are the VK based?"

"East Texas and Louisiana. They're not huge, but they're bleeding-edge violent. Bigger on ideology than most other clubs." Kaiser points at two Nazi lightning bolts stitched onto the jacket. "SS sig-rune insignia. Typical Aryan bullshit."

"Why would these guys help Snake, though? Is he paying them?"

"Doubtful. The lightning bolts can mean Klan, as well. The new Klan, of course, not the original. I think it's the Kennedy angle that gives Snake his cachet."

"How so?"

Kaiser clucks his tongue as though trying to decide how much to reveal. "I haven't told you a lot of this . . . you had enough on your plate."

"Well, I need to know it now."

"Not long after Snake disappeared, we started seeing some blog chatter about the JFK assassination, and it tracked pretty closely with what Sonny Thornfield told you and me in the Concordia Parish jail on the day he was murdered."

"About Frank Knox being the second shooter in Dallas?"

"Right. Lots of the same details. That's like blood in the water to conspiracy theorists, and it made the rounds of all the hate-group websites. There's no doubt that groups like the VK would have seen it. Snake would be a hero to those guys. And the Knoxes being Louisiana boys would have gotten them really interested. VK bikers meeting Snake would be like stoners meeting Ken Kesey. He was *there*. Present at the creation. Snake could tell them about all the Double Eagle murders, plus God only knows what bullshit he spun them about the Martin Luther King assassination."

"So Snake might be hiding out in Texas or Louisiana."

"It's possible. But I don't think so."

"Why not?"

Kaiser hesitates once more, then continues. "Because a ghostwriter named Blair F. Edelman has spent the last two weeks in Andorra."

Andorra is a small republic on the mountainous border between France and Spain, a notorious tax haven that conveniently has no extradition agreement with the United States. Forrest, Snake, and Billy Knox had always planned to run there if their drug operation ever came under attack, and the FBI has a record of Snake and Billy entering the country by car under their own names. But as soon as they did, Snake promptly disappeared.

"You ever heard of Edelman?" Kaiser asks, leading me back around to the front of the station.

"He's written some big celebrity bios, right?"

"That's him. I think he's been meeting with Snake in Andorra. We only picked up that he was there four days ago, and we're watching him now. But I think he's onto us. We've seen him with Billy Knox, but Billy claims to have no contact with his father."

"You think he's writing about the Kennedy stuff?"

"Has to be. No Double Eagle book would interest Edelman without that. He's used to seven-figure deals. And Snake wants to make the biggest splash he can. Some of the blog chatter made it into the *National Tattler,* but that wouldn't satisfy Snake. I think he wants to go mainstream and take all the credit he can for killing Kennedy."

"That's practically begging to get caught."

"What else does a bitter old bastard on the run have to do with his remaining time? There's no deal he can cut that wouldn't involve him dying in prison. This way, he makes a martyr out of his brother, Frank, and grabs some immortality for himself. And if he *does* end up going to prison, the Aryan Brotherhood will receive him like a god."

I think about my experiences with New York publishers. "And someone will publish it, all right."

"You bet your ass they will. After forty years, the definitive truth about Dallas comes out at last? Mobster Carlos Marcello uses ex-Klansmen to kill John Kennedy? Teenage Lee Harvey Oswald sexually exploited by David Ferrie? That's number one for months."

"Do you have enough evidence to debunk the story?"

Kaiser takes a deep breath and sighs heavily. "Penn . . . I think the goddamn story is true."

A chill races over my skin. "Then why not beat Snake to the punch? Go public with it?"

"For one thing, the Bureau can't make pronouncements like that without rock-solid evidence. Snake, on the other hand, can say any damn thing he feels like. He's not even worried about libel—hell, he's wanted for multiple murders. But we've drifted afield." Kaiser wipes his hands on his jacket. "What matters tonight is that the VK involvement is a gift to us. Up to this point, Snake's been moving completely underwater. But now we can start pressuring the VK. Bring in every member that's got an outstanding warrant and squeeze them, hard. Sooner or later, somebody will talk."

"That's what you said about the Double Eagles."

"These guys aren't the Double Eagles. They're hard-core by today's standards, but not one VK in fifty could have stood toe to toe with Frank Knox."

"I hope you're right this time."

Kaiser motions for my bodyguard to join us. Tim sidles over and waits to hear what the FBI man has to say.

"I'm afraid these VK assholes are all about payback," Kaiser tells him. "The fact that you and Penn put down two of them isn't going to be forgotten. They'll try to hit back. You need to double up on security for a while. I might be able to augment what you're doing, but in the end it's going to come down to more money for private protection."

"Caitlin's dad will help out," I say. "Tell Tim what you think we need. I'm going to get back to Annie and Mia."

"I'll handle it," Tim says. "You take care of those girls, Penn."

I walk a couple of steps toward the glass door, but before I get out of earshot, Kaiser calls, "Are you sure the guy said nothing else to you before he died?"

I look back at the corpse lying in the dark. "Positive, John."

After a long look, Kaiser says, "Okay. You're good to go."

I walk back into the station, where Annie and Mia sit drinking Diet Dr Peppers. Both have been seriously shaken, but as usual, Mia is doing a good job of managing Annie's anxiety.

"You guys ready?" I ask wearily.

"Way past," Mia says. "Let's get this girl home."

HOURS LATER, DESPITE my exhaustion, I find it almost impossible to sleep. When I do, I dream of helmeted men on black horses pursuing me through dense fog. After I can stand no more of lying restless in the dark, I get up and go down to the kitchen, where I fix a bowl of raisin bran and watch the second half of *To Have and Have Not* with the volume set low.

As I watch Humphrey Bogart and his alcoholic first mate suffer through a hellish fishing charter, a dark memory rises into my mind. It wears the face of Lincoln Turner, my half-black half brother. I've only seen Lincoln three times since he confronted me in the Adams County jail, where I was being held on suspicion of murdering Forrest Knox. Twice from a distance, without him seeing me—not that I could tell, anyway. But the third time I realized he was following me across town in his truck. With the confidence imparted by the pistol under my seat and the bodyguard in the car behind me, I called Tim Weathers and told him what I planned to do. Then I pulled into a barbershop parking lot on Homochitto Street and waited to see if Lincoln would follow me.

He did.

He pulled his Chevy F-250 alongside my Audi, rolled down his window, and waited for me to do the same. In the truck, he was three feet higher than I off the ground, and his eyes smoldered with anger. My right hand gripping my pistol in my lap, I lowered my window with my left as crazy scenarios swirled through my brain. For some reason I was thinking of Cain and Abel, only I had no idea which of us was Cain and which was Abel. Maybe that would depend on who fired first—for I was strangely sure that Lincoln, too, had a weapon in his hand.

"You have something to say?" I asked, searching, as I always did in his presence, for my father's face in his—or even for traces of my own. I saw none, and once more, I could not get over how dark he was. Passing him on the street, I would never have suspected a high percentage of Caucasian blood. But my skepticism was moot: a DNA test had proved Dad's paternity beyond all doubt.

"So they let you out of jail," Lincoln said in his deep bass voice. "You killed a state police officer with a spear, and they let you right out. So sorry, Mr. Mayor, all just a misunderstanding. It must be nice to throw that kind of weight."

"I'm late for an appointment. If you have something to say, say it."

The dark eyes regarded me with discomfiting intensity. "We got the same blood running through our veins, Penn Cage. So answer me this. How come you got everything and I got nothing?"

My half brother's face was hard, but his curiosity seemed genuine. How could I answer his question? Summarize five hundred years of tragic history? Or would that simply be an evasion? Was the fault my father's alone? I thought back to the report I'd received from the Chicago private detectives I'd hired three weeks before. Their information was sketchy, but what it revealed sobered me. In almost every way, Lincoln Turner and I are mirror opposites. While I was reared as the son and heir of a highly respected physician and a mother who could have modeled for a poster from the Eisenhower era, Lincoln grew up in government-subsidized housing on Chicago's South Side, with an alcoholic mother and a brutal con man stepfather always in trouble with the law. Statistically speaking, my success and Lincoln's failure were practically foreordained. While I was striving for a baseball championship and attending American Legion Boys' State, Lincoln was scrapping in the streets and running from the Chicago PD. When his stepfather—whom Lincoln had believed was his real father—wasn't in prison, he was gambling away his wife's salary. It was a miracle Lincoln made it through law school without being convicted of a felony himself. And while I was transitioning from a successful legal career to a more lucrative one as an author of legal thrillers, Lincoln was slaving in a small firm, chasing small-time cases until he was finally busted for embezzling escrow funds from a client trust account. According to my sources, he did this in a desperate attempt to save his "father" from a long prison term, but that didn't stop the Illinois State Bar Association from suspending his license.

Was it any wonder, then, that the eyes watching me from the truck window burned with such resentment? What galling rage must eat at his insides every time he thinks of the married white Mississippi doctor who impregnated his mother and abandoned her to the frozen Chicago ghetto? What must he see in my soft white skin and expensive clothes? In my reputation and my political power, however modest? In my lovely daughter with her blessed future? What did he feel, I wonder, when he heard that Caitlin had been murdered? One atom of sympathy? Or did he revel in unexpected schadenfreude and see Caitlin's death as a gift in his quest to tear down all that my father has built in the years since he abandoned Viola Turner?

"You got a mama," Lincoln said bluntly. "My mama's dead."

"I'm sorry."

Contempt curled his upper lip. "Sorry don't help her. Sorry don't help nobody."

"Are you sorry that my wife is dead? Or my fiancée?"

"I didn't know the ladies. They were both rich, though, from what I hear. They had their time."

"You think money takes away the pain of life?"

He barked a laugh, harsh and derisive. "Only somebody who's got money could ask that."

"Is that what you want out of all this? Money?"

"Everybody wants money. But there ain't enough money in the world to take away my pain."

"What do you want, then?"

"Justice."

"That's a big word. It means different things to different people."

Lincoln shook his big head. "Only means one thing to me."

"What's that?"

"Payback."

"You want our father to suffer the way your mother suffered."

Lincoln smiled then, and his smile was more frightening than anything he'd ever said to me. "The Bible says the sins of the father will be visited upon the sons, even unto the seventh generation. You and your little girl ain't but two generations. But that's a start, I guess."

My hand tightened on the pistol in my lap. "Are you threatening my daughter?"

"Man, I don't have to threaten nobody. Karma's on its way around, all by its own self." He glanced away, at the cars passing on the road beside us, then behind my Audi at the big Yukon. "Got your muscle back there, huh? You keep on paying him. He can't protect you from what's coming."

"I wouldn't go back there and test him."

Lincoln's laugh was deep and jolly. "You know, most of our lives, you and me didn't know each other existed. But it's like I told you in that juke joint out by Anna's Bottom. We've been tied together as sure as twins separated at birth. We come from the same pair of balls, but you got blessed and I got cursed. Maybe you come from the left nut and I come from the right. What you think?"

"This isn't getting us anywhere."

"You're wrong, *bro*. Hey, you ever been diving?"

"Diving?"

"Scuba diving."

"A few times."

"You and me . . . we're like two divers tethered to each other, dropping down into an underwater cave. What they call a blue hole. Down, down into the dark, to a place nobody's ever seen and lived to tell, where there's no light and no oxygen, nothing but the bones of those who went before."

"You're losing me, Lincoln."

"Oh, you're with me. You know what's at the bottom of that hole?"

"What?"

"The truth."

This got my attention. "And what's the truth?"

"Another big word, like justice. Maybe the biggest one of all. One truth is, you spent your life trying to measure up to a father who was a liar. And I spent mine trying to save a piece of shit I *thought* was my father, but he dragged me down with him like a drowning man."

I didn't know what to say to this.

"But that ain't the *bottom* truth," Lincoln said. "That's just currents in the water."

"What's the bottom truth?"

"Oh, no, my brother. You don't learn that till you get to the bottom." He held up a thick forefinger. "And we ain't near 'bout there yet."

"I'll tell you what. Why don't we go somewhere and sit down, just the two of us? We'll drop the bullshit and come to some rational accommodation. How about it? These kinds of situations have been around for centuries, and people found a way to live with them."

"You mean bastard sons and *rightful heirs* sitting down and working shit out?"

Money again. "I wouldn't put it that way."

His eyes hardened into dark gemstones. "Man, you better wake the fuck up. It's *way* too late for that."

"Is it ever too late to do the right thing?"

"Ask my mama that."

This silenced me. I thought about driving away, but something held me in the parking lot, under that smoldering gaze. The anger in Lincoln Turner was to the hatred of men like Snake Knox as a blowtorch to liquid nitrogen. If Lincoln wanted Annie dead, he would cut her throat on the steps of a church and feel justified in the eyes of God. Snake might do the same, but he would do it in cold blood.

"What did you say to my father when you visited him in jail?" I asked.

"*My* father, you said? You mean *our* father, don't you? As in, *'Our Father, who art in prison, cursed be thy name . . .'*?"

The malicious edge in his voice sent a shiver along my arms.

"What would *you* say?" he asked. "What would you say to a man who'd left you and your mother to die on the side of the road?"

"Lincoln . . . he didn't even know you existed until a few months ago."

His eyes blazed. "Boy, you're like a blind mole burrowing through rich soil. Don't know what's behind you, above you, or beneath you.

You're fat and happy, right up till the moment the patient farmer hammers a spike through your head."

This image made my heart flutter. "Who's the patient farmer? You?"

Lincoln laughed once more, big rolling waves of sound that rebounded between our two vehicles. "*Daddy,* bro. Who else? *Big Daddy.* You and me, we're out here suffering, not knowing shit. And he's over there in a federal country club being protected by the FBI. You *'splain* that to me, huh?"

I said nothing. Lincoln had no interest in the agenda of John Kaiser or the FBI. He cared nothing about the Double Eagles or the Kennedy assassination.

"But in three weeks," he went on, "they gonna move him back here to the Adams County jail—to that cracker Sheriff Billy Byrd's jail. *Then* ol' Pop's gonna get a taste of real prison life. Yes, sir. It's gonna be sweet. Karma sho' is a bitch. You think about that, my brother from a different mother." Lincoln stabbed a thick forefinger at me. "And you have a *blessed* day."

He reached out and waved at Tim Weathers with mock friendliness, then put the truck in gear and peeled out of the parking lot with a shriek of rubber.

I don't remember what Tim said when he walked up to check on me. Even now, sitting at my kitchen table with an empty cereal bowl staring up at me, I'm not sure why this confrontation returned with such vividness. Maybe because I know that the message I was given by the VK biker will have to be transmitted to my father. And the only person who can do that is me. If I'm going to visit Dad tomorrow, after not speaking to him since before Caitlin's death, a lot of memories like this are going to boil up out of the darkness at the bottom of my mind. I suppose Lincoln Turner came up first because he's the living symbol of my father's sin. His sin, yes, and perhaps also his crime. It was Lincoln who set in motion the murder investigation that ultimately led Shadrach Johnson to charge my father with first-degree murder. And now Lincoln haunts my city—and my family—like some dark, retributive spirit.

"Penn? Are you okay?"

I look up to see Mia Burke pad into the kitchen wearing yoga pants and a T-shirt that falls to midthigh.

"I heard somebody moving around a while ago," she says. "I thought it might be Tim or one of the guys."

"No. I just couldn't sleep."

She gives me a knowing look. "How could you, after what happened tonight?"

When I don't answer, she picks up my bowl, takes it to the sink, and begins washing it. In the half light she reminds me of my wife, though Mia looks nothing like Sarah did. Mia is dark-haired, compact, and muscular, where Sarah was light-haired, lithe, and tall, just as Annie is growing to be.

"You been watching that movie?" Mia says, not looking around.

"Not really."

"There's hardly any of the original Hemingway story left in it. But Faulkner wrote a lot of the script, I think. It's kind of a poor man's *Casablanca*."

This is typical Mia, who often sounds thirty rather than twenty, and sometimes a lot older than that. I cannot imagine how I would have handled Annie's crisis without her.

"I guess I'm going up," she says, leaning back against the sink. "You want me to fix you some coffee or something? It's not that long till sunup."

I give her a smile filled with more gratitude than an offer of coffee demands. "No, thanks. I'm coming up, too. I need the rest. I'm going to see my dad tomorrow."

This stops her cold. "Really?"

"Yeah. It's time. But I'm not taking Annie with me. I'll need your help to make that work out."

"Sure, no problem."

"Thanks, Mia."

She walks into the hall first, and I switch off the TV and the light as I pass. We mount the staircase together, her a little in front, treading quietly so as not to wake Annie. At the top we pause, the moment slightly awkward, then with tight smiles we separate and go to our rooms.

As I lie back down, I remember that once, long ago, Mia told me how Humphrey Bogart and Lauren Bacall met and fell in love on the set of *To Have and Have Not*. He was forty-four, she nineteen. They married and remained happy until he died from cancer twelve years later. Tonight Mia did not remind me of that, but I do remember. It's a strange life we have here, Mia and Annie and me. On some level, despite the disasters that made it necessary, I have enjoyed my time in this cocoon. But one thing is certain: it can't go on forever. And something tells me that tomorrow, my visit to my father may set in motion the next act of our family tragedy.

Unless the bullets I fired earlier tonight already did that.

CHAPTER 4

I DON'T REALLY want to see my father, but I don't see that I have much choice. There are two federal correctional institutions at Pollock, Louisiana. One is a medium-security facility that houses violent felons. The other is a minimum-security country club for nonviolent offenders, and this is where John Kaiser chose to house my father during his period of protective custody.

Relaying Snake Knox's message to Dad meant driving back along the same rural roads Tim Weathers and I drove last night when the two VK bikers followed us, and where we ultimately killed them. Tim insisted on riding with me this time, and also on putting a chase car behind us with two more security men. Tim said he didn't fancy being surrounded by a hundred Harleys on a country highway with only the two of us to make a stand. The guys in the chase car had some heavy weaponry that a motorcycle gang would not be expecting.

I didn't ask for details.

After what seems an interminable drive, Tim turns the big Yukon into the prison entrance, we pass the gate, and I remember that Pollock's not that bad, as prisons go. Nothing remotely like a state facility—Parchman, for example, which for a visitor is a shitty experience from start to finish, and for a prisoner can be hell on earth. The Pollock FCI feels more like an inexpensive but clean motel, one that happens to have bars, barbed wire, or mesh over every opening big enough for a human hand to pass through.

Being processed in reminds me of my years as a prosecutor, and it also makes me wonder how Annie has felt going through this, week after week. But if experience has taught me anything, it's that kids seem to do very well handling prison visits; it's the adults who seesaw between high anxiety and depression.

Before long, I find myself seated alone in a room the size of a large office cubicle. I was searched twice, despite my father being supposedly held in *protective* custody. But prisons have their procedures, and woe betide any guard who dares to break them—at least publicly. Annie and my mother must be very familiar with this sterile room.

I've visited a lot of witnesses in a lot of prisons, but seeing my father in this place will not be easy. When I hear the door open, I turn, my neck and back painfully stiff from last night's action.

But it's not my father who comes through that door.

First I hear an electric whir. Then a wheelchair scoots through the opening, bearing a man who was six feet four inches tall when he still had his legs. Now a crocheted comforter covers his lap, and also the space where the lower extremities that diabetes took from him would normally rest.

I wasn't expecting Quentin Avery, since he divides his time between Washington, D.C., and a palatial home in Jefferson County, Mississippi, which is a good hundred miles away. But something obviously drew Quentin here today, and I'm pretty sure it was me.

Expertly manipulating the wheelchair's joystick, he rolls to within inches of my chair and gives me a fond smile. The tight white Afro and skin light enough for freckles always give his face a friendly cast, and his greenish eyes often have a twinkle in them. But I have also seen those eyes blaze with fire, and ice over into opacity. The voice usually emerges as a soft southern drawl, but this man has argued landmark cases before the Supreme Court, and in such venues he can call forth a booming God-from-the-burning-bush bass that shakes judges in their seats. Today, though, he's my benign uncle Quentin, ready to dispense wise advice for those smart enough to take it. Or so he would have me believe.

"I heard you had some trouble last night," he begins, with a wink in his voice.

"Little bit."

"You're turning into a regular cowboy this year."

"I'm not here to see you, Quentin. Where's Dad?"

"Easy, Trigger. He'll be out in a minute. I thought we ought to have a word first. What prompted this visit after all the distance?"

"The guy I shot gave me a message last night. A message for Dad. And for you."

The green eyes register surprise. "A message from . . . ?"

"Snake Knox. And I did *not* tell the FBI that."

Quentin rolls his tongue around his mouth, then swallows, as though drinking down this information. "What's the message?"

"Word for word, he said, 'Your daddy's nigger lawyer's gonna try to blame that old woman's death on Snake.'"

"Colorful. Reminds me of my youth."

"Then he gave me Snake's message: 'Wives and children have no immunity.'"

Quentin reflects on the words.

"What does that mean, Q?"

"It's a threat, obviously. Against Peggy and Annie, I imagine."

"That's all? Nothing more?"

Now he looks blank. "Like what?"

"I don't know. This was almost the last thing this guy said on earth. And I felt like there was more to it than a simple threat. He wanted to be sure I got the exact words."

Quentin reaches out and squeezes my hand. "You were in the heat of action, boy. You'd just shot a man. Your neurons were firing at a thousand times their normal rate. Don't read too much into it."

I think about this for a while. "Is it true, what he said? Are you going to try to blame Viola's death on Snake Knox?"

Quentin looks down at the floor and sighs. "Penn . . . I have been specifically instructed not to talk to you about my case strategy."

"By Dad."

A nod.

"Jesus Christ. Do you have evidence that Snake killed Viola?"

He looks up again, empathy and regret in his face. "I *can't talk about the case.*"

"If you have such evidence, why not give it to the police or the FBI?"

"I can't discuss it, Penn. But I will tell you this: There's no way in hell that Snake or anybody else could have any idea of what my strategy is. Because I don't know myself yet."

This silences me for a few seconds. "Then why is Snake afraid that you might try to pin Viola on him? If Snake's afraid of that, that must mean either he killed her, or he was there on the day of the murder and he's afraid you can prove it."

Quentin pushes out his lower lip. "All food for thought."

"Okay, Quentin. Okay. I get your position. But I have to ask you one thing. Given all the physical evidence I know about, I've worked through every imaginable scenario of what could have happened in that room on the night Viola died. Natural causes, suicide, physician-assisted suicide, and murder. And I know one thing for sure: unless the videotape stolen from Henry Sexton's camera recorded the *actual* murder—and it exists somewhere and is played in court for the jury—nobody can say for sure how Viola died. Which gives you reasonable doubt. If you paint a convincing enough story, the jury should have no trouble voting to acquit."

Quentin is enjoying this like a law professor watching a student wrestle with a difficult case. "And which story would you choose, Counselor?"

"Easy. Viola tried to inject herself with a lethal dose of morphine but only partially succeeded, due to physical impairment. That explains the botched injection. Maybe Dad was there when she did that, maybe not. But once he *was* in her presence, she suffered a heart attack. Naturally, Dad used adrenaline to try to revive her. In his zeal to do everything possible to save her, he administered a fatal overdose. Maybe that was excessive zeal, or maybe he picked the wrong syringe. But either way, if you tell that story right, no jury in Natchez is going to convict him of murder."

Quentin has steepled his long fingers. "You might be right about that. But here's the problem. If that's the way things happened, then why the hell didn't Tom say that immediately after her death? Why didn't he sign Viola's death certificate and call for the ambulance or the coroner? Why refuse to speak? And worse . . . *why skip bail*?"

This, I have no facile answer for. "Can you tell me?"

"I'm afraid not, my young brother."

"Do you *know*?"

"I do not."

"Good God, Quentin. What is he playing at? Is he really on some self-sacrifice trip?"

"For the last time, Penn . . . I can't discuss it."

"What about change of venue? Surely you can tell me about that. Have you made your motion?"

Quentin shakes his head.

"Why the hell not?"

"Because Judge Elder let me know in no uncertain terms that he would deny it."

"Without even considering it?"

This earns me a sober nod. "Joe's being surprisingly difficult. Like backing up Billy Byrd on not letting Tom attend Caitlin's funeral. If I didn't know him pretty well, I'd be worried about judicial bias going forward."

"So you know Elder?"

Quentin chuckles. "He's a black Mississippi judge, ain't he? Joe worked for me one summer when he was in law school."

"Well, surely he's cut from better cloth than Shad or Billy Byrd."

Quentin clucks his tongue. "Joe's a good boy. We'll get a better idea of where he stands when he starts ruling on pretrial motions."

"But you can't afford to wait on the change-of-venue motion. You should at least file and make him deny it."

"I know that. My problem is my client. Tom actually believes that Natchez is where this case needs to be tried. Natchezians are the people most affected by the case, and he's content to put his fate in their hands."

More suicidal logic. "Then why did you discuss moving the case with Elder at all?"

Quentin's eyes harden. "Because I'm worried about Tom's safety once he's moved to the Adams County jail."

"No shit. That alone ought to be grounds for a change of venue."

"Joe Elder promised me Tom would be at no risk while in Billy Byrd's custody."

"He can't guarantee that!"

Quentin shrugs, then touches his joystick and spins his wheelchair ninety degrees left. "Listen," he says, his face in profile, "your father's gonna be escorted through that door in a minute. You've had a lot of experience in the criminal courts. You've seen a lot of men and women in jail. Put a lot of them there yourself. But seeing your father in jail is a whole different thing."

"I know that."

"No, you don't. This would be like Tom having to operate on you in an emergency. He might think he could handle it, but once he stuck that scalpel into your body, I promise you, his hands would be shaking. This kind of situation hits you in a soft place, where you ain't ready for it. And I want you to *be* ready when Tom comes in here."

"I can handle it, Quentin."

The old man's eyes soften, but the look in them is not comforting. "It's not you I'm worried about. I don't want Tom thinking you're coming apart because of this situation. While he's locked in this place, he sees you as the head of his family. And if he's going to last until the trial, he's got to know you can hold everybody together. Keep them safe."

"He knows that."

"Reinforce it."

There's so much gravity in Quentin's voice that I find myself peering deep into his eyes for some clue to his thoughts. Rather than endure my gaze, the lawyer looks down at the comforter draped over his knees.

"I had to go see my daddy in jail once," he says softly. "He was a sharecropper, you remember?"

This tale has long been a staple of Quentin's courtroom repertoire, and I'm not sure I have the patience to listen to it today. "I know this story, Q."

"Not all of it, you don't. The landowner claimed Daddy had stole something, so the sheriff jailed him for a month. Bread and water, just like the old saying. The strap, too." Quentin taps the right arm of the chair with his long fingers. "Seeing Daddy locked in that jailhouse cut me to the bone, Penn. I've never felt more helpless than I did then. That's probably the reason I'm a lawyer today."

"Quentin—"

He reaches out and grabs the sleeve of my jacket. "I know I've told that story to juries before—milked it when I had to—but I always held something back."

Something in his voice catches my attention. "What's that?"

"Daddy didn't go to jail just once, Penn. And most times, when they took him . . . he was guilty."

"What?"

Quentin nods soberly. "He stole things from the boss man. Pilferage, you know? Some tack here, a hog there. Sharecropping was practically slavery back then. I think it was Daddy's way of fighting the system—a corrupt, dehumanizing system. Usually they only kept him in the pokey a couple of weeks. But one time they kept him ninety days. We nearly lost everything that year. Truth be told, we damn near starved. Me and my brother couldn't hardly get the crop in. We ate our animals and our seed corn. You'd think the neighbors would help out, but they had too damn little themselves, and nobody wanted to risk helping somebody who'd upset the boss man."

Quentin lets out a bitter chuckle. "Daddy had an attitude, now. Mama was always scared he'd backtalk some gunbull and they'd shoot him. 'Shot trying to escape.' You know how it went in those days."

I nod. "The Ray Presley solution."

"You got it. I was about twelve when he went in that time. I was so mad I wanted to kill somebody, and so scared I wanted to hide in my mama's skirts. But no matter how I felt, I couldn't change how things were."

There's a note in his voice that puzzles me. "Why are you telling me this? Are you saying Dad's guilty?"

"No, goddamn it." Quentin glares at me like an impatient father himself. "I'm saying you've been doing all you can to keep your distance from your father, and I know why. He's hurt you. *Bad.* But when you see him in here, something's gonna break in you. You're gonna revert back to Penn Cage, crusader for justice. But boy . . . in this situation, you can't do anything to save your father. This time, that's my job. *Your* job is to give him the strength to get through the month we have until the trial. Can you do that?"

Because Quentin seems so upset, I give his question some real thought. "To tell you the truth, I don't know how I'll react until he walks through that door."

After a while, Quentin says, "Just leave the past alone. If you still blame your father for Caitlin's death, you're way behind Tom himself. It damn near killed him when he heard that girl died."

I fold my hands on the scarred table. "Yeah, well. That's between him and me."

Quentin reaches out and catches my sleeve again. "Just remember one thing. We're all mortal. We all sin. We're all guilty. That's why I could never be a prosecutor."

"Unlike me, you mean."

"Just don't be too quick to judge, that's all I'm saying. Or too harsh." He releases my sleeve. "By the way, I want you to know it was me who leaked the DNA test proving Tom's paternity of Lincoln Turner."

A sudden numbness comes into my face.

"You know why I did that, right?" he asks.

My answer is automatic, a law student's reply. "You didn't want Shad dropping a big revelation on the jury. Goes to motive. If Shad had sprung that during the trial, the effect would have been explosive. You wanted the shock to dissipate during the months of lead-up."

Quentin gives me a grateful nod, as if I've absolved him. "I know the publicity couldn't have been easy for you."

"I hope you gave Mom some warning, at least."

"Tom spoke to Peggy before I let it out."

"Small mercy." Suddenly, I'm almost boiling with exasperation. "Do you two really plan to keep up this closemouthed, blood-brothers act all the way to the trial?"

Quentin shrugs. "Tom's my client. I have to be guided by his wishes. If you can change his mind, I'm happy to have you on the team."

"Screw it. I'm through trying to convince him to do the right thing. Or anything. I'm here because Annie is at risk—end of story."

Quentin studies me a few moments with deep sadness in his eyes. Then he says, "I love you, Penn. Don't ever forget that."

He touches the joystick on his chair arm, whirs to the door, and knocks twice on it. A corrections officer opens the door and holds it for him to exit.

After Quentin disappears, the officer continues holding the door for a tall, emaciated man with white hair and a beard who shuffles unsteadily into the room, his hollow eyes squinting at me.

My father.

CHAPTER 5

"YOU'VE LOST WEIGHT," my father says, shuffling to the table where I sit. "A lot of weight."

"About twenty pounds," I say awkwardly. "Don't have any appetite."

"Me either."

His progress toward me is shockingly slow. The arthritis in his feet must be worsening. Despite aging rapidly over the past few years, due to various comorbid conditions, my father has always projected a deep vitality that patients sensed and drew on for comfort. But now he seems shrunken, gray and desiccated, like a monk emerging from a solitary cell, unused to human contact.

"Jewel Washington's been bringing me casseroles about every other day," I tell him. "Melba, too. Annie and Mia and the security team have been living off them."

"At least the food's not going to waste. Jewel and Melba are good women."

He grips the back of the empty chair with his clawlike right hand, then slowly lowers himself toward the seat. With ten inches to go, his knees give out and he drops into the chair with an explosive grunt.

"A lot has happened since we last saw each other," he says.

"There's no need to get into all that."

His eyes find mine and peer deeply into me. "Maybe not. But I want you to know something about Caitlin."

I hold up my hand in the universal sign for STOP. I cannot bear to talk about Caitlin's death with my father.

"Son," he goes on, "I need you to know I did everything I could to save her. I had no instruments, my hands were cuffed, but still we came close, working together. Caitlin did things some soldiers couldn't have done—"

"I know all that," I cut in, my voice cracking. "Look—I'm sure you did everything you could. But that's not the point, okay? *She shouldn't have been there in the first place.* It was the choices you made early on—refusing to speak about Viola's death, jumping bail—*that's* what killed Caitlin. Not failing to drain her goddamn pericardium."

Dad stares back at me, his mouth and chin quivering. "All right," he says finally. "You're right. But no matter how you feel about me, we have to talk. For the family's sake."

"I'm here, aren't I?"

"Yes. And I'm glad. Also surprised."

"Snake Knox sent you a message. Through me."

"John Kaiser told me that. But he said you never got the message."

"Huh." I give Dad a subtle wink. "He must have forgotten."

Dad blinks slowly, then motions for me to come closer and whisper. Leaning forward, I tell him exactly what I told Quentin.

Dad looks perplexed by the words. "Wives and children?" he echoes. "No immunity?"

"That's what the biker said. And he seemed especially concerned that I get the exact words. I figured you might get more out of the message than a simple warning."

"No. That's what it sounds like to me. A threat."

"Yeah. Except when did the Double Eagles ever shy away from hurting wives? They raped and beat women as a standard tactic."

"Black women," Dad says. "Maybe that's the difference. He's talking about *our* wives. White women."

I watch him in silence for several seconds. "Maybe."

"What did you and Quentin talk about?" he asks.

The change of subject irritates me. "Not his damn trial strategy, that's for sure."

Dad makes a sound of contempt. "Don't worry about the trial. The trial isn't important."

This statement is so patently absurd that it takes me a few seconds to respond. "If you're convicted, you will die in the Parchman penitentiary. How is that not important?"

My father winces, then begins scratching at a scaly patch of psoriasis on his arm.

"Penn, what if the charges against me were dismissed today? What would that accomplish?"

"You'd be free."

"True enough. But as long as Snake Knox is breathing and roaming loose, we live under threat. All of us."

"Why is that, Dad? Because you and Viola killed his brother?"

For the first time, he looks surprised.

"Yes, I know about that. Caitlin mentioned it in the phone recording she left behind at the Bone Tree."

He sighs, then shakes his head. "Snake doesn't know about Frank. He couldn't."

"Are you sure?"

"Yes. Because if he did, he wouldn't have simply left me at the Bone Tree to die. He would have put a bullet in me. Or worse. Torture is his specialty, remember."

Dad's mention of the Bone Tree forces me to think of Caitlin's last hour on earth. "Then why does Snake want you dead?"

"I don't know. He's afraid of me, for some reason." Dad jabs a crooked finger at me. "But you're a target, too. Don't forget that. You killed Forrest Knox. And Snake knows that. That means anybody and everybody you hold dear is in Snake's sights. Annie, Peggy, Jenny—even Mia Burke."

"Wives and children don't have immunity," I murmur.

"Exactly. God, I wish Daniel Kelly were still around. You know what he would call Snake. Remember?"

"A one-bullet problem."

"Damn right. Kelly's still MIA in Afghanistan?"

"Presumed dead."

"That is a tragedy on so many levels."

A thought from a dark place rises to the surface. "Since we're talking about this kind of extremity . . . what about Walt Garrity?"

A pensive look comes over Dad's face. "On the morning of Caitlin's funeral, I told Walt the time had come to kill Snake. I was certain that was our only option. Walt agreed, in principle, but he said he couldn't risk the rest of his life to do it. I understood. He loves that Mexican wife of his, and he's only been with her a little while."

My father's eyes brighten a little. "That's one reason I turned myself in. I half hoped that when I showed up at Henry's funeral, Snake would raise his head and take a shot at me, and Kaiser and his team might get him. But Snake was too smart for that."

"He's no fool. Snake had an old Double Eagle murdered after planting a ton of evidence in his house. Framed him for knocking down that FBI jet."

"I know. Silas Groom. He was one of my first patients in Natchez."

"Snake killed about a dozen birds with that stone. Now every other Eagle is scared to death of meeting the same fate."

Dad chews his bottom lip as though silently trying to work out a problem. "I've been over everything I ever knew about those bastards," he says, "all the way back to my days as company physician for Triton Battery. Partly for Kaiser and the Bureau, but also for myself. I remembered one case I'd forgotten, a young woman from Athens Point. She was raped by some white men down in the Lusahatcha Swamp in the midsixties. They killed her husband in front of her. Lynched him. It was a terrible case, but it got very little attention. The young wife never really recovered. Her mother-in-law brought her to me for help, but I couldn't break through her depression. Eventually, she left town and committed suicide. I always felt like the Double Eagles had been behind that. They had a strong presence in Lusahatcha County, even back then."

"Shit. When did this happen, exactly?"

"Oh, 1965 or '66. But I can't even remember the mother-in-law's name. They wanted it kept quiet. They were afraid of retaliation, and rightfully so. All the law down there was Klan back then. Even now, I think the sheriff is in with the Knoxes. Or was, anyway."

"Billy Ray Ellis," I mutter in agreement. "So, what are you thinking? You want me to kill Snake Knox?"

Dad gives me a tired smile. "Hell, no. I wouldn't ask that of you. What I would like you to do is go back over Henry Sexton's footsteps. Go see the old Double Eagles—and not just them. Go see their wives, ex-wives, their children. Talk to them—really talk. If you'll do that, I believe you'll end up convincing one of them to testify against Snake."

His suggestion has stunned me. "Testify in open court? You've got to be kidding. The FBI has been working that angle all along."

"You're not the FBI. You're my son."

"Do you think that grants me some kind of superpower? These aren't grateful black patients, Dad. These are pissed-off, defiant old rednecks."

Dad's eyes flicker with conviction, even excitement. "I believe you can do it. You've got a gift with people."

"Hell, *you* couldn't even do it! You got up at Henry Sexton's funeral and asked everyone in the community to break their silence and tell what they knew about the Double Eagles. But *nobody* has come forward. Have they?"

"They're afraid, Penn. And rightly so. Afraid for their wives, their children, afraid for themselves. But they can be turned. I treated most of those people at one time or another. They're human beings. They have consciences. And they have vulnerabilities, just like we do."

His request has jarred something deep within me. "Why do you want me to do this? Seriously. It's a fool's errand."

"I don't believe that. It *will* be dangerous, though. I've heard you're wearing a bulletproof vest when you go out, and that's good. But you should take a bodyguard everywhere you go. Don't relax your vigilance for even one second."

I'm incredulous that he would assume my assent to this plan. "Dad . . . I'm not doing this. You haven't given me a thing to work with."

With a long sigh he looks down at the floor. Then he looks up and almost inaudibly whispers, "I'll give you something. On the night Viola died, there was a pickup truck parked in the trees on her road. There was a Darlington Academy sticker on the back windshield."

This stops me. Darlington Academy was one of the "Christian schools" founded in response to school integration during the 1969/1970 school year. Darlington's financial backers had been members of either the White Citizens' Council or the Ku Klux Klan. Maybe both.

"Whose truck was that?" I ask.

"Walt did some digging, and our best guess is an old Double Eagle named Will Devine."

"I remember Devine. He was in the jail on the day Sonny Thornfield was killed."

"That's right."

"Kaiser told me Will Devine agreed to turn state's evidence after Sonny's murder, but after the FBI jet went down, he backed out."

"But that proves he's conflicted! You should start with Devine."

"Why did *Walt* dig that up? Does Kaiser know about the Darlington Academy truck?"

Dad shakes his head.

"Why the hell not?"

Another sigh. "I can't tell you that, son."

"Oh, for fuck's sake."

"We're wasting time, Penn."

Anger flashes through me. "Why even tell me this? What the hell do you think I can do?"

"Put pressure on Devine. Squeeze him and see if you can make him pop. Walt tried, but Will wouldn't talk to him. Slammed the door in his face."

"I'll bet he did."

Dad's hollow eyes implore me across the inches that divide us. "I'm not asking for myself, Penn. It's for the family."

"Sure it is. Like everything else you've done, right?"

"No. Not everything. Most of this happened because of something selfish I did long ago. I fell in love with another woman."

"Like I said, no need to go into all that."

"I won't. All I'm saying is this: If you do what I ask, then one of two things will happen. Either someone will agree to testify against Snake, or Snake himself will raise his head."

"And then what?"

"If we're lucky, somebody will stomp on him."

"Who? Kaiser?"

"Maybe."

"One of my guards?"

Dad turns up his palms. "There's no way to know. You killed a man last night. An hour before it happened, you couldn't have conceived of doing that, could you?"

He's right, but this only makes me angrier. "How many men have you killed, Dad?"

After a long silence, he says, "More than I like to remember."

"Where?" My father has never told me a single war story about Korea. "In the war?"

"Yes."

"But you were a medic."

"That's right."

I wait, but he doesn't elaborate. "Jesus . . . okay. I'm going to think about what you've told me. Or asked me, I guess."

"Are you going to be coming back? Next time Peggy and Annie visit, maybe?"

"I don't know."

"I understand."

"Listen, Mom's terrified that something will happen to you once you're transferred to the Adams County jail."

Dad dismisses this with a wave of his crooked hand. "Billy Byrd won't murder me in his jail, or even have me killed by an inmate. He wants to see me convicted. He wants a public downfall and he's sure it's coming. He and his deputies gathered the evidence themselves. To Billy, it's an open-and-shut case."

"It looks that way to me, too, honestly. How the hell can you get any semblance of a fair trial with those guys in charge of the evidence?"

"A fair trial?" Dad smiles strangely. "I never expected one. Any evidence that might even have muddied the water disappeared that first day. Probably never even reached the evidence room. But it doesn't matter."

"Why the hell not?"

Dad looks at me as he would a slow child. "Because I'm guilty, son."

I must have misheard him. "What?"

"I killed Viola."

His simple, declarative confirmation knocks the breath out of me. I search his eyes for some clue to a deeper message, but I see none. It takes a moment to get my voice working. "Are you speaking literally? Or . . . in some larger moral sense?"

A sad smile touches his mouth. "This isn't a philosophy symposium, Penn. I killed Viola. The *why* is nobody's business. That's between her, me, and God."

I am gobsmacked, as the Brits say. And utterly bewildered by the casual tone of his confession. "Dad, I'm feeling a little lost here."

"Because you're overthinking things. I worked in a movie house in the late forties, when I was a teenager. Do you remember me telling you that?"

I cannot find words to answer.

A look of nostalgia comes into his face. "The Rialto in DeRidder, Louisiana. I saw a lot of pictures in that grand old dame of a theater. Good ones, bad ones, just okay."

A worm of fear is turning in my belly. *Has my father lost his grip on reality?* "Dad, what the *fuck* are you talking about?"

"I'm trying to set you straight, son."

"About what?"

"You're confused about what kind of movie you're in."

"What kind of *movie* . . . ?"

"Yes. This isn't a mystery. It's not a whodunit, with Margaret Rutherford playing Miss Marple. I'm the killer."

"Dad, for God's sake—"

"This isn't even film noir," he goes on. "It's a *western,* Penn. It always was. With black hats and white hats. Well . . . maybe my hat is gray. Like Henry Fonda's in his later years."

I get up from the table and walk toward the door. His words are so maddening that I want to get physically away from him. Halfway to the door, I stop and turn back. "If you killed Viola . . . why even go through this trial? Why not plead guilty, take your sentence, and live out your last year or two of life in jail?"

He apparently takes my question very seriously. "I've thought about that. A great deal, in fact. But I can't do that to your mother. Or to Annie. What I do now, I'm doing for them."

Right. Tom Cage, the family martyr.

"You said your motive was between you, Viola, and God. But you don't believe in God."

This time his smile is sad. "That was only a figure of speech. What I meant was, it's between Viola and me—and she's gone now. When I go, my motive will be lost to history, just as it should be."

Maybe I'm not listening with the proper detachment, because his words hit me like a slap in the face. "That's great, Dad. Only you don't live in a vacuum. The decisions you make have consequences for the rest of us. Terrible consequences."

"I know. I've learned that, if nothing else. If you'd let me—"

I hold up my hand again, and this time, mercifully, he stops. But when the doorknob is in my hand, he says, "I'm so sorry for everything, son. I mean that."

Without turning back, I say, "Is that what you said to your other son? To Lincoln?"

When he doesn't reply, I look back.

"Yes," he says finally, and then he shakes his head in resignation.

At these words, something in my mind simply shuts down. There's only one thing left to say.

"Good-bye, Dad. I won't be coming back before the trial."

And I leave him.

THURSDAY

CHAPTER 6

IT TOOK TWENTY days for the VK motorcycle club to hit back in revenge for Tim and me killing their members, and what they did was something I had not imagined in my most horrific nightmares. What they did proved John Kaiser's classification of the Double Eagle group as a domestic terror organization completely justified. What they did was obscene.

And it happened only yards from my front door.

I spent the twenty days between those two violent episodes doing what my father asked me to do—visiting Double Eagles, their wives, their children, and where possible their ex-wives and known associates—and I hated every minute of it. Of course I told myself I was picking up the torch Caitlin had dropped, not fulfilling the charge that my father had laid upon me at the federal prison. But whatever I was really doing, it didn't work.

Nearly everywhere I went, I was walking in the footsteps of John Kaiser's FBI agents, and not one of them had gleaned even a seed of valuable information from those sources. This was probably because all those agents had been walking in the footsteps of Henry Sexton, and Henry had died in a ball of fire in Brody Royal's basement. Everyone I visited knew that. They knew, too, about Glenn Morehouse and Sonny Thornfield. And Silas Groom. And every person I talked to had fully absorbed the object lesson: if you go against Snake Knox's Double Eagle group, you die.

My quest through Concordia Parish and the outlying neighborhoods of Adams County was like a journey through my distant childhood. I'd played Dixie Youth baseball with kids from those neighborhoods: freckle-faced, pale-skinned, buck-toothed, bruised-and-scabbed-over kids who could have sprung fully formed from a Norman Rockwell painting. Most had lived the first decade of their lives with big grins; too many had lived the remainder with a confused scowl and a diminishing sense of control over their futures.

Those kids were in their midforties now, and I hardly got a sympathetic echo at a single house. Children of Double Eagle members had picked up the code of silence by osmosis, and they observed it faithfully. Suspicion was the order of the day. A couple threatened me, but most were simply uncomfortable or resentful—uncertain how to behave when torn between the southern compulsion to be hospitable and the instinct to push away all inquiry about their families. I took someone along on every visit, even to see the women. Usually Tim Weathers, but sometimes Kirk Boisseau. Kirk didn't have the training the Vulcan guys did, but my old school buddy had an asset they did not—intimate knowledge of the local population. As a former marine working in the landscaping business, Kirk had become familiar with this segment of society that I hardly knew anymore, if I ever really had.

I didn't question Will Devine—the probable owner of the Darlington Academy truck—right away. But the day after visiting my father, I called Keisha Harvin and begged for everything she could tell me about Devine and his family. The young reporter came through for me within hours. Like most original Double Eagles, Devine had spent his working life employed by the Triton Battery Corporation, just south of Natchez, on the Mississippi River. In age, Devine fell between Frank and Snake Knox. For the past five years he'd been suffering from a chronic lung disease and didn't leave the house much. According to Keisha, Henry Sexton's journals didn't supply much detail on Devine regarding the Eagles' modern-day criminal activities, but Henry had believed the man played a major role in some of the 1960s murders.

According to Dad, Walt Garrity had visited Devine at home. A retired Texas Ranger, Walt can be pretty persuasive with white guys from his own generation, but Devine had slammed the door in Walt's face more than once. John Kaiser's FBI agents must have gotten the same treatment, because if Devine came close to turning state's evidence back in December, John wouldn't have let up the pressure on the old Double Eagle.

I first tried Devine at his house on a Sunday morning, thinking maybe he'd be in a Christian frame of mind. From behind a screen door, he told me that if I didn't get off his property, he'd give me a blast from the double-barreled shotgun he was aiming at my belly. The fat old bastard was huffing while he threatened me, and he looked like he could barely hold himself on his feet. But he also looked like he would shoot if I provoked him further. The bug eyes behind big plastic glasses held a mixture of outrage and fear. It was then I realized that to Will Devine I probably appeared to be an incarnation of the retribution he had dreaded since his violent youth.

An old woman was talking low in the shadows behind him. I couldn't make out her words, but her tone seemed less bellicose than that of her husband. I considered asking Devine about the pickup truck with the Darlington Academy sticker—which was parked in a driveway thirty feet to my left—but then I thought better of it. As I drove away from the house, I started going down the list of the man's children and grandchildren.

Will Devine's sons proved to be less combative than their father, but they also claimed to know nothing substantive about his involvement with the Double Eagles. They knew I would happily jail their father if I could, but they seemed to accept this as simply the way of things. Like most Double Eagle kids, they remembered the barbecues where the fathers had drunk beer and blown up stumps and junk cars, but claimed they'd believed the men were just horsing around. If they had known that their churchgoing father had been rehearsing bomb attacks on local blacks, they said, naturally they would have . . . well, they didn't know what they would have done, but you know . . . *something.*

I didn't mention that the mothers had obviously known what those exercises were for, yet not one ever called the FBI to warn anybody. The longer I spent with Will Devine's boys, the more I saw guilt in their eyes. Not personal guilt—not the shame of conscious collusion or conspiracy—but a knowledge that they *had* heard and seen enough to know that Daddy meant to harm somebody with those "big fireworks," and that "somebody" was a different color than they were.

When I left those grown-up boys, I had the feeling that if I'd met them a little earlier in life—before so many people died—they might have been glad for the chance to confide to me the secret fears of their childhoods. Both Devine sons revealed that their father had beaten them ruthlessly for the slightest misbehavior. But that, they insisted, was common among their friends' families. "It was a different time," they said. "Tougher. Children were there to be seen, not heard. That was just the way it was, and maybe ought to be again."

When they spoke of their mother, Nita Devine, both men got soft looks in their eyes. One even wept as he spoke of her selfless devotion. Nita was, it turned out, the woman I had heard speaking from the shadows behind old Will. When I asked if the sons thought they could get me some time alone with their mother, both clammed up instantly—obviously equating my suggestion with betrayal.

The younger son, Deke Devine—named for an astronaut—gave me a lot of information about other children of Double Eagles. Most had settled within ten miles of their childhood homes. A few had gone into the military, but most worked in the oil fields, plus a smattering of small-engine mechanics, arc welders, electricians, taxidermists, or farm chemical salesmen. I wrote down as much information as I could before a feeling of betrayal shut Deke Devine up again, and I left on relatively good terms. As I drove out to Highway 65, I made a mental note to return and delve deeper into the younger son's conflicted mind.

For twenty days I crisscrossed the parish with my list, moving from houses to trailers to apartments in the hope of persuading a living Double Eagle or one of their children to talk to me. I wasn't even sure what I most wanted to know; I simply had to poke at the hornet's nest until something came swarming out. But nothing did. Going through the motions of my former career as an assistant district attorney partially restored my sense of order, and with it my connection to the world. But by the time the morning of the VK's retaliation rolled around, I was still suffering from a fundamental sense of dislocation.

I awakened to the scent of coffee coming from the kitchen, which told me that Mia was up, and probably Annie, too. Most mornings I find Mia at the kitchen table, reading a novel or working at her Mac-

Book while Annie takes her shower. That morning, Annie poked her mother's face through my door and said, "Eggs and toast or oatmeal and blueberries?"

"You pick."

"Both. You need to get some weight back."

"How about some garlic cheese grits?" Mia called. "That'll put some meat back on your bones."

"I'll give the oatmeal a shot, if you put brown sugar in it."

With a groan I rolled out of bed, stretched, then went into the bathroom and turned on the hot water in the shower.

KEISHA HARVIN HAD fallen in love with Caitlin Masters's house the first night she stayed in it, and in the months since, she'd only grown to love it more. A three-story Victorian on Washington Street, directly across from the mayor's house, it was the kind of place Keisha might never be able to afford on her own. Every morning she awakened in the cavernous house, she smiled, then rose and padded like a princess across the hardwood floor and down the stairs to the gleaming kitchen, feeling all the while as though she were acting in a movie.

Sabrina, she thought sometimes. *I'm the black Audrey Hepburn.*

And yet . . . Keisha never could get quite comfortable in the house. Wherever she walked, she felt Caitlin's unquiet ghost hovering nearby. Keisha had no sense of any malevolent spirit, only one that hated to let go of the world of light and life. Keisha told herself that since she devoted almost every waking hour to completing Caitlin's work on the Double Eagle cases, Caitlin's ghost would forgive a sister for trespassing in her home.

This morning Keisha had meant to get to work early. She'd set an early alarm, but for some reason she slept through it. Whenever that happened, she always felt as though some cosmic force were trying to sabotage her plans. She'd skipped her shower to make up time, and now she stood hunched at the back door, fumbling with her keys, trying to cram the flat metal into the lock while her backpack and purse dragged her right shoulder earthward and threatened to upend the jellied toast balanced in her left hand. Stuffing the toast into her mouth, she finally slid the key into the lock, turned it, then yanked it out and trotted awkwardly toward her Prius, which was parked in the narrow driveway beside the house.

Keisha thanked God for her keyless remote, which she clicked with an immense sense of relief. As she tossed her purse across the driver's seat, someone called to her from her front yard. Keisha forced a smile as she turned, expecting her elderly neighbor—who was always watering his flowers—or even maybe Penn's daughter, Annie. What she saw instead was an old white woman wearing a leather jacket and holding a McDonald's cup in her hand.

"Can I help you?" Keisha asked.

"I hope so," said the woman, who had stringy gray hair and a harsh edge to her voice. "Here's a present for you, pretty girl!"

Then she threw the contents of her cup in Keisha's face.

The shock of the liquid hitting her skin and eyes made Keisha gasp and drop her backpack. She shook her head like a dog trying to dry itself, then held up her hands in case the woman meant to physically attack her.

No attack came.

Keisha didn't realize her eyes were closed until she heard laughter, and some part of her brain registered that the laughter was receding.

The woman was retreating, thank Jesus.

"God*damn*," Keisha sputtered, pulling the tail of her blouse from her jeans and using it to wipe her face and eyelids. "Crazy bitch."

As she wiped, her eyes began to burn.

She blinked several times, then tilted her head back, but this did nothing to relieve the burning, which seemed to be worsening.

Shit, she thought as the pain rapidly grew intolerable.

Keisha gasped, then cried out and wiped harder. The pain kept ratcheting up the scale. Then she realized her face was burning as well.

Panic detonated in her chest, robbing her of breath and judgment. By the time she thought of her garden hose, she could barely see. Stumbling across the St. Augustine grass, Keisha began to scream.

"WHAT'S THAT?" ANNIE asked sharply.

I stopped with a spoonful of oatmeal nearly to my open mouth. "What?"

Mia froze halfway to her feet. "Somebody screamed."

When the second scream came, Mia bolted from the kitchen, Annie on her heels.

"Wait!" I yelled. "Damn it! Tim's not out there! He's in the bathroom! *Wait!*"

By the time I got outside with my pistol, I saw Annie and Mia racing across the street toward Caitlin's house. In the front yard, Keisha Harvin was stumbling around like Patty Duke playing Helen Keller. At first I thought it was some kind of prank, so clumsy and strange did Keisha look, but with the next scream I recognized genuine pain and horror.

Scanning the street for threats, I leaped down the steps and sprinted across the pavement, praying Tim wasn't far behind. Mia was trying to question Keisha, but the reporter only sobbed and babbled unintelligibly. I knew only one thing: Keisha was in terrible pain, and her face and eyes seemed to be the source of it.

"This is Penn, Keisha! What happened?"

She screeched for a couple of seconds, then said, "She threw Coke in my face!"

"Who threw a Coke in your face?"

"White lady!"

Looking closer, I saw that Keisha's blouse was wet, as was the skin of her upper chest. As I noted this, my gaze locked onto the skin itself, which did not look right at all. Something corrosive had gotten at it—

"Oh, God," I breathed. "Mia! Did you touch her?"

"I don't think so."

"Go rinse your hands with the hose."

"Make it stop!" Keisha screams. "It's *burning*!"

"Annie, did you touch her?"

"No! Daddy, what's the matter with her?"

"Run home and call 911! Then get me the rubber gloves out of the washroom."

Annie stared transfixed at Keisha's pouring eyes.

"Annie, right now! We need an ambulance and police!"

"I'm going!" she cried, sprinting back toward the house.

"I can't see!" Keisha wailed. "All I can see is light. What did she do to me?"

"Breathe, Keisha," I said in a level voice, fighting the urge to take hold of her and comfort her. "Stop talking, just breathe. I want you to sit down where you are. I'm going to get the garden hose. Do you hear me?"

Her fingers found her reddening cheeks. "Oh no—my face . . ."

"Sit down, right here. Or better yet, lie on your back."

"On the ground?"

"Yes. *Mia, bring the hose!*"

A sprinter in high school, Mia covered the distance to me in three seconds and clapped the hose into my hand. Keisha was still sobbing, but I figured the tears were good for her eyes.

"Keisha, I'm going to rinse your face, your eyes, everything. I need you to help me by staying calm. There's going to be water in your face—a lot of it—but just keep breathing through your mouth. We're going to rinse your skin until the ambulance gets here. Even under your eyelids."

"Hurry, hurry—"

I turned the thick, clear stream of water on her face and brought the hose to within three inches of her skin. In the sluicing torrent I could see the beginnings of some sort of deep burn, but with her dark skin it was hard to tell how bad it was.

"What can I do?" Mia asked, staring at Keisha with horror.

"Call Drew and tell him we have a severe acid burn, a facial burn. Tell him we're going to need an ophthalmologist as well."

"What else?"

"Get Tim over here to cover us. This might not be the end of it."

FOUR BLOCKS FROM Washington Street, Wilma Deen opened the door of a Toyota club cab pickup and climbed into the backseat. Alois Engel hit the gas before she even got the door closed, which told her he was overly keyed up by the proximity to violence, as usual.

"Did you get her?" he asked, glancing back over the seat.

"Watch where you're going!"

"Goddamn it, did you get her?"

Wilma thought back to the confusion in the young girl's face when the acid hit her, before she realized how much pain and suffering had been flung from that go-cup. "I got her, all right. She'll never be the belle of the ball again."

"Holy *shit.*"

Wilma felt the truck speed up as they moved toward Canal Street, which would take them to the Louisiana bridge.

"Slow down, Alois. I don't want to spend ten years in Parchman."

"I hear you, don't sweat it. Gimme some details, though. I didn't get to see shit."

Wilma slid down until her face was below window level and closed her eyes. She wasn't thinking about Keisha Harvin, but her own brother, Glenn. How he had looked when he realized his sister had sided with Snake and the Double Eagles over her own kin. That decision had been a revelation to Wilma, too, but she hadn't regretted it. Not often, anyhow.

She'd spent nearly three months in hiding, and truth be told, she'd gotten cabin fever. Living on the run was Shitsville, as her daddy used to say. One of the few things he'd been right about.

"FBI's gonna go batshit over this," said Alois. "The mayor, too."

"Good. I'm tired of hiding every goddamn day. I needed some action."

Alois nodded and took a long, gradual right turn, which meant he must be following the ramp down to the twin bridges over the Mississippi.

"We're about to get all the action we can handle," he said. "It's about damned time, too."

Wilma settled back in the seat and closed her eyes, but she didn't see darkness. She saw the colored girl's mouth fly open in shock as the acid hit her. By now she was suffering the torments of hell. Deep in her chest Wilma felt a twinge of something she'd thought was dead. It was empathy. But she gritted her teeth against it when she remembered her brother's eyes while she helped Snake and Sonny inject him with a lethal dose of fentanyl. Once you'd gone that far . . . there was no going back. You could only go forward.

What had most appealed to her about the acid attack was that by carrying it out, she would earn the respect of the VK club, who'd been handling their concealment from the FBI. And not only of the mamas—who were catty, slutty bitches—but the bikers themselves. The leader of the VK, a tough old Vietnam vet named Lars Dempsey, reminded Wilma a little of Frank Knox, or what she remembered of Frank, anyway. She wasn't sure how Snake kept Lars doing his bidding. In that world, the big ones ate the little ones, and she couldn't see a man of Snake's age surviving for long. But she had to give him his due: it had been almost three months since Forrest died, and the VK were following Snake's orders like an obedient army.

I guess the Knoxes are just born leaders, she thought, half resentfully. *And I reckon that's a good thing, 'cause without Snake I'd be in jail or dead in a ditch right now.*

CHAPTER 7

"YOU DID WELL, washing her face and eyes so thoroughly," says Drew Elliott, holding a penlight to Keisha Harvin's cheek. "You mitigated some of the external damage."

My father's younger partner has been working over Keisha for half an hour, but he only let me into the St. Catherine's ER treatment room two minutes ago. He's been applying a solution of something called calcium gluconate to every affected surface of Keisha's skin. To my relief, he's given her an IV narcotic for pain, and she appears to be unconscious, which makes it easier for me to remain calm while he examines her facial skin under the light.

"Will she suffer any permanent vision loss?" I ask.

Drew looks up at me, apparently confused. Then softly he says, "She'll probably lose her sight, Penn. Forever. We won't know for a few hours yet. I've called in Pat Crosby for an ophthalmological consult. But her corneas are already cloudy. It doesn't look good."

This recalibration of my worst-case scenario starts my heart thumping again. "How bad will the facial scarring be? She's a pretty young girl."

Drew moves the beam of light down to her neck. "That's not my main concern. The question is, will she survive?"

This jars me to the core. "*What?* She's twenty-five years old. I realize she'll never be on the cover of *Vogue* after this, but . . . you're saying it could kill her? Was there poison in the acid or something?"

"No, but there doesn't have to be. The acid in that cup wasn't hydrochloric or sulfuric—which would have been bad enough, but mostly limited to skin and eye damage. It was hydro*fluoric*. Hydrofluoric acid bonds with calcium ions, which means it passes through the skin and goes deep into the body, all the way to the bones."

My face feels cold. "What happens then?"

"The resulting reaction releases a flood of calcium into the bloodstream. And if you get enough calcium in your blood, it stops your heart. Permanently."

"But . . . surely you can do something to counteract that?"

Drew bends to get a better view of Keisha's neck. "Not enough, I'm afraid. It comes down to how much acid got into her. I just read about a case where a guy in a college laboratory spilled about a cup of hydrofluoric acid onto his lap. He jumped into a nearby swimming pool and stayed there for thirty minutes trying to wash himself. They initially thought he was okay, but a few days later they had to amputate both legs."

"Oh, God."

Drew clicks off the light and sets it on the instrument tray. "Ultimately he died. Heart damage."

I turn away and walk over to a sink, trying to wrap my mind around what Drew has said. Standing in the cold air of the ER, I remember the message Snake Knox sent to my father three weeks ago: *Wives and children have no immunity.* A wave of nausea rolls through my belly, and I'm thinking of darting into the toilet when Drew removes his gloves with a pop, drops them in the trash can, then lays his hand on my shoulder.

"Who would do that to this girl? The Double Eagles?"

Wives and children have no immunity. "Had to be. Keisha's been pretty hard on them in the newspaper."

"Penn . . . what if that had been Annie?"

"Don't even say that, man."

Drew drops his hand from my shoulder and looks me directly in the face. "I know you're thinking it. If you're not, you're crazy. Maybe it's time you get her out of town. Out of the country, even. Mia, too. And maybe you should go with them."

I haven't heard Drew sound this serious since he was jailed on a murder charge himself. "I don't know if I can do that right now. Leave, I mean."

"Because Tom's going on trial? Hell, you haven't even been to the prison to see him, have you?"

"Once."

"Are you planning to attend the trial, then?"

"I don't know. The issue is my mother. I think I've got to be here for her."

Drew studies me for some time. "I understand. But think about moving Annie and Mia. Anybody you or your father care about is a target."

"You're right. I will."

He gives me his professional smile. "I've got to get over to my office."

I look back at the table, where Keisha lies peacefully, at least for the moment. "Please keep a close eye on that girl, Drew."

"I intend to. I've told the nurses to call me if any family members show up. But if she gets any worse, I may have to send her up to University in a chopper."

"I understand."

He gives me a fraternal flick of his head in farewell, then heads for the big double doors.

JOHN KAISER IS standing with Annie and Mia when I come out into the waiting room. As soon as he catches sight of me, he tells the girls he needs a minute with me in private. I tell them that Keisha is resting quietly and that Drew has done everything possible for her, that now all we can do is wait. Then I give Annie a hug and follow Kaiser into an alcove where three vending machines stand humming.

"Did she say who attacked her?" he asks.

"She said it was a white woman—older, she thought—but she couldn't give any real description. Black leather jacket was all she remembered. Sounds like the motorcycle gang, doesn't it? The VK?"

"That's the obvious assumption. I'd like to know where Wilma Deen is. She was present the night her brother was murdered, and she vanished right after Snake did. That tells me she's capable of something like this."

"I hope it was her. I don't want to think this was payback for Tim and me killing those two VK guys."

"You realize they could have hit you the same way, Penn. Or Annie."

"No, they couldn't," I think aloud. "We have protection. She didn't. That's why they hit Keisha."

The FBI agent considers this. "Your father's trial starts in four days.

Could be the VK are sending him and Quentin another message with this attack. Maybe somebody's getting nervous."

"Snake?"

"Who else? But why, I don't know. Only your father knows that."

I wave my hand, too upset even to discuss that issue. "Still no leads on Snake's whereabouts?"

"You think I've been holding out on you? We've got nothing, Penn. Forrest and Snake had a long time to prepare for an emergency exit. And Forrest knew what he was doing. I've reached the point where I think the only thing that's going to give us Snake Knox is luck. And he's been a lucky son of a bitch all his life."

"Everybody's luck runs out eventually. And remember, Snake is his own worst enemy. He likes the spotlight. Once this trial starts, he may not be able to control himself. You think he can just sit somewhere and let this circus unfold? With national TV coverage every day? I don't know how Snake was tied in to Viola—or even to my father—but sooner or later, he's going to come sniffing around that trial."

"We'll be watching."

"Meanwhile, I'm going to try to think of a way to draw him out."

Kaiser looks worried. "Don't do anything stupid. Use your brain, not your heart."

"Go in there and look at that girl, John. She's twenty-five, and she's going to be blind for the rest of her life."

"Christ."

"Drew says she may die. It was hydrofluoric acid."

"Goddamn. I know what that can do."

"She's one of the good guys, man. One of us. A *kid*. Are we just going to sit here and take this shit?"

Kaiser reaches out and squeezes my upper arm. "Sometimes that's our only choice. That's part of being the good guys."

I say nothing.

"I'd like nothing better than to go to war with these assholes. But we can't even be sure who did this."

I do not share Kaiser's view. In my mind I see the smug visage of Snake Knox while Kaiser and I tried to interrogate him in the Concordia Parish Sheriff's Office. He made us look like fools that day.

"Penn?"

"I'll see you, John. Please let me know if you learn anything."

The FBI man watches me carefully as I walk away, headed for the corner that will lead me to my car.

"Hey!" he calls. "Don't you have a bodyguard?"

"Tim's with the girls. I'll text him to meet me at the car."

"Are you carrying?"

The reassuring weight of my pistol rides my left ankle as I walk. "Never without it now."

Kaiser nods, then sends me off with a mock salute.

I DO TEXT Tim, but not to meet me at my car. I tell him that I'll be busy with Kaiser for some while, and that I want him to take Mia and Annie back home for the time being. As his reply comes in, I spy Jamie Lewis, the editor of the *Natchez Examiner,* about twenty feet from my Audi, walking toward the hospital.

"Jamie!" I call.

He waves and approaches me. "I've been on the phone with Caitlin's father. He's going to up the security for all of us. He's flagellating himself for not doing it sooner."

I can't imagine what kind of agony John Masters must be putting himself through over this attack.

"Seeing Keisha like that is going to kill her brother," Jamie says.

"The Auburn football player? You know him?"

"I met both her brothers at an Alabama football game. Roosevelt Harvin isn't a guy you forget. He played defensive tackle. The oldest brother didn't play college ball, but the dad played at Mississippi Valley State."

"Are they coming to Natchez?"

Jamie nods. "The brothers are. The dad's sick, apparently. They should be here late tonight. Early tomorrow morning at the latest."

"This is going to be so bad. She may die, Jamie."

His face goes pale. "What?"

"It has to do with the type of acid. It screws up your calcium and causes potentially fatal systemic problems."

"Oh . . . fuck, man."

"I'm sorry to be the one to tell you. Look, I need to get going."

I start to leave, but Jamie appears to be in shock. He's shaking his head like I've just told him the world is about to end.

"Keisha's special," he says. "You know? Fearless. Pure. Somebody's going to pay for hurting that girl, I'm telling you."

"If they ever find out who did it."

"I'm not talking about the cops."

"Don't talk crazy," I tell him, echoing Kaiser.

"I'm not talking about myself. I mean her brothers."

I shake my head. "That wouldn't help Keisha any. But take it from me, as a former prosecutor. Relatives swear they're going to kill the perps in these situations all the time, but they almost never do."

"Really? Why is that?"

The fifteen years of difference between the newspaper editor and me suddenly seems an eternity. "Because the terrible truth is, all anyone accomplishes by doing that is getting himself sent to prison. I've seen it happen."

Jamie thinks about this. "Well. I hope that's enough to settle the Harvin brothers down. But I wouldn't count on it. Are you coming back later?"

"I'll be back. You keep your eyes open, Jamie. Your name's on the website, too."

The editor nods, then sets off again, slowly meandering toward the hospital entrance.

Climbing into my Audi, I start the engine, then switch on the AC and sit with my face near the central vents until my skin feels cold.

Will Keisha Harvin ever feel that again? I wonder.

Closing my eyes, I reach out and turn on the CD player by touch. Soon the cabin fills with "*Capriccio Primo,*" a solo cello piece played to perfection by Elinor Frey. As she bows the heavy strings, my pulse slows and my blood pressure falls. But deep within me, something like a motor has begun spooling up. I recognize the feeling now, from the day I heard Caitlin speaking from the grave, on the last recording she made before she died.

The day I killed Forrest Knox.

As the end of the piece approaches, I open my eyes, reset the track, and put the car in reverse. *Don't talk crazy,* I told Jamie Lewis. But giving advice is a lot easier than taking it. Sometimes to move forward, we have to go back first.

I'M PARKED OUTSIDE the Kuntry Kafé, the seedy diner where last December I confronted Randall Regan, who after our conversation ambushed me in the restroom. I don't remember driving here. I do remember crossing the river, looking down at the muddy, majestic current of the Mississippi moving slowly toward Baton Rouge, New Orleans, and finally the great dead zone in the Gulf that lies off the mouth of America's largest sewage canal. The warm spring sun made the river look red, and the ethereal cello coming from my speakers held my darker thoughts at bay as I rolled over the bumpy span joining Mississippi and Louisiana.

Unlike the stylish villains' lairs portrayed in Hollywood thrillers, the dens of some of the most evil men in the world are surprisingly mundane. Carlos Marcello, the Mafia don who ruled New Orleans for decades, regularly met his minions in the Morning Call Coffee Stand in Metairie, one table away from silver-haired matrons having their morning café au lait. In the 1960s, the Double Eagle group met daily in the little restaurant of the Shamrock Motel in Vidalia. And according to John Kaiser, some of the old Double Eagle members still hang out in the Kuntry Kafé, which is the dining appendage of the Kuntry Inn, and not far from the old Shamrock. The diner is clearly a cousin of its predecessor, but it's a dump, stinking of grease and sour milk.

I wonder if there are still Christmas bells hanging from the door . . .

If I were prudent, I would have asked Tim Weathers to meet me here, or Kirk Boisseau. But if they were here, they would limit my options. Unlocking my glove box, I take out the Springfield nine millimeter I keep there and shove it into my waistband, then pull out my shirttail so it hangs over the butt. With this addition I feel less naked than I would have with only the .38 on my ankle.

Five more seconds of the cello sets me up just right.

With the cooling fan of my Audi still running, I get out and walk up to the glass door. The diner is mostly empty, but three old men and a long-haired blond kid sit mumbling over mugs of beer at the back table.

One of the men is Will Devine. They look up as I yank open the door, but they say nothing. As I move toward them, the blond kid stands and squares up to me like he means to fight. My shirttail still hangs over the butt of my Springfield, but I figure the old men at the table picked out the concealed weapons within two seconds of seeing me.

"Look here, boys," says one of the white-haired men, a wiry old guy who reminds me of the deceased Sonny Thornfield. "We got the mayor of Natchez paying us a visit. To what do we owe the honor, Mayor?"

Earl Tarver, says the lawyer in my mind. *Double Eagle, born 1936. Which makes him sixty-nine years old . . .*

"Yeah," says another man with a grin. My memory offers up a second name: *Buddy Garland.*

Will Devine says nothing. He's staring down into his beer mug.

"I think he's come over for an ass-whippin'," says the blond kid, who is two inches shorter than I but has twenty years of youth to his advantage. With his light blue eyes, he looks like a recruiting poster for the Hitler *Jugend.*

Earl Tarver's eyes travel up and down my body, then settle on my face. "Ease up, Alois. You don't want to tangle with the mayor today. He's got his dander up."

"Like I give a fuck."

"Look at his hands," Tarver said.

I don't look, but I can feel my hands quivering.

"Sit down, Alois," Tarver commands.

The boy reluctantly obeys, his eyes electric with hatred.

"What you want, Mayor?" Tarver asks. "Where's your buddy, the FBI agent?"

When I don't answer, Tarver says, "That Kaiser got his nose rubbed in it by his boss, didn't he? After that fuckup at the Concordia jail back in December, I ain't surprised. I believe he told the Justice boys in Washington that Sonny was about to bust open every unsolved case left over from the Klan years. And then"—Tarver snaps his fingers with a pop—"Sonny went and hung hisself. Ain't that somethin'? Couldn't stand the guilt, I reckon. Turning traitor will do that to a man."

I look slowly around the café. The only other patron is a thin, pale-skinned man in a booth in the back corner. He has black hair and he's wearing a leather jacket with the letters VK visible on the arm I can see.

"I'm here because somebody threw acid in a young woman's face today," I say, my eyes still on the biker. "Blinded her."

Nobody at the table looks surprised.

"Is that right?" asks Tarver. "What girl was that?"

"Nigger gal, I heard," says Garland. "Nosy gal who worked for the Natchez paper."

"That really why you're here?" Tarver asked. "You running interference for the colored now? That what they pay the mayor for on your side of the river?"

I fix my eyes on Tarver's. "Your old boss killed somebody that meant a lot to me."

He sniffs and looks at his compatriots. "I think he's talking about that newspaper publisher."

Garland snorts a laugh and ducks his head in agreement, a grin on his face. "His old lady, Earl."

"I heard a nigger done that, too," Tarver goes on. "A poacher from down in Lusahatcha County. Found him dead behind a crack house in Baton Rouge, didn't they?"

Garland lifts his mug and drains half the beer in it. "Yup. One less to worry about."

While these comments ricochet around my neurons, I draw the Springfield from my belt, pull back the slide, and lay the barrel against the comedian's temple.

"Say that again, Mr. Garland."

Devine's chair scrapes the floor as he shoves back from the table and gets to his feet, wheezing from the effort. The kid looks like he wants to jump me, but Tarver just laughs and says, "Damn, I wish I had a camera."

"I got one on my cell phone," says the blond kid.

"Don't worry, Buddy," Tarver says calmly. "Cage won't shoot. He's the fuckin' mayor."

"Don't do nothin', Alois," says the man with the pistol against his head. "Don't *touch* your phone. Please."

"He ain't gonna shoot," Tarver insists. "Take the picture, Alois. If we get a picture of this, Sheriff Dennis will have to throw him in jail. It'll be front page news."

As the blond kid digs into his pocket, the empirical reality of the situation finally registers in my brain. Tarver *wants* me to shoot. The life of the man at the end of my gun barrel means nothing when weighed against the prospect of me sitting on death row in Angola Penitentiary—which is where I'll wind up if I kill a man on this side of the river.

As the blond kid holds up his cell phone, I lower the gun and take the empty chair at the table, concealing the gun below its Formica surface.

"I came over here to tell you guys something," I say softly.

"What you waitin' for?" asks Tarver.

"Snake sent me a message about three weeks back. Through a biker. He said, 'Wives and children have no immunity.'"

The old man squints as though laboring to understand the words. "That don't sound like Snake to me."

"Yes, it does. It sounds like all you fuckers. I know you, Tarver. You're the kind of backshooting coward that stands in the dark and executes a man who's lying in a hospital bed, or throws a cup of acid into a young girl's face. You're the kind of shithead who kills an old lady who remembers being raped by you back when you could still get it up."

Tarver's head jerks at that, and his eyes fill with hatred.

"Oh, yeah," I tell him. "I know all about that machine shop."

Will Devine swallows audibly.

"But the thing is," I go on, "guys like you and Snake, the ones who did the beatings and killings back in the sixties? You were nothing but pawns in the hands of the rich boys. White trash. Flunkies. In the grand scheme of things, you were only one cut above a nigger yourself. That's why civil rights scared you so bad. You talked loud and wore your bedsheet proud, but if you ever really got out of line—or got ideas above your station—the boss in the big house would trim your wick so fast your head would spin."

The blond kid looks like he's about to have a stroke, but the truth of my words is written on the faces of the older men.

"My dad started as poor as every one of you," I go on. "But he worked his way up and out. Now, sure, I'm the one living in the big house on the high side of the river. But I've never forgotten where I came from."

I hear a siren in the distance. *Did a cook in the back dial 911?*

"Cops on the way," says Alois, an edge in his voice.

"Just say your piece and get the fuck out," Tarver mutters.

Sliding the Springfield from beneath the table, I lay it flat on the

Formica in front of me, the barrel pointed at Tarver's belly, my finger on the trigger.

"Back during the Civil War in Tennessee, there was a man named Jack Hinson. Came from Highland Scots stock. Hinson tried as hard as he could to stay out of the war. But one day, a Union patrol killed two of his sons, then had the heads mounted on Hinson's gateposts. After that, Hinson had a special rifle made. Then he went to war against the Union army. He killed the lieutenant who murdered his boys first. But before he was through, he killed more than a hundred soldiers."

The old men are watching me with rapt attention; this is the kind of story they would normally love.

"The point is, I come from Highland Scots stock on my mother's side. And if the girl who got acid thrown in her face today had been my little girl . . . I wouldn't have walked in here like I did. I wouldn't have sat down to talk. I'd have walked in and shot you in the face."

Tarver blinks slowly, appraising my words.

I look next at Garland, then Will Devine. The fat man looks afraid.

"Then I'd have shot these two. Center mass while they were still pissing themselves. And no jury within five miles of Natchez would convict me."

The old men are watching Tarver now.

"Aren't you the badass all of a sudden?" Tarver says softly.

"Why don't you ask Forrest Knox that question?"

The old Double Eagle's mouth drops open.

"Let me fuck him up, Earl," says the blond kid. "Let me cut him."

Suppressing the urge to smash the heavy Springfield against the kid's skull, I stand and back slowly to the door. The siren is louder now.

"Remember what I said about my little girl. And make sure Snake gets the message."

My last image is Will Devine's face, white with fear, and behind it, the tall man in the leather jacket speaking into a cell phone. Reaching behind me, I open the door and walk swiftly to my car, then drive back up to the bridge over the Mississippi, the cello slowly pulling me earthward, stemming the tide of endorphins rushing through my blood and brain.

The man I was six months ago would never have done what I just did.

That man is dead now.

Maybe this is what it means to be born again.

CHAPTER 8

TWO HUNDRED MILES from Natchez, just north of Sulphur, Louisiana, lay a thriving sod farm that ten years earlier had been a struggling horse farm. Being that Sulphur was one of the most polluted places in America, with twelve chemical plants pumping out toxic by-products twenty-four hours a day, the horses hadn't done too well, so the owners had sold out to a nice fellow with a ponytail from Beaumont, Texas. That fellow was Lars Dempsey, founder of the VK motorcycle club.

Dempsey rarely brought club members to the sod farm, which he operated as a legitimate front business. When he did bring them, they weren't allowed to ride their hogs in, or even to wear their jackets. This was because the fifty-nine-acre complex sometimes served as a storage and distribution depot for the VK's meth and gun-running operations.

What had drawn Snake Knox to the sod farm was not only its relative isolation, but the fact that it had an airstrip. Parked out on that airstrip now was an Air Tractor crop duster, probably the least suspicious aircraft in the American South. Its tiny cockpit could hold only a pilot, which suited Snake down to the ground. If he had to make a quick getaway, he didn't have to worry about taking anybody with him. And anywhere he flew between Texas and South Carolina—or even to Mexico—cops would assume he was only a crop duster ferrying his plane to a job.

Just now, though, Snake didn't plan on flying anywhere.

He'd traveled a long way to get to this place, modest as it was; six different countries in eleven weeks, and none particularly enjoyable. Andorra had been the best of them, mainly because that had been the original emergency sanctuary set up by Forrest. Billy was still living there and grateful for every bit of luxury and security that Forrest's planning had provided. But Snake had no intention of lolling around a

French-Swiss tax haven with a bunch of expatriate millionaires. He'd actually felt happier when he was sneaking through Honduras on a third-rate fake passport bought in Mexico. For him, every place he'd been through had been but a waypoint on his journey back home.

The reason was simple: unfinished business.

That was why he was sitting on a tall kitchen stool in front of a mirror while Junelle Crick, one of the VK "mamas," worked on him with an arsenal of beauty salon chemicals that smelled fouler than some of the poisons Snake used to spray on summer cotton.

Well past fifty, Junelle sported fried blond hair, bright red lipstick, and dark blue eye shadow, and she had a Salem Menthol 100 perpetually hanging from her bottom lip. She had pendulous breasts, a flat butt, a round paunch, and wore stretch pants. Snake couldn't have felt any more at home if he'd been in Vidalia.

Junelle had set a piece of poster board in front of the mirror so that Snake couldn't see himself until she had finished her makeover. While she tortured his eyebrows with tweezers, Snake reflected on the past three months.

With epic daring he'd brought down an FBI jet loaded with evidence against the Double Eagles. Then, despite relentless pursuit by the FBI, he had held the gang together and silent. One of his most effective moves had been to kill Silas Groom and frame him for the downing of the jet. Groom's death had shaken every living Eagle, each of whom had assumed that old Silas had been betraying the group by ratting to the FBI. Frank would have been proud of Snake for that one.

More impressive still, in the midst of a crackdown by Colonel Griffith Mackiever's Louisiana State Police, Snake had managed to forge an alliance with one of the most feared and powerful motorcycle clubs in Texas and Louisiana. He'd done this by offering the VK access to Forrest's network of corrupt cops and judges. Snake could only offer that protection because he'd salvaged and maintained enough of the Eagles' meth trade to keep paying about a third of Forrest's network. That had been a tough trick. The files discovered in Forrest's Baton Rouge storage unit had resulted in several statewide investigations, some into district attorneys and judges. Snake had held on to a handful of DAs by blackmail rather than continued bribery, but all that mattered was he still had them.

Still, it was a dangerous game to play. The VK naturally wanted the name of every contact at once; so far Snake had managed to dole out a few at a time. But the endgame was inevitable. Once the bikers had all those precious contacts, they wouldn't need him anymore.

Snake did have some genuine support within the VK ranks. Some of the older members treated him like a rock-and-roll star. The JFK story had obviously made the rounds, and this earned a lot of respect among the guys who remembered the 1960s.

"All right, hon," Junelle said, stepping back from the stool. "You ready?"

Snake nodded. "Let's see the damage."

When she yanked the poster board away, Snake didn't recognize himself in the mirror. His long white rat's nest was gone, replaced by perfectly trimmed black hair combed straight back from his face. And Junelle hadn't stopped at his scalp. She'd dyed his eyebrows, too. Combined with the new dentures Snake had bought off an Indian dentist up in Shreveport, the total effect was stunning. A complete transformation.

Snake whistled long and loud. "I'll be damned. I look like Ronald Reagan at the Neshoba County Fair."

"Better, darlin'," croaked Junelle, sending ash floating from the tip of her cigarette onto his lap. She snipped an errant hair above Snake's left ear. "Did Reagan go to the Neshoba Fair?"

Snake turned around on the stool. "Did he *go* there? Baby doll, when Reagan first ran for president, he got up on a platform five miles from Philadelphia, Mississippi, and gave a talk about states' rights. Summer of 1980, and I was there. He put it right in their faces, boy. States' rights, and the hole where they buried them three civil rights workers not a stone's throw away. The country responded, too. They knew what he was talkin' about. Nobody left like Reagan these days. No, sir. Or it don't seem like, anyway."

"Well," Junelle said, her head tilted to one side as she assessed her handiwork. "I think you may be my masterpiece."

Snake gazed into the mirror like a septuagenarian Narcissus. "I'll be dogged," he marveled. "If those Arabs are as good with passports as you are with hair dye, I might just buy me an antebellum home in the middle of Natchez and sit on my veranda all day sippin' bourbon."

"I'm not sure I'd try that."

"I might, though," Snake murmured. "I *just might*. After my book advance comes in, that is."

He felt his newest burner phone buzz in his pocket. Getting to his feet, he took out the phone and clapped it to his ear.

"Yeah?"

"It's Toons."

Terry "Toons" Teufel was the SA, or sergeant at arms, of the VK motorcycle club. Snake didn't trust the man—who seemed like a nut job—but under the present circumstances he had no choice but to rely on him for protection.

"Yeah," Snake said again.

"I think we got a problem."

"I'm listening."

Ever attuned to the needs of the men around her, Junelle signaled that she was going into the kitchen so Snake could have some privacy.

"The splash went perfectly today," Toons said.

"That don't sound like a problem."

"But an hour later, somebody showed up at the Kuntry Kafé with a hard-on for you and your buddies."

"Who? That FBI man, Kaiser?"

"No. The doctor's boy. The mayor."

Snake went still. If he remembered right, Penn Cage had faced off with Randall Regan in the Kafé. "Is that right?"

"Yeah. I had a guy in there, sitting in the corner booth. Cage walked in with a pistol and held it to one of your guys' heads."

Snake tried out a couple of different expressions in the mirror. When he scowled, he looked like a banker who'd missed a putt on the eighteenth green. "And?"

"One of your guys told him, 'Ain't you a badass all of a sudden.' Then the mayor said something that you might be interested in."

"Which was?"

"He said, 'Why don't you ask Forrest Knox that question?'"

Snake went still. As he stared blankly into the mirror, acid flooded into his belly. He suddenly looked like a clown to himself.

"You need to dump your phone after using that name," he said in a monotone. "And I gotta dump this one."

"Relax, man. That's what we use 'em for."

"Don't fuckin' tell me when to relax."

"Take it easy, pops. Look, I'm gonna be comin' by soon. You and me got something to talk about."

"News to me."

"I'm gettin' tired of waitin' on those names you promised us."

Snake kept his voice cool. "You'll get 'em when I said you'll get 'em. Not an hour before."

"We need 'em now, Knox. We got guys coming up for trial in St. Tammany Parish. One in St. Landry, too."

"Talk to Lars. He'll set you straight."

"I'm always talkin' to Lars. He told me I should ask you about it. The names, man."

"*After* you've fulfilled your half of the bargain. That's when you get 'em. Then and only then. That's the deal. I'm hangin' up now."

"Wait. That woman of yours, the one who did the splash? She wants to come to where you're at."

"Tell her forget it. Nobody comes here. Not till the new passports come in. She's gotta stick to the rules like everybody else."

"That's what I told her. But her and that boy of yours don't seem to care much for rules."

"Are you saying you can't handle them?"

"I'm saying if I have to handle that boy, don't bitch at me if you have to pay to have him fed through a tube for the rest of his life."

Snake scratched at his hairline. The dye seemed to be irritating his scalp. "Do what you gotta do. But you'll want him around later, when the shootin' starts."

"I got plenty of gun hands, Grandpa."

Snake laughed softly. "Alois is more than a gun hand. He's a mechanical genius. You'll see what I mean pretty soon."

"Yeah, yeah, I can't wait. I'm out."

Snake hung up. Then he switched off the cell phone, removed its SIM card, and dropped it in the bowl of hair dye Junelle had left on the nearby card table. As he looked down at the black fluid, Penn Cage's words echoed in his head: *Why don't you ask Forrest Knox that question?*

"Everything copacetic, Daddy?" Junelle asked, easing back into the room.

Snake looked into the mirror at the handsome stranger staring back at him. "What do you think about Toons, Junelle?"

She took a deep breath, then gave Snake a sidelong glance. "Just between you and me?"

He nodded.

"He's a mean son of a bitch. Paranoid. Which I guess is sort of his job. But Toons takes it too far, you ask me. He's a fuckin' psycho. The younger girls say he's sick in the bedroom, too. Which in this club is sayin' something."

"I'm a psycho, too, June-bug."

Junelle gave him a knowing grin. "Yeah, but you're my kind of psycho."

Snake gazed back into the mirror and forced a smile so that he could examine his new teeth. Damn, but they were white. Like Chiclets. Yeah . . . the new look would take some getting used to. He looked more like Brody Royal than himself.

"You okay, Daddy?" Junelle asked, lighting a fresh Salem with a kitchen match, then shaking it out and drawing deep on the cancer stick. "You look tense."

He grunted, turning left to examine his profile.

"You want me to suck it for you?" she asked, blowing out a long stream of blue smoke. "Take the edge off?"

Leaning away from the menthol cloud, Snake turned back to the glass, thinking about his unfinished business. *I wonder how far this face can take me? I wonder how close it can get me to Penn Cage—*

"Daddy?"

"Later," he snapped. "After dinner. Jesus."

"Okay, okay. Don't get pissy. I'm just tryin' to help."

He felt a flash of anger. "You wanna help?" He started to tell her to get the hell out, but upon reflection he unzipped his fly and hung his dick out instead. "Help."

Junelle laid her cigarette on the edge of the card table and dropped to her knees with a contented smile. *Hell,* he thought as he disappeared into her bright red mouth. *She's probably been doing that since she was thirteen. Happier sucking dick than doing anything else.*

While Junelle fulfilled her destiny, Snake thought about the Cage family.

CHAPTER 9

WHEN I GOT home, I told no one what I'd done at the Kuntry Kafé, but on my way into the house I told Tim Weathers to keep his men especially alert tonight. After the acid attack, my warning was redundant. On the orders of John Masters, Tim had already posted extra men outside. They'd come on a plane with eight others from Dallas, the contingent sent to guard the reporters of the *Natchez Examiner*. There's nothing like shutting the barn door after the horse has bolted.

Once more my family has been thrown into shock. Annie tried to put up a good front, but I saw right through it. By the time I got home they had heard through the rumor mill how serious Keisha's condition was. And they weren't the only ones receiving updates by text message. Mia's mother, Meredith Burke, called me and demanded that I release Mia from her employment and send her straight home. I didn't blame her one bit. The problem was, Mia refused to leave. I must admit I was glad, because if she'd simply left, Annie would have fallen to pieces. But obviously changes must be made. I invited Mrs. Burke—who has been a single mother for the past sixteen years—to come by our house and discuss the situation with me and John Kaiser about seven P.M.

An hour before she arrived, Drew Elliott stopped by and delivered six tubes of 2.5 percent solution of calcium gluconate, the only known treatment for hydrofluoric acid burns. I'd called Drew at his office and asked if he could get us enough for the girls to carry some at all times, and he was glad to do it. Watching him instruct them on how to use it brought home the danger like nothing else had. Drew answered several tough questions from Mia and Annie about Keisha's prognosis, then hugged them both and left.

I took that opportunity to discuss the possibility of moving one or both of them to another city, or even another country. I also raised the possibility of my going with them, though none of these options seemed practical. Where could Annie go that she would feel safe and secure? Not England. My sister, Jenny, is flying in for Dad's trial. My mother isn't about to leave Dad during this crisis. That leaves me to take Annie somewhere "safe." But can I flee Natchez while my father stands trial for murder and my mother walks a tightrope between hysteria and catatonic despair?

I voiced none of these concerns, of course. And despite the danger, Annie made it clear that she had no intention of leaving her home, especially while "Papa" was about to be tried for murder. Mia took her own counsel for some time before answering. Then she grasped my daughter's hand and said that Annie needed her, and she had no intention of abandoning her job. Since Mia is only twenty, I wasn't about to leave it at that. But when Kaiser arrived, he surprised me—and also Mia's mother—by telling us that the safest option, without question, was for Annie and Mia to remain where they were.

"You see, Mrs. Burke," Kaiser explained, "as unpleasant as the thought is, by working with this family for the past three months, Mia has already made herself a target. If she were to go home to your house, for example, what protection would she have? Here, she's got former Navy SEALS guarding her around the clock. Plus police patrols and some FBI protection. Even if she went back to Boston, she wouldn't be nearly as safe as she is here."

Meredith Burke began to sob quietly. Her daughter took her hand and squeezed it. "We'll be okay, Mom, really. Keisha had no protection this morning. But they guard us like the royal family."

"But when will this *end*?" asked her mother. "When Dr. Cage's trial is over? Or will it just go on?"

"If I have anything to do with it," Kaiser said, "the danger will end before the trial does. Jury selection begins Monday—four days from now—and the trial proper will be under way by Tuesday. Between you and me, I believe Dr. Cage's trial is going to function like a baited trap.

Snake Knox is the source of all this violence, and one way or another the trial is going to bring him to us. Once we have Snake, we'll roll up the rest without any problem."

Kaiser's plan sounded good, in theory. It was the execution I doubted. But I didn't raise my doubts then. What I wanted was to get Annie and Mia safely and peacefully into bed.

After I'd accomplished that, I went down to my basement office and paced the floor for a while. On some level, I'd been expecting retaliation for my visit to the Kuntry Kafé—a drive-by shooting or Sheriff Billy Byrd's deputies pounding on the door with an arrest warrant. But either Earl Tarver had decided not to report what I'd done, or my friend Sheriff Walker Dennis had encouraged him not to make a fuss, because by ten P.M. nothing had happened. At eleven Tim Weathers texted me that everything outside was quiet.

Once I began to believe we were in the clear, I started to reflect on what I'd done after leaving Keisha in the ER. As potentially self-destructive as that confrontation was, it broke something loose in my congested soul, a dense impaction of hate, shame, and impotent rage that only action could remedy. This brought fresh clarity to my mind, and I found myself pondering the most puzzling mystery of the past three months—the location of Snake Knox. Unlike Kaiser, who seems willing to accept the proposition that Snake has fled these parts for a life of expatriate comfort, I'm convinced that, like any predator, the old Double Eagle could not bear to be away from his home territory for long.

Despite the hour, I picked up the house phone and called Carl Sims, my good friend and a deputy for the Lusahatcha County Sheriff's Department. I asked him to keep his eyes and ears open for the slightest sign of unusual activity down his way. The Knox family, while Louisiana natives, had become deeply embedded in Lusahatcha County, Mississippi, over the years, and I had no doubt there were dozens of people down there who would gladly shelter Snake from the FBI. More disturbing still, Carl's boss, Sheriff Billy Ray Ellis, had been a frequent guest at the Valhalla Exotic Hunting Reserve, and he wouldn't be particularly zealous in following up tips about Snake Knox sightings. Carl said he'd been thinking the same thing, but so far he'd had no luck along that line.

While I had him on the phone, I told the former marine sniper that my father had known a woman from Athens Point who lost her son to a lynching in Lusahatcha County in the mid-1960s. I didn't know her name, but her daughter-in-law had supposedly been raped the same night. She had ultimately committed suicide, but I hoped that if we could locate the mother, she might remember something damning about the Double Eagles—in particular Snake Knox. Carl told me he'd put his father on it. Reverend Sims knew everybody in Lusahatcha County, and if the woman was still around, he would know her. The question was, would he reveal what he knew?

I thanked Carl and hung up.

I was about to switch off the lights and go upstairs when my cell phone rang. When I looked at the LCD, I was surprised to see the name of my literary agent displayed there.

"Peter?" I said, after pressing SEND. "What in the world?"

"I'm sorry it's so late, Penn. I called to ask you a favor, and for someone else, if you can believe it."

"That doesn't sound like you."

He laughed. "I know, right? I assume you know who Serenity Butler is?"

Serenity Butler. "She's a black Mississippi writer. Nonfiction. Just won the National Book Award, right? For a memoir?"

"That's right. *The Paper Bag Test.* They sent you an ARC about a year ago, hoping for a blurb, but I don't think you got around to it."

"Things were pretty crazy around that time."

"I know. The reason I'm calling is, it turns out that Serenity was close to the reporter who was attacked in Natchez this morning."

"Keisha Harvin? Really?"

"Serenity teaches journalism at Emory in Atlanta. Apparently Harvin took two of her classes and really impressed her. The girl has been sending Serenity copies of every story she's written on the Double Eagle stuff."

"Okay."

"Anyway, the point is that Serenity is driving to Natchez tomorrow."

"What?"

"Yep. She's taken a leave of absence from Emory. She's coming back to Mississippi to find out what happened to Keisha and why. I know because her editor called me. She asked if I could set up a meeting between you two. I told her you were probably buried under the stress of the upcoming trial—"

"Shit. You think?"

"I know, I'm sorry. But my friend says Serenity is totally sincere in her feelings for this girl. And I tell you . . . I read her book. It's breathtaking."

This stopped me. I hadn't heard Peter Smith use language like that about a writer in a long time. While I ruminated over my answer, I walked to my bookshelf and scanned the bottom row, where I tend to stuff galleys sent by hopeful writers, agents, and editors. There it was.

The Paper Bag Test.

I bent and pulled the volume from the shelf. The galley had a plain white front with the title and author's name, but on the back was a color photo of a remarkably pretty black woman in her midthirties. She was light-skinned, about the color of a paper grocery bag, and her features proclaimed a provocative mixture of Caucasian and African blood. She had luminous eyes, even in the flat photograph, and her camera-ready looks made it hard to believe the bio beneath the photo, which stated that Corporal Serenity Butler had served as a line soldier for the U.S. Army in Iraq during Operation Desert Storm.

"Penn? Are you there?"

I swatted the galley against my thigh. "Yeah, Peter. I've got the ARC right here."

"Well. What should I tell them?"

"Tell them you couldn't reach me."

I heard him sigh in disappointment.

"I'll take a look at the book tonight and give you a call in the morning. Things are insane down here, you wouldn't believe it. But if I like what I read, I'll carve out fifteen minutes for her."

"Oh, man. That's great, Penn. I know you're going to love it."

"You're that certain?"

"She's a Mississippi girl, down to the bone. I can't believe you haven't met her before now."

"She's from Laurel, Peter. Other side of the state. Not a lot of interaction between Natchez and Laurel."

He said nothing for a few moments. "Are you sure that's it?"

I felt the sting of indignation. "What does that mean?"

"Nothing, bro. Just give me a call tomorrow. And I'm sorry things are so tough. I'm praying for your father."

"If you don't hear from me tomorrow, that's a no."

I hit END and walked over to the lamp beside my desk. I had told Peter the truth about Laurel. I know a hell of a lot of people from Mississippi, but I don't think I've ever known more than one from Laurel. Compared to Natchez, it's like another planet over there.

As I stare at Serenity Butler's photograph, Peter's voice echoes in my mind. *I read her book . . . It's breathtaking.*

I wasn't lying when I told Peter things had been crazy around the time I was sent this galley. But was that really why I never got around to reading it? Jealousy is a powerful and stubborn emotion, and maybe the literary buzz that began as soon as this new writer's manuscript began to circulate in New York had awakened that poisonous feeling in me. The critics had hailed Butler as a wunderkind, a raw new voice of realism on race, one that might someday rival that of Toni Morrison. That kind of hyperbole was sure to put off most veteran writers, and at forty-five, I am certainly a member of that club.

Almost resentfully, I flipped open the book, which revealed the dedication page. The dedication read: *For my mother, who died bringing me into this world; and my father, whoever he might be.*

I swallowed once, reread the lines, then turned the page.

I'm a big believer in first lines. If a writer doesn't grab you with their first sentence, even in a literary novel, they might need to think about another line of work. As my eyes sought out the first line of Serenity Butler's memoir, I realized she had a killer.

Not every child has a father, nor every mystery a solution.

When my eyes reached the period, I realized I wasn't breathing. In eleven words, Serenity Butler had reached through my chest wall and tapped her fingernail against my heart, like an archaeologist searching for an echo. As my eyes retraced the line, I backed over to my Eames lounge chair, collapsed into it, adjusted the lamp, and began to read.

FRIDAY

CHAPTER 10

KEISHA HARVIN'S BROTHERS arrived from Alabama in the small hours of Friday morning. Despite the time, John Kaiser arranged for them to see their sister in the St. Catherine's ICU. I didn't see the two brothers until later that morning, when I went to check on Keisha. Both were big men, but it was obvious which one had played defensive tackle for Auburn. Everything about Roosevelt Harvin was round: head like an oversized bowling ball, arms like anacondas, thighs like live oak trunks. The man's hands defied description: they weren't simply huge; he looked as if he could open the valve on a fire hydrant without a wrench. His brother, Aaron—who was maybe thirty—was big by conventional standards, but at least he fell within the normal frame of reference. He had a close-trimmed mustache and looked like a ladies' man.

When I saw the two of them standing over their sister's hospital bed, Roosevelt's big tears falling on the sheet beside Keisha's scarred face and taped-shut eyes, I had no idea what to say. After I quietly introduced myself, Aaron shook his head and said, "I'd cry, but I done cried all my water out."

"Look what they done to her, Mr. Cage," said Roosevelt, his hand on her upper arm. "Why they did that?"

My deepest fear was that Keisha's attackers had chosen her because they could not get to me or my family. But I couldn't bring myself to voice that here.

"They didn't like the stories she was writing."

"She was writing the truth, wasn't she?"

"These assholes don't like the truth. Pardon my language."

Roosevelt nodded.

Aaron said, "They killed your fiancée a few months back, huh? Keisha's boss?"

"That's right."

"I seen you got bodyguards around your family now. I met your little girl earlier this morning. I like her."

"Thank you. Yes, the Double Eagle group has made several death threats against us."

Both men stared at me for a while without speaking. Then Aaron said softly, "Keisha thought maybe after Ms. Masters got murdered, you, uh, maybe took things into your own hands. Killed that Knox fella. That dirty cop."

I looked back at them but acknowledged nothing.

"Li'l K didn't want to make a thing out of it," Aaron went on. "That's what we call her in the family, Li'l K. She said guy killed your fiancée, and if you'd wasted him, you was right to do it."

I communicated as much as I could to them without speaking.

Roosevelt nodded, then squinted and said, "The man who owns the newspaper don't pay no security for my baby sister?"

I felt my cheeks redden. "He paid for additional security at the paper, but he didn't cover all the reporters at home. I told my guys to watch out for Keisha when she left in the mornings, and most times she'd text them and say she was leaving. But yesterday she was running late and didn't text anybody."

"Sounds just like Li'l K," Aaron said. "Always in a hurry."

Roosevelt reached out with one of his enormous hands and gently patted his sister's leg. Then he looked up at me again. "Do you know who done this to Keisha, Mr. Cage?"

"I don't. Keisha said in the ER that a woman threw the acid, an older woman, but that's all she knew. Yesterday I went to a restaurant where some of the old Double Eagle guys hang out, and I got in their faces pretty good. Pulled my gun on them. But I don't think I accomplished much."

The two brothers shared a look. "How about you show us where that place is?" Aaron asked. "Maybe we'll get further than you did."

"I'm afraid you'll get yourselves thrown in jail."

"I been in jail before," Roosevelt said. "Ain't the end of the world."

"What about these motorcycle guys we hear been hangin' around town?" Aaron asked. "Keisha wrote about you and one of your guys shooting two of them a few weeks back. You think this was some kind of payback for that?"

Aaron Harvin spoke without rancor, but he sounded very familiar with the concept of payback.

"I'm afraid it could have been, yes. That's my deepest fear."

Both young men nodded sadly, but neither implied that their sister's present condition was my fault.

"If there's anything you guys need," I said helplessly, "anything I can do—"

"You can tell us where those crackers hang out at," Aaron said. "Ain't nobody else done no good around here, seems like. Might as well let us try."

So I told them what I knew. The three of us spoke softly across the sedated body of their sister, our voices barely audible amid the hum and beeping of the medical machines. After we finished, both men took hold of my hands, forming a rough circle over their sister.

"We gon' pray now," Roosevelt said. "Aaron, you do the talkin'."

When I left that ICU room, I had for the first time some small inkling of the guilt my father must feel over Caitlin's death. When I could stand the guilt no longer, I allowed a different feeling to rise and take its place. Dread. Dread, and pity for the people who committed that outrage upon Keisha Harvin. Standing joined in that prayer circle, my hands dwarfed by those of the Harvin brothers, I felt immeasurable fury seething within both men. No power on earth is going to stop Aaron and Roosevelt from making someone wish they had never taken it into their fevered brains to attack a vulnerable young woman trying to make her way in the world. Whether it's the Knox clan or some faction of the VK motorcycle club, they should consider themselves beneficiaries of divine deliverance if they live to be arrested by the FBI.

WHEN I GOT home from the hospital, I called Peter Smith and told him he could give Serenity Butler my cell number. After reading her memoir, I realized I had been an ass not to read it on the day I received it. I told Peter that Serenity could call me whenever she arrived, and we'd have coffee waiting for her at my house. Peter told me that would probably be after five, and he would update me if he learned anything more specific.

Mia and Annie overheard this call, and I thought nothing of it until Mia began to question me while Annie watched a DVD of *Grey's Anatomy* in the library.

"What's the story on Serenity Butler?" Mia asked, tapping away at her MacBook. "Google says she won the National Book Award last November."

"She did. For a memoir."

"Ever met her?"

"Nope."

"She's pretty." Mia rotated her computer so that I could see a shot of Serenity standing in front of a huge pine tree. "Like model pretty."

"I know. But in the book she explains how that's been more of a liability to her than an asset. In the army, and also when she was a little girl. It drew too much attention to her."

"This woman was in the army?"

"I know. It seems weird, doesn't it? She grew up dirt poor outside Laurel, Mississippi. Never knew her father. Her uncles were in the pulpwood business, which is a damn tough life. She enlisted to get money for college. She was in when the first Gulf War broke out. Served in both Kuwait and Iraq during Desert Storm. She saw a lot of stuff."

"Wow." For once, Mia looks impressed.

"The book is structured around her search for her father in Philadelphia, Pennsylvania. He was a white man."

"Obviously. Her mother never told her who her father was?"

"Her mother died in childbirth."

"Man. She's, like, out of Dickens or something."

"Alexandre Dumas, more like. It's an amazing story. Her mother hated Mississippi. She was ten years older than I am, born in 1950. Her name was Charity. Charity took off across the country when she was eighteen, aiming for California. She was in Kansas City during the riots after Martin Luther King was assassinated. She was in Los Angeles when Bobby Kennedy was killed. She even got involved with some Black Panther actions. She knew Bobby Hutton and Eldridge Cleaver."

"Who's Bobby Hutton?"

"The seventeen-year-old treasurer of the Black Panthers. He's dead. Shot by a cop in 1968. Anyway, after all that fell apart, Charity managed to get a music scholarship to an arts college in Philadelphia. She hitchhiked across the country and stayed there two years. Then she got pregnant by somebody—Serenity was never able to discover who—and rode a Greyhound back to Mississippi during her eighth month of pregnancy. She died from preeclampsia right after giving birth to Serenity."

"That definitely sounds worth a book. Was it more the story that won the award, or her writing?"

"Both, I'd say. Her writing's first-rate. She has an unbelievable eye for detail, and she's psychologically incisive as well. Ruthless, really, with both herself and others. But her life is the amazing thing. Apart from being a soldier, she's worked as a journalist, a teacher, a dancer, and a singer. She's been married twice, she kicked a drug problem . . . and she's only thirty-five."

"Any kids?"

"None mentioned in the book."

Mia is watching me with an appraising eye. "I don't think I've ever heard you this impressed with anybody before."

"It's the military service. Combat service."

"Why?"

"Well . . . guys in my generation got really lucky. We were too young for Vietnam, and by the time the next war rolled around, we were too old, unless you were already in the service."

"So?"

"Military service is a rite of passage for men. A big one. My father served in Korea. My mother's father and uncles fought in World War Two."

"I would think you'd be glad to miss the chance of getting killed or crippled."

"Sure—on one level. But it's not that simple."

A deep curiosity lights Mia's eyes. "Why not? Not some Hemingway trip, surely?"

I wonder if I can explain this to a twenty-year-old girl without sounding like a testosterone-driven idiot.

"I remember when Desert Shield was going on, the prep operation that led up to the first Gulf War. Things seemed rational enough. But then the bombs started falling on Baghdad, and everybody knew we were going to war for real—the first large-scale war since Vietnam. One night I was watching the news, and they ran a story on a female soldier who'd been ordered to ship out to the Gulf. They showed her at home with her family—a husband and two kids. Her children were crying, and her husband didn't know *what* to do. He was about to be living with two crying kids who missed their mother, and *she* was the one going off to fight. And . . . I don't know. Something welled up in me that I couldn't keep down. Tears came into my eyes, my throat closed up. Sarah grabbed my hand and asked me what was wrong. I jumped up out of my chair and said, 'By God, if they're shipping mothers over there to fight, something's *wrong*. I need to get over there.'"

"Are you serious?" Mia asked.

"You're damn right. When I saw that girl packing up to leave her kids behind, I was filled with shame. I felt an absolute conviction that it was time for me and every boy I'd grown up with to get a rifle and pair of boots and go take care of business."

"Jesus, Penn. That's a natural reaction, I guess. But also childish. You never trained as a soldier."

"Maybe not. But I know how to fight. And that wasn't George W's war, which was bullshit. It was the first one. Anyway, I guess on some level, when I was reading Serenity's book, I kept seeing that mother from that newscast."

"Was she black? The woman in the news story?"

"No, white."

Mia nodded but said nothing further. It was strange to realize that by suppertime we might be sitting at the table with the young celebrity on Mia's computer screen, a woman who has done far more dangerous—and traditionally masculine—things than I, a man ten years her senior.

"Well," Mia said finally, turning her computer back around. "I can't wait to see what all the fuss is about."

CHAPTER 11

WALT GARRITY WATCHED Tom Cage shuffle into the visiting room at the Pollock federal prison and carefully take a seat at the empty table. The two men said nothing at first. They didn't need to. They had survived the hell of Korea together. Heat, snow, VD, the Chinese coming over the wire in suicide waves . . . even the Bugout. Once you shared history like that, speech tended to be redundant.

"How you makin' it?" Walt asked finally.

"Can't complain," Tom said. "Beats a sleeping bag in forty below."

"Scraping ice out of the men's noses."

Tom chuckled. "Hypodermics taped under both armpits?"

"And your mouth full of morphine ampoules."

Tom lifted his arm to take in the prison visiting room. "Luxury by comparison."

Thirty seconds passed, during which Tom looked over at the window in the door to see if anyone was observing them.

"I'm glad to see you, Walt," he said finally. "Something happen?"

Walt shook his head. "Nothing on my end."

"Shit."

"Yeah. Is it safe to talk in here?"

Tom nodded. "Within reason."

"I heard about that colored reporter. The one who got acid thrown in her face yesterday."

"People don't say 'colored' anymore, Walt."

"Well, I do. Among friends, at least. No harm done. Anyway, it seems like an escalation. I'm afraid that acid attack is just the beginning of something."

"You and me both. Kind of puts teeth in Snake's message about wives and children."

Walt grunted. "That old boy makes it easy to pick a side, don't he?"

A shadow came into Tom's face. "Not for you. Not when the stakes are what they are."

"The stakes are what they always were, pardner."

"Walt. Carmelita wants you home, and don't try to sell me anything else. She feels lucky to have you, and you're damn lucky to have her. You keep this up for me, and you could get killed. You might not get home to her."

The old Texas Ranger sat in silence for half a minute. Then he said, "I reckon I'll stick a while longer."

"Walt—"

"I figure I owe it to you."

"You don't owe me a goddamn thing. We're even. We've been even since Korea. We each of us saved the other."

Walt smiled in a way that cut right through Tom's assertion. "No, sir. When we escaped from that Chinese patrol, you should have left me behind."

"*Left* you? Go to hell, Garrity."

"You know I'm right. My leg was broke. I couldn't walk for shit. If you hadn't carried me down that mountain, I'd have spent the past fifty years buried in North Korea."

"Well. Whatever you think you owe me, you paid off last December, with change to spare."

Walt shook his head. "Maybe that's not even it now. Sometimes during the long nights, I get to thinking about Knox and his bunch. They've outlived their time, you know? We have that in common with them. And I think maybe they're our burden to bear. Our evil to deal with."

Tom nodded. "I can't argue with that. But we haven't exactly done a bang-up job so far."

"Sometimes it takes a while to stir a rattlesnake out of his hole. Sometimes you gotta smoke him out."

"I thought Penn was going to do that for us."

"Give it time, buddy."

Tom winced in pain as he shifted on the chair. "I don't know how much time we have. My trial starts in three days."

Walt tapped his fingernails on the table. "I look for something to happen before then. But I tell you, things would be a damn sight easier on me if I could tell Penn what I'm doing. I wouldn't have to spend so much time hiding from him and his bodyguards."

Tom thought about this for a while. Then he said, "No. Penn can't know about this. First, he's got to be able to deny all knowledge. Second . . . the people he's talking to might sniff it on him."

Walt squinted at his old friend. "Are you sure that's it? Or do you just not want to tell your son he's playing bait?"

Tom's face hardened. "This is war. You know that."

Garrity held up his hands. "Let's not plow the same field twice. I'm just making sure you face this straight-on."

"Don't worry about that. Look, are you sure you haven't noticed anything? *Sensed* anything?"

"Not even a rustle in the tall grass."

"But you're ready?"

Walt didn't bother to answer this.

"You're settled with it, I mean. In your soul?"

Walt stretched his creaky frame, then looked back at the window in the door. "Believe it or not, I talked to Carmelita about it."

Tom blinked in disbelief.

"Don't worry about her," Walt said. "She saw some rough stuff in Juarez before she moved up here."

"What did Carmelita say?"

"She talked to her brother. He's a priest down there still."

"Jesus, Walt—"

"He's a priest, goddamn it. He can't say nothing. Anyway, Carmelita told him a bit about the Knox family history."

"And?"

"He quoted some scripture, but I can't remember the exact words. What it came down to was this: in a just war, certain things are permitted."

"Would he call this a just war, I wonder?"

"Given the facts he knew, he did. He gave me his blessing."

"Well, I'm glad to hear it." Tom rubbed his forehead, then said, "*Damn,* I'd give my left arm for a cigar."

Walt smiled. "Can't help you there, bud. Got some chaw in the truck."

"God forbid." Tom looked over at a cabinet mounted to the wall. "How about a game of gin?"

Walt grinned. "Penny a point?"

CHAPTER 12

BY THE TIME our doorbell rings at 6:35 P.M., Annie and Mia have combed through everything available on the Internet about Serenity Butler, including a video of her acceptance speech for the National Book Award. They're particularly excited that she spoke fondly of Mississippi rather than trashing it, which would have been easy for a black writer to do.

When I answer the door, I find Tim Weathers standing beside one of those rare authors who looks like her jacket photo come to life. Serenity's eyes hold a steady light, and her smile is quick and broad. She's wearing jeans and a white tank top, and her hair is gathered in a low ponytail at the back of her neck. She might be a little thinner than in her photograph, but her arms are full and muscular.

"You guys have some serious security here," she observes, sticking out her hand. "Tee Butler."

I recognize the nickname from reading her memoir. Shaking her strong hand, I pull her into the house. Tim Weathers gives me a wink as I shut the door.

"After what happened to Keisha," I say, by way of explanation.

"Oh, I get it. I wasn't criticizing."

"My daughter and a friend are in the kitchen. They can't wait to meet you."

"Great," Serenity says, following me down the hall.

I lead her into the kitchen, where Mia and Annie stand like the children in *The Sound of Music* waiting to be presented to the baroness.

"Annie, Mia, this is Serenity Butler. Serenity—"

"Hey, Annie," Serenity says, stepping forward and giving my daughter a high five. The writer glances back at me. "I saw who was who by the timing of their smiles." Serenity turns to Mia and points at the T-shirt she's wearing. "UCA, huh? You a cheerleader?"

"Used to be," Mia says awkwardly.

"Me, too. Waaay back. Hey, I know 'Serenity' is a mouthful, okay? My friends call me 'Tee' for short. Why don't you guys call me that?"

"Tee," Annie says, testing the name. "That's cool."

"In South Louisiana 'Tee' means 'little,'" Mia says. "They use it instead of 'Junior.'"

"You mean like 'Tee Neg' or 'Tee Jean'?" Serenity laughs. "You got people from South Louisiana?"

Mia's blushing now. "Some cousins."

"Me, too. But my 'Tee' is just a diminutive."

The conversation falters for a few seconds, and in that span I notice a keloid scar a little in front of Serenity's left ear—a dark, U-shaped ridge at the hinge of her jawbone, about the size of a half-dollar. It's not a bad one, but most women would try to minimize it with makeup. Yet Serenity leaves it exposed for the world to see. Since keloids are characteristic of African-Americans, perhaps she uses the scar as a badge to confirm her race beyond doubt? As I wonder about this, I realize I'm not the only one staring at our visitor's face. Mia is gazing at Serenity as though confused by something.

"Mia," I say softly.

Mia snaps out of her trance and blushes even deeper red.

"It's okay," Serenity says. "When you title your book 'The Paper Bag Test,' once people find out what it means, they all stare."

"What's the paper bag test?" Annie asks.

Serenity smiles patiently. "In the black community, back in the day, people with lighter skin tones were looked at as higher on the social scale."

"By white people or black people?"

"Both. But it was black people who created the test. It started down in New Orleans. If you were going to an exclusive party, or thinking about joining a sorority, say, they would hold up a paper bag by your face and check your skin shade. If you were lighter than the paper bag, you were considered suitable. If you were darker, you didn't get in."

"Gyahh," Annie says. "That sucks."

"You said it. And I'm exactly the color of the average bag. Which caused me no end of problems. When you live on a borderline, nothing's ever easy. Sometimes I was in the cool group, sometimes I was untouchable. I got to know both sides."

"That's kind of cool, actually," Mia says. "For a writer, I mean."

"I guess," Serenity concedes. "But for a young girl trying to find her way, it sucked."

Annie laughs, proud of having chosen the proper description of Serenity's plight.

To change the subject, I say, "So, you taught Keisha in college?"

"As an undergrad. She had a lot of fire in her, even then."

"Keisha's so awesome," Annie says. "She isn't afraid of anything."

Serenity smiles with her mouth closed, but I can read her response in her eyes. *That's probably not true anymore.*

"Okay, guys," I say, clapping my hands to punctuate the end of this exchange, "Serenity and I are going down to my office. I'm going to give her some background on Natchez and the Double Eagles."

The disappointment in their faces contains more than a little resentment, but I'll have to endure it. Annie's not ready for the conversation Serenity and I are likely to have.

MY BASEMENT OFFICE suite is centered around a twenty-by-twenty room, with brick pillars replacing a load-bearing wall I removed during the remodel. Two doors lead off to rooms I use for storage, printers, and the like, but now those rooms have cots in them, for the security guys to catch naps when they need them.

"Thanks for being so nice to Annie," I say as Serenity walks to the bookshelves that line one wall and begins perusing spines.

"I like her," Serenity says. "She look like her mother?"

"Spitting image," I confirm, but I add nothing more on that subject. "I read your book last night."

"Yeah?" She looks back over her shoulder at me. "What'd you think?"

"Honestly? I was stunned. I didn't expect that kind of mastery in a first book."

Serenity moves slowly down the row of books, dragging a forefinger along the spines. "What was your favorite line?"

Not many writers would ask this. Is she testing me? To see whether I really read her book?

"There were lots of good lines. True insights. One of my favorites was something your uncle said. The one they called Catfish? About how being from Mississippi makes you different."

She smiles. "Mississippi blood. That part?"

"That's it."

A distant fondness comes into Serenity's eyes, and she quotes her uncle word for word: *"I been all over the South, man. Cutting pulpwood and playing the blues. Mississippi blood is different. It's got some river in it. Delta soil, turpentine, asbestos, cotton poison. But there's strength in it, too. Strength that's been beat but not broke. That's Mississippi blood."*

"That says it, right there," I tell her. "'Beat but not broke.'"

"It's a lot more poetic than 'Mississippi exceptionalism.'"

We share a laugh, and somehow this mutual appreciation of our common history banishes the awkwardness of being alone without really knowing each other.

"You remind me of another writer," I tell her. "He's not from the South, but he had a black father and a white mother."

"James McBride?"

"How did you know?"

She clucks her tongue once. "A lot of people say that. If McBride wasn't so damned good, I'd be offended."

"Because my first point of comparison is a mixed-race writer, and not just Carson McCullers or Eudora Welty?"

"Of course. But I get it. I'm not naïve."

"It was McBride's prose I was thinking of. The gift for detail."

"You don't have to dig yourself out of a hole."

"I wasn't . . . shit, okay."

Serenity stops her slow progress along the shelf and takes out a volume by Shelby Foote. She looks at the title page, then slides it back in.

"So how does it feel to win the National Book Award?" I ask.

"Pretty damn good, I won't lie. How does it feel to sell millions of books?"

"Not bad." We share another laugh. "Maybe we all want what we don't have," I suggest.

"Touché."

At last she turns away from the bookshelf and sits down in the Eames chair where I read her galley last night. After testing the cushion, she lifts her shapely legs onto the ottoman and crosses them.

"I guess you're wondering what I'm doing here, right? Natchez, I mean."

"Well . . . you're friends with Keisha."

"I am. But that's not all of it. Maybe not even most of it. I want to get justice for Keisha, yes. But I'm really here because of the larger story."

"Which story, exactly?"

Her dark eyes focus on mine to the exclusion of all else. "Your story. Or your family's. Your father and Viola. Does that surprise you?"

"Ah . . . yes. A little."

"Keisha's been sending me her stuff all along. Since before your fiancée was murdered. And I see a lot of parallels with my mother's story in the relationship between Viola Turner and your father. And I see myself in Lincoln Turner, of course."

"I can see that, at least in the abstract. But in your book, you made it sound like you'd put your quest for identity behind you. 'Not every mystery has a solution,' you said."

Serenity's gaze moves off of me. "Right. Well, on that point . . . there's been a development."

"What kind of development?"

"A candidate has come forward. For my paternity."

This is the last thing I expected to hear. "Who is he?"

"A retired art professor in Philadelphia. He's sixty-nine years old. He's already offered to take a DNA test. I'm pretty sure he's the guy."

She's speaking with cool detachment, but I don't buy it. "How do you feel about that?"

"I'm not sure. He just contacted me last week. You read my book. I spent a lot of time up in Philadelphia, trying to trace who my father was. And I actually talked to this guy. He wasn't one of my main candidates, but I did interview him. He denied even remembering my mother. I knew she'd been in one of his classes, I had the records. But he claimed he'd taught too many students to remember individuals."

Having seen a photo of Charity Butler inside Serenity's book, I doubted this. "Even those as striking as your mother? Doesn't sound like any professor I ever had."

Serenity clucks her tongue again, this time making it sound like a guilty sentence from a judge. "Exactly."

"So why the change of heart after all this time?"

"Two reasons. First, his wife died."

"Ahh. And the second?"

"Come on. I just won the National Book Award. I'm famous."

"And he's an academic." I shake my head in disgust. "He wants the world to know that half your genes came from him."

"You got it, Mayor. No heart involved. It's all ego."

"Well, what are you going to do?"

"Haven't made up my mind. I don't really like the guy. But I suppose I want to see whether I can recognize what my mother saw in him. I didn't the first time."

"What about your own connection to him? Your future?"

Serenity's mouth twists with deep displeasure. "That man's not my father. My grandparents raised me. My aunts. Uncle Catfish. I don't plan to get warm and fuzzy with my sperm donor."

Sensing deeper anger in her voice, I decide to change the subject.

"That thing your uncle used to say about Mississippi blood. The strength in it. 'Beat but not broke.' Do you think he was only talking about black people?"

My question proves sufficient to distract her. "I asked him that once," she says. "Catfish actually liked white folks, especially the working people. He thought they'd been manipulated by the moneyed class to resent blacks, but he respected their honesty. Said he always knew where he stood with white southerners, that they always lived up to their word. Uncle Catfish never trusted Yankees. He was like Charles Evers that way."

"And James Brown."

"There you go. Now, Catfish *did* say that Mississippi had always bred a special strain of asshole. The Ross Barnett types. We've still got a few of those around, I think."

"Especially up at the state capitol. Hypocrisy is their wardrobe of choice."

"*Lawdy, lawd,*" Serenity says in a Butterfly McQueen voice. "Looks like I've found me a bona fide progressive household. Yes, *suh,* Mr. Rhett."

"Guilty as charged." As I watch her watch me with what I know is a ruthlessly unsentimental eye, I say, "Where are you planning on staying while you're in town?"

"I booked a room at the Eola Hotel."

"Have you checked in yet?"

"No. I came straight here."

I take a quick mental inventory of the house. "Look, I want to make you an offer."

Her eyes twinkle. "I'm all ears."

"If my instinct about you is correct, you're going to lose no time making yourself a target of the same bastards who attacked Keisha there. In fact, by coming to this house you might already have done that. So I think you ought to stay here with us. At least for your first couple of days."

"Seriously? In this house?"

"Well, Caitlin's house is right across the street, but you know what happened to Keisha there. We've got enough room, plus a truly badass security team. You won't find that at the Eola."

After a few seconds of reflection, Serenity takes a deep breath, purses her lips, and sighs. "Mr. Mayor, I accept your offer. I don't fancy getting acid thrown in my face. Or worse."

"Good." Her answer gives me a deep sense of relief. "Why don't you get your stuff from your car, and Mia and Annie will help you settle in."

Serenity tilts her head as though pondering something. "Hey . . . I don't want to pry, but what exactly is the status with you and the cheerleader in there?"

"Cheerleader?"

"The girl with the UCA T-shirt."

"Oh. Mia takes care of Annie."

"She looked a little old for that."

"She's only a sophomore in college."

A faint smile touches Serenity's lips. "My mother was a sophomore when she got pregnant with me."

Hot blood rushes to my cheeks. "Good Lord . . . *no.* It's nothing like that. Mia was Annie's babysitter a couple of years ago. After Caitlin was murdered, Annie kind of lost it. My mother's living near the prison where my father's being held right now, so Mia offered to help."

"I see." But Serenity's eyes say the opposite.

"Do you?"

She pooches out her lower lip. "Aren't we in the middle of a semester? There isn't a college in Natchez, is there?"

"Mia goes to Harvard. Everything blew up during her Christmas break. She took off a semester to help."

This time Serenity's nod is slower but more definite. "*Now* I see. Well. Did I just ruin my invitation?"

"No, no, it's fine. You're just wrong about Mia. You'll see after you've been here awhile."

"I'm sure you're right."

She gets up lightly and heads for the stairs. "I'll just grab my bag."

"You need any help?"

"Nope. I travel light."

WHILE SERENITY RETRIEVES her bag, I run upstairs to the kitchen to work out her sleeping arrangements with Annie and Mia. Annie is overjoyed to hear that she'll be staying with us—Mia, less so.

"With Mom coming in Sunday night, you guys will have to double up, and the biggest room is the old master bedroom on this floor. Are you okay with that?"

"Yeah!" Annie says, not even looking at Mia, whose mouth has tightened. "Tee's probably going to need the bodyguards. Especially if she picks up where Keisha left off."

"Mia?" I ask. "I know that's asking a lot, you giving up your privacy. You could use the sofa bed in my office in the basement."

"With the security guys on cots down there?" Annie asks. "No way."

"That old master bedroom is plenty big enough for Annie and me," Mia says, covering her displeasure so that Annie won't pick up on it. "Where will you put Serenity? The upstairs guest room at the end of the hall? By your room?"

"Gram needs that one," Annie says. "It's closest to the hall bathroom."

"Serenity can take the small room on the other side," I decide. "Hell, she'd probably be happy with the basement. She lived in a tent in Iraq."

Annie laughs. "We need to put sheets on that bed upstairs. I'll do it." She slaps Mia on the arm and runs into the hall.

"Right behind you," calls Mia, who continues to stand at the counter, watching me, as the drumbeat of Annie's feet on the stairs resounds in the hallway.

"What is it?" I ask, a little uncomfortably. "You need your own room?"

"No. I'm such an ass. I can't believe I was staring at Serenity like that. Because of the skin color thing."

"It's okay. Seriously. I was staring, too."

"Did she say anything?"

"About that? No."

Mia's eyes narrow. "Bullshit. I can tell you're lying. What did she say?"

"You really want to know?"

"Yes."

"She said you have a thing for me."

"She—did *not*." Mia blushes deeply again.

"She implied it."

An angry sigh escapes her mouth. "Well, she's definitely not a genius. That's a relief." Mia walks to the kitchen door, then looks back at me. "By the way, I'm not buying that whole 'paper bag test' suffering shtick. Any woman as hot as she is didn't suffer *too* much exclusion in high school or college."

I think about this. "That's the pot calling the kettle black, isn't it?"

"I'm just making an observation."

"Would you have guessed a woman as pretty as she is would have joined the army? As a private?"

"No. That stumps me, I'll admit. That's why I'm going to read her book."

"I'll be interested to hear your conclusion." I raise my hand in farewell.

Mia gives me a fake smile, then disappears into the hall.

CHAPTER 13

IN THE DARK sprawl between Vidalia and Ferriday, Louisiana, two men wearing black leather chaps and jackets staggered out of the Steel Tiger bar and headed into the oyster-shell parking lot. Stump Seyfarth had been drinking enough that he listed to starboard as he scanned the lot for his hog.

"Where's our bikes?" he bellowed indignantly. "Didn't we park right there by the sign?"

"God*damn*, son," said a laughing Jimmy Gunn, still reasonably sober. "You must have your beer goggles on." Jimmy shielded his eyes against the lone streetlight, then bent his knees and peered into the mostly empty lot. "Mother*fucker*!" he shouted. "I'm gonna *kill* somebody."

"What is it?" Stump cried. "Whassa matter?"

"Somebody tipped our bikes over!"

Jimmy ran clumsily to where the Harleys lay in the gravel and dirt, looking like chromed black rhinos felled by a game hunter's rifle.

"They scratched my Road King to hell and gone!" he shouted, his ears pounding with rage. "Looks like they beat in the tank with a wrench or something. I'm gonna *waste* the fuckers that done this, I swear."

Stump finally caught up. He stood panting over the wrecked bikes, his hands on his big hips. "How you gonna find 'em?"

"Had to be local thugs," Jimmy reasoned. "Unless Cage and his friends did it. Nobody else would have the balls."

"Could have been some Bandidos or Vinlanders passin' through, huh? Saw we were inside, so they kicked over our rides and split?"

"I seriously doubt it."

"FBI, maybe?"

Jimmy considered the possibility, then dismissed it. "Naaah. This ain't their style." He bent over and took hold of his handlebars. "Help me pick this bastard up. Jesus *Christ.*"

He waited for Stump to get his hands beneath the seat, then heaved upward with all his strength. The two men grunted and strained until their lungs and bladders were near to bursting. They'd just about cleared the sixty-degree point when someone with a deep bass voice shouted, *"Look out!"* from the darkness behind them.

Stump lost his grip, backpedaled, then fell on his butt with a grunt and a curse. His hand shot into his leather jacket, but before he could grab the gun in the holster he wore against his ribs, a hand caught the collar of his jacket and snatched him to his feet. Another dug inside the jacket and yanked out his pistol.

Jimmy Gunn made the mistake of trying to hold the Harley erect by himself, which probably gave him a hernia before he let the eight hundred pounds of metal drop to the shell gravel. The ground shuddered from the impact. Jimmy, too, reached for a weapon—a butterfly knife in his boot—but before he could get it, someone caught him in a headlock from behind. Jimmy tried to twist, but the man behind him was too strong. He was black, though. Jimmy could tell by the smell. Not bad—just different.

"What the fuck?" gasped Stump, trying in vain to free himself from the giant who had grabbed him from behind.

Jimmy gaped in disbelief at the size of the forearm locked around Stump's neck. The big head whose chin pinned the crown of Stump's head was deep black, and the whites of its eyes shone with a bluish light. When the giant spoke, his voice was so deep and resonant that Jimmy felt the air in his own chest move.

"Ya'll the ones messed up my li'l sister?" asked the giant.

Jimmy felt his face get hot. "What?"

"Don't play, now. Ya'll's crew messed up my sister. She worked over in Natchez, at the newspaper."

Stump's eyes went wide. Jimmy prayed his friend wasn't so drunk that he'd be unable to lie. Stump wasn't the sharpest tool in the box when sober, and for the last hour he'd been laughing about the colored girl that Snake Knox's bitch had splashed with acid.

Stump croaked, "We din't have shit to do with that. We just heard about it on the radio."

"Doc say she might not live," said the giant.

The huge spade had the kind of face Jimmy could imagine smiling from ear to ear, his eyes twinkling with delight, his big belly shaking with joy. But he wasn't smiling now. "Aw, come on now," Jimmy said, watching Stump's eyes. "That's bullshit. I mean, we didn't have nothing to do with it, but I know acid in the face don't kill nobody."

"You're wrong there," said a voice in Jimmy's ear. "That kind of acid eats down to the bone. Messes up your heart."

Panic flared in Stump's eyes. Jimmy didn't sense even a millimeter of room for negotiation in the men who had bushwhacked them. Surely these guys didn't mean to kill them, though? Niggers preferred drive-bys, lots of noise and attention. Even in prison, they always used shanks. And Jimmy had yet to see a weapon.

"Listen, bro," said Stump, and Jimmy cringed. "We ain't the guys you want. We didn't have nothing to do with that business. Some oilfield boys were talking about it in the bar earlier, but we don't know shit."

"You're lying," said the voice in Jimmy's ear.

"That's God's truth, I swear!" Stump cried.

"It don't matter," said the giant. "You part of the same poison. And I'm tired. You'll do."

Just then Jimmy realized that the giant was wearing gloves. Leather work gloves. *Where the hell did he find gloves to fit those monster hands?* he wondered.

Then Jimmy saw the hand at the collar of Stump's jacket move up and close around the top of his skull like a five-point vise.

"Oh Jesus," Stump groaned. "Aaaggghhh . . . don't do that!"

"Ain't done nothing yet, mister. You'll know when I do."

Panic tore around inside Jimmy's chest like a crazed rat.

"They got security cameras here, man! If you hurt us, the law gonna get you for sure!"

"No cameras," said the voice in his ear. "We already checked."

"Please," begged Jimmy. "Let us go. You can have the bikes. I got nothing against brothers, myself. I had a bunch of black friends in Angola."

"What that VK on your jacket stand for?" asked the voice in Jimmy's ear. "Viking something? That's what the FBI man told us."

"Varangian Kindred. 'Varangian' means Vikings, though, yeah."

"That a prison gang?"

"No, no. A motorcycle club. One percent."

The giant reflected on this for some time. "They told me in college that the Vikings settled America before Columbus ever got here. Hundreds of years before."

Jimmy felt a flicker of hope. "That's right, man! What college did you go to? You play ball? You must have, big as you are."

"You reckon them Vikings ever got to Africa?"

Jimmy couldn't think. Stump had shut his eyes, and Jimmy knew his old buddy was praying silently for mercy.

"If they didn't," said the hot breath in his ear, "I'd say they were lucky. What you think?"

Jimmy nodded, believing it.

"So . . . my sister," said the giant, giving Stump's head a squeeze, like a man checking a melon. "Time to pay. Make your peace with God."

"Hold on!" Jimmy shouted. "You want us to give a message to somebody?"

"You are the message," said the voice at his ear.

"Wait!" Stump shrieked.

But the big hands had begun their work, as slow and sure as if the giant were trying to twist free a bolt that had rusted to a metal plate.

"Oh, Lord," Jimmy moaned, as infantile shame flooded through him. "I shit myself."

"Don't worry," the giant said gently, his jaw muscles clenching with effort. "All be over in a minute."

SATURDAY

CHAPTER 14

SATURDAY MORNING BROUGHT bad news. Keisha's condition had worsened, and Drew Elliott was considering having her flown to University Medical Center in Jackson. At the hospital, John Kaiser informed me that two damaged Harley-Davidson motorcycles had been found in the parking lot of a dive bar on the Louisiana side of the river, their license plates removed. Kaiser pointed out the strangeness of someone stealing the license plates but not the bikes themselves, and of no one claiming two motorcycles. Then he asked me if I knew the whereabouts of Keisha Harvin's brothers last night. Thankfully, I did not.

At the prompting of Serenity Butler, I negotiated a limited period of freedom from my security team, then drove Tee across the river, through Vidalia, then Ferriday, and on to Clayton, where the church that hosted Henry Sexton's funeral stands. There we met with Reverend John Baldwin and his son, who is also a preacher. Serenity introduced herself, then spent an hour patiently questioning the two pastors about their lives in Clayton. The elder Reverend Baldwin is in his nineties, and he told Tee about serving in the navy during World War Two, then returning home to help found the Deacons for Defense. Baldwin's son served in Vietnam and still suffers from PTSD as well as an autoimmune disease he believes to be linked to Agent Orange. Like most people, the Baldwins were surprised to learn that Serenity had served in a war, but that common thread quickly established a bond of trust between them.

As we left their church sanctuary, Tee gave the preachers a card with her cell phone number and told them she'd welcome a call at any hour of the day or night—especially one regarding information that might help in the quest for justice for Keisha Harvin, or in the larger battle against the Double Eagles. Then she hugged both men and led me out to the Audi, which was parked near Henry's grave.

"Where next?" I asked.

"We've touched base on the black side. Let's see if we can stir whitey up a little bit."

"What?"

Tee grinned. "Which of the Double Eagles do you most want to talk to you?"

"Doesn't matter. None of them will talk. And with you there, they might get crazy. A couple have already pulled guns on me."

"We'll see, then. Give me a name."

Against my better judgment, I said, "Will Devine. He's one of the original members. He might know something about Viola's death."

"Will Devine it is." Serenity slapped the roof of the S4. "Let's move."

WILL DEVINE LIVES on the western edge of Vidalia, not more than a couple of blocks from the houses of Snake Knox and Sonny Thornfield. During the drive over from Clayton, I give Serenity a briefing on my history with the Devine family and what I hope to learn from him or his sons.

"So Devine probably took part in the murder of Sonny Thornfield," she says. "Inside the Concordia Parish jail?"

"If he didn't take part, he saw it happen."

"And Snake Knox was in there at the time?"

"Yes."

"Well, damn. Let's get this redneck talking."

"I don't think you appreciate the reality of this situation. The two times I've been there, Devine met me at the door with a double-barreled shotgun."

She laughs. "Maybe you need lessons in sweet-talking, Mr. Mayor.

Your history as a prosecutor obviously didn't give you the proper skills for this kind of work."

"Okay. We'll see how you do. Devine weighs about two seventy, and he's ugly as an albino sea lion."

"Then attention from a sister like me ought to be even more welcome."

I PARK IN Will Devine's driveway, just behind the pickup that was parked near Viola's sister's house on the night Viola was murdered. As we walk to the front door of the small 1950s ranch house, Serenity points a finger and cocked thumb at the truck and says, "There's the Darlington Academy sticker."

Just before we reach the screen door, the wooden door behind it flies open and Devine barks, "Ya'll get away from here! I done told you twice now. I'll shoot. I will!"

The voice seems too high-pitched to come from such a big man. Devine sounds panicked, and I can see that Serenity instantly picked up on this.

"Mr. Devine," she says in an official voice, "I'm Corporal S. T. Butler. I'm here concerning your affiliation with the terrorist organization known as the Double Eagle group."

Through the fine wire screen, I see Devine blinking in confusion. "What are you, some kind of cop?"

"If you refuse to cooperate, Mr. Devine, you will wish that I was a cop. This is a terrorism investigation. Is that clear?"

"No. What the hell you want with me? I ain't done nuthin'."

"If that's true, then you'll have no problem putting down that firearm and stepping out here for a word."

As on my previous visits, I hear a female voice murmuring behind Devine's bovine silhouette. Squinting, I can just make out the shoulder and hair of a dark-haired woman behind him. His wife, surely, Nita Devine.

"If this is a terrorism investigation," he says, repeating his wife's words, "what the hell is the mayor of Natchez doing with you?"

"That's privileged information, Mr. Devine. Now, please step outside. Without the firearm."

Devine uses the shotgun barrel to knock the latch up and then shove open the door, and steps outside, pushing Serenity backward with the muzzle of the gun.

"I've about had it with you smart-ass colored," he growls. "This is my property, and I know my rights. You can't do shit to me 'less you got a warrant. And I ain't seen one yet."

"Mayor Cage," Tee says, standing her ground and turning to me, "call Special Agent Kaiser and tell him to send a polygraph team to this address."

"Hey, now," Devine begins, "what the—"

Faster than I can process the motion, Tee pivots toward Devine while doing something with her hands that results in the fat man gaping at her in astonishment and pain. Somehow she twisted the shotgun out of his hands before he could fire it. After a second's hesitation, she inverts the weapon and drives the butt up toward Devine's chin for a butt stroke, but at the last instant she stops. Devine throws up his hands about two seconds too late to stop the blow that would have broken his jaw, if it didn't kill him.

"Do you see me, mister?" Serenity asks. "Do you see what's in my eyes?"

He nods, cringing from the gun butt.

"You ought to be ashamed, pointing this gun at strangers who knock on your door. I *ought* to beat you with this thing. You deserve it."

"Call the sheriff, Nita!" Devine yells.

"Yeah, do that," I tell him. "Walker Dennis and I are old friends. We've been working this case together from the start."

Nita Devine hesitates. She must know I'm telling the truth.

"Who the hell are you?" Will asks Serenity. "Are you a goddamn cop or what?"

"I'll tell you what I'm not, Mr. Devine. I'm not a naïve girl trying to make the world a perfect place. I'm a soldier. I've seen the same shit your buddies saw decades ago, but *you* missed out on. That's right, I know your record. You fell between the wars. Got lucky, didn't you? Well, I didn't. You hear me, Mr. Devine? You *feel* me?"

"We don't want no trouble, now."

"Well, you've got it. I've read every word Henry Sexton ever wrote about the Double Eagles. And I am honing in on you bastards. On you in particular. And that truck with the Darlington Academy sticker on it."

Devine cuts his eyes at the truck.

"And don't bother trying to take it off, 'cause we've already got two dozen pictures. My message to you is this, sir. Pretty soon, I'm gonna have all the evidence I need. And then the dominoes will start falling. And as Mayor Cage can tell you, if you know what's good for you, you'll be the first to fall. Because everybody else gets crushed."

The fat man's jaw juts out in defiance. "I ain't no rat."

"Snake Knox wouldn't give up one day of freedom to protect you, Will," I tell him. "And he murdered your buddy Silas Groom to get himself off the FBI's wanted list. A Double Eagle, just like you. Or maybe *you* killed Groom, for Snake."

"That's a lie! That's a *damn* lie!"

"Well, somebody killed Groom. And whoever it was, they're going to ride the needle in Angola."

Through the screen door, the woman says, "That's enough, now. Come inside, Will."

"I'm not finished with him," Tee says.

"Yes, you are." The woman steps forward and opens the screen door, and in her sullen, wrinkled face I see twice the intelligence present in her husband's eyes.

Serenity removes the shells from the shotgun, then hands the weapon back to Devine, who makes no move to go inside.

"I'd reload as soon as we leave, Mr. Devine. Once it gets out that I was here, Snake may put out the word to drop the hammer on *you*. A couple of those skinhead motorcycle freaks might pull up here around two A.M. to pour acid down *your* throat."

She turns and walks back toward the car. As I follow, Nita Devine says, "Wait up, Mayor. I want to ask you something."

I turn and wait for her. Nita steps outside and lets the screen door clap shut. Tee starts to join me, but Mrs. Devine jabs her finger and says, "Not you, missy. Just him."

Tee stands her ground long enough to save face, but after a couple of seconds, she heads back to the car.

Nita Devine looks like she hasn't slept for days. Her hair is unkempt, and the circles under her eyes are so blue they look black.

"How can I help you, Mrs. Devine?"

In a low voice, she says, "If somebody was to talk to the FBI—one of the original boys, I mean, from the group . . ."

"The Double Eagle group?"

She nods. "What kind of deal could they get?"

While I try to decide how best to respond, she says, "What I mean is, can the government really protect Will? And his family?"

"Of course. They do it all the time. Just like in the movies. Witness protection program."

"They didn't protect Sonny Thornfield too good."

She's right about that. "That was Sonny's fault, ma'am. Sonny made demands that the Bureau couldn't possibly meet fast enough to save him."

I glance at her husband, who's staring at the concrete under his feet. "Will, you were in the jail when Sonny was killed. Can you tell the FBI who did that? Because that would buy you one hell of a deal."

Devine's mouth begins working as though around a plug of tobacco. "Who says Sonny was murdered?"

I shake my head, then turn and walk toward the car.

"Wait!" calls his wife.

I look back, skepticism plain on my face.

Nita says, "What if a man was, uh—"

"What if your husband was there when Sonny was killed?" I ask. "Took part, maybe?"

Dark blood comes into her cheeks.

"Can he still turn state's evidence?" I go on. "Could he still get a plea deal that would protect him? Is that what you want to know?"

Without looking at her husband, Nita Devine nods slowly.

"Speaking as a former prosecutor, I can tell you that the answer to that question is an unequivocal yes. The best witnesses are almost always accomplices to crimes."

I'm not sure if what I see in her face is relief or despair. But behind whatever that emotion is, I see what looks like surrender. It's time to leave them stewing in their fears, and in this life they have made together.

"SO THAT'S WHAT sweet-talking looks like," I say as I get back into the Audi.

Serenity laughs softly, but I hear satisfaction in her voice.

"He's going to talk," I tell her.

"Did he say that?"

"No. But he's more than halfway there. The wife is past ready."

"You sure?"

"Yeah. The question is, how long will it take them to come to it? If it takes too long, they'll be the next ones to get measured for caskets."

"They've gotta know that," Serenity says.

"The wife knows. That's why it'll be sooner rather than later."

"We gonna sit here all day?" she asks.

"You didn't have to tell him about the sticker on the truck."

"Do you not have photos of it?"

"I don't know. But since Walt Garrity was here before us, I'm ninety-nine percent sure we do."

"Then let's go. I'm thirsty. I need a beer."

As I pull onto the narrow street and drive slowly between the bass boats and empty trailers parked against both curbs, I say, "You got a little radical back there. But it made all the difference. That shotgun move scared the shit out of Devine."

"Just basic close-quarters combat drill." Serenity does some sort of kung fu move with her hands, then laughs again. "It's like Eddie Murphy said in *48 Hours*. I'm your worst nightmare—a nigger with a badge."

"Except you don't have a badge."

"Neither did Eddie." Tee winks at me. "Perception is everything, right?"

CHAPTER 15

Sulphur, Louisiana

SNAKE KNOX STOOD with his back against the interior wall of the sod farm's administrative office, his arms folded across his chest. Opposite him stood Toons Teufel, sergeant at arms of the Varangian Kindred, and three muscular club members in riding leathers. Snake figured they did the strong-arm work that had always been part of the gun and drug businesses. Rocket scientists they were not.

To Snake's left stood Wilma Deen and his bastard son, Alois, who'd been staring dumbfounded at Snake ever since they were brought in. The transformation Junelle had worked on him was that profound. Snake didn't like that Toons had brought Wilma and Alois to the farm. The only reason he could see for it was that Toons wanted to be able to kill all three of them at the same time. He figured the arrogant shit was trying to get up the nerve to do exactly that now.

"Four men," Toons repeated. "We've lost *four men* because of you, and for what?"

Snake said, "You choose a rough business, you take casualties sometimes."

"Two men at the gas station," Toons said, counting on his fingers. "Two men outside the Steel Tiger. And what the fuck have we got out of it?"

"The names of two friendly judges, a bent DA, and a dozen dirty cops."

"That ain't a quarter of what you promised us!"

Snake offered nothing.

Toons raised his right forefinger and shook it, then kept shaking it as he walked toward Snake. Snake kept his eye on Toons's other hand, in case he made a move for the gun at his side or one of the two knives he wore at all times. Toons also carried a sap, Snake knew, something you didn't see much these days, but which could be a hell of a weapon in the hands of a skilled man.

"I'm tired of you stalling," Toons said, his wide eyes looking like he'd been sampling some of the gang's product. "We didn't lose anybody doing *our* business. We were doing *your* business. And I don't understand your business."

"You don't have to. Lars does, and that's all that matters."

Toons grimaced at the mention of his boss's name. "I'll tell you what Lars understands, Grandpa. You promised us the remains of Forrest's network. You promised us ranking officers in the drug units. The HIDTA, for example. And you promised us judges, Snake. *Judges.*"

"I've already given you two, plus I got two of your mules out of trouble down in Iberia Parish."

"We're supposed to get *direct access* to all Forrest's judges."

"If I give that to you, you'll cut my throat the first time I go to sleep."

Toons tried to keep a straight face, but a near hysterical smile broke through, and his eyes danced. "Now *that's* an idea, Snake man. I must confess, I have thoughts about that."

Snake pushed himself off the wall and spat into a trash can by the crappy metal desk. "I tell you what, Toons. You keep on fantasizing. Go choke your chicken while you think about cutting my throat. And I'll keep focusing on my business. Because that's what businessmen do."

Snake started to walk out, but Toons moved in front of him.

Snake fought the urge to jerk the gun from his belt.

"I don't like it when you don't show me the proper respect," Toons said.

"Then act like you deserve it."

"You know what my name means, Snake?"

"Yeah. You're Looney Tunes, like the cartoon."

"My last name. Teufel. It means 'devil.' You think Lars made me SA because I'm a fucking comedian?"

"I stay out of Lars's business, Toons."

"See, that's where you're wrong. You're all up in our business. You're getting my men killed. And I—don't—like it."

"Your men are getting themselves killed. Which don't inspire confidence."

Toons went into his pocket and brought out a butterfly knife, which seemed to be the bladed weapon of choice among a lot of the VK.

Snake forced himself to breathe slowly, and he didn't move one centimeter. He didn't look at the knife, either. He looked straight into Teufel's glinting eyes.

"Lars may buy your dime store psycho act," he said. "But I know the truth. You ain't no devil. I've *seen* the devil, boy. I've shaken his hand and supped with the motherfucker on many a dark night. And I'll tell you this for free. You and your gorillas here wouldn't last two days in the Marine Corps. Now, get the fuck out of my way."

The man tasked with enforcing security for the VK stared into Snake's eyes for fifteen or twenty seconds. Then he decided to pretend he'd been joking all along.

When Snake walked out of the office with Wilma and Alois on his heels, he looked down at his right hand to be sure he wasn't shaking.

He wasn't.

"That's telling that asshole, Pop," Alois crowed. "Hey, let's go over to that barn for a minute. I want to show you something."

Snake looked back at the office, then over to the old horse barn that now served as a warehouse for the sod farm. "Wilma, you go into the house with Junelle. Act like you're glad to be here, even if you can't stand the bitch."

Wilma spat on the grass. "I want to cunt-punt that cow every time she opens her mouth."

Snake shook his head. "Get on in there. We'll see you in a minute."

Wilma expelled a stream of profanity under her breath, but she went.

Snake led the way out to the horse barn, which no longer smelled like manure and leather but like the toxic ag chemicals Snake had spent his life around.

"That son of a bitch thinks he's the devil?" Alois said as they passed into the shade under the broad roof. "He's a fuckin' joke."

Snake stopped just inside the barn and turned. "What are we doin' out here, boy?"

"I told you, I got something to show you."

Snake suppressed a scowl. He'd had to learn to get used to Alois treating him like a real father. "What?"

"A little toy I been workin' on."

"Well, where is it?"

Alois reached into his pocket and brought out a dull metal cube about an inch and a half square. Using his thumbnail, he flipped a tiny catch, and one side of the cube slid halfway open.

"What is it?" Snake asked. "A Rubik's Cube or something?"

Alois handed the cube to his father as though passing him a rare and fragile relic. "Look inside, but don't touch anything in there. Seriously."

Snake gingerly moved the little cube up and down until he got it the proper distance from his aging eyes, then backed to the edge of the shade and turned the gadget until the sun shone into its tiny opening.

What he saw appeared to be the works of a mechanical watch. In front of the watch sat some sort of compressed spring. Snake squinted into the tightly crowded space. Rising out of the mouth of the spring was a thin sliver of metal, like a needle. But Snake had no idea what the function of the mechanism might be.

"What *is* it?"

"I call it the Needle Box," Alois said proudly.

"And what the fuck does it do?"

"It kills."

"Kills what? People?"

Alois gave him a strange smile. "Anything. Any mammal, for sure."

"How?"

"Simple. Inside there is a spring-loaded hypodermic needle. Attached to the needle is a tiny rubber bladder. The trigger is attached to a timer right now. But the whole thing is mechanical. Doesn't put out any electrical field."

Snake turned the gadget in his hand again. On the opened side he saw a tiny hole, which must be where the needle would emerge if triggered.

"What comes out of the needle?" he asked.

"Anything you want. Cyanide. Ricin. Thallium. The quickest killer's cyanide, obviously. I already killed a pig and two dogs with it. Killed them so fast you wouldn't believe it."

"Huh," Snake said, still studying the toylike device. "Could you rig one to trigger remotely?"

"Sure, yeah. It's the poison that's tricky. Ricin or thallium's the way to go if you want somebody to suffer. Thallium's the worst. That's a living hell, and the best doctors in the world can't save you."

"Where do you get thallium?"

Alois smiled with wicked pleasure. "It's gettable."

Snake nodded in appreciation of the skill that had gone into building the little machine. Alois had obviously inherited the aptitude that had made Snake a dab hand with improvised explosives. "And how do you plan to use this thing?"

Alois reached out and lifted the Needle Box from his father's hand. "How about this? I could make one cut in a motorcycle seat—very carefully—and plant this baby right under someone's butt cheek. Toons, for example. And anytime I wanted over the next twelve hours . . . he'd get a shot of cyanide. And *tha-tha-tha-that's all folks!*"

Deep pleasure spread through Snake's belly and chest. But his mind was moving so fast, he stifled the laugh he felt rising and took back the box from his son.

"Where else? Could you put it in a car seat?"

"Sure. Any kind of seat that's got enough padding."

Snake looked back toward the office and shook his head. Then he released his laugh, a sudden expulsion of triumphant glee.

"What you thinking, Pop?" Alois asked.

Snake laughed until he'd caught his breath. "I'm picturing Toons with the red-ass, boy."

Alois laughed, too, so happy was he to have earned his father's respect.

"The Needle Box," Snake said. "How many of these little boogers you got?"

"A couple. But I can build more. All you want."

"Two'll do." Snake winked. "For a start."

CHAPTER 16

WE SPENT A lot of the afternoon cleaning the house in preparation for my mother moving back in tomorrow. Annie especially wants the house to be in perfect condition, and she took quite a while arranging things just so in the guest room where Mom will be staying. Mom would probably prefer to sleep in her own house, but there's no question of that while Snake and his VK soldiers are on the loose, especially after the warning he sent to Dad.

About an hour ago Tim and I drove down to C&M Seafood and bought twenty pounds of huge crawfish that had just come off the heat. Now we're all gathered around the kitchen table—even the security guys—cracking shells and sucking heads while Annie yells *"Gross!"* every minute or so. Serenity's been trying to get her to suck the meat from a head, but Annie steadfastly refuses.

A loud knock at the door causes Tim to get up a little more swiftly than the average person might, but he's calm about going to check who's there. When he returns, a handsome black man of about twenty-five is following him. Because Carl Sims isn't wearing his Lusahatcha County deputy's uniform but a light blue polo shirt and jeans, it takes me a second to recognize him.

"Carl!" I cry. "What are you doing here, man? Not official business, I hope."

"Nah, man," he says. "I got a little news for you, on that thing you asked about, but it's nothing urgent."

The woman whose son was killed at the Bone Tree . . .

"I see y'all got some mudbugs!" Carl says, laughing. "Big ones, too."

"Sit down and make a plate."

"I won't say no to that."

As Carl grabs two paper plates to make a stable shelling and eating platform, I notice Serenity watching him with a level gaze.

"Oh, Carl," I say, "the lovely lady to Mia's left is Serenity Butler. She's a writer from Atlanta. But she's a Mississippi girl at heart."

"That right?" Carl's eyes are bright with interest. Clearly he did not fail to notice Serenity when he first came in.

"You two have something in common," I tell him. "Can you guess what it is?"

He looks at her for a while, and for a moment I think he might guess the truth. But when he finally speaks, he says, "I can't imagine, I'm sorry to say."

"Serenity was in the Gulf War. The first one."

"Embedded reporter?"

Serenity laughs. "Army corporal."

Carl's grin loses its levity. "Seriously?"

"Nine months in Iraq."

"Glad to know you, Serenity."

"Tee." She holds her butter-slick hand over the table. "Just Tee."

Carl takes her hand and shakes it. "Okay, Ms. Tee."

"Carl was in the second war," I tell her.

"Army?" she asks.

"Marines."

"Iraq or Afghanistan?"

"Fallujah. First and second battles."

"Regular grunt?"

"Sniper."

Serenity looks at Carl with new eyes, as if to say, *Okay . . . I see you now.* Carl practically glows from her attention.

Annie cuts her eyes at me and squeezes her lips together in a way that tells me she's noticed the chemistry between them.

"I was in Fallujah," says one of the younger security guys. "I was glad to get out, too."

The subtext of that comment was *Not everybody did.* This makes me want to hear his story, but Tim Weathers silences any elaboration with a single glance that is impossible to misread. *There will be no war stories in front of eleven-year-olds.*

We attack the steaming red piles of crawfish for another half hour, and then Carl and I go down to my basement office with a couple of beers.

"I'm glad you came in person," I tell him.

"I didn't want to call you about this."

"You still don't trust everybody in your department?"

"Billy Ray Ellis is still sheriff. That ought to tell you all you need to know."

I nod dispiritedly. "What have you got?"

"My dad knows the woman you asked about. The one whose son got lynched. His voice had a real funny sound when he told me. He said this lady knew the worst story in the world."

"*The worst story in the world?* Coming from your father . . ."

"That means something, brother. I'm not sure I even want to know. You know?"

"Yeah. But to nail Snake, maybe we have to know."

Carl nods soberly. "Her name is Cleotha Booker. She's a widow. Long time now. She's real old and mostly keeps to herself. Daddy talked to her about you. She refused to speak to you at first, but then she found out you were Dr. Cage's son. She said if you were willing to drive down to Athens Point, she'd talk to you. But she told Daddy right up front that she doesn't know anything about who killed her boy."

"Damn. And her daughter-in-law?"

"She passed way back in '67 or '68. Committed suicide up north somewhere."

"That's what my dad remembered, too."

"Don't sound like much of a lead, Penn."

I shrug. "You never know. I've broken cases with less."

Carl takes a long swallow of Corona. "So, Mr. Mayor. *Who* is that hot thing upstairs?"

"Serenity? She's a writer, like I said. She's in town doing research."

Carl manages to hold a neutral expression for about two seconds. Then he breaks into wild laughter and slaps his thigh with his free hand. "*Lord,* is she hot! Ain't no *way* that girl was in the army. No army I was ever in, anyway."

Carl has got me chuckling with him. "She's not hard to look at, I'll grant you that. She is about ten years older than you, though. I figured you'd see her as an old lady."

Carl draws his head back like I'm a drunk driver who just swore he's sober. "Get *out* with that shit. I'd trade ten college girls for a night with that lady up there. That's a real woman. You can tell."

"I think you're probably right. You ought to read her book."

Carl's serious look returns, but then he breaks up again. "I *might* read a chapter if it'll get me a chance to talk to her."

"Hell, you can go up and talk to her right now."

"Penn, Penn, Penn—I mean *talk* to her. Man, you're old sometimes."

FORTY-FIVE MINUTES LATER, Carl looks well on his way to getting his wish. The off-duty security guys are sitting on the back porch drinking beer. Annie is doing something on her computer, and Mia looks content reading on the sofa with her feet kicked up on the arm. I'm putting away dishes when I decide to ask Carl something about the sheriff in Lusahatcha County. Before I go looking for him, though, he and Serenity appear in the kitchen doorway.

"I'm gonna take Tee to see a couple of things before the sun goes down," Carl says, looking innocent as a choirboy.

"Great," I reply, just as innocently. "Get her to tell you about our visit to some Double Eagles this morning."

"The mayor is easily impressed," Tee says from behind Carl. "Let's go. Sun's going down."

Ten seconds later the front door slams.

Standing at the sink, I survey the kitchen, which is pretty clean, considering. Annie's lost in her computer. Looking past her to the den, I see Mia reading her book on the sofa. I may be wrong, but there appears to be a trace of a smile on her lips. Though I watch her for some time, she never looks up at me. She merely licks one finger and turns the page, the faint smile still in place.

ABOUT TEN THIRTY P.M., Serenity texts me that she wants to drive down to Athens Point to see Cleotha Booker in the morning, if I have time. So . . . she wangled that private information out of Carl without any trouble. I text her that I do have time, if we leave early. She sends another text saying that she's talking to Keisha Harvin's brothers and won't be back for some time yet. It's then I realize that I've been waiting for her to return so that we can discuss the Athens Point issue as well as what happened at the Devine house.

Once I know Tee will be late, I decide to go upstairs and try to get some sleep. As I say good night to the girls, Annie looks up from the TV and says, "Is Serenity coming back tonight?"

So I'm not the only one waiting for Tee's return. "Yes, but not for a while yet."

My daughter looks worried. "Is she okay?"

"Oh, yeah. Carl will take good care of her."

Mia glances up at me then, but she makes no comment.

"I'll see ya'll in the morning," I say.

"'Night, Dad."

AT THE FOOT of the staircase, I realize I'm not really ready to sleep. Instead, I text Tim and ask if he'd like to take a walk with me. He's been doing some paperwork on one of the cots in the basement, and he's happy for a chance to get some exercise in the night air. The only caveat: he insists that I put on my bulletproof vest—*with* the ceramic inserts—which goes a long way toward turning our outing into a good walk spoiled.

As we start toward the river, I spy an old man walking his dog in the distance, where Commerce Street meets Orleans. The animal seems to be pulling its master along, impatient at being constrained by age or infirmity. Something about the old man looks familiar, but I say nothing to Tim, who is also watching the pair. Natchez is a small town, and if I don't know the dog walker well, I've certainly seen him many times in my life.

We walk down to the bluff and stand looking at the muted sheen of the river in the darkness two hundred feet below. Then we check the doors and windows of Edelweiss, which Quentin Avery and his wife, Doris, will be moving into tomorrow for the duration of the trial. As we head home, I think about walking up State Street to take a look at the jail that tomorrow will become my father's home until his case is judged. But in the end, I decide I don't want that image in my mind while I try to fall asleep tonight.

We walk up Washington instead, and Tim smokes a cigar on the way. As we near the top of the incline where the public library, the Episcopal church, Temple B'nai Israel, and majestic Glen Auburn face one another from four corners, Tim stops to stub out his cigar. While I stand looking at the steps of the church, where I stood after graduating from high school, Tim looks back down the long grade we just walked.

"There's that old man again," he says. "Walking his dog."

I peer down through the sporadically lit darkness until I see man and beast slowly cross Washington on Wall Street. "Looks like the dog is walking the man."

"I just realized something," Tim says. "Those Double Eagles are all old guys. Maybe we need to have a word with our dog lover down there."

"Next time," I tell him, sweating under my bulletproof vest. "I'm ready to hit the rack."

"Okay," he says after a few seconds. "Tomorrow."

SUNDAY

CHAPTER 17

SERENITY AND I got up early to make the drive to Athens Point. We don't have all day to spend following this lead. According to John Kaiser's latest call, my father is scheduled to depart the Pollock FCI for the Adams County jail at two P.M. He'll be transferred in an FBI vehicle, which should put him at the sheriff's office for the handover and processing at about three. Mom will be following in her own car, with an FBI vehicle bringing up the rear. I plan to be back to Natchez to get Mom settled in at my house.

Serenity has said nothing about her late activities last night, and I haven't asked. Our breakfast conversation consisted of arguing with Tim Weathers until he agreed to let us make this trip without bodyguards. Tim didn't like it, but Serenity forcefully persuaded him that she could not only spot a tail from a mile away, but kill any civilian foolish enough to try to ambush us on the road or in Athens Point.

South of Woodville, we turn east off Highway 61 and head toward the Mississippi River, devouring the bends of the serpentine road that leads to the old logging town. I drove these curves back in December, and at a much higher speed, while searching for Caitlin. Not far to the east lies Valhalla, where I killed Forrest Knox, but I don't mention that to Serenity. The swamp where Caitlin died lies to the south, in the lowland between the green hills and the river, and I can feel it pulling me, like some low-frequency magnetic field that tugs at flesh and bone.

"This is pulpwood country," Serenity says in a hushed voice. "I feel it. A lot of shortwood came out of these forests. A lot of men lost fingers and hands up in here, or had their legs and backs broken."

"They still do a lot of logging down here."

She cuts her eyes at me. "I thought you read my book. Pulpwooding's not logging. It's nigger logging."

I look sharply over at her, but she's staring out the window at the virginal green of early spring. Pine and hardwood trees cover the hills from here to the Mississippi River, and most observers would think the sight beautiful. But Serenity Butler sees only suffering in those trees.

"You saw the Bone Tree, right?" she asks, still looking out the window. "When you found Caitlin and your father there?"

Her forwardness in asking about the place my fiancée was murdered surprises me, but it's also refreshing. Serenity simply doesn't worry about things like propriety.

"Yeah," I say quietly, recalling the shock of leaping out of the helicopter into the swamp, fighting my way toward Caitlin's bloody body. "I saw it."

"Keisha told me they burned it."

"Only partially."

"I'd like to see what's left someday."

"Why?"

She raises a finger and taps the window beside her cheek. "Do you think some places are inherently evil?"

I want to answer no, but in truth I'm not sure. "Do you?"

She tilts her head, watching the forest rush past, then begins to speak softly. "I've stood on the sites of massacres. I've pulled my boots out of the sand in a mass grave. And I felt strange things there. But I think that feeling of wrongness came from inside me. From my knowledge of what had been done there. The land has nothing to do with it. The buildings, either. Nuns and children have been slaughtered in churches, schools, fields of flowers. It sucks, but that's the human species."

"I agree in principle. But the Bone Tree . . . people have done murder beneath it for centuries. Rape and torture, too. Why?"

She shrugs. "It's isolated. Ancient. Different. Humans have always attached a totemic significance to that kind of thing. But in the end, it's just an old tree. Right?"

"Kaiser isn't sure the Bureau ever found all the bones in the mud beneath it. And Reverend Sims told Carl that Mrs. Cleotha Booker knew the worst story in the world. Maybe we should ask her about that tree."

"If she's really the one. And if she doesn't have Alzheimer's or something."

"To tell you the truth," I say bitterly, "if I went back to that tree, I'd dump five gallons of high-octane gas over it and burn what's left down to the ground. Like St. Boniface felling Thor's oak."

Serenity finally turns from the window and gives me a long look, as though she wants to ask me another, more personal question. But in the end she looks through the windshield and watches the blacktop being swallowed by the car.

WE FIND THE house Carl Sims described without too much trouble. It's more shack than house, really, standing alone at the end of a dirt road, just as Carl's father, Reverend Sims, said it would. The road itself doesn't register on my GPS unit, but it's there nonetheless. Mrs. Booker's home leans like a listing ship or a house drawn in a Dr. Seuss book, but no canted house in Whoville ever looked so poor. I can see cracks between the unpainted barn boards of the front exterior wall, and the patched tin roof has been dented by a hundred fallen limbs. Behind the dwelling lies a junk-filled gully spiked with trees being slowly strangled by kudzu.

The raised porch is the kind that often shelters a mean dog who will attack anyone who approaches, but no animal emerges as Serenity and I walk up the steps. No one answers our knock. Then a curtain flutters in the window to our right, and a gray cat leaps onto the sill and regards us with intense curiosity.

"What do you think?" I ask. "Does this look like the place where you hear the worst story in the world?"

"Maybe."

"Do you think there's anyone inside?"

Serenity nods. "She's in there."

I hear a strange clump and shuffle that reminds me of someone walking on crutches, or on a walker with tennis balls on its feet. Then the door opens, and I see what looks like the oldest woman in

Mississippi standing before us, gripping a dented aluminum walker. Sure enough, the ends of its four legs have been jammed into slits in faded green tennis balls. The old woman blinks at the daylight with yellowed eyes set in a head that trembles constantly on her neck.

"Mrs. Booker?" I ask.

"Sho' is. And you're Dr. Cage's boy. I can see it in your face."

"Can you really?"

She nods. "You've got his eyes. Kind eyes. Dr. Cage was a true healer."

"Thank you, ma'am. This is my friend, Serenity Butler. She's a writer, too."

"Is that right? Well, I can't read no more, since my eyes gone bad. I used to take the *Reader's Digest*. But ya'll come on in. And please be patient. I can't get around like I used to."

The old lady stumps toward a battered La-Z-Boy recliner. "If any of my babies get in your way, just give 'em a shove with your foot."

Only now do I realize the house is full of cats. Felines of all sizes occupy every horizontal surface. At least a dozen animals are perched on various pieces of furniture, and two sit atop an ancient Frigidaire visible through a door at the back of the front room. I smell at least one litterbox, but the house doesn't actually stink, as I would have expected. Maybe Mrs. Booker spends what energy she has cleaning up after the cats rather than doing housework. I don't relish the prospect of sitting on what looks like flea-infested upholstery, but I do. The cat in my chosen chair seems ambivalent about moving, but it finally surrenders and concedes its territory.

"The chil'ren 'round here call me the Cat Lady," Mrs. Booker says. "You can see why. Nobody loves these babies but me. I don't understand why. They don't ask much from you, and they can just about take care of themselves. That's what's special about a cat. A dog'll love anybody, but a cat's love is a gift."

I'm not sure how to start a conversation about a lynching, but Serenity takes care of that. She walks over to a photograph of a strapping man in blue overalls with a bandanna on his head and asks, "Is this your son, Mrs. Booker?"

The old lady laughs. "Lord no, that's my husband, Lemuel."

"He's a handsome man."

"Yes, indeed. Lem was a good man, too, but he's gone more than forty years now. Got crushed by a log, loading a pulpwood truck. Chain broke."

"I'm sorry," I say automatically.

"My family were pulpwood cutters," Serenity says. "Cutters, haulers, you name it, they did it. Bleeding for turpentine, if you go further back."

Mrs. Booker has gone still. Then she squints at Serenity. "Is that right? Where you from, girl?"

"Up around Laurel. Longleaf pine country, back in the old days. All those old trees are long gone, though."

"Sho' is, baby. Long gone. And the men who cut 'em gone, too. Pulpwoodin's a dangerous business, but that's about all the work there is down in these woods for a black man. Or workin' at the sawmill. White men do the proper loggin' 'round here. Always have. Ya'll push them cats out these chairs and set down. Tell me what you come to find out from the old Cat Lady. Lots of bad things happened 'round here back in my day. Nobody cares about that now, though. Nobody even remembers."

"We care," Serenity says. "Do you remember?"

The watery eyes close, and the lined face tightens with grief. "Oh, Lord, yes. I wish I didn't. But I'll never forget." She nuzzles the chin of a thin calico with her foot. "You want to know about my real baby, Sam."

"We do," I tell her.

"That's Samuel over there," Mrs. Booker says, pointing to a framed photo on a table near the wall. Serenity goes over and looks at the photo, then picks it up and brings it to me. It shows a young man of about twenty holding a .22 rifle in one hand and a mess of squirrels by their tails in the other. Sam was thinner than his father, but just as handsome, and his eyes are bright with intelligence.

"That boy started putting food on the table when he was twelve years old," Mrs. Booker informs us. "Take a seat, baby," she says to Serenity. "Over here where I can see you."

Serenity nudges an orange tomcat off an old club chair and perches on the edge of it.

"Have you two had happy lives?" Mrs. Booker asks, her eyes filled with concern.

"I suppose so," I tell her, looking around the room. "I feel pretty lucky."

The old woman smiles. "Have you seen bad things?"

Serenity and I share a quick glance.

"You can't go through life without seeing some bad things," I say. "Can you?"

"No, no. But I mean *evil* things. Because there is real evil in this world." She turns to Serenity. "What about you, darling? You look too young to have seen much wickedness."

"I fought in a war, Mrs. Booker. And I covered the crime beat in a lot of urban housing projects. I've seen some of the worst things people can do to other people."

The old lady nods soberly. "Then you've seen him."

"Who?"

"*Him*. The serpent of old."

We share another uncomfortable glance. "If there is a devil," Serenity says, "I've seen him all right. In every country in the world."

The Cat Lady nods. "He can move anywhere, child, anytime. But at least I know I won't be putting something in your mind that it can't handle."

I say, "Why don't you tell us what happened to your son, Mrs. Booker?"

"He was killed by demons. White demons."

"Do you mean the Ku Klux Klan?"

"No. The Klan wore white robes back then. These demons wore black. Black or green."

Serenity cuts her eyes at me. She's wondering whether Mrs. Booker is in full possession of her faculties.

"And this happened at the place people call the Bone Tree?"

The old woman crosses herself. "That's the place. A pagan altar, that's what it is. Ask any of the old folks down around that swamp. They'll tell you."

"Will you tell us what happened?"

The persistent calico jumps soundlessly into Mrs. Booker's lap and settles there. The old woman sighs in surrender and scratches the animal between its ears.

"Sam was a hardworking boy," she says. "Lots of ambition. He left

Athens Point and moved north just as soon as he was old enough. He worked in Detroit, Michigan. Sam didn't like being too far away from me, but work here was slow. After he'd had enough, he came back home. But he wasn't alone. He had a woman with him. A wife, I should say. Dolores. We all called her Dee. Sam had married her up there. She was young and pretty, which was all fine and good. But she was also white, which wasn't."

This catches Serenity's interest. "Your son married a white woman up north?"

"Well, I *thought* he had. And so did everybody else 'round here. Dee's skin was so light, and her hair so straight, that she could pass, you know? Without even trying. Much lighter than you, baby. Up in Detroit, most people just treated her white, and she didn't bother correcting them. Didn't hurt nobody, did it? But Dee was proud of her family, and she didn't mind saying she was black. Her daddy was black, and she loved him. Though I don't think she quite knew what it was to be treated black. Not Mississippi black, you know?"

"Oh, I know," Serenity says softly. "Did Dee tell people here in Athens Point she was black?"

Mrs. Booker nods sadly. "That's where the trouble started. Dee lived black here from the start—went to the colored church and doctor—but the fact was, nobody believed her. Not even black folks. She wasn't even high yellow, to look at. Dee was so fair, people just thought we was lyin' to cover up the truth. White folks started sayin' my boy didn't know his place. Said he'd gone off north and come back with biggity ideas."

I'm suddenly sure I don't want to hear the rest of this story. But I can't see how to avoid it. Nothing would make Serenity leave this house now.

"First, they fired him from the sawmill," Mrs. Booker goes on, "even though the foreman said Sam was the best man he had. But the klukkers had a lot of power then. So Sam went back to hauling pulpwood, like his uncles. Dee went to work, too, at the dollar store. But she caught a lot of trouble there, from the other women. They were all jealous of her. The men wouldn't leave Dee alone, either, white and black. Always trying to touch her and stir up trouble. Sam should have taken her back to Detroit right then, but he had too much pride. He didn't like to back down, and back then that was usually a fatal condition for a black man in Mississippi."

I can tell from Serenity's gaze that she feels bonded to this woman in a way I never could.

"It was my fault, much as anybody's," she goes on. "If I'd told Sam to go, he probably would have. But I didn't. I was selfish and wanted him close to me."

Serenity says, "When did the demons come into the picture, Mrs. Booker?"

"Pretty soon after that. They took Sam and Dee right out their house one July night, just up the road from here. It happened so fast I didn't even hear a dog bark. Turned out later they'd killed Sam's dog. Cut its throat. Anyway, I didn't know anything was wrong till dawn the next day, when poor Dee came stumbling up my steps in a bloody slip and nothing else. No shoes . . . nothing."

Serenity is staring at the old woman with hypnotic intensity. "What happened to her?"

"The devils came in black masks and knocked Sam out. Then they loaded him and Dee into a panel truck and drove them to the edge of the Lusahatcha Swamp. The men blindfolded them and tied their hands. Then they put them in a boat. There was three, she said. Three boats. They set out through that damned swamp with lanterns on the bows, Sam and Dee in different boats. They trolled slow for a long time, and then they hit land. When they pulled off Dee's blindfold, she saw a cypress tree bigger than any she'd ever seen before. She said one of the men showed her old rusted chains hanging down from one of the limbs. Said they'd been hanging there since slave times."

In the pause that follows this statement, Serenity shudders.

"Sam had come to by that time, but his hands were tied, and he couldn't do nothing. They started beating him. Dee screamed, but the devils just laughed. Said there wasn't nobody to hear but snakes and alligators."

"Were they still wearing masks at that time, Mrs. Booker?"

"I believe so. They started beating on Sam, kickin' him, and callin' him all kinds of names. Crazy religious names, Dee said. Some of it she didn't even understand. Lord, they were filled with hate. One was howling scripture during all this."

"What did they want from Sam?"

"*Want?* Vengeance, baby. They said he'd married a white woman, and there was only one penalty for that crime. Death. *Mis-ce-genation,* they called it. I looked it up in the big dictionary at the church. Race-mixing is what it means. They said Sam was guilty of defiling a white woman, and he couldn't be bringing no mud babies into the world. *Mud babies.* Which is just pitiful, when you think how many white men fathered babies on black women. Probably some of those very men doing the beating."

"You know they did," Serenity whispers. "What happened next?"

"When Dolores realized why they was beating Sam, she started screaming then that she wasn't white. She told 'em her daddy was as black as Sam, and she hadn't ever pretended to be white. But it didn't do no good. They didn't believe her, see?"

The old woman shakes her head, then raises one hand to wipe her eyes. "Dee realized then that they meant to kill Sam. And she was right. Somebody got a rope out the boat and slung it over a limb. Sam was only half-conscious by then, thank Jesus. Dee begged and pleaded, 'Why do you have to kill him?' she kept asking. Finally, one of them turned to her and said, 'Because he's a nigger. And he defiled your womanhood, you whore.'"

"Jesus," I breathe, barely able to believe this happened less than forty miles from my childhood home.

"You know what Dee did then?" Mrs. Booker asks.

"Tell me," Serenity whispers.

"She broke loose and threw herself down over Sam to protect him. They started beating her, but when they stopped to catch their breath, she said, 'He hasn't broken your law! Can't you see what's right in front of you? I'm a nigger, too, you damn fools! *I'm a nigger, too!*'"

Neither I nor Serenity speaks while the old woman takes a Kleenex from the table beside her and dabs her watery eyes. Then at length Serenity says, "Dolores told you all this?"

"When she got to where she could talk straight, she did. It took most of a day to get her in her right mind."

"How did she get away from them?"

"They dropped her about a mile from my house when they was done with her."

I close my eyes, wanting not to ask, but I know Serenity won't let it go any more than Caitlin would have. "What else did they do to her?"

The old woman's eyes seem to deepen with infinite sadness. "You know what men like that do. They had their way with her. That's what they wanted all along, I think. Sam was just in the way."

"Why did they let her live?"

The old woman takes some time with this. "I've asked that very question for years and years. Maybe they were so arrogant that they didn't think anything could happen to them. And they were *right*, weren't they? Maybe they figured if they let her live, they could take another turn with her on down the road."

"Did they hang your son?" Serenity asks.

"Yes, ma'am. Right in front of his wife. Lynched him. Happened no more than ten miles from here."

"What year was this?"

"Nineteen sixty-six."

The summer of my first-grade year. "Did you report it to the police?"

The old woman stares at me as if I'm crazy. "Baby, like as not, some of the men behind those masks *were* po-lice."

"What about the FBI?"

"The FBI got wind of what happened some way, and they sent two men to talk to me. One was very kind. But I couldn't tell him anything. What he most wanted to know was where to find that Bone Tree, but I didn't know, and Dolores had no real idea where those devils had taken her. Of course, I heard they found that tree back around Christmas time. A girl died over there, finding it."

"That was my fiancée," I say softly.

"Oh, no. Lord Jesus." The Cat Lady lowers her head. "Now I see. So much pain in this world."

"But you knew something," Serenity says in an incisive voice. "Didn't you? Dolores remembered something about those men, or she saw something, and you kept it from the FBI."

Mrs. Booker watches Serenity for a while without speaking. Then she says, "The FBI told me they found some of Sam's bones under that tree. They used DNA to identify them. My pastor's gonna do a pretty service at the church after they get released to me."

"Mrs. Booker," Serenity says insistently. "Miss Cleotha. You know something, don't you?"

The old woman just stares straight ahead.

I take a folded page from the *Examiner* from my pocket, then get up and kneel beside her. "Mrs. Booker, there are over a dozen unsolved murders from the 1960s in this area, including your son's." I unfold the page, revealing headshots of Snake Knox, Brody Royal, Sonny Thornfield, and half a dozen Double Eagles. "These men are suspected in many of them. I think they might have been behind those masks the night your son was murdered."

The old woman doesn't look down at the page.

"My fiancée and a very brave journalist did a lot of work to try to punish the men who committed these crimes, Mrs. Booker. They died for it. And a young woman was hurt the other day for trying to carry on their work."

"I believe I heard about that, yessir."

"Will you look at these pictures? I know you're afraid, and you've had reason to be afraid for a long time. But things are finally changing, Mrs. Booker. Several of these men are dead already. I killed one myself, though I can't say that outside this room. Maybe the worst one."

At last she turns to look at me, piercing brown eyes set in sclera so yellow they look jaundiced. "God bless you, child."

"But that man's uncle is still alive. He's still hurting people like that young reporter."

The old woman closes her eyes, then gently pushes the calico off her lap and fixes me with an unsettling stare.

"I know things are changing," she says. "But they don't change everywhere at the same speed. Down here time moves on a different clock. Down here it's still forty years ago, in some ways. Back then, I knew if I told those FBI men something, and they started questioning people around here—or up at Natchez, or across the river at Ferriday—word would get out that somebody had talked. And sooner or later, those devils would come back around here. The FBI men always promised protection, but they couldn't protect anybody. They weren't gonna move into this house with Dee and me. And Lem was already dead when all this happened. If we'd told anything, we'd have died within a month. And nobody would have made a fuss, either. In white folks' minds, Sam and Dee had upset the natural order of things, and they got what they deserved."

I remember my father telling me how his fear of retaliation kept him from telling the FBI things he'd known about the Double Eagles. If a white physician couldn't summon the courage to talk to the FBI, how could anyone expect a poor black woman to do it?

"What happened to Dolores?" Serenity asks. "Did she go back north after that happened?"

Mrs. Booker pets the cat distractedly. "Eventually. I tried to get her help here." She nods at me. "I took her to several doctors, but she wouldn't open up to any of them. Not even Dr. Cage. Your father tried hard, son . . . but nobody could break through that darkness. Dee finally went back to Detroit, with her parents. But she never really got away from that tree. She was beyond mortal help, you see? And she'd given up on God. She had no way back to the light." The old woman lowers her head. "Dee took her own life about a year after she got back home. Laid down in a hot bath and slashed her wrists. I got a telegram from her daddy. Two lines, that was all. Her family never forgave Sam for bringing their baby south."

I look at Serenity, who, to my surprise, has tears pouring down her face.

"Why don't we talk about something else?" I suggest. "We shouldn't have put you through this for so long."

"Oh, don't worry about me, baby," the Cat Lady says, laying her other hand over mine. "It's Sunday. Pastor Sims will come by and check on me this afternoon. And I've got my babies to talk to." She makes a cooing sound in her throat, and a large gray cat silently springs from some unseen shadow into her lap, taking the calico's place. The big cat seems to land with purposeful gentleness, as though aware that its owner can't take much weight.

Serenity gets to her feet, then leans over and kisses the old woman's hair. "You take care, Auntie. We're going to leave you in peace."

Mrs. Booker looks up at Serenity with more alertness than I've seen in her eyes for several minutes. "You children are doing good work," she says. "I can see that. But please be careful. Justice is God's business. Nothing ever balances out equal in this world. Only in heaven."

"We'll be careful," Serenity promises, and she starts to turn, but the old lady holds her hand tight. "And take a little advice from an old country woman. Most people get snakebit because they tried to kill a creature they should have left in peace. You think about that when you make your plans."

As Serenity and I walk to the car, the Cat Lady stumps out onto her porch, gripping her walker. Surrounded by circling felines, she watches us like a mother making sure her children are safe until they leave her sight.

After I shut my car door, I say, "The worst story in the world?"

"Not even close," Serenity says, buckling her seat belt. "But for something that happened in the good old U.S. of A., it's right up there."

"I don't think Mrs. Booker heard the whole story. I think Dolores spared her a lot. The Double Eagles were cruel sons of bitches. They liked to take trophies from their victims."

Serenity looks at the old woman watching us from the rickety porch. "Too bad Dolores offed herself."

The coldness in Tee's voice puts me off, but I sense that she meant no harm by it. Brutal frankness is just her way. I wave at the Cat Lady, then turn the key and start the engine.

"What is it?" Serenity asks. "Why aren't we leaving?"

Cleotha Booker is still standing on her porch, watching us like she plans to spend the rest of the day standing there.

"Penn?" Tee prompts.

"Give me a second," I say irritably. "I've interviewed a lot of witnesses in my time. After a while . . . you develop an instinct about people."

"And? What are you saying?"

"Why is she still standing up there?"

"Because she's a lonely old lady. And we made her think about some horrible shit."

I shake my head, still focused on the old woman's hollow eyes. "She's afraid."

"Of course she is."

"Not of the Klan, though. Or the Double Eagles. She's afraid of *us*."

"What do you mean? Why would she be afraid of us?"

"Because she's hiding something." A surge of certainty blasts through me, and I switch off the engine. "Let's go find out what."

The second I start back up the gravel drive, the Cat Lady's composure collapses in on itself. The mask of the doddering old woman falls away, and fear and calculation flash from her eyes in equal measure. By the time we reach the porch steps, her whole body is quivering.

"Don't come back up here," she begs. "Please."

"Why not?" Serenity asks from beside me.

Mrs. Booker sighs wearily, almost in surrender. "I knew you'd come back. Dr. Cage was no fool. Still, I fooled him like the rest. But maybe the son's just a little sharper than his father."

"What are you talking about?" Serenity asks. "What did you do?"

"Dolores isn't dead," I say, keeping my eyes on the Cat Lady. "She never killed herself. They told everyone that to protect her. So the Eagles would never go after her, the way they did Viola. Right?"

Serenity is staring at the Cat Lady in disbelief.

"Right?" I press.

"It was the only way to be sure," the old woman says. "God forgive me, but I'd do the same thing again."

"Where is she?" I ask. "Still in Detroit?"

"I'll never tell you. Never."

But I know she will. I have a secret weapon to make people talk. Her name is Serenity Butler.

CHAPTER 18

DESPITE SERENITY'S BEST efforts, Cleotha Booker did not tell us where her daughter-in-law is living. But she did eventually agree to contact Dolores by phone and ask if she'd be willing to talk to us about what happened at the Bone Tree back in 1966. During the ride back to Natchez, I can tell that Serenity has developed a new respect for me, and I feel some pride at that. It's good to know my instincts about people haven't completely deserted me during my long night of grieving Caitlin.

By the time we reach home, my mother has arrived from Pollock. We find her sitting at the kitchen table with Annie and Mia, looking more frazzled than I've ever seen her. She has swollen bags under her eyes that makeup can't fully mask, and a look of bone-deep fatigue that can only be the result of severe sleep deprivation. When I hug her, she feels as though she's lost five more pounds in the week since I've seen her.

When I introduce Serenity, Mom nods courteously, but she doesn't manage to raise a smile. This, more than anything, tells me that her dread of what might happen to Dad once he falls under the control of Sheriff Billy Byrd in the county jail is consuming her like a disease.

Sheriff Byrd forbade Mom from being present in the ACSO building during the transfer, claiming that would constitute special treatment. Byrd told Quentin Avery he didn't want anyone getting the idea that a physician would be treated any different than a yard man in his jail. This is likely only a hint of things to come. Annie and I have passed a few hours trying to keep Mom calm, with Annie carrying the bulk of the load, but nothing short of my father's acquittal is going to ease her burden, and the trial is sure to last at least a week, if not longer.

Quentin Avery and his wife, Doris, arrive in Natchez about four. Serenity and I drive down to the bluff to help get them settled in Edelweiss, which I offered to Quentin as a base of operations during the trial. Despite having three stories, the house is perfect for him, because the widow I bought it from installed an elevator a couple of years before she moved to a group care facility. It's a primitive, wire-cage-type lift, but it will hold the weight of Quentin's motorized wheelchair, and that's all that matters.

At Quentin's request, Doris makes Serenity some coffee in the kitchen while he and I go out to the broad front gallery "to discuss strategy for tomorrow's voir dire," according to Quentin. Quentin rolls his wheelchair to the rail, from which you can survey fourteen miles of the Mississippi River. I sit in one of the large rocking chairs Caitlin always said she wanted up here to watch the sunsets.

"Are we really going to discuss the voir dire?" I ask. "Or do you have something else to tell me?"

A faint smile touches the old man's lips. "Still quick as ever. We'll get to the jury list. Housekeeping first. I'm officially listing you as part of your father's defense team. Your father doesn't want that, but your mother insists, and you know who wins that argument."

Oh, yeah.

"Peggy wants to know you can check on your father at any hour of the day or night, and with Sheriff Byrd being a prick, the only way to accomplish that is for you to be one of your father's lawyers."

"I get it." I try to keep my tone neutral, but I know Quentin's powers of perception.

"Penn, you're a great lawyer," he says. "I'd give my left arm to have you sitting with me at the defense table. But your father wants you excluded. I'm sorry, but that's the way it is. There's nothing personal about it."

"It's *purely* personal. And I don't get it."

"I know. But your father's the client, and I'm following his wishes."

I sigh heavily. "Is there anything else?"

"A couple of things, actually. First, this case isn't going to be like any I ever tried before. I'm going to take a very unconventional approach to get your father acquitted. I might even get a little crazy."

"What does that mean?"

"I'm not a hundred percent sure myself yet. But whatever I do, I won't be able to explain my strategy to you. So I'm asking you to promise me now that whatever I decide, you won't be pestering me every minute to explain my tactics."

"I'm not going to be your main problem, brother. Mom is going to expect me to explain every step of the trial to her. And if you keep me in the dark, then you do the same to her. And you know that's not going to fly."

Quentin gives me a look of world-weary confidence. "You let me handle Peggy."

"You're welcome to it."

"So we're good?" Quentin asks, a note of challenge in his voice.

"Actually, no. But what the hell can I do about it?"

"Hell, boy, can you think of anybody you'd trust more than me to defend your father?"

In truth, I know some genius-level criminal attorneys much closer to the primes of their careers than the legless old man sitting in the wheelchair beside me. But in a murder case involving race in Mississippi . . . those lawyers would be like novice sailors adrift in a hurricane compared to Quentin Avery.

"No," I concede after a resentful silence.

"Just keep the faith, Penn. No matter how crazy you think I might be. We have a deal?"

Something keeps me from giving him my unqualified trust. "What about Judge Elder? Are you still worried he's leaning to Shad's side in this thing?"

This question Quentin actually considers. "I don't want to get into legal details, but I've tried to get some special considerations for Tom at the jail, considering the severity of his health problems—not to mention my worries about Billy Byrd—and Joe hasn't been any help."

"You should have filed that damned change-of-venue motion."

Quentin looks upriver, where a string of barges is making its way down from Vicksburg. "You got any boiled peanuts? I could really use some."

"No boiled peanuts, Q."

"Damn. How 'bout you send that pretty writer out for some? Or one of them bodyguards you got?"

I stand in exasperation and walk to the rail. "Do you want to go over the jury pool or not?"

He waves his hand. "Nah. I just want *you* to go over it, so you can give me a thumbs-up or thumbs-down during the voir dire. I choose by instinct, you know that. But you might know some info on locals that somehow escapes my Sherlockian skills." The old lawyer gives me a self-mocking grin. "I'm not perfect. Not quite, anyway."

"That's for *damn* sure," says Doris Avery, stepping onto the gallery with Serenity in tow.

Doris is thirty years her husband's junior, which puts her close to my age. She's also a lawyer, and a beautiful woman. In the afternoon light, I can't help noticing the difference in skin tone between her and Serenity. Though lighter than Quentin, Doris is darker than Serenity, and thus solidly on the wrong end of the paper-bag-test spectrum.

"What have you ladies been talking about inside?" Quentin asks. "The handsome menfolk out here, I trust?"

"Delusional," says Doris. "That's what you are. And you'd better watch your mouth around this girl, Q. She won't put up with your sass for five seconds."

Quentin grins, then winks at Serenity. "I'll look forward to being reprimanded."

Doris snorts. "What have you two been talking about? The voir dire, I hope."

"Boiled peanuts," Quentin says. "I got a serious jones for some right now."

"Well," Doris says with infinite patience, "let me get cleaned up a little, and then we'll take a ride and see if we can find some in this town. These two have more important things to do than listen to your bullshit."

Serenity and I leave them smiling on the gallery, slapping it back and forth like a couple married for fifty years.

"She's worried about Quentin," Serenity says as we get into the Audi. "She said he's been going down fast since he lost his second leg."

I shift the car into gear and loop around by Rosalie, where the French settled Natchez back in 1716. "He'll make it through the trial," I say, sounding like I'm trying to persuade myself. "This is his swan song."

Serenity nods, but she doesn't look convinced.

As I turn left into traffic on Canal Street, she lays her hand over mine where it rests on the emergency brake lever. She squeezes lightly, then lifts her hand and puts it back in her lap.

A shiver goes through me at her touch, but upon reflection her gesture didn't seem sexual in any way. It was more an unspoken acknowledgment of something we both sense. *Bad times coming.* Beyond that, she might have meant to add, *And I'm here with you.* But who knows?

The moment's passed.

CHAPTER 19

BY EIGHT P.M. we've still heard nothing from Cleotha Booker. An hour ago, Serenity retired to her room to make some calls, which meant reaching out to friends in Detroit to have them ask their elders about any Dolores who got married in the 1960s and moved to Mississippi for a while, then returned. This kind of effort sounded absurd to me, but Serenity told me I might be surprised by the way information moved in the black community—even in a large city like Detroit. While she put out her feelers up north, I watched television with Annie and my mother. I paid no attention to the programs, and Mom didn't, either. But sitting there served to begin the process of our coming back together as a family before the trial starts tomorrow.

During a commercial break, Annie muted the volume to raise the question of whether she'll be allowed to go to court. I'm open to the idea, but Mom is dead set against it. She told Annie she doesn't want her hearing any of the "scandalous lies" that will doubtless be told about her grandfather. Annie reluctantly accepted this—for the time being—but I know the real reason for my mother's resistance. She doesn't want Annie hearing the truth about her grandfather.

About eight thirty, I decide to walk the three blocks down to the courthouse and get a look at the field of battle. Tim walks with me through the darkness, and he's perceptive enough not to talk beyond the first twenty steps. The scent of flowers is on the air: azaleas, Confederate jasmine, and my favorite—sweet olive—but the sweetness only serves to remind me how transitory all happiness tends to be.

The Natchez courthouse stands two blocks from the bluff, directly opposite the sheriff's department and jail. On one side of State Street, set on a small hill, the classic Greek Revival building rises above the majestic oak trees that surround it. On the other side of the street squats a brick Stalinist version of a medieval pile, with slit windows on the jail floors piled atop one another to compete with the white columns and airy cupola facing them. The architect probably copied those windows from a castle in a book. My father is behind one of those slits, but I can't tell which. If I stand here long enough he might look out, for like me, he doesn't usually go to sleep until long past midnight.

Tim has given me about thirty yards of space, which is more than he usually does. Tonight I'm thankful for the separation. As I stare at the ugly, sodium-lit building, it suddenly strikes me that Dad hasn't excluded me from this case to hurt me. Rather, he has cut himself off from us all, like a father in the Middle Ages infected with plague, crawling off into the forest to die before infecting his family. The only person he's willing to talk to is an ailing peer: Quentin Avery.

Turning to face the courthouse, I reflect on the fact that I have tried more than a thousand criminal cases in my life—many of them murder cases—but tomorrow I will be only a spectator. I will carry Quentin's water during the voir dire, but once the real action starts, I'll be relegated to the gallery. Many lawyers would probably be content with this; Quentin's courtroom skills are legendary. But that is cold comfort tonight. To my knowledge, he has no investigators, no co-counsel, not even assistants working for him (other than his wife). How in God's name does he plan to break down the nearly impervious forensic case built up by Shadrach Johnson and Sheriff Byrd over the past three months? I suppose I'll find out at the same time as everyone else in the courtroom. I can only pray that the old fox lives up to his legend one last time.

"Mr. Mayor?" calls a soft voice.

I squint and see the courthouse janitor—an old black man, naturally—walking down the concrete steps.

"Is there anything I can help you with?" he asks.

"Actually, I was thinking about going in and taking a look at the courtroom. But I guess it's too late for that."

"I'm afraid so. I just locked up, and the sheriff took my key. Normally I could take you in, but this trial's different. The FBI was down here with dogs all evening, sniffing all over the building."

I'm actually relieved to hear this. "It's all right. I'm fine out here."

"You could probably call Sheriff Byrd to let you in," he suggests.

"I'd rather not do that."

"No, sir, I didn't figure."

So even the janitors know there's bad blood between Billy Byrd and my family.

"If you really want to get in, there is a way. But you've got to climb up onto the roof from the fire escape. It's pretty dangerous."

"No, no. I was about to head home. Haven't we met before?"

The janitor smiles without making eye contact. "You've said hello to me a couple times. I'm Noel Shelton."

The name sounds familiar. "I knew a man with your last name," I think aloud. "He helped me find some files a few years ago. Important files. They helped me on a civil rights case."

White teeth show in the darkness. "That was my brother, Leon. The Del Payton case, right?"

"That's right! Does Leon still work here?"

"No, sir. Leon done passed. Three years ago, now."

Though it's night, the shadow of mortality falls over us. "I'm sorry. He was a good man."

"Yes, sir. And . . . I know it's none of my business, but please tell Dr. Cage to hold his head high tomorrow."

This takes me by surprise. "You know about his case?"

"Shoot, everybody 'round here know."

"What do you think about it, Noel?"

The custodian shrugs, his gaze focused over my shoulder, on the sheriff's department. "I can't speak for nobody else. But I know this: when Leon was sick, he like to broke the family with doctor bills. Lab bills, X-ray bills, surgeon bills, anesthesia bills, the home health. After he died, we had people calling ten times a day, and collectors coming from the hospital in Jackson. It was terrible. Me and my two sisters paid and paid, but we couldn't begin to cover it all."

It's an old American story. "I'm sorry, Noel."

"You got nothing to be sorry about. The onliest bill I knew I wanted to pay was your daddy's, 'cause he took such good care of Leon at the end. But we paid the pushiest people first, you know? Had to. We went to see Dr. Cage at his office, to ask for some time, 'cause of the load and all. You know what he said?"

I suspect I know the answer, but I shake my head.

"Doc took his bill and studied on it for a minute. Then he folded it up and dropped it in the trash can. He said, 'Your brother was a fine man, Mr. Shelton. Ya'll git on home now. Don't worry 'bout that bill no more.'"

My throat tightens, preventing me from replying.

At last the janitor's eyes find mine, and they are filled with unspoken feeling. "I ain't exactly clear on what they think your daddy done, Mr. Mayor. And I'm just a custodian, like my brother. But if you need somebody to stand up in that courthouse and tell the truth about Dr. Cage, I'd be proud to do it. Ain't no better man in my book. My sister, too."

I want to say, "Thank you, Noel," but all I manage to do is shake his callused hand and turn back up the dark street, my eyes stinging with tears of confusion.

"Hey, Penn," Tim calls, closing the distance to me with a graceful economy of motion that belies the speed involved. "You've got an audience over there."

Following Tim's hand, I look across the street and see a brown-shirted figure with his arms folded standing before the glass doors of the sheriff's department. Billy Byrd. Over his big belly and burly forearms, the gold star gleams on the sheriff's chest. His satisfied grin reaches toward me like a slapping hand. Then he calls, "I see you're out mixin' with the quality, as usual. Looks like you forgot your mop, though. We can get you one from inside."

A deputy standing behind him laughs.

"There's no upside to me going over there," I say softly. "Right?"

"Absolutely none," Tim agrees.

"You wanna come in and say hello to your daddy?" Byrd taunts me. "He's a sad sight, Mayor. But I'm doin' all I can to keep him comfortable, yes, sir. Lots of special attention."

"How about we go kick their asses?" I suggest.

Something like harsh laughter sounds in Tim's muscular chest. "I'd like five minutes with that bastard in a locked room. That grin would be on his asshole, not his face." Tim takes hold of my arm and leads me up State Street. "But it'll have to be another time. Unless you do want to check on your father?"

"Byrd wouldn't let us in now."

"Hey!" Sheriff Byrd calls after us. "Why don't you two lovebirds get a room? We don't like a lot of PDA between men around here."

Their laughter echoes after us between the buildings, sounding exactly like that of the boys I used to play against in the cow pasture football fields of the "Christian schools" in the 1970s.

"Another time," Tim repeats, like mantra. "Another time."

ABOUT A MILE outside Athens Point, Mississippi, two men sat smoking in a pickup truck near a crooked old shack at the edge of the woods. The driver was in his midforties, his passenger twenty years older.

"Tell me again what Kenny told you," said the driver.

"He was passin' by here going to check a well, and he saw the car parked here. It was an Audi S4. The one with the big engine."

The driver nodded. "That's the car, all right. The mayor drives it. Cage. I've seen him in it up on the bluff in Natchez. At the balloon races. What the hell would he be doin' here?"

"Talkin' to the Cat Lady, what else? Ain't nobody else around here."

The driver scratched his beard and looked around the car. The only visible light was a dim glow against the curtains in the rightmost room.

"You know who the Cat Lady is, don't you?" asked the older man.

"Just an old colored woman with about a hundred cats. Why? Somethin' special about her?"

"Not really. But a long time ago, somebody lynched her kid."

"Klan?"

"Word was, it was the Knox brothers. The Double Eagles."

"Huh. I never heard that."

"Why don't we go in there and find out what the mayor was doing here? Might just get us a fat reward. Or huntin' rights out at Valhalla, at the least."

The driver grunted, still thinking. Athens Point had changed a lot since Forrest Knox was killed at Valhalla.

"If we're gonna do something, let's do it," said the older man. "I'm tired of sittin' here."

The driver took a deep drag on his cigarette. "Let's not get hasty," he said, smoke drifting from his mouth. "I'm gonna make a phone call."

DEEP IN THE well of the night, I sit up from a sound sleep with the certainty that something is terribly wrong. I listen intently but hear nothing amiss. Nevertheless, I throw off the covers, take my pistol from the bedside table, and walk out into the hall.

My mother is lying on the floor, staring blankly up at the ceiling.

"Mom!" I cry, dropping to my knees. "What happened?"

She blinks her right eye repeatedly, as though trying to clear something from it. Then she speaks in a guttural voice: "I was trying to get to your room. Penn, I can't . . . I think I'm having a stroke."

Adrenaline flushes through me, bringing me fully alert. "Why do you think that? You're not slurring your speech. What's going on?"

"My right arm . . . numb. My foot, too. And . . . I can't see out of my right eye. I'm sorry."

Jesus Christ. "When did this start? Just now?"

"No. I was seeing flashes of light earlier, when we were watching TV with Annie."

Frustration balloons in my chest. "Why didn't you say anything then?"

"I thought it was stress. I didn't want anybody telling me not to go to the courthouse tomorrow."

"Mom, I'm calling Drew."

"No!"

"I'm going to pick you up and carry you into my room."

"Don't. I'm too heavy. You'll hurt your back."

"Here we go." Sliding my arms beneath her, I lift the woman who brought me into the world into the air and carry her bodily to my room. There I set her on the foot of my bed, grab my cell phone from the bedside table, and dial Drew Elliott's cell phone. I do not pray, as a rule. Like my father, I don't believe there's any deity out there to hear such things.

But I am praying now.

MONDAY

CHAPTER 20

AT FIVE THIRTY A.M., my cell phone rang at the hospital. Serenity had just received a call from the Cat Lady, during which the old woman asked for Serenity's word that neither she nor I would ever reveal the name or location of her former daughter-in-law, if she passed it to us. Serenity instantly agreed, and thirty seconds later she had a name, a time, and a New Orleans address.

I spent Monday morning at St. Catherine's Hospital with my mother while Drew ran a battery of tests to confirm or rule out a stroke, including an angiogram and an MRI. Throughout this process—which was mostly hurry-up-and-wait—I received a steady stream of updates from the courthouse describing the voir dire process. The texts were authored by Rusty Duncan, a local lawyer whose friendship with me dates back to nursery school at St. Stephen's Prep. Rusty's a funny son of a bitch, as well as smart, and he peppered his texts with quips and sarcastic commentary about Quentin's unusual questions for the potential jury members. The basic picture Rusty painted was of a circus in which citizens who normally tried everything short of self-mutilation to avoid jury duty were lying through their teeth to get a chance to hear the lurid details of my father's case and ultimately decide his fate.

About midday Drew Elliott came to me in the cafeteria with what he believed was good news. "Earlier I believed Peggy had a TIA," he said, "a transient ischemic attack. But now, believe it or not, I'm thinking her symptoms may have resulted from a complex migraine headache. They can mimic the symptoms of stroke. Peggy has no history of migraines, but God knows she's under unbearable stress."

Despite his optimism, Drew insisted on additional tests, and also on keeping Mom in the hospital overnight. When Mom told him she planned to be in court tomorrow for the beginning of the trial proper, Drew absolutely forbade it.

"Peggy, I could be wrong about the migraine," he said. "And if there *was* a clot—and we missed it or it was reabsorbed—then there could be another one coming down the pike. And statistically, the next one would be bigger and more damaging."

"I don't care," Mom said flatly. "And if the big one is coming, what's the difference if I'm lying in bed or sitting in court downtown?"

"Your odds of survival. That's the difference, Peggy."

Even this made little impression on my mother, of course. I almost wept with relief later, when my sister arrived after her drive up from the Baton Rouge airport. Jenny was jet-lagged from her London flight, but she agreed to stay with Mom while Serenity and I flew to New Orleans to interview someone I described as "an important witness who might be able to help get Dad acquitted."

After an exhaustive discussion of the risks, Tim Weathers and one of his men drove us to a grass airstrip south of Natchez, where Danny McDavitt's Cessna 182 awaited us. Tim had bought into the notion that Serenity and I flying secretly to New Orleans while our security team remained on station in Natchez might provide the best possible cover for our trip.

I'd gotten to know Danny McDavitt through Carl Sims, and the pilot has proved invaluable to me more than once. It was Danny who dropped Carl and me into the swamp beside the Bone Tree during our attempt to rescue Caitlin. While he helped Serenity get aboard, I got another call from Rusty, who was leaving the courthouse.

"They finished the voir dire," he said, panting as befitted his bulk.

"And?"

"For a while I was worried it would go into tomorrow."

"What was the delay?"

"Well, like I texted you, we had a reversal of the usual dynamic. We've got thirty-five thousand people in Adams County, and every damn one apparently wants to serve on this jury. They think it's going to be the biggest show of the decade."

"Great."

"Judge Elder took more time than usual to cull out the 'habitual drunkards' and 'low gamblers.' Shad burned a couple of peremptories to cut out preachers. He doesn't want anybody especially forgiving of human frailty on that panel. And he tried his best to cut older black women. He got right up against the Batson rule. He knows those black ladies love your daddy."

"Yeah, but do they still love him after this Viola-Lincoln thing?"

"Come on, man. Outside kids ain't no big thing to them."

"I'm not so sure, Rusty."

"I couldn't tell who Quentin's ideal juror was. And he didn't ask my advice a single time. At one point he muttered something about Mississippi needing a set of peremptory challenges for white men with big silver belt buckles. I think I saw Judge Elder smile at that, but he coughed to cover it, so I'm not positive."

This prompts a favorable grunt from me.

"Anyway, after they narrowed it down, Quentin started checking family relations. He told the crowd he once tried a murder case in which the opposing lawyer—who was from out of state—hadn't realized until the trial was over that four of the jury members were cousins. He got a big laugh. He's a natural with juries, Penn. A real performer."

"No doubt. So, how'd it wind up?"

"They settled on seven blacks and five whites, with one alternate from each race. Four of the blacks are women, and three whites."

Seven women and five men. "What do you think, Rusty?"

"Hard to know with this case. I don't know what else might come out that we haven't heard yet. Has your daddy got any other big secrets that could break in the next week?"

"Who the hell knows? Not me."

"I hear you. You gonna be in court tomorrow?"

"Barring unforeseen emergencies—which have been the rule up till now."

"Okay, then. I'll see you when I see you."

That was eighty minutes ago.

The sky has been clear for our southward flight, and on final approach to New Orleans Danny gives us a good look at the state of the city six months after Katrina. As mayor of Natchez, I know the statistics well, but they pale in comparison to what we can see on the ground. Bed frames and masonry piled in the streets. Overturned boats lying in yards. A telephone pole sticking up through a wrecked house. An upside-down school bus. A pack of dogs loping along the Seventeenth Street Canal.

As Serenity drives our rental car into the city, negotiating a depressing number of uprooted trees, I tell her some of the stats I know. More than half the homes in the city are still without electricity. Three hundred thousand people have yet to return. Eighty-three thousand families are living in asbestos-filled FEMA trailers. Serenity nods through my recitation. Then, when I pause, she says, "Were you down here during the storm?"

"No. It hit Natchez, too. I was trying to hold things together up there."

Another nod. "I came down and worked a boat with a rescue crew."

Of course she did. I should have guessed by now.

"I have some cousins here," she explains. "Distant. We spent two days pulling people off roofs and out of trees. Then I helped with some recovery work. The bodies, you know. Man, in some ways this place was worse than Iraq. *Way* worse."

"What was your takeaway?"

A bitter laugh escapes her mouth. "Politicians don't give a shit about the South. Except at election time. If Katrina would have hit the East Coast, most of this shit would never have happened the way it did."

By the time we reach the Garden District, the light is fading. Here on the high ground the houses have power, and as the lights come up, it's easy to tell myself that the storm had never happened. But then the wind changes, and I catch the funk of rotting wood and black mold.

To my surprise, Dolores St. Denis lives in a mansion only two blocks from St. Charles Avenue, on Dufossat Street. Set behind ivy-covered brick walls, the cream-colored three-story château is fronted with pine trees, and heavy wrought iron spans the spaces between all the columns.

We use an intercom to announce ourselves, and Mrs. St. Denis herself buzzes us inside. When the huge cypress door opens, I find myself looking at a remarkably striking woman in her midsixties. As expected, her features are almost entirely Caucasian—far more so than Serenity's—but there's a subtle darkness to her skin that no one who knew her background would mistake for a suntan. When she speaks to introduce herself, her diction is not only perfect but refined, and I know with certainty that this woman could "pass" for white in any environment she chose.

"I've gone by Dee for decades now," she says, leading us deeper into the house, which is furnished with a mixture of antiques and modern pieces. "But you may call me Dolores. I rather like hearing it again, actually."

"What does your husband do?"

"Maurice was an executive for an insurance company. He passed away three years ago. I'm alone now."

She seats herself in a burgundy velvet chair, then motions for Serenity and me to sit on a low-slung sofa that looks like a Roche Bobois.

"Mr. Cage, I agreed to see you because of your father. When I was in a very dark place, he tried to help me. He really tried. But I was beyond help at that time."

"I appreciate that. It's my father who's in serious trouble now. Anything you can tell us might help him considerably. I know that your—your time in Mississippi was very difficult. And I'm sorry to have to ask you about it."

Dolores St. Denis folds her hands in her lap, then looks up at me with startling intensity. "Mr. Cage, I know you were once a lawyer. Do you have any experience with violent crime?"

"A great deal, ma'am. I was an assistant district attorney in Houston for eight years. I worked the most violent cases that came through our office. Gang murders, serial killers, everything."

"Sexual assault? Gang rapes?"

"That, too, I'm sorry to say. Group assaults on both women and men."

She sighs and shakes her head, and I notice that her hair is very straight and fine. "Then you have some idea of what I was trying to deal with back then."

I nod. "We're here because I believe some of the men who killed your husband may have been the ones who ordered the murder of my fiancée."

She blinks in surprise, as if she's only just put together my deepest personal connection to the case. "I see. Well . . . what would you like to know?"

"I've been wondering whether the woman who suffered the horrific assault Mrs. Booker described might remember a lot more detail than she confided to her mother-in-law."

After a few moments, Dolores nods. "I didn't tell her everything, of course. I couldn't. It would have broken her. I didn't want her suffering as I was. I didn't have any peace after that night. Not one night of peace, for the dreams."

I don't want to hear worse than I heard in Mrs. Booker's house, but this is what we came for. "What did you dream, Dolores?"

"They . . . they did terrible things to Sam that night. They mutilated him. In my dreams, early on, he came to me without his eyes, and his privates gone. He still does sometimes, even today. Oh, dear Lord. Why would men do that?"

"Some of the Double Eagles are sociopaths. Sadists, more than racists. They used war and the violence of the civil rights struggle to cover their natural predilections."

She considers this for a while. "That makes complete sense to me."

"How many men were there altogether, Dolores?"

She shudders and closes her eyes. "Six."

I want to ask her to look at some photographs of the Double Eagles, but instinct tells me not to—not yet, anyway.

"Are you here because you want me to testify against those men?"

"We're here first because we want to know if you even have information that could positively identify any of the men who killed your husband."

She nods slowly, warily.

"Is that a yes?" Serenity asks.

Dolores doesn't reply.

Something tells me to get off the couch, kneel before her, and promise not to divulge anything she might tell us. But I remain where I am. Serenity cuts her eyes at me, and what I read there is: *Don't say anything. She's coming to it in her own way.* Then Dolores begins to speak in a soft, hoarse voice.

"As for identification . . . one of the men had a stutter. He was a big man, very big, and he was drunk. He had trouble getting an erection when he tried to take his turn, and he almost killed me by beating me, all the while yelling it was my fault."

I nod encouragement, but my mind is racing.

"That triggered something," she guesses. "Didn't it?"

"Your description fits Glenn Morehouse, the Double Eagle who first broke their code of silence and talked to Henry Sexton. The FBI thinks he was murdered by his old comrades. His sister may have helped to kill him."

Dolores shakes her head in amazement.

"What else do you remember?"

"There was a blond man who howled scripture during the assault. I saw the hair underneath his hood. He quoted scripture even while he raped me. It terrified me that he blasphemed like that while he was . . . doing what he was doing. But it almost seemed he was doing it to mock someone."

"If that was who I think it was," I tell her, "his father was a lay preacher, and a completely evil man."

"What other details do you remember?" Serenity asks.

"The blond man had scars on his stomach. On his lower abdomen. They looked serious. Like something you'd get in a war."

"Most of the Double Eagles were combat veterans," I temporize, trying to mask my excitement. "Can you describe the scars?"

"I don't . . . they were darker than the other skin. Raised. They didn't look like bullet holes. They looked like . . . like little pieces of hot metal, maybe?"

"Shrapnel," said Serenity, touching the scar in front of her left ear.

"That's it."

"What else?" I ask softly as my pulse races.

"One of them was just a boy. A teenager, but barely. He was quiet through most of it, and I thought he was just going to watch. But then the leader told him to take his turn. He was darker than the rest, far darker than me. Two of the men were dark-skinned for white men, but this one especially. I noticed because the ones watching were holding up lanterns beside me, all throughout."

"I'll bet anything that the young one was Forrest Knox. And the older dark one was his father, Frank."

Dolores's face remains impassive.

"Did you read any of the stories about the Double Eagles in the *Times-Picayune*?" I ask. "Last December? Forrest Knox was a ranking officer in the state police."

"I can't bear to read about crime and violence."

Serenity and I share a look. This woman is very fragile, and pushing her too hard might well silence her forever. Looking down, I see her hands quivering.

"That dark young man you remember was Forrest Knox. He was killed in December."

"Really?"

"Yes, ma'am."

"How did he die?"

I glance at Serenity, who raises her eyebrows, giving me the choice.

"Violently, Dolores. He murdered my fiancée. And he died with a spear through his throat."

Dolores St. Denis studies me in silence for half a minute. Then she says, "I see."

"His father was almost certainly the other dark man you remember. He was the founder of the Double Eagle group. Frank Knox. He was killed in 1968, only a couple of years after your husband was murdered."

Dolores goes pale at this. "Really?" she whispers.

If I had to guess, she is thinking about decades of nightmares she might have been spared had she known that the demon in them was dead. "Yes, ma'am," I say again. "He died on the floor of my father's medical office. His chest was crushed in an industrial accident."

Relief shines from Dolores's eyes.

"Would you be willing to look at some photographs?" I finally ask.

She instantly draws back from me. "I'd rather not. Do you really think any of those men are still alive?"

"I'm afraid so."

"Which ones? Not the blond man."

I dread answering her, but I have no choice. "He might be, yes. He might be just the man we're after."

She closes her eyes once more. "Oh, God. I knew it."

"What?" asks Serenity, leaning closer. "What is it?"

"They were all bad . . . but in some way, he was the worst. Not the most brutal, but . . . the most twisted. It was him who turned me over, who—"

"It's all right," I say quickly. "You don't have to tell us that right now."

"I'd rather get it out. I never thought I would, you see. But now . . . maybe because of what you've told me, I feel I can."

"What did the blond man do?" Serenity asks softly.

"He sodomized me. Several did, after that. But that wasn't the worst of it. The blond one used a stick on me. A piece of bamboo. He said something about the Japanese doing the same thing in China. He called them 'Japs,' of course. I—"

Dolores's voice dies suddenly, as if her air has simply run out.

"Are you all right?" asks Serenity, starting to her feet.

"I thought I was going to die that night," she whispers. "They tore me up so badly. That's why I have no children. I couldn't conceive after that."

"That had to be Snake Knox," I say with conviction. "He's the missing piece in that scene. Frank and his buddies took trophies off the Japanese during the war. Snake probably did the same in Korea. They were obsessed with that kind of thing." And Snake used a bottle on Viola during the machine-shop rape . . .

Serenity has reached out and taken hold of Dolores's hand. "I'm right here with you," she almost croons. "They can't hurt you now."

"I need to find out if Snake Knox was wounded in Korea," I think aloud. "Or if he had any sort of abdominal scars at that time."

"No, you don't," says Dolores.

I look up in surprise. *Did I go too far?* "I'm sorry, Dolores. I've just been hunting this guy for so long. You don't want me to pursue this?"

She shakes her head. "You don't need to worry about the scars. Because I saw his face."

This revelation hits me like a lightning flash. "You saw the blond man's face?"

"Yes. While the others were raping me, he and the older dark one shared a bottle of whiskey off to the side. They didn't think I could see them, I guess. Or they weren't planning on letting me live, maybe."

"May I show you some photographs?"

Dolores takes a deep breath, then nods.

I take out the folded page from the *Examiner* that I showed her mother-in-law in Athens Point. On it are headshots of most of the Knoxes, Glenn Morehouse, Sonny Thornfield, and several other Double Eagles. Dolores scans the page for about ten seconds, then reaches out and lays the nail of her right forefinger on the face of Snake Knox.

"That's him. That's the blond man with the scars. He and the dark man killed my husband."

I close my eyes with enervating relief. "Jesus God."

"Thank you," Serenity tells her. "You don't know what you've done."

Getting slowly to my feet, I look down at Dolores. "I promise you this, Mrs. St. Denis. That man is going to die in Angola Prison."

She glances over at Serenity, then back at me. "Even without me testifying in court?"

I force myself to take a deep breath, then sit back down in front of her. I came to this fork in the road a thousand times as a prosecutor. Nobody wants to sit in open court and point their finger at a violent killer.

"Dolores—"

"I can't do it," she says quickly. "I know what you want, and I wish I could help you. But I can't sit in the same room with him. I can't."

Serenity nods with understanding, but I know she's going to try to bring the woman around. "Dolores—"

"Can't you just use what I've told you?" she cuts in, her voice high and unsteady. "Like an anonymous tip?"

"I'm afraid that won't work in a murder case," I explain.

Dolores looks into her lap and begins to sob quietly. I look to Serenity for help, but even she doesn't seem to know what to do. While we stare at each other, Dolores's house phone begins to ring. The bell is soft, but Dolores's head snaps up so fast that it scares me.

"It's okay," I assure her. "Nobody knows we're here."

"Maybe it's Cleotha, checking on me."

"I'm sure it is. Why don't you answer it?"

She gets up, walks to an occasional table near the door, then picks up the phone and says, "Yes?"

About five seconds pass. Then she says, "Hello? Hello . . . ?"

As she hangs up, her face drains of color.

"They said my name," she says dully. "They said 'Dolores Booker?'" Suddenly her eyes go wide. "They've found me. After all these years . . .

oh, dear God. I should have never—oh, *Lord*. What do I do? Call the police?"

My heart is pounding, but my brain is working fine. "I'd rather call the FBI. They have a field office in New Orleans, and I know a guy who can get a team here fast."

"'Fast' is a relative term," Serenity says. "Their field office is out by Lake Pontchartrain, isn't it? That's what I remember from Katrina. We need help *now*."

Serenity is assuming that Snake or the VK have already got people coming to this house. Is she right? We can't afford to hope otherwise. "Then let's help ourselves. What's the address of this house again?"

Dolores is too frightened to answer, but Serenity says, "2304 Dufossat."

I pick up the phone and hit 911.

"Nine-one-one emergency," says the dispatcher.

"There's a home invasion in progress at 2305 Dufossat! I heard shots, right across the street! And there's a man carrying a TV out of the house. Two more are carrying a generator. Hurry, please!"

I slam down the phone. "It's going to ring again, but we're not going to answer. Dolores, this is a big house. Is there any way out that nobody would know about? Or think of?"

"I can't think!" she cries, holding her hands to her cheeks.

"Breathe, Dolores. Think about how you leave the house."

You never know how someone will hold up under stress. Dolores St. Denis looks like she's on a one-way trip to infantile helplessness. But just when I think I'm going to have to heave her over my shoulder and carry her out, she says, "I can't let them take me."

"They're not going to," I assure her. "But we need a way out. A way nobody would expect."

She nods jerkily, like someone trying to convince themselves they're still alive and capable of movement.

"We're with you," Serenity tells her. "*Think*, Dolores. How do we get out?"

"There's a side door," she whispers. "Right up against the hedge."

"Show us."

CHAPTER 21

WE EXIT DOLORES'S house into near darkness from a side door that opens onto a shrub-lined fence. With less than eighteen inches of clearance between the wall and the hedge, I pray that if anyone has already come for Dolores St. Denis, they'll be unlikely to try this side of the mansion first.

Without any discussion Serenity rushes past me and takes point, leading us toward the backyard, away from our rental car, which has probably already attracted attention out front. Tee has a pistol in her hand, a black semiauto that looks like a .40 caliber. Dolores is hyperventilating, but something keeps her moving—probably her memory of what she experienced in the Lusahatcha Swamp back in 1966.

As we pass the back corner of the house, I find myself wishing I'd called Kaiser for help. He could put an FBI tactical team around this house capable of stopping a frontal assault by a crazed mob. The question—as Serenity realized—is how fast could he do it?

Tee's left hand whips up to stop us, but not quickly enough to prevent me from colliding with her back. When she turns, I see her frustration at dealing with untrained civilians.

"Stay here," she says.

Before I can argue, she sprints to the stucco wall that borders the back of the property, leaps up and catches the top with her fingers, then pulls herself up and looks over it. After about twenty seconds, she slowly lowers herself, then runs back to where we await her.

"There's an alley back there," she whispers. "There's a motorcycle parked in the alley, and there's a guy on the motorcycle."

"VK?"

"It ain't Steve McQueen."

She must have watched The Great Escape *with her uncle Catfish,* I think crazily. I don't relish getting into a gunfight, especially with Dolores in the middle of it. "Should we wait for the cops to respond to my home invasion call?"

Serenity clearly doesn't like this option. "I don't hear any sirens yet," she whispers. "I don't want to sit here waiting for the NOPD. They might not show for half an hour."

"What, then?"

"His kickstand isn't down." She bites her bottom lip, then gives me a hard look. "I can take him out."

"You mean *kill* him?"

"No. Neutralize him."

Before I can give any opinion, Serenity unbuttons her blouse, then yanks out her shirttail. "If you hear me shoot, I had no choice. Okay?"

"Jesus, Tee. Are you—"

"*Listen.* When I yell 'Now! Now!' you bring Dolores through the back gate and get right on my heels. Got it?"

"Yeah."

Serenity squeezes my hand, then turns and sprints far out to her right. This time when she reaches the wall, she climbs it and drops over to the other side.

"Where's she going?" Dolores asks. "Why aren't we following her?"

"We're going to in a minute. Just wait. I don't see the gate."

"There's a Judas gate over there in the ivy, to the right. I have the code."

A little good news. Unable to stand waiting in the dark, I lead Dolores forward to the wall, then pull myself up and peek over.

What I see astonishes me.

Serenity is sashaying up to the biker like a drunken crack whore, cooing something that sounds like sex slang from the hood. It's gibberish to me, but the biker seems to understand well enough. He sits up straighter on his Harley and waits for her to reach him. I can clearly see the VK patch on the arm of his jacket. When Serenity is close enough to touch, he reaches out and takes hold of her left breast.

Tee lets him get a good feel.

After he samples the merchandise for a few seconds, she unzips her jeans, digs her hand into her crotch, pulls out her Glock, and cracks him across the face with it. Before the biker can recover, Tee raises her right foot, jams it against the gas tank, and kicks out with all her strength. The Harley teeters, then crashes over on the VK man's leg.

"NOW! NOW! NOW!" Tee yells, waving her Glock at me.

Dropping to the ground, I grab Dolores's arm and run to the Judas gate to our right. With shaking fingers she punches in the code, and then we run into the alley where Serenity waits. Tee makes a point to keep us away from the trapped biker, but as we pass I see him yank his leg clear of the Harley.

As Dolores and I run down the fence-lined alley toward a proper street, I hear the *pop-pop-pop* of a semiautomatic pistol. My heart stutters, and I pull Dolores to a halt. She doesn't want to stop, so I hold her in place with one hand and aim my pistol back toward the way we came with my other.

The seconds between that moment and seeing Serenity come tearing down the alley are some of the scariest of my life. But ten seconds after Tee reaches us, we emerge on Soniat Street, look both ways, then race south to Baronne. When we reach the corner, we veer right on Robert Street and sprint south again, to the broad thoroughfare of St. Charles Avenue.

"Call a cab," Serenity snaps, pulling Dolores into a shadowy doorway. "Won't be any cruising down here. If you don't get one in two minutes, we'll jump the next streetcar."

"No streetcars," I say breathlessly. "All the lines are still down. Did you shoot that guy?"

The whites of her eyes flash in the dark. "I just scared him. Let's move, or there'll be more shooting to come."

IN THE END, we took a cab.

We had to hide awhile waiting for it to arrive, but forty minutes later we were airborne again, flying north toward Natchez. I sat up front with Danny McDavitt, while Tee sat in back with Dolores. I called ahead and told Tim to have at least three men and the Yukon waiting at the Natchez landing strip. I wasn't sure how the VK had traced us to Dolores's house, and I didn't want to take any chances. I very much wanted to call John Kaiser and tell him who we had with us, but something told me that if I did, Dolores would deny everything she'd told us.

I thought that once the lights of the city had vanished beneath us, Dolores might calm down, but she didn't. She was certain that the only way the VK could have found us was by torturing it out of Mrs. Booker in Athens Point. I finally eased her mind by persuading Danny to fly low over Doloroso, where I knew a cell tower stood on the high hill there. Dolores called her mother-in-law, and she nearly collapsed when Mrs. Booker told her she was fine and had received no visits from anyone.

"They couldn't have followed this airplane down to New Orleans," I told Tee quietly. "They must have found out we visited Mrs. Booker and traced her calls to Dolores afterwards."

When Dolores finally leaned against the cabin wall and closed her eyes, I discovered I'd received a text from Drew Elliott. It read: *99% sure now Peggy did not have a stroke. Likely complex migraine. We got lucky, Penn. Keeping her 24 hours for observation, abundance of caution. She doesn't want Tom knowing anything about it. Talk to you soon.*

I sighed heavily, closed my eyes, and settled lower in my seat.

Ten minutes later, Danny landed us on the same grass strip from which we had taken off four and a half hours earlier. Tim and his team stood waiting beside the armored Yukon, and they took great care to be sure that Dolores felt safe during the transfer to the vehicle.

Once we reached my house, I showed Dolores to the last upstairs guest room. I offered to move her to my mother's room, which was now empty, but Dolores wouldn't hear of it. I offered her food, but this she declined also. She did accept some green tea, and then she asked if I might have any Xanax or Valium. I pilfered a couple from my mother's stash, gave them to Dolores, then left the poor woman alone with her nerves.

Downstairs, Annie and Mia insisted on hearing a blow-by-blow account of our trip. They were munching on hot popcorn, and Serenity was gobbling it down faster than either of them. I edited out the worst of Dolores's traumatic memories, but they could tell that Serenity and I had both been rattled by our experience. While Tee gave them an almost comedic version of our escape from the Garden District,

I called Carl Sims and asked if he could check on Cleotha Booker for us. When I described the situation, Carl told me he'd feel better parking his cruiser in front of her house for the night. I thanked him, then pointed upstairs and held out my sweaty shirt to let the girls know I'd be taking a shower. Serenity kept talking, but a split second before I passed through the door, she looked over Annie's head and gave me an almost imperceptible nod. Annie was laughing out loud as I climbed the stairs, and I said a silent thank-you to Tee for shielding her from the reality of our New Orleans experience.

AS THE STEAMING water washes away the sweat of our trip to the hurricane-ravaged city, I think again about calling John Kaiser. But doing that at this juncture would risk destroying Dolores's faith in me, and that I cannot do. Now that she's been reassured that Mrs. Booker is okay, Serenity and I will have time to work on her. The only problem is that Dad's trial proper begins tomorrow.

As I rinse the shampoo from my hair, I see Serenity once more, sashaying into that alley like a strung-out prostitute and kicking over the VK biker's Harley. From the safety of my bathroom it seems funny as hell, and I laugh aloud. After the water begins to cool, I get out and quickly dry off, then pull on some warm-ups and a T-shirt. I'm about to head down to check on the girls when a soft knock sounds at my door.

"Yeah? Mia? Annie?"

The door opens, and Serenity steps into my room.

"Cool to talk in here?" she asks.

"Sure. Are Mia and Annie okay?"

Tee shuts the door behind her. "I told them I needed a shower, too."

Which means Annie could knock on my door at any time. "How do you feel about Dolores's condition?" I ask.

"She's scared to death. I think I'd better stay here with her tomorrow. During the trial, I mean. Otherwise she might bolt."

"Agreed."

Serenity sits on the chair beside my dresser. Then she drops her head between her knees, sighs heavily, and rubs her scalp hard. After twenty seconds of this, she straightens up, shakes out her hair, then smiles strangely.

"That was *wild,* wasn't it?" she says.

I laugh once more. "I don't think that biker will ever forget you."

"I'm just glad I didn't have to shoot him!"

This time we both laugh, knowing beneath the laughter that we were damned lucky to get out of New Orleans without getting hurt—or worse.

"You think she'll talk to the FBI?" Serenity asks, all seriousness again.

"Maybe. The problem—from my point of view—is that while Dolores can almost certainly put Snake Knox on death row, she can't do anything to help my father get acquitted for murdering Viola."

"I was thinking about that during the flight back." Serenity stands and walks toward me. "Penn, all you can do is what you can do. You know? I had to learn that in the army. It's a tough lesson. And hey, putting Snake Knox on death row is more than the FBI ever managed to do."

"I know. But . . ."

She gives me a chiding look. "I want you to kiss me," she says quietly.

The heat in her eyes stuns me more than her words. "You do?"

"Don't you know that?"

"But I thought you and Carl—"

A faint smile spreads her lips. "Are you that blind, boy?"

Holy shit. "I guess I am."

She closes the distance between us, then rises up on tiptoe and presses her mouth against mine. Gently at first, then harder. Her hands slip around my waist, her fingers digging into my back, and then her mouth opens.

I hear an almost feline sound deep in her throat.

My fingers slide into the damp hair at the base of her neck, and my right hand flattens against the small of her back, pulling her against me. As we kiss, I feel a flexed thigh and calf mold themselves around my left leg. In seconds she's panting against my mouth.

We break apart suddenly, as though prompted by the same impulse, still holding each other at the waist but looking feverishly into each other's eyes.

"What's the matter?" she asks.

"Nothing. I just—"

"I know."

"I guess it's everything we've been through?"

"Doesn't matter what it is."

She laughs, a sharp sound of release. But then her eyes darken. "Oh, wow," she breathes. "Oh *shit*. Do you believe this? Do you see who we are?"

It takes me about three seconds. "My father?"

She nods twice, then shakes her head. "And my mother. Or Viola. Same difference. Christ, you see how easily it must have happened for them? With the strain they were under back then?"

For the first time I have some inkling of how powerfully my father must have been pulled into Viola Turner's arms. As Serenity and I process this realization, our hands fall away from each other. Self-consciousness is anathema to spontaneous sex.

She raises her right hand and runs it through her hair where I was holding her. "I really want you," she says. "I mean, I want to sit on you right now."

I swallow hard. Maybe the only thing keeping me separated from her is my acute awareness of Mia and Annie one floor below. "But . . . ?"

"But I feel like I'm acting out some weird Jungian script. You know?"

"Yes."

Tee laughs again. "Why aren't we welders and not writers?"

"I'm not sure that would make much difference."

"You know what?" she says, her tone that of a professor analyzing an obscure Greek play. "We're *not* like your father or my mother. And I'm not like Viola, either."

"Why not?"

"Because we're free agents. *They weren't.* If you and I want to hook up, there's nothing stopping us. If we want to go down to the courthouse tomorrow and get fucking married, there's nothing stopping us."

"You might be rushing things a little."

Serenity flips me off. "What I'm saying is, when you're like our parents were—when you're tasting the forbidden—at some level you know there's no real future. You're like married people having an affair. Unless you're caught, you pretty much know the relationship is stillborn."

She's right. "Even if you kid yourself about it," I think aloud, "and fantasize about a future together, you know there really isn't one."

"Exactly. But for you and me, the future *is* out there. It's real. If we make love right now, then tomorrow we'll be forced to confront the reality of it. Your daughter, my job in Atlanta. This act would have consequences. Whereas if this were 1964—"

"We'd do it in a bubble of secrecy, and it would stay in the bubble."

Serenity smiles. "Exactly. We'd have no choice."

She walks to my dresser and lays her hands on it, breathing with conscious rhythm. There is a woman in the throes of sexual heat and emotional confusion. Despite her thin frame, Tee's taut haunches fill out her jeans in a profoundly erotic way. The powerful curve of her thighs below the buttocks sends my blood pumping southward.

"So, now that we've analyzed ourselves," I say. "What do we do?"

Tee straightens up and looks back at me, clearly undecided. "You tell me."

"Dad, are you finished yet?"

My daughter's voice, right on cue . . . "I guess I am," I say softly. "Right?"

Serenity puckers her lips in thought, but after a few seconds, she nods. "We have some thinking to do. And thinking usually stops this kind of foolishness."

I take a deep breath, then let it out slowly. "I'm sure you have somebody in Atlanta. Right?"

She sighs. "I'm not a nun, Mr. Mayor."

"Okay. I haven't been with anyone since my fiancée was killed."

Tee looks back at me in silence for several seconds. "Not even the cheerleader?"

"No joke. It's only been three months."

"I'm sorry."

I can't blame Serenity for her suspicion. After all, I'm up here kissing her. "I'm going to head back down."

"Hey, I said I was sorry."

"It's okay. I just don't want Annie running up here and feeling weird."

"Oh. Yeah." She raises her hand in a wave of regret. "It sucks doing the right thing, doesn't it?"

"Almost always."

SNAKE KNOX ROLLED over in the dark of his room at the sod farm in Sulphur. His burner phone was vibrating. He shook himself awake and checked the text, which read: *Call this number: 601-304-0095.*

Snake felt under his pillow for his pistol, slid it to within easy reach. Then he dialed the number.

"You answered quick, Grandpa," said Toons Teufel. "You nervous?"

"Did they get the bitch?"

"No." Toons hawked and spat. "They were too late."

"What do you mean?"

"Somebody got her out."

Snake rubbed his eyes and sat up. "Who did?"

"Don't know. Only person my guys saw was a woman. Young. Black. Armed."

"A black woman made fools out of your boys? I shoulda sent Wilma."

"Fuck you, Knox. I'm just lettin' you know. Had to be FBI, a black chick who knew how to use a gun like that? She played it like an undercover."

Snake thought about this. "Penn Cage is tight with some FBI. If he got what I think he got from this Cat Lady, he might have brought the Bureau in."

"Hey, I don't know what you wanted with that woman. She lived in a goddamn palace, I heard. Rode out Katrina like Marie Antoinette. But they didn't even have time to empty the mansion. Somebody called in a home invasion across the street, and the NOPD showed up for once."

"No idea where she is now?"

"Nope."

"Thanks for nothin', Toons. Jesus."

Snake clicked off, but he didn't lie down again. He lit a cigarette and sat smoking in the dark, his mind spinning outward like a hawk flying over dark trees, till the oak and hickory and pecan that covered the hills gave way to cypress and black water. He saw boats in the dark, arrowing through the night, lanterns in their bows. And he saw taut skin that looked golden in the flickering light. He closed his eyes, and the vision grew clearer. With it came sounds: laughter and screams and grunts in the humid dark. And then he heard it, the strangest claim he'd ever heard a human being make: *I'm a nigger, too . . . I'm a nigger, too!*

Snake wondered if the throat that screamed those words still really drew breath on the earth. If so, the woman who owned it had more power over him than almost anyone alive.

And she had vanished.

I WENT TO bed two hours after my shower, but sleep has proved impossible to find. Tonight's events, both in New Orleans and in my bedroom, have left me a twitching bundle of tension and hyper-arousal. I told Serenity the truth when I said I hadn't been with a woman since Caitlin died. If I'm honest with myself, I haven't felt pulled toward anyone with enough intensity to take that step.

But I am no ascetic.

Serenity was right about one thing. During the past weeks, I've sometimes lain in bed so tight with sexual tension that my mind runs through every past experience and every possible one as well. And living in close proximity with Mia Burke has pushed me there more than once, at least in my mind. I'd like to deny it, but even two years ago, when we worked together to save Drew Elliott, Mia let me know in no uncertain terms that she was a sexual being and was open to a relationship with me. I was sane enough then not to test her, and I still am—even with her sleeping down the hall every night. But in the sanctuary of my mind I have been with her many times, and nothing has made me more conscious of this fact than the arrival of Serenity, who has utterly changed the sexual dynamic in this house.

Tee was right about the Jungian thing, too.

She and I have been walking in the footsteps of our parents, and every bit as blindly as other human beings repeating the mistakes of their pasts. When I think of how self-righteously I've condemned my father, and of how quickly I reached for Serenity . . . when I'm not under a fraction of the stress he must have been in 1968. Of course, my father was married at the time, and I'm not. But despite Caitlin's death, I have *felt* married right up until tonight. And yet . . .

Did I think of Caitlin even once as I pulled Serenity against me? *No.*

Lying in the cool darkness with only the hum of the air conditioner for company, I try in vain to erase the faces and figures materializing behind my eyes. Maybe the only answer is to embrace the visions and relieve myself. As I slip my hand beneath the covers, I wonder if Serenity is lying awake in similar torment in the guest room down the hall. She was shaking with desire when she stood over my dresser. Did she find sleep more easily than I? Or is she too touching herself at this moment?

As I follow that thread in my mind, a shaft of light cuts through the dark and falls across my bed. Turning, I see a shadow pass quickly across the light—then my door closes. I tense for a couple of seconds, but something tells me I need not be afraid.

The floorboards creak once, then again. A soft curse floats through the dark. Then a dark hand splays itself against my white sheets, and two dark knees depress the mattress. I can't see a face, but the unfamiliar scent tells me it must be Serenity.

Rising up on one elbow, I try in vain to make out her features in the darkness. I reach for the lamp on the bedside table, but she says, "No."

Then she pulls my hand to one breast and flattens my palm over it.

"Tee," I whisper. "What about—"

"Don't talk," she says in a low, insistent voice. "I mean it."

After a few seconds without breathing, I begin kneading her breast. A purring sound escapes her throat. Then she presses me onto my back and hikes one knee over my hips, reaching between us, searching.

"Jesus," I gasp.

"I warned you," she says, settling her weight upon me. "If you say one more word, I'll stop."

TUESDAY

CHAPTER 22

AT 6:14 TUESDAY morning, my mother checked herself out of St. Catherine's Hospital against her physician's advice. The fact that her physician was her husband's partner gave Drew Elliott no special power to hold her; all Drew could do was call to give me a heads-up. Forty minutes after one of Mom's friends drove her to my house, she was being helped to bathe and dress by Annie and Jenny. Nothing on God's earth, she said, was going to stop her from sitting in the first row in the courtroom during her husband's trial. *If the Lord wants me that badly,* she said, *he'll have to take me from the courthouse, not the hospital.*

Once Mom was ready, we ate a light breakfast, then Tim Weathers talked us through the departure procedure he expects us to follow every morning of the trial. The armored Yukon is too wide to fit the narrow driveway beside my house, so we are to gather at the front door, then at Tim's command move swiftly down the steps and into the safety of the big SUV, shielded by the bodies and weapons of the operators from Vulcan Asset Management.

I stand at the door with Annie and Mia, who are highly irritated about being forbidden to attend the trial proceedings, while Tim and his guys do a recon outside. Jenny has accompanied Mom to the upstairs restroom for a final pretrial stop. Serenity is upstairs, too, doing what she can to make Dolores feel at home. When Mom appears at the top of the stairs, Jenny is not beside her, so Annie races up the steps to help her down.

Left alone with Mia, I suddenly register that she's wearing sunglasses inside, which is unusual for her. Before I can ask if she thinks Annie is doing all right, she says softly, "So, are you a southern gentleman now?"

"What?"

"I noticed a new vibe at the breakfast table this morning."

"What kind of vibe?"

Mia lowers her chin and looks at me over the sunglasses. "Between you and our houseguest?"

The blood rushes to my cheeks as I finally grasp her meaning.

"Do you think Annie noticed?" I whisper, looking quickly at the staircase. Annie and Mom are halfway down already.

"I don't think sex is on her radar quite yet. But if you keep it up, she'll sense the connection."

Mia pushes the glasses back up on the bridge of her pert little nose, covering her eyes once more. As Mom's feet reach the ground floor, I find I'm still looking at Mia. "What did you mean by southern—"

"Tim's coming back up," Mia says, and sure enough, the front door opens behind her as if at her command. "Time to go, everybody!"

I'm inside the Yukon and halfway to the courthouse before I understand what she meant by her "southern gentleman" comment. I first heard that saying back in high school. They probably started saying it in these parts about 1805, and apparently they're still saying it two hundred years later.

You ain't a southern gentleman till you've dipped your pen in ink.

For a twenty-year-old, Mia Burke sure knows how to stick the knife in. I guess she has learned some things up at Harvard.

JUDGE JOE ELDER'S courtroom isn't large by urban standards, but it's spacious for Mississippi. The walls are cream, the curtains and chairs blue, the wood stained oak and pine. Once the judge enters and takes his throne, he will sit high above everyone except the spectators in the balcony. The witness stand isn't really a stand at all, but an enclosed box raised a single step above the floor. The people in the second row of the jury box sit higher than the witnesses. A large balcony hangs over the gallery, with a staircase in the left rear of the courtroom leading up to it. Portraits of past circuit judges adorn the walls between high windows streaming spring sunshine, and all but one of those judges are white. Above the judge's bench hangs the state seal, but the most iconic—and ironic—artifact in the courtroom is the Mississippi state flag, which, despite hanging in the court of an African-American judge, still bears the Confederate battle flag in its upper left quadrant.

I tried nearly a thousand criminal cases during my legal career, and I spent countless hours doing just what I'm doing now: waiting for a judge. At most of those trials, I was sitting at the prosecution table, representing the State of Texas. Today I'm sitting in Mississippi, and I am only a spectator. Today the man who sits in my customary place is one of my mortal enemies: Shadrach Johnson.

The district attorney of Adams County waits at the prosecution table like an actor in his prime waiting backstage at a Broadway theater. In five minutes, Shad will deliver his opening statement in the most important trial of his life—up to now, anyway. Unusually, he sits alone at the table. His assistant DA, a young male lawyer in his midthirties, sits in one of the chairs behind his table, backed against the bar.

Twenty feet to Shad's left, Quentin Avery sits behind the defense table in his motorized wheelchair, a crocheted comforter tastefully covering his legless lap, a gray Armani jacket on his shoulders. To Quentin's right—directly in the sight line of the jury—sits my father, as close to ramrod straight as he can manage with his arthritis and his osteoporotic spine. After three months in jail, Dad has lost twenty pounds. He'd already lost a good bit after the October heart attack; now his suit hangs off him the way suits do on fading men who don't want to waste their children's money on new clothes.

Doris Avery sits in one of two chairs placed several feet behind the defense table, her back against the bar. Most spectators probably assume she is a secretary rather than an attorney in her own right. And though I'm nominally part of the defense team, I'm sitting in the first row of the gallery *behind* the bar, between my mother and Rusty Duncan. My sister, Jenny, is sitting at Mom's other shoulder. A helpful circuit clerk saved us seats immediately behind the defense table, which provides good optics in terms of supporting Dad but also limits our view of him to the back of his head.

Three months of sensational pretrial publicity have ensured that the opening of the trial proper is a standing-room-only event. With Caitlin's sister running the *Natchez Examiner,* local newspaper coverage has been evenhanded, but the Jackson and Baton Rouge papers have had a field day with the lurid aspects of the case, and even the national media have run stories on the "landmark" trial. TV cameras are generally forbidden in Mississippi courtrooms, but I've heard that Judge Elder has been flooded with requests to make an exception to that rule. All it takes is a whiff of 1960s-flavored racism to bring the network hounds running. Thankfully, Joe Elder has so far denied all such requests, and instead allowed a half dozen pool reporters to make digital audio recordings of each day's proceedings for accuracy, so long as they do not broadcast them. I've worried constantly that the judge would cave under pressure to allow the cameras in, but I suspect that Judge Elder knows Shad Johnson well enough to know he would play to the cameras every chance he got, and as for Quentin Avery: any lawyer nicknamed "Preacher" would be bound to find a way to use TV cameras to his advantage.

In truth, it wouldn't have mattered if not one word had been printed or spoken about this case in the media. With a beloved white physician accused of murder, and wild rumors flying about him having several illegitimate black children, Natchez folks alone would have filled this courtroom twenty times. As we were ushered into the courtroom by the circuit clerk, he told me that people began lining up at six A.M. in hopes of getting a seat in the gallery. The judge has even allowed a certain number of people to be admitted without seats and stand at the back of the chamber. Amazingly, the eight chairs between the windows on the left wall are filled with ranking deputies, when normally five or six would stand empty.

Looking over my shoulder, I see a crowd that's about 50 percent black, and 50 white. A little ominously, the races seem to have segregated themselves, like boys and girls at a junior-high-school party. The self-segregation isn't absolute: the black section is salted by a few white faces, the white section peppered by a few African-Americans, but I can't escape the feeling that deep currents of emotion seethe beneath the muted roar of expectant conversation in this room.

To my surprise, I see several faces that belong to potential witnesses—at least, they would be witnesses if I were defending my father. Viola's sister, Cora, and Lincoln Turner are the most obvious examples. Quentin could easily clear them from the court by "invoking the rule," which any competent criminal lawyer would do to prevent witnesses from adjusting their stories based on the testimony of others. Yet for some reason Quentin has not done so. *What kind of crazy game is he playing?* I wonder. *And does he truly understand the stakes?*

My mother is squeezing my hand so hard that my fingernails are turning blue, but I don't protest. Wearing a dove-gray dress and gloves—yes, gloves—she looks like a first lady facing a congressional hearing in which her husband could face evidence for impeachment. But Mom came from far humbler origins than Hillary Clinton. Born on a subsistence farm in Louisiana, she picked cotton from the time she was old enough to drag a sack until she left for college, the first person in her family to attend one. Educated in a two-room grade school, she read seventy-five novels the summer after her senior year and ultimately graduated first in her college class. After teaching in the slums of New Orleans to put my father through medical school, she served several years in Germany as a military wife, among women who spent more on their spring wardrobes than she'd spent on clothes since her wedding day. Yet despite her marital "success," Mom never basked in the glow of being a doctor's wife, which confers considerable status in a town like Natchez. Nor did she have patience with the ex-sorority girls who ran the garden clubs, though she joined one for a while and worked tirelessly at whatever projects she was assigned, so that her children would become part of the social fabric of the town.

How must it feel for her to sit here and watch a black judge, two black lawyers, and a predominantly black jury decide the fate of her husband, whose alleged crime is killing a black woman to whom he once turned for romantic comfort? Twelve citizens of Adams County, Mississippi, seven black people and five white. And no matter how noble their intentions might be, no matter how objective they've told themselves they can be, such detachment is not possible. The people on this jury represent a divided city, a fractured state, a wounded nation. Evidence will be presented to them, but they will not see that evidence the same way. Arguments will be made to them collectively, but they will not hear the same words. Those jurors will be like men and women in the middle of a divorce. The facts at issue may be as clear as glass to neutral observers, but the principals will see only reflections of their own fears, hear only echoes of their own prejudice, act only out of anger and wounded pride.

I'm surprised Mom can sit here without a toxic level of Xanax or Zoloft in her system. Though she may be seventy, Peggy Cage is still the farm girl whom her mother called to kill the copperheads and rattlesnakes that sometimes slithered up onto the porch while the men were away in the fields.

The small hand now gripping mine—the hand that once gripped a hoe handle just as hard—is damp enough to wet the glove that covers it, and its nails dig into the back of my hand like knife points. Leaning close to Mom's ear, I whisper, "The judge will be here any minute. Then Shad will give his opening statement. It'll be tough to listen to, but Quentin will make up whatever ground we lose as soon as Shad sits down."

"Penn," she whispers, "I know people on that jury. Third from the left, second row, that's Edna Campbell. And the man two seats down from her. He worked at a service station I used to patronize. He was always rude. And—my God, that black woman on the other end, first row . . . she used to cook for Margaret Corwin over in Glenwood, at parties."

"Mom, that's how it is in small towns. Take a piece of advice: Try not to think about the jury. Don't even look at them. You'll drive yourself crazy analyzing every twitch and raised eyebrow, and in the end all you'll do is miss half the testimony."

"But your father's fate is in their hands!" she hisses with urgency.

"Yes and no. It's Quentin and Shad who'll determine Dad's fate, far more than those twelve people. And Dad himself, maybe. So save yourself the aggravation."

Mom doesn't answer, but her grip tightens another notch, and my hand begins to go numb. As I try to ignore the pain—and wonder whether I can take my own advice—it hits me just how historic this trial really is. Natchez has a distinguished judicial history: the first bar association in the entire United States was founded here in 1821. Most recently the Justice Department decided to relocate a federal district court to Natchez, which over two hundred years ago was the capital of the Mississippi Territory. Between those two historic benchmarks lie several notable trials, some of which are best forgotten. But my father's trial is certain to be remembered for more than the matter at issue before the bar. A trial in which not only the judge but also both principal attorneys are black is as rare as snow in Mississippi—rarer, in fact, since it actually snows in Natchez every couple of years. Black district attorneys are thin on the ground in my state. Since each judicial district has only one DA, whereas many districts have multiple judges, gerrymandering has carved out a significant number of "black" posts, making black judges quite common.

Judge Joe Elder is one of those smart lawyers who, around the age of fifty, realized that the state retirement system was one of the best around and decided to run for the bench. He has fulfilled most of his first four-year term, and by all measures he's been an exemplary judge. A native of Ferriday, Louisiana, Elder attended historically black Alcorn State University, where he played basketball, then Howard University School of Law in Washington, D.C. He joined a corporate firm in D.C. for a few years, but then returned to Mississippi and set up shop on Lawyers' Row in Natchez. Like most local attorneys, he handled whatever walked through the door, and he was overqualified for most of the work. He often trounced the white Ole Miss law school graduates whom he faced in court, and I suspect that gave him more than a little enjoyment.

To my immediate left sits one of those Ole Miss lawyers. Rusty Duncan has practiced almost every kind of law imaginable, but it's plaintiffs' cases and divorce work that pay his four kids' tuition at St. Stephen's Prep. Fifty pounds heavier than when we graduated from St. Stephen's together, the unrepentant cynic has the lobster-red skin of a guy who spent the past week water-skiing on Lake St. John with his belly hanging over his 1970s-style cutoff blue jeans. But his appearance is deceptive: Rusty can still water-ski barefoot if challenged, and he's got as keen a grasp of courtroom psychology as any lawyer I know.

"All rise!" cries the bailiff. "All rise for the Honorable Joseph D. Elder of the Fifth Circuit Court of the great State of Mississippi!"

Conversation dies as Judge Elder, all six feet six of him, strides into the courtroom from a side door and climbs the stairs to his lofty seat. Still trim and fit, Elder moves with athletic grace, and his shaved head makes him look ten years younger than his true age, which is near sixty. His deep-set eyes radiate authority; he doesn't need to speak to make clear that he will brook no nonsense from anyone. Judge Elder is darker than Quentin Avery, whose skin is the color of shelled pecans; and compared to Shad—who's as yellow as a Cotton Club chorus girl—Elder looks like a Masai warrior. As the judge leans over some papers on his desk, a few brave souls in the crowd begin to whisper to each other.

"You know how I think of them?" Rusty Duncan says in my ear.

"Who?" I ask.

"Shad, Quentin, and Judge Elder."

"How?"

"Shad is Sidney Poitier, Quentin's Morgan Freeman, and the judge—"

"Shut up, Rusty."

"Aw, come on, Joe's busy." Rusty bumps my shoulder with his. "Look, George is talking to him now."

Sure enough, the circuit clerk has climbed up to confer with the judge about something. "Shad Johnson reminds you of Sidney Poitier?" I ask with astonishment. "That's like saying Rush Limbaugh ought to be played by Gregory Peck."

"I know, I know. Poitier would have to play against type, but that always works for great actors. When Sidney was young, he had that same striving intensity Shad has, the Mississippi black boy who made it all the way to Harvard."

"I'd cast Poitier as Judge Elder. He'd have to wear elevator shoes, though. Who would you cast as Judge Elder?"

"Isaiah Washington."

"Who the hell is that?"

"The black surgeon on *Grey's Anatomy*." Rusty gives me a sidelong look. "I thought Annie was a fanatic for that show."

"She is, but I don't watch it that closely. It's just the time with her I like."

"Oh. Well, Quentin's definitely Morgan Freeman. He's got the white kinky hair, the Visa-commercial voice, and that held-in temper, like he might go off if you push him too far. Like Crazy Joe Clark, remember?"

"At least Morgan Freeman's from Mississippi."

Though Rusty has too much tact to mention Lincoln Turner, I turn and look to my left, past my mother, to where my half brother sits behind the prosecution table. Lincoln looks like exactly what he is: a man involved in a blood feud, waiting for the law to punish the cruel father whom he believes killed his mother. The hard-set jaw and sheen of sweat on Lincoln's face give me the feeling that if the impaneled jury doesn't deliver the verdict he desires, he'll gladly carry out the appropriate sentence himself. Perversely, I find myself trying to mentally cast an actor who could embody the malevolent emotions radiated by Lincoln Turner.

"Clarence Williams the Third," Rusty whispers in my ear.

"What?"

"To play Lincoln. Clarence Williams played Prince's father in *Purple Rain*. He was Linc in the old *Mod Squad,* too, but he was a pretty boy then. As he got older, he developed that barely restrained rage that's steaming off your brother over there."

"*Half* brother. Damn it, Rusty, my father's on trial for murder, and you're ready to turn it into a TV miniseries."

"Let me agent the deal, and I *will*." Like most plaintiff's lawyers I know, Rusty Duncan has no shame. "Did I tell you I met Morgan once, up at his blues club in Clarksdale? I wonder if he remembers me." Rusty elbows me again. "This is big, buddy. Why do you think Court TV and CNN are outside on the steps?"

"Because Joe Elder has more sense than to allow them in here."

"Don't get too comfortable with that setup. Joe's liable to cave on that any minute. That's probably what George is talking to him about now."

Fresh anxiety brings on a sudden urge to urinate. "Bullshit. How can they pressure a judge?"

"Elected judges are politicians, my man. And what politician doesn't want to be on TV?"

"Me."

Rusty pulls a wry face. "You're an aberration. Mark my words: the first big revelation that comes out of this trial, we'll have cameras inside the court."

"The court will come to order!" cries the bailiff.

This time the hum dies more slowly, slowly enough that Judge Elder pans his eyes across the crowd like a machine gunner sighting his weapon.

"Before we begin," Elder says in a deep baritone, "let me be clear about something. Because of the notoriety of this trial, people may feel that the normal rules of decorum do not apply." He glances down at the lawyers' tables. "Some *attorneys* may even feel that way. But let me assure everyone in this room: If you cause trouble in this court—if you make undue displays of emotion or cause a disturbance of any kind—you are going to jail. You will not pass Go, nor will you collect two hundred dollars."

If this is a joke, nobody laughs.

"Ladies and gentlemen," Judge Elder says gravely, "a distinguished member of the community stands accused of first-degree murder, and the sharks are circling outside. Media people, political fanatics with their own agendas. Some may even have made it into this room. So I say it again: There are deputies present who will enforce my commands without a moment's hesitation. I won't lose five minutes' sleep over jailing *anybody in this courtroom*. I can't be clearer than that. Don't say you weren't warned."

The spectators have drawn back from Judge Elder's daunting presence, and while they're still pressed into their chair backs, the judge says, "Mr. District Attorney, you may begin your opening statement."

Shadrach Johnson has prepared his whole life for this moment. Now forty-four years of age, he hasn't risen nearly as high in the world as he once believed he would have by this time. Shad believed, in fact, that he would be governor of Mississippi by now. That was the goal he set himself when he first returned to Natchez from Chicago and ran for mayor of this city, seven years ago—or nearly eight now, I guess. And rightly or not, Shad blames me for the most crippling setbacks in his quest. In some cases he's right, others not. The black community here wasn't nearly so quick to accept an ambitious "outsider" as Shad assumed they would be—not even a prodigal son—but most of their reluctance was based on a collective assessment of Shad as a man bent on furthering his own cause, and not that of his people.

But today offers an opportunity to wipe all those setbacks away. In the three to five days that this trial is likely to take, Shad can revenge himself against me, redeem himself in the eyes of the more resentful faction of his people, pile up a mountain of political capital, and—best of all—strut in the media limelight for a few precious hours. Shad's vanity is considerable, but not so great that he takes anything for granted. He's learned a few lessons from dealing with me. And he knows better than to underestimate Quentin Avery. At Harvard they still cite cases Quentin tried before the nation's highest court as landmarks of jurisprudence.

Quentin knows better than to underestimate Shad Johnson as well. He also feels a great animus toward Shad, for complex racial reasons I can only partly understand. Quentin once tried to explain them to me, and while I understood his reasoning, I cannot feel the same emotions he does. What I do know is that Quentin—the black Mississippi lawyer who helped to conquer Jim Crow with practical idealism and unshakable fortitude—looks at Shad Johnson with sadness and more than a little anger. Quentin understands selfish impulses; he himself endured withering criticism during the 1990s for defending drug dealers and trying several class-action suits in Jefferson County, greatly enriching himself in the process. But Quentin senses a different sort of greed in Shad—a hunger to be admired, revered, even worshipped, but without putting in the trench labor usually required to earn those things. Quentin also believes that Shad, having attained those things, would be the last man ever to give back anything to the community or to his own people. In my judgment, Shad feels only envy of or contempt for others, and nothing in between. What made him that way I do not know, nor does Quentin. What I do know is that Shad's ambition and anger make him a dangerous adversary, and his first order of business this week is revenge.

He plans to get it by making sure my father dies in prison. As Shad rises and walks to the podium in his $2,500 suit, I sense his barely disguised lust for retribution running like an electric current through the courtroom, setting everyone's hair on end before he speaks a word. This may not be a capital murder case, but when a seventy-three-year-old man goes on trial for murder, everyone understands the reality:

My father is on trial for his life.

CHAPTER 23

"NOTHING ABOUT THIS trial is normal," Shad begins. *"Not—one—thing.* We have one of the most respected white physicians in this city accused of premeditated murder of a black woman by the State—"

"All right, Counsel, both of you approach right now," bellows Judge Elder. *"Now."*

Shad freezes for a moment, then moves toward the bench, but Quentin's wheelchair remains silent.

"Your Honor," Quentin says with supreme confidence, "there is no issue from our side as regards the mention of race. We have no concern about the prosecutor using race to inflame the jury, and thus we see no need for a sidebar. The defense is ready for the State to proceed as it began."

Judge Elder blinks in disbelief, and probably on two counts: first, that Quentin would consider allowing Shad to begin his opening statement with the mention of race; second, that Quentin would dare to contradict his instruction to approach the bench. I can hardly believe it myself. Any Natchez attorney worth his fee would have been yelling to the rafters the second the words *black woman* escaped Shad's lips. Quentin's entire approach to this trial has been unconventional, to say the least, but with this step he is veering into the radical. Joe Elder studies his former mentor with what looks like suspicion. Maybe he's asking himself—as others have—whether the old lawyer has finally lost his grip on reality. But the longer I look at Judge Elder, the more I think he senses a deep strategy concealed behind Quentin's aged face, the genius of a chess master playing a very long game.

"Dr. Cage?" says Judge Elder. "Do you agree with your attorney that a frank discussion of race and what part it might have played in this crime will not prejudice the jury against you?"

"I do, Your Honor. I fully understand the implications, and I am fine with them. All I want from these proceedings is the truth."

Judge Elder frowns at this. "Very well, it will be noted. The jury will disregard the defendant's last statement. Mr. Johnson, you may proceed."

"Thank you, Judge," Shad says, looking at Quentin like a man studying a familiar dog that has begun acting strangely.

Turning back to the jury, Shad says, "Think about what I said before, ladies and gentlemen. Not many years ago, this trial would not even have happened. Dr. Thomas Cage would not even have been *accused* of this crime by the State. Viola Turner would have been buried under the ground, and that would have been the end of her. But today, in this room, we are living out the progress that this nation, and hopefully this state, has made since the 1960s. Here in this courtroom, we have a black judge, two black attorneys, and seven black jury members. And I tell you now: *Nothing* will be hidden. Before we are through, all will be revealed."

This obviously rehearsed statement comes off as anticlimactic after what my father said moments ago. But this is what the crowd has come to hear, both black and white. They want to know what secret history underlies the scandal that has swept through Natchez like an unquenchable fire during the past few months. Shad acknowledges this by addressing not only the jury, but also the assembled audience.

"Some people may be upset that I'm speaking so openly about race. We're supposed to be living in a color-blind society, aren't we? But we all know that we do *not* live in such a society. I keep hearing about a *post-racial* society. Whatever a post-racial society is, we're still decades away from it. In Mississippi, and in Washington, D.C., too. And make no mistake: race lies at the very heart of this case. Were it not for the fact of race—the perceived difference between people of different colors—Viola Turner would not have been murdered."

This statement brings a hush over the crowd. Judge Elder looks right at Quentin as if expecting an objection, but Quentin appears unperturbed, even carefree.

Shad holds up his forefinger like a passionate professor. "Let me explain something to you. As a prosecutor, I normally stay away from the issue of motive during trials. Everybody who watches TV is familiar with the terms 'motive, means, and opportunity.' But in this room, means and opportunity carry a whole lot more weight than motive. Why? Because the State is not required to prove *why* anybody did anything. What the State *is* required to prove is that a given person did on a certain day, at a certain time, with malice aforethought, kill a particular person. That's all. The *why* doesn't come into it. That's for the *Law & Order* writers to worry about."

Soft laughter reverberates through the room.

"But this case, ladies and gentlemen, is different. This case is *all* about motive. The question we must answer is 'Why?' And the answer lies in the relations—both public and private—between black and white. Which happens to be the two colors we have sitting in the gallery, in the jury box, and standing by the hundreds outside this courthouse. Well, you lucky few are inside. And you're going to hear a remarkable tale over the next couple of days. A brutal and tragic story. So, let me play storyteller for a few minutes and set the stage for you."

Shad leaves the lectern and steps into the well, which is a presumptuous habit of his, and to my surprise Judge Elder doesn't stop him.

"Who was Viola Turner?" Shad asks. "She was a woman who lived a tragic life. Though Viola spent most of her years in Chicago, she was born right here in Natchez, the former slave capital of the South. She was educated at Sadie V. Thompson High School. She married at the Holy Family Catholic Church, where she was a devoted and outstanding member of the choir. But in 1967, Viola's husband was killed in Vietnam, before she could have any children by him. From the age of twenty-three until she was twenty-eight years old, Viola worked for the defendant, Dr. Thomas Cage. In her twenty-eighth year, in 1968, she suddenly moved north to Chicago without telling anybody why. After she moved to Chicago, Viola remarried." Shad pauses for effect. "But not before she had a son."

In the gallery audience, several women audibly catch their breath.

"As the evidence will show, that child was fathered by Viola's employer, Dr. Thomas Cage, before she ever left Natchez."

This is old news by now, but to hear it spoken in court, and entered into the record, gives the clinical fact a denser reality.

"You will hear testimony from that child," Shad promises (like a good showman). "He is now thirty-seven and can speak for himself. But let us return to Viola. After leaving Natchez, she lived and worked in Chicago until four and a half months ago, when she returned to her hometown. Nine months earlier, she had been diagnosed with lung cancer. She began treatment in Chicago, and she exhausted all viable treatment options before she left. Make no mistake about one fact: When Viola arrived in Natchez, she knew there was no hope of a cure. Only palliative care, until the end. Viola Turner came home to die."

The grim finality of these words deepens the silence in the courtroom.

"As soon as she arrived here, Viola placed herself under the care of Dr. Thomas Cage, her former employer, former lover, and father of her only child. The evidence will show that at least a month before her death, Viola made a pact with the defendant to help her end her life. And there, ladies and gentlemen of the jury, lies the heart of this case.

"There's a certain perception in our community that what happened to Viola Turner was not murder at all, but what is colloquially known as a 'mercy killing.' I discussed this concept during the voir dire, but I want to be sure we're all clear on this point. Legally, the act that laymen refer to as 'mercy killing' is known as *assisted suicide*. Assisted suicide is a felony, and a separate one from murder. In the simplest terms, assisted suicide means you help someone to die. Either a doctor or a layman can be guilty of this crime. If a layman hands a depressed paraplegic a loaded shotgun, or a doctor hands that same man a lethal dose of morphine, and the paraplegic kills himself, they are both guilty of assisted suicide. This is a controversial subject, and people's deepest feelings come into the debate. Most often, religious feelings. Some people feel that assisted suicide is justified in some cases; others think it's outright murder in every case.

"What's important today, in *this* case, is that you understand that what happened in Cora Revels's house on December twelfth of last year was *not* assisted suicide. It was *murder*. Murder in the first degree. That is the issue before the jury. You need to understand something else, too. Assisted suicide can very quickly slide over into murder. If the layman who gave the depressed paraplegic the loaded shotgun pulled the trigger himself because the man in the wheelchair was unable to do it, that layman committed murder, not assisted suicide. Likewise, if a physician in Mississippi injects a patient with a lethal drug because the patient is unable to do so, he has committed murder under the law—even if that victim desired his or her death at the time. *Murder.*

"Many people might sympathize with the case I just described, so I want to clarify further. Dr. Thomas Cage did not inject a dying woman with morphine because she was too helpless to do it herself. He did inject morphine into Viola Turner, as he had on almost every day prior to her death. And he did inject a lethal dose. But morphine is not what killed Mrs. Turner. Due to Dr. Cage's severe arthritis, and probably stress, he only injected a part of the lethal morphine dose into his victim's vein. The remainder went into the soft tissue beneath the vein, where it was rendered essentially harmless because of how slowly it would be absorbed into the patient's bloodstream.

"The evidence will show that Viola Turner actually died of a massive overdose of adrenaline, causing a terrifying and painful death. By pure chance, or perhaps fate, that agonizing death was recorded on a computer hard drive attached to a video camera left in the victim's room by a journalist. I can assure you that, after seeing that video, you will be under no illusions that what happened to Viola Turner could be described as a mercy killing."

Word of Henry Sexton's video recording leaked out weeks ago, but thankfully the file itself has not leaked, to pop up on YouTube or some similar site. With Shad Johnson and Billy Byrd in charge of the evidence, I'm more than a little surprised. Shad must have decided that he'd rather handle the premiere of that footage himself. Looking away from the large, flat-screen TV on a cart against the wall, I glance up at the balcony and see Miriam Masters, Caitlin's older sister, leaning on the rail, looking into my eyes. Miriam and Caitlin did not much resemble each other. They were both thin and strong, but where Caitlin had jet-black hair, pale skin, and green eyes, Miriam has sandy-blond hair and gray eyes that hold a different sort of intelligence than her sister's did. Caitlin was lightning quick on the uptake, while Miriam has a slow-burning intellect that suits itself to the siege-type litigation that until five years ago she handled for her father's newspaper chain.

"If you feel confused by what I've just said," Shad says to the jury, "I sympathize. At the simplest level, a person might ask, 'How can you murder somebody who begged you to help kill them?' On one level, that's easy to answer, if we use the example I gave of the depressed paraplegic and the shotgun. But there the motive is still to end pain out of mercy, something reasonable people can argue both ways. What makes *this* case unique in the annals of jurisprudence is that we have a willing victim—a woman who wanted to die, and who'd asked her physician to help her do that as a mercy—but a physician whose motive for agreeing to end her life was the moral opposite of mercy or compassion. Dr. Cage's motive was not to help Viola Turner end her pain, but *to silence her forever*." Shad's eyes move from one face to the next in the jury box. "Tom Cage acted ruthlessly to protect himself from a woman who was about to shatter the reputation he had spent decades building, and to destroy the family he had chosen over the victim herself, and the son she had borne by him."

Shad folds his hands and looks at the floor. If anyone had any doubts about how aggressively he would go after my father, Shad has laid those doubts to rest.

"The question," he goes on, "is not whether or not Tom Cage killed Viola Turner—he did. Evidence will show that Dr. Cage was alone with the victim in the hour prior to her death. Fingerprint evidence recovered at the scene proves that Dr. Cage injected Viola Turner with morphine on that night. The autopsy proved it was a lethal dose. Both the syringe and the morphine vial were recovered by law enforcement. The autopsy also proved that Viola was given a lethal dose of adrenaline. The adrenaline ampoule was not recovered, but evidence will show that Dr. Cage had ready access to untraceable stocks of adrenaline and was known to keep ampoules at home, in his office, and in his emergency medical bag."

After this recitation of facts, Shad raises his head and moves on to what the jury is really interested in. "Right now, I'd like to dispel one misconception: the video recording I just mentioned does not show Dr. Cage injecting Viola Turner with adrenaline, as some rumors have claimed. It shows only the results of that injection, which are horrifying enough. Mrs. Turner probably triggered the camera during her death throes, when she was trying to reach her telephone to call for help. But regardless of this omission, the critical facts are not in doubt."

Shad nods toward my father with almost casual condemnation. "That man sitting there killed Viola Turner. The question is, *why?* And the answer, ladies and gentlemen, is depressingly simple. For most of her life, Viola Turner had known things about Tom Cage that no one else in the world knew. The most dangerous of those secrets was a staple of Southern gothic fiction: Tom Cage, the beloved white physician, had fathered a black child. I feel strange saying that, I don't mind telling you. Because in point of fact, Lincoln Turner is *half* black, and half white." Shad's voice drips sarcasm as he pays off his setup line. "But as we all know, it only takes one drop of black blood to make you a nigger."

No exclamation of horror follows this word, but a state of hyper-alertness has taken possession of the people in the room. Tactically, Shad's choice of words was a blunt announcement that no punches will be pulled during this trial, that the euphemistic language of political correctness will not be used to mask painful truths. In my experience, juries appreciate such frankness, and my lawyer's instinct tells me that Shad has stolen a march on Quentin.

"I'm sorry if I offended anyone by saying that," he says, "but anyone easily offended by such language would be well advised to leave this courtroom and not return. For race and racism, as I said, lie at the very heart of this case. Let us be honest here together. Everyone in this room has heard the word 'nigger' more times than they could count. We've heard it said in anger and in jest, in casual discourse, and in flaming rhetoric. But the important thing to recognize about the statement I made—that it only takes one drop of black blood to make you a nigger—is that a horror and hatred of what was once called miscegenation was part of the world Tom Cage grew up in. Even if Dr. Cage himself did not share the deepest prejudices of many whites—and I'm not saying he didn't, for many a white racist loved to bed black women—Tom Cage knew that he lived in a town filled with people who did. *This* town. And after a lifetime of building a reputation for integrity unsurpassed in this city, Dr. Cage could not stand to see that reputation shattered, his children disillusioned, his son's political career damaged, his personal legacy destroyed.

"And what of Viola Turner? For four decades she had dutifully concealed his darkest secrets. But when she returned to Natchez, this poor woman was staring at death's door, and she was ready to unburden her soul. Ready to do right by her child. She could no longer stand to carry Dr. Cage's lies within her like a second cancer. Hiding those lies had forced Viola to enmesh herself in a web of deceit so complex that no one knew the whole of her terrible life story. Tragically, Viola believed that Tom Cage had enough integrity and responsibility to live up to the actions of his past. But he did not. Faced with the choice of telling the truth or committing murder, Dr. Cage chose to kill. And how easy it must have been. For evidence will show you that Tom Cage was no stranger to murder."

This assertion stuns me like a blow. First, because my father *is* connected to a murder some years ago—an accidental killing that resulted from a beating Ray Presley carried out in Mobile, Alabama, in 1973, against a dirty cop who had threatened my aunt's life. I can't imagine that Shad would know anything about that, and even if he does, such information would not be admissible in this trial. But therein lies the rub. "Prior bad acts" are generally not admissible in a criminal trial, and Quentin should have raised the roof the instant Shad declared his intention to bring up such. Yet Quentin still sits at the defense table like a placid old man on a town square bench. Judge Elder clearly expected some sort of protest, but Quentin offers none. *What the hell was Shad referring to?* I wonder. There's no way he could know about Dad helping my wife to pass when she lay on the verge of death from cancer.

Perhaps surprised not to be interrupted, Shad says, "Ladies and gentlemen, the details of this case are complicated, but the heart of it is simple. This is the tale of a saint who turned out to have feet of clay. Worse, a saint who made a pact with the devil. Make no mistake, this trial is the final act in the public and professional life of Dr. Tom Cage."

If Shad stops here, he will leave the jury awestruck and Quentin Avery almost no chance of retaking the emotional ground gained in the collective mind of the jury. But Shad does not stop.

Why, I'm not sure. Is it the packed courtroom? The distinguished members of the audience? The historic nature of the trial? All of that goes into it, certainly. But the most likely reason Shad doesn't have the good sense to sit down is his knowledge that the moment he does, Quentin is going to stand up. Not literally, of course. But Quentin is going to nudge his joystick and roll that wheelchair out in front of the jury, and from that moment on, facts will have only secondary importance. On a good day, Quentin Avery in front of a jury is a combination of Martin Luther King Jr. preaching in Selma, Sam Cooke playing the Apollo Theater, and Harry Houdini escaping from the most diabolical restraining devices known to man. Facing that kind of oratorical firepower might keep me talking when I ought to sit down, too.

And keep talking Shad does. He launches into a long, sequential outline of the facts of the case—who did what, and when; who knew what, and when—when he should be saving all that for his case in chief. Most of these facts are already known to me, through my illegal contact with Jewel Washington, the county coroner and a loyal supporter of my father. (Jewel has friends in the sheriff's department, the police department, the courthouse, and every other institution that matters in this county, thank God.) As Shad laboriously guides the jury through a timeline involving Viola and her sister, Cora, my mind begins to wander.

I can't count the times I've done what Shad is doing: outlining the facts of a murder to a jury that is sometimes bored, other times riveted by what you have to tell them. The only thing different about this case is that everyone in the jury box is already familiar with the facts to some degree, and every one of them knows or knows of my father. One might think that would be grounds for a change of venue, but in Mississippi only the defense can request a change of venue, and Quentin made no such request. And as with every other facet of my father's defense, Quentin did not seek my opinion on this.

The most alarming thing Quentin has done to date, though, is fail to request "discovery" from the State. In most states, the defense is entitled to examine any and all evidence against the accused in possession of the prosecutors, including exculpatory evidence, as well as a list of all witnesses the State intends to call. In short, the defense is entitled to see everything the State has, in advance. Likewise, the prosecution is entitled to see whatever the defense has, as well as a list of witnesses the defense intends to call. In Mississippi, however, nothing about this process is automatic. The defense attorney must request discovery, and by so doing, he agrees to reciprocally show the State the same courtesy. It's the adult version of "I'll show you mine if you show me yours." Yet even though this process is not automatic by law, in practice it has become so, because no defense attorney would dare enter a courtroom to face the vast power of the State without having the most complete possible inventory of what he was up against.

Except Quentin Avery.

During the past three months, that lion of the law has not asked the State of Mississippi to provide *any* information about the case against my father. I only learned of this professional negligence from Caitlin's sister, Miriam, just prior to her reporting it in the *Natchez Examiner,* and I nearly exploded when I did. Before I spoke to Quentin about it, I was certain he was going senile. After I talked to him, I wasn't convinced I was wrong, but rather that he had some arcane strategy he was not going to share with me no matter how loudly I demanded it. My father clearly agreed with his strategy—which appeared to be legal suicide—and that left me no option but to consult a couple of older criminal lawyers in town about the matter. As it turned out, both recalled rare cases in which a defense attorney had declined to request discovery in order to conceal a surprise witness from the State. I can only hope that this method lies at the heart of Quentin's apparent madness. If so, however, he has not confided it to me.

"*. . . above the law*!" Shad cries with startling vehemence.

These three words, uttered with an icy edge of indignation, break through my anxious reverie.

"That's what we have here!" Shad declares, in the tone of a self-satisfied prosecutor headed home to the barn. "A privileged white physician who believed that nothing he did on that night would be *questioned,* much less raised against him as an accusation. Because, ladies and gentlemen, Dr. Tom Cage was not doing anything he had not done before, as you will see."

There he goes again, I think, with a nightmare vision of former patients' family members parading through the witness box with horrifying tales of unwanted euthanasia. *Tom Cage as Dr. Kevorkian . . .*

"This time, he was merely doing it for a *different reason,*" Shad says.

"In this case, to silence a dying woman he had once claimed to love, and by so doing, to hide the fruits of his sin from the eyes of a world that had revered him for most of his life."

Ten minutes later than he should have, Shad points at my father with the accusatory fire I always summoned in the courtroom. "*That man there,*" he says with what sounds like genuinely righteous anger, "held the power of life and death over a powerless patient—a patient he had exploited in the most shameful way possible—and he exercised that power solely to protect himself. He chose to take her life. He meticulously planned the crime, and he ruthlessly carried it out. Were it not for the conscience of Viola's sister, the anger of Viola's son, and the random chance of an accidental video recording being made, Dr. Cage would have gotten away with it. But if we do our duty here this week, he will *not* get away with it. Before this trial is over, you will know in your heart that Tom Cage committed murder in the first degree, that he is as guilty of that crime as any man can be."

While Shad stands with his finger still pointing at my father, I turn slightly to my right and see that Mom has gone pale, so pale that I worry she might slide off her chair onto the floor.

"Mom?" I whisper. "Do you need to leave?"

She shakes her head, but her color does not return. While I try to figure out how to help her, my cell phone vibrates in my pocket. As covertly as possible, I take it out. It's Serenity. Her text reads: *You need to get home. Dolores is losing her shit. She can't reach Cleotha Booker by phone.*

The heels of Shad Johnson's Italian shoes click on the hardwood floor as he walks back to the prosecutor's table. As quickly as I can, I type: *Can u handle her for 20 minutes? I need to hear Q's opening statement. Call Carl Sims and have him check on CB.*

Judge Elder says, "Mr. Avery, you may begin your opening statement."

Tried Carl already, Serenity replies. *Got voice mail. Trying him again. FYI Dolores freaking out is upsetting Annie. Mia handling that.*

"Mom, I have to help Serenity with Dolores," I say into her ear. "Don't lose your faith. Quentin is worth ten of Shad Johnson. They don't call him 'Preacher' for nothing. He's going to stand up and pull that whole jury right into the palm of his hand."

"I don't know," Mom whispers. "I'm frightened, Penn."

"Don't be. Quentin can talk to a jury like a father to his adult children, and thunder like Moses come down from the mountaintop. You watch. Shad Johnson won't ever forget this day."

"Mr. Avery, are you ready?" Judge Elder repeats.

The click of an electric brake echoes in the courtroom, and Quentin's wheelchair whirs softly for about three seconds. Then the legendary voice speaks in a soft and passionless tone.

"Judge, the defense elects to defer its opening statement until prior to presenting its case in chief."

While the puzzled crowd tries to work out what this means, my blood pressure plummets. For a few seconds I fear that I and not my mother might faint to the floor. Just as with the issue of discovery, Quentin has exercised a little-used prerogative of the defense, which is to make no opening statement until after the prosecution has presented its entire case. There's a reason this option is seldom used. Almost no defense attorney believes his client can withstand several days of unopposed accusations and damning evidence without sustaining devastating damage in the minds of the jury.

No attorney except Quentin Avery.

"Penn, what's happening?" my mother asks with barely restrained panic.

"Wait a second," I temporize, certain that Quentin must be stalling for some reason.

Judge Elder is staring down at Quentin with one eyebrow raised, but Quentin appears to be intent on something on his table.

"Mr. Avery?" asks Judge Elder. "For the record, are you sure about that?"

Quentin looks up and answers with the same lack of passion. "Positive, Judge."

"Well, then. All right."

My pulse is somewhere north of 110 beats per minute when my cell phone buzzes again. This time the text is from Mia Burke: *You need to get here. Serenity just reached Carl, and he's 20 minutes away from old lady's house. Dolores is losing it. Premonitions of disaster. Annie is freaking out because of D. Come NOW.*

"Mom, I have to go," I whisper.

"*What?* Penn, what's happened?"

"Dolores is so upset she's freaking Annie out."

"Oh, God. But what about your father? Penn, why didn't Quentin argue with everything Johnson said?"

"I don't know, but I promise I'll find out. Stay here and remember every word that's said. Rusty will keep me posted via text. I love you, Mom."

Before I can rise, Judge Elder says, "Mr. Johnson, please call your first witness."

"Your Honor, the State would like the jury to see the video recording of the death of Viola Turner, which has been stipulated into evidence as State's Exhibit One."

While the crowd thrums in anticipation, I rise into a crouch and start moving toward the aisle, grazing knees and thighs, triggering protests and even muffled curses from those I pass. It would have been better to wait until the room was darkened for the playing of the video, but Mia's SOS sounded desperate. Praying for leniency from Judge Elder, I push into the aisle and start toward the back door.

"Mayor Cage," booms the judge. "What do you think you're doing?"

I freeze in the aisle like a schoolboy caught trying to sneak out of assembly.

"No one enters or leaves my court except during a recess."

Turning toward Joe Elder, I speak with all the conviction I can muster. "Judge, I have a family emergency. I implore the court for understanding."

The judge looks back as if to say, *That's obvious, and your emergency's right here in this courtroom.*

"It's a medical emergency, Judge. My daughter. I apologize."

"Go, then. But you won't be readmitted until after the lunch recess."

"Thank you, Judge."

"Bailiff, please dim the lights so that the jury can see the videotape."

As I hurry toward the door, I wonder whether Quentin has truly begun going senile. *I need to research the mental complications of diabetes . . .*

I'm almost running when the courtroom goes dark behind me.

CHAPTER 24

SERENITY WASN'T EXAGGERATING about Dolores. Her anxiety has almost escalated into full-blown panic by the time I reach home. The elegant and decorous woman I met in New Orleans has become a quivering, wild-eyed wreck. She's convinced that Cleotha Booker—the Cat Lady from Athens Point—has been murdered.

"Carl will be at Cleotha's house in fifteen minutes," Serenity assures her. "I'm sure he's going to find her working in her garden or something."

Dolores shakes her head like a mental patient who thinks you're trying to convince her that grass is blue. Annie, by contrast, settles down to something like normalcy within two minutes of my return. Mia walks her into the den, leaving Serenity and me to sit with Dolores at the kitchen table, waiting to hear from Carl.

When my cell phone pings, Dolores nearly jumps out of her skin, but it's only a text update from Rusty. As I switch my phone to silent, I read a message that's not very uplifting.

> 8:36 A.M. *Shad just played the vid of Viola dying. Can't believe Q stipulated that into evidence! Not challenging the chain of evidence, authenticity, nothing. Wow . . .*

I didn't think about it before, but why wouldn't Quentin challenge the video recording? I guess since he knows it's almost certainly authentic, he doesn't want to go through the vain hassle of trying to suppress it. Nevertheless, most defense lawyers would. What worries me more is that Shad has apparently made no mention of the videotape that should have been in Henry Sexton's camcorder when the police arrived—the one whose removal made the hard drive the default recording medium. Did the sheriff recover it at the scene, or maybe locate it elsewhere? If Quentin had filed for discovery we would know that, but since he didn't, that hypothetical tape waits like a buried land mine somewhere in the unknown terrain before us.

When another text flashes up, I excuse myself and walk into the den, promising to come right back if I hear from Carl.

8:53 A.M. State pathologist on stand. Confirms V had terminal cancer. Describes botched morphine injxn. Cause of death adrenaline overdose. Resulting death terrifying and painful, as video showed. Jury horrified by CSI-type detail. Good bang for the buck, if ur Shad.

As Annie realizes what's going on, she begins to hover around my chair, waiting for updates, but I shoo her back to the television.

"Why doesn't Mr. Rusty just call you on his cell and leave the line open?" she suggests.

Not a bad idea, I think. But then the likely reason hits me. "I think that would technically be breaking the law, or at least the judge's order about media in the courtroom. Rusty would technically be broadcasting the trial."

"That's called *narrowcasting,*" Annie corrects me.

Jesus. "Okay, but you know what I mean. The judge has only allowed six pool reporters into the courtroom, and they can only make audiotapes for their records, not for broadcast."

She shrugs and looks back at the television, but I sense that her attention has not left me.

8:55 A.M. Shad questioning M.E. n detail bout why adrenaline injected. Complicated. Going to record voices on my dictation recorder. U listen later.

For the next few minutes no texts come in, and anxiety begins to rise in me. Not only because of Quentin's apparent unwillingness to act like a lawyer, but also because Carl should have called by now. Glancing back into the kitchen I see Serenity sitting with an arm around Dolores's shuddering shoulders. Tee looks at me and shakes her head. I decide to give Carl one more minute.

My mind shifts straight back to the trial. In his opening statement Shad offered no explanation for why Dad would have chosen adrenaline to kill Viola if he botched the morphine injection. Convincing the jury that this was a plausible choice under the circumstances is critical to Shad's case, and as a former prosecutor, I can see problems with it. But there's no point in speculating. If Rusty succeeds in his covert recording, I'll hear Shad's examination of the pathologist soon enough.

My phone vibrates powerfully in my hand, signaling an incoming call. Checking the LCD I see CARL SIMS. A premonition of death passes over me, leaving a sense of dread behind.

"Hello?" I say quietly.

"Penn, I'm at Mrs. Booker's and it's not good."

"Tell me," I whisper, having struggled mightily not to say, *Is she dead?*

"I found the old lady lying on the ground beside her porch. She's alive but unresponsive. Looks like a fall to me. Serious head trauma."

I close my eyes, overwhelmed by horror and guilt. "That was no fall," I whisper. "That's a crime scene, Carl."

"I'm afraid you're right. I've got paramedics on the way, so I'm about to be real busy. Can you inform the St. Denis woman?"

"Yes. She's right here."

"I'm sorry, man."

"Thanks. We'll talk later."

Hanging up the phone, I quietly ask Annie and Mia if they'll go downstairs and give me some time to talk to "Mrs. Dolores." They know instantly that something terrible has happened, and I couldn't have concealed it no matter what I told them. As they walk into the hall, Mia looks back at me with her lips closed tight. Beyond her, I see Annie raise a hand to the back of her head and pull at the hair there.

Any hope I had of breaking the news gently is shattered when I turn back to the kitchen. The second Dolores St. Denis sees my face, she begins to shriek.

TEN MINUTES LATER, we've gotten a Valium down her throat and Drew Elliott is on the way. At first Dolores wanted to drive straight to Athens Point, but we convinced her she could accomplish nothing there, except putting her own life at grave risk. Somehow Serenity convinced her to lie down upstairs. After they went up, I sat in the kitchen waiting for Drew and reading Rusty's texts as they arrived from the courthouse. When I wasn't trying to work out what hidden logic might lie behind Quentin's seemingly incompetent behavior, I began to realize that I'm going to have to bring John Kaiser into the Dolores situation, whether she wants me to or not. But that can wait until Drew examines her.

Meanwhile, the ping of my cell phone has become my Pavlovian master.

> 9:07 A.M. *Shad just tendered the witness. Quentin said No questions. He apparently doesn't intend to cross-examine the pathologist. WTF?*

WTF indeed. No competent defense lawyer would let the autopsy findings go unchallenged, especially since several aspects of the post-mortem offered fertile lines of inquiry.

> 9:11 A.M. *Shad called Cora Revels to the stand.*

> 9:13 A.M. *Cora explaining she's Viola's sister, describing childhood. Compelling witness.*

At 9:18 Tim Weathers escorts Drew into the house, and I gratefully direct him upstairs. I'm happy to see an old-school black bag hanging from his right hand, because it offers the promise of effective sedation. There's nothing like having doctors "in the family." After Drew and I separate, I return to my text updates like someone watching a slow-motion disaster.

> 9:19 A.M. *Cora affirms existence of asst. suicide pact. Q. doesnt object on hearsay grounds. Id at least object and make judge overrule. I got a bad feeling about Q, man . . .*

The rules governing so-called hearsay evidence are complex; some scholars believe they exist to prevent a defendant from being accused of crimes without being able to confront his accuser. The exceptions to hearsay are several, but any good lawyer would have objected to

Cora's statement so that the issue could be preserved for review on appeal to a higher court. By Quentin's failure to object, Dad loses that right. So the question is . . . what the fuck is Quentin doing sitting on his ass like a brown Buddha?

> 9:22 A.M. *Cora establishes your father in her house that night. She went to nearby neighbor's house to rest. Often did that. Left Tom alone with V, that night n others.*

> 9:25 A.M. *Cora says V's son Lincoln was on way from Chicago that night. Says she told Tom Lincoln was close to Natz, but didn't tell V. Cora didn't want Tom to go thru with pact while Lincoln on way home. Didn't want Tom and Lncln to meet 1st time over Viola's dead body.*

> 9:28 A.M. *Next thing C remembers is getting call from Tom asking how V doing. C trotted home & found V dead. She thought then the pact had been fulfilled, even tho Tom acted like V was alive when he left.*

> 9:31 A.M. *Cora had mixed feelings about asst. suicide pact. Religious guilt. She Catholic like V. Cora claims Lincoln was coming because she told him death was close, but nothing about death pact b4 L arrived. Shit, my fingers spazzing out. I may call you and sit here with the line open.*

I type: *Can you do that w/o getting caught?*

> 9:34 A.M. *Less obvious than txting. U may not be able to hear tho. Let's test it in a bit. Still text 4 now*

I hear Drew's heavy tread descending the stairs. I meet him in the hall, and I can see instantly that the news isn't good.

"Well?" I prompt him.

"Mrs. St. Denis is going to need a psychiatric consult. She's been living with a repressed trauma for decades, as I'm sure you know. The assault on her mother-in-law has triggered an unbearable level of terror and guilt. I think she's a suicide risk, Penn. I sedated her. She doesn't seem to have any family she feels comfortable having handle this. I met Serenity, and Dolores seems to trust her, but that's no long-term solution. Do you have any sort of plan?"

"I'll do whatever you advise, Drew. But I'm going to have to bring the FBI into this. There's the question of her personal safety. That woman up there can put Snake Knox on death row in Angola."

Drew nods, but I see more than a trace of judgment in his eyes. "If you're waiting for her to sit in a courtroom with Snake Knox and tell a jury that he raped her and murdered her husband, you're going to be waiting a long time. That's my feeling, anyway. But you're right to call the FBI. We've had enough innocent people hurt lately."

"Speaking of that, how's Keisha doing?"

He shakes his head. "I shipped her up to UMC in an ambulance this morning."

The weight of this news, on top of Cleotha Booker, is almost too much.

"One more thing," says my old friend. "Annie is having a significant anxiety reaction. She's trying to cope, but down deep I think she's regressing to the state she was in after Caitlin was killed. I think death is the trigger, Penn. She simply can't deal with loss, not even the aura of it. Which shouldn't surprise us, given how she lost her mother, and others in her life."

"Drew . . . goddamn it. Tell me what to do."

He lays a hand on my shoulder and looks into my eyes. "Forget about going back to the courthouse. Annie needs you here, within reach. You understand? Mia alone is not enough."

"I understand. I'll stay."

"And you'll call the FBI?"

"The second you leave."

"Okay. I'll check back in about three hours."

When Tim pulls the door shut after Drew, I take out my cell phone and, ignoring the latest texts from Rusty Duncan, speed-dial John Kaiser.

"Penn," he answers. "What's up?"

"John, listen. Are you in Natchez right now?"

"Yeah. What's going on? I heard you left the courtroom."

"Buddy . . . I've got an eyewitness who can testify to Snake Knox committing rape and murder. The victim was her husband."

First there's only silence. Then Kaiser says, "Who the hell are you talking about?"

"I can't tell you that unless you promise to go very easy with this woman. She does *not* want me to call the Bureau. In fact, she's told me she would recant everything if I did."

"Are you sure she's on the level?"

"John, if she ever decides to testify, she'll be God's gift to whatever prosecutor gets Snake's case."

"If she didn't want you to call me, why did you?"

"Her life's in danger. I think her mother-in-law was assaulted last night. She's probably close to death now, if not dead already."

"Good God. Where's this woman now?"

I hesitate, then decide to trust him. "At my Washington Street house. But you may not be able to talk to her for a while. Drew just sedated her. This is the witness you've been looking for from the beginning, John. Don't blow it by rushing her, okay? If you come, come alone."

"Message received. I can be there in . . . is an hour okay?"

"Two might be better. I told you, she's out for now. And I need to figure out how to explain you showing up."

"I'll see you around lunch, then. Just me."

I hit END, then text Serenity: *Are you okay?* She's only upstairs, but something tells me that Dolores St. Denis might not want me barging into her room.

The reply comes in twenty seconds: *D finally sleeping for real. I'm going to stay with her for now. Worried she might harm herself if she wakes alone.*

I type: *I just talked to FBI. They're going to have to be involved. If only for protection, not testimony. John Kaiser will come alone. Will not pressure D. Think about how we can convince D she'll be safe with them.*

This time there's a delay. Then Serenity types: *You mean how we can lie?*

NO, I answer.

We killed Cleotha Booker, Penn. We led them to her.

Serenity is obviously overcome with guilt.

She's not dead yet, I type. *I'll talk to you in a while. Let me know if I can bring anything up.*

I wait for an answer, but my phone remains quiet.

Walking back to the kitchen, I take out a cold Tab, drink half the can in one fizzy rush, then sit down and scan Rusty's most recent messages. They seem like missives from some faraway proceeding to which I'm only incidentally connected. I suddenly realize that I'm using them to escape the guilt I feel at what's happened to the Cat Lady.

9:37 A.M. *When Cora found Viola dead, she panicked. Felt like "man walking in space." She called Lincoln, not Tom, and then told Linc about suicide pact. Linc furious. Almost in Natz by then. Told Cora call 911, ask for paramedics and ACSO.*

9:39 A.M. *Lincoln arrived on scene just after Sheriff's Department.*

9:45 A.M. *Shad tenders witness, reserves right to recall Cora.*

Shad is reserving the right to recall Cora because he wants to stay focused on the forensic case and not disturb the timeline he's engraving in the minds of the jury. But she will be back, and her testimony will likely be the stuff of daytime melodrama.

9:46 A.M. *Holy shit! Quentin said "No questions" AGAIN! Not going to cross! WTF?*

Now my pulse is picking up. I can't imagine any possible reason that Quentin would let Cora Revels leave the stand without cross-examining her.

9:48 A.M. *Shad looks like the cat who ate canary. He can't believe his luck. I can't either. Why is Q lying down? Alzheimers for real???*

9:53 A.M. *Shad called Sheriff's Detective Joiner to stand.*

10:06 A.M. *Joiner says deputies assumed they working asst suicide case. Found morphine vial, syringe, hairs and fibers, yadda yadda. Bagged and tagged all. Found camcorder on tripod, no tape.*

10:19 A.M. *Shad tenders witness and . . . NO FUCKING CROSS! You gotta get down here man. You have 2 fire Quentin. Obvs malpractice! Shad dragging your dad to Parchman with nobody pulling the other way on the rope.*

In less than an hour, my bewilderment has escalated to anxiety, frustration, and now outright anger.

10:24 A.M. *Sheriff Byrd on stand now.*

10:32 A.M. *Byrd testifies Shad showed him the tape of V's death at 1:07* P.M. *Monday 12-12 and said he was first person other than Shad to see it. Shad explained Henry Sexton provided camera, recording made accidentally. Sexton pointed out existence of recording. Shad, Byrd put tape into evidence, later had copy made by pro.*

10:44 A.M. *Shad tendered Byrd, reserved right to recall. No cross from Quentin. No surprise. I need some f'ing Xanax.*

Rusty doesn't even bother to raise hell this time. Every lawyer in the courtroom must be about to burst, but of course no one can say anything.

10:49 A.M. *Fingerprint expert on stand. Prints on syringe and vial your dad's. Immediate AFIS match based on your dad's gun carry permit. Yawn.*

11:01 A.M. *Shad tenders witness. No cross. u surprised?*

11:08 A.M. *Hair and fiber xpert. Your dad's hair all over the scene. DNA match. Carpet fibers from your dad's house all over. Shad tenders . . . no cross. Too depressing to watch, man. This is going to be a conviction in world record time. Q's lost it. I'll take over if u want. It's that bad.*

I'm definitely panicked now. My heart is headed into tachycardia, and it's all I can do to keep Annie from realizing how upset I am.

11:10 A.M. *More hearsay now. Judge unfazed. Shad says his office contacted by Lincoln Turner and told about suicide pact. He called the mayor and asked him to speak to his father about what happened.*

It's improper for the DA himself to read something like this into the record, but Judge Elder seems to be proceeding on the premise that Quentin's failure to object waives Dad's right to keep it from the jury.

11:14 A.M. *Later same morning, Henry Sexton informed DA that a camera he left in decedent's room had a hard drive on it. They checked said drive and found the tape you watched, showing the death of VT 5:38* A.M.

Monday, December 12th. Dr Cage refused to answer questions on any of those events.

11:18 A.M. *Judge mentions lunch, but Shad calls one more witness. Leo Watts, asks to treat him as hostile. Elder grants.*

Leo Watts is a local pharmacist and longtime friend of my father's. By asking to treat Leo as a hostile witness, Shad will be allowed to ask him leading questions on the stand. Furthermore, the jury will know that they are hearing testimony from someone predisposed to view my father in a favorable light.

11:23 A.M. *Leo says your dad prescribed morphine for V ever since she got back. Lethal amounts. Big whoop. Most terminal cancer patients have that. Q must bring this out on cross! Shad asking about adrenaline. Leo admits your dad has written adrenaline scrips for himself. Not in long time though. Says many docs with heart disease keep adrenaline vials around house, in car, but Shad cuts him off.*

11:34 A.M. *Leo reluctantly admits Tom prescribed potentially lethal amnts drugs to people w endstage cancer, AIDS, etc. if patient were to take overdose. Says not uncommon, but Shad cuts him off again. Pray Shad doesn't have disgruntled patient family ready to testify to asst suicide in past. Tho I guess would b better than murder 1.*

I type: *If he doesn't, it's not for lack of looking.*

11:37 A.M. *Shad just let Leo go. Quentin HAS to cross here, let Leo say what he wants, undo damage.*

11:39 A.M. *No questions from Q! I'm in shock. Lawyers in crowd freaking out. This is an emergency.*

11:44 A.M. *Recessing for lunch. On my way 2 your house. We gotta stop this circus!*

"Daddy?" Annie asks, and her voice startles me so badly that I shove the kitchen table forward with a screech.

"I'm sorry," she says from just inside the kitchen door. "I just wanted to let you know I'm okay. For real."

Mia stands in the hall behind her, looking far from certain of that.

I reach out and pull Annie to me for a hug. "I'm glad, Boo." I glance up at Mia over her shoulder. "How's Dolores doing?"

"Serenity's still in her bedroom with her."

After a few seconds, Annie pulls back and looks into my eyes. "Daddy, you look almost like you did when you heard Caitlin's phone message at the church."

Can I tell my eleven-year-old daughter the truth? That I feel as though my father is dying of some terrible disease, and I've turned him over to a renowned surgeon who seems to have forgotten basic anatomy and whatever surgical technique he ever possessed.

"It's just the trial, Annie. From what Rusty tells me, Mr. Quentin's not doing what he should be doing in the courtroom. He's not doing what I would do, anyway."

Annie sticks out her lower lip. "I told you in the beginning you should be defending Papa."

"I'm afraid that's not really an option. But Mr. Rusty's on his way here. He and I are going to talk about what to do. I may need to go down to my study with him for a while."

She nods quickly. "It's okay."

"And John Kaiser's going to be coming over as well. To try to help Mrs. Dolores."

"Good. I'm really okay, Dad. You do what you have to do."

CHAPTER 25

TAKING ADVANTAGE OF Annie's temporary calm, I climb the stairs to meet Serenity outside Dolores's guest room. I wait for half a minute, and then Serenity slips through the door and leaves it cracked enough so that she can monitor her charge. Through the opening I see a woman lying on her side beneath white bedclothes, her arms clenched around a pillow. Even from this distance I get the sense that she is twitching and jerking in her drug-induced sleep.

"How is she?" I ask.

Tee just looks back at me with sadness and anger in her eyes.

"Has she been conscious at all since we talked?"

"Twice. I mentioned the FBI to her. I didn't want to, but we obviously need some help. Somebody tried to kill that old woman, Penn. All I can see when I'm sitting in there is that shack full of cats waiting for a woman that'll never come home."

"I know."

"That's on us, Penn."

"I know it is." After a few moments of silence, I say, "What do I tell Kaiser when he gets here?"

Serenity bites her lip. "Send him up and tell him to knock very softly. I'll handle it from there."

"Okay."

I hear a rustle from the bedroom.

"Later," Tee says, and the door shuts in my face.

BACK IN THE kitchen, I speed-dial Quentin's cell phone, but it kicks me straight to voice mail. He's probably piloting his wheelchair through a gauntlet of cameras waiting outside the courthouse, with Doris walking point for him. I know better than to worry that he'll reveal his strategy to reporters, but since he's doing almost nothing in the courtroom, maybe he plans to try the case in the media?

Our house phone rings, startling me. The caller ID shows my mother's cell phone.

"Mom?" I answer.

"No, it's Rusty! We're stuck in traffic near the courthouse. It's insane. I've got everybody in my Town Car. Tim's guys are behind us in the Yukon. We won't have much time when we get there, so I'm going to play you what I recorded of the pathologist's testimony over your mother's phone. Then you'll be on the same page with us."

"Okay, go."

"It's on my little Sony microcassette. Forgive the crap sound."

After a high-pitched howl of feedback, two voices begin speaking through a digital hiss. One belongs to Shad Johnson, leading the witness so egregiously that I can't believe Quentin is not objecting; the other to a Dr. Adam Phillips, the state medical examiner.

> *"Could an elderly physician with severely restricted hand mobility make such a mistake with a simple injection, Dr. Phillips?"*
>
> *"Of course. Even young physicians with healthy hands miss veins, or punch through them. Especially veins that have been worn out by toxic chemotherapy agents."*
>
> *"Do physicians under great stress tend to make more mistakes than those who are not?"*
>
> *"The statistics support that. But physicians are trained to operate under stressful conditions. That's the nature of the job."*
>
> *"What if the stress were psychological and deeply personal? Unrelated to the job?"*
>
> *"Severe stress of that type would increase the odds of making a mistake for any physician, as it would for any professional attempting to do his job."*
>
> *"But Dr. Cage would have seen that the morphine was not killing his patient, would he not?"*
>
> *"If he stayed at the scene. Did he stay at the scene?"*
>
> *"Let me ask the questions, Dr. Phillips. Would it have been to*

Dr. Cage's advantage to stay at the scene? If his goal was to murder the patient and not be found out?"

"Well, of course. If he had stayed at the scene, then Mrs. Turner would have died under a doctor's care. No autopsy would have been required. If he wanted to kill her, or murder her, he'd have been home free. Unless the family raised a stink."

The question of whether or not Dad was present at Viola's house during her death comprises the central hole in Shad's case, and to my knowledge, no evidence proves that he was. The idea that Quentin would let this kind of leading questioning proceed without objecting is simply beyond me.

"How long after the botched morphine injection would it have taken for a doctor at the scene to realize the drug was not killing his patient?"

"That's hard to say. It depends on a lot of factors, and a patient's morphine tolerance can't be determined after death."

"Can you make an educated guess?"

"Between ten and thirty minutes. With as little morphine as got into her bloodstream, Mrs. Turner might have remained conscious the whole time, or she might have awakened after only a few minutes of sedation."

"All right. Why would a doctor administer adrenaline after seeing that the morphine was not having its intended effect? Would he do it to resuscitate her? To try to bring her back to life?"

This question is improper on so many grounds that I wouldn't know where to begin to object. Shad is obviously implying to the jury that Dad injected the adrenaline, when he has presented no evidence that he did so. Yet Quentin does not object!

"A knowledgeable physician would not use adrenaline in that situation, no. He would know that adrenaline does not counteract the effects of an intravenous morphine overdose. For that he would need naloxone. I suppose that if he were desperately trying to save the patient, he might

> *hope it would help keep her alive until paramedics arrived to take her to the hospital. But the evidence shows that a lethal dose of morphine never reached Mrs. Turner's brain, so why would he try to resuscitate her? She could not have been dying from the morphine."*

What if she were dying of something else? I make a note to ask on cross, as if I will actually get the chance to question this witness.

"Precisely," says Shad. *"And in this case, no paramedics were called, Doctor. Furthermore, we know from the hard drive recording that the doctor was not performing chest compressions on the patient subsequent to the adrenaline injection. What does that suggest to you?"*

"Object, Quentin," I mutter, "you son of a bitch."

> *"Medically, I can't make sense of it. Not if his objective was to save the patient. But then, why would he be trying to save her at all if she had signed a DNR directive? Adrenaline is used to yank patients back from the precipice of death. A DNR order is signed for the specific purpose of preventing the use of such drugs."*
>
> *"Think about the facts as they've been explained, Doctor. Can you come up with any theory that might explain them, short of Dr. Cage intentionally giving the adrenaline to murder the patient?"*
>
> *"Well . . . a doctor helping a patient to die might feel some regret in the midst of the act. It's conceivable that he might try to resuscitate her with adrenaline, and accidentally kill her with it. Due to allergy or simple overdose. The effects of epinephrine can vary widely from patient to patient."*
>
> *"Epinephrine and adrenaline are the same drug, correct?"*
>
> *"I'm sorry, yes. But again, a competent physician would know that adrenaline wouldn't specifically counter the depressive effects of morphine. And finally, again, the evidence shows that a lethal dose of morphine never reached her brain. Why would anyone try to resuscitate a conscious person? It makes no sense."*
>
> *"I suppose he might have tried to resuscitate her in that ten- to thirty-minute window of unconsciousness, if he were suddenly filled with remorse, as you suggested."*
>
> *"Yes, but if so, then why didn't he call paramedics?"*
>
> *"Oh, yes. Thank you for reminding me. Doctor, given the forensic evidence, let me suggest a hypothetical scenario to you, as a forensic expert."*

At this, I almost throw the kitchen phone onto the floor. Even Judge Elder must have been tempted to step in here, yet the questions roll on, as if Shad is directing this movie as well as acting in it.

"Our physician means to kill his patient with morphine by injection of an overdose. The patient submits voluntarily, as it was her intent to commit suicide. Due to stress and arthritis, the doctor botches the injection. Soon he realizes that the morphine is not killing the patient. He has no more morphine. The doctor is under a time constraint to leave the house. His patient has been partially sedated by the morphine, so he decides to use what he has on hand to finish the job. He decides to inject her with IV adrenaline, which will send her into cardiac arrest. Because of his profession, and his standing in the community, he's virtually certain that no questions will be asked, so long as he remains at the scene to call the coroner. He can sign the death certificate himself. It will still be a perfect murder, as he'd planned. Are you with me so far?"

"Yes."

"The problem begins when the adrenaline hits the patient's system. She does not die quickly. She panics, cries out, flails about. Despite his plan, the doctor is horrified by what he's done. He might even be afraid that the neighbors or relatives will hear and become alarmed. In his panic he flees the scene, knocking the telephone onto the floor. He knows that by leaving the scene, he is risking an autopsy. But if the adrenaline is detected, he can simply say that he resuscitated the patient and left her alive. That he was in a quandary about what to do. He had to say that, you see? Otherwise he could not explain his failing to report her death.

"Do you see any problems with this scenario so far?"

"Only that adrenaline has limited therapeutic value in counteracting a morphine overdose, if he intended to claim he had resuscitated her with it and left her alive."

"Might not a general practitioner plead ignorance on that point? Ignorance and desperation?"

"No. But you're forgetting the DNR order. Why would he say he had tried to resuscitate her, since she was DNR?"

"I'll ask you to answer your own question."

"I don't know."

"Think about it."

"Well . . . he might claim that, since the woman was his former nurse, and he had great affection for her, he disobeyed the DNR order and saved her."

"That would make sense, wouldn't it?"

"But then why didn't he also do chest compressions?"

"You're jumping back into what we know now. The doctor's intent at that point was simply to say he left his patient alive. He had no idea that the woman's dying agony was being recorded on video. No idea that we would see that he didn't perform chest compressions or any other lifesaving measures. He intended to claim that he had performed chest compressions, and that she survived. That she must have died subsequent to his intervention."

"If he'd performed chest compressions on an elderly woman, the evidence would be obvious. Severe bruising, broken ribs even. But that brings me back to my original problem with the whole scenario."

"Which is?"

"Why did he leave the scene? As I said earlier, if he'd stayed at the scene, no autopsy would have been required."

"Exactly. I've asked myself the same question many times. Why did he leave the scene? There are three possible answers. One, as he watched Viola die, Dr. Cage was overcome by the horror of his act and could not stand to remain at the scene of the crime."

"Right now the jury's thinking about that video recording," I say into the phone, "and how Viola was panicking and begging for Dad's help."

"Yep," Rusty says, pausing the tape. "We're getting close to your house now. Keep listening. Not much left."

"Two, there was something at the scene the doctor needed to destroy as soon as possible."

"The videotape Viola made for Henry," I say.

"Bingo," says Rusty.

"Why hasn't Shad mentioned that specifically? He didn't even bring it up in his opening statement."

"He will, don't worry. Listen to the end."

"Three, someone arrived on the scene, or was about to arrive—a family member who would 'raise a stink,' as you suggested—and the doctor didn't have the nerve to brazen it out in front of that person."

"Lincoln," I mutter. "Cora testified that Dad knew Lincoln was on his way to Natchez from Chicago."

"Yep," Rusty says in an emotionless voice.

"Do any of those scenarios sound reasonable to you, Doctor?"

"I wouldn't know about the doctor needing to destroy anything. But the other two scenarios sound reasonable. I've seen families accuse a doctor of murder after a death. But still, this doctor would know that once he ran, an autopsy would almost certainly be performed. That's a big risk."

"Is it? If he claimed that the adrenaline was used to resuscitate her? Used successfully?"

"It would be a stretch, medically speaking. I still think the easiest and smartest thing by far—for a doctor meaning to kill his patient—would be to stay on the scene, call the ambulance after the patient expired, and brazen it out. That would almost certainly be the end of it—legally speaking."

"But that would require a great deal of nerve, Doctor. And the physician in this case is no longer a man in his prime with little to lose. Further, his reasons for panic fall outside the realm of your medical expertise, so I'll now turn you over to the tender mercies of the counsel for the defense."

"Do you believe this?" Rusty says angrily. "He's *daring* Quentin to cross-examine the guy. But by now he's positive that Quentin won't. Shad is mocking Quentin Avery, man! I could never have imagined it. We're a block away from your house. There's only one thing left."

"Let me hear it."

"Your witness."

"Mr. Johnson, one other scenario just occurred to me."

I can tell by the delay before Shad's reply that the medical examiner has jumped off script. But if Shad doesn't let him say whatever he wants to say, Quentin might well roll out from behind his table and offer Dr. Phillips the opportunity. Any competent attorney would. I've been in this situation myself, and I know Shad has little choice but to let his witness speak, and hope for the best.

> *"What's that, Doctor?"*
>
> *"If Dr. Cage meant to murder Mrs. Turner, as you've postulated, and he ran out of morphine, which the evidence indicates—"*
>
> *"Proves."*
>
> *"Yes, all right. Well, even if everything went as you've suggested, once the whole thing went wrong and the doctor knew he was going to be charged with first-degree murder . . ."*
>
> *"Yes?"*
>
> *"Why didn't he just say, 'All right, yes, we had an assisted-suicide pact. I provided the morphine for her to euthanize herself, but she botched the injection, so I let her inject the adrenaline to stop her heart. It wasn't ideal, but it was all I had.'? Why didn't he say that? The penalty for physician-assisted suicide is ten years, isn't it? A murder conviction means life in prison."*

Shad takes so long with this question that I find myself hoping the pathologist has stunned him into losing his composure. But then Shad comes through with his customary tactical proficiency.

> *"He may well intend to say that when he testifies, Doctor. Or if he didn't intend to say that, he may decide to now. But the fact is, when questioned by the authorities, Dr. Cage said nothing of the sort. In fact, he refused to say anything at all. And that is why we find ourselves here today. I tender the witness."*

Less than five seconds pass before Quentin Avery says, "No questions, Your Honor," and I shut my eyes with the dread of a man watching a replay of a fatal accident.

"We're here," Rusty says in my ear. "Finally."

"Good."

CHAPTER 26

I'VE JUST MADE a round of all the security guards, making sure they know to expect John Kaiser and that he could appear from anywhere. Tim and I are standing near the back door, discussing the possibility of bringing more men from Texas, when Rusty marches halfway up the hall and waves at me.

"Dude. I've got the whole crowd in there, and we need to get the Quentin issue sorted out before your mom has a real stroke and your dad gets sent up the river."

Following Rusty to the den, I find not only my mother but Jenny, Annie, and to my surprise, Miriam Masters. Everyone's talking at once, but the theme is universal: Quentin Avery has lost his mind.

"Penn, I can't calm down," Mom says in a quavering voice. "My hands have been shaking for the past hour."

"Take it easy, now." I lean down to hug her, but she pushes me away.

"Take it *easy*? You've got to fire Quentin, son. You've got to take over Tom's defense!"

"Mom, I can't fire Quentin. Only Dad can do that."

"Then somebody take me to the jail, and I'll tell him he's got to do it. Is that where Tom is now? Or do they give him lunch in the courthouse?"

"There's a holding cell in the courthouse," Rusty says softly, "but if I know Billy Byrd, Doc's back in his cell."

Annie's standing by the television, taking in every word. Few things disturb children more than frightened adults, and Annie was upset before anyone got here. I go over and put an arm around her, telling her softly that things are going to be all right, that everybody's just upset by a mistake Mr. Avery made. But I can feel her shivering against me.

"Let's all calm down," I say firmly. "There's got to be some rational reason Quentin is doing what he's doing. We've got three lawyers in this room. Let's figure it out."

Mom suddenly realizes that she's let herself go in front of her granddaughter. She gets up and leads Annie over to the love seat in the corner, murmuring so softly I can't make out her words.

Rusty is watching me expectantly, but it's Miriam I turn to first. She may be a glorified corporate accountant in her normal life, but she graduated fourth in her class at Stanford Law School, and she did two years in the public defender's office in San Francisco.

"What do you think?" I ask.

She sucks in her lips and shakes her head, obviously as bewildered as the rest of us. "Penn, I've never seen anything like it before."

"Rusty? You ever see any backwoods Clarence Darrow try something like this?"

Rusty shakes his head in a perfect imitation of Miriam. "I kept wondering, 'Is this like a slowdown offense in basketball? Where it looks like the coach is an idiot and the team is shit, even though they're playing smart?' But this ain't no basketball game, bubba. Quentin hasn't invoked the rule to keep his witnesses sequestered. *He didn't even file for discovery.* I've *never* seen that happen in a murder trial. The guy even deferred his opening statement, and let Shad have all the momentum from the word go! I've seen that maybe once in my career. He hasn't made *one* objection or cross-examined a single witness. And every time Quentin lets some trademark Shad Johnson bullshit pass without objecting, that's one more thing that'll never be reversed on appeal."

"Bingo," says Miriam. "That jury has already heard things it never should have heard. Those images will never leave their minds, no matter what instructions the judge gives. I can't believe Judge Elder isn't worried about getting reversed based on ineffective assistance of counsel."

"It's *Quentin Avery,*" Rusty says, stating the obvious. "Lawyers don't come any more experienced than that. Not in these parts. Not anywhere."

"Maybe that's the problem," Miriam says, voicing our common fear.

"Alzheimer's?" Rusty asks, looking for confirmation in our eyes. "I mean . . . surely it's in the realm of possibility. The guy's lost both legs to diabetes already. Could he have had, like, mini strokes or something? Something not obvious, but still incapacitating?"

"I'm no doctor," Miriam points out, "but from what I saw this morning, I'd say it's possible. Penn, did you notice anything worrisome when you spoke to him prior to the trial?"

"When I saw him at the prison, he did tell me to expect an unconventional strategy. But we've hardly talked to each other since. This is his and Dad's show, and I'm not part of it."

My mother cuts her eyes at me, the old maternal reproach.

"Have you tried to *call* Quentin?" Rusty asks.

"At least ten times before you guys showed up. His mobile keeps kicking me to voice mail."

"We've got to fire him," Mom insists from the corner. "I don't see any other way."

This draws every eye in the room to her.

"Nobody can fire Quentin except Dad," I repeat. "And Dad won't do it. I wasn't in the courtroom. Did he look panicked by what Quentin was doing? Or not doing?"

"All I could see was the back of his head," Mom says with frustration.

"He's not scared," Jenny says from the sofa. "He just sat calmly through it all. But I don't know what that says about *his* mental state."

"That could just be resignation. Fatalism."

Everyone suddenly looks at me, as though I have the answer to the riddle of Quentin Avery.

"Whatever Quentin's doing, " I think aloud, "it's been part of his plan all along. As I said, he told me three days ago that he was going to take an unconventional approach to Dad's defense."

"Unconventional," Rusty grunts. "Like driving thirty miles per hour is an unconventional way to win the Daytona 500."

In the wake of this comment, the front door opens and closes softly. A moment later John Kaiser leans past the door frame, acknowledges me with a quick salute, then vanishes. The next thing I hear is his feet padding softly up the stairs.

My mother is gazing curiously at me, but I ignore her.

"I think we've done what we can here," I tell them. "Which is basically nothing. I'll keep trying to reach Quentin. You guys need to eat something. There are sandwiches in the kitchen fridge."

"I can't eat," Miriam says miserably.

"I can," Rusty growls, getting up and lumbering toward the kitchen. "My fingers have about seized up from texting you all those updates."

Mom catches my eye over Annie's shoulder. "Penn, you need to go back to court for the afternoon session. I'll stay with Annie."

I shake my head. "No way. The jury has to see you there, supporting Dad."

"Then let's take Annie with us."

Annie claps her hands with relief and excitement. At last we've arrived at the simple solution she proposed in the beginning.

"Boo, go help Rusty find the sandwiches."

She starts to argue, but today my look is enough to propel her into the kitchen. As she vanishes, Mom says, "Penn, what is John Kaiser doing here?"

"It's nothing to do with Dad's trial. Now, you need to brace yourself for the next session. Based on what Shad has done so far, I expect him to recall Cora Revels to the stand, or else he'll call Lincoln. And they'll dive straight into the issue of motive. We're going to hear all about Dad and Viola's relationship. *All* about it."

My mother's jaw clamps shut, and her eyes glaze over with suppressed rage. But at whom? Shad Johnson? Or my father?

"All right," she says in surrender. "You stay here."

I hit speed dial for Quentin's cell and wait for the automated voicemail message, but the sound of repeated ringing rocks me back on my heels. I hold up my left hand sharply, and the resulting silence brings Rusty and Annie back from the kitchen.

"Hello?" says Doris Avery.

I feel an alarming pressure in my chest, like something's trying to burst out of it through my constricted throat, but I force myself to be calm. "Doris, this is Penn. Could I please speak to Quentin?"

"He's trying to eat lunch. It took us forever just to get to Edelweiss."

Edelweiss is only four blocks from the courthouse, but they probably had a harder time getting clear of the courthouse than my crew did. Still, they could easily have answered the phone while stuck in Quentin's converted van.

"I really need to speak to him, Doris. You must know that, after what happened in court this morning."

Mom's eyes blaze. She's about two seconds from snatching the phone out of my hand and reminding Doris who's paying her husband's fee.

"Are you calling to ruin my lunch?" Quentin growls in my ear. "I hope not, 'cause I ain't got much time to eat before the afternoon session."

It's a shock to finally have Quentin on the phone, but I recover quickly. "Quentin, I've got my mother and sister here, and we're more than a little concerned about your courtroom tactics thus far."

Rusty pokes his head through the door and makes a horrified face.

"Or your lack of them, rather," I clarify.

"What are you talking about?" Quentin asks as he noisily chews what sounds like a salad.

I hit the speakerphone button so that everyone can hear. "The fact that you haven't made a single objection or cross-examined a single witness."

"Don't worry about that. Everything's going according to plan."

As I shake my head in disbelief, Rusty twirls his hand in a circle around his ear. "And what plan is that?"

Quentin barks a short laugh, then continues chewing. "You're an old prosecutor. What plan does it look like?"

"It looks to me like the Mahatma Gandhi plan. Nonviolent resistance. Turn the other cheek until you're lying dead in the gutter."

This earns a belly laugh from the old lawyer. "That shows what you know, big shot. I'll tell you what my plan is—the Leonardo da Vinci plan. I'm the master, and you're watching me paint my Mona Lisa. Come back for the afternoon session, if you can, but don't worry if you can't. And tell Peggy not to worry."

"It's too late for that, Quentin," Mom says in a serrated voice.

"Hello, Peg," Quentin says in a softer tone. "Don't worry about Tom and me. We know what we're doing."

"If that's true, I wish you'd let the rest of us in on it."

"I wish I could, darling. But you'll see soon enough. Have faith."

When Mom's hand touches her cheek, I realize she's very close to breaking down.

In the resulting vacuum, Quentin says, "Penn, tell your buddy Rusty to come back for the afternoon session. He can consider it free remedial education."

Rusty's face goes red as the old man cackles, and I know then that Quentin's about to hang up.

"Quentin, wait!" I say, but I'm too late. We're all staring at a dead phone.

"Out of his effing mind," Rusty says. "Certifiable."

I meet Miriam's deep gray eyes.

"I don't know," she says. "It comes down to how much faith you have in your father's judgment."

"Temporarily impaired," Mom says in a soft voice. "Tom's not thinking straight. I've got to talk to him."

"You won't get to him before they start up again," Rusty says, looking at his watch. "Not for more than a couple of minutes, anyway. Can you convince him to fire Quentin in two minutes?"

Mom looks at Annie, then smiles wretchedly and wipes a strand of hair from her eyes. "I doubt it."

"Who takes Quentin's place if Dad does fire him?" I ask. "Who walks in there with the score twelve–zip and tries to pull out the game?"

"*You do,*" the four answer in unison.

"Sounds like a plan," Mia says from the kitchen doorway.

As my friends and family look into my eyes with emotions ranging from hope to desperation, I think about Quentin and my father. Dad always taught me that fear is contagious, and disastrous to decision making. Three days ago, Quentin told me I probably wouldn't understand his strategy in this case, and he made me promise not to run to him every five minutes for an explanation of his tactics. Does what happened this morning constitute genius or incipient dementia? I don't have enough information to answer that question. In the last analysis, with Quentin Avery pulling the strings, I'm willing to bet on the former—at least for a little bit longer.

"No," I tell them. "Quentin and Dad have information we don't. We can't even guess what that might be. And even if Dad were *willing* to fire Quentin right now, there's not enough time for me to prepare for the afternoon session. Tomorrow would be the earliest I could start."

"Your dad could be toast by tonight," Rusty says with brutal frankness. "He's halfway to Parchman already."

I spear my old friend with a glare for saying this in front of Annie and my mother, but he only shrugs. *The truth is the truth,* say his eyes. *What's the use in sugarcoating it?*

"Let's give Quentin the afternoon. If he goes any farther off the rails, Judge Elder will have to shut the thing down anyway."

"Declare a mistrial?" Miriam asks.

"Elder won't do that," Rusty argues. "He knows nobody's going to reprimand him for letting Quentin Avery run his own show."

"I'm not so sure. But the point's moot anyway. You barely have time to finish eating and get back."

"Jesus," groans Rusty.

"You guys go play your roles. Annie and I will be here. And try to get closer to the bar, if you can, so I can hear better."

Rusty rolls his eyes, but in the end he gobbles down the remains of a sandwich and walks into the hall. As the women file past Rusty toward the front door, he looks back with a pragmatic tilt of his head.

"Start warming up that pitching arm, Counselor. Avery's coming off the mound."

"Get out of here."

THIRTY SECONDS AFTER Rusty's Town Car pulls away from the curb, followed by the Yukon, two black sedans glide into the space. Four FBI agents get out, and there's absolutely nothing casual about their movements. I nearly jump out of my skin when John Kaiser touches my shoulder from behind.

"Let's go in the den," he says, his eyes troubled.

"What is it?" I ask once we're clear of the hall.

"Dolores St. Denis has agreed to enter protective custody."

"What's the status of Cleotha Booker?"

"She's unlikely to regain consciousness."

His answer covers me like a shadow. "Is there any chance it was a real fall?"

"About one percent."

"No," I breathe, pushing my fingers back through my hair.

As we stare at each other, the door opens and the four agents move swiftly up the staircase.

"You need to go?" I ask.

"They'll wait for me. This is a bad situation, Penn."

"You think that's news to me?"

I know Kaiser's grinding his teeth, because his jaw is flexing, hard. "Who is Serenity Butler?" he asks.

"A friend. A writer."

"Why is she taking care of Mrs. St. Denis?"

What can I say? "They're both women? They're both black? She got elected because Dolores trusts her."

"You brought Mrs. St. Denis up here in an airplane?"

"It seemed like the safest method."

Kaiser shakes his head. "This was right on the borderline, man. You really pushed it. You should have called me yesterday, before you ever went to see her."

"You and I have different objectives, John."

"There were gunshots reported within one block of that woman's house last night. Also a false report of a home invasion."

I say nothing to this.

"Penn, you don't have the legal authority to do *anything* like that. Do you understand? If this were anyone but me standing here, you'd be in federal custody."

"And if I hadn't done what I have," I say in a low voice, "you wouldn't be about to interview a witness that the Bureau should have found *forty years ago.* One who can put Snake Knox in line for a lethal injection."

Kaiser holds up his hands, but before he can speak I say, "And she was living right in New Orleans—*your home base.*"

He grinds his teeth again. "What's your point?"

"My point is, you're welcome."

CHAPTER 27

SERENITY HAS VACATED the house. When I asked where she was going, all she said was, "I need some motherfucking *air*." When I called after her to ask whether she would take one of Tim's guys along, she pretended not to hear me. To some extent, I was glad for the break. I didn't want to spend the afternoon hearing Serenity tell me how culpable we are in the attack on Cleotha Booker and the suicidal ordeal of her daughter-in-law.

I already know.

Settled in the den with Annie, who seems to be contentedly watching television with the volume low (Mia has gone upstairs to take a shower), I am thankful for the "distraction" of my father's trial.

Shad Johnson's first witness after lunch is neither Cora Revels nor Lincoln Turner, but my father's personal nurse for the past fifteen years, Melba Price. This choice surprises me. Melba will project a symbolic power from the stand, because she is the modern version of Viola. She loves and respects my father, and she will help him if she can. Moreover, she is beloved in the town, much as Viola was in her day. No matter what the facts may seem to say, Melba's belief in my father's innocence, if she expresses such faith, will carry a lot of weight with the African-American women on the jury. So why does Shad take the risk of putting her on the stand?

It's the adrenaline, I realize. One weakness of Shad's forensic case is that no empty adrenaline ampoule was found at the death scene, unlike the morphine vial with Dad's fingerprint on it. Leo Watts, the pharmacist, proved that Dad had written adrenaline prescriptions for himself in the past, but not anywhere near the date of Viola's murder.

Shad must be confident that Melba will prove that Dad had ready access to the drug, and in the time frame of Viola's murder.

As Rusty's texts start to trickle in, they verify my instinct. Judge Elder grants Shad permission to treat Melba as a hostile witness, and soon the DA is leading her like a child. To Rusty's horror, and mine, Melba gets no protection from Quentin, who ought to be objecting to some questions, if only to break up Shad's rhythm. Rusty's furious texts come through as the modern-day equivalent of a Morse code SOS, but I can easily imagine the damage Melba is doing, even as she tries her best to save the man that she's served and respected for so long.

Through Melba, Shad establishes that my father keeps a supply of adrenaline at his office to resuscitate coding patients, even though they don't have a true crash cart there. Melba also reveals that the record keeping at the office is not detailed enough to know for sure whether any adrenaline might be missing. Dad's clinic is not like a hospital with strict accounting and supply procedures—except with narcotics—and adrenaline, while potentially dangerous, is not a narcotic. In a bid to bypass the marital privilege, Shad asks Melba (rather than my mother) whether she has personal knowledge of Dad keeping adrenaline at his residence, but she evades this trap with a simple "I don't know." But when asked directly whether Dad regularly kept adrenaline in his "black bag," the kit he used during house calls, Melba concedes that he did. What else could she say? Any competent physician would stock adrenaline in the bag he carried with him to handle potential emergencies, and she makes this point before Shad can shut her down.

Having established this critical fact, Shad shifts gears and begins questioning Melba about Dad's health, particularly his psoriatic arthritis and how it has affected his hand function. In this matter Melba is fairly truthful, if more general than Shad would like, but in the end she admits that for the past year Dad has been getting Drew Elliott to perform all prostate exams required in the office, because he can no longer use his fingers effectively enough to do them himself. She probably knows that if she is evasive about this, Shad could simply call Drew to the stand. Also, like me, Melba knows that Shad has spent the past three months trolling among Dad's patients for whatever negative information he can find, and she wouldn't want to open the door to putting any of them on the stand.

About the time I expect Shad to release Melba, he begins probing potentially more vulnerable spots. Melba admits that she knew Dad was treating Viola during the last weeks of her life, but denies knowing that any sort of assisted-suicide pact existed between them. She claims she didn't know that Dad and Viola had been lovers in the past and says it wouldn't have mattered to her if she had.

At 1:32 P.M. Rusty sends two text messages saying that Shad has decided to gamble that Melba might be shocked or shamed into saying something incriminating about Dad.

Shad ques: Did Dr. Cage ever behave improperly towards u in sexual way? Pls remember u r under oath. Answer: No. Never. Shad looks smug, like Melba's lying, but female jury members glaring at him.

Ques: Do you believe Dr. Cage ever helped any patient to die? Ans: I don't know about anything like that. But I think a lot of doctors around here have done it. In some cases, it's the only decent thing.

Melba's courageous assertion gives me a guarded feeling of hope. By bringing Melba Price onto the stand, Shad has given Quentin a golden opportunity to allow a highly credible witness to say wonderful things about Dad. And Melba is clearly ready and willing to do all she can for him, which might be a lot. If she speaks with the full force of her character, she could look those women on the jury in the eye and convince at least one of them that her employer would kill himself before he would harm a patient under his care.

But the next message that comes through sends me into shock.

1:34 P.M. *Shad looked worried when he tendered Melba, but he shouldn't have. Leonardo's reply? No questions, Your Honor.*

"Oh my God," I murmur. "Oh, no."

"What is it, Daddy?" Annie asks from in front of the television. "Did Mr. Quentin do more bad stuff?"

I sigh so heavily that I feel dizzy, the way I do when I stand up too suddenly.

"*Daddy?*" Annie jumps to her feet.

"I'm okay, Boo."

My phone pings again as I pull her against my side.

2:07 P.M. Shad just recalled Cora Revels.

A few seconds pass, then Rusty types: *Fuck this shit. My fingers about 2 fall off. I'm just going to open the line & take my chances.*

"Annie, we're going to have to turn off the TV," I say in a taut voice.

"Why?" she asks, but before I can answer, her eyes widen with prescient knowledge. "Mr. Rusty's calling from court!"

I nod, and she clicks off the TV with the remote.

"Can I listen?" she asks. "I won't make a sound, I promise."

"You can't, baby. This is grown-up stuff, as grown-up as it gets. I need my earpiece from my desk in the basement. It might be in—"

"I know where it is!"

Annie races into the hall, and I hear her feet banging down the narrow steps to my office. In less than a minute she's back carrying my wired earpiece.

"All right," I concede, thankfully plugging in the jack. "You can stay in here with me, but don't even breathe loud, okay?"

She grins. "Okay."

CHAPTER 28

WHEN THE CELL phone rings in my hand, I press the button to answer, then press MUTE on the microphone on my earpiece cord so that nothing can be transmitted from our end. Then I lie back on the sofa and close my eyes, my ear tuned to the distant human voices reverberating through a thick mist of low frequency.

"When Lincoln was born," says an elderly female voice I've never heard before, *"Vee told me that his father was a black man she'd met when she first got to Chicago, when she was homesick something terrible. She said she'd gone with him just once, and got pregnant. I didn't really believe her. Viola had never been easy like that, and Lincoln was born only eight and a half months after she got to Chicago. He was a big baby, too. Wasn't no preemie."*

Shad Johnson's more educated voice cuts through the hiss of the phone. *"Who did you think the father was?"*

"Somebody from Natchez. Had to be."

"Did you have someone in mind?"

"I had several," Cora says in a snippy voice.

"More than one?" Shad asks with feigned amazement, and I know then that Cora Revels has been coached, and closely. *"I thought you said your sister was not a woman of easy morals."*

"She weren't."

"I don't understand, Miss Cora."

"You will. About two weeks before Viola left for Chicago, she was raped by some Ku Klux Klansmen. Several at one time."

A sudden roar comes through the phone.

"Did you witness that attack?"

"No, sir. Nobody did but them dirty men."

Objection! shouts a voice in my head. *Hearsay!* My heart is pounding so hard I feel loopy, but Quentin's voice is not to be heard.

"Did Viola tell you what happened to her?" Shad presses.

This time when Quentin fails to object, I know Rusty is right: Quentin Avery, the legal legend, has lost it. He's got to go. I only hope that Dad's fate isn't sealed before the end of Cora's testimony.

"Not at first," says Cora. *"First a rumor went around town. I think them men was bragging about what they done. Anyway, I asked Vee about it, and she finally broke down and told me it was true. I know now they done it to her to get our brother, Jimmy, to come out of hiding, where they could take him and kill him. Jimmy was hiding down in Freewoods, but when he heard what happened to Viola, he come looking for them that done it."*

As Cora Revels's voice breaks, I wonder why Shad has led her to reveal this long-buried event. Surely by doing so he risks the jury realizing how deep the hatred must have been between Viola and the Double Eagles, even to the day she died.

"So you believed Viola's child was a result of this rape?" Shad continues.

Leading the witness! I want to scream, but Quentin says nothing.

"Yes, sir."

"How long did you believe that?"

"Twenty-eight years."

There's a pause during which I suspect Shad is making a show of calculating Lincoln's age by the elapsed time. *"So, from 1968 until 1996 you believed that Lincoln had been fathered by Klan rapists?"*

"Yes, sir."

"Did you tell anyone else about your suspicion?"

"No."

"Did you ever tell Viola's second husband, the man whose legal name is Junius Jelks, about your suspicion?"

"Not before thirty-some-odd years passed. Viola wanted me to lie about how Lincoln was fathered. She didn't want her new husband in Chicago, Mr. Jelks, thinking that boy was fathered by klukkers from Mississippi. She told him Lincoln's father was her first husband, James Turner. A dead war hero."

An audible murmur of many voices comes through the earpiece.

"Did you support her story?"

"I did. It troubled me, and I confessed it to the priest, but I stuck to that story for a long time. A mighty long time."

"When did you stop?"

"In 1996, when our mother died. Vee had came down to help take care of Mama for the last month—being a nurse, you know—and Mr. Jelks came with her."

"Where was Lincoln at this time?"

"Lincoln had just got out of law school the year before, so he was working in Chicago."

"How old was he then?"

"Twenty-eight. He got a late start in law school."

"All right, Miss Cora. Why did you stop telling the lie about Lincoln's birth?"

"Well . . . the day Mama died, Vee and me was settin' with her body, and Vee just started talking. About things, you know. The future, what was gonna happen to the family, like that. And she told me then that Dr. Tom Cage was Lincoln's true father."

A low murmur swells, like hornets waking in the ground.

"How did you feel about that?"

"Oh, believed it the second I heard it. I was shocked, because I'd never suspected they were going together at the time. But I knew she was telling the truth. I knew she'd loved and admired Dr. Cage. I just didn't think they would ever have crossed that line. Neither of them."

"Did your sister tell you anything else that day?"

"She begged me not to tell her husband about Dr. Tom."

"You mean Junius Jelks?"

"Yes, sir. Junius had a bad temper, and he was drinking pretty heavy at that time. He'd been in and out of prison, so he could be a hard man. Sweet, sometimes, but I knew why Vee was scared."

"Do you think Viola was afraid that Junius Jelks would hurt Lincoln, who was a full-grown man by then?"

"Not physically. But he might say something to hurt him. Junius knew just how to hurt people with words. No, I think Vee was more afraid that Junius—or even Lincoln, if he found out about his real father—would do something to mess up Dr. Cage's life back here. That was the last thing Viola wanted. She knew she'd sinned, having that affair. And even though Dr. Cage was the one married, Viola felt the guilt for it. She couldn't have lived with destroying a family."

"I see. Well, on that day your mother died, did Viola also tell you whether or not Dr. Cage knew he was Lincoln's father?"

All this is patent hearsay, of course—not even admissible under exceptions—but without Quentin objecting, Cora's story seems to carry the weight of a deathbed confession. After a seemingly endless pause, Shad says, *"Miss Cora?"*

"Yes, sir. On that day, Viola told me that Dr. Cage had been sending her money every month since she left Natchez."

"Are you saying that Tom Cage had been sending your sister money for twenty-eight years?" Shad asks as though astounded.

"Yes, sir."

Cora's reply hits me like a line drive in the solar plexus. I can only imagine the horror my mother must be feeling now, for if this is true, who can believe that Dad wasn't sending that money to take care of an illegitimate child? A married man might send his old lover money for a few months, maybe even a year or two. But nearly thirty years? My God. Even with Mom's iron constitution, how can she sit in that courtroom without staring at Dad in shock and fury? After what he told me about being ignorant of Lincoln's existence until the night Viola died, I know I couldn't.

"There was many a month that Viola and that boy would have gone hungry without that money," Cora goes on. *"Later on, it helped with Lincoln's schooling. Sometimes Junius drank up every cent Cora earned as a nurse. Or used it in some scam of his, some get-rich-quick scheme. That was probably the thing that made me keep the secret so long. I thought if it ever came out that Dr. Cage was Lincoln's father, that money might stop coming. So I kept quiet."*

"I understand, Miss Cora. Lord, Lord. Any sister would have done the same."

Shad's attempt to emulate Quentin's folksy manner is clumsy, but without the genuine article to compare him to, the jury might just be buying it. How the hell can Quentin sit quiet through all of this?

"So when," Shad asks, *"did Junius Jelks learn that Lincoln was not the son of a Vietnam war hero, as he'd been told?"*

"Oh, that was a few years after Mama passed. About 2001, or the year after. Junius found an old newspaper notice of James's death. Maybe somebody from Natchez sent him one, I don't remember. Anyway, Junius knew right away that James Turner couldn't have fathered that boy. James had been killed eighteen months before Lincoln was born.

"What did Mr. Jelks do when he learned about this?"

"First, he beat Viola, for lying to him."

"Did Viola tell him the truth at that point?"

"No, sir. She tried to tell him that old story of a one-night stand, but Junius didn't believe it. He just kep' on beating her."

"What did she tell him then?"

"She told him about the Klan rape back here in Natchez."

"And did Mr. Jelks believe that story?"

"Yes, sir. He did."

"Did he come to you for confirmation?"

"Sho' did."

"What did you tell him?"

"I stuck by my sister. I told Junius that Lincoln had been fathered by a black man in that one-night stand. And Lincoln was always pretty dark-skinned, so Junius couldn't be sure. Vee was terrified of what he might do to Lincoln if he really thought he'd been tricked into raising a boy with Klan blood in him . . . Junius couldn't abide that." There's a pause, then Cora says: *"I wish now that I'd just told Junius the truth about Dr. Cage right off, because what he told Lincoln in the end caused him terrible pain. But Lincoln can tell you about that better than I can."*

"And he will," Shad promises the jury. *"But before you step down, tell us this, if you will. Why would Viola fall back on the Klan rape rather than admit Lincoln had been fathered by a reputable white doctor? Did she do that only to protect Tom Cage?"*

"For God's sake," I mutter. Any prelaw student would know to object at this point. Cora Revels cannot read minds and consequently cannot testify to what her sister might have been thinking when she made any given decision. But the hissing silence of the cell connection tells me that Quentin Avery is sitting as mute and motionless as an Easter Island statue.

"I've thought about that a lot," Cora says. *"Maybe you got to be a woman to understand this, but . . . as bad as that rape story was, one thing would have torn up Junius Jelks even more than that."*

"What's that, Miss Cora?"

"Knowing there was a white man somewhere that Viola had loved in a way she could never love him. And if Viola had said Dr. Cage's name out loud just once, Junius would have seen the truth in her eyes. He was quick that way.

So she buried it down deep, deep as she could, and told a terrible lie that was partway true."

Several seconds of silence follow this. Then Shad speaks in a mournful tone. *"That's a hard story to listen to, Miss Cora. You look worn out. I'm going to let you go in just a minute. But first tell us this. Did Junius Jelks never hear that rape rumor himself?"*

"No, sir. He never spent much time in Natchez."

"Lots of black folks moved up to Chicago from here during those years."

"Yes, but they didn't want to tell such a terrible tale on Vee, and nobody knew for sure it had happened. The Klan might have spread that tale just to get Jimmy, which they did. No black folks wanted to help the Klan spread lies."

"Except maybe the person who sent Mr. Jelks the Killed in Action notice of James Turner?"

"Yes, sir. Could be."

There's a fairly long pause, during which I hear some throat clearing and the sound of heels on hardwood. Then Shad says, *"Miss Cora, in all our talk about family and the past, I forgot to ask you one thing. We all saw the video recording that was accidentally made on the hard drive on Henry Sexton's camera. But let's talk about the camera that hard drive was attached to. When did Mr. Sexton put that into the house?"*

"About a week before Viola died. Just after his second interview with her."

"Did he tell you why he was leaving the camera there?"

"Yes. He wanted Viola to be able to record her recollections about the old days, if the mood struck her. That's why he gave her that remote control."

"Did she keep the remote control by her bed after Mr. Sexton left?"

"Yes, sir."

"All that week?"

"That's right."

"And was there a tape in that camera?"

"Yes. I saw Mr. Sexton put one in it."

"Do you know if your sister made any recordings prior to the day of her death?"

"I didn't see her do it. But I know she did. Sometimes when I'd come in, that remote would be laying on her blanket. I think she was recording whenever I wasn't around. One time she even asked me to leave, and I saw her pick up that remote."

"I see. What about the day she died?"

"Well . . . that day was different. Late in the afternoon, Viola asked me to go out for a while. And she gave me some instructions."

"Which were?"

"She said I should make sure Mr. Henry came back and got his camera the next day."

"Is that all?"

"No. She told me Dr. Cage would be coming by later, but I shouldn't say anything about her making a tape for Mr. Henry."

"Did you do as she said?"

"I was going to. But then she changed her mind."

"What do you mean?"

"When I got back—before Dr. Cage came that night—Vee told me she'd decided to ask Dr. Cage to give the tape to Mr. Henry."

"Viola was going to give this videotape to Tom Cage?"

"That's right. She said it was going to be like a test. That tape had things on it that would be painful for him, and she wanted to know if he'd do what she asked him—pass it on to Mr. Henry—in spite of that."

"I see." There's another pause, and I sense Shad is about to try to draw blood. *"Miss Cora, did your sister tell you anything about what she had recorded on that tape?"*

The next sound I hear should be Quentin yelling "Objection!," but all I hear is Cora Revels softly answering her coach's question.

"She told me a few things. Mr. Henry wanted to know everything she remembered about Jimmy and Luther, before they disappeared. Especially things they had done for the Movement. Viola told me she knew a lot she'd never told anybody, and she wanted Mr. Henry to know it. She also talked about Lincoln, and how she wanted Dr. Cage to acknowledge him. To give the boy his name. She wanted Lincoln to be able to tell the world that his father was Dr. Cage, not that no-good Junius Jelks. She told me that being pregnant with Lincoln was tied up in why she'd left Natchez in the first place—after Jimmy disappeared—and to understand it all, you had to understand some terrible things."

"Did she explain what she meant by that?"

This time Cora Revels is the one who pauses. Maybe Quentin figures Judge Elder would allow all this under the "declarant unavailable because of death" exception to the hearsay rule, but he should at least object for the record.

"Miss Cora?" Shad prompts.

"It's hard for me to say this. But Vee told me she had been troubled by something for a long time. Years and years. She said she'd committed a terrible sin a long time ago. Not just a sin, like adultery, but a crime. And the older she got, the more it weighed on her."

My heartbeat is picking up.

"What did you think of that?" Shad asks gently.

"Well, I couldn't think of a crime Viola would commit. When we was little, we used to shoplift things on a dare sometimes. Chewing gum, fishin' corks, little stuff like that. But Vee wouldn't even do that. She said stealing was wrong, no matter how small a thing was. That was Vee."

"Did you believe that she'd committed this crime she spoke of?"

"Oh, yes. 'Cause I could see how it was weighing on her."

"Was Viola the only one who knew about this crime?"

"No. Whatever it was she'd done, Dr. Cage knew about it. She told me that much. But Doc hadn't turned her in for it. And she said that made him as guilty as she was."

A slow accumulation of heat in my face tells me I've stopped breathing. Cora can only be describing one event: the murder of Frank Knox in my father's medical office.

"And did she speak about this crime on the videotape for Henry Sexton?"

"Objection!" I snap, and Annie looks up sharply from the floor. "Contents of writings, recordings, and photographs," I add, holding my finger to my lips to keep her from distracting me with questions.

But Quentin does not object, and Cora Revels hammers another nail into Dad's coffin.

"She did. Viola was conflicted about how much to say, though. Whether she should tell the truth about Dr. Cage's part."

"Did she tell you anything specific about this crime?"

"No, sir."

"All right, then. Was the tape Viola made for Henry in the video camera when you went to your neighbor's house to rest?"

"No, it wasn't. It was in the drawer of the bedside table, by Viola's bed."

This answer takes my breath away. I've always assumed that this tape was the one removed from the camcorder on the night Viola died.

"I see," Shad says, obviously aware of every answer he's leading her to.

"Daddy, are you okay?" Annie whispers.

Without a sound, I nod and mouth, *Everything's okay* to my daughter.

"After you got home and found your sister had passed away, did you think about the video camera at all?"

"No, sir. It flew plumb out of my head."

"When did you next think about it?"

"A little while later, when Lincoln asked me about it."

"What did you tell him?"

"Why Henry Sexton had put it there on the tripod."

"And what did your nephew do then?"

"He opened up the camera to see if there was a tape inside."

"And was there?"

"No, sir."

"I see." Shad pauses to let this sink in. *"To the best of your knowledge, had there been a tape in it when you left for the neighbor's house earlier that evening?"*

"I know there was. Because Viola asked me to put one in before I left."

My heart is hammering now.

"Why did she do that?"

"I don't rightly know. But it took me about five minutes to load the thing. I'm no good with that kind of gadget. Cell phones and such."

"I'm not either, Miss Cora. So there was no tape in the camera when you returned?"

"No, sir."

"And so far as you know, no one else but Dr. Cage visited your house in the interim?"

"The what?"

"The period in between the time you left, and then returned to find Viola dead."

"Right. That's right."

"So, the tape had been removed from Henry Sexton's camera, leaving only the hard drive, which was set to record if the tape ran out."

"Yes, sir. Whoever killed my sister stole that tape for sure."

Now the courtroom sounds like a swarm of hornets taking flight. Judge Elder silences them with a single warning.

"Miss Cora, I'm going to let you go now, but I may have to call you back up later. Is that all right?"

"Yes, sir. Thank you. I feel better gettin' all that family business off my chest after all these years. It's a sore trial, carrying those kinds of secrets alone."

"Tender the witness, Judge."

"Come on, Quentin," I murmur, hoping against hope. "Get up, damn it."

"Daddy?" Annie whispers. "Are you sure everything is okay?"

I signal yes and motion for Annie to stay where she is.

My earpiece hisses as though transmitting from a deserted Arctic weather station; nothing gives me any clue as to what Quentin might be doing. By now the lack of cross-examination has become so routine that no one expects anything but a curt "no questions" from Quentin, followed by the district attorney calling his next witness.

But by the odd acoustics of cell-phone microphones, I hear the high-pitched whir of Quentin's wheelchair in the pine-floored courtroom, which for a moment confuses me as much as it must everyone else. Then a warm, southern-accented baritone that makes Shad Johnson's sterile Chicago voice sound like a resentful little boy's says, *"Ms. Revels, I can't tell you how my heart goes out to you and your family for all these tragedies. I just have one or two questions for you, and then I'll let you go."*

"Oh, thank God," I breathe, making a fist with my right hand and pumping it in the air.

Annie stares at me like I've gone crazy. "What happened?"

"Rip Van Winkle just woke up."

CHAPTER 29

"DO YOU BELIEVE *that Dr. Tom Cage murdered your sister?"*

The first question of Quentin's cross-examination of Cora Revels is spoken in a gentle voice, but it comes through my earpiece with electric effect. The collective intake of breath in the courtroom sounds like a rush of wind. I'll bet in all his coaching, Shad never prepared Cora Revels for that one.

After a long silence, Viola's sister says, *"I do believe Dr. Tom killed her. I don't believe he wanted it to hurt like it did, like what we saw on that film. But sometimes even doctors don't know what a drug will do. A nurse friend of mine told me that."*

"She's absolutely right," Quentin says. *"I can tell you that from experience. I've taken medicines that make my legs hurt, and I don't even have any legs."*

The crowd laughs hesitantly.

"Would you answer me this, Cora? Do you believe that Dr. Cage killed your sister to fulfill their suicide pact, out of mercy? Or did he do it to stop her from revealing the truth about their affair and the birth of that child? Or—did he do it to cover up whatever crime Viola seemed haunted by? The one she said Dr. Cage had helped her cover up?"

Quentin's questions nearly knock me out of my chair, so it's no surprise that Cora seems to be thrown off balance by his apparent willingness to admit that his client might have killed her sister.

"Well, I think . . . both. All of it, I mean. Maybe Dr. Cage didn't know himself which it was at the time. That's how people are. I know he loved my sister. But he'd gone a long time without doing right by that child. Lincoln, I mean. And everybody 'round here had thought so highly of him for so long. I think the idea that Natchez would learn the truth about everything was too much for him. Maybe he told himself he was helping Viola out of her pain.

But a man that mixed up about what he's doing ain't got no business giving suicide drugs to people."

I can imagine Quentin absorbing this answer like a dutiful soldier standing resolute in the face of cannon fire. Then I hear the high-pitched whir again.

"When Mr. Johnson asked you whether Tom knew that he had a son by your sister, you did not actually answer the question. You said that as of 1996, Dr. Cage had been sending money for twenty-eight years."

"That's right."

"That doesn't necessarily mean Dr. Cage knew he'd fathered a son by Viola. Does it?"

"Well, sure it does."

"Your Honor?" says Quentin.

"Ms. Revels, forget the money. Did your sister tell you specifically that Dr. Cage knew he had a son by her?"

The pause that follows this must be killing Shad—to the same degree that it's sparked hope in my heart—but then Cora says, *"Of course she did. The night Mama died. She told me all of that."*

"I see," Quentin continues. *"Cora, did any strange white men visit your house in the weeks before Viola died?"*

"What do you mean, 'strange'?"

"White men you'd never seen before?"

"Your Honor!" Shad cries. *"Mr. Avery is blocking my witness!"*

Quentin was a tall man before he lost his legs, and with Shad seated, he could easily interpose himself between the eyes of the DA and Cora.

"I'm sorry, Judge," Quentin says. *"I didn't realize Mr. Johnson was so sensitive about having eye contact with his witness."*

Having made his point that Shad might be signaling his witness, Quentin quickly says, *"You were saying, Miss Cora?"*

"Well, I wasn't there all day every day . . . but I didn't see any men like that."

"Did your sister tell you that men claiming to be members of the Ku Klux Klan or the Double Eagle group had visited her while you were gone? Threatened her, even?"

"Your Honor!" Shad shouts. *"Counsel is blocking my witness* again*! This is flagrant abuse!"*

A broad smile stretches my mouth. Quentin's gamesmanship with

Shad gives me the first real confirmation that he has a strategy and is carrying it out.

"Mr. Avery," Judge Elder says in a chiding tone, *"you do seem to be playing games with your wheelchair. Please move aside."*

"Thank you, Judge," says Shad.

"Now, the witness will answer the question, whether she can see you or not."

"No, sir," says Cora. *"Viola didn't say nothin' about strange white men comin' to the house. Any white men, except Mr. Henry. God rest his soul."*

"Miss Cora, earlier you testified that Viola returned to Natchez in 1996 to care for your mother. Do I have that right?"

"Yes. Mama was dying, and we needed her."

"I see. And did Viola take a tour of her old hometown? Did she go out and see the sights of Natchez? Visit some old restaurants? Or maybe new ones?"

"No, sir. No indeed."

"Objection, Your Honor," Shad interrupts. *"Relevance."*

"Overruled."

"Please continue, Miss Cora," Quentin says gently.

After a pause, Cora Revels says, *"Vee and Junius flew into Baton Rouge, then drove up in a rental car after dark. Vee didn't leave our house the whole time she was in Natchez. She even stayed out of sight when anybody who wasn't family visited. That way word never got out that she was home. Not out to any white folks, anyway."*

"And why did Viola take those precautions?"

"She didn't want any old klukkers finding out she was here."

"Because she was under a standing death threat?"

"Objection, Your Honor. Leading the witness."

"Sustained."

"I don't know about any death threat," Cora says. *"But Vee sure didn't want anybody on the other side of town finding out she was home."*

"By 'the other side' of town, did you mean the white side of town?"

"That's right."

There's a silence in which I hear nothing, not even Quentin's wheelchair. Then, in an incisive voice, he says, *"Regarding this crime Viola told you had been bothering her. When was your impression that this had occurred?"*

My pulse is still accelerating. Why the hell is Quentin pressing an issue that could lead to new murder charges against his client?

"Oh, long ago. Back before she left Natchez, when she was working for Dr. Cage."

"I see. Did Viola tell you why she hadn't told anyone about it before?"

"Judge, I'm forced to point out that counsel is purposefully blocking my view of the witness again."

"Please return to the podium, Mr. Avery," Judge Elder says wearily.

This time I don't hear a whir, but Cora Revels goes on without prompting. She sounds as though she wants to be done with this topic. *"Whatever it was, she said the law might have taken her away from Lincoln for it, and that terrified her. They could have hurt Dr. Cage, too. But now that she could see the end coming, she felt like it needed to be told."*

"You had the feeling there was still risk in telling what she'd done?"

"Oh, yes, sir."

"What about the risk to Dr. Cage? He wasn't facing a terminal illness. He would have to live with the outcome of whatever Viola got off her chest."

"I think with all that had happened between them, she felt like she'd protected him long enough. All she really cared about at the end was Lincoln, and getting out the truth about how and why Jimmy and Luther were killed."

"I understand. But Viola did tell you that Dr. Cage was as guilty as she was?"

This time Cora pauses, and my lawyer's instinct tells me it's the pause of a deceptive witness trying to be sure her lies dovetail before she answers.

"I can't rightly say. Whatever it was, Dr. Cage had been involved somehow, but more in the way of covering up what Viola had done."

"Your Honor, may I approach the witness?"

"You're fine where you are, Counselor."

Quentin's brake clicks and his wheels squeak, as though he's stopped suddenly or made a sharp turn.

"Cora, you testified to being shocked at the idea that your sister could be guilty of a serious crime, yes?"

"Of course I was."

"Because she didn't steal, not even candy as a child?"

"That's right."

"And she was most assuredly not the type to cheat, counterfeit, assault, forge, or kidnap?"

After a few seconds of what must be shocked silence, Quentin says, *"I need you to answer out loud, Cora."*

"Vee wouldn't do nothing like that."

"Objection, Your Honor," Shad says angrily. *"These questions are patently absurd. Irrelevant. Insulting. Take your pick."*

"Judge," says Quentin in a folksy voice, *"I've given opposing counsel a remarkable amount of latitude during his examinations, and I'm afraid I must note that he has not returned the courtesy. He's as jumpy as a puppy who needs a newspaper."*

"Mr. Avery," Judge Elder says sharply, *"just because you've been lazy with your objections doesn't mean the district attorney should hold himself to the same standard."*

"Ouch," I say aloud, wishing I could see Quentin's face.

"Miss Cora," Quentin resumes, *"do you realize that we are now left with only one crime on which the statute of limitations has not run out?"*

"I don't know much about the law, sir."

"My point, Cora, was that after six or seven years, the only crime your sister, as we know her, would have had to fear being punished for was murder."

I can sense the shock of the spectators even through the phone.

"Oh, Lord. That can't be right."

"I'm afraid it is. Can you think of anyone whom your sister might have had reason to kill in 1968?"

"No, sir! Good Lord. I can't even imagine such a thing!"

"But you're sure that Viola had been raped by Ku Klux Klansmen that year. 1968?"

"Yes, sir. I do know that."

"Cora, have you ever heard the name Frank Knox?"

I feel light-headed enough to pass out. If Quentin establishes that Dad and Viola shared complicity in a secret murder, that gives Dad *more* motive to have killed Viola, not less. On the other hand . . . it would also give Snake Knox and the Double Eagles an even more personal motive: revenge.

The silence after the Knox question lasts so long that I wonder whether my phone battery has gone dead, but then Quentin's grandfatherly voice says, *"Miss Cora? Frank Knox?"*

Even the hiss from the earpiece sounds brittle with expectation. Nearly everyone in that courtroom has heard of Frank Knox.

"The name sounds familiar," she says finally, *"like from a long way back."*

"Objection," Shad says. *"Irrelevant."*

"Your Honor," Quentin responds, *"I am going to be delving very deeply into the history of the Double Eagle group during this trial. This is only the beginning."*

After a long delay, Joe Elder says, *"I'm going to allow it, but this line of questioning had better lead somewhere quick."*

"Yes, Your Honor. Cora, Frank Knox was a former Ku Klux Klansman who founded a terrorist group called the Double Eagles. They were the leading FBI suspects in the rape of your sister in 1968."

"Lord Jesus."

"Did Viola ever mention that name to you?"

"I don't recollect that. Like I said, that was a long time ago."

"But you seem to remember everything else very clearly. I was hoping that name might not have escaped you. Do you remember a man dying in Dr. Cage's office that year?"

My hands are quivering the way they used to before I went into court to cross-examine a critical witness.

"I don't . . . know," Cora says almost inaudibly.

"He was a factory worker, badly injured at the Triton Battery plant. He was taken to Dr. Cage's office, where your sister was helping to stabilize him for transport to the emergency room. But he died in Dr. Cage's surgery room. Viola was treating him when it happened."

"You know, it seems like I do remember somethin' 'bout that. Vee must have told me about it."

"That man was Frank Knox, Cora. The founder of the Klan offshoot group that specialized in terrorizing and murdering African-Americans in this area. They burned buildings, beat black people, killed black people. They also raped black women."

"Mm."

"And you remember Viola telling you that she was haunted by a terrible crime? One that had happened before she left Natchez?"

The pause is almost painful. *"Yes, sir."*

"Thank you, Cora. No further questions at this time, Your Honor."

Out of the empty hiss, I hear Rusty Duncan whisper, "Holy shit. Did you hear all that?"

Unmuting my phone, I whisper, "I heard it."

"Did you know about any of it?"

"Some."

"Am I wrong, or is Babe Ruth back and swinging for the fence?"

"I don't know," I confess. "I don't know what the hell he's doing. I think my blood pressure's about two hundred over one hundred."

"I'm hanging up. I'll text you in a minute."

The phone goes dead in my ear.

"What happened?" Annie asks from the floor. "You look happy."

"I'm not sure. But things might look a little better than they did before. I think."

"Did Mr. Quentin do something right?"

My cell phone pings in my hand. "I sure hope so."

Rusty's text reads:

3:12 P.M. Shad just recalled Billy Byrd. Elder asked if questioning would take long. Shad said no. Elder taking 15 minute break. Bathroom, probably. You should feel the vibe in here, man. Feels like 1965. It's like the Klan's in here with us.

Billy Byrd? I say to myself. *What can Bill Byrd testify about beyond the forensics?*

"What, Daddy? What did Mr. Quentin do?"

"I'm not sure," I say, still dazed by Quentin's cross. "But I know what he didn't do."

"What?"

"He didn't ask about the videotape."

"What videotape?"

"The one in Henry's camera."

"Daddy, I don't understand."

Annie is trying hard to help me, despite being confused.

Fifteen minutes, I think, my heart kicking in my chest.

"What was on the tape, Daddy?"

"Annie," I say, sitting up and taking one of her hands in mine, "there's one more witness against Papa today, and Mr. Rusty says Quentin needs my help to handle him."

Her eyes widen.

"Do you think you can do without me for an hour?"

She bites her lip for about three seconds, then nods.

"Mia must still be around, right?"

"She is. She probably just wanted us to have some time together." Annie smiles with conscious bravery and gets to her feet. *"Miiiaaaa?"*

Quick footsteps sound on the staircase, then Mia's head pops through the door. "What's up, kid?"

"Daddy's got to run to court for one more witness."

Mia smiles a little too quickly and brightly, and I realize she's working hard to adapt to whatever comes next.

"We're good, no problem," she says, glancing at her watch. "You'd better hurry, huh?"

"Yeah. I'll get Tim to drop me. I'll see you guys in an hour."

CHAPTER 30

A DEPUTY LETS me into the courtroom just as Judge Elder's recess ends, and his friendly scowl makes it obvious he's only doing it because he knows me. As I move to the front of the gallery, I realize there's not a single open seat behind the bar. For a moment I consider taking one of the chairs immediately behind Quentin's table—beside Doris—but that would draw too much attention to me. In the end, I return to the back of the room and lean against the wall with my arms folded. Quite a few people in the courtroom have recognized me, and they're not shy about staring. A photographer I don't recognize snaps my picture with a zoom lens.

When Sheriff Billy Byrd's name is called, he rises from the line of deputies' chairs against the left wall and makes his way toward the witness box. Byrd looks like a drugstore cowboy with a beer belly, or a used car salesman got up in a sheriff's costume. He settles into the witness box with the confidence of a man who's been there hundreds of times. As they swear him in, Shad Johnson stands up from the prosecution table with a Ziploc bag in his hand. Looking closer, I see a mini-DV tape inside the bag.

I hope Quentin isn't as frightened by the appearance of that tape as I am. But from the back wall, I see what looks like tension in his posture.

"Sheriff Byrd," Shad says, "this morning your chief investigator testified that on the morning Viola Turner died, you found a video camera in her sickroom, and that this camera was found to belong to the reporter Henry Sexton. Is that correct?"

"It is."

"Your investigator testified that no tape was found in the camera."

"That's correct."

"Were any other tapes found in the house?"

"Two blank tapes sealed in their original packages. Mini-DV type, brand Sony. Mr. Sexton informed us he had left four blank tapes for Mrs. Turner when he delivered the camera. All new and sealed."

Shad holds up the Ziploc bag. "I have here one of those two sealed tapes, which were stipulated into evidence as State's Exhibits Eleven and Twelve.

"Sheriff, Cora Revels told us that there was a tape in the camera when she left for her neighbor's house, but none when she returned."

"Ms. Revels made a statement to that effect when we interviewed her the day of her sister's death."

"What did you and your investigators surmise from this?"

"Whoever killed Mrs. Turner took the tape with him."

"Why would the killer do that?"

Quentin could object here, but he doesn't.

"Could be lots of reasons," Byrd says, working his jowls like a man pondering this question for the first time. "Maybe the tape showed him injecting the lethal drug. Or maybe the victim had said things on the tape that he didn't want anyone to know."

"Did you search extensively for that missing tape?"

"Yes, sir, we did. We put our full effort into finding both that and the tape that Mrs. Turner had made for Henry Sexton. We searched the Revels house from top to bottom, and grid-searched the property. We searched Dr. Cage's residence and office. But we still couldn't find it."

"Did you give up?"

Billy Byrd's offended sneer makes plain that giving up is not a permissible action in his book of procedure. "No, sir. We did not."

"What did you do?"

"Well. During the multistate manhunt for Dr. Cage, we figured out that he'd been moving around with Mr. Walt Garrity, an old army buddy from Texas. That was how he'd been evading capture. Garrity had brought an RV van over from Navasota, sleeps four. Got a kitchen and shower and everything in a tight little space. High-end thing. They'd been staying in that."

I haven't seen Walt in court, but I know he's here somewhere. He told my mother that John Kaiser had informed him he was unlikely to be arrested if he kept a low profile, although Billy Byrd could arrest him at any time for aiding and abetting a fugitive. Knowing Walt, he's up in the balcony behind Serenity, wearing some kind of disguise.

"What's the significance of that vehicle?"

"Well, after Dr. Cage turned himself in to the FBI, I figured we ought to search that vehicle, if we could find it, on the off chance that he might have left something incriminating in there. Dr. Cage was the primary suspect by then, of course. He'd skipped bail with Mr. Garrity's aid, and the two had abandoned the vehicle a day or two earlier, so we decided to try to find it."

"And how did you proceed?"

"Carefully. We had some jurisdictional issues relating to that search. Mr. Garrity had some law enforcement contacts on the Louisiana side of the river, where they'd mostly been hiding, and those agencies weren't too keen on helping us. But after putting out the word sort of quietlike, I got a call from a Concordia Parish deputy who'd located the Roadtrek van."

"And where was it?"

"Parked in the garage of a lake house owned by Dr. Cage's younger partner, Drew Elliott."

A buzz of conversation fills the room, but a glare from Joe Elder kills it.

"What did you do then?" Shad asks.

"I consulted with you, the district attorney."

"And what did I advise?"

"You said that since Garrity had been in law enforcement, we ought to be a little cagey about our search."

"And what plan did we agree on?"

"We asked a Louisiana judge to write a search warrant on that van, specifying videotapes among some other articles."

"And then?"

"A Concordia deputy searched the van right there in the garage."

"And what did he find?"

"Several articles, among them one Sony mini-DV videotape, pressed up under one of the cushions that serves as a mattress in that vehicle. A Sony videotape that had been used but recorded over. Erased, in other words."

"What did you do then?"

"I went down to the Ferriday Walmart and bought some Sony tapes exactly like those Henry Sexton had delivered to Viola Turner's house."

I'm not quite sure what's coming, but a dizzy sensation of falling tells me that it won't be good.

"And what did you do with those tapes?"

"I opened one and recorded sixty minutes of footage with the lens cap on."

"Just what you would have done if you were going to erase a prerecorded tape."

"Yes, sir."

"And then?"

"I gave it to the CPSO deputy who had conducted the search. He removed the tape from Mr. Garrity's van and bagged it as evidence. But he left the new erased tape in its place. We also left the van in place, as though it had never been searched."

"Why did you do that?"

"So that Mr. Garrity wouldn't realize that the tape hidden in his van had been found by the authorities."

Shad turns away from Sheriff Byrd for a few seconds, giving the jury time to think about what has become a television cop show.

"Was there anything special about the tape you replaced Mrs. Turner's tape with?"

Byrd tries and fails to conceal a smile of satisfaction. "Yes, sir. I planted a little GPS tracking device in it, so we could know where that substitute tape was at all times. We also planted a similar device on Mr. Garrity's van, one that worked on a different frequency."

"I see. Did you learn anything else from the videotape?"

"Yes, sir. Our fingerprint man determined that there were two sets of fingerprints on the tape."

"To whom did they belong?"

"The majority belonged to Henry Sexton, but there were several others that belonged to Dr. Tom Cage."

A hundred heads in front of me turn and look at the person next to them.

"And how did your expert match those?" Shad asks.

"The same way he matched the ones on the morphine vial. From the prints Dr. Cage gave in Jackson when he applied for his concealed-carry permit back in 1991."

"I see." Shad looks at the jury as he asks his next question. "When did all this take place, Sheriff?"

"The day after Dr. Cage turned himself in to the FBI, which was the day of Henry Sexton's funeral. We didn't know where Mr. Garrity was at the time, but he had a motel room in Vidalia. I learned later that he was actually staying at Dr. Cage's home in Natchez."

"While Dr. Cage was in custody?"

"That's right."

Quentin should be objecting all over the place, but he sits like a man who's been punched so hard he can no longer hold up his hands to guard his chin.

"So, Sheriff, is that the end of the saga of the missing videotape?"

"No, sir."

"What happened next?"

"The next night, Mr. Garrity showed up to retrieve his van from Dr. Elliott's lake house. We began tracking our devices at that time and also put visual surveillance on him. He visited a couple of places of interest."

"Which were?"

"One was the CPSO jail, where he visited Dr. Cage, who was there under FBI protection. This was when the Bureau had temporarily taken over that facility."

"I see. What was the other place?"

"Well, later on, after dark, he drove over the bridge to Mississippi."

"And you were tracking him via the GPS devices you'd planted?"

"Yes, sir. Both of them. The one on the van, and the one in the videotape."

"What happened next?"

Billy Byrd can't contain his pleasure; a smarmy smile breaks out on his heavy face. "When he started over the bridge, we were tracking both signals. But when Garrity was a little over halfway across, only one signal kept coming, while the other stayed fairly static."

"How did you account for that?"

"Well, about this time, our tailing unit had seen Mr. Garrity's arm flick something out of his window, in the direction of the left-lane bridge rail."

"And what did you observe on the tracking unit?"

"The GPS signal from the tape stayed in midriver for about fifteen seconds, then went dead. The one in the van kept right on driving, all the way to Ryan's Steak House."

"And what did you conclude from this?"

"That Mr. Garrity had dumped what he thought was the tape from Viola Turner's house into the Mississippi River. I deduced that he had done that on Dr. Cage's order, probably passed to him during the jail visit only hours earlier."

After about five seconds, during which time I am silently screaming at Quentin to object, Shad says, "Thank you, Sheriff. No further questions, Your Honor."

The click and whir of Quentin's motorized wheelchair comes so fast it's as though Shad's voice triggered it. He cannot allow that testimony to go unchallenged. He rolls right past the podium and up to the witness stand, speaking in an incisive voice.

"Sheriff Byrd, do you realize that Dr. Cage's fingerprints on a blank tape found in Mr. Garrity's RV in no way prove or even indicate that this tape came from the house of Viola Turner?"

"Yes, I realize that."

"Then what makes you think that was the tape Viola had made for Henry Sexton?"

"The lot number."

At the back wall, I cringe as though I've taken a sharp blow. I know what's coming now.

"The lot number on that tape proved it was from the same lot as the two tapes we found in Mrs. Turner's house. That meant they had been sold in the same store at about the same time."

"Very well," Quentin says, trying to cover as best he can. "Do you have any film of Walt Garrity driving that van that night?"

"Yes, sir."

"Does it show his face?"

"Well . . . I don't know. We have film of the van. I don't know if it shows him driving. It was a dark night. But my men tailed him from the lake house."

"Mississippi deputies working in Louisiana?"

"Uh, no, these were Louisiana officers."

"Sheriff Walker Dennis's men?"

"That's right."

"Working under Sheriff Dennis's orders?"

Sheriff Byrd is slow to answer. "Not exactly. The mess they had over in Louisiana after that Forrest Knox was killed caused a lot of problems over there. Some interagency problems, as well."

"But those men will swear under oath that they saw Captain Garrity get into the van?"

"They absolutely will."

"Sheriff, I have to say, this entire episode sounds like something out of *Mission: Impossible* rather than a small-town murder investigation."

"We do what we can to stay on top of technology."

"I'm sure. But to what purpose, Sheriff? If you'd found the tape Mrs. Turner supposedly made, why go to all that trouble to pretend you hadn't?"

"May I answer that, Judge?" Shad asks.

Judge Elder leans forward and says, "The witness will answer, Mr. Johnson."

"Well . . . being as the tape we'd found had been erased, the district attorney figured we might learn a lot more about what Dr. Cage and Mr. Garrity was up to if they didn't know we was onto them. We thought the adrenaline ampoule might have been in that van as well. If Garrity was going to try to destroy it at some later date, we wanted a record of that."

"And was the adrenaline ampoule in the van?"

"Not that the deputy could find."

"Yes or no, Sheriff?"

Byrd grits his teeth. "Negative."

"Sheriff Byrd, if Dr. Cage was guilty of murder, why do you think he would keep a very incriminating piece of evidence for, let's see, seven days? And keep it where it could easily be found?"

The sheriff shrugs. "Guilty folks do crazy things all the time. They're under stress."

"So you assumed at that time that Dr. Cage was guilty?"

"Well . . . yeah. He looked guilty as hell, pardon my French."

A couple of people chortle in the gallery. From behind, Shad Johnson looks like a man trying hard to keep control of himself.

"Look," says Sheriff Byrd, "Doc Cage had probably erased the tape on the first day. He probably knew it couldn't really hurt him much—since erased videotapes can't be restored—and he had other things on his mind."

"Like trying to find out who had really murdered Viola Turner?"

"That's not what I meant."

"I find that very easy to believe, Sheriff." Quentin touches his joystick and executes a quarter turn away from Byrd. "Let me suggest another scenario to you. One that might easily explain the fingerprints and the lot number."

Byrd looks at Shad, but Shad doesn't risk trying to send him any signals.

"Henry Sexton leaves a camcorder at Viola Turner's house, hoping she will record memories from her past. Viola tells Dr. Cage, who visits her almost every day, about this arrangement. She does just as Henry Sexton suggested and makes a tape. But perhaps one day she decides she has said too much—more than she might ever want to become public, even after she's gone. So she asks Dr. Cage to erase it. In his fiddling with the camera, he removes the tape, leaving his fingerprints on its plastic case. Quite possible, yes?"

"I suppose. But that's not what Miss Cora said happened."

"True enough. But another scenario occurs to me, Sheriff, one that better fits testimony we've already heard. Let's assume Viola did make the tape for Henry that Cora Revels described, one filled with potentially embarrassing material for both herself and Dr. Cage. All right?"

"Uh-huh."

"She initially plans to keep the tape secret from her old lover, but in the end she tells him about it. As a test, as Cora suggested. On the night of her death, she tells Dr. Cage to take the tape with him when he leaves, and to give it to Henry Sexton. Viola is alive when he leaves, mildly sedated by morphine, as usual. After leaving the house, Dr. Cage watches the tape—a natural impulse, and something most of us would do. On it are very personal things that he appreciates, but that he would prefer that his wife and children not have to deal with. Dr. Cage now has a moral dilemma.

"Only hours later, he learns that Viola is dead and that he may be charged with her murder. Shortly after this, he realizes he has become the object of a witch hunt by your department. So he packs the tape into his bag and leaves with Mr. Garrity."

"I don't have to take that," Byrd growls. "The man jumped bail. He was a fugitive."

"Please bear with me, Sheriff. You'll get your chance to respond, I assure you. Yes, Dr. Cage did jump bail, but he did *not* flee the jurisdiction. In fact, he spent every day trying to track down members of the Double Eagle group, whom he believed to be responsible for Viola Turner's death. Further, he eventually attended the public funeral of Henry Sexton—the man who provided Viola the tape in the first place—and then turned himself in to the FBI. And all the while that videotape was in his van. Do those sound like the actions of a guilty man?"

"Hell, yes. He was a fugitive on a murder warrant."

"On a charge that never should have been made."

"Objection," Shad interjects. "Badgering the witness."

"Sustained."

"If the doc was innocent, why did he erase the tape?" Byrd demands.

"We have no evidence that he did that," Quentin says with conclusive authority. "Moreover, you just testified that the tape sat in an unattended van for, what? At least two days? Possibly three?"

Sheriff Byrd isn't used to this kind of treatment in a courtroom. "This is ridiculous," he says angrily.

"Further," Quentin goes on, "since the tape is blank, the only indication we have of what might have been on it comes from the testimony of Cora Revels."

"So?" Byrd violently turns up his palms as though weary of dealing with a fool.

Quentin answers with a lazy cadence that easily blunts Byrd's anger and frustration. "So the veracity of her statements depends totally upon her credibility as a witness. And I will be returning to that subject in greater detail later."

Billy Byrd looks at the prosecution table and swallows. Shadrach Johnson offers him no help.

"Sheriff Byrd," Quentin says in the tone of a regretful headmaster to a student, "I have been told that prior to this case, relations between you and Dr. Cage were not exactly friendly."

Byrd's porcine eyes snap back to Quentin. "We spoke when we passed."

"That's not what my client told me. In fact, after learning the history between you two, I've had to ask myself whether, given the past friction between you, there's any way you could deal impartially with him in this case."

Shad could object here, but he doesn't want the jury to spend a half hour listening to tales of Billy Byrd's domestic abuse if he can avoid it. I'd like to see Quentin explore just that, but he doesn't.

"For example," he continues, "do you dislike Dr. Cage enough to have your men stage this deep-six incident over the Mississippi River in order to make Dr. Cage look guilty?"

Byrd's face goes dark with blood. "I don't have to sit here and listen to that!"

"I'm afraid you do, Sheriff. You're no more immune to the judicial process than Dr. Cage or myself, or even Judge Elder. And at this point, I have to ask the simplest question of all: Was that tape ever in the bedside table of that sickroom in the first place, as Cora Revels suggested? And if so, was there ever really anything on it?"

Byrd's enraged eyes narrow. "You're trying to get me all turned around!"

"On the contrary, Sheriff. I'm trying to strip away all conjecture and assumptions and leave only facts. And what we know is that, even if there *was* a tape in that bedside table, no one can say what happened to it. Certainly no one saw Dr. Cage remove any tape from that house."

"Well, who else could have done it?"

At this point Quentin is turned in profile to me, and I see him smile. "*That,* Sheriff Byrd, is a very good question. One I think you should have been asking from the very beginning. But you didn't feel that was necessary, did you? Lincoln Turner told you who his mother's killer was, his suspect suited you just fine, and you never looked seriously at any other possibility."

"But his prints were on the tape!"

"His fingerprints are on *a* tape, Sheriff. A *blank* tape. An erased tape that you say a deputy working surreptitiously for you supposedly discovered in an abandoned van."

Sheriff Byrd shakes his head in impotent rage.

Quentin looks up as though about to ask another question, but then he simply says, "No further questions, Your Honor."

As Quentin rolls back to the defense table, Sheriff Byrd growls, "You think you're so damn smart. What about the other tape? Why don't you ask me about that? Huh?"

Quentin's face is toward me as the words leave Byrd's mouth, and I see him lose a shade of color. *Oh, no,* I groan silently, bracing for the worst.

If Quentin doesn't respond to Byrd's parting shot, then Shad will happily lead Byrd wherever it is he wants to go on redirect. Except . . . Shad's suddenly rigid posture tells me he might not be happy about Byrd's little taunt.

"Your Honor," Quentin says, turning his chair again, "in light of the witness's outburst, may I continue my cross-examination?"

"You may, Counselor."

Quentin drives his chair back up to the witness box. "What tape were you referring to, Sheriff?"

"The tape that was in the camera that night."

"What about it? Are you saying that you believe you found that tape as well?"

"You're damn right we did."

Shad Johnson comes to his feet. "Your Honor—"

"Yes, Counselor?"

Quentin looks over his shoulder at Shad. "Is the prosecutor objecting to his own witness, Your Honor?"

"I'm not sure," Joe Elder says. "Mr. Johnson?"

"I beg your pardon, Your Honor."

Shad returns to his seat slowly enough that I can tell his witness has gone off script.

"Tell us about this other tape," Quentin says.

"We found it in the hospital Dumpster," Billy Byrd says in a defiant voice.

For a couple of seconds I stop breathing.

"What hospital?" Quentin asks.

"St. Catherine's, where Dr. Cage puts his patients."

Oh, man . . .

"And when was this?"

"The day after Viola Turner was found dead. As I said earlier, we made a maximum effort to find those tapes. We covered every place Dr. Cage might have been, and one was the hospital. And we found a Sony mini-DV tape in that Dumpster."

I'm balling my fists so hard that my right tricep starts twitching. As I suspected all along, Quentin made a suicidal mistake in electing not to request discovery.

"And did the tape have anything on it?" Quentin asks.

Billy grimaces like a man with an ulcer. "No. It had been erased, just like the other one."

Hell, yes! shouts a voice in my head, and my hands relax. *Lost in the sands of time.*

"I see," Quentin says. "And did it also have Dr. Cage's fingerprints on it?"

My right hand clenches once more.

"No, it had no fingerprints. It had been wiped clean."

"Clean," Quentin echoes. "No prints. On a tape found in a Dumpster."

"You know what I mean."

"I know what you're assuming. But in this case, I see no connection whatever between that tape and my client."

"You will."

"What does that mean?"

"The lot number on that tape matched the one that had the doc's prints on it and the two that we found sealed in Ms. Revels's house. And Dr. Cage had gone to the hospital the morning of Viola Turner's death. I know that for a fact. He also went the next day, before skipping bail."

This time Billy silences Quentin, and the pleasure in his face is almost sexual. After about ten seconds, Quentin says, "But there was nothing on the tape, correct?"

"That's right."

After several seconds of absolute silence, Quentin turns his chair and drives back to the defense table. "No further questions at this time, Your Honor."

The courtroom feels as though some machine just sucked half the air out of it. No one knows quite what to do. In this strange silence, Judge Elder looks at his watch, and I do the same. It's 4:09 P.M.

"Mr. Johnson," says the judge, "do you have another witness?"

Shad comes to his feet and speaks in a measured voice. "I do, Your Honor. I had intended to call Lincoln Turner. However, in the heat of cross-examination, Sheriff Byrd mentioned evidence that I had not intended to bring forward until tomorrow. That has created a difficult situation."

Judge Elder doesn't look very sympathetic. "Explain, Counselor."

"The tape he referred to was indeed found, but at this time it is undergoing complex forensic analysis and processing."

"Of what nature, Counselor?"

"Your Honor, only very recently I was told that technology exists that might allow a partial restoration of the videotapes in question. I queried the FBI about this, and I was told that my best bet was to contact the manufacturer. I did so. At this time, those two tapes are being worked on in a California lab owned by the Sony Corporation . . ."

The acid flooding my stomach is probably minor compared to the reaction Quentin Avery must be enduring.

". . . if I may beg the court's indulgence," Shad continues, "I could call Mr. Turner at this time, but my direct examination could take quite a while. And since Sheriff Byrd brought up the tape found in the hospital Dumpster, I would prefer to enter both it and the tape found in Mr. Garrity's van into evidence and deal with them before examining any other witnesses."

"And will you be ready to proceed with that evidence first thing in the morning?"

"I believe so, Your Honor."

"Very well." Elder looks at his watch once more. "Court is adjourned until nine A.M. tomorrow."

The crowd comes to its feet as one, like a human hive about to set out on an evening hunt. I need to talk to Quentin, but rather than try to buttonhole him in this mob, I'll wait a bit, then get Tim to run me over to Edelweiss.

Joining the river of people sweeping through the back doors, I text my bodyguard to pick me up on Market Street. As I cut that way to make my exit, I realize that while it's only two blocks from the courthouse to the bluff, the trial has brought chaos to the one-way streets of downtown Natchez. It could easily take Quentin and Doris half an hour to make it to Edelweiss in their van.

"Penn!" shouts a male voice. Tim Weathers's voice. "Down here!"

The armored Yukon is parked in the middle of Market Street, blocking traffic like it's waiting for Jay-Z and his entourage. I dart around a man trying to negotiate the steps in front of me with a walker, then race down to the street and jump into the backseat.

"Where to?" Tim asks, only half turning his head.

"I need to talk to Quentin, but we've got thirty minutes to kill. How about we take Annie and Mia to get a hamburger?"

"Sounds good to me."

As we roll up Market Street, we pass a half-dozen TV satellite trucks, with reporters doing stand-ups under the courthouse oaks. Undoubtedly they are trumpeting to the world the existence of two videotapes that might be miraculously restored from oblivion. If they are—if the Sony Corporation's wizards can perform a digital resurrection—what truths will those tapes reveal?

I don't want to think about it.

CHAPTER 31

AFTER SHARING HAMBURGERS and shakes with Annie and Mia, I convinced Tim to let me drive my own car down to Edelweiss. I'm sure he's not far behind me, but it feels good to escape the shell of the close-protection drill for even a few minutes. Downtown traffic is still congested, but my Audi is small enough to dart between disoriented drivers on Washington Street.

Seeing an opening between an SUV and a Honda, I gun the S4 through the narrow gap and race for Broadway, which runs along the river. Eighty feet before I reach it, I pull the Audi between two crape myrtles on the right and drive across the grass to a hidden garage in the backyard of Edelweiss. Peering beneath the massive ginkgo tree that dominates the backyard, I can just see the nose of Quentin's white Mercedes van sticking out from the corner of the house, parked on Broadway. A cable TV van with a big dish on its roof has set up base camp on the bluff side of the street, so reporters must be lurking nearby.

Using the ginkgo trunk for cover, I move stealthily toward the house. The broad gallery that wraps around the old chalet makes Edelweiss seem to float about ten feet above ground level. A line of green pickets shields the brick-pillared ground floor on all four sides, but there's a gate in back, and a single stair leading up to the gallery. After unlocking that gate, I run up the stairs and reach the kitchen door without any media hounds sniffing me out.

I knock gently several times, but no one comes to the door. There's no glass set in the back door, so I can't see anything. Moving to my left, I look through a window and see Quentin and Doris in the kitchen, Quentin in his wheelchair talking on the phone while Doris peers toward the front of the house. A plate of Ritz crackers lies on the counter, beside it a jar of peanut butter and a can of Corona.

I tap gently on the window.

Quentin and Doris both jump as though someone fired a shot. I point to the door to my right. As Doris moves toward it, Quentin hangs up the phone and angrily shakes his head. Doris walks to the window, leans up to the glass, and says, "I'm sorry, Penn, he doesn't want to be bothered right now. He needs to stay focused on the case."

"*What* case?" I ask, too loudly. "If you don't let me in, the reporters will hear me and come running."

Through the glass I hear Quentin cursing behind Doris. "I'm sorry," she says again. "There's nothing I can do."

I'm about to bang on the window when Doris very pointedly looks downward. Following her eyes, I see her hand at her waist, beckoning me inside. At first I think she means to let me in, but then I realize that since she was hiding the gesture from Quentin, that's unlikely. Then it hits me.

Taking my keys from my pocket, I simply unlock the back door and walk into the kitchen.

"You're trespassing, goddamn it!" Quentin snaps.

"I own this house."

"We'll move to a goddamned hotel, then!"

"We're not moving anywhere," Doris says firmly, "unless it's back home."

I try to catch her eye, but Doris Avery is far too smooth a customer to let her husband detect conspiracy between us. I'm happy to have this woman as my ally. I met Doris two years ago, but I still don't know how she wound up married to a man my father's age.

"What do you want?" Quentin demands. "You ruined my lunch. Have you come to ruin my dinner, too?"

Before I can answer, he says, "The least you could have done is brought a couple of those bodyguards of yours with you. We need the help. The tourists are bad enough, trying to walk in the front door every ten minutes, but now we have the media maggots all over this case."

"I'll see about getting a man for your door."

"Make sure he'll protect me from you, too."

"I'm surprised, Quentin. You usually like holding forth to the press."

He gives me a quick glare, then rolls away and starts eating Ritz crackers from the plate on the marble island. Doris walks into the doorway that leads to the front room, then leans against the casing and waits to see what I've come to say.

"Quentin, I'm here because my mother wants to fire you."

"Is that all?"

"No. Every lawyer in the courtroom thinks you're suffering from dementia."

He actually cackles at this. "Yeah, I see all those hacks out there second-guessing me. Armchair quarterbacks. Your fat pal Rusty's been staring a hole in my back all day. I've been worried he might have a stroke."

"Do you blame him? I'm surprised the judge hasn't stepped in from being worried about being reversed on appeal."

"On what grounds?"

"Ineffective assistance of counsel."

He chuckles with defiant pride. "I'd like to see the judge with the balls to say that of me."

"Joe Elder's no pushover."

Quentin's eyes glint with emotion I cannot read. "No. But he's not about to stop this thing. You know why?"

"Why?"

"Because he wants us to lose. He's *enjoying* this."

This takes me aback. "Why do you say that?"

"When you've spent as many years in court as I have, you sense things. Hell, he's practically acting as co-counsel for the prosecution. I just don't know whether Joe wants to see me lose—you know, the Freudian kill-the-father thing—or whether he has some kind of grudge against *your* father. But it's one or the other. You ought to do a little digging and find out which."

"I will. Is that why you're not objecting? Because you think Elder will overrule?"

Quentin doesn't deign to answer. Spreading peanut butter on his Ritz seems to interest him a lot more.

"If that's it, at least make him overrule you. Then it'll be preserved for appeal."

His eyes flick my way for a second. "I'm not worried about the appeals court, man. I'm gonna win this trial."

I look to Doris for help, but she only shrugs.

"You haven't said what *you* think of my strategy," Quentin says in a teasing voice.

"Strategy? You let Shad make his entire forensic case with no opposition. You haven't challenged any evidence or objected to patently inadmissible testimony. You didn't even make an opening statement!"

"Are you finished?"

"Quentin, you only cross-examined two witnesses out of eight."

"It ain't the quantity of the questions, Grasshopper. It's the quality."

"You let Shad convince at least half the jury that the killer removed both videotapes from Cora's house. Most of the jury believes Dad took those tapes."

Quentin waves away my points as though I'm raising trivial issues.

"What the hell are you going to do if Shad walks in tomorrow with digital restorations of those tapes?"

"I'm not worried about those tapes."

"Why not? Have you spoken to Dad about them?"

"I just did."

"Do you know what's on them?"

He smiles like a Jamaican handing out joints on a beach. "No idea, brother."

I take a deep breath and try to rein in my anger. "Quentin . . . those tapes could destroy you tomorrow. And send Dad to Parchman."

At last he fixes me with a serious gaze. "Are you that sure your father is guilty?"

"What the hell am I supposed to think at this point?"

"I guess you've given up, then."

Doris's presence should hold me back, but I can't keep from demanding one specific answer. "Man . . . why the hell were you probing at the Frank Knox business with Cora?"

"It's central to the Double Eagle thread of the narrative."

This direct answer is such a novelty that it brings me up short. "Do you have proof of what you suggested about the Double Eagles threatening to kill Viola?"

Once again he exercises the royal prerogative not to answer.

"I'm not talking about in 1968," I press. "I'm talking about the present day. Since Viola came back from Chicago. Do you know that white men came to see her? Threatened her?"

Quentin turns his wheelchair and runs his long fingers over the stainless steel face of the refrigerator. "All-Viking kitchen, baby. Me and Doris got the same thing at home. Made in Mississippi, just like the best music, the best women, the best—"

"Quentin! Do you have proof of any Double Eagle threat in the present?"

With a flick of his joystick, he whirls on me and yells: "If I had that, this case wouldn't even have come to trial!"

"Then what *do* you have? A surprise witness? Is that why you didn't request discovery? So Shad wouldn't know you have a secret weapon?"

He laughs with scorn. "Surprise witness? Secret weapon? Man, what you think this is? *Ironside*? *Matlock*?"

"Quentin, for God's sake. Dad's life is at stake. You can't simply imply that because he and Viola may have killed a Double Eagle, the Eagles took their revenge forty years later. Tell me you've got more than hints and ancient history."

Quentin finishes chewing a cracker with angry force, then sets his jaw and stares back at me without a word.

"I'm only asking," I tell him, "because I happen to have checked the alibis of Snake Knox, Sonny Thornfield, and every other Double Eagle whose identity is known to the FBI for the night Viola died. John Kaiser helped me. And all those bastards have alibis. Sonny, Snake, and three others have a rock-solid one."

Quentin chuckles softly. "That bullshit about playing cards all night at Billy Knox's hunting camp?"

"That's right."

"You know that's a lie. That's just the guilty parties covering each other's asses."

I don't mention what Dad told me about Will Devine's pickup truck. "Camp employees swore they were there."

"And every damned one of those Mexicans earns his living from Billy Knox. What else they gonna say?"

"Quentin . . . this is a criminal trial. What we *suspect* doesn't mean shit. You know that better than anybody. If you think Snake and Sonny killed Viola, you've got to prove it."

Quentin smiles as though from some inward pleasure, then steeples his fingers before him. "Penn, what do you think a murder trial is?"

"Please don't start with the Will Rogers legal philosophy."

"I'm not. Just tell me the fundamental essence of a murder trial."

"The State attempts to prove beyond a reasonable doubt that the defendant committed murder, and the defense tries to prevent that by every means at its disposal."

Quentin is still smiling like a Socratic professor. "If this was grammar school, I'd give you a gold star."

Doris shakes her head from the door.

"I can do without the condescension, Quentin. I've tried more murder cases than you ever did."

"But always as a prosecutor. Penn, you spent a decade working to prove your cases so thoroughly that twelve jurors would vote unanimously for conviction. That's a tough job. But me? I've spent my whole life as a farmer."

"What are you talking about?"

"Planting seeds. That's my job. Seeds of doubt. I plant a tiny seed, water it a little—with words, not H2O—and then I patiently tend it, nurse it to life. Most times, the seed dies aborning. But now and then, that doubt grows so strong in the soil of some sympathetic heart that one person finds the courage to stand against the combined anger and prejudice of eleven other people. And when that happens . . . my client goes free."

"Poetic," I mutter, "but not particularly helpful in light of today's disaster."

"One juror, Penn. That's the business I'm in."

"That's not enough. Eleven to one, you hang the jury, and there's a retrial."

Quentin's beatific smile becomes still more serene. "Even the longest journey begins with one step. An avalanche can start with one snowflake. One whisper, my brother. One word."

I hold up both hands to stop his flow. "Preacher Avery," I mutter, "the evangelist of reasonable doubt."

"That's right. And in this trial, I've got the dream client. Your father's done so much good in this town, somebody on that panel's got to be yearning for a way to let him go home to his family. All I've got to do is give them a hook to hang their doubt on."

"You've got a long way to go. You let Shad dig a mighty deep hole today."

"A circumstantial hole."

"And the tapes?"

This time he drops the smile, but he lets me know he resents me forcing him to be so pragmatic. "Look, on the way over here, I called a forensic guy I use in New York, top of his field. He tells me there's less than a ten percent chance that Sony can restore the data on those tapes to any usable form. I'll take those odds any day."

Relief floods through me with surprising power. "That's good to know. But even if the tapes stay erased, the forensics aren't your only problem. Shad's outflanked you on race."

"How you figure that?"

"He didn't sidestep it. He shoved race right onto the front burner. And not even the great Quentin Avery can predict how a jury of seven blacks and five whites is going to react to evidence of an interracial affair, a mixed-race baby, and a white man killing a black woman to keep her quiet. The blacks may want to punish Dad for not acknowledging that baby, and the whites might crucify him for letting down his own race and his legal family. Hell, Shad could argue that every good thing Dad has done to help blacks since 1968 was a pathetic attempt to expiate his guilt over Viola and her child."

"Is that what you'd argue in his place?"

"You're damn right."

Quentin nods slowly, as if listening to me for the first time. "Do you think Shad's smart enough to do that?"

"Harvard Law isn't a charm school."

"No. But it's the kind of place that turns out lawyers so clever that sometimes they outsmart themselves."

"That's wishful thinking, Q. Look, either you give me some sort of substantive outline of your strategy, or a change is going to have to be made."

He glances back at Doris, but she's looking at the floor. "You hear that, baby? Penn's talking like he's my client."

"I heard him," she says softly.

The old man turns back to me with hardened eyes. "Boy, you know only your father can fire me."

"Quentin, Dad may be your client, but Mom's paying your fee."

"Bullshit."

"He put his assets in her name long ago."

The old eyes flare with indignation. "I'll handle the case pro bono, then."

This brings a faint smile to my lips. "Will you?"

"You're damn right I will. I'm rich as Croesus, goddamn it!"

"It may come to that, buddy. But it doesn't have to."

"So long as I run every step of my case by you for approval? No, thank you. Hey, what have *you* been spending your time doing? You made any progress convincing a Double Eagle to flip?"

This stops my train of thought. So Dad told him about our conversation in the Pollock FCI.

"What about Will Devine's truck?" he asks. "The Darlington Academy sticker?"

I glance at Doris, who looks confused by this conversational turn.

"I've made some progress," I tell him, thinking of my last visit to the Devine house and of Dolores St. Denis. "But until you show me more than you have today, I think I'll keep it to myself."

"How's that supposed to help Tom?"

With a quick glance at Doris, who seems to be silently pleading with me for something, I say, "How did Dad feel after court adjourned today?"

"He knew what to expect."

"He wasn't ready for the news about that Dumpster tape. I can't believe today's events didn't shake him."

"Go see him, if you don't believe me. You can tell Peggy you tried to convince Tom to fire me. But it's a waste of time. Your father knows exactly what I'm doing, and why I'm doing it."

"Then why the hell don't you enlighten me, so I can keep my mother from having a stroke?"

"You're mother's a lot stronger than you think, boy. She'll be fine."

"She's strong, all right. But today . . . she just about gave out."

He jabs a finger at me. "Then you find a way to be in that courtroom for her tomorrow. Because things are likely to get worse before they get better."

A pall of dread settles on my shoulders. "How could they get worse?"

"Things can *always* get worse. If you came from the same generation as your father and me, you'd know that."

A flash of anger makes my face hot. Having lost one wife and one fiancée, I feel I've endured my share of grief. "I know how bad life can get, Quentin."

He snorts. "You've lost two women, Penn. I feel for you. But you ain't sick or in jail, and you still got a beautiful little girl to raise."

With shaking hands I take a step back toward the door, looking over Quentin's head at Doris, who is shaking her head as though in apology.

"You've got half a day," I tell him. "If you don't start turning things around tomorrow morning, I'll find a way to stop this circus. And I think I know somebody who can help me."

"Yeah? Who's that?"

I tilt my head toward Doris. Fear and anger flare in her eyes, but I'm past caring about marital intrigues. "If Doris and Mom get on the same side, you'll be back in Jefferson County before Judge Elder even notices you're gone. You and Dad won't have a thing to say about it."

This gives him pause. "And what if that happens? Who's gonna take my place? *You*?"

"I don't want the job. But I'll take it before I let you sabotage the trial."

"You might as well put your daddy on that old gray bus to Parchman this afternoon."

"Quentin, I'll put a night-school ambulance chaser in that courtroom, so long as he knows when to yell 'Objection' and he can tell hearsay from legitimate testimony."

Doris marches out of the doorway, circumnavigates the island, and interposes herself between Quentin and me, then begins speaking softly to him, so softly that I can't make out her words. I start to leave, but in a much more restrained voice Quentin says, "You don't know anything about the Impressionists, Penn?"

My hand is on the back doorknob. "Some. What's your point?"

"Only this. When hack artists looked over the shoulder of Monet, all they saw was a man painting dots. Daubs and dots."

"But when they took a few steps back, they saw the whole picture?"

"You got it."

"I need to get home. I'm sorry, Doris."

"Come on, my brother!" Quentin says, as though I'm taking all this too seriously. "I'm just tryin' to make you feel better."

I walk out onto the gallery, then look back at him through the half-open door. "You get Dad acquitted, you can tell me what a genius you are all day long. Until then, why don't you try to remember a little basic legal procedure?"

He shakes his head as though I'm a hopeless case. "Why don't you get out of my light, hack?"

"Half a day, Quentin. Then you get your walking papers."

As I shut the door, I see Doris watching me over her shoulder, her dark eyes inscrutable as ever.

ONE BLOCK AWAY from my house, my cell phone rings. It's Rusty, of course.

"What did Quentin say?" he asks.

"It's going to get worse before it gets better."

"Fuck."

"At least he dropped his Leonardo bit. Now he thinks he's Monet."

"I think he's freakin' Big Bird. He's got to go, amigo. When court opens tomorrow, you've got to be standing at the defense table. You, your father, and nobody else. That's something the jury can believe in, right there."

"I gave him half a day, Rusty."

"You *what*? Q can sink your old man in less time than that."

"I went with my gut."

"Well, usually that's a good thing. But not this time."

"I'll tell you what scares me most. There's some kind of split between Quentin and his wife. I think Doris is worried Quentin's out of his league, too. Something's messed up. I don't know what."

"Go talk to your father."

"There's no point. He won't fire Quentin. Whatever's at the heart of this case, Dad won't confide it to me."

"Shit, man. Is he that embarrassed about all this? So he tagged Halle Berry, and she got pregnant. That's no reason to go to jail."

"I'm glad you're not making the closing argument."

"Better me than Quentin Avery. Dude, I've known your mom a long time, and she's close to cracking. She doesn't care who Tom nailed back in the Dark Ages, she just wants him out of jail. Why can't he see that?"

"Maybe Dad really believes the Knoxes will kill Annie or me unless he takes the fall."

Rusty breathes into the phone for a few seconds. "Well . . . if that's it—"

"I know. Nothing's going to change his mind."

"Where's Ray fucking Presley when you need him? Or your blond buddy from the Special Forces?"

"I know what you mean."

"Call me later."

"Yeah."

CHAPTER 32

SNAKE KNOX CROUCHED behind the desk in the sod farm office, his mouth open and his hands lightly over his ears. Junelle Crick stood over him, begging him not to go through with it. Snake told her to shut up and get down.

His fling with the VK mama had paid off in spades. This morning she'd told him that his passport and other ID had been delivered two days ago, but that Toons Teufel had locked both in the company safe. Toons had also ordered two of his men to stay behind and make sure Snake didn't leave the compound. After hearing this, Snake had lost no time liberating enough plastic explosive to blow the safe with a shaped charge. He'd planted the charge five minutes ago, after the security guys jumped on an ATV and went out to help change a PTO implement on the farm's main tractor.

Snake glanced at his watch. At the last instant, he reached up and snatched the babbling Junelle down behind the desk, saving her from the flash and possible mutilation by shrapnel. It wasn't gratitude that had prompted this action, but his awareness that he might yet need an ally in this location, despite his immediate plans.

While Junelle shook her head in shock at the explosion, Snake got up, walked through the smoke, and crouched before the open safe. He found his new ID documents in a manila folder with Chinese characters on it. He laughed cynically as he got up. To get these documents, the white-supremacist bikers had dealt with local Arabs who then procured the desired articles from a Chinese supplier.

As he walked past the desk, Snake picked up the flight bag he'd packed earlier and headed toward the door. At that point, Junelle finally figured out that he was leaving, and what his departure was likely to mean for her future. As she begged him to take her with him, he said, "Sorry, hon, my plane only holds one."

"But—but they'll kill me," she said. "Toons will kill me!"

"Tell him I made you tell me about the IDs."

"He won't believe me."

"Yes, he will." Snake drew his pistol from the holster on his hip and cracked her across the face with it.

Junelle dropped like a sack.

He kept his pistol out as he left the office and crossed the open space between it and the airstrip, listening for the sound of the ATV's engine returning. He knew they had tried to sabotage his plane, but the bikers were amateurs when it came to that kind of work. Snake had slipped out before dawn and repaired the wires they'd cut.

He climbed into the Air Tractor and started the engine, then turned the plane and taxied into the wind, building speed as fast as he could. When the plane's wheels left the earth, he felt a wild laugh building in his chest, the same one he'd felt when Alois showed him the Needle Box.

As the plane climbed, Snake banked and flew over the sod field. Three hundred feet below him, the blue ATV was parked beside the big orange tractor. The men by the Kubota looked up, looked down, then looked up again and began pointing and yelling.

"Adios, assholes!" Snake yelled, even as the men drew handguns and began firing at him.

He wished he had a load of herbicide to dump on them as a parting gift. Talk about fucking up somebody's day . . .

As Snake climbed away from the futile bullets, he felt his burner phone vibrate in his pocket. Taking it out, he yelled, "Toons? That you?"

"This ain't Toons," said a woman. "You know who this is?"

Wilma Deen. Wilma and Alois had headed back to Natchez a few hours ago. "I do. What's going on?"

"I heard some taped testimony from the trial. The dead nurse's sister testified today. And you should have been there to hear it."

"What'd she say?"

"Your brother didn't die from them batteries fallin' on him. That nigger nurse killed him."

Snake flew right through a pillar of smoke spewing from one of the chemical plants near Westlake. "Hold up. Cora Revels said that?"

"Not willingly. That Quentin Avery pulled it out of her. But it sounded pretty conclusive. She killed him while he was waiting for treatment back there in Dr. Cage's office. And Dr. Cage likely covered it up for her. I mean, he had to, didn't he? He was dickin' her."

Snake felt acid flood into his gut. "That nigger murdered Frank?" he said dully, not really believing it. He thought back to the day that pallet load of batteries had tumbled off the forklift and crashed into his brother, crushing bones and opening his chest. And how Sonny and Glenn had rushed him to Tom Cage's office rather than the hospital, because that was what Frank wanted . . .

"If Tom Cage knew all along that bitch killed Frank . . ."

"What'd you say?" Wilma shouted. *"All I can hear is a roaring!"*

"I said, *Ya'll get that place we talked about ready! I've got my papers and I'm on my way."*

"You mean it?"

"Do what I told you, goddamn it! Out."

Snake rocked back and forth in the small cockpit, fighting a compulsion to throw the phone out of the plane. He felt like his brain was on fire. His beloved brother had not died in an accident; Frank had been murdered. Using all the skill he had, Snake lifted the AT-501 to its operational ceiling and then beyond it. The flat land of Louisiana drifted beneath him like a slow-motion film, unrolling endlessly. Snake never looked down, only forward. He was watching for the most familiar landmark of his flying career, the great brown serpent of the Mississippi River. The only fluid that could quench the fire in his head waited on the far bank of that river, pulsing with ignorant hope.

The blood of the Cage family.

CHAPTER 33

IT'S NIGHT, AND Annie is watching our DVD of *To Kill a Mockingbird,* searching for clues to the legal system and ideas on how to defend her grandfather. She has long known that Atticus Finch inspired me to become an attorney—as he did thousands of other lawyers—and that in many ways, *To Kill a Mockingbird* inspired me to write my first novel. The irony is that, for most of my life, I believed I was raised by a father who was as close as you could come to Atticus Finch in the real world. Dad might have been a doctor rather than a lawyer, but people still looked at him the way they looked at Gregory Peck in that film, and the way most citizens of Maycomb looked at Atticus in the novel: as a paragon of honor, courage, and rectitude.

More to the point, the black people of my little Mississippi town seemed to honor my father with the same respect shown to Atticus, as when the old preacher says: *"Jean Louise, stand up. Your father's passin'."* But tonight, all I can think about as Annie watches the old black-and-white classic is what Scout would have thought if, at age forty-five, she'd learned that she had a half brother fathered by Atticus on Calpurnia, their maid. Such things seem unimaginable in the idealized world of the film, but in Lee's novel, Mr. Dolphus Raymond married a black woman and fathered interracial children, thus earning social exile for himself, his morphine-addicted wife, and his children.

What does Annie see, I wonder, as she watches the movie trial and thinks about her grandfather? Does she see how much the world has changed since 1960? Or does it look essentially the same to her, with the colors of the accused and accuser inverted? In the film, a black man is unjustly imprisoned by whites. In Annie's world, her white grandfather has been unjustly imprisoned by a black district attorney. Does she see race behind my father's indictment? Annie attends private school with quite a few black children—the offspring of black physicians and attorneys (plus a few exceptional athletes)—but the public schools are almost entirely black. More telling still, we could dine out in restaurants every night for a year and not see a mixed-race couple. We see them other places now and then—at Walmart or the baseball field, for example—but in what passes for "society," such things remain unseen, if not unknown.

Something else struck me at the beginning of the film: the first time we see Atticus—always remembered as a man who regards violence as the desperate tactic of lesser men—he's revealed to be the "best shot in Maycomb County," and he actually kills a rabid dog before his children's eyes. What could more firmly establish the credibility of an action hero than this? And if we didn't know that Atticus was willing to be ruthless when necessary, would we so readily listen to his homilies about honor and fairness?

I also wonder what Atticus Finch would have done if the woman he loved had been murdered on the order of a man beyond the reach of any court. Surely the "best shot in Maycomb County" might be tempted to use his rifle to eliminate Forrest or Snake Knox? At the end of the film, Sheriff Heck Tate leaves us in no doubt that if rough justice happens to strike down a monster like Bob Ewell—who tried to kill the Finch children—it's best to simply look the other way. In the spirit of Sheriff Tate, Rusty Duncan today mourned the fact that Ray Presley or Daniel Kelly isn't around to neutralize the Knoxes by whatever means necessary. Would that moral trade-off buy us freedom from fear? If Snake Knox turned up dead tomorrow morning, would my father still sit silent in court while Shad Johnson ushers him toward Parchman Farm?

"Daddy?" Annie says as she watches the credits roll.

"Mm-hm."

"Is Mr. Quentin Avery like Atticus?"

"Ahh . . . yes and no."

Annie rolls off the pillow she's been lying on and looks back at me, and I get one of those unexpected blasts of déjà vu, when her mother's soul looks out of her eyes. "Quentin is actually more heroic than Atticus," I tell her, trying not to think about her mother. "Atticus Finch is always seen as brave, and he was. But Atticus was white. Part of the dominant class. All he really risked by defending Tom was being spit on by trash like Bob Ewell, or not being invited to some fancy parties. But when Quentin was a young lawyer, he literally risked his life every time he took on the system. That took real bravery."

"And what about now? Is Mr. Quentin brave now?"

I'm not sure I know the answer to this question. "Well . . . the world has changed a lot. Quentin's made a lot of money, and in some ways that makes him part of the dominant class. Although to some people, he'll always be just a black man, no matter how rich he gets."

"But as a *lawyer,* I mean. Is he as good as you?"

"That's hard to say. I was a prosecutor, but when Quentin took on criminal cases, he mostly defended people."

Annie groans in frustration. "Could you *beat* him? That's all I'm asking."

"I never had to go against him, so I don't know. I'm glad I never had to. I think the outcome would probably have depended on the evidence. Whose side it favored."

"Whose side does it favor in Papa's case?"

"That's hard to say, since nobody's sure exactly what all the evidence is. There may be witnesses none of us knows about."

Annie crosses her legs Indian style, then props her elbows on her knees and her chin in her hands. "Well, I know something's wrong. Ya'll can't hide that from me. Mr. Quentin's upsetting everybody. Gram and Miriam, but you especially. I can tell. And I think there's only one thing to do about it."

"What?"

"You have to take over Papa's case, like Mr. Rusty said. You *have* to defend Papa."

"Why?"

"Because I know you'll do the right thing. Like Atticus."

"Annie, these days, a lawyer like Atticus Finch wouldn't be able to win many cases. These days it takes a smart, slick lawyer like Quentin to do it."

"But Atticus *didn't* win his case, Daddy. He just did the right thing. My teacher would call that a moral victory."

This simple assertion of what should be obvious stuns me with the force of an epiphany. "Have you thought about what you're saying, Boo? Atticus didn't just lose his case. He lost his client. Tom Robinson died."

"But only because Tom hung himself. Papa wouldn't ever hang himself."

I wonder if that's true . . . If Dad could hear the faith in his granddaughter's voice, he certainly wouldn't—

"Even if you lost this first trial against Mr. Shad," Annie goes on, "you could appeal, and eventually you'd win."

"What makes you so sure?"

"Because Papa would never do the wrong thing! He might do something that *looked* wrong. But if we could know all the things he did before he did it—and feel them—then we'd know it wasn't wrong."

The logical gymnastics of a child can be amazing.

"All you have to do is get the jury to see and feel everything Papa knew and felt before he did whatever it was he did. And then they'll find him innocent. And I know you can do that."

It suddenly strikes me that Annie might have stumbled onto Quentin's strategy at last. *Could that really be what Quentin intends to do?*

"I'll think about it, Boo."

"Don't take too long. I heard Mr. Rusty say Papa doesn't have much time."

Is she old enough to hear the truth? "Annie, I'm glad you have so much faith in me. But thinking I can save Papa is like saying Mama wouldn't have died if Papa had treated her from the start. Papa's a good doctor, but he couldn't have saved her. No one could."

She knits her brows and focuses all her intelligence upon me. "Are you saying no lawyer can save Papa?"

"No. But I'm saying that right now his best chance is Quentin Avery—even if the rest of us don't understand what Quentin's doing. I'm a good lawyer. Quentin is like a magician with rabbits up his sleeve. You just wait."

"If I have to wait, can I *please* do it in the courtroom?"

I groan with exasperation. "Boo, we've been over this a hundred times."

"So this makes a hundred and one! Daddy, ya'll think I don't hear things, but I do. I hear *everything*. I know how bad things are. I know nobody's perfect. Nobody tells the truth all the time. I've lied before. Everybody does, when they don't want to hurt people."

"And?"

"Don't you see that going to court isn't going to scar me for life? Papa needs me there! If he sees me, maybe he'll realize he needs to tell you whatever it is he's been keeping to himself."

Again I wonder if Annie could be right. Perhaps. But I'm not going to sit an eleven-year-old girl in a courtroom where my father's bastard son might accuse him of God knows what.

Catching Annie under the arms, I pick her up and hold her face close to mine. "I'm sorry, but you're just not old enough. I'll stay with you tomorrow, and Rusty will keep us up to date by hook or by crook."

As she rolls her eyes with theatrical exaggeration, female voices drift down the stairs. A few seconds later, Mia and my mother walk into the den together.

"Well," Mom says to Annie, "have you had any more little episodes like you did this morning?"

Annie's cheeks turn apple red. "I wouldn't have had any *episode* if you and Daddy had taken me to court with you."

"Oh, now, come on." Mom reaches out and pulls Annie to her. "Let's go in the kitchen and get some ice cream. Your father's had a monopoly on you long enough."

As they head into the kitchen, I give Mia a questioning glance. "Didn't she go visit Dad earlier?"

"She did."

"Usually she comes back feeling low."

Mia shrugs. "I perked her up a little."

"How did you manage that?"

"Mad skills." She gives me a self-deprecating smile.

Two years ago, Mia and I went through a series of events that rocked the whole town. People lost their lives, and reputations were damaged beyond repair. Mia Burke forever changed my view of high school girls, and with that change came a melancholy realization that my own daughter will likely lose her innocence sooner than I hope, and probably in ways I could never foresee.

Mia walks over to the sofa against the wall and tucks her legs beneath her. She's left room for me, but I sit in the chair opposite the TV.

"Are you holding up okay?" she asks.

"It's harder than I thought it would be."

She looks over toward the kitchen door. "Can I ask you something about Caitlin?"

"Sure."

Almost inaudibly, she says, "Is it true that she was pregnant when she died?"

Why is she asking me this now? "Yes. How did you know that?"

"It was in a story I read in a Jackson paper. About the autopsy report."

I nod in silence.

"Your mom just mentioned it to me, though. A few minutes ago."

This surprises me. "Really?"

Mia nods, her eyes still on the kitchen door. "Did Annie ever find out?"

"Not so far, thank God."

"Okay. So . . . your mother also told me your father's not handling this very well. That he's pulled inside himself. That he's not telling you guys anything. Only Quentin."

"I'm surprised Mom told you that much. By her law, nothing is ever mentioned outside the family circle."

Mia's eyes flicker with something I can't interpret. "Maybe I'm inside the circle now. How much faith do you have in Quentin?"

"It comes and goes."

"Options?"

"Annie thinks I need to be defending Dad."

"From the mouths of babes—"

"Comes baby talk."

Mia shakes her head, then stretches as though tired. "Don't you think maybe you should go see your father?"

"Did Mom push you to get me to visit him?"

"She didn't push me at all. But it seems clear that your father's silence is crippling his defense. Are you sure he's even talking to Quentin?"

"I'm not. I'll tell you something, though. Quentin's erratic behavior has distracted our family from a very simple fact."

"What?"

"From a prosecutor's standpoint, Shad Johnson made his case today. A very compelling forensic case, right down the line. No matter what Miriam prints in the *Examiner,* after hearing today's testimony, nobody can deny that Dad had the motive, the means, and the opportunity to murder Viola Turner. And so far as anyone knows, he has no alibi. When you add the bomb Sheriff Byrd dropped about that tape they found in the Dumpster . . . things look pretty grim."

Mia gets up from the couch and comes to sit on the ottoman in front of me. "Look at me," she says, taking my hand. "Do you think your father killed Viola?"

"He told me he did."

Her face drains of color. "What?"

"When I visited the Pollock FCI that one time."

Mia is finally at a loss for words.

"Truthfully, I don't think he murdered her. But did he kill her? It's possible. And I'm scared as hell of those videotapes."

"If he did kill her, do you think he would have told your mother?"

"No. God, no."

Mia nods. "Agreed. Peggy believes he's innocent, straight-up, no doubts."

"Oh, I know that all too well. She still worships him."

Mia squeezes my hand, then releases it. "Listen . . . your mom thinks you blame your father for Caitlin's death. And she's right, isn't she?"

"Yes, to a point. But to tell you the truth . . . right now I'm worried about his sanity. I'm thinking of asking Drew to go talk to him. Evaluate him."

Mia folds her arms across her chest and looks at me with a familiarity I haven't experienced since Caitlin was alive. "I'm going to go out on a limb here," she says, "because somebody needs to."

"What do you want to say?"

"Do you think Caitlin blamed your father for her death?"

"What?" I ask, unsure whether I've heard her correctly.

"I mean out there in the swamp, when she was dying. Did she blame him?"

A blast of anger surges through me, and I want to snap back at her. But then I remember Caitlin's voice during her Treo memo, telling me not to blame anyone but her for her solo trip to the Bone Tree. An electric tingle races along my arms. It's not as if any of this is new information, but—

"Stop blaming your father," Mia advises. "At least until you know all the facts. Caitlin and I weren't exactly BFF, but the lady had her shit together. She was the closest thing to a role model I could find in this town. And I think that's what she would say to you now, if she could. Cut your father some slack."

The ring of my cell phone spares me from having to respond to Mia's plea—which in truth sounds like Caitlin speaking from the grave.

I'm half expecting the caller to be Serenity, but the phone says UNKNOWN NUMBER. Usually I don't answer such calls, but with the situation this fluid and the stakes so high, I can't afford to ignore this one.

"Penn Cage," I answer.

"Penn, it's Doris Avery."

A premonition of danger moves through me. "Is everything all right?"

"There's no emergency, if that's what you mean. But I was wondering if you could come by for a brief talk."

"With Quentin?"

"Quentin's asleep."

I look away from Mia's questioning eyes and try to guess what has prompted this call. "Are you at Edelweiss?"

"Yes. I'm out on the gallery."

"I'm only a few blocks away. I'll be there in a minute."

"Hurry, Penn. Please."

CHAPTER 34

EDELWEISS HAS TWO staircases that ascend to the gallery like the legs of a capital A. As I climb the right staircase in search of Doris Avery, the orange eye of a cigarette appears from the darkness under the north gallery above me. I smelled the tobacco smoke from half a block away, but the overhead lights are off, so I didn't see Doris. Even now, her coffee-colored skin seems to drift in and out of the dark. Only her eyes, which catch the light from the streetlamp on the bluff, remain constant in the gloom.

Her low voice, taut with tension, says, "I hoped that after lunch today, you'd feel it was worthwhile to come down here tonight."

"How long have you been out here?"

"Long enough to smoke too many cigarettes."

"What's going on, Doris? Quentin didn't want me in this house today, but you did. Why?"

"Something's wrong."

"Obviously. But what?"

She takes a quick drag on the cigarette, then blows the smoke away from me. "I'm not sure."

"Is something wrong with Quentin? Health-wise?"

"*Health*-wise? Of course. Where do you want to start?"

"I meant mentally."

She takes some time with this. "Is he mentally competent? Yes. Is he as sharp as he used to be? Sometimes I think he's even sharper."

"Then what are you talking about?"

She walks to the rail and gazes off the bluff toward the great twin bridges to the south, their silver metal glowing like an erector set project spanning the dark river. "I was third in my law school class at Emory, Penn. Did you know that?"

"I didn't."

"I'm not surprised. I live in a mighty big shadow. I worked for the U.S. attorney in Atlanta as well, on a federal task force."

Her revelation amazes me. "Why have you never told me?"

"You never asked. You just assumed I was the trophy wife. Which I am, to a degree."

"But Quentin—"

"He never told you either, right? There are good and bad reasons for that. I do a lot of work for my husband, but sometimes it suits his purposes for juries to see him struggling alone against a battery of corporate sharks. David and Goliath, right? That's why I sit behind his table, and sometimes even behind the bar. He lets them think I'm his trophy wife, and I let him let them think that."

These revelations have scrambled my assumption that Doris is an essentially powerless bystander to what's been going on. "Well . . . Jesus. As a lawyer privy to the defense, can you tell me what the *hell* Quentin was doing in court today?"

She sighs heavily. "What people saw in court today was a horse with hobbles on. You ever seen that?"

"I've always heard the term. I've never seen it, though."

"Hobbles are like handcuffs for a horse. Keeps them from walking away."

"Who's handcuffing Quentin?"

She shrugs her shoulders, and in her eyes I see pain. "I don't know. But *that's* what's wrong. I usually know everything about his cases. Quentin bounces ideas off me all the time. *Every* case. I've won more than a couple for him, I can tell you."

"But this one's different?"

Doris blows out a stream of smoke as she nods. "He's walled me out completely."

A worm of fear begins gnawing at my heart. "Just like my father and me."

She nods with the weariness of someone who is far ahead of me in her fears. "They're like two old lions who've crawled into a thicket to lick their wounds."

"And Quentin hasn't told you why."

Doris goes rigid; then I see she's pointing into the shadows beneath the crape myrtles on Washington Street. A deep, man-shaped umbra is just discernible against the dark background.

"He's with me," I tell her, laying a hand on her arm. "Protection."

The tension drains out of her as if from an uncoiling spring.

"Surely you have some theory about what's behind Quentin's reticence?"

"All I know for sure is that he's scared. And if he's scared, it's because your father's scared."

"What are they scared of?"

Doris shakes her head like someone who's been trying to answer this question for months. "Your father wouldn't act out of fear for his own life. That I know. Quentin wouldn't, either. Sometimes he doesn't want to go on living anyway."

"Has he said that to you?"

She looks me fully in the eyes at last, and I realize how beautiful she really is. Her eyes are large, though filled with sadness, and her jaw is perfectly curved, the line of bone as clean as a strung bow.

"You think a man with Quentin's vanity can lose both legs and keep going like it's nothing? Quentin Avery used to be tall and strong—vital even at seventy. Now he has to look up to everybody he meets. How do you think he handles that?"

"I'm sorry, Doris."

She leaves those bottomless eyes on me for a couple of seconds more, then turns away. "This, too, shall pass."

After staring out at the dark river for a while, she says, "Penn, I think we're all hostages, even though we're walking free. Annie, you, me . . . all of us."

"You mean literally? Hostages to the Double Eagles?"

She nods. "Quentin's dealt with death threats all his life, especially back in the sixties. But the thing is, very few people follow through on death threats. Even hardened criminals. A few racists did, and those are the stories we remember. But nobody shot Jackie Robinson. I'm sure you were threatened plenty of times as an ADA."

"Sure." *And a few tried to make good on their threats.* "I'm listening."

"But in *this* case, the men we're talking about are racists *and* criminals. Terrorists, really. Two or three generations of tightly knit sociopaths, committed to violence and involved in the drug trade. Anybody with any sense knows they were behind the killings that happened before your father was arrested. They killed Caitlin. These men kill their *own,* Penn. Do you think they would hesitate to kill you or me? Or Annie?"

"Have you talked to Quentin about this?"

"Sure. God forgive me, I tried to get him to walk away from your father's case. I knew right away it meant trouble. Most of the world has moved past all this hatred. Even in Mississippi. And Quentin doesn't have much time left, Penn. Whatever he does have, he deserves to live it out in peace."

"Doris, the world hasn't moved past any of this. Bosnia? Rwanda? It's the same atavistic horror. Tribalism. But I hear what you're telling me."

"I feel for Viola Turner. She led a tragic life. But God knows her time had come. Why can't we let the dead bury the dead this time?"

"Look . . . I don't know what the hell Dad and Quentin are up to. Shad Johnson was never going to let Dad plead down to no jail time, but I know this jury can be sold on reasonable doubt. At least I believed it until I heard about those tapes."

A flicker of fear shows in her eyes.

"Was Quentin as shocked as I think he was to hear about that Dumpster tape?"

"I think he was. But what shocked him most was that Sony has it."

"He hasn't given you any idea what might be on it?"

"He hasn't even conceded that he knows anything about it."

As I look at her distraught features, a deeply unsettling thought awakens in me. I lay my hand on her shoulder, and she leans toward me, not away. "Doris, would Quentin intentionally lose a case in order to protect our lives? Yours? Mine? Annie's?"

She mulls the question for a bit. "If your father asked him to, he might."

"Jesus."

"That would be the only reason, though." She stubs out her cigarette on the rail, then flicks the butt out onto the sidewalk and looks up into my eyes. "There's something else that worries me. I don't even know how to put words to it. But there's something dark at the heart of this case. Something we don't even begin to see . . . but *they* know. Quentin and Tom. I don't know why they're keeping it from us. How could it be worse than what we know already?"

"Things can always be worse, Doris. There's no use speculating about that. Just tell me this. Does Quentin have any surprise witnesses lined up?"

"If he does, they'll be a surprise to me, too."

In this moment I'm suddenly certain that Quentin has no secret plan, no masterfully subtle strategy, that he is not in truth a magician but a frightened old fool. "My God," I breathe. "Don't you see? Quentin's throwing the case."

Though I spoke softly, Doris brings up both hands and waves them before me as though trying to calm a spooked animal. "Don't jump to conclusions, Penn. I didn't say that."

"What else could it be? And what's the dark thing you're worried about? You must have some idea."

She reaches into her pocket and brings out her cigarettes and a lighter. The flame illuminates her smooth skin for a few moments, and I fight the urge to cough. "I don't want to speculate," she says, smoke drifting upward from her lips. "But I guess we have to."

"Go on."

"Do you think your daddy killed Viola?"

I turn away from her and gaze off the precipice of the bluff, into the vast, dark stream that divides the continent. "I don't know. He once told me he did, but I'm not positive that he meant it literally. If he did kill Viola, it wasn't for the reason Shad claims—to keep her quiet. It was a mercy killing. A mercy killing gone wrong somehow."

"I feel just the opposite," Doris says. "If Tom really loved Viola, I don't believe he could have put her down like a lame horse. She was a *nurse,* Penn. She could have injected herself, if she really wanted to die that badly."

"Maybe that's what the botched morphine injection was about. A failed attempt."

Doris shakes her head stubbornly. "I've seen the medical reports. Viola was in bad shape, but not so bad that she couldn't have injected the deep vein in her thigh. She knew how to do that."

"Okay, then. What are you telling me?"

Doris takes a long drag on her cigarette, like a diver taking a deep breath before plunging off a cliff. "When I was nineteen years old, I got involved with a married man. One of my college professors. I was crazy in love. He made me promises, and I believed them. Maybe he meant them when he said the words . . . I don't know. But anyway, one night I told a girlfriend about him. Lord, her eyes lit up like I'd told her the secret of eternal youth. I knew right then that I'd made a mistake. She was going to tell somebody the first chance she got. But I'd been drinking too much, and so had she. When I first told her, I may have halfway hoped she *would* tell. But later that night, I panicked. I realized how terrible the consequences would be for his family if she told anyone. For me, too. If my father and mother ever learned what I'd done, it would break their hearts. They'd never let me come home. Well . . . my friend had passed out by that time. She was lying on the floor, so drunk she couldn't have woken up if the fire alarm went off."

Doris is clearly reliving the moment as though she were there. "And?"

"For a few minutes . . . Penn, I thought about holding a pillow over her face until she stopped breathing."

A chill rushes over my skin. "*What?*"

She nods slowly, almost defiantly. "Smothering the life out of her."

"Bullshit."

"I swear to God. In those few moments, I couldn't bear the idea that the world would know what I'd done. My mother and father . . . my lover's wife and children."

"What stopped you?"

"Fear. That's all. And maybe my upbringing. But that pillow was in my hands, boy. You hear me?"

I shake my head in denial, but Doris reaches out and squeezes my arm hard enough to hurt. "Listen to me. *Any human being* is capable of killing to keep their darkest secret from coming to light. Don't lie to yourself about that."

"So, you believe Dad could be guilty."

"Of course. But Quentin's job isn't to find out whether or not Tom's guilty. It's to make sure he doesn't go to jail. The rest is up to God."

"You mean the jury."

Doris shrugs like that's the same thing.

A car drives slowly past on Broadway, headlights slicing through the mist gathering on the bluff. Tourists frequently cruise this street to look at Edelweiss, the Parsonage, and Rosalie, but when I glance down to my left, I see Tim writing down the license number.

"I kind of wish you hadn't told me that story," I murmur.

Doris releases my upper arm and pats it. "Don't say that. Lying to yourself is the worst thing you can do when you're at war."

"Spoken like a true soldier," I say with a hint of mockery in my voice.

"Look at me," she says, stepping in front of me. "I'm forty-one years old. Quentin is thirty-two years older than I am—eight years older than my father. But that's who I sleep with, every night. And each day, sickness takes something else away from him." Her eyes blaze with the anger of a woman on the edge of despair. "You think I'm not in a war right now? *You ain't payin' attention.*"

When I draw back from the intensity of her bitterness, Doris shocks me with a laugh, full-throated and filled with pleasure. "You know what I'd like more than anything right now?"

"To go home to Jefferson County?"

"Nope. To get in your car and drive to some club where they don't care what color we are and dance all night. Dance till the sun comes up."

"Are you serious?"

Her eyes are glowing, but the weight of her sadness is still plain in the slope of her shoulders. "Do you know how long it's been since I've danced like that?"

"A great dancer I'm not, Doris."

"Oh, baby. You've still got both your legs, and you ain't a bad-lookin' man."

Her words make me feel like Quentin could be listening from the third-floor window.

"Quentin's sound asleep," she says, reading my mind. "Today wore him out. But he doesn't have to eavesdrop to know my mind. Quentin can read thoughts, Penn. Don't think he can't."

"You really believe that?"

All humor leaves her face. "You watch him with that jury. With hostile witnesses."

"Are you really that confident? A lot of people believe Quentin's losing it. My mother, for one. Several attorneys, as well. They say he's not the man he used to be."

Doris reaches out and pokes my stomach with her finger. "Are you the man you used to be? Could you please me the way you could have twenty years ago?"

"I'm not talking about the body."

"You can't separate the two! Mind and body are like flame and candle. But as for Quentin's competence . . . his body may be falling apart, but his mind's still a straight razor. That's the tragedy. He's like that physicist with Lou Gehrig's disease. But don't lie awake tonight thinking he couldn't handle this job if he wanted to. Compared to Shadrach Johnson, Quentin's got X-ray vision."

"Superman, huh?"

"I'd never say that to his face, though." She laughs softly, but underneath the laughter I hear her strangling tears.

Glancing down to where Tim waits in the shadows of Washington Street, I realize time is passing quickly. Serenity must be back at my house by now . . .

"I should probably get going, Doris."

"Wait." She takes another drag, then turns her face and blows out the smoke. "I wasn't going to tell you this, it's scared me so deep."

Fresh fear makes my face feel cold. "Doris, for God's sake—"

"Remember when I said Quentin and Tom are like two wounded old lions who've crawled into a thicket together?"

"Yeah."

"I'm afraid they've made a bargain with each other."

"What kind of bargain?"

"Like the one Tom made with Viola."

Horror prickles the hair on my neck. "Doris—"

Her eyes go wide with confessional urgency. "I'm afraid Quentin has agreed to throw the trial if Tom will pay him back by helping Quentin pass without any pain."

At first I don't grasp what she's suggesting. But then I get it. On its face, the idea seems crazy . . . and yet a strange sense of déjà vu has started a thrumming in my chest. "Doris . . . that's impossible. If Dad were convicted of killing Viola, he'd never be free to fulfill his half of the bargain."

She counters this argument with eerie certainty. "Tom could make it happen, if he wanted to. He knows a lot of people. Doctors, druggists . . . nurses. People who'd do anything he asked."

"Do you really think Quentin's that depressed?"

"Oh, yes." At last the tears come, wet streaks glinting in the streetlight's spill. "I try, Penn. I do everything I can to keep his spirits up. But Quentin's sin is pride. He'd be the first to tell you that. The problem is simple: He can't do what he used to do. You know what I'm talking about. Survival means more than that to most men, I guess. But Quentin's an all-or-nothing kind of man. And he can't abide pity. He *won't*."

I take Doris in my arms and pull her tight against me. "Stop thinking about it. Just shut your mind off."

"I wish I had a shot of morphine myself. Enough to knock me out for twenty-four hours. Just to *catch my breath*."

"What if I take you dancing instead?"

She laughs, but then her bosom begins to heave and shudder against my chest. All I can do is hold her tight. After a while, she draws back her head and fixes me with her liquid brown eyes, now shot with blood. "I guess we'll just have to see what happens in court tomorrow."

"I guess we will."

She walks with me to the head of the near staircase, then lets her hand trail down my arm as we separate. When I'm halfway down to the sidewalk, she says, "You told Quentin earlier you'd give him half a day to turn things around. What will you do if he keeps going the way he has so far?"

"Whatever it takes to have him removed from the case. Help me help him, Doris. Any way you can think of. Can I count on you?"

After several seconds of what must be agony, she nods three times. Then she turns and walks to the tall doors that lead back to the bed where Quentin Avery sleeps.

CHAPTER 35

WALKING BACK UP Washington Street, I pass between the courthouse and the sheriff's department once again. I hope Dad has found a way to sleep in his cell three floors above Billy Byrd's office. He's never slept much, and with his joint pain he needs a lot of medication to find any rest. Medications and dosages have become a source of squabbling between Quentin and the sheriff, and I'm betting Dad is sitting up there pondering dimensions of this case that remain unknown to me.

The specter that Doris raised—that Quentin might allow Dad to be convicted in exchange for a painless death—has stuck with me. I'm tempted to go in and ask to see my father, if only to confront him about that. But even if she's right, he would never confess it. The real question is why he would want to be convicted in the first place.

The lesser of two evils, answers a voice in my head.

"Did you say something?" Tim asks from behind me.

"No." Taking out my phone, I check for text messages, hoping for word from Serenity. But there's nothing. "Let's get home, man. You want to run it?"

Tim grins. "Oh, yeah! Let's do it."

He breaks past me, then spins and starts backpedaling, waiting for me to come after him. Filling my lungs with cool night air, I dart forward and pass him, sprinting like I once did on these same streets when I was a much younger man. Tim's footsteps pound up behind me, and I know he could easily pass me, but for a few seconds I enjoy the illusion that I'm winning, that I'm actually outrunning the darkness that has followed me for as long as I can now remember.

AFTER LETTING MYSELF into the house, I walk through to the den and find Mia lying on the sofa with a hardcover book propped on her stomach. I say hello, and she answers, but ten seconds later she's back to studying the pages like Champollion over the Rosetta Stone.

"What you reading?" I ask, walking closer.

She holds the book higher for me to see. The jacket is from an old first edition I bought in England, *The Eagle Has Landed,* by Jack Higgins.

"That's not your kind of thing. You couldn't find something more your style in my office? Or have you read everything in there already?"

"I actually like this. Was Doris okay?"

"She's worried about Quentin's health. I think they're both depressed."

"I'm not surprised," Mia says without looking up.

Sensing that she wants me to leave her alone, I start to walk into the kitchen, but then I go back to the sofa. "Is Annie asleep?"

"No, she's up in your mom's room. Peggy and I talked while Annie was taking a bath, but I wanted Annie to get some alone time with her."

Before I can thank Mia, my cell phone rings.

"It's Jenny, calling me from upstairs," I say, looking at the LCD. "Probably wants to talk about the trial."

Mia clucks her tongue critically. "High maintenance, man."

I could go upstairs to talk to Jenny, but I'd rather not. She will have a dozen points to make, most of which are irrelevant to the core issues of the trial, and mostly she'll want reassurance. I call her back and do my best to sound attentive, but plead that I need to do some legal research downstairs. While my sister chatters on, I walk a slow circuit around the main floor, keeping a good distance from Mia. But as I extricate myself from the conversation, I pass back into the den and steal a glance at the running heads on the two exposed pages of the book in her hands. The left-hand one reads: *Serenity Butler.* The right-hand one: *The Paper Bag Test.*

"Oh, boy," I say, trying not to laugh as I hang up. "Why didn't you want me to know you're reading that?"

Mia slams the book shut and drops it on the floor, her cheeks pink. "Hell, I don't know. I guess because I was catty this morning. I'm embarrassed now. It's a damn good book."

She sits up and gives me an abashed smile, but it fades quickly.

"Mia, do you regret taking this semester off? Maybe it isn't what you thought it would be."

"Nothing ever is, in my experience." She looks up with eyes much older than her years, but it's clear she's not complaining or looking for sympathy. "But I don't regret it. Annie needed me. She still needs me. And whatever this is, it's sure as hell not boring."

"Nope. It's like living in the eye of a storm. With people getting hurt all around us."

Mia nods. "To that point, Serenity's still not back. You think she's okay?"

I give it a few moments' thought. "Serenity can handle herself in most situations. Maybe she's with Carl."

Mia laughs, but it sounds forced. "He was sure into her, anyway."

With that she scoops up the book and slips her feet into a pair of sandals that she'd slid under the sofa.

"I'm going up," she says, bouncing to her feet. "See you tomorrow."

I raise a hand to wave, but she's already turned away, and she doesn't look back as she passes through the door. The quick beat of feet on wood tells me her young legs swallow the long staircase without effort, and then I'm alone in the silence.

I'VE BEEN LYING in bed about five minutes when a soft knock sounds at my door. I hate to admit it to myself, but I'm hoping it's Serenity. I can't imagine why she wouldn't have texted me that she was okay, even if she's lying in bed with Carl somewhere. With all that's been happening, surely she knows I'd be worried.

"Come in," I say, sitting up against the headboard.

A vertical bar of light appears at my door, and then I hear my mother's voice in the darkness. "Penn? Are you awake?"

"Yeah. I just laid down. Come in."

Mom slips through the door and pads over to my bed, then sits on the edge of the mattress, a silhouette in the dark. I'm about to switch on the bedside lamp when she touches my hand and asks, "Did you see your father tonight?"

"No," I tell her, leaving the light off. "Doris Avery called me. I had to go hold her hand for a while."

"Oh. Did you learn anything? Something that could help?"

I'm not about to let my mother in on Doris's worst-case fears. "I'm afraid not."

After a period of silence, Mom says, "I noticed that Serenity's not back. Is she staying here tonight?"

Something in my mother's tone sounds more than concerned for Serenity's safety. "I thought she was. I'm not sure, though."

Mom makes a noise I can't interpret. Then she says, "You've been very nice to take time out to help her with her research."

"She's helped me too, Mom."

"Oh, I'm sure. She's had quite an exciting life."

"Mom . . . what do you want to say?"

"Nothing, really. I just hope you're not getting too attached to her. I know she seems glamorous, winning that award and everything. But she's a troubled soul, Penn. I sense it. She's seen a lot more of the world than you. And I just don't want—"

"Mom, I'm forty-five. You don't need to run interference for me."

In the dim light spilling from the door, I see the trace of a smile, but it quickly vanishes. "I know. But I also don't want Annie to feel uncomfortable in her own house."

When I switch on the bedside light, Mom shields her eyes from the sudden brightness. "Do you think she does?" I ask. "Feel uncomfortable."

"Well, she's certainly having a tough time right now. And I know Mia senses something between you and Serenity."

I chuckle at this. "I think Mia's got a little crush on me, Mom."

"Well, there's nothing wrong with that. She's working wonders with Annie, and she's whip-smart. And you're a single man with a good—"

"Mom, this isn't a Jane Austen novel. She's only twenty years old."

At this, my mother actually says, *"Pshaw,"* or something similar. "Twenty-year-olds today know more about life than I knew at thirty. Most girls these days are on the pill by fifteen. Girls from good families, even."

The subtext of this is painfully clear: *A twenty-year-old white girl is a more suitable choice than a thirty-five-year-old black woman.*

"It's bedtime, Mom."

"All right. I don't have to be told twice."

She gets up with a soft groan, and just as I think she's about to close the door, she says, "Will you promise me something, Penn?"

I sigh. "Sure."

"Don't give up on your father."

Jesus. "I won't, Mom."

"I know this is hard. It is for me, too. But Tom has always stood by us. He's always taken care of us. Now we have to take care of him."

"I understand," I tell her, trying to keep the resentment out of my voice. "But it would be a lot easier if he would help."

There's a long silence. Then she says, "You can do it, son. I know you can."

Desperate to change the subject, I ask if she's had any more migraine or stroke symptoms.

"Not one," she assures me. "Now that the battle's been joined, I think I'm going to be fine. It's the waiting that kills me."

There's a lot more waiting to come. "I'll see you in the morning, when we board the tank."

"Good night, Penn."

The door creaks, and the bar of light vanishes.

ONE RESTLESS HOUR after my mother left my room, something prods me to get up, put on a robe, and walk down to the kitchen. I'm not sure whether I heard something or nervous hunger is driving me. As I move up the hallway in my bare feet, I hear tapping coming from the kitchen. Sliding left, I slip into the dark den and peer through the far door at the kitchen table.

Serenity Butler is sitting at the table with a cup of steaming coffee, her eyes locked on her computer screen. Seeing her bent over the machine, her fingers flying faster than mine ever do when I'm writing, I wonder if she's somehow found her way onto the same trail where Caitlin fell, just as Caitlin stepped into Henry's footsteps after he was nearly beaten to death. Serenity's passion for her work burns as fiercely as Caitlin's, and this frightens me. I can't let this young woman lose herself in those old cases and go rogue the way Caitlin did. As tough as Tee is, she might just stumble upon her own Bone Tree in the forests that line the Mississippi River . . . and meet a similar fate.

"You gonna stand there in the dark all night?" Tee asks, never lifting her eyes from the computer. "Or come in here and have some coffee?"

"Can you see in the dark?" I ask, walking into the kitchen.

She holds up her coffee mug. "You want a sip? Just made it."

"No, thanks."

Without missing a beat she goes back to typing.

"Something inspired you?" I ask.

"Not exactly. Just getting down some notes and observations. I like to do it when they're fresh."

I smile, but I'm envious of her work habits. "So where have you been? I was worried. I think everybody was."

"Sorry about that. For a while I was where I couldn't text, and then my battery went dead."

A teenager's reply. "I see."

She glances up, still typing, then suddenly stops and leans back in her chair, faintly amused. "Look, I was out interviewing some people."

"Hey, I don't want to pry."

"You deserve to know. But you won't like it. I was talking to Lincoln Turner. And his aunt, Cora."

Nothing she could have said would have shocked me more. "Seriously?"

"You think I'd kid you about that?"

"I guess not." I reach and turn on the sink tap, then turn it off. "What the hell, Tee?"

She slides her chair back with a screech. "Penn . . . I don't know what idea you have about me, but I'm not here to tell your family story the way *you* see it. I'm here to find out the real story—the truth, whatever that is. And to find that, I have to go where the story takes me. You're a writer, for God's sake. Do you disagree with that?"

I take a deep breath and try to push down all the anger that's built within me today. "No, I get it. It's just hard, from where I stand. What did Lincoln have to say?"

"A lot. That's one angry man. And he has reason to be."

She said this with a note of challenge in her voice. "Yes," I concede.

At last Tee gives me a reprieve from her stare. "I could relate to some of what he went through growing up, but I tell you, my childhood was *The Cosby Show* compared to his."

I try to look interested, but the truth is, I'm not.

"I'll tell you something, though," she goes on, her eyes lost in the middle distance. "Him and Aunt Cora . . . they're lying about something."

This makes me stand up straight. "What do you mean? About what?"

"I don't know. A lot of what they told me was straight from the heart. Lincoln's pain is genuine, but . . . he's holding something back. Something big. Him more than her, but they both know whatever it is."

"But you don't have any idea?"

"Not yet. But I'll get to it." Tee looks up again, her eyes less accusing than before. "Heck, I'm liable to wake up in the middle of the night and just blurt it out."

This image actually brings a smile to my face.

"Anyway," she says, her eyes almost elfin, "I'm thinking maybe you ought to be there in case that happens."

For a couple of seconds I'm not sure she said what I think she did. Then she reaches out with her left hand, her forefinger slowly turning in the air, beckoning my hand to hers. When I raise mine, she touches the tip of my forefinger with hers, then hooks her finger around mine.

"What you think, mister?" she says, flexing her finger and pulling my hand back and forth like we do this all the time.

Her unconscious echo of Doris Avery gives me a strange chill. "Um . . . I figured after you disappeared like you did, you wanted to give it a break. Process everything."

Serenity clucks her tongue twice, her eyes never leaving mine. "I've processed it. In fact, I've been thinking about it all night. What about you?"

"I've thought about it. I guess maybe that's the real reason I came down here."

At last she breaks eye contact and uses her free hand to take a sip of her coffee. "Well, then. Let's not overanalyze. The way I figure it, I can go upstairs and take care of things myself, or you can come up with me and show me how creative you can be."

"Do I get a vote?"

"I'm afraid you do."

WEDNESDAY

CHAPTER 36

AT 9:02 WEDNESDAY morning, Judge Elder asks if the prosecution is ready to proceed on to the matter of the videotapes. Shadrach Johnson answers in the affirmative, and then—by some logistical machinations that must have cost the taxpayer dearly—enters into evidence the two videotapes that were yesterday evening in the hands of the Sony Corporation. For the trial, the tape found in Walt's Roadtrek becomes State's Exhibit 15, and the hospital Dumpster tape S-16. While I stare in dread—and the people in the gallery wait with bated breath—Shad recalls Sheriff's Detective Robert Joiner to the stand and begins weaving a net that will tie my father to what I still think of as the Dumpster tape.

Shad is wise not to recall Billy Byrd on this subject. The black jury members aren't fans of the sheriff, and they'll be much more amenable to the younger and more professional-looking detective. Joiner begins by confirming what Byrd blurted out yesterday: that a search team led by himself discovered a Sony mini-DV tape in a Dumpster behind St. Catherine's Hospital on the afternoon of the day after Viola was found dead. While Joiner speaks, I look for signs that the tapes are about to be played for the jury, but I see no media cart, no screen or TV being set up. Detective Joiner establishes that the tape found in the Dumpster came from the same lot as the two sealed tapes discovered in Cora Revels's house, and also the tape allegedly found in

Walt's Roadtrek (and surreptitiously taken by the Adams County Sheriff's Office). Finally, he reports that his investigation determined that Dr. Tom Cage had made rounds at the hospital the previous morning between eight and nine o'clock. Hospital employees also reported seeing Dad in the hospital parking lot on the afternoon of the following day. When Shad tenders the witness, Quentin rolls forward and asks only one question: Were my father's fingerprints found on the tape discovered in the Dumpster?

"No, sir," Detective Joiner answers.

"No further questions, Your Honor."

The air of expectation in the courtroom has diminished somewhat. Shad is trying everyone's patience by putting off the playing of the tapes. Next, Shad calls an Atlanta-based expert in video forensics named Joseph Chin and begins to qualify him as an expert. Quentin has stipulated the man's expertise, earning brownie points with the jury.

"Mr. Chin," Shad begins, "what is your connection to my office?"

"I've been acting as a forensic video consultant. I have also acted as liaison between your office and the technical division of the Sony Corporation."

"Thank you."

As Shad starts to ask his next question, my faith in Quentin Avery's instincts crumbles under the weight of the DA's relentless work ethic and hunger for revenge. We are about to learn whatever information those "erased" tapes contained.

"And what can you tell us about the type of videotape in question?"

Chin answers with the dry precision of an engineer. "Digital videotape of the kind found in the cassettes in question—mini-DV tapes—is much more difficult to erase than other types of tape, such as VHS, reel to reel, or the cassette tapes of the 1970s. It uses evaporated metal technology, and devices like bulk degaussers—popularly known as demagnetizers—will not erase them with any degree of completeness. Sometimes they won't even affect them."

"But can mini-DV tapes be erased?"

"Oh, yes. Recording over their length in real time will realign the magnetic particles on the tape—permanently, for all practical purposes."

"But in some cases such tapes can be restored?"

"I have never seen it myself. But in a very small number of cases it has been accomplished."

Shad lets this statement hang for a few seconds.

"And what about the two tapes I sent to the Sony lab for this purpose?"

Mr. Chin nods once, then lifts a piece of paper from his lap. "The Sony technicians were unable to restore the data on the videotape taken from the RV belonging to Mr. Walter Garrity. The magnetic content was permanently altered when the tape was reloaded into a camcorder and put in record mode for its entire one-hour length. The original data could not be recovered."

It takes a couple of seconds for me to register what he said. Then a voice in my head says, *One down, one to go.*

"What about the other tape?" Shad asks, voicing the crowd's thoughts.

"The tape found in the hospital Dumpster was a different matter."

Oh, God . . .

"That tape was erased using a different method."

Shad nods soberly, as though learning this information for the first time.

"And was the Sony team able to restore this tape?"

Everyone in the courtroom leans forward.

"No, sir. They were not."

The crowd's expectation becomes shock, then disappointment, then tangible frustration, even anger at Shad Johnson for toying with their expectations. For *teasing* them. But true to his nature, Shad presses doggedly forward.

"Did you learn any useful information from their report on the videotape taken from the hospital Dumpster?"

"Yes, sir. The magnetic data on that tape was actually far more scrambled—disrupted—than the data on the tape taken from the RV. It had been passed through a magnetic field of enormous power."

"Will you elaborate, please?"

Even before he answers, I feel nausea in the pit of my stomach.

"Yes, sir. The effects noted on that tape were almost certainly produced by a magnetic resonance imaging device."

"Are you referring to an MRI machine?"

"Yes, sir. The kind of device hospitals use to image soft tissue."

"I see. Thank you, Mr. Chin. Tender the witness."

The familiar click and whir sounds as Quentin drives himself toward the witness box.

"Mr. Chin, you testified that these two videotapes were erased by two different methods, yes?"

"Yes."

"So the State would have us believe that some person used two completely different methods to erase two videotapes in his possession?"

"That's what the facts show. In my opinion—"

"I'm sorry, Mr. Chin, you're an expert in videotape restoration, and not a criminologist or psychologist, correct?"

Joseph Chin's disappointment is plain; he was salivating over the prospect of giving his theory on why a murderer might choose different methods to erase two tapes. The obvious answer—at least to me—is that the tape exposed to the MRI machine contained more sensitive or incriminating information than the one erased in the camcorder.

"I'm not a criminologist or a psychologist," Chin admits with regret.

Quentin gives him a conciliatory smile. "So, to summarize, the technicians were unable to reconstruct *any* data from the tape erased in the camcorder, correct?"

"That's correct."

"So, why should a person with something to hide risk being seen doing something suspicious or even as risky as gaining access to an MRI machine when he could erase both tapes in complete privacy using a camcorder?"

"Uh . . . maybe he didn't know the camcorder method was just as thorough?"

Quentin appears to consider this answer. "All right. Just to be absolutely clear, Mr. Chin, *no* usable information has been recovered from either videotape you were asked to help analyze, is that correct?"

"That's correct."

"So those tapes can give us zero information about what happened in Cora Revels's house on the night Viola Turner died?"

Chin glances uncomfortably at Shad, then says, "Well . . . by the strict criteria of the data they contain, that's correct."

"Can your analysis, or that of the Sony technicians, prove that the tape was ever in Cora Revels's house at all?"

"The fingerprints—"

"Fingerprints are not your domain, Mr. Chin. Can any analysis conducted by you or the Sony techs prove that those tapes were ever in Cora Revels's house?"

"No, sir."

Quentin touches his joystick and turns dismissively from the witness. "No further questions, Judge."

While Quentin returns to his table, Shad calls a man named Byron Reed to the stand. A thin black man with gold spectacles gets up and walks to the witness box to be sworn.

I don't know Mr. Reed, but I can guess what he's here for: to confirm something that most people in the courtroom already know—that St. Catherine's Hospital has an MRI machine. In short order this witness—who works as an MRI tech at St. Catherine's—does just that, but Shad does not release him. Instead Shad walks over to the jury, looks back at the witness box, and asks, "Mr. Reed, on the morning Viola Turner was found dead, did you see Dr. Thomas Cage in St. Catherine's Hospital?"

"Yes, sir."

"What time was that?"

"Between eight thirty and eight forty. I can't be any more specific than that. I was between patients."

"And where did you see him?"

"In the hallway on the first floor."

"And how far was he from the room housing the MRI machine at that time?"

"Um . . . about sixty feet."

I close my eyes and force myself to breathe deeply. As I exhale, I feel my mother's hand grip mine. She's not looking for comfort, I realize. She's trying to comfort me.

"And what was Dr. Cage doing there?"

"I don't know."

"Did you speak to him?"

"Yes. I always speak to Dr. Cage. He always has a word for everybody."

"And how did he seem on that day?"

Reed takes his time with this question. "About like any other day, I'd say."

"He didn't seem preoccupied?"

"Objection," Quentin says. "Leading."

"Sustained," Judge Elder declares.

"Withdrawn. Mr. Reed, did Dr. Cage have patients anywhere in the area of the MRI unit?"

"Ah . . . not really, no. But Dr. Cage is the kind of doc who's all over the hospital all the time. Old school, you know? Visiting techs and nurses, other people's patients. You might find him fiddling with a microscope in the lab, helping the techs try to fix it."

"So, in your experience, Dr. Cage was handy with technology?"

"Oh, yeah. A lot of doctors know medicine but don't know anything about the technology that gives them the data to make their diagnoses. A lot of docs couldn't shoot an X-ray if they had to."

"But Dr. Cage is different?"

"Yes, sir. When it comes to lab tests, X-rays, surgical equipment, rehab stuff, he can tell you the way they did it in the Civil War, World War One, World War Two, and right on up to now."

Shad is working hard to conceal his pleasure. Byron Reed doesn't seem to understand that by his enthusiastic praise of my father, he is damning him further with every word.

"Thank you, Mr. Reed."

Quentin declines to cross-examine Byron Reed, and Judge Elder releases him. Then Shad calls a man I do know to the stand, an X-ray technician named Gerald McGraw. Gerry McGraw is about sixty, with a bald head and a salt-and-pepper beard. A Vietnam vet, the X-ray tech has been a friend of my father's for years. As the clerk swears McGraw in, I realize exactly what Shad is doing. Having been deprived of the content of the videotapes, Shad means to demonstrate that Dad had both the opportunity and, more important, the technical know-how to erase them so thoroughly (and exotically, in the case of the Dumpster tape).

Though obviously reluctant to hurt my father in any way, Gerry is forced to concede that the basis of their friendship centered around shared enthusiasm for various technologies. McGraw is a ham radio operator, and Dad loved to stop by his house and help him tinker with his setup. Both Gerry and Dad had photographic darkrooms in the late 1960s and early 1970s, and this memory makes me remember standing in our bathroom/darkroom as a boy, counting seconds as my wet hands moved between the trays of developer, stop bath, fixer. The pungent smell of those chemicals comes back in a powerful rush, and with it a sense of oneness with my father that I haven't experienced in a long time.

Somehow Shad has even dug up the fact that both Gerry and my father were hi-fi fanatics, and built Heathkit receivers and speakers at home. Gerry is forced to concede that Dad was as good with a soldering iron as he was with a suturing needle, and even more damaging, that both men were familiar with—and owned—"bulk degaussers" used by enthusiasts to erase old reel-to-reel tapes.

By the time Shad releases Gerry, the damage has been done, and Quentin elects not to cross.

Judge Elder looks at his watch, then says, "Mr. Johnson, it's almost eleven o'clock. Can you examine your next witness in an hour?"

"I believe so, Your Honor. The State calls Lincoln Turner."

As Lincoln enters the courtroom wearing a sport coat and tie, I realize that things are about to get worse, not better.

CHAPTER 37

WHEN LINCOLN TURNER enters the witness box to be sworn, every eye in the courtroom but my mother's follows him, and every head but hers strains forward so as not to miss anything he might say. For if anyone knows the truth or the cost of Tom Cage's past sins, they reckon, it is the big black man facing them now.

My half brother looks out over the assembled citizens with something between detachment and disdain. While the bailiff gives Lincoln the oath, I think back to last night, when Doris Avery revealed to me her darkest fear: that her husband and my father have bound themselves in an unholy bargain to provide services that only they could give each other. If my father will give Quentin a painless escape from this life, then Quentin will allow Dad to be convicted. This scenario only makes sense to me if my father believes he's protecting one or all of us from pain or death by his sacrifice. If that is the case, then the evil he fears can only be Snake Knox and his henchmen. I know far better than to discount this threat, yet I can't help but hope that Dad has not despaired of saving himself altogether.

As the bailiff takes back his Bible and Shad rises from his table, my sister, Jenny, squeezes my left wrist hard enough to bruise. She's fidgeting and sweating as though unconsciously trying to prove she's my mother's opposite.

"You were sworn in as Lincoln Turner," Shad says, standing about ten feet from his witness. "Who is your biological father?"

"That man sitting right there," Lincoln says, pointing at my father. "Dr. Tom Cage."

"How do you know that?"

"A DNA test proved it."

"That DNA test has been entered into evidence and marked State's Exhibit Seven, Your Honor." Shad spreads his hands, touches his fingers together, and addresses Lincoln like a more restrained version of Dr. Phil. "When were you first told that Tom Cage might be your father?"

"I wasn't told. Not really. I had to dig that information up myself."

"And how did that come about?"

"About six months ago, I discovered some checks and letters in my mother's personal effects in her Chicago apartment, plus a photograph of Dr. Cage and my mother in a state of undress. My mother finally told me the story then. Up to that time, she had lied to me."

"From 1968 until 2005 she had kept this information from you?"

"Yes, sir. She'd been lying about who my father was ever since I was born. And not just to me. She lied to everybody."

Shad pauses to let this tragedy—or outrage—sink into the minds of the jury members.

"Will you tell us what your understanding of your paternity was, from the earliest time you remember?"

Quentin should object that the defense has already stipulated that Tom Cage fathered the witness and no further questioning on this point is necessary.

But Quentin says nothing.

"From the time I was a little boy," Lincoln says, "I believed my mother's husband was my father. The man I called Daddy. That's what she told me."

"What was that man's name?"

"His legal name was Junius Jelks, but I didn't know that for a long time. In my first memories, my last name is Taney, which was the name Daddy was going by then."

"Excuse me, let's be clear for the jury. Whenever you say 'Daddy,' you're referring to Junius Jelks, and not Tom Cage, your biological father?"

"That's right. I'll try to call him Mr. Jelks, but it gets confusing when I think back to different times."

"I think we can all follow you. Please just tell us what you knew and when. And, Judge, let me state for the record that all relevant documentation such as birth certificates, adoption records, et cetera has been stipulated into evidence."

Judge Elder glances at Quentin Avery as though wondering why he didn't challenge some of the documents to which Shad refers, but Quentin seems oblivious to this.

"I was born in December of 1968," Lincoln begins, "in Charity Hospital in Chicago. When I first went to school, our family went by the last name of Taney. But I know now that was just an alias."

"And how do you know that?"

"Daddy had a lot of jobs over the years, but the truth is, he was a con man. A grifter. Because of that, he always went by different names. Aliases. That goes with that kind of work."

"Where is Junius Jelks now, Lincoln?"

"The Illinois State Penitentiary at Joliet, serving a fifteen-year sentence for fraud."

"Go on."

"When I was six years old, Mama moved me to a different school. She told me then that our last name was going to be Turner from then on. She said that had been our real name all along. Which was true, in a way. It turns out that Turner was the name on my birth certificate."

"Can you explain that?"

"At the time I was conceived—probably March of 1968—Mama's first husband, James Turner, had been dead for nine months. Killed in Vietnam. When Mama went to Chicago, she was pregnant by Dr. Cage. But when I was born, she put down James Turner's name on the birth certificate. She told them her husband was still over in Vietnam. They didn't have computers back then, so I guess that wasn't hard. Anyway, a year later, when Mama married Daddy—Mr. Jelks—she believed he was an insurance man. But by the time I was five, she'd figured out different. Junius Jelks made his living breaking the law. Mama almost left him then, but she really wanted me to have a father, so she made a deal with him. If Mr. Jelks would legally adopt me, she would stay his wife."

Lincoln's Dickensian narrative has everyone in the room enthralled. Looking behind me, at the balcony, I see Serenity writing in her notebook, her rapt eyes on the witness box.

"Mr. Jelks agreed to this arrangement," Lincoln goes on, "but they still had a problem. Daddy didn't have a good enough ID to adopt me under the name of Taney, and he was wanted for several crimes under his legal name, Jelks. Then he hit on the idea of using Mama's first husband's ID papers to adopt me. It's kind of sad to say it out loud, but Mama agreed to the plan, and that's what they did. Junius Jelks became James Turner, Vietnam vet and war hero, and I went from being Lincoln Taney to Lincoln Turner."

Shad pauses to let this sad and complex tale sink into the minds of the jury.

"How long did Junius Jelks succeed in passing himself off as James Turner?"

"Several years. He went by James Turner when he did anything legitimate, but he had a lot of other aliases for criminal activities."

"How do you know that?"

"Because he used me in his cons. From the time I was little. People will believe almost anything when you've got a child with you. And if you teach that child to help you, the marks are like fish in a barrel."

"When did you learn that James Turner was not your father's true name?"

"We got arrested when I was thirteen. A vice cop recognized Daddy's face. He'd arrested him before, down in Minooka. That cop didn't care what the driver's license said; he knew he'd collared Junius Jelks. Daddy had to do another stretch in jail, and I was lucky not to go to the reformatory."

"How did your mother explain the problem with the names to you?"

"Mama told me we'd had to use the name Turner because Daddy had been framed for something a long time ago. She had no idea that I'd been helping Daddy work cons for years. He'd take me out of school to do it. I was his meal ticket for a while. All Mama did back then was work and drink. I think she suspected how bad things were, but she couldn't face it. She was depressed. They didn't have drugs for that then, so she just drank and chain-smoked her Salems.

"I was pretty confused by then," Lincoln goes on. "I made decent grades, but I was in and out of trouble all the time. I had anger problems. Fought a lot. I was lucky that Child Protective Services didn't take me out of the home during that period."

"But still you managed to attend college."

"That's right. Mama had always worked hard, and she managed to hide a lot of her money from Mr. Jelks. She had a decent little nest egg put back for me."

"Enough to pay for four years of college?"

"No. But she'd worked for the same doctor for seventeen years, and he put up some money for me to go. Whatever Mama didn't have, he paid."

"Was this doctor black or white?"

Lincoln seems almost reluctant to answer. "White."

This answer obviously resonates with the jury, who now realizes that Viola went to Chicago and put herself into a situation almost identical to the one she'd left behind in Mississippi. At least some jury members must be wondering whether Viola might have been sleeping with that doctor, too. A smart defense lawyer would bring this up during cross-examination, subtly suggesting that Viola Turner had a very practical—perhaps even predatory—side when it came to survival. But of course Quentin will suggest no such thing. He probably won't even bother to question Lincoln.

"What was Mr. Jelks doing during your teen and college years?"

"Messing up like me, only worse. Mama got him a few legitimate jobs—the doctor she worked for did, too—but Jelks always managed to get himself fired. He still tried to rope me into cons, but by then I knew that if I was convicted of a felony, I'd never be a lawyer, and for some reason that was what I'd made up my mind to be."

"Why did you want that?"

"I guess Mama put it in my head. She was tired of all Daddy's lies and crime. I think she wanted something she could be proud of. She'd named me after Abraham Lincoln, you know."

Shad vouchsafes the witness a supportive smile, and he makes sure he's facing the jury when he does it.

"And did you go to law school?"

"Yes, sir. Night school. It took me longer than most, because I had to work my way through. But I passed the Illinois State Bar in 1995. I was twenty-seven years old."

"How did your legal career go?"

"Pretty good, for a while."

"And today?"

Lincoln looks into his lap like a sinner in church about to come to Jesus. "I no longer have a license to practice."

Shad feigns surprise. "Why is that, Mr. Turner?"

Like any good prosecutor, Shad is removing all chance of Quentin making capital out of forcing Lincoln to admit he's been disbarred.

"Daddy did a stretch in prison from 1997 to 2001," Lincoln says quietly. "After he got out, I got him a legit job as a runner with a law firm."

"Excuse me? A runner? Do you mean a gofer?"

"Uh, no. In some places, a 'runner' is somebody who recruits clients for attorneys. Hangs around ERs and places like that, drumming up business."

"I see."

"Well, Daddy managed to stay straight for almost three years. Or at least he didn't get caught during that time. But then he got busted for a big con. It was either the public defender or me, so I defended him in court."

"How did that go?"

"Not well. He was a three-time loser, and the prospects for acquittal were zero. I was hoping for a reasonable plea deal, but the ADA was being a hardass—excuse me, Judge."

"Keep it civil, Mr. Turner."

Lincoln ducks his head like a disciplined child. "Well, not long before Daddy's trial date, he told me he'd got word through a contact in the courthouse that we'd hit the jackpot with the judge we drew. For seventy-five thousand dollars, our judge would supposedly see that Daddy did no more than a year behind bars, then a year of house arrest, and the rest on probation. At that time he was looking at fifteen years without parole, so this deal was like a gift from the gods."

"You're talking about bribery, Lincoln."

"I'm talking about the Chicago judicial system. I know it sounds bad, but this was a *judge* asking for the money. This was the real world, not some moot court."

"So, what did you do?"

"I tried to find that seventy-five thousand dollars."

"How did you go about that?"

"First, I asked Mama for it. I was pretty sure she still had some money squirreled away. But she wouldn't lift a finger to help Daddy, not by then. After her mother died in '96, she lost a lot of empathy for Mr. Junius Jelks."

And why was that? I wonder. But Shad doesn't ask the question.

"So where did you get the money for the bribe?" he asks instead.

"From the escrow account of one of my clients."

"You embezzled the money?"

"Yes, sir."

A collective grunt of judgment comes from the gallery, but the tale is far from over. Redemption is still possible for our abused urchin.

"And what happened when you tried to pay the bribe?" Shad asks.

"The judge's bagman took the money. But just by bad luck, my client learned I had dipped into his account, and he went after me. Before I knew what had happened, I'd been suspended, and Daddy had been sentenced to fifteen years without parole."

"What happed to the money?"

"What do you think? The judge and his bagman played dumb. They're probably still laughing today."

"You must have had some hard feelings toward Junius Jelks by that time."

"Not really, to tell you the truth. Not then. I thought we'd both been screwed by the system. I mean, he was guilty of fraud, sure, and I of embezzlement. But in my eyes, what that judge did was ten times worse. Abusing the public trust for his own gain?"

"Will you ever be allowed to practice law again?"

"Maybe. I hope so. First I have to pay restitution, but that's hard to do when I can't practice law to earn the money. It's a catch-22."

"Your mother wouldn't help you pay the restitution?"

"No, sir. She thought I would just give the money to Daddy. Which he was asking me to do. He wanted to hire another lawyer and try to go after that crooked judge."

"But you did ask your mother for the money?"

"Yes, sir. She flew into a rage. She said she wouldn't waste one dollar trying to help Junius Jelks. They'd found her cancer by then, and she was pretty depressed. I think she blamed Daddy for most of the bad that had happened to us. She was screaming that he'd ruined my legal career."

"Did you not blame Junius Jelks for that?"

"Not like she did."

"Why not?"

"I don't know. I felt like there was something wrong inside of Mama. She had some kind of hate for Daddy that I didn't understand. I thought it was her hate that had cursed us, somehow."

"How did Jelks react when you told him you couldn't get money for an attorney?"

"He went crazy. He was facing fifteen years of hard time."

"What did he say to you?"

"He told me I was useless. A waste of good air. Then he said that didn't surprise him, 'cause I wasn't no son of his anyway."

"How did you react to that?"

"I thought he was kidding. But then something happened to his face, and I knew he wasn't. It was like the mask came off. The last one. He'd worn masks all his life, conning people. He was a master of disguise, never showing who he really was. But that day I saw the real Junius Jelks. And there was nothing in his eyes but anger, fear, and hatred."

"Did you ask him who your real father was?"

Lincoln nods.

Judge Elder says, "Please give a verbal response."

Lincoln looks up at the judge. "Is it all right to use profanity?"

"You can repeat what he told you."

"He told me that Mama had been raped by a bunch of Ku Klux Klansmen back in Mississippi. He said one of those cracker bastards was my father."

"Oh, *Lord,*" cries an older black woman from behind me, and a dozen other people join her.

"Junius said he'd lied to me all those years because Mama wanted him to, but he was done with her now, and me, too. He didn't want me thinking he was my daddy anymore. He said it made him sick to look at me. Every time he looked at me, he saw some dirty-ass klukker. Said he always had."

Murmurs of sympathy and condemnation rise in volume behind me.

"Did you believe what he'd told you?" Shad asks.

"Not at first."

"Why not?"

"Well . . . because I don't look white. Or even half white."

"Did you ask your mother about the Klan story?"

"Yes. She denied it. She told me that the rape had happened, but that none of those men were my father. She said my father was a man she'd met when she first got to Chicago."

"Did you believe her?"

"I wasn't sure. *I wanted* to believe her. I asked if he was white or black. She said black. She said he'd been a married man, but he was dead by then, so there was no use telling me his name."

"Did you believe her?"

"I believed her about the Klan part. But I didn't believe my real father was dead, whoever he was. I sensed she was lying to me. To protect me, maybe, but lying all the same."

"How did you sense it?"

"I can always tell when people are lying. It's something I learned working cons with Junius Jelks. Don't ever try lying to a grifter. They always know. That ability helped me a lot in court."

"But, Mr. Turner, you've already told us that your mother had been successfully lying to you throughout your life, and you didn't know it. Now you say you always know when someone is lying? How do you account for that?"

Lincoln's eyelids slide halfway down over his eyes as he ponders this. After about twenty seconds, he blinks and looks around like a man awaking from a trance. "I'll tell you. When a woman who never lies tells her *first* lie . . . nobody questions it. Nobody catches on, because they can't even imagine that person trying to deceive them. It's the Big Lie. But inside a family, see? And that's why I never caught on. My mama *never* lied. So the one thing she did lie about, I never picked up on—even though she had lied about it every day of my life."

Shad nods soberly. "Now, to clarify, Lincoln, this conversation with your mother about the Ku Klux Klan rape took place how long ago?"

"Seven months ago. About four months before she died."

"And your mother had already been diagnosed with lung cancer?"

"That's right."

"How did you react to all she'd said?"

"I started pulling away from her. Pushing her away, I guess."

"Even though she was terminally ill?"

"Yes. I'm not proud of it, but I couldn't get over the fact that she'd been lying to me since I was a child. My whole life had been a lie."

"What was your next clue to your true paternity?"

"As Mama got sicker, I had to start taking over some of her affairs. That's when I discovered a box hidden in her apartment, filled with old records, souvenirs, and memorabilia. James Turner's war medal was in there, the real James Turner. There were a couple of letters, too, and some photocopies of checks from the 1970s."

"Were the letters signed?"

"No."

"What name was on the checks?"

"Thomas Cage, M.D."

At least a dozen people behind me mutter "*Mm-mm-mm*" under their breath.

"Let the record show that these checks were stipulated into evidence on Monday," Shad says. "Now, were there any other clues in the box?"

"There was a Polaroid snapshot of Mama with a man."

"What man?"

"That man right there. Dr. Tom Cage."

"What did it show?"

"They were standing in a room with a sheet wrapped around them."

"Were they clothed beneath the sheet?"

"They didn't appear to be, no."

"Judge, we'd like to enter this photograph into evidence and let the jury examine it."

If Quentin is ever going to object, now is the time. But he doesn't. Even as Joe Elder looks expectantly at him, Quentin simply watches Shad carry the old Polaroid snapshot over to the jury and give it to the woman seated at bottom left in the box. Her eyes narrow, then widen, and then her whole face goes red. I can't bear to turn and look at my mother's face. Ahead of me, my father simply stares straight ahead, at the judge's bench. My mother might as well be a mannequin posed beside me, for all the life she shows.

"What did you do with what you'd found in the box?" Shad asks.

"I confronted my mother with it."

"How did she react?"

"She finally told me the truth. The real truth."

"Which was?"

"She said my father was Dr. Tom Cage, from Natchez, Mississippi. She'd known it from the beginning. She'd been protecting him all those years. That was why she'd lied to me, and to Jelks."

"Did she say anything else about Dr. Cage during that conversation?"

"She told me that a lot of the money that put me through school had come from him."

"This is very important, Lincoln. Did she say whether or not Dr. Cage knew he was your father?"

Lincoln's brown face darkens with blood. "Of course he knew!"

"Did your mother tell you that?"

"Yes. That's why he sent the money all those years. Mama said Dr. Cage had kept us going during the times that Daddy was spending every dime she made. And she begged me not to do anything to disrupt his family life."

"He's lying," Mom whispers in my ear.

"About what?"

"Tom never knew he had a son by that woman."

Shad says, "How did that make you feel?"

"Sick," Lincoln replies. "That man had ruined our lives, and Mama still worshipped him. She said most other men would have left her high and dry with her baby, but Dr. Cage had always provided for us. I couldn't make her see different."

"Can you prove Dad didn't know about the child?" I whisper to Mom.

"How can I prove a negative?"

"You can't. And the jury will see him sending that money for so long as proof."

Mom's voice grows louder in my ear. "Tom could have been sending that simply out of guilt over the affair! Or because she was raped and had to leave town. It doesn't mean he knew."

She sounds so certain that a question occurs to me. "Mom . . . did you know Dad was sending that money?"

My mother gives me a glare that could freeze vodka, and I face forward again.

Shad has moved closer to Lincoln, and now he really does his best to imitate Dr. Phil. "How did that make you feel, Lincoln?"

Again Quentin should be objecting—feelings have little to do with facts—yet again he remains silent.

"I hated her," Lincoln says bitterly. "I never wanted to see her again. That's what I thought then, anyway."

"Did you tell your mother that?"

He nods, and tears run down his face. "I told her I was glad she was dying."

Lincoln Turner may be tailoring the truth to fit his goals, but on this point I believe he is telling the truth.

"How did you feel about Dr. Cage at that time?"

"I wanted to kill him."

If I were about to cross-examine Lincoln, I would begin by creating the impression that by pushing hard for a murder charge against Dad in the beginning, he was attempting to use the legal system to carry out this desire for revenge. But will Quentin do the same?

"What did you actually do?" Shad asks.

"I broke off all contact with my mother."

"Even though she was dying?"

"Yes. I told you, I've got some anger issues. Back then, I blamed her for everything bad that had ever happened to me." Lincoln's dark eyes move from the district attorney to the defense table, where my father sits beside Quentin. "And *him,* of course. Dr. Cage."

"Did you have any idea how your mother's illness was progressing?"

"After she came back to Mississippi to die, my auntie—Cora Revels—would call and tell me how she was doing."

"Did you tell Cora that you knew Dr. Cage was your father?"

"I did after she told me it was Dr. Cage taking care of Mama down here."

"Did you ever come visit your mother again, Lincoln?"

"No, sir. But I got to feeling worse and worse about the things I'd said to her. After a while, I wanted to tell her I'd forgiven her before she passed—even if it wasn't quite true. I knew it would make her passing easier. Personally, I think it was telling all those lies for so long that gave her the cancer. It poisoned her."

"Did you get to tell your mother you'd forgiven her?"

"No."

"Why not?"

"One night, Auntie Cora called and told me she thought Mama didn't have much time. She didn't tell me about the assisted-suicide pact, but she told me she was pretty sure Mama wouldn't last more than twenty-four hours."

"What did you do?"

"I jumped into my truck and drove straight through from Chicago to Natchez."

"Where were you when your mother died?"

"Thirty minutes north of Natchez."

Shad bows his head and lets this terrible irony sink in. After a few seconds, he says, "Why didn't you call your mother during that long drive?"

"I was getting updates from Cora, telling me to hurry, you know? Then suddenly she stopped calling me. I called Cora a few times, but I kept getting her voice mail."

"But you didn't call Cora's house and talk to your mother?"

"No, sir."

"Why not?"

"Part of me was afraid *he* would be there. Dr. Cage. Another part wanted him to be there when I got there."

"Is that the only reason you didn't call your mother?"

"No, sir. You don't say the kind of things I needed to say to her over the telephone. Not to your mama. You need to hold somebody's hand to say that."

Several women in the jury nod, both black and white.

"Do you wish now that you had called her that night?"

"Yes, sir. I do."

"What would you have said?"

Lincoln Turner swallows hard and looks toward the ceiling. "Hold on just a little longer, Mama. I'm coming home."

Three women in the jury box take handkerchiefs from their purses and wipe their eyes. The rest are looking daggers at my father. The men don't look too happy with him, either.

"Wouldn't have done no good, though," Lincoln says in despair. "He'd given her the morphine by then, and Cora was passed out at the neighbor's house."

Shad bows his head again, as though gathering himself after being wrung out emotionally. "Let's clarify something. Junius Jelks, your mother's husband and widower, never knew who your real father was. Is that correct?"

"That's right."

"All right. Now . . . what did you find when you arrived at Cora Revels's house in the wee hours of December twelfth?"

"By then, Auntie had come back home, and I told her to call 911. The paramedics were there."

"Did your aunt mention Dr. Cage to you?"

"Not at first. But within an hour, she told me about the assisted-suicide pact."

"Yesterday Cora Revels testified that, at that point, she believed that what had taken place was an assisted suicide."

"She told me the same thing."

"But you didn't believe her?"

"The scene looked chaotic to me. It didn't look like the scene of an assisted suicide."

"Do you have enough experience to make that judgment?"

"I'm no expert. But it didn't look as though Mama had died peacefully. I didn't know the Mississippi law on assisted suicide, but I knew that if Dr. Cage had given her the injection himself, he was guilty of murder."

"I see." Shad starts to walk back to his table, but then he turns back to the witness. "Tell me this, Lincoln. Did you hope that Dr. Cage had given her the injection? That he was guilty of murder?"

"At that time? Yes, sir. I did."

The silence that follows this statement is absolute.

"And now?"

"Now . . . I just want to know the truth."

"Thank you." Shad gives Lincoln a sympathetic smile, then walks to his chair and sits down. He doesn't look at Quentin when he says, "Your witness."

Judge Elder is looking at his watch and probably thinking of his stomach when the click and whir of Quentin's chair announces that he will indeed cross-examine Lincoln Turner.

Quentin's chair rolls up to the lawyer's podium, then past it, and stops about ten feet from Lincoln, who stares back with sullen defiance.

"Hello, Mr. Turner," Quentin says in his warm baritone.

Lincoln nods warily. He is facing a man whose cases he probably studied in law school.

"That's a mighty sad story you just told."

Lincoln offers no comment.

"Judge," Shad complains, "is there a question on the horizon?"

Joe Elder gives Shad a dark look. "Mr. Johnson, Mr. Avery just allowed you to conduct a fireside chat with your witness. Be patient."

"Yes, Your Honor."

Quentin hasn't broken eye contact with Lincoln since rolling up to the witness box. But now he looks down, touches his joystick, and makes a quarter turn toward the jury. "Before we get into any of the substantive issues you raised, Mr. Turner, I want to get my chronology straight. I find that it sometimes helps me—and also jury members—to work backwards from the present rather than forward from a past event. All right?"

"Whatever you say."

Quentin gives a tight smile. "You stated that you did not see your mother from the time you had the confrontation over Tom Cage until she lay dead in her sister's home. Is that correct?"

"Yes."

"And you never got to tell your mother you'd forgiven her, because you didn't arrive from Chicago in time. You were still thirty minutes outside of town when she died."

I can see the lawyer in Lincoln trying to figure out where Quentin is going with these questions, but Quentin's casual tone gives no clue to what he considers important.

"That's right," Lincoln says.

"All right. Now, you stated that you wanted to kill Tom Cage after you learned he was your father."

"That's right."

"And you only learned that fact three months before your mother died?"

"Yes."

"Do you still want to kill Dr. Cage?"

Lincoln looks like he'd prefer to kill Quentin Avery right now, but the blaze of anger in his eyes slowly subsides. "No, I don't want to kill him. I don't want nothing from him."

Quentin draws back his head in surprise. "You want him to go to jail, don't you?"

"If the jury believes he should."

Quentin smiles at this. "Come now, Mr. Turner. Don't you believe that Tom Cage murdered your mother?"

"Yes."

"And didn't you prompt the DA to begin the investigation into her death?"

"Any son would have done the same."

Quentin nods agreeably. "But you never wanted anything from Dr. Cage, you said?"

"You mean money? Or something like that?"

"I mean anything."

Lincoln looks down into his lap, as though genuinely lost in thought. Then he looks up and says, "I wanted his acknowledgment. When Mama told me he was my father, what I really wanted was to hear that he wasn't ashamed of me. That I meant something to him. But that ain't nothing but a little boy's dream." Lincoln gives me a baleful glare. "Tom Cage had his white son over there, the mayor. What would he want with me? The truth is, he wished I'd never been born—and he still does."

A pall of ill will toward the Cage family falls over the court. I can feel it like a sudden drop in temperature, like the shadow of storm clouds passing overhead.

Quentin regards Lincoln for several seconds in silence. Then, after glancing up at Judge Elder, he rotates his chair and whirs back toward the defense table. Just before reaching it, he rotates to face Lincoln again.

"If you didn't want anything from Dr. Cage—nothing but his acknowledgment, as you claim—then why do you think your mother hid his identity from you all those years?"

Lincoln blinks slowly in the face of Quentin's question. At length, he says, "I think she was more worried about protecting him than helping me. But I don't know for sure. And thanks to Tom Cage, I never will."

Quentin smiles faintly, as though in appreciation of a fine line heard at a play. "No further questions, Judge."

"Redirect?"

"No, Your Honor," Shad replies.

Quentin's suddenly truncated cross-examination leaves everyone perplexed, including Lincoln Turner.

Judge Elder recovers first, and says, "It's past twelve o'clock. Let's all have some lunch. We'll resume at one fifteen."

CHAPTER 38

RUSTY AND I are escorting my mother and sister out of the courthouse through the side door that leads to City Hall when my cell phone pings to alert me to a text message. Checking the screen, I see DANFORTH WASHINGTON on the LCD. Dan Washington is Jewel Washington's son. I hate to be rude to my own mother, who is talking, but I can't afford to ignore a message from the county coroner, a staunch ally of both me and my father.

"Just a second, Mom. This is important."

Darting through the jostling people to the wall, I read Jewel's text.

Urgent we talk f2f. Mrs. Petros is out of town. I'll be in the courtyard behind her house in five minutes. Can u get there?

The antebellum home Jewel is referring to stands only two blocks from the courthouse. I type: *On my way,* then press SEND.

"What is it, Penn?" Mom asks, reaching the wall at last. "Not trouble, I hope?"

"No, I just need to talk to somebody. I'll be home soon," I promise. "Let Mia take some time for herself, if she will."

Mom nods, but she can't manage a smile.

Rusty looks back with an inquisitive arch of the eyebrows.

"This is chaos," I tell him. "Find Tim and his guys, and don't leave Mom's side until you do. Tell Tim I'm fine alone for a half hour."

"I've got her, buddy. Who you meeting?"

"Jewel," I whisper.

Rusty's eyes widen, but he says nothing, and I jog down the steps to Washington Street, ignoring the reporters and texting Serenity as I run.

hav 2 meet somebody. tlk2 u soon as i can.

AT THE CORNER of Washington and Wall stands a house that was built in 1735. When I was a boy, it was owned by a man who operated a rare bookstore out of it. My father would spend hours browsing through the dusty shelves or digging through boxes of the latest acquisitions while I toyed with more esoteric merchandise. The book dealer owned a gold-headed cane that had belonged to George Washington Cable when the writer lived in New Orleans. I often pretended that the cane had a sword tip concealed in it, and the dealer would play the role of villain for me. When he died, the old man left that cane to my father. Now it lies in a treasured place on one of the bookshelves in my father's study.

Jewel chose this house for its proximity to both the courthouse and her office. She had to walk only one block to reach it. Behind the two-story colonial is a courtyard bounded by a high, ivy-covered wall of crumbling brick. One gate opens onto the street, and it's this that I slip through, into a fragrant, verdant world of flower beds and hanging plants.

The county coroner sits at a wrought-iron table in the corner of the courtyard, smoking a cigarette with intense concentration. I walk over and sit far enough away that I don't have to breathe the smoke as she exhales it.

"Mrs. Petros would kill you if she saw you smoking out here."

"She's on a bicycle trip in France. I don't think her eyes are that good."

"What's going on, Jewel?"

"I'm not sure, but something's rotten in the sheriff's department. And you need to know about it."

"That's not exactly news with Billy Byrd wearing the star."

"How about tampering with evidence?"

"Talk to me."

Jewel takes one last drag, then stubs out the cigarette, stands, and throws the butt over the high wall behind her. "About an hour ago, I ran into a deputy down at the convenience store. A black deputy."

"Okay."

"He's kind of been giving me the eye for a while, so when he pulled me aside, I figured he was trying to flirt with me. He wasn't. He told me he had overheard two white deputies talking about your father's case in the locker room. They were laughing about how slick they had done something."

"What?"

"He didn't hear enough to be sure. But they were joking about hair and fiber. He thinks they were joking about 'losing' some potential evidence. That, and maybe substituting random hair and fiber for some left by a potential perp."

"Shit. That's serious, but pretty vague. Would the guy be willing to talk to me?"

Jewel moves her head slowly from side to side. "He's scared of losing his job already. And don't tell me you can get him on at the police department, because the benefits over there *suck*."

"I hear you. Would he try to find out more than what he has already?"

"I told him to. We might get lucky, but he's not going to risk his career for me. I'm still hot for my age, but not *that* hot."

I take a good minute to think this over, and Jewel doesn't interrupt me.

"If they're screwing with evidence," I think aloud, "that means they know Dad's innocent."

"Not necessarily. They may just be piling on, trying to make sure he doesn't skate thanks to Quentin's courtroom tricks."

"What tricks? I'm not sure he has any left."

Jewel gives me a sharp look. "Don't be too quick to judge him. He's a sly old fox, is Quentin."

When her smile turns wistful, my eyes widen. "Don't tell me . . . you and Quentin?"

She laughs softly. "Ol' Q got around in the old days. When I was a nurse, I was a witness in a malpractice case he was handling. I caught his eye, just like every other pretty young thing. He took a couple of depositions from me. No assistants present."

I shake my head in wonder, amazed by the connections we go through life without seeing.

"Jewel, Dad's hair and fiber were all over Cora Revels's house. From what you've said, those deputies must have destroyed evidence that would incriminate someone else—someone who stands a reasonable chance of being accused of the crime. Because otherwise, even if we had whatever hair and fiber they destroyed, we wouldn't know whose hair to compare it to."

Jewel gives me a slow nod.

"What kind of hair would stand out in that house?" I ask.

"Caucasian, baby."

"Exactly. Apart from Henry Sexton and my father, how many white people visited that house in the past few weeks, or even months?"

"Not many. And the most likely in my book would be Snake Knox and his buddies."

"Goddamn it," I mutter, surprised to feel a blossom of hope in my heart. Despite all my anger and resentment at my father, some part of me still desperately longs for him to be innocent. "I think Cora Revels knows they were there, and she's flat-out lying about it."

"Wouldn't surprise me."

"But why should she lie about that?"

Jewel shrugs. "Fear of the Knoxes?"

"Maybe. Jewel, if your deputy would go on the record, I could—"

"Forget it, Penn. He won't do that unless he's got harder evidence than he has now. A lot harder. So don't be jumping the gun and telling anybody about this."

"Then what the hell can I do with it?"

"Use your head. I figure maybe you've got some connections of your own inside that sheriff's department. Somebody who owes you a favor. Or your daddy. He's bound to have patients on Byrd's payroll. Maybe they can find out what went down with the evidence."

"Okay . . . I hear you."

Jewel stands and lays her hand on my shoulder. "There's one other thing."

"What?"

"My friend says Billy Byrd is better friends with Billy Knox than he ought to be."

"Billy Byrd and Billy Knox know each other?"

"Are you kidding me? Byrd's daddy worked at the Triton plant with Frank Knox back in the day. And the sheriff goes on vacations over to Billy Knox's fishing camp in Texas. Strange bedfellows, wouldn't you say?"

"No, it makes sense."

The look in Jewel's eyes tells me she hasn't confided everything that's worrying her.

"Come on, Jewel, give me the rest. And don't sugarcoat it."

"I'm worried about your daddy. He's segregated in his own cell over there, but that don't mean he doesn't come into contact with other inmates at times. Or that the guards aren't with him out of sight of the cameras now and then."

"Are you saying Billy Byrd might try to kill Dad while he's in custody?"

"I didn't say that. But I am saying that if *somebody* wanted to hurt him, it might not be as hard as it should be."

If Jewel is worried about this, then the danger is real.

"So whatever stroke the title of mayor gives you," she goes on, "I'd use it to make sure your daddy's under surveillance at all times in there."

"Being mayor of this town is like trying to run a company with Monopoly money."

She shakes her head sadly. "I can't believe Quentin hasn't found some way to spring Doc out of that jail anyway."

"That's up to Judge Elder. And Quentin says he's got something against either him or Dad, but he doesn't know which, or what it could be. Even Dad claims not to know."

Jewel is clearly pondering this question. "I never heard much trash about Joe Elder, so I never looked at him too close. He's from across the river, though, in Ferriday, same as those Double Eagles."

"But he's . . ."

"What?" The coroner gives me an expectant look. "B-L-A-C-K?"

"Yeah."

"Maybe he's color-blind."

"What do you mean?"

"Maybe he only sees green." Jewel gives me a wink. "I'll ask around."

I give her a hug, then head for the courtyard gate. As I touch the rusted handle, she says, "I don't know if you know, but Shad's about to call an out-of-town witness."

I stop and turn back. "Who?"

"I don't know. But he's an old guy, and he flew in from Ohio."

"Is he some kind of expert?"

Jewel turns up her palms. "No idea. I'm just giving you what help I can."

"Thanks, Jewel."

She blows me a kiss, then picks up her cigarettes and lighter from the table. She won't leave until I've been gone at least five minutes.

After exiting the courtyard, I stand on the sidewalk of Washington and try to decide my next move. If I walk two blocks west, I'll be at Edelweiss, and I can relate Jewel's information to Quentin face-to-face. If I walk five blocks east, I can be home with Annie. After a few seconds' deliberation, I turn east and dial Doris Avery's cell phone. She answers on the second ring.

"It's Penn," I hear her say.

"Is he calling to congratulate me," Quentin asks, "or to bitch at me some more?"

"Did you hear that?" Doris asks.

"Yep. But I'm not calling to either bury or praise him. This is kind of an emergency."

I hear a clatter as she hands the phone to Quentin. He protests a little, but at last he comes on the phone. "What is it?"

"You know the county coroner, I believe? Better than most?"

This kills Q's attitude in a hurry. "I seem to recall that case, yeah."

"She just passed me some disturbing information, and I'm not talking about your cocksmanship."

"Let's hear it."

As quickly and obliquely as I can, I relate everything Jewel told me about what the deputy overheard, and the conclusions I have drawn. Quentin listens without interrupting, but when I finish, he says, "What do you want me to do with that?"

"I just thought you should know."

"Well, now I know."

"Aren't you pissed off about it?"

"I'm not going to raise my blood pressure over something I expected from the start of this case. Billy Byrd's the kind of throwback who'd beat a prisoner with a phone book, open his cell, then shoot him in the back and say he tried to escape. Tampering with evidence is nothing to that jackass. And we both know the DA's not above holding back exculpatory evidence. So, what's new about this?"

"Well, this obviously means they're trying to conceal someone's involvement in the crime. And Jewel says Byrd is tight with Billy Knox."

"And?"

"Well, that would mean Billy Byrd is up on the stand trying to convict Dad while privately trying to protect a wanted criminal who probably murdered Viola."

"You're right. But you'll never prove that. Whatever hair and fiber evidence supported that is obviously gone. Jewel's deputy friend isn't going to testify, so that's the end of this discussion."

"But . . . you're telling me Dad's definitely innocent?"

"Isn't that the case I'm making in the courtroom?"

"You haven't done a goddamn thing in the courtroom!"

"Be patient, my brother. The hardest part of anything is waiting. But my day's coming."

Dealing with Quentin is beyond exasperating. "By the way, Shad's about to call some old guy from Ohio to the stand. Any idea who that might be?"

"Possibly."

That's clearly all Quentin's going to give me.

"Are we through, Penn?"

"No. Jewel's afraid for Dad's physical safety in Byrd's jail. So am I."

"I've thought a lot about that, and I've discussed it with Tom. We feel like the isolation procedures are sufficient to protect him."

"You know that's bullshit. I think we need to call the state attorney general and have him crawl up Billy Byrd's ass."

"Don't do that, Penn."

"Why not? At least Byrd would be too scared to let anything happen to Dad under that kind of microscope."

"Byrd's already under a microscope. Penn, I'll be frank with you: this case isn't about any goddamn hair and fiber. You need to let that go."

"You don't know that."

"You don't know what I know, boy. Now, don't talk to anybody about what Jewel said. All you'll accomplish is to put her life at risk. I'll talk to your father about the security issue, too."

"Get back to me after you do. I mean tonight, Quentin. If you don't, I'm calling the AG."

"Good luck with that. I'm hanging up now."

And he does.

CHAPTER 39

BY THE TIME I reached home, I only had ten minutes to gobble down a sandwich and give Annie a hug before it was time to head back to the courthouse. Yet again she pleaded to be allowed to accompany us, and behind her I could see that Mia would give almost anything to attend the trial rather than sit in the house behind armed guards. But after Lincoln's damning testimony about my father's secret life, I don't have to take the heat for refusing. My mother tells Annie she's absolutely forbidden from attending court.

"Ninety percent of what's being said in that building is lies," she declares, and neither Jenny nor I challenge her.

Eight minutes later, Tim delivers us to the courthouse steps, where he turns the wheel over to one of his associates and escorts us through the milling throng to our seats inside.

Serenity has reclaimed her seat in the first row of the balcony; or perhaps she didn't leave during lunch. If she had, she'd never have gotten that seat back. A pang of guilt hits me for not bringing her a sandwich. As I wave at her, she holds up a brown paper bag and gives me a quick grin.

Of course. Leave it to an ex-soldier to come prepared.

A sudden hubbub tells me Judge Elder is making his entrance. The tall robed figure looks neither right nor left as he makes his way to the bench. Once he's settled and everyone takes their seats again, he says, "Call your next witness, Mr. Johnson."

Shad rises. "The State calls Major Matthew M. Powers, United States Air Force, Retired."

This time, when the back door of the courtroom opens, my father turns in his chair and rises to see over the crowd of spectators. The bloodless cast of his face looks like that of a man who has seen the dead walk.

Powers must be the man from Ohio, I think.

Though he must be over seventy, Major Powers strides to the witness box with the assured gait of a man ten years younger. He still has all his hair, close cropped and iron gray, and his eyes are clear and blue. He wears a gray suit over a white dress shirt and narrow black tie.

As he's sworn in, I sense that my father has been bowled over by his appearance. Twice Dad has bent his head and whispered something to Quentin, but Quentin just patted his arm in reassurance. I have a feeling that Quentin—along with my father—is about to pay the price for not requesting discovery.

"Major Powers," Shad begins, "do you know the defendant in this case, Dr. Tom Cage?"

"I do. Or I did, long ago."

"When did you meet him?"

"On one occasion. November thirtieth, 1950."

"And where was this?"

"Beside a road in North Korea, southwest of the Chosin Reservoir."

Even before Major Powers finishes his answer, I know that nothing he could tell us about something that happened during the Korean War is admissible as evidence in this case. It must fall under the heading of "prior bad acts." Yet Quentin shows no sign of preparing to object. It's all I can do not to get to my feet and do it myself.

"What were you doing there at that place and time?" Shad asks the major.

"I had been flying a Lockheed Shooting Star for the air force. The F80 was designed as an air-to-air fighter, but on November twenty-fifth the Chinese troops that had secretly flooded over the border hit the Second Division and overran all the American positions, so we were pressed into service in a ground support role—"

"Penn?" whispers my mother. "They shouldn't be able to bring Korea into this trial, should they?"

"No."

"Then why doesn't Quentin stop Johnson?"

"I don't know."

"Why doesn't Tom tell him to stop this?"

Mom's right. Quentin should be objecting like crazy. Yet even though Judge Elder knows this testimony should be inadmissible, he wants to hear what Major Powers has to say. The jury does, too. That's why Quentin isn't objecting. He doesn't want to be seen as trying to hide any part of the truth. By refusing to protest, he's saying, *We're all here to get to the bottom of things, so to hell with the rules. We're not afraid of what anybody has to say.*

"I think Dad and Quentin are on the same page, Mom."

"Then *you've* got to stop it."

"I *can't,*" I whisper.

"You're on the legal team, aren't you?"

"Technically."

"Then object!"

"Dad doesn't want me to do that."

"*I* want you to. I'm telling you to do it. Your father's not thinking straight."

"And how did you come to meet Dr. Cage in Korea?" Shad asks from the podium.

"Mom, I'll help you get Quentin fired at the next recess, but I'm not going to create a scene that might be damaging to Dad by getting into a fight with Quentin in front of the jury."

She closes her eyes as though to block out the exchange occurring before her.

"On November twenty-eighth," answers the major, "my aircraft was hit by ground fire, and I had to crash-land the plane. Chinese troops were trying to get to me when some stragglers from a shattered American infantry unit pulled me out of the cockpit and took me with them.

"I'd sustained serious injuries to my legs, but with the massive attack under way, there was no way to get me to a MASH unit, or even a collecting station. The marines had been hit at Chosin Reservoir by this time, and they were holding up pretty well, but the army was in chaos across the peninsula. There was only one road leading south through the mountains from the Eighth Army's Ch'ongch'on River positions. After some hours, I was loaded into a box ambulance that was part of a massive convoy trying to retreat down that road. We could only move vehicles in small groups because the Chinese controlled the high ground on both sides of the pass, which had become known as the Gauntlet."

"Please continue."

"Dr. Cage was the medic tending the wounded in the back of the ambulance. Conditions in the vehicle were pretty horrific. Men lying above were defecating and urinating on the men below them. Not what you'd expect in the American army. There were seven other wounded, plus myself. They were from two army units that had been virtually wiped out. Anyway, our turn to run the Gauntlet came after midnight on November thirtieth. I guess that makes it December first. About ten minutes into our run, Chinese machine guns opened up from both sides of the road. Our driver was hit, along with some of the wounded, and the ambulance went over the shoulder and rolled two hundred feet into a gorge."

Major Powers has the jury; nothing rivets civilians like a true war story. But I have a feeling my father isn't the hero of this tale.

"Were any soldiers killed during this incident?" Shad asks.

"Yes. Two by gunfire, and two more by the subsequent crash. The driver sustained serious injuries and was trapped under the steering wheel."

"Do you know what the driver's name was?"

"Yes. Private Walter Garrity."

Shad glances over his shoulder as though looking for Walt. Major Powers follows his gaze. I do, too, but I see no sign of my old friend.

"What happened after the ambulance came to a stop?" Shad asks.

"When the smoke cleared, five men were left alive in back, including myself and Private Cage. Cage checked the condition of the driver, who was screaming in pain."

"What was the condition of the other men?"

"Dire. They were moaning more than screaming, I guess. They'd all been gravely wounded before being loaded into the ambulance. The accident only aggravated their injuries."

"But they were conscious?"

"All but one. He had a head wound, and he was in and out. Everyone was in shock at this time."

"What happened next?"

"Private Cage freed the driver from the front, which was a painful ordeal. Private Garrity turned out to be a medic as well. At this point, both medics climbed into the back and assessed the wounded. It was obvious that none of the survivors could move under our own power, or bear stretchers. One of the boys' legs had been shattered by bullets. Another was paralyzed from the waist down. Private Cage then told Private Garrity that he was going to try to climb back up to the road and get help. Private Cage had some minor wounds from an earlier engagement, but he was the only man healthy enough to make the attempt."

"What happened next?"

"Cage left the ambulance, then returned approximately forty minutes later. He said that the only American vehicles left on the road were wrecks filled with dead, and the Chinese on the heights were still firing at anything that moved."

"Did you believe him?"

"Frankly, I've never been sure he went up that cliff at all. But that's just my opinion."

"What happened then?" Shad asks.

"Private Cage asked Garrity to go outside to hear his report, which he did. For privacy, I'm sure, but we all heard it. The two medics decided that help was unlikely to arrive before the wounded in the back expired."

"You heard this conversation clearly?"

"Yes."

"Could the other wounded men?"

"Yes. The iffy one had slipped into a coma while Cage was gone."

"What was the reaction of the conscious soldiers?"

"Panic, among the two who were alert."

"And your reaction?"

"I was praying, to be honest. Praying for strength. For myself and the medics."

"What happened then?"

"One of the wounded called out to Private Cage. He begged not to be left behind."

"Had Private Cage or Private Garrity made any mention of leaving the ambulance at that time?"

"No. But the situation was clear to everybody. I had a broken femur, and the others were worse off than I was. Climbing a cliff was out of the question. The medics were the only men who had a chance of getting out of that gorge under their own power."

"All right. Go on."

"The medics climbed back inside and gave us their version of the situation."

"Which was?"

"Help was unlikely to arrive before the men died of their wounds or hypothermia. Capture by the enemy was highly likely. That might mean torture, if the rumors we'd been hearing were correct."

"What happened next?"

"Both medics stated that they intended to leave the ambulance and try to reach an American unit. Their stated goal was to bring back assistance."

I hear a collective intake of breath from the crowd behind me.

"*Both* medics?" Shad asks. "Not just one?"

"That's correct."

"Wasn't it their duty to stay with the wounded?"

"I thought so. They obviously didn't."

"So they meant to abandon you where you lay?"

Powers sniffs. "They did offer to instruct me on how to inject morphine, which I already knew from survival training. They said they would place the other wounded within my reach."

"That was nice of them."

"Wasn't it?"

When Quentin doesn't object to this obvious sarcasm, I almost come out of my chair.

"What happened next?"

"One boy kept begging not to be left behind, but the other one had calmed down. He told the medics he'd rather be killed by his own men than captured by the enemy. I could tell that a lot of stories about torture had circulated among the ground troops."

"So this soldier asked to be killed?"

"Yes, sir."

"And the other?"

"I could see that once the idea was broached, the second boy began considering the same desperate choice."

"What happened then?"

"I told the medics that I knew what they were thinking, and that they couldn't do it. It would be murder. Cold-blooded murder."

"What was their response?"

"Private Garrity said it was up to each soldier to make his own choice."

"And then?"

Major Powers shakes his head slowly. "The two conscious boys chose to be injected with a fatal dose of morphine."

Shad nods as though in grave appreciation of Powers having to relive this moment. "And the unconscious one?"

"He was from the same unit as one of the conscious boys. The same hometown. That boy said the one in the coma would choose the same fate if he could. Private Cage didn't want to inject an unconscious man, but the two others persuaded him to do it. My words counted for nothing. I quoted scripture to them, but it fell on deaf ears."

A black woman in the jury utters a sound I can only describe as lamentation.

"Were the soldiers in fact given a lethal dose of morphine?"

"They were."

"Who injected them?"

"Private Cage."

A muffled groan comes from someone in the jury. This time Judge Elder throws a glare at the jury box.

"All three men?" Shad asks.

"Yes. Garrity had a broken shoulder and felt he couldn't do a professional job. But he was in full agreement with the decision."

"Did the medics leave the ambulance immediately after Cage gave the injections?"

"No. They waited until all three men fell unconscious."

"Did they say anything to you?"

"They said that if they made it out alive, they'd come back with help."

"Did you say anything to them?"

"Yes."

"What?"

"I told them they were both going to burn in hell, but that I would see them in Leavenworth first."

Shad turns and looks straight at the jury, as though to be sure they have understood the full import of what has been related to them. "All right. What happened to you after Cage and Garrity left?"

"I watched those poor boys die. Then I slowly froze for about ten hours. Cage had piled some blankets on me, but I ended up losing four toes to frostbite anyway."

"Who got you out?"

"The Chinese finally sent a patrol down to check the wreck. They hauled me up the cliff with a rope rig, then slowly passed me up the line to a Chinese prison camp for interrogation."

"All right, Major. Were there ever any repercussions for what had happened in the ambulance?"

"Yes. After about a month in captivity, I was traded back to our side for a Chinese MiG pilot who'd been shot down. As soon as I got back to South Korea, I reported what had happened to my commander and filed a formal complaint against both Cage and Garrity."

"What was the result of your efforts?"

"Nothing."

Shad looks incredulous. *"Nothing?"*

"A lot of angry phone calls passed between the air force and army brass, but the long and the short of it was, the whole episode was swept under the rug for political reasons."

"What political reasons?"

"General MacArthur had made a terrible blunder by pushing his forces so far north and triggering China's entry into the war. His whole command was in disarray. He wasn't about to let a scandal like what happened in that ambulance break in the stateside press. So he buried it. Cage and Garrity got off scot-free, and I was told to forget it ever happened."

"And did you?"

Despite his rigid composure throughout his testimony, the major's chin quivers now. He has been waiting fifty-five years for this moment. "I'll see those poor boys on my deathbed, Mr. Johnson."

Shad looks over at the jury as though asking if they have any questions, but the horror and disgust on their faces is plain. They have heard all they need to, it seems. I have questioned many witnesses in my time, and a few were like Major Powers. They'd lived for decades with a memory that had festered in them like an abscess, and then, unexpectedly, a chance presented itself for them to walk into a witness box and have a prosecutor lance that abscess for them. And in most of those cases, the testimony that came pouring out was devastating.

"Your witness, Mr. Avery," Shad says, unable to disguise the triumph in his voice.

Quentin is whispering something in my father's ear.

Judge Elder says, "Mr. Avery?"

Quentin looks up as though surprised. "Your Honor?"

"Do you have any questions for this witness?"

"No. No questions, Judge."

As the whole crowd murmurs in amazement, Judge Elder looks down at Quentin as though he has truly lost his mind.

Why has Quentin allowed this? I wonder. For the first time I consider standing to cross-examine a witness. Could I possibly make up some ground with Major Powers? How? I've had no time to prep, and my father never told me anything about the episode in the ambulance, or anything else about his wartime experience. Besides, once Quentin allowed Powers's story to be told, the damage was done.

"You're free to go, Major," Judge Elder says.

Major Powers gets to his feet and marches toward the center aisle with military precision. As he passes the defense table, he pauses, looks down, then hawks and spits on my father's chest.

No one makes a sound. No one except my mother, who emits a soft and desolate cry.

Major Powers stands his ground, as though daring Dad to rise and fight him, but my father merely looks back at him and says, "I'm sorry, Major."

The pilot shakes his head with contempt, then walks down the aisle as though he can't wait to get out of the state of Mississippi.

As Quentin takes a handkerchief from his coat pocket and begins wiping my father's coat and shirt with it, pandemonium erupts in the courtroom. In the balcony I see Serenity on her feet, both hands on the rail, her eyes locked on mine as she slowly shakes her head. When Judge Elder orders a ten-minute recess so that my father can clean up, my mother sags against me, but I jump up and pull Jenny into my seat to support her. I have time for only one thing now.

Firing Quentin Avery.

CHAPTER 40

THE CROWD OF spectators stunned silent by Major Powers spitting on my father are now on their feet and swirling in place like too many cattle forced into a pen. My first instinct is to pass the bar and go straight to Quentin, but a sheriff's deputy blocks my way. Over his shoulder I see the bailiff leading Quentin and my father out of the courtroom through the judge's chambers. With the chaos behind me, it's not hard to see why. As the jury members file into the jury room, George Dobson, the circuit clerk, calls something to the deputy blocking my way, then beckons me into the well of the courtroom.

"What the hell's going on in this trial, Penn?" he asks in an urgent whisper. "Thurgood Marshall's just about got your daddy in the penitentiary. Two days ago I didn't think Shad had a chance in hell of convicting Doc. But if that jury had to vote right now . . . Is Avery all there, or is it time for the nursing home?"

"I'm afraid it's the latter." I grab the clerk's forearm. "If I can get to him before this break is over, I'm going to fire him. Can you get me out through the judge's chambers? If I have to fight my way through this crowd, I'll never catch Quentin in time."

"I'd call that a critical mission." Dobson looks over his shoulder at the guarded door. "Give it fifteen more seconds, then I'll take you through."

"Thanks, George. I owe you."

EVEN AFTER BEING led to the broad hallway between the circuit court and the chancery court via the judge's chambers, I find myself in the midst of a milling crowd. Rising onto tiptoe, I catch sight of Quentin's wheelchair rolling into the tax assessor's office, a deputy walking escort. Casting aside the good manners I was raised with, I bull through the crowd and cover the distance to the door of the tax assessor's office. Through the glass in the door I see a secretary I've known since I was a teenager. Spying me, she tilts her head toward the door to the assessor's private office.

As I reach for the knob, the deputy who escorted Quentin starts to challenge me, but after recognizing me and seeing the look in my eye, he backs off.

"Mrs. Evans," I say, "we might get loud in there."

The secretary picks up her purse and comes around the desk. "Of course, Mr. Mayor. I have an errand to run anyway. Please just lock the door when you leave."

"I will."

Opening the inner door, I see Quentin seated at the window of the private office, looking out at the Eola Hotel four blocks away.

"I told you it was going to get worse before it gets better," he says. Then he turns to me, and I see fatigue and pain in his eyes. The shock of white hair looks less theatrical from up close, and more the result of old age.

"Go ahead," he says with resignation. "Speak your piece."

Only then do I notice Doris standing in the corner of the office, looking as though she's been crying.

"I gave you half a day," I say evenly. "Your time's up."

"I haven't even given my opening statement."

"You're not going to give it. You're done, Quentin. I'm sorry." I look over at Doris, who appears profoundly shaken. "That man should never have been allowed on the stand."

"That depends on your point of view," Quentin says.

"Well, from the point of view of a *lawyer,* the sum total of Major Powers's testimony was inadmissible. And you could have stopped it with a single objection."

"Your father won't fire me, Penn."

I move to my right, demanding that he look me in the eye. "I hope I won't have to ask him to. I'm asking you to step aside, as a point of honor."

Quentin takes a long breath, sighs heavily. "Tell me something. If you take over Tom's case, how are you going to begin?"

"By finding out what happened that night, and building a case from there."

"Tom won't tell you."

"After what just happened in court, he might."

"You're wrong. A little spit isn't much to a man who's faced gunfire."

"That wasn't just spit. That was contempt. And contempt can maim a man like Dad worse than bullets can."

With his trademark click and whir, Quentin backs up and rotates his chair to face me. "I shouldn't have to tell a big-shot prosecutor this, but juries don't like being excluded. They don't like lawyers trying to keep witnesses from saying what they want to say. They don't like judges and lawyers whispering where they can't hear, and they *hate* it when you go back into chambers. As you told me yesterday, we're dealing with an interracial affair, a mixed-race child, a possible mercy killing, even murder of a patient by a doctor. Those are tantalizing issues. And the jury isn't going to take kindly to a slick lawyer saying, 'I'm sorry, you can't see this bit here, as juicy as it may be. Yes, there's a tape of the victim's death, but by exploiting a technicality I'm going to stop you from watching it.' That's not the way I'm going to run this case, my brother. And that's not the way your daddy wants it run."

"He wants the whole truth out there. That's the deal?"

"That's the deal."

"That's quite a change of heart after lying for thirty-eight years, wouldn't you say?"

Quentin dismisses my implication with a wave of his hand. "The jury wants the truth, Penn. And I've finally got a client who's willing to stand by everything he ever did."

"So to hell with the rules of evidence?" I glance at Doris, who obviously shares my confusion. "Let's join hands and listen to Dad's life story from the age of one, then let the jury decide his fate?"

"If that's the way Shad wants to go, so be it."

"What?"

"I trust the jury, Penn. Even at my age. You're still a prosecutor at heart. I don't think the jury's so quick to cast stones."

"But they *are,* Quentin. It's human nature. With some jurors, the higher up you are, the more pleasure they take in pulling you down. With others, the more they worshipped you, the more furious they are when they find you're not who they thought you were."

"That's a sad way to look at the world, brother. You should have a little more faith in your fellow man."

"I'm sorry. I've been through too many murder trials for that."

Quentin shrugs in his wheelchair. "If you think your father's ready to trade me for you, go up to the men's room by the holding cell upstairs. That's where he is. Give it your best shot. I'll abide by his decision."

I'm reaching for the door when Walt Garrity crashes through it, a look of fury in his eye. "I've been looking all over for you," he bellows. Then he looks past me, at Quentin. "You've got to put me on the stand! That goddamn pilot didn't tell half the story."

"Sorry, Captain," Quentin says. "I don't need you."

Incredulous, the old Texas Ranger looks at me, his face almost purple.

"It's not Quentin's decision anymore," I tell Walt, taking hold of his arm. "Or it won't be in five minutes. I'll be calling you to the stand myself in about ten minutes."

"Goddamn right!" Walt throws a glare at Quentin as he leaves the office.

As I follow him, I look back at Doris. "Please answer your cell when I call."

She nods once, and I go.

SHAKEN BY MY confrontation with Quentin, and speeding from adrenaline at the prospect of taking over Dad's defense, I experience the walk to the upstairs restroom in slow motion. As I pick my way through the crowd, an old filmstrip of images flashes like a Super 8 movie projected onto my retinas. I see my father as a younger man, wearing sunglasses and a short-sleeve no-iron shirt in glaring sunlight, looking down at my outstretched hands as I beg him to come into the pool with me. So many summer activities revolved around water in Mississippi, but Dad rarely ever went into pools or ponds, or even the ocean. I can still hear my mother telling me, "Daddy doesn't like to swim," or "Daddy doesn't like the sun." In my mind, this explained why he was always pale, why he never took his shirt off, even when the other dads waded in to lift us onto their shoulders to fight battles in the shallow end.

But a few times, on vacation, Dad did go swimming. Maybe five times in my entire childhood. The time that remains indelible is the summer our parents took us to Hot Springs, Arkansas, for a medical conference. Dad had bought me a toy submarine, a sleek gray plastic model that could actually submerge by means of a dissolvable tablet that trailed bubbles behind the sub. I was having so much fun that I repeatedly begged him to come in, and to my amazement, he finally relented and went back to the room to change into a bathing suit.

When he returned, I saw puckered purple scars on his shoulders, belly, and thighs. Time had faded the marks, but his general color was so pale that they stood out like night crawlers on his skin. Before I could think much about them, Dad splashed into the water and started a game of submarine warfare with me, and I forgot the scars. After we ran out of submerging tablets, he set aside the toy and gave me "real submarine rides" underwater. I'd hold my breath and cling to his neck, then stare at his big freckled shoulders as he frog-kicked between the forest of white legs in the blue-green water of the hotel pool. Looking back now, that might have been the best day of my childhood—the day my daddy did something he hated so that I would be happy. The livid bumps on his shoulders and stomach did little to dampen my fun, but I didn't completely forget them. Later I asked Mom about them, and I saw sadness come into her face.

"Daddy got those in the war," she said.

"How?" I asked. "Did the Germans shoot him?"

"A different war. Koreans shot him, I guess, or Chinese. I don't really know. Daddy doesn't like to talk about it. So don't ask him, all right? Not until you're older."

I promised I wouldn't, and for a long time I didn't. When I finally got up the nerve, at fifteen, Dad shrugged it off and said he'd been hit by shrapnel in Korea, but it was nothing to write home about. Those were his exact words. But if that was so, why did I always perceive a sense of shame when I saw him without his shirt, or wearing short pants? It was like walking into a room and seeing your father's genitals, only a lot more awkward. Like Dad, I had a penis of my own. But I didn't have war wounds. Even now, as a man, I have no firsthand knowledge of war. But after hearing Major Powers's account of what happened in that ambulance, I finally have some idea of what my father did in Korea. Perhaps I also understand the sense of shame that went with his wounds.

Pushing through the men's room door at last, I find Dad leaning over the sink. He looks like a man who's been beaten by someone who knows how to hurt you deep without leaving marks on the surface.

"I'm sorry you had to see that," he says. "I hoped you'd never have to hear that story. Korea wasn't all like what happened in that ambulance."

"It doesn't matter. Nothing will ever change the way I feel about you. But right now's not the time to talk about that. We have to move fast."

"What do you mean, son?"

"Dad . . . Quentin can't represent you any longer. I know you had your own reasons for hiring him, but if you let him continue like this, you'll never hold Annie in your arms again outside a prison."

He blinks as though this prospect has finally begun to sink in. "What would you do if I fired Quentin?"

"Ask for a mistrial. If I don't get that, I'll cross-examine every witness and keep out all inadmissible testimony. The jury should never have heard Major Powers's story, and Judge Elder knows it. The circuit *clerk* just told me we need to fire Quentin."

"But Shad's almost finished his case."

"Has he? I'm afraid he's going to parade a dozen relatives of dead patients through there and have them accuse you of euthanizing their sainted mothers. And Quentin will *let him do it*."

Dad shakes his head. "There won't be any of that."

"How do you know?"

"Because by the time a patient reaches the point where they need some help crossing over—in those very rare cases—the family wants it, too. Often the patient's too far gone to know. And those times . . . well, they're sacred. Nobody's going to come in here and talk about that."

A cautious sense of relief eases some of the pressure in my chest. "I hope you're right. Tell me this. If Walt were called as a witness, could he provide any details that might make the two of you look better than you did in Powers's account?"

While Dad thinks about it, I say, "I think Walt would have killed Major Powers if he met him in the hallway after his testimony."

"Walt suffered a lot that night, and the days after. A lot more than Powers did."

"So, could Walt make up some of that ground in the courtroom?"

Dad finally shakes his head. "No. What happened that night happened pretty much the way Powers described it. But it doesn't matter. Quentin's not going to call Walt as a witness."

"Forget Quentin, Dad. Given his erratic behavior up to now, I'm sure Judge Elder would give me at least a day to prepare a proper defense. Every lawyer in that courtroom thinks Quentin has either lost his mind or is throwing the case on purpose."

Dad looks away.

"Which is it? I know you know."

"He hasn't lost his mind."

"Then he's throwing the case?"

"He's doing what he has to do. What I've told him to do."

"You wanted Major Powers to say those things he said in there today?"

"No. I would have preferred that bit of history stay buried in the snows of Korea. For the sake of those boys' families. Now the media won't stop digging until they figure out who died in that ambulance. I'm sure their parents are all dead, which is a blessing, but there'll be brothers and sisters who'll suffer when they learn what happened."

"Dad, this isn't going to sound noble, but you've got to start thinking about yourself. And if not yourself, then the rest of us. Your family is suffering. Do you understand that?"

"I do."

He's still not looking at me. I hear my voice rising, but I can't stop myself. "If the Double Eagles have threatened us, *tell* me. I'll get us protected until I find a way to put them behind bars."

"You can't protect your family against men like that. Life doesn't mean the same thing to them that it does to us. They'll take risks normal people won't. They know people who'll kill Annie in exchange for a day's supply of methamphetamine."

"So that's it, then? That's the reason you're doing all this? You're exchanging your life for our safety?"

I don't realize how badly I need to hear a yes to that question until he says, "If my going to prison ensures that you and Annie and Jenny and your mother will be safe from now on . . . I'm happy to go. I almost died last October, Penn. I'll be lucky to live another year, even with the best care."

"Stop talking like that! This is like committing suicide because you can't take the pain when a cure might be possible."

As my voice reverberates in the tiled bathroom, Dad steps away from the sink and squeezes my upper arm. "No, it's not. I can endure pain. But there are things I couldn't endure. I've had three months to think about all this. The hardest thing has been not being able to tell you the whole truth. I hope that by the end of this ordeal, you'll understand. But right now, I can't go beyond a certain point."

"Even with all that's at stake?"

"No. Because of it."

A deputy bangs on the door, then opens it a crack. "One minute till the recess is over, Doc."

Dad grabs my arms with surprising strength. "No matter what happens in that courtroom, remember this. What matters is you, not me. You and Annie. Jenny, too. But here, now, alone, I'm going to tell you something, and you don't ever forget it. You *are* me. You hear?" Dad shakes me bodily, his eyes burning into mine. "The older I get, the more I see myself in you. Do you know how that feels? To look at the man you've become, and know I had a part in that? To know I didn't survive that war for nothing? Long after I'm gone, you'll be here, and I'll be alive in you. And in Annie." A smile lights his whole face. "That girl's a Cage through and through."

Hot tears slide down my cheeks. I've been preparing for my father's death for a long time, but to see life and death as he does now . . . it's more than I can take.

"And Lincoln?" I ask softly. "He's your son, too."

Dad winces as though from physical pain. "Lincoln has my genes, yes. But I had nothing to do with shaping him. And all the regret I feel doesn't help him one iota. From what Viola told me, the father Lincoln had was worse than none at all. But let's not dwell on what we can't change."

"And Mom? What about her?"

"There's no time, Penn. But however rough this seems on her . . . this is the bargain Peggy made. I let her down with Viola, God knows, but Peggy fell short, too—in her own eyes, I mean. But I stayed, and to Peggy that's what counts. You hear me? To her people, children are what matter—period. You do what's necessary to protect the next generation. Your mother may not know exactly why I'm doing this, but she knows I've got my priorities straight. And she has enough faith in me to let me do it."

"She doesn't let you see how hard it is on her."

"I know, believe me. But she can take it."

Jesus, the hardness of their generation. "I'm not so sure. If you're convicted . . . she might do something desperate."

Dad actually smiles at this. "Not a chance, boy. Don't give that another thought."

"Time to go, Doc!" cries the deputy, holding open the door.

As he turns to shoo away some rubberneckers in the hall, I force my cell phone into Dad's hand. "Doris and Quentin are waiting for your call. Tell Quentin it's over. Let me defend you, Dad."

He pushes away the phone. "It's too late, Penn. I'm sticking with Quentin. We'll take the hill together or go down fighting."

"But he's *not fighting*."

Dad takes hold of my right wrist and squeezes. "He will. You just keep coming to court. We'll see how much damage a couple of old men can do."

The glint in his eye almost makes me believe, but then I remember how the jury looked when Major Powers spit on his chest. Before I can speak again, he turns to the deputy and says, "Let's go, Jimmy. Back to the trenches."

"Stay right on my ass, Doc. Whole courthouse is full of freaks today."

"I'm with you. Lead on."

CHAPTER 41

WHEN COURT RESUMES, Shad stuns me by calling Walt Garrity as his next witness. It takes a few seconds for me to realize the brilliance of this move, but I do, just in time to explain it to my mother.

"Shad expects Quentin to call Walt to refute Major Powers's account of what happened in the ambulance, so he's doing it himself. This way he can guide the questioning. See? Judge Elder just gave Shad permission to treat Walt as a hostile witness. That means Shad can lead Walt where Shad wants him to go. Plus, Shad can make it painfully clear that Walt's on Dad's side. The irony is, Quentin had no intention of calling Walt."

"But Quentin *can* cross-examine him, right?"

"Quentin could have cross-examined Major Powers, too."

Mom closes her eyes and braces herself for whatever is coming.

"Captain Garrity," Shad begins, "you heard the testimony of Major Powers about what happened in that ambulance on the night of November thirtieth, 1950."

The weathered old Ranger looks as though he is bursting to tell his version of what happened that night. "I did."

"And does your recollection of that night differ in any significant way from the account Major Powers related?"

"As to the sequence of events, no. The *character* of events was a bit different than he portrayed."

"How so?"

"The major's story reminded me of our old reports in the Texas Rangers."

"Back before computers?"

"Back when we rode horses."

Several spectators laugh, but Walt wasn't trying to be funny.

"A typical report might read: '*Pursued robbery suspect south-southeast for three days. Cornered him near Terlingua. Shot suspect next day after altercation with associates. Returned to El Paso.*' It hits the high spots, but it don't exactly cover the subtleties of the thing."

"Well, that's why I've called you up here."

"Is it?" Walt looks skeptical.

"Yes, sir. Please feel free to add anything you believe Major Powers should have included."

"Well, first off, the major wasn't in a position to make the same judgments Tom and I were about those men. Powers had no medical training, beyond survival school for pilots. Even if he'd had training, he had limited mobility, and he suffered a concussion when the ambulance went over the cliff."

I can see the jury warming to Walt's delivery, but Shad seems willing to pay the price to get what he wants from Dad's old friend.

"Second, the major said Tom had only minor wounds himself. In fact, Private Cage had sustained serious shrapnel wounds from fragmentation grenades on the night of November twenty-fifth, when the Chinese first attacked our position."

Shad looks a little disconcerted by this correction of the record. "Go on, Captain."

"Well, we started with eight wounded soldiers in that ambulance—it was an old Dodge WC54, World War Two vintage—which meant we were double loaded, plus me driving and Tom in the back. Most of those boys was wounded so bad they wouldn't have made it to a surgeon even if the ambulance hadn't gone off the road. The accident only caused additional casualties and shock, like the major said. Two GIs were killed by machine-gun fire during the ambush, and two more died during the roll down the cliff. One might have reached the hospital in decent shape if we hadn't been ambushed, but he sustained a skull fracture during the crash. He was in and out briefly, then fell unconscious. But here's my point: as bad as those two conscious boys were hurt—mortally wounded, both of them—they fully understood the situation. No help was coming."

"How did they come to understand it? Through what you and Private Cage told them?"

"Lord, no. The whole damned division was bugging out, and they knew it. All discipline had broken down; the army was in full retreat. I don't like saying it, but wounded were being abandoned all over the place. We could hardly get *tanks* down that road, much less stop and mount a rescue operation. Nobody was going to take time to winch an ambulance back up onto a road that was nothing but a kill zone. And those boys knew that. We all did. Even Powers."

"Let's get back to the wounded men," Shad suggests.

"Let's," Walt says icily. "So . . . I was trapped in the driver's seat, but I could hear fine, better than I wanted to. One boy was crying for his mother; another was screaming in pain. He quieted down when Tom gave him some morphine. That's when Tom came forward and freed me. He did that by breaking my shoulder, by the way. Broke it with an entrenching tool."

A soft gasp sounds in the courtroom.

"Weren't no other way," Walt said. "There wasn't no Jaws of Life down in that godforsaken gorge. Tom told me what he'd have to do to get me out, and I said 'Get on with it, then.' I'd have let him cut my arm off to keep from being captured by those Chicom bastards."

Shad probably figured he had an idea what was coming, but the jury members are hanging on Walt's brusquely delivered words in a way they did not when Powers spoke.

"After Tom freed me, we climbed in the back and tried to figure a way to get those boys back up to the road. We saw right quick we couldn't manage it, so Tom decided to climb the cliff to see if he could get help. We'd heard screaming up there earlier, but that had stopped. Tom's climb took a while, and the wounded didn't get any better during the wait. I did what I could to treat them, but they bled more and went deeper into shock. The one who was in and out went into a coma and stayed there. I had to shoot myself with morphine just to stand the pain from my shoulder. We was a pitiful bunch, I tell you. We tried to laugh about it, but it was twenty below zero. Hard to see the funny side when you're that cold.

"Anyway, our column had taken off hell-for-leather when the ambush started. Some of our boys got knocked off the tanks when the gunners rotated their turrets to fire back at the Chinese, and some got crushed flat by the treads. Piss-poor planning, I'll tell you. By the time

Tom got up to the road, there was nobody there but dead GIs and Chinese waiting to ambush the next column. That's when he got grazed by another bullet. And that's another thing the major left out. If you don't believe me, get him to strip down and take a look at his scars."

Shad forces a respectful smile. "We'll take your word for it, Captain."

Walt looks hard at Shad, then continues, his eyes on the faces in the jury box. "After Tom got back, he asked me to come outside the ambulance to hear his report, but the boys heard it anyway, like Powers said. The next column to come down the road was going to catch the same hell we had. Tom and I were hurt too bad to move the wounded, who couldn't ethically be moved anyway—so there we were. Rock and a hard place, literally."

"Why couldn't you stay where you were and wait for relief?"

Walt looks at Shad like he's an idiot. "Did you not hear me say it was twenty below zero? We had two boys bleeding out and one in a coma. There was no heat and no hope of help. Plasma was frozen solid in the *aid stations,* and we had none in the ambulance. The only thing we had enough of was morphine."

"Go on."

"That's when the first boy begged us not to leave him."

"Had you told the wounded you intended to leave them?"

"Not at that point. But every GI north of the thirty-eighth parallel knew the Commies' prisoner policy. No quarter given. The North Koreans had been mutilating POWs before executing them. A couple of ambulances filled with wounded had been burned out with flamethrowers. And we were even more afraid of being captured by the Chinese."

Shad takes a moment before going on. "Wasn't it your duty to stay with the wounded, Mr. Garrity?"

"Mr. Johnson, that might be a thorny problem in some philosophy book, or even a field manual. But in real life . . . no soldier is obligated to wait for certain death unless ordered to, and we hadn't been. Tom and I had a tough choice. We were medics, and dedicated to our work. We could stay there and be captured—which meant death or worse—or we could try to climb out and bring back help, if we could somehow hook up with an American unit in time. We knew the odds were low. We told those boys how things stood. We said, 'We'd take you with us if we could, but we can't move you without killing you.' And that's when one of them, a tough little fella from Idaho, said, 'Kill me now, then. Better you than them devil monkeys.' That's what some guys called the gooks—the North Koreans—back then. I don't think he even knew it was the Chinese who'd knocked us off the road. Anyway, I looked at Tom, he looked at me, and we knew each other's minds. It was either put them boys out of their misery or leave them to a terrible fate."

"And Major Powers?"

Walt sniffs as though he has just detected a noxious odor. "Major Powers. Well . . . early on, the major had been praying, like he said. But about this time he chimes in and says, 'I know what you men are thinking, and you can't do it. No matter what these boys say, it's wrong, and you know it.'"

"How did you respond?"

"I told him I thought what he was saying was fine for a church meeting, but not much use down in that gorge. I'd gone to church most every Sunday growing up, but my heart told me it was up to them boys to decide how they wanted to meet their maker."

"And?"

"They decided. They told us to give 'em enough morphine to go to sleep and not wake up. And that's what we done." Walt sniffs a couple more times, like a man with hay fever, but then I realize his old slit eyes are welling with tears.

"Another thing the major left out . . . them two boys held hands while we done it. Held hands and prayed till they fell unconscious. Not one day of my life has passed that I don't see those boys in my mind. But I'll tell you this: Even if the Lord sends me to everlasting perdition for what I done that night, I know I did right by 'em. Tom, too. I know that in my heart. Their own mamas wouldn't have done no different."

Shad looks astounded by this assertion. "Do you really believe that, Captain Garrity?"

"Son, if I didn't believe it, I'd have shot myself in the head thirty years ago."

Shad appears to have no idea how to respond to this. "Permission to approach the witness, Your Honor?"

Judge Elder nods.

Shad walks away from the podium and circles slowly toward Walt. "You said 'we' during that description. But did you inject either soldier with a lethal morphine dose?"

"I offered to, but my dominant hand was numb from the broken shoulder. Tom volunteered to do it, to make it easier on the boys. And on me, too, probably."

"I see. And the unconscious man?"

"Like the major said, Tom didn't want to inject him. But one conscious boy knew that fella and said the boy wouldn't want to wake up alone with a North Korean's bayonet in his gizzard, if by some miracle he did wake up. I agreed with them, and Tom finally went on and did it."

"I see. So . . . you don't believe that Tom Cage committed murder on that night?"

"No, sir. I mean, yes—that's right. It wasn't murder. It was like putting down a horse with a broken leg. Three horses. They were hopeless cases."

"Yet Major Powers survived that night."

"Yeah," Walt says with what sounds like resentment. "That's another thing."

"What do you mean?"

"Another thing the major left out."

Shad looks wary now. "I think we've heard enough to clarify what happened in the ambulance."

"Well, I think you're missing a key detail, Mr. Johnson."

I remember Quentin's insistence that the jury hates to be denied any part of a story. Shad knows trouble is coming, but he also senses that he shouldn't resist. Now that the door is open, Quentin can easily bring out whatever Walt wants to say during cross. Better to bring it out himself and try to steer the questioning. "Please enlighten us, Captain."

Walt gives a tight smile. "Major Powers wasn't like the other wounded in that ambulance."

"How do you mean? He had the lightest wounds?"

"No. He *did* have the lightest wounds, but since he couldn't walk, that wouldn't have mattered. Except for another fact."

"What's that?"

"He was air force. The other wounded were all army. And Powers wasn't just air force. He was a *pilot*. A jet pilot. And all field officers in both the North Korean and Chinese armies were under orders not to harm captured American pilots. Pilots were considered the highest-value American prisoners by the Chinese, because it was their MiGs we were fighting in the skies over Korea. Even the Korean civilians had been ordered not to hurt our pilots if they parachuted down or crash-landed. Pilots were passed back up the chain until they were taken into China for questioning. My point is, a lot of them survived. So, while Powers surviving to live fifty-five more years to come here and testify might make it seem like Tom and I acted hastily that night, the fact is, those army boys were as good as dead the minute we went off that road. In that ambulance, only Major Powers had a get-out-of-jail-free card."

While Shad tries to find a way to gracefully get Walt off the stand, the old Ranger says, "World War Two was the same. Hermann Goering had been a pilot in World War One, so he set up special camps for airmen in the next war. In some wars, being a pilot is kind of like being in an international gentlemen's club. Not that some didn't suffer—they did. But that's not like having your eyes gouged out with a sharpened spoon, or having your balls cut off before they bayonet you through the mouth."

Shad stares at Walt like a man watching an unpredictable dog.

"You know who *really* killed those boys in that ambulance?" Walt asks pugnaciously.

"Who?"

"Douglas MacArthur. The Chinese had said they would enter the war if we marched too far north, but MacArthur didn't believe 'em. We'd been seeing troops wearing quilted coats and tennis shoes for three weeks, and finding perfectly square foxholes—which is textbook Chinese discipline—but our brilliant leader ignored the intelligence. He sat over in the Dai Ichi building in Tokyo, wearing his kimono, and sent thousands of boys to their deaths. That bastard should have been court-martialed the week after the Bugout. I don't know why it took so long for Truman to fire him. If he was here now, I'd spit on *him*."

"On Douglas MacArthur? An American hero and legend?"

"You're damn right. Men have to die in war, but those poor boys died for MacArthur's arrogance. For no other reason."

"I suspect you're oversimplifying matters, Mr. Garrity."

"No, that's what *you're* doing. Hindsight's always twenty-twenty, ain't it, Mr. DA?"

"Whether it is or not, Major Powers's vision was twenty-twenty when he watched Tom Cage kill three soldiers by lethal injection in 1950. You saw the same thing, correct?"

"I did."

"Then we've heard all we need to on that subject. Let me ask you about one other thing. It's a small matter, but very important."

Walt says nothing.

"When Tom Cage was apprehended outside Henry Sexton's funeral, after jumping bail, he had been driven to that church by you, had he not?"

"He had."

"In fact, you had been driving him around ever since he skipped bail. Aiding and abetting a fugitive, as it were."

"You could call it that, if you had a mind."

"Well, Mr. Garrity, you spent decades serving as a Texas Ranger. What did you call men who skipped bail?"

"Depended on the man. Some were outlaws, and some were good boys caught in a misunderstanding. That's why Rangers were taught to use their judgment."

Shad gives Walt a sidelong glance that lets him know he does not appreciate the sparring. "Were you in court during Sheriff Byrd's testimony that the night after Dr. Cage turned himself in to the FBI, you threw a videotape from your RV into the Mississippi River?"

"Yes, sir, I was."

"Was the sheriff's account accurate?"

Walt leans back in the witness chair and folds his arms. Once more he sniffs, then gives the jury box an appraising glance.

"Captain Garrity?" Shad presses.

"Yessir?"

"Will you answer the question?"

"The sheriff's account was accurate enough."

"You threw that videotape from your RV into the river?"

"I threw *a* tape into the river, along with some other stuff."

"Are you saying you didn't know what was on the tape?"

"That's right."

"Had you visited Dr. Cage earlier that afternoon in FBI custody?"

"I had."

"At that time, did you discuss the videotape in the van?"

"No, sir."

Shad looks skeptical. "Dr. Cage did not tell you where to find that tape and ask you specifically to destroy it?"

"How could he, if we didn't discuss the tape?"

"Yes or no, Captain."

Walt is starting to lose patience with Shad. "The answer is no."

Shad lets the jury see an exaggerated look of incredulity. "If you knew nothing about the tape, not even what was on it, then why would you get rid of it?"

Walt gives Shad a bitter smile. "Because you and your wannabe-cowboy sheriff had been trying to frame my best friend for a week. After Tom turned himself in to the FBI, I stayed a night at his house to make sure his wife was okay. The next day, I decided to go back to Louisiana and get my van. Given the situation, I figured the Roadtrek might draw some unwelcome attention from Sheriff Byrd when I crossed back into Mississippi. So I searched it, just to be careful. I found that tape under a seat cushion. I also found a half-empty bottle of Maker's Mark and a video camera. I'd never seen the tape before, so I put it in the camera and fast-forwarded through it. Wasn't nothing on it. In the end, I decided to stuff everything in the bag and toss it when I drove back over the bridge. If you want to charge me with littering, go ahead. But I wasn't going to help anybody frame my best buddy for something he didn't do."

An odd smile touches Shad's lips, and the sight of it strikes fear in my heart.

"Captain Garrity, did Tom Cage ever tell you that he killed Viola Cage? As a mercy killing, even?"

Walt's face darkens. "No, sir. He did not."

"I see. Did he ever tell you specifically that he did not kill her?"

"Yes. He did."

Shad takes a step toward the jury and looks back at Walt. "Captain, is it your deepest conviction that Tom Cage is innocent of the murder of Viola Turner?"

Walt leans forward. "Absolutely."

Shad nods slowly, then turns to Judge Elder. "Your Honor, at this time I would like to enter an audio recording into evidence as State's Exhibit Seventeen."

"What is the nature of this recording?"

"It was made in Navasota, Texas, under a warrant duly ordered by a Texas circuit judge."

The blood has drained from Walt's weathered face. Navasota is where Walt lives, where his wife lives. And in this moment Walt is asking himself the same question I am: *What the hell has Shad done?*

In a short enough span of time for me to know this has been rehearsed, Shad's assistant rises from the chairs behind him and goes to the side of the courtroom to load a tape into a player.

Quentin could object to this recording and stop it from being played until its authenticity is verified. But I guess he figures it's going to be admitted in the end, and if he's going to keep up the appearance of Dad having nothing to hide from the jury, better to let it be played without argument.

Walt must be losing it up there, but he's been in the witness box enough times to know better than to let anyone see him sweat.

"Ready," says the ADA.

"Ladies and gentlemen of the jury," Shad says, "you are about to hear a brief portion of a recording of a conversation between the witness and his wife, Mrs. Carmelita Cruz Garrity. It was made four days after Tom Cage turned himself in to the FBI, and three days after Captain Garrity threw the videotape into the river."

Walt leans forward, his face expressionless, his mind spinning through every conversation he had with his wife during that period.

A female voice with a heavy Mexican accent says, *"How long are you going to stay in Mississippi, Walter?"*

"I'm not sure," Walt answers in an exhausted voice. *"As long as they need me."*

"They?"

"Tom and his family."

"And you're staying at Tom's house? With his wife there?"

"I have to, darlin'. Peggy's in bad shape. She puts on a good show, but this is a tough situation."

"Oh, I'm so afraid. What if they arrest you for what you did last week? For driving Tom around while he was wanted?"

"I don't think they will. I've been helping the FBI and the Louisiana State Police with some important cases. They don't want me in custody. The sheriff in Natchez could give me some hassle, but I don't think he wants to get crossways with the feds over one dried-up old Texas Ranger."

The hiss of bad connection comes over the speakers. Then Carmelita says, *"Walter, I'm so worried. You've risked so much for Tom already. I know he's your friend, but . . ."*

"But what, darlin'? Spit it out."

"Are you sure Tom didn't hurt that nurse? Not even as a—how you say, mercy?"

"Mercy killing."

"Sí. Are you certain, in your heart?"

This time the silence drags so long that my pulse begins pounding in my ears. Then Walt speaks words that I know he will regret for the rest of his life.

"Carmelita . . . the truth is, I don't know what happened in that house that night. And part of me doesn't want to know. The truth is, even if he did kill her, I wouldn't do anything different than I've done. I know you don't understand it, but the man is my friend. And I owe him. From Korea, and for a lot more."

"I know," Carmelita says. *"I'm not trying to nag you. I just worry."*

"I know. Everything's going to be okay."

Shad raises his hand, and his assistant stops the tape.

Beside me, my mother has lowered her head, surely to mask tears. In the witness box, Walt looks out over the crowd with the same iron self-control he always displays. But inside he is dying.

"Your Honor," Shad says, "I have no further questions for this witness."

Walt starts to get up, but Judge Elder says, "You haven't been released, Captain."

Judge Elder looks at the defense table. "Mr. Avery?"

"No questions, Your Honor."

Walt just manages to hold himself in the chair until Judge Elder says, "You may step down."

Joe Elder watches Walt walk away like a weathered statue of a cowboy brought to life: his chin held high, his eyes scanning the crowd, zeroing in on anyone who stares at him. I suspect that, like most men in the room, Joe Elder is wondering just what he would have done had he found himself in that ambulance on that freezing night.

At first I can only see the back of my father's head, but then he turns to watch every step of Walt's journey out of the courtroom. As Walt passes the bar, pain flickers in his face, but beyond him I see my father's eyes, and they are filled with forgiveness.

"Mr. Johnson," prompts Judge Elder. "You may call your next witness."

Shad comes to his feet, his hands at his side.

"Your Honor, the State rests."

MY FIRST REACTION is relief—pure, unbounded relief that Dad is not going to be subjected to a parade of relatives of deceased patients claiming that he helped to kill their loved ones. But before I can think too much about this, Judge Elder looks down at Quentin and says, "Mr. Avery, are you ready to proceed with your opening statement?"

"Your Honor, I am. But I have two issues. First, I'm having some medical issues, and I'd like to deal with those before my opening statement. Second, my first witness is flying in from out of state, and he only landed in Baton Rouge a half hour ago. He's at least forty-five minutes away. Further, I only intend to make very brief remarks in my open. For those reasons, if the court is amenable, I would prefer to make my opening statement tomorrow morning, and then proceed directly with my first witness."

Many judges would agree to this, but Joe Elder says, "Is your medical problem acute, Mr. Avery?"

Quentin seems surprised by the question. "It's . . . well, more of a chronic issue, Judge."

"It's not yet four o'clock, Mr. Avery. Unless you have an acute emergency, we can't afford to waste the court's valuable time due to inadequate travel arrangements for your witness."

Quentin appears so shocked by Elder's response that he's at a loss for words.

In the resulting vacuum, the judge says, "I will grant a ten-minute recess if you need to take medication or deal with any physical needs. But after that, you will proceed with your opening statement."

To my surprise, Quentin actually turns and looks back at me, but I can't read his eyes. Is he asking me to help him decide what to do?

"No, thank you, Judge," he says, turning back to the bench. "I'll proceed with my statement now."

"Very well." Elder gives Quentin a suspicious look. "You may begin."

And with that, "Preacher" Quentin Avery whirs around the defense table, stops beside the podium, and faces a jury that, like me, must wonder just what this unpredictable attorney's idea of an opening statement might be.

CHAPTER 42

"LORD, OUR DISTRICT attorney likes to talk, doesn't he?"

Quentin has stationed his wheelchair beside the podium, but I'm sure this is only his initial position. He will almost certainly move around the courtroom during his statement, seizing and releasing the territory between judge, jury, and the spectators like a wily field general, pressing home every advantage that his handicap gives him. "I guess when you graduate from a high-dollar law school like Harvard, you just can't resist exercising all those fine, big words they teach up there."

"Mr. Avery," Judge Elder breaks in, "you know better than that."

"My apologies, Judge. In my younger days I used to pride myself on my own verbal facility, but I've gotten so old now that I have to get straight to the point. When you're liable to have to run to the restroom any minute, like me, you can't take time to gild the lily."

Quentin rolls his chair out into the open space before the jury box and smiles at them like a kindly patriarch about to address his relations at a family reunion.

"Where do I begin, ladies and gentlemen? To tell you the truth, my head is spinning. As best I can remember, we started out yesterday morning in Natchez, Mississippi, in 2005, and we ended up this afternoon by the side of a road in North Korea in 1950. I can hardly get my bearings. So while I try, I'm going to tell you a story about my daddy.

"Yesterday and today, while the district attorney's witnesses paraded in and out of that box, I kept thinking back to my childhood. World War Two was going on, and I was nine or ten years old. This was a frightening time in the world, with nobody quite sure what was true and what wasn't. Well, I got into trouble at school with some other boys, and then I managed to get out of it. I did that by using my quick wits and quicker tongue. I was pretty proud of myself, yes sir. Downright smug, probably. But you couldn't keep nothing from my daddy. By four thirty that evening, Daddy knew everything that had happened. And he sat me down on our old porch and said something I never forgot. He said, 'Son, *half the truth is a whole lie.*'"

Quentin falls silent, seemingly lost in a reverie about his father.

"Mr. Avery?" prompts Judge Elder.

"'Half the truth,'" Quentin ruminates, "'*is a whole lie.*' These past two days, I've been noticing that some people didn't have the benefit of my daddy's instruction."

Shad starts to object, but there's a long-standing tradition that lawyers do not interrupt each other's opening statements.

Quentin rolls closer to the jury. "You folks may not know it, but we have a mess of lawyers sitting in this courtroom with us. Yesterday, too. This is a historic trial. And I'll tell you right now, a lot of those lawyers think I'm crazy. That I'm going senile. Why? Because I've let the DA get away with murder for a day and a half. He's bent the rules every which way, and I've done nothing to stop him. I haven't even tried to slow him down. I've let Mr. Johnson present patently inadmissible testimony without objecting to it . . ."

Shad's face is rapidly darkening, but Quentin pushes on, as though oblivious to the effect of his words on opposing counsel. As outrageous as they sound, they are also true.

"I've listened to hearsay, irrelevant evidence, testimony about prior acts that can't legally be held against my client in the present, and I didn't object to any of it. I'll tell you something else. By *not* objecting, I lost my ability to appeal a guilty verdict based on that testimony. That's right. If you convict Dr. Cage of murder, I cannot appeal your verdict based on any of the legal flimflam that Mr. Johnson has pulled, because I didn't object to it *when he did it*. If I didn't have the long experience that I do, I believe Judge Elder himself would have dragged me back to his chambers to ask me if I ever graduated from law school."

As I scan the faces in the jury box, it seems to me that they are grasping Quentin's point. Whatever his strategy might be, it's an all-in bet.

"So *why*, you must be wondering, would I do that? Why would I give Shadrach Johnson an inch and watch him take a mile? I'll tell you. In the Book of Matthew, Jesus said, 'If a man asks you to walk a mile with him, walk with him twain.' 'Twain,' for those of you who don't read your Samuel Clemens, means 'two.' Well, while Mr. Johnson put on his case, I tried to follow Jesus's exhortation. It's been difficult, but early on, Dr. Cage and I decided that, since he has nothing to hide, we would not attempt to stop anybody from saying anything they wanted to on that witness stand. We're not going to try to 'game the system,' as the young folks say, or manipulate it to our benefit. We want the same thing you good people do. We want the truth to come out. The whole truth, and nothing but.

"That's a novel strategy, believe me. Even Dr. Cage's son, our distinguished mayor, is worried that I'm getting old-timer's disease. But I told the mayor what I tell you now: my faith in his father's integrity is such that I have *no fear* about letting any man say what he will in this court."

Quentin lets the silence stretch out, so that his words will sink into the collective mind of the jury.

"Half the truth is a whole lie," Quentin repeats, as though for his own benefit. "The Good Book says, 'Thou shalt not bear false witness.' Well, I promise you that, before my case is done, you will see that the Ninth Commandment has been broken by more than one witness for the State. And I'd like to remind some of the people in this room that in our modern age, that biblical proscription has been codified into law. The offense is called perjury, and the sentence is grave: *not less than ten years.*"

The jury seems appropriately impressed, and Shad looks downright worried by the turn Quentin's open has taken. The DA must be wondering which of his witnesses lied, and if they did, whether Quentin has evidence to prove it.

Taking a small piece of paper from the crocheted comforter on his lap, Quentin says, "During his opening remarks, the district attorney said an interesting thing. To paraphrase, he said, 'Were it not for the fact of race, Viola Turner would not have been murdered.' That's provocative, isn't it?" Quentin rolls back to the defense table and puts his hand on my father's shoulder. "Ladies and gentlemen, let me tell you about this man and *race.*

"Tom Cage was the first doctor in this town to integrate his waiting room. He did that against the wishes of his boss, Dr. Wendell Lucas. Tom Cage made house calls at night on the north side of town when it was still called the colored section—or Niggertown—and other white doctors thought he was a fool."

The courtroom feels as though its barometric pressure has suddenly dropped three points, into the storm zone. Quentin Avery is about as predictable as a tornado, and there's no telling what might come out of his mouth.

"For forty years," Quentin continues, his hand still on Dad's shoulder, "this man treated black folks as he would his own family. In an era when white *children* called black men of seventy by their first names only, Tom Cage called his black patients mister and missus. Back then, any white male might say to a black stranger walking down the road, 'Hey, Mose, get over here and fix my flat tire.' And old Mose went." Quentin lets his hand fall from my father's shoulder, then shakes his head like he remembers fixing the tires of more than one white man in his youth. "But in Dr. Cage's office, it was, 'How are you feeling today, *Mister* Jackson? Let me palpate that liver for you, Mrs. Ransom.' I'm talking about *respect,* folks—plain good manners. And if a man couldn't pay his bill from Dr. Cage, he knew he could drop by the Cage house with a mess of collards or a bucket of catfish, and that would stand as good as cash money."

This is the unadorned truth. I remember countless visits like that, and the shy expressions on the faces of the men who brought the buckets and boxes.

"And if you couldn't manage that," Quentin says, "you knew no debt collector would be coming to your door to embarrass you in front of your wife and children. Because in those cases, more often than not, Dr. Cage just *let it go*. Why? Because he knew how it was for black folk in Mississippi. Tom Cage knew how it was for poor folks, because he'd grown up poor himself. He knew what it was to do without. And he didn't want to be the cause of anybody else's children suffering."

Rusty Duncan nudges my knee and nods toward the prosecution table.

To my amazement, Shad Johnson is actually pretending to play a violin, which tells me that he's grossly misjudged his jury. But Quentin has not. In less than five minutes, the old fox has turned aside the juggernaut of momentum that Shad painstakingly built up over the past two days and convinced at least half the jury that they'd be lucky to have an uncle or a father as honest and fair and understanding as Quentin Avery. A closer look at Shad tells me that he's making his satirical gesture to conceal the rage threatening to boil out of him at Quentin's folksy performance. For a performance is what it is. No one knows better than Shadrach Johnson that the man in the wheelchair talking like a cross between Will Rogers and Martin Luther King Jr. has argued landmark cases before the Supreme Court, and on those occasions Quentin did not speak like a man who'd just walked out of a Delta cotton field. But galling though it might be, Shad is bound by custom to silence.

"I could parade five hundred people through this courtroom to verify my assertions," Quentin continues, "but I don't need to do that. Because most everybody in this room already knows they're true. The black folk here know there ought to be a *monument* in front of the old house on High Street where Dr. Cage had his clinic. Where other whites saw a Negro, a nigra, a nigger, a buck, a *boy*—Tom Cage saw a human being. When most everybody else treated you like a servant, Dr. Cage treated you as an equal. Black folk knew they could go to his clinic and get help, no matter how much trouble they were in." Quentin raises his forefinger and tilts it just enough that it's pointing at a pair of black women sitting in the jury box. "How can I put a price on what that meant to people in this town? I don't know a number that high. And yet"—he sighs as though he can hardly bear to go on—"here sits Tom Cage, accused of premeditated murder of a patient under his care. Here he sits, stoic and silent, while low men and women lie under oath and slander his name." Quentin hangs his head, as though he can barely endure the injustice of the situation. "Do you know what I say to that, ladies and gentlemen?"

The jury collectively leans forward.

The white shock of hair comes up. "Do you know what I say to the State of Mississippi? To the high-and-mighty district attorney?"

Several jury members actually cock their ears toward Quentin to be sure they don't miss his answer.

Quentin turns to Shad, his eyes burning with what looks like contempt. "Have you no *shame,* brother?"

Shad finally explodes, which is exactly what Quentin wanted. "Judge, this is outrageous! Opposing counsel isn't making an opening statement. He's delivering an oral hagiography of his client and slandering the district attorney!"

"Oral hagiography?" Quentin echoes, as though mystified. "Isn't that illegal in Mississippi?"

Half the lawyers in the room burst into laughter, prompting Judge Elder to come down hard on Quentin.

"Mr. Avery, attorneys are permitted considerable leeway in their opening remarks, but you're not only exceeding the agreed-upon speed limit, you're driving on the wrong side of the yellow line. Confine yourself to the facts of the case, or move on to your case in chief."

Shad is livid, but he can do nothing more to slow Quentin's flow.

"Members of the jury," Judge Elder continues, "please disregard the defense attorney's last comments."

"Thank you for putting me back on course, Judge," Quentin says, all amicability again. "Let's get down to the *facts* that Mr. Johnson has been making such a fuss about. We all know by now that a romantic relationship existed between Dr. Cage and Viola Turner in February and March of 1968. The district attorney has done his best to make that relationship sound sleazy, as though Tom Cage were the kind of slavering, lecherous white man who liked a little dark meat on the side when he could get it."

The crowd gasps, and the judge steps in again. "Watch your language, Counselor."

But Quentin refuses to back off. "Judge, can we not be frank in this forum? We're all adults here. Can we not use the language that accurately portrays the situation?"

The jury clearly agrees with Quentin, but Joe Elder says, "Mr. Avery, you'll remain within the bounds of propriety or suffer the consequences."

"All right, Judge. Well . . . we all know the kind of man I was talking about. But Tom Cage *ain't that kind of man*. In forty-five years of practicing medicine, not one sexual harassment claim has ever been made against him. And during all those years, he's had several black female employees, all of whom are willing to come forward and testify to his good character.

"So. What caused this illicit relationship? Do we need Sherlock Holmes or Sigmund Freud to figure it out? No. I doubt anyone knew

Tom Cage better than Viola Turner, the exceptional nurse who worked at his side during the troubled 1960s. Now, I don't know what problems might have existed in Dr. Cage's marriage." At this point, Quentin looks pointedly at my mother, who stares straight ahead like a graven image of the long-suffering but loyal wife.

Was that look prearranged? I wonder.

"All marriages have their strains," Quentin says with regret, "and we never know what's cooking in someone else's pot. But take a moment to imagine poor Viola Turner learning that her young husband had been killed in Vietnam. Imagine that young widow enduring a year of terrible loneliness while her brother did dangerous work for the civil rights movement. Picture this dedicated young sister working at Dr. Cage's side each day, witnessing his unique commitment to helping people. *Her* people. And not with cocktail party rhetoric, mind you, but down in the trenches, where it mattered. Is it not easy to see how strong feelings might develop in that kind of situation?"

It would be just as easy, I realize, for a modern-day jury to read that situation as sexual harassment. But today Quentin will benefit from Mississippi always being ten years behind the times.

He makes eye contact with several women on the jury. "I'm not condoning an extramarital affair, ladies and gentlemen. We all know that adultery is wrong. But in extraordinary circumstances, the heart will seek its own comfort. And the flesh is weak, as the Good Book tells us.

"We can't shy away from human truth in this court, however painful it might be. We have been called here specifically to uncover the truth. But Tom Cage is not on trial for adultery. And he has never denied that he had a relationship with Viola Turner. He didn't *advertise* it, mind you, and I don't blame him. In 1968, a revelation like that would have put his whole family in mortal danger. But neither did Dr. Cage try to deny that he might be Lincoln Turner's father, once he'd been told of the child's existence. Why didn't he try to evade that responsibility? Because he's *not that kind of man*. Tom Cage loved Viola, and she loved him in return. Theirs was a tragic affair. They were two good people caught in a bad situation. But whatever sins Tom Cage may have been guilty of in 1968, they have a lot more to do with the Seventh Commandment than the Sixth, which is not, by the way, '*Thou shalt not kill,*' as most people quote it, but '*Thou shalt not do murder.*'"

While most people in the court try to remember what the Seventh Commandment was, Judge Elder says, "'*Thou shalt not commit adultery.*' That's the Seventh Commandment."

"Thank you, Judge," Quentin says to the younger man, like a Sunday school teacher complimenting his favorite student.

Before Joe Elder can find a way to put Quentin back in his place, the click and whir of the wheelchair sounds, and Avery rolls out from behind the defense table. He steers toward the jury box, but stops a few feet short of it and speaks in a conspiratorial voice.

"Ladies and gentlemen, I'm going to let you in on a secret of the legal profession. There's an interesting test that district attorneys apply when they decide whether or not to prosecute a murder case. They ask themselves two questions. One: *Did the victim need killing?* And two: *Did the right person do the killing?*" Quentin pauses to let these questions sink in. "If the answer to both those questions is yes, most DAs won't touch the case with a barge pole."

While the jury members ponder this, Quentin says, "That logic might seem cynical to laymen, but there's a sound reason for it. And the reason is, sometimes judges don't fully define reasonable doubt, and sometimes jurors follow their hearts instead of their heads to find it. We lawyers call that gut sense of right and wrong the Unwritten Law. Why? What is the Unwritten Law? Well, it's exactly what it sounds—"

"Not another word, Mr. Avery!" erupts Judge Elder. "Against my instincts, I have been patient with you, but you just walked up to the precipice of a mistrial. And what's worse, you know it."

Quentin's embarrassment looks genuine enough, like that of an elderly man who momentarily forgot he was in church and started discussing sexual intercourse. But I'm not buying it, and neither is Joe Elder. Quentin was purposefully leading his jury to the prosecutor's worst nightmare: jury nullification. Jury nullification occurs when a jury disregards all instructions and votes with what some people call its "collective conscience," but which could more accurately be described as its collective gut instinct. Less charitable critics would call it "frontier justice."

In a bass voice that could have come from Zeus on Olympus, Judge Elder says, "Mr. Avery—*you have been warned.*"

"My sincere apologies, Your Honor." Quentin looks back at the jury. "Let's return to those two cynical questions I mentioned for a moment. First: *Did the victim need killing?* Let's say our murder victim was a foulmouthed, hyena-headed, belly-dragging baboon who beat his wife, cuckolded his neighbors, and abused his children. Everybody who knew him agreed that the world was better off without him in it. So . . . did he need killing? *Yes.*"

A white man in the jury actually laughs, earning a baleful glare from Judge Elder. I'm sure Shad has been wanting to shout in protest throughout Quentin's open, but since he liberally abused the rules himself, he hasn't got much of a foundation for it.

"Question two," Quentin pushes on. *"Did the right person do the killing?* Well, if the killer was the victim's battered wife, his abused son, or his cuckolded neighbor, the answer is probably yes again. And under those circumstances, it's doubtful that any jury would vote to convict the killer, no matter what instructions the judge gave them. And the DA knows that. So, what happens? He finds a way to avoid going to trial.

"But let's look at a different set of circumstances. What if the victim was an elderly black woman with terminal cancer? A woman beyond all hope, suffering agonizing torment, and ready to leave this world of toil and tears? Question one: *Did the victim need killing?* Well, according to the State, the victim herself believed she did. The assisted-suicide pact proves that. What about question two? *Did the right person do the killing?* If the State is to be believed, the man who took the victim's life was her personal physician and former lover, a man beloved by the community and trusted by thousands of patients. Now, *if* that man did the killing, I'd say that by the standards of the Unwritten Law, he was the right man for the job."

The jury seems stunned by this assertion, but Shad Johnson looks positively apoplectic. The DA can already feel the foundation of his carefully constructed case shifting on sand, where he thought he'd built on bedrock, and Quentin hasn't even called his first witness. Worse, because Quentin didn't request discovery, Shad has no idea who Quentin's witnesses might be.

"Given what I've told you," Quentin says, "I find myself wondering why this case was brought before the bar at all. Don't you? Why are we sitting here today, ladies and gentlemen? The answer has nothing to do with justice, I assure you. That shouldn't surprise you. A Natchez judge whose picture hangs on that wall used to tell juries that the court system wasn't about justice, but compromise. 'Justice,' he said, 'is when everybody gets exactly what they deserve—and Lord knows none of us wants that.'"

As hesitant laughter echoes through the court, Quentin's voice drops into the register of a man dealing with the gravest matters. "My friends, we are gathered here today because of the broken heart of a fatherless child."

After looking at Lincoln with sympathy, Quentin shifts his gaze to Sheriff Byrd, who now sits against the wall with a couple of his deputies. "We are also gathered here because of the envy, hatred, and ambition of powerful men." Then Quentin's eyes fall on Shad Johnson. "Ultimately, we are here because of the base human desire for revenge at any cost."

Even Judge Elder looks shocked by this statement, but if Quentin intends to prove that my father has been framed, he has the right to say these things.

"Ladies and gentlemen of the jury," he intones, "this may not be a capital trial, but make no mistake: a man's life is at stake here. Tom Cage is seventy-three years old. His health status is grave. If he's sentenced to spend even a year in jail, he's unlikely to survive. So I humbly ask you to bear with me as I present my case. Your time is precious, and public service a dying virtue. But with the stakes so high, I implore you to persevere until the truth lies naked before us all. For only then can we say that we have done our duty, and that justice has been served."

After a full visual survey of the jury, Quentin rolls back toward his table. But before he reaches it, he stops and looks over his shoulder as though troubled by some thorny moral dilemma.

"Ladies and gentlemen, I can't leave it at that. I have a confession to make. During the 1960s I was known as a crusader for justice, a defender of human rights. But I tell you now, I have represented guilty men. Every defense lawyer has. A client never tells you he's guilty, and you don't ask. But deep in your soul—in your inmost heart—you know. Nevertheless, you hold your nose and remind yourself that you're serving the Constitution, which was written by men a lot wiser than yourself. Men who believed it was better that ten guilty men go free than one innocent man rot in prison."

Quentin rolls himself slowly back toward the jury. "Why am I telling you this? Because I want you to know that *today* I came into court with a clear conscience. Today I am *not* holding my nose, or willfully blinding myself to some dark truth. Because on *this* day, in *this* trial, my client has more integrity in his little finger than I have in what's left of my whole body."

Now I'm the one left breathless by Quentin's audacity. With an overwhelming sense of déjà vu, I watch him point at my father in exactly the same way that I, as a prosecutor, often pointed at murderers. With almost religious conviction Quentin says, "That man—Dr. Thomas Jefferson Cage—is *innocent*."

Shad leaps to his feet, yelling something I can't make out over the roar of the crowd, but it doesn't matter. There's no rule that prohibits a lawyer from saying that his client is innocent, but few take that risk. Quentin has just done so with devastating effect. Shad might be able to call into question the way Quentin prefaced his statement, but right now that doesn't matter. Both the jury and the spectators have been knocked out of their socks. It's as though a football team trailing in the Super Bowl suddenly followed a ninety-seven-yard touchdown run with a successful onside kick, and the momentum shift was enough to give the spectators whiplash.

Judge Elder bangs his gavel, calling for order, and the crowd settles back into a resentful but expectant silence.

"Overruled," Judge Elder rules with obvious reluctance. (I never even heard what Shad's objection was.) The judge would clearly like to make Quentin pay a price for his boldness, but he can do little other than give the old lawyer a reproving glare. "Please conclude your remarks, Mr. Avery."

Quentin looks pointedly at his watch, as if to say, *I'll take my full allotted time and no less, thank you.*

"I'll tell you something else," Quentin says defiantly. "My client is not required to defend himself against these malicious charges. He's not required to take the witness stand and testify to his innocence. He is *presumed* innocent. The burden of proof lies with the State of Mississippi. Dr. Cage is protected by the full power of the Constitution of the United States. Nevertheless, Mr. Johnson over there is salivating in the hope that an old country doctor just *might* be proud enough, or foolish enough, to give a Harvard-trained prosecutor a chance to go after him with his sharpest legal scalpels. Well"—Quentin turns up both palms and gives Shad a beatific smile—"I have good news for Mr. Johnson. He is going to get his chance."

An electric buzz ripples through the courtroom, and my heart starts to pound.

"At the conclusion of this case, Dr. Tom Cage will walk into that witness box and tell you all what happened on the night Viola Turner died. And I will make you all a promise." Quentin glances at Shad, then turns slowly to the audience, which includes not only Sheriff Byrd, but probably also some corrupt law enforcement officers and even survivors of the Double Eagle group. "When Dr. Cage finally speaks, men sitting in this room now will *tremble*."

The silence that follows this prophecy is like the vacuum of deep space. There's only the soft whirring of Quentin's wheelchair as he rolls back behind the defense table and lays a comforting hand on my father's arm.

"Thank you, Your Honor."

As the silence grows, Doris Avery scuttles forward and whispers in her husband's ear.

"Your Honor," Quentin says in a surprised voice, "I've been informed that my first witness has arrived outside the courthouse. I'm ready to proceed with my case."

Judge Elder looks at his watch.

Shad Johnson stares at Quentin like an animal trying to determine whether another is predator or prey. The DA is desperate to know whom Quentin, after two days of sitting mute during devastating testimony, intends to call as his first witness.

"Call your witness," Judge Elder orders.

"The defense calls Colonel Karl V. Eklund, U.S. Army, Retired."

"Objection!" Shad cries.

"On what grounds?" Judge Elder asks.

"We've had no notice of this witness."

Judge Elder looks conflicted about his ruling. At length, he says, "You've had no notice of any witnesses, Mr. Johnson. Nor will you get any."

While Shad tries to appear unfazed, Judge Elder takes it upon himself to explain to the jury the concept of discovery and the rules pertaining to it in Mississippi. When he concludes, Colonel Eklund still has not appeared.

"Mr. Avery," says the judge, "is your witness ready to be called?"

"I believe so, Your Honor. But the colonel is over seventy, and he's from out of state. I'd better send somebody to find him."

"Before you do that, tell me, will you be examining this witness at length?"

Quentin smiles affably. "I will, Your Honor. Since the district attorney saw fit to end his case with Korea, I thought I'd start mine there. So we could be here for some while."

Shad sits blinking like a blindsided driver after a minor collision. "Objection, Your Honor. Irrelevant. The State has no record of a Karl Eklund being present in or around the ambulance where the events Major Powers testified about occurred."

"That's because Colonel Eklund was not present in the ambulance," Quentin says, "or anywhere near it."

"Then how is his testimony relevant?" Shad asks in a challenging tone.

Quentin's smile broadens. "You'll find out soon."

Doris Avery is heading down the aisle toward the door when Judge Elder says, "Mr. Avery, I've reconsidered your earlier request, and I think we should adjourn for the day. Tomorrow we can be assured that your witnesses will be present and ready to testify, that the jury will be fresh, and that your health needs will be attended to."

Quentin is taken aback by this decision, but he recovers quickly. "Thank you, Judge. I know the jury will appreciate the break as much as I do."

Shad says, "Your Honor, as I said before, if Colonel Eklund wasn't present in the ambulance, his testimony is obviously irrelevant to the present case."

Every lawyer in the courtroom looks at Shad, amazed that he would have the nerve to say this when the entirety of Major Powers's testimony should never have been allowed.

"Mr. Johnson, you opened the door to Korea. How do you suggest I stop Mr. Avery from walking through it?"

"But Your Honor—"

"I'll rule on relevance as his testimony proceeds," Judge Elder says ominously. "Court is adjourned until nine A.M. tomorrow."

CHAPTER 43

SNAKE KNOX STOOD on wet sand just south of Rodney, Mississippi, and watched a fiery sun slip into the river. Sky and wind told him there would be rain tomorrow, and that suited him fine. It had taken most of the day to set up a secure hideout and redundant escape routes, but Snake no longer settled anywhere, not even for a day, without doing both. His Air Tractor was chocked under some trees in a field one mile north of Rodney. Across the river, just west of St. Joseph, Louisiana, was a Cessna 182 he'd had a share in for the past twenty years. And thirty feet away, tied to a cottonwood tree, floated a twenty-four-foot Four Winns Horizon speedboat. The city of Natchez lay only twenty-five miles to the south by river. Snake could get there in forty minutes in the Four Winns, and he was only thirty minutes from Natchez by road, if he used the old pickup he had borrowed from Red Nearing, who owned the little farm they were using at Rodney.

Snake could scarcely imagine a safer hiding place. In the early 1800s, this little town had nearly become the capital of the Mississippi Territory. Though small, it had been a famous crossing point of the Mississippi River since Indian times, and it was surrounded by wealthy plantations. But a sudden shift in the course of the river had changed all that, and by 1870, Rodney had become a ghost town. Today about fifty people clung to their old houses, but they were ghosts themselves. Nobody came here but a few tourists, to stare at the Yankee cannonball that had stuck high in the brick wall of the church during some brief shelling by an ironclad during the Civil War. It wasn't even the original cannonball, Snake knew, the real one having been stolen long ago. Rodney's surviving public buildings were falling to pieces, and you could barely see most of the houses, thanks to the chest-high weeds choking the yards. The main traffic was hunters, and most of them had Confederate flag decals behind the gun racks in their pickups.

Rodney was friendly territory.

Alois and Wilma had wanted to stay by the boat and watch the sunset, but Snake had told them to get back up to the house. He was sick of listening to them yap. They wanted to know what he was going to do next, but if he'd learned anything from Frank, it was keep your plans to yourself until the last possible moment.

Being forced to leave the sod farm at Sulphur hadn't sat well with Snake at first, but once Wilma had told him about Viola Turner killing Frank in Dr. Cage's office—and Tom Cage likely covering it up—Snake had been glad to get closer to Natchez. The truth was, while Forrest was alive, Snake had had to be careful about how he approached Dr. Cage's situation. Forrest believed violence was bad for business, except where it was a direct requirement of business, and he wanted it minimized. But with Forrest's death at the hands of Penn Cage, Snake had gained the freedom to deal with Dr. Cage as he wished, though being hunted as a fugitive had limited his options.

Initially, he'd been content to let Dr. Cage be convicted of murder and die in Parchman. Snake had meant to let the son endure this heartbreak, then suffer his own retribution for killing Forrest. That would likely involve the death of his daughter first, and only later the death of the mayor himself. But the revelation that Dr. Cage had covered up Frank's murder for his nurse had scrambled Snake's thinking. His sense of being in control of events had slipped.

Worse yet, he'd received a report from someone attending the trial that Quentin Avery had got up on his hind legs and shocked the court with his opening statement. That meant that Tom Cage might mean to make a fight of it after all. Snake had been trying to figure out why Cage would do that, and he couldn't. He'd put out all the feelers he safely could, and as yet no answer had come back to him.

As the upper rim of the flaming sun sank below the horizon, Snake turned to go, but before he took two steps, his burner phone rang.

"Yeah?" he said.

"This is BB," said a voice Snake recognized as coming from a mouth stuffed with chewing tobacco. He also heard wind roaring in the phone. He could picture Sheriff Billy Byrd driving down the highway in his cruiser, sticking his big head and Stetson out the window to spit.

"About fuckin' time," Snake said. "What you got?"

"It ain't good."

"Let's hear it."

"That nigger girl those VK boys thought must be FBI?"

"Uh-huh."

"She's a friend of the mayor's. Another writer, believe it or not."

Snake had already learned that Cleotha Booker had been visited by Penn Cage and a young black woman, but he'd assumed the girl was one of Kaiser's FBI agents. "A *writer*? You're telling me this gal going around bending her pistol over bikers' heads is a *writer*?"

"Truth is stranger than fiction, man. She apparently served in Desert Storm. Army."

"I'll be goddamned. What about the older woman? Dolores?"

"I sent patrols up Washington Street as many times as I could today"—Byrd spat loudly in the rushing wind—"helping out with security, don't you know. Turns out Kaiser and four of his agents went crashing into Cage's house after lunch yesterday and got the St. Denis woman out of there. One of my deputies talked to a neighbor who saw it happen. So the St. Denis woman had probably been staying in Cage's house since Monday night."

"Son of a *bitch,* Billy. Any idea where they took her?"

"None yet."

Snake sighed and looked out over the darkening water. Dolores St. Denis could put him on death row at Angola, and he had no desire to test the ability of the Aryan Brotherhood to protect him from the most violent niggers in America.

"Billy, I got to know where that high-yellow bitch is being hid."

"I know it, bud. But I don't know how I can help you. John Kaiser ain't gonna tell me shit about that kind of thing. She's in the hands of Uncle Sam now."

Snake made a fist and squeezed it tight. As much as he'd wanted to cut the cord with the VK, he was going to need them still. "Okay. Tell me about Tom Cage, then."

"What about him?"

"I heard his lawyer said today they're gonna make a fight of it."

"Sure sounded like it to me. But they got their asses handed to them all day long in court. If the jury could have voted right after that air force major spit on Dr. Cage, he'd already be in the bus headed for Parchman."

"Yeah, but that's *not* when they vote."

"I don't think it matters, buddy. That Avery's been acting like he's gone senile."

"'Acting' is right," Snake muttered. "Quentin Avery is the craftiest spade you ever come across in your life. You can bank on that."

"Well . . . what do you need from me?"

Snake closed his eyes and made a command decision. "Tell me about Dr. Cage's jail routine."

"Ohhhh, shit now. Come on. Don't go there. We got media from all over the world in town!"

Snake winced and spat into the river. "Start talking, Billy boy."

As the sheriff reluctantly complied, Snake turned and walked up into the dark trees between the river and Rodney. A cloud of mosquitoes instantly swarmed his head. He cursed and swatted until they were a bloody paste on his cheek and forearms. He had no intention of becoming one of the ghosts of this forgotten town.

CHAPTER 44

AN HOUR AFTER nightfall, we finally caught a break. The one-sided nature of today's courtroom action had an unintended consequence: after seeing how badly things were going for my father, Reverend John Baldwin and his son Reverend Richard, whom Serenity and I visited on her first full day in Natchez, knocked at my front door and asked to see us. With them they carried something Henry Sexton would have seen as the holy grail of local journalism: two photocopied pages from the journals of Albert Norris.

According to Henry, Norris's journals disappeared from his music store on the night it was burned by the Double Eagles. Some investigators had even theorized that Norris had been murdered over the journals themselves. A set of accounting ledgers, these apocryphal volumes supposedly contained records of all the trysts Albert had arranged over the years between mixed-race couples, as well as records of bootlegging sales, loans, and many other activities that fell on the wrong side of the law. Henry had once told me that anyone in possession of those ledgers would never have to worry about money again, so valuable would they be as a blackmail tool.

Tonight I learned that Reverend Baldwin personally salvaged those ledgers from Albert's floor safe on the night he was burned out. Baldwin had served with Albert in the Deacons for Defense, and he knew his friend wouldn't have wanted those records to fall into the wrong hands—especially those of the KKK or the Double Eagles, where knowledge of interracial relationships would likely have resulted in reprisal murders. For this reason, too, Baldwin did not risk bringing the journals to my house, but only two photocopied pages.

"We've been attending the trial, you see," the elder Reverend Baldwin explained. "And it's pretty clear to me that Judge Elder is biased toward the prosecution."

"Quentin Avery believes the same thing."

"Well, I don't think that's fair to your father. And I don't think it's accidental."

"What makes you say that?"

That was when Baldwin brought out the photocopied pages. And what they showed was that in 1954, a black woman named Fannie Elder had been secretly meeting a white man with whom she was sexually involved. Most times she met him in his office, but a few times she met him in the back of Albert's store. When I saw the man's name, I was speechless for a few seconds. When I finally found my voice, I said:

"*That* son of a bitch?"

Reverend Baldwin nodded and said, "Is Judge Joe Elder's real father."

The man whose name was written in Albert Norris's book was Claude Devereux. Claude Devereux, the Cajun lawyer who had defended both Ku Klux Klansmen and Double Eagles during the worst years of the 1960s. Claude Devereux, the lawyer to whom Albert Norris's doctor had confided Albert's dying accusation against Brody Royal, and who had then betrayed that information to Royal, resulting in the murder of that doctor by Snake Knox. Claude Devereux, the lawyer in a photograph with my father, Brody Royal, and Ray Presley during a deep-sea fishing excursion with a Frenchman who likely had been involved in the assassination of John Kennedy. The lawyer who three months ago fled the country to escape RICO charges stemming from his illegal business activities with Brody Royal, and for criminal acts committed on behalf of the Knox family.

"Does Judge Elder know this?" I asked.

"He does," said Reverend Baldwin. "And I believe that's the reason for his bias against your father. When he thinks about your father and Viola, he sees Claude Devereux and his mother."

I thanked both men profusely, as did Serenity, and then we led them back to their car. I found that I was shaking with excitement, if only because the revelation that those ledgers still exist would have been such a triumph for both Henry and Caitlin.

"What do you want to do with this?" Serenity asked.

"We have to take it to Quentin. Joe Elder clerked for him. He'll know how to handle it."

"I guess we made a good impression when we went to see the Revs," Tee said.

"I think we can chalk this windfall up to you."

She grinned then. "I'll take that. I only wish my efforts in the redneck quarter had been as effective."

Less than five minutes later, we discovered that they had been. Before we could leave the house to visit Quentin at Edelweiss, my cell phone rang. The caller was Deke Devine. The younger son of Double Eagle Will Devine—the son named after a Mercury astronaut—Deke told me that he and his mother wanted to speak with me privately about a possible deal for his father. Will Senior, he said, would not leave the house because he believed that he—like every other surviving Double Eagle—was being watched by members of the VK motorcycle club. When I asked how we could meet, Deke told me that he and his mother would drive up my street—Washington Street—in one hour in a Winnebago motor home. He would stop at the corner of Washington and Union long enough for me to climb inside. When the meeting was over, he would return me home. I didn't like the sound of it, but Devine said those were the only circumstances under which his mother would meet me. I told him to be at that corner in one hour, and I would hear what he had to say.

"Why is everybody helping us all of a sudden?" I asked the air.

"Because your dad's getting his ass kicked?" Serenity suggested.

I laughed, but I knew that explained only the Baldwins' visit. The only thing that could be driving old Will Devine to cut a deal was the raw fear of death. For himself or his family—or both. And even then, betrayal is an almost incomprehensible step to take. For to date, every Double Eagle who even tried to betray his "brothers" has died for it, and died badly.

DESPITE THE FACT that Serenity and I come bearing gifts, Quentin lets us no farther into Edelweiss than the main hall, which irritates me more than a little, since I own the house. He's wearing a robe cut off and hemmed just below his stumps, and a crumpled comforter lies in the front part of his wheelchair's seat. Doris stands far down the hall behind him, just outside the door to the kitchen. She's wearing a translucent nightgown that leaves little to the imagination, even in the faint light spilling onto her from the kitchen.

Quentin is studying the first photocopied page in his lap, after grumpily chastising me for bothering him at this hour. I don't know why he's taking so long to speak. I highlighted the names of Fannie Elder and Claude Devereux in yellow, with the dates of their rendezvous. But Quentin is staring down at the photocopy like a doctor deciphering a litany of lab test results.

"You see those names, right?" I ask. "The highlighted ones?"

He doesn't look up. "I'm not blind yet, goddamn it."

"You get the significance, right?"

At last he raises his head, his face dark with frustration. "Reverend Baldwin's out for blood, isn't he? Forty years of sitting on this, and now he's ready to blow the whole city wide open. I've known Fannie Elder for fifty years. And yes, I know that coonass snake-in-the-grass Claude Devereux. Did Reverend Baldwin tell you that Devereux is *definitely* Joe's father?"

"He did."

"Damn." Quentin folds the sheet and slips it into his wheelchair pocket. "I guess he would know, if anybody would. He's Fannie's pastor. Goddamn it."

"Don't you think this could be grounds for a mistrial?"

"A *mistrial*?" Quentin looks at me like I'm crazy. "Man, I don't want a mistrial! I want a *fair* trial."

"But Quentin—"

"This isn't the easy call you seem to think it is, Penn. Judicial bias is a funny thing. For one thing, all judges are biased, some way or other. That's human nature. You start trying to prove it, though, and you'll run out of friendly jurisdictions quick."

"You're not worried about that. Not anymore."

"Because I have one foot in the grave? Is that what you're saying?"

"All I'm saying is, look at the situation for what it is."

"And what is the situation, my brother? As you see it?"

It takes a lot of will to control my frustration. "Judicial bias in a trial is like a rock under a rushing stream. You can't see it, and you might get through the rapids without hitting it, but that rock is steering the current the whole fucking time. The rock itself doesn't even know what effect it's having. But in the end, it's decisive."

Quentin smiles. "That's a pretty good analogy, boy. You've got a way with words. But don't start kidding yourself that you're a voting member of this defense team. You're on it because your mama wanted you there. Now, if that's all, I've got things to do."

"Surely you're not going to just *sit* on this."

The old lawyer takes a deep breath, then blows out all the air in one long rush. "Doris?" he says over his shoulder. "Bring me my cell phone, please."

The shadow behind him disappears, then quickly returns with the phone.

"Dial Joe Elder for me."

As Doris does his bidding, Quentin looks at Serenity and says, "I've been reading your book. To help myself sleep."

Tee doesn't rise to his bait.

"Turns out it's not as boring as I hoped it would be."

Doris hands him the phone. While Quentin awaits an answer, he looks up at Serenity again and shakes his head. Then I hear a tinny version of Joe Elder's bass voice saying, *"What the hell are you doing calling me, Quentin?"*

"Joe, this is important. . . . Yes, I know. I taught you that, damn it. . . . No, it's nothing about the trial. It's personal. . . . No, not about me. About you. I need to give you a heads-up, brother, and you *don't* want me to talk about this on the phone. . . . How about you meet me on the bluff, down by the old pecan factory? . . . Listen, Joe. This is no game. This is brother to brother. . . . Right. Thirty minutes'll work. See you soon."

Quentin clicks END and hands the phone back over his shoulder to Doris, who retreats down the hall in her nightgown.

"Anything else?" he asks in a challenging tone.

"Yes. What if I told you I may have a Double Eagle ready to turn state's evidence?"

To this, at least, Quentin has no sarcastic reply.

"This man has almost certainly committed murder with Snake Knox. He probably participated in the rape of Viola Turner, as well. The one at the machine shop."

"Who is it?" Quentin asks, his eyes as serious as those of a man contemplating a duel.

"Will Devine, the man whose truck was parked near Viola's house on the night she died. The truck with the Darlington Academy sticker on it."

Quentin whistles long and low. "How'd you pull off *that* trick?"

I tilt my head at Serenity, and Quentin gives her a knowing leer. "I might have guessed Wonder Woman here had something to do with it. Well. That changes things a bit. You said you *may* have a Double Eagle. What exactly does that mean?"

"We're going to meet his wife and son in a little while. We won't know for sure what we have until then."

Quentin is obviously working something out in his mind. "Devine's going to want a plea deal before he testifies in open court and implicates himself. And he's going to want protection. What are the odds you can get a federal plea deal done in time for Will Devine to help your father?"

"How long does that give me?"

"Hell, Penn, I need him by tomorrow."

"Tomorrow!"

"Boy, how many rabbits you expect me to pull out of my ass?"

"I see your point. Well, I can sure as hell put John Kaiser on it. And I know the U.S. attorney for the Western District of Louisiana. It's certainly possible—in theory."

Quentin nods slowly. "All right, then. You get to work on Devine. Just don't get killed. You could go to a meeting like that expecting fat Will Devine and arrive to find Snake Knox waiting—like finding a timber rattler where you expect a box turtle."

"We'll be careful."

"I'm guessing Ms. Butler there can take care of herself. Maybe she can take care of you, too."

"Kiss my ass, Quentin."

"Are we done?" he asks.

"You never got back to me about what Jewel Washington told me."

"About Byrd's deputies possibly tampering with evidence?"

"Yes! The hair and fiber evidence."

Quentin turns up his palms. "Have you got me any proof?"

"No."

"Then get out of my face and go find me some!"

"Jewel's trying. But I've thought about it, and one thing seems clear. If those guys did any kind of tampering with hairs taken from the scene, the hairs had to be Caucasian."

"Why?"

"Because that house would have been full of African-American hairs. From fifty different people, I'd bet. And Sheriff Byrd's priority is nailing Dad. We know Dad was there, so what kind of tampering could those deputies have done?"

"I'm too tired to guess."

"They'd have destroyed other Caucasian hairs found at the scene. There wouldn't have been many, not in Cora Revels's house. I'm guessing they got rid of some Caucasian hairs and, if necessary, replaced them with others, maybe even their own, which wouldn't raise any red flags."

"Why replace them?"

"Even in Billy Byrd's sloppy operation, there might have been some written or photographic record of Caucasian hairs being found. Records Jewel had seen and would remember."

Quentin's eyes look a little brighter now. "They replaced hairs belonging to Snake Knox and Sonny Thornfield. That's what you're thinking?"

"If those bastards were in that house, they left trace evidence. Unless they wore hairnets, they would have left hairs at the scene."

"Gray hairs," said Quentin, grinning. "Maybe the deputies substituted their daddies' hair for Knox's and Thornfield's."

"Maybe so. But it certainly seems worth pursuing."

Quentin nods noncommittally. "I'm going to see your father once more tonight. There's a deputy there who'll let me in. You met him when you were in the jail." Quentin cuts his eyes at Serenity. "As a *resident*."

"Are you going to talk to Dad about the hair and fiber stuff?"

"Yes. I'll call you when I leave the jail. Now, get out of here. I've got a meeting to go to, thanks to you."

"How about we give you an escort?" I ask, not joking at all.

Quentin shoos us toward the door. "Didn't you hear what I said to Joe? This is brother to brother. No honkies allowed. Now if you want to send Miss Black Universe here with me for protection . . ."

"*That's* not happening," Doris says from the shadows behind him.

"Then I'm going alone."

CHAPTER 45

DEKE DEVINE'S WINNEBAGO squeaked to a stop at the end of my block just as promised, and Serenity and I stepped through the side door into the cramped RV. Deke sat behind the wheel, and his face darkened when he saw Serenity climb the steps.

"You were supposed to come alone!" he snapped.

"I'm not walking into a meeting with any Double Eagles—or their families—alone. You're lucky I didn't bring my main security team."

"Get somebody else," said his mother from our left. "Not her."

Nita Devine stood in the narrow aisle of the RV, clinging to a handle above her head to maintain balance.

"Mrs. Devine," I said evenly, "the federal government—including the Justice Department—is staffed with thousands of black employees. If you plan to cut a deal to save your family with witness protection, you'd better get used to black faces."

She chewed her lower lip for several seconds. Then she said, "Get moving, Deke. Head for the bypass."

As the RV lurched forward, Nita steadied herself, then squeezed herself into the space between a leatherette bench and a removable table attached to a post stuck into the floor.

"Well, sit down," she said. "Let's get to it. They'll get suspicious if I don't get back quick."

"Who will?" I asked.

"Those motorcycle gangsters. They're watching our house again. All the Eagles' houses. They switch up."

"Your husband is at home?"

She nodded. "My other son's with him. You met him."

We pulled two small plastic chairs from the "den" of the RV up to the little table. Nita Devine took a pack of cigarettes from her purse and lit one without asking if we minded. Her hands shook, and her eyes held more emotions than I could separate—chief among them desperation.

"You told me the government would give Will a good deal. That they could keep him safe. Keep us all safe."

"I'm reasonably sure of that, yes. But it always depends on the information the witness can provide."

"You don't have to worry about that. Will knows everything. About the Double Eagles, I mean. He was there from the beginning. Or almost the beginning."

"He saw them kill people?"

A bitter laugh comes from her throat. "He still has nightmares to this day. The older he gets, the worse they get."

Serenity holds up her hand and says, "Why is your husband suddenly willing to talk after all these years?"

At first I don't think Mrs. Devine is going to deign to speak to the black interloper in her Winnebago. But at length she says, "Because he finally knows what I been telling him all along is true. Snake Knox don't give a damn about Will or any of the others, except to the degree he can use them. Him and Sonny killed Glenn Morehouse, their childhood friend. Then Snake killed Sonny—his best friend—in the Concordia jail. Strangled him with a towel while they all held him still. *Then* he ordered Silas Groom killed to frame him for bombing that FBI plane, when we all know Snake done that."

"You know that for a fact?" I ask.

"Will does."

"What else does he know? Does he know anything about Viola Turner?"

Nita grimaced and blew out smoke. "He knows everything, I told you. Most all the Double Eagles raped that woman, you know. Two different times. The first time it was just a small group, at her house. Snake and Frank and Forrest, a couple more. But that second time, in the machine shop . . . Lord, they tore that girl up. If Ray Presley hadn't got her out and back to Dr. Cage, she'd have died up in there."

I feel as though Serenity's body temperature has dropped ten degrees. I don't risk turning to look at her. I need to hold Nita Devine's gaze to my own. If she feels Serenity's fury, she might clam up.

"Will said that himself?"

"The machine shop? Oh, yeah. He took his turn like all the rest. Cheatin' bastard."

"What else do you know about Viola?"

"Dr. Cage got her out of town somehow, but Snake and Sonny found her in Chicago later. They wanted to kill her, but the big boss said no."

"The big boss?"

"Carlos Marcello. The mob boss of New Orleans. I think he had some kind of understanding with Dr. Cage. Marcello said they couldn't kill Viola unless she broke the deal she'd made and came back to Natchez."

My heart begins to pound. "Will told you that?"

She nods, then takes a long drag from her cigarette. Smoke floats slowly from her mouth as she continues speaking. "They told her then they'd kill her if she ever came back."

"What about later?" Tee asks. "After she got back here? Did they threaten her then?"

"He doesn't know that for sure. He says they went to see her at least once, during the day, he thought. He doesn't know what they said. But they borrowed his pickup on the night she died, and he didn't have no option to say no, if you get my meaning."

"What exactly do you mean?"

"I mean, they wanted it because they was going out to do something illegal. And they didn't want to use their own vehicle."

"But why use your husband's truck? He's also a Double Eagle."

"Because they're lazy shits, that's why. They didn't have to walk but two streets over to get Will's truck. And they didn't ever expect to get caught. So they figured that was enough insulation."

That's enough, I think. *If Devine will testify to this in Dad's trial, he will guarantee an acquittal.*

Nita Devine raises her finger and shakes it at me. "But none of this even begins to count all the nigras they beat and burned out and killed back in the day. Or the women they messed with. Hell, for Snake and his bunch, that was just fun and games."

Serenity's breathing has gone shallow, and I worry she might lash out at Devine's wife.

"Mrs. Devine," I say quickly, "do you have any idea where Snake is now?"

She shakes her head. "No. And you won't find him easy. Snake's a survivor. And people are scared to death of him. He could be living next door to them and they know it, and they won't tell you nothing."

"But your husband will," I say softly.

"If the deal is right. It wasn't easy, I tell you. Frank Knox brainwashed all those boys, way back. Made them think they were heroes. They thought Frank was a hero, and maybe he was, but he made them think they could be like him. Bigger than life, you know? But Snake Knox ain't bigger than life. He's lower than snake shit. He's the spawn of the fuckin' devil, sure as I tell you. And that Wilma Deen is just as bad. Helped him kill her own damn brother. How low can you fuckin' get, I ask you?"

Nita stubs out her cigarette and lights another, blows the smoke over Serenity's head.

A thought strikes me. "There's a young guy I've seen around, blond. Looks like he's in the Hitler Youth or something. Do you—"

"Alois Engel. That's Snake's bastard son. Had him off a woman over in Texas. Never did a damn thing to take care of the kid, but now the little bastard worships him. And he's just like a baby rattlesnake. Smaller in size, but the poison's twice as deadly to make up for it."

Great.

"Now," Nita says, "I've shown you mine. Time for you to pull down your drawers and show me yours. Let's talk about the deal."

I nod, thinking hard. "Deke can start back toward my house. This won't take long."

"Did you hear that, boy?" she calls.

"I heard him. I'll take the Liberty Road turnoff and head back downtown."

I wave my hand in thanks.

"Okay, Mrs. Devine. What you're almost certainly looking at is full protection for your family. A move to another part of the country, and—"

"Can we pick where?"

"Ah, you might be given two or three choices. But you can't just pick a city off the map."

"Okay."

"They'll either get Will a job or provide him a pension sufficient to support you in your present standard of living."

She makes a sour face. "I guess we haven't won the lottery, huh?"

"No. But you'll be surprised at how well they'll take care of you. *If* Will keeps up his end of the deal. Why don't you let me talk to my FBI contact before we get into any more details? Then you can speak to him directly."

"Sounds good to me. I like to get it from the horse's mouth."

I almost laugh picturing John Kaiser dealing with this woman.

"There is one thing," I tell her, leaning forward. "For me, it's the most important thing."

"What's that?"

"The FBI's primary goal is nailing Snake Knox and the remaining Eagles for their 1960s murders. But my main concern is saving my father."

Mrs. Devine nods but says nothing.

"From what you've told me, Will has the power to get my father acquitted, by making reasonable doubt impossible to ignore. But to do that, he'd have to testify in my father's trial within the next two days. Possibly even tomorrow. And I doubt Will's plea deal can be completed by then."

The fear in her eyes rises to the surface again. "So he wouldn't have the federal protection?"

"Oh, he'd be protected. Absolutely."

She begins chewing her lip again. "I know Dr. Cage is a good man. He took good care of Will when he worked at Triton, and my sister and aunts all go to him. They swear by him."

"Do you think Will would be willing to help my father, if I help him arrange this plea-bargain deal? I'll tell you right now, the feds won't consider it a priority. Your husband will have to insist on it."

Nita takes another drag with her quivering hand. "We ain't no fans of the government. I just want to know Will is safe."

"I can guarantee that, Nita."

A new glint shines in her eyes. "If he does that, you reckon you could sweeten the pot a little? You personally, I mean. We ain't greedy. Just something to help with the transition."

I take a deep breath before answering, and in the silence I hear Serenity grinding her teeth. "How much were you thinking?"

"Well . . . twenty-five thousand?"

I look down at the table, taking my time with this. I expected her to start much higher, and of course there's always time for them to go up, once they know they have me over a barrel.

"It's a big risk," I tell her. "The FBI would flip out if they knew we did something like that. They might revoke the agreement."

She's watching me like a hungry dog waiting to snatch a piece of food from my plate.

"But I could probably find a way to get that to you in cash. But—"

"Fifty," she says suddenly, looking almost defiant. "Fifty cash, and I'll guarantee Will stands up for Doc Cage in court."

This kind of agreement breaks so many laws I don't even want to think about it. "Tomorrow? He'll testify tomorrow for fifty?"

"You get me the money and guarantee his safety, and it's a deal."

"Don't ask me for a dollar more later. You do that, and I'll tell the FBI. And it'll blow your deal."

She holds up both hands and grins. "Fifty's it, baby doll. Fifty's good."

FIVE EXCRUCIATING MINUTES later, they let Serenity and me out on the corner of Washington and Union again. Tee looks like she's about to throw up. After the Winnebago rumbles away, she hugs herself and shivers.

"I feel like I need a *bath*," she says, her voice dripping with disgust.

"That's your KKK elite right there."

"Did you hear her talking about what they did to Viola? All she cared about was that her fat-ass husband cheated on her to rape a black woman."

"I thought you might lose your cool, but you stayed cold. You were like an ice statue."

Tee's eyes flash with fury. "Not on the inside. Man, when she said 'nigras' I nearly went across that table and snatched her tongue out of her head. It was worse than any time I ever heard 'nigger.'"

"I knew it would be bad. But you insisted on going."

"Oh, I'm glad I went. Some things you can't learn any other way. And that was one of them. Penn . . . think about spending tax dollars to protect that trash. I say give them to Snake. Or better yet, throw them in Angola and let the black gangs eat 'em up. That'd be fair payback right there."

"I think somebody needs a drink."

She catches my upper arm and squeezes hard. "Boy, you read my *mind*."

"I have to call Kaiser first."

"I'm good," she says, glancing up at my town house in the middle of the block. "I'm actually glad to be out of the house for a while. Cabin fever, you know?"

I already have my cell phone out. Speed-dialing Kaiser, I have to wait only two rings.

"Penn?" he says. "What's up?"

"Are you alone, John?"

"Give me five seconds."

I hear shuffling and rustling, then Kaiser says, "Go."

"Think about Dolores St. Denis and her potential as a witness against the Double Eagles. Are you doing that?"

"Uh . . . yeah. What kind of game is this?"

"Now multiply that by ten."

Kaiser says nothing for several seconds. Then he whispers, "You son of a *bitch*. You flipped an Eagle."

"Affirmative."

"Where are you?"

"Don't even think about coming to me. I'm busy. And this witness is not, repeat not, with me. Not even close to me. But he is going to make you the most famous FBI agent in recent history."

"You know I don't give a damn about that."

Kaiser's telling the truth about this. "I know. But there's nothing wrong with a little well-deserved acclaim. Especially for someone in trouble with his bosses."

"You're right. Thank you. Now, why do I feel like you're applying Vaseline all of a sudden?"

"Because I have one condition."

"Oh, shit. What's that?"

"Before he testifies for you, he testifies for my father. Tomorrow."

This time the silence lasts so long I think we've dropped our connection. But then Kaiser says, "There's no way in hell we're going to get a plea deal negotiated by tomorrow. Not in time."

"This witness is sui generis, John. He can bring down all that remains of the deadliest domestic terror cell in U.S. history. You can sell that. I know you can."

"Then I'd better get started. I need the guy's name."

"Not over the phone."

"Of course not."

"Serenity and I are headed to a bar. Say . . . the Corner Bar. You know it?"

"I've enjoyed many a scotch there since my confinement in Natchez. Me and my boys also get to steak night there now and again."

"We'll be there in ten minutes."

CHAPTER 46

QUENTIN AVERY HAD driven his wheelchair down the sidewalk that ran along the bluff from Edelweiss to where the old pecan-shelling plant used to stand. He'd thought of getting Doris to drive him to the meeting, but he knew that Joe Elder would feel safer with no one else around. Too, he'd wanted to feel the wind that raced up the face of the bluff after crossing the whole flat plain of Texas and Louisiana. The first part of his journey had been well lighted, and he'd passed a few lovers strolling along the fence back toward the center of town. But the streetlights grew farther apart out by the old pecan plant site. He was glad to see Elder's tall silhouette waiting for him when he arrived.

"That you, Quentin?" Joe called.

"It is."

"Where'd you come from?"

"Edelweiss. Penn Cage's house down by Silver Street."

"All that way in your wheelchair?"

"I've got good batteries. And I'm not an invalid yet."

"I didn't mean that. It's just late for a . . ."

"A stroll?" Quentin said with a bitter chuckle.

"Yeah."

Elder had been gazing out over the river, but Quentin turned toward what was left of the foundations of the old plant. "You know, when I was a boy, I used to sell pecans to this place. We'd sneak onto people's land and pick up what we could before they chased us off. Then come sell them here."

"Nobody ever arrested you?"

"I got bit by a couple of dogs, but no cops got me."

"What a loss that would have been to the legal profession."

Quentin laughed at Elder's sarcasm.

"What are we doing out here, Quentin?" the judge asked. "This is improper as hell."

Quentin then took a folded piece of paper from beneath the comforter on his lap. He unfolded the paper and held it out to Judge Elder. "Joe, this is a photocopy of one page taken from a ledger kept in the early 1960s by Albert Norris. You remember him, don't you?"

"Of course. Albert used to give me jellybeans when I walked by his store as a kid. What the hell is this about, Quentin? Ancient history?"

"Just look at the page."

Elder regarded the paper as though it might bite him. As a judge, he knew that a document could be as dangerous as a venomous snake. After leaning down and squinting in the dark, he took the page and moved closer to the streetlamp on the edge of the bluff.

"You see the names on the third line?"

Elder didn't answer at first, but Quentin could see that his hand was shaking.

"Are you trying to blackmail me, Quentin?"

"You know better than that. It's just something I thought you should be aware of."

"You have the original?"

"No. There are several ledgers, but they're not in my possession. You're looking at a copy of the only page with those two names on it. But the rest of the story is on the following page."

"Who has the originals?"

"I'd rather not say. He can be trusted, though."

"I don't know any mortal who fits that description."

"The man who possesses those ledgers could have turned the towns on both sides of this river upside down any time during the last forty-one years, but he never has. He hasn't exposed a single person named in them."

"He must be a saint to fight that temptation."

"Close to it, Joe."

"White or black?"

"Black."

Elder nodded. "I repeat my question. Why are you showing me this?"

"Joe . . . to be frank, I've sensed some bias from the bench during this trial. I'm not alone in that, but I doubt the general public perceives it. And I was puzzled by it myself, until I read this entry in that ledger."

"What do you think it means?"

"Come on, brother. I watched you when you read those names. You weren't surprised at all."

Impatience tightened Elder's expression. "What do you *want,* Quentin?"

"Only what every defendant is entitled to under the law. A fair trial under an impartial judge."

"No court of appeals would say you're not getting that. They might say you've got Alzheimer's disease, but that's not my lookout."

Quentin just waited.

"Why are you defending Tom Cage?" Elder asked finally. "A man like that, who took advantage of a sister back in those days?"

"My brother, you need to take a couple of steps back from this case. All you see in it is your mama and yourself. Or Claude Devereux."

"It's the same damn situation!"

"No, it's not. Devereux is a lying bastard who defended mobsters and Klansmen, cheated his partners, dishonored his robe when he was a district judge, and probably paid for a murder by contract. He did have charisma, though, and I imagine that's how he convinced your mama to go with him for a while. But that's got nothing to do with Tom Cage. Dr. Cage is one of the finest men I've ever known, black or white. And that's saying something."

Elder snorted with contempt. "From the evidence I've seen, Tom Cage may have broken his medical oath, dishonored his profession, and committed murder himself."

"You haven't seen all the evidence. I haven't even begun my case."

"*What* case? Shad Johnson's already got your client boxed for transport to Parchman, with a red bow wrapped around him."

"Joe, you worked for me. Do you really believe that? This trial's only half over. And that's why I'm here tonight. I can't fight Shad and you both."

Elder shook the paper in his hand. "What's going to happen to the original of this page, Quentin?"

"I'd like to say it could just disappear. But the journals of Albert Norris belong to history. Norris was murdered by the Double Eagle group, and his murder must be solved. His killers must be punished, and publicly."

"You're saying those journals will be evidence in a future murder case?"

"They'll probably have to be, Joe. They're filled with information about the Double Eagle group. Of course, I hope your part of the story never comes up."

"Hope ain't much to hang a hat on."

Quentin let him think about that for a few seconds. Then he said, "I can give you a little more than that. As far as I can see, if there were a page or two missing from Norris's journals, that wouldn't change the outcome of a major case. What's a couple of pieces of paper in the sands of time?"

The judge looked off toward the river, as though he couldn't bear to look Quentin in the eye. "Would you do that for me?"

"It's not completely up to me, but I'll do all I can to ensure it."

"Who has those damned journals, Quentin?"

"I can't tell you that. But I will tell you, the page came to me through Penn Cage."

"Shit! This *is* blackmail."

"No! It's not. The saint who kept the ledgers secret all these years gave them to Penn Cage because he trusts Penn to do the right thing. He did that because, after watching the trial, he thinks you're not being fair. He thinks you're trying to convict your own father by helping Shad Johnson convict Tom Cage."

"Shad doesn't need any help from me. Not on this case."

"All I want from you is impartiality, Joe. Let the jury decide this case on their own."

"I don't trust Cage to keep quiet. Not if his father is convicted."

"Have a little faith in your fellow man, Joe. It's like trusting a jury."

Elder was about to reply when a skinny black boy of about eighteen stepped out of the shadows and approached them along the fence. He wore unkempt clothes, and his pants were hanging off his behind in the current fashion.

"He's not out here for exercise," Quentin said softly.

"Have a little faith," Judge Elder said in a mocking tone. "Isn't that what you just told me?"

The stranger stopped about three feet from the judge. "Yo, brother," he said. "You got a couple dollars for a man in trouble?"

"Not tonight," Elder said. "We're talking here, and we need some privacy."

The stranger's head ducked and weaved as he looked back toward the road. Then a glittering knife appeared in his hand.

"I'll give you privacy, after you give me all yo' shit. The crip, too."

Judge Elder stared at the man in amazement. "Boy, do you have any idea who you're pointing that knife at?"

"A richer man than me. That jacket you're wearing would rent my crib for six months."

Elder straightened up and shook out his arms like a center about to defend the lane against an All-American forward. "So, you're gonna rob a man in a wheelchair?" He looked down at Quentin, who was watching the knife warily. "Jesus wept, Quentin."

The mugger looked back at the road again. "Hey, homes, I gots to live, too."

"Nigga, *please,*" Elder snapped. "You listen up. I'm Judge Joe Elder, and if you don't get straight back to your crib and stop hassling people, I'll put you *under* the fucking jail. You hear me?"

The mugger's eyes widened, revealing bloodshot sclera in the dim light. "Man, you crazy? Don't you see this knife?"

"Do you see this gun?"

Elder and the mugger whipped their heads toward Quentin, who had taken a small black automatic from beneath the blanket on his lap.

"You just do what the judge told you to do," Quentin said. "And pray he doesn't remember your face the next time you show up in court."

The mugger didn't look frightened. "You gonna shoot me, old man?"

"My little brother, I will shoot you in the balls, and after you go limping away, I'll plug you in the ass. Now drop that knife!"

Two seconds later the knife hit the ground.

"Listen to me, boy," Joe Elder said. "You need money? There's a bunch of nice ladies who work hard to keep up an old cemetery on Watkins Street. One of your ancestors might be buried there. You show up there next Wednesday afternoon. I'll pay you to cut grass and help those ladies."

The boy stared at the judge like he was crazy.

"If you *don't* show, and you ever come before me in court? Boy, you'll need diapers the rest of your life 'cause your asshole won't close back up after your time in jail. You feel me?"

The boy bolted into the dark.

Judge Elder leaned over, picked up the knife, then threw it off the bluff into the kudzu below. "Jesus, Quentin. What's this world coming to, when you can't walk through a small town without getting mugged?"

"That's pretty rare here, actually."

"Not in Ferriday." He blew a long stream of air from his cheeks. "You don't carry that piece into court, do you?"

"Not yet."

"You're full of shit about me showing bias in the courtroom."

"We'll see how it goes tomorrow."

Elder leaned on the fence and looked out over the gleaming river. Then he bent and pulled a weed stalk from the ground and stuck it between his teeth like a farm boy.

"You know, when I was growing up in Ferriday, folks used to say 'Thank God for Mississippi,' just so we wouldn't be last in everything. But I believe Concordia Parish in those days was worse than any county in Mississippi. Except maybe the Gulf Coast."

"Carlos Marcello had his hand in both places. Between his outfit and the local rednecks, it was pretty bad, Joe."

Elder pushed himself off the fence and squatted in front of Avery's wheelchair. "Quentin, what kind of crazy-ass game are you playing in my courtroom?"

Quentin smiled at his old protégé. "A long one."

"Well, you'd better get your shit together quick. Or Dr. Cage is going to spend whatever time he's got left in one of the worst prisons in America."

Quentin's eyes twinkled in the dark. "O ye of little faith. You've got no more confidence in me than that?"

"I've seen you work magic, all right. But this case reminds me of that crazy motorcycle jumper back in the seventies, Evel Knievel. He kept on adding more cars to the line he had to jump. And then he tried to jump a canyon. I think you've set yourself up the same way. There's a limit, Quentin, even to genius. And you've got to drag that jury over the canyon with you."

"You know what I say about that?"

"What?"

"Ain't no hill for a stepper."

Joe Elder looked at the place where Quentin Avery's legs should have been. "Speaking metaphorically, of course."

Quentin raised his forefinger and shook it at his old clerk. "What did I used to tell you before we walked into a trial?"

Elder laughed heartily for the first time. "Watch and learn, Joe. Watch and learn."

Quentin smiled. "I knew I'd taught you something."

CHAPTER 47

SNAKE KNOX STOOD in darkness amid the twenty-three surviving columns of the Windsor Ruins and listened to the rumble of approaching motorcycles. It sounded like at least four to him, but he kept calm and focused on the business at hand. He'd placed lookouts on the highway covering both approaches, and now that was paying off.

5 Harleys, read the text from one of the Quince twins, two quiet but eager nineteen-year-olds enlisted by Alois.

Stay on point till I clear you, Snake texted back.

He'd chosen Windsor because of its isolation and its proximity to Rodney, but also for its history. Built only four miles from the river, the mansion and its third-floor cupola had served as an observation post for Confederate forces until the Vicksburg Campaign, when Ulysses Grant took over the 2,600-acre plantation and converted the house to a Union hospital—and observation post. Snake figured if it was good enough for the Blue and the Gray, it was good enough for him.

Tonight the ornate capitals of the great Corinthian columns stood out starkly against the moonlit clouds, giving the scene a ghostly aura that appealed to his sense of the dramatic. He wondered if the Varangian Kindred would appreciate the ambiance.

Snake had parked Red Nearing's pickup in the turnaround in front of the ruins, to give Lars and his VK boys the impression that he was trapped here, if they chose to believe that. But Alois and the Quinces had parked three ATVs in the trees on the north side of the ruins. If Snake needed to make a quick getaway, he could do it—so long as he reached the ATVs. To that end, he'd posted Alois in a nearby tree with a rifle and a night scope, while Wilma Deen waited behind one of the massive plinths that supported the forty-foot columns. Armed with a pump shotgun, Wilma could provide a hell of a lot of covering fire in the event of a hasty retreat.

As the bikes approached, Snake felt his burner phone vibrate against his leg. He'd instructed Lars not to use phones out here, so he wasn't surprised to find it was Billy Byrd calling him back.

"You found that high yellow yet?" Snake said by way of answer.

"Not yet."

"Then why are you bothering me?"

"Two preachers showed up at Mayor Cage's house. Nigger preachers."

"What preachers?"

"The Baldwins, from Clayton, Louisiana."

Snake knew them well. Old man Baldwin had been tough as nails back in the day. He'd served in the navy during the war, and when he came home, he hadn't planned to stand at the back of the line. When things had heated up in '64, he'd formed the Deacons for Defense and helped arm the local black community against the Klan. Even though Snake had been his enemy, he'd respected the man for fighting instead of lying down.

"After they left," Byrd went on, "Cage went to where Quentin Avery's staying, on the bluff. Then Avery goes out to the bluff and meets the trial judge, Elder."

This surprised Snake. "And?"

"And he gave Elder something. Papers, it looked like. I'm guessing he got something from the preachers."

"What would Avery go to Elder about?"

"Are you kidding? The trial, I imagine. But that's nigger business. I ain't got the first idea."

"You're a big help, Billy."

Byrd grunted. "You know, watching those two uppity bastards standing on the bluff together, I couldn't help but think how easy it'd be for one man with a shotgun to do the world a favor. One blast of buckshot."

"It ain't 1964, Billy."

"That's for damn sure. It's okay to kill a white man but not a black one? World's upside down."

"You do what I tell you and nothing more."

"I know. I know."

"Keep your eyes on the mayor. And don't forget what I told you about tonight. Surest way to head off any surprises in court."

The sheriff sighed and hung up.

Twenty seconds later, five headlights slashed the darkness of the dirt turnaround, and five big Harleys rolled right up to the cable that prevented vehicles from riding among the columns. Snake watched the VK dismount and take weapons from their saddlebags, fought the urge to draw his own pistol.

Lars Dempsey himself led the group. Snake could pick him out, even in the dark. Dempsey's long blond hair, gone to gray, was pulled into a ponytail. Behind him Snake recognized Toons Teufel. No mistaking the arrogant strut. The other three looked like members of Toons's special security unit. They walked to within five yards of Snake, their heads swiveling slowly as they scanned the footprint of the old plantation house.

"You got a lot of sack," Toons said from Dempsey's right shoulder. "Dragging us all the way out here."

Snake said nothing. He would not speak until Lars Dempsey did. All five men wore riding leathers: chaps and jackets, and each of the jackets had VK emblazoned on the right arm.

The founder of the Varangian Kindred scratched his beard and said, "You blew up my safe."

"The retard there hid my passport in it."

"What if he did that on my orders?"

"Then you blew up your own safe."

Lars sniffed and thought about this. "Why'd you split the sod farm?"

"I got tired of this fool playing with his knife. If I'd stayed any longer, I'd have cut his nose off with it."

Toons took a step forward, but Dempsey stopped him with a raised hand.

"What do you want from us?" Lars asked. "You must have a reason for this meeting."

"I need what I needed from you at the start. Manpower. Troops."

"For what?"

"Are you still watching the old Eagles for me?"

"Some. Not so much, since you bugged out."

"I need you to get back to it. ASAP."

"Why would we do that?"

"To get what you got into business with me for in the first place."

"You've been kind of slow coming across with that."

"Let's get something straight," Snake said. "You ain't a high school quarterback and I ain't no cheerleader. We got a deal. You're gettin' itchy. But you've moved more weight over the past two months than you did in the six months before that. And I've taken a ton of heat off your gun trade. You've probably doubled your profits there, too."

Lars said nothing, which told Snake he'd been dead-on.

"It's not just the surveillance," Snake said. "I need some soldiers. And not the guys trained by this clown. I need shooters. Guys who've been in the shit and know how to stay cool. Who can hold their fire until it's time and won't piss themselves when things get dicey."

"You mouthy old fuck," Toons said, lunging forward with a flash of steel.

"Freeze!" Lars barked.

Toons froze. "Why?" he asked, panting with rage. "We don't need this old fool."

"Because he's no fool," Lars said quietly. "Are you, Snake?"

Snake reached into his pocket and took out a quarter. He held it out to Toons.

"What the fuck is that?" Toons asked.

"Your life."

"What?"

Snake tossed the quarter on the ground between them. Two seconds later, a rifle shot cracked through the darkness, and all five men in leathers hit the dirt. When no further shots sounded, they got to their feet, nervously looking around.

"Where's your quarter, Toons?" Snake asked.

Toons looked down at the ground, then bent at the knee and plucked the deformed piece of metal from the dirt.

Snake felt a little twinge of pride at his son's marksmanship. *Blood always tells,* Frank used to say. "You can have the next one through your eye, if you like," Snake said.

"You made your point," Lars muttered. "Who you planning on killing tomorrow?"

Snake wasn't about to answer this question. "That's my business."

"Not the way things are going. We've got the FBI shaking us down from here to Texas. I don't want you using my men to hit FBI agents."

This ponytailed bastard has good instincts, Snake thought. "I may not be killing anybody. I just need to remove a certain threat."

"And for that you need shooters?"

"Have you got 'em or not?" Snake snapped, hoping his exasperation would forestall further inquiry.

After a long look, Lars nodded. "You'll get your men. Where?"

"Here. Tomorrow, eleven A.M. I'll need them for twelve hours."

"No problem. But let me ask you something. That trial. How come the mayor isn't defending his father? I heard he was a hotshot prosecutor when he lived in Houston."

"His daddy don't want him," Snake said.

"Why not?"

Snake considered how much to tell Dempsey. At length, he said, "Daddy's got secrets he don't want his boy to know."

Lars nodded. "Don't we all. Do you know what his are? The doc's?"

Snake smiled. "Good night, gentlemen."

Dempsey reached out and tapped Toons on the shoulder. "Let's go."

Lars turned and started back to the turnaround, but Toons didn't follow. He remained rooted to the ground, scanning the tops of the great columns for any sign of a sniper. When he failed to find one, he jabbed a finger at Snake.

"You and me ain't finished, old man."

"You're begging for a bullet, retard. Take some advice. Don't be with the group coming tomorrow. You're not cut out for real action."

Snake turned his back on the VK security chief and walked between two plinths into the darkness.

CHAPTER 48

SERENITY AND I are sitting up in the kitchen, drinking tea and waiting to hear from Quentin. Jenny just went upstairs with a migraine; Mom and Mia are watching television with Annie in the den. I'm trying to decide whether they smelled liquor on Tee and me when we came in from our meeting with Kaiser in the Corner Bar. I know Annie smelled smoke, because she mentioned it. If anyone smelled alcohol, it would have been Mia.

"What's the deal with Jenny?" Tee whispers, twirling her forefinger in her mug, from which she has not removed the tea bag.

I shrug, my mind on the likelihood that the FBI will allow Devine to testify in Dad's trial—and in time. "She gets migraines."

Serenity glances at the door to the den, as though Mia or Annie might hear her. "I mean, of everyone in your family, she seems the least like she fits." Whatever my facial reaction, Serenity feels encouraged to go on. "And why does she live in England?"

"It's complicated. Jenny was seven years ahead of me in school, and she was a star. But she didn't want to teach back then. She wanted to write. She majored in English lit and spent her first four postgrad years writing two novels that together sold about three hundred copies. I, on the other hand, never set out to be a writer. It was simply something I stumbled into after tiring of my career as a prosecutor."

"Oh boy."

"You can imagine the rest. When my first novel sold at auction, then hit the bestseller lists, Jenny began taking visiting professorships overseas. Ultimately, she married an Englishman and remained over there to raise her children. Jenny would say 'rear' her children, of course, but that kind of grammatical precision will get you a cup of coffee if you add three dollars to it."

"Do you feel guilty about that? Her reaction?"

Before I can answer, my mother appears in the door that leads to the den. "How are you two doing? Is there anything going on with Tom's case that I don't know about?"

Serenity and I share a look. Though she doesn't change her expression, I sense she's telling me to come clean with my mother. Without giving her too many specifics, I tell Mom that an original Double Eagle is about to turn state's evidence against his fellow criminals, and there's a chance that he could testify tomorrow in Dad's trial.

"If the U.S. attorney completes the plea deal and allows it," I conclude, "I think that man's testimony alone could constitute reasonable doubt and result in Dad's acquittal."

Mom stares at me in silence for several seconds. "Is your tea still warm?" she asks.

I pick up my cup and hold it out to her. "I've hardly touched it."

When she takes the cup, I see her hand shaking. Serenity gives her an encouraging smile, but in this moment I realize that my mother is barely holding herself together. She takes a long swallow of tea, then focuses in the middle distance.

"Quentin did a fine job with his opening statement, didn't he? He floored that jury. I—I think we're going to have to trust that Quentin is still the legal lion he was when the whole world knew his name."

"He stunned them, all right," I reply, and leave it there. I'm not about to make Mom face how risky Quentin's strategy is.

"I think I'm going up," she says. "It's been a *long* day. May I keep your tea?"

"It's yours now."

She gives me a guilty smile. "Good night, Serenity."

To my surprise, Tee gets to her feet. "Actually, Mrs. Cage, I think I'll go up with you. It *has* been a long day." She looks back at me. "And Penn needs a little time with Annie."

My mother nods pointedly, and I know then that Serenity has scored a point with her.

"Good night, you guys," I say wearily.

They turn and walk into the hall together, without Serenity giving me the slightest signal that I might see her later. I can't believe she's going to go to bed without hearing Quentin's report of his meeting with Judge Elder. And *that,* I suddenly realize, was her signal. She knew she'd never slip a wink or an intimate wave past my mother.

She left it to me to figure out the obvious.

AN HOUR LATER, I'm staring up into Tee's eyes as she labors above me with quiet persistence. Then she closes them, which I regret, but this allows my own eyes free rein over her body, which is miraculously new and strange. Her skin is indeed the color of a paper bag, but her nipples and areolae are the color of Hershey's Kisses.

"I—don't—like—being—*quiet,*" she whispers with rhythmic frustration, working toward her second release. In the moment of cresting, her eyes flash open and find mine, and the urgency behind them pours into me, or rather, seems to pull something *from* me. Serenity's orgasms, while long and powerful, seem not to satiate a deeper need that I feel within her, a hunger for connection that is only partly physical.

As she shudders above me, closing her eyes once more, then falling forward until her face is pressed into my neck, I think of all the places she's been, the experiences she's had, so many of which she described in her book. All that—a story known to hundreds of thousands of people—is contained within the mind and flesh of the woman molded against me now, breathing deeply in my ear.

"What is it?" she asks in a sleepy voice.

"What?"

"You want to ask me something."

"No, I don't."

Her eyes open. "Liar."

I feel such an eerie sense of having my mind read that I grasp desperately for any subject other than the one I was thinking of.

"I was just wondering," I begin blindly, "why . . . you haven't asked me if you're the first black woman I've slept with."

"Hah!" Serenity rolls onto her back and spits a sharp laugh at the ceiling. "Baby, please. I *know* I'm your first."

She's gone from somnolent to wide awake in less than a second. Boy, did I pick the wrong question. "How do you know?" I ask.

"The way you look at me, smell me, touch my hair. It's a good thing your writing's more subtle than your game."

"I'm sorry I brought it up."

She rolls onto her side and runs her finger over my chest. "'Course, I'm just *half* black," she says in a teasing tone. "Unless we're going by the one-drop rule. Then I'm *all* black. But I don't know if you could handle the real deal."

"Can we just skip it?"

She runs her fingertip down to my abdomen, then farther still. "Next thing, you're gonna ask me about penis size. That's the next white-boy question."

I try to keep my face impassive, but Tee just laughs harder. When she finally stops, she says, "You want me to just *tell* you?"

"I don't know."

She pokes me in the side, a mischievous glint in her eyes. "*Well.* Just between us girls . . . beyond a certain minimum, it's not how big it is. It's how *hard* it is."

For some reason, this doesn't comfort me much.

"It's killing you not to ask me, isn't it?" she presses, her eyes filled with mirth.

"Don't know what you're talking about."

"Oh, yes, you do. That *certain minimum.*" She reaches down and closes her hand around what is commonly called my manhood and whispers, "You made the cut, Mr. Mayor. *Just.*"

While I process this answer, she squeezes me and says, "How 'bout you finish what you started?"

Before I can do that, my cell phone rings. Serenity groans, then rolls over and grabs it off the bedside table.

"Quentin," she says, handing it to me.

I click SEND and say, "You took long enough, didn't you?"

Tee presses her lips to my ear and hisses, "*Speakerphone.*"

I hit the button.

"Is anybody else with you?" Quentin asks.

Serenity shakes her head.

"Just you and me and God, Q. Or was that redundant?"

Quentin chuckles. "I'm surprised. Where's that hot little Nobel Prize winner you had with you before?"

Serenity snorts a laugh, and Quentin says, "I thought so. I caught some vibe earlier tonight. You're a lucky man, Penn Cage."

Tee rolls her eyes, but the smile doesn't leave her face. "Did *you* do any good tonight," she asks, "you old hound dog?"

"Judge Elder and I had a frank and honest exchange of views. I think we'll find him a little more amicable in court tomorrow. What about my potential star witness? Have you two been hanging with the Klan?"

"We have. Everything may depend on John Kaiser at this point. They've promised to testify for Dad, but the witness is scared to death of Snake Knox."

"Rightfully so."

"I've promised to guarantee their security. I'd be more confident if Kaiser and the U.S. attorney could get a deal signed. Kaiser is grateful to us for turning the witness, so he's glad for him to help Dad out. But there are a lot of moving parts."

"Always, always."

"What about Dad? Did you talk to him?"

"I'm just leaving the jail now. I told Tom everything you told me—the possibility of deputies tampering with the hair and fiber evidence, everything—and he agrees with me. Don't make any accusations against the sheriff's department."

Serenity squints at me as though something is wrong.

"Dad said that?" I ask.

"Yes, and more. Tom said, 'We have no proof of anything, and even if we did, it would only create a distraction.'"

I'm incredulous. "Wait a minute. Dad said that even if we have *proof* of tampering, we should do nothing?"

"Correct."

"Quentin, what the hell?"

"There's more. Tom also said to tell Jewel Washington to stop digging into whatever those deputies might have done."

"*Why?*"

"You lost your fiancée, Penn. Do you really have to ask me that?"

A wave of heat passes over my face. "Are you saying those deputies might kill the county coroner to cover up what they did?"

"I'm saying it's reckless to pretend we're not in a very dangerous situation."

"Christ, man. If we could get proof that Billy Byrd's deputies suppressed evidence implicating someone else in Viola's death, that alone—"

"Boy, listen to me! This case ain't about hair and fiber. Do you hear me?"

Serenity's brow is knitted tight in concentration.

"What's it about, then?"

"For me? Representing your father's interests to the best of my ability. Now, I've got to go. Doris is waiting. The best thing you can do is get the U.S. attorney to close that plea deal and clear—"

"Don't say the name!"

Quentin curses in frustration. "I was going to say clear *my witness* to testify tomorrow. But don't make any other moves without checking with me first."

"Bullshit I won't. Don't you want me to come down there and brief you on what the witness knows about Viola?"

"No. I'm not going to start getting excited about a witness who may or may not appear tomorrow. I'd be a fool to rely on that. Good night."

As I drop the phone on the sheet, Serenity says, "Did that sound right to you? About the hair and fiber?"

"It sounds like the same bullshit Quentin's given me from the start."

"I just don't see the logic of your father's position, other than he's acting out of fear. And that doesn't fit with what I know of him."

"I know. It's not fear for himself, though. It's fear for others."

I can tell Tee is ready for an intense discussion, but after today, I simply haven't the patience or stamina for it. What I want to do is what she suggested before Quentin called—finish what I started before. Luckily, Tee is quick to read my mood, and once more she climbs astride me, this time sitting on my thighs so she can use her hands first.

"Any more silly white-boy questions before we resume?" she asks with a teasing smile.

"I learned my lesson."

"Good."

She reaches between us to slide me into her, then freezes.

"Penn?" says my mother. "I couldn't sleep for thinking about—"

At that moment I realize Mom isn't outside the door, but inside the room with us. Whipping my head left, I see her standing motionless with one hand on the doorknob, her mouth hanging slack, her eyes glassy. All three of us seem transfixed by some external force. The first person to move is Serenity, who reaches down and raises the comforter to cover her gently swaying breasts.

"I should have *knocked*," Mom cries, snapping out of her trance like someone hit her with heart paddles.

"Mom, it's okay!" I call, but the door closes on my words.

Cursing under my breath, I lift Serenity off my midsection, roll out of bed, and grab for my pants, but she catches hold of my arm and says, "Penn, don't do it."

"Don't what?"

I look back angrily, but Tee's face holds only sadness and warning.

"Your mama didn't see us just then," she says softly. "She saw your father and Viola."

Her words suck the breath out of my chest. Thinking about the pain my mother must be enduring right now is almost impossible to bear. On top of the trial and the gossip and all the rest of it—

"Don't," Tee whispers. "Don't do that to yourself. You can't change their past. You can only change the future. Your future. Come back to bed."

"I don't think I—"

"Yes, you can." Her dark eyes are no longer trying to pull something from me. They are pouring something into me. She reaches out and takes my hand, pulls me back onto the mattress. "Remember how we started?"

"How?"

"No talking."

After a few seconds I nod, not at all certain that we want or need the same things in this moment. But she pulls me to her, threading one leg around mine and running her fingers through my hair, her eyes never leaving my face. "Tonight let's try something new," she says, softly kissing my shoulder. "Tonight, you talk all you want."

She pulls the covers up to our necks, then over our heads.

THURSDAY

CHAPTER 49

ON THURSDAY MORNING, when Judge Elder asks Quentin to call his first witness, a retired army colonel named Karl Eklund walks into the courtroom from the back door and strides to the witness box with a soldierly bearing that would put Major Matthew Powers to shame. Eklund stands about an inch under six feet, but he has the chiseled features of a martial bust whose sculptor left no spare material on his work, and the colonel's eyes have plainly seen more than most men ever will. It's only after looking at Eklund for half a minute that I realize that something isn't quite right about his face. It's been worked on extensively by plastic surgeons, not to enhance his beauty, which is limited, but to reconstruct whatever existed before whatever happened to it happened. When Colonel Eklund takes the oath with his hand on the Bible, he gives the impression of a man who would cut off his right arm before breaking a vow.

I half expect Shad to try to disqualify Eklund at the start, but the DA seems to sense that he would lose more points with the jury by trying to silence this man than by letting him speak. As Quentin rolls toward the podium, Shadrach looks worried.

Looking from Shad back toward the witness box, I happen to catch sight of my father. For most of the trial I've seen only the back of his head, but now he has turned to face Quentin by the podium, and his face is almost bloodless. Dad knew that Colonel Eklund would be testifying this morning, yet he looks like he never expected to see the man walking and talking again.

"Colonel Eklund," Quentin begins, "do you know the defendant, Dr. Thomas Cage?"

"Yes, sir. I do."

"How do you know him?"

"He served under me in Korea."

"Was he a physician then?"

The colonel gives a soft chuckle. "No, he was a private. An eighteen-year-old medic, fresh out of high school. I was twenty-three."

"During this trial, we've heard a lot of testimony about Private Cage's actions on the night of November thirtieth, 1950. Were you with him on that night?"

"No, sir. I'd been wounded and flown to a hospital in Japan."

"I see. So when was the last time you saw Private Cage?"

"The night the Bugout began."

"I'm sorry? The Bugout?"

"The American retreat from the Yalu River area in Korea. It started the night of November twenty-fifth, when the Chinese revealed their true strength and went through our lines like Hitler's panzers through the Polish cavalry."

"I see. What was your rank and assignment on that night?"

"I was a second lieutenant in charge of J Company, one of the northernmost American units in Korea. Love Company was stuck out the farthest. They were an all-black unit commanded by a Japanese-American officer. Love Company usually got the most dangerous probing assignments, for the obvious reason. And then there was us, Company J, to the east on Hill 403."

"What was your assignment on that night?"

"To hold the hill."

"Did you succeed?"

"No, sir."

"Why not?"

"Because at midnight the Chinese People's Volunteer Army attacked us with overwhelming force. The odds were in the neighborhood of fifty to one. We weren't dug in very well, either. I'd been on Peleliu in the Pacific, so I knew how important good foxholes were, but the men were wet and tired when we got to the hill, and the ground was frozen. Deeper holes wouldn't have mattered, though, given what the Chicoms threw at us that night."

"Was Private Cage on Hill 403 that night?"

"He was. He served as one of my company medics."

"Do you remember how he performed his duties during the Chinese assault?"

"I'm not likely to forget it."

"Why is that, Colonel?"

Colonel Eklund is searching for my father, I realize. He probably can't quite grasp that the old man sitting at the defense table is the young medic he commanded in Korea. But then he does, because a look of wonder and sadness comes into his eyes.

"Colonel Eklund?" Quentin prompts. "Why won't you forget Private Cage's actions on Hill 403?"

"Because I recommended him for the Medal of Honor for what he did that night."

"Objection!" Shad barks into the shocked silence. "This can have no relevance to what happened in an ambulance five nights later."

Without waiting for Judge Elder to rule, Quentin says, "I'd like to let the jury decide that, Your Honor. But I believe you'll see the relevance in a few moments."

At last I understand why Quentin allowed Shad to call Major Powers to the stand with his tale of mercy killing in the ambulance. The moment Powers began to testify about what happened in 1950, the Korean War became fair game in this trial. Elation—and resentment at Quentin—are flooding through me in equal measure. Quentin claimed that my hope of him having a surprise witness in his back pocket was juvenile, yet true to his reputation as a courtroom magician, he has produced one.

Judge Elder looks hard at Shad. "As I said yesterday, Mr. Johnson, you opened the door to Korea. I can't very well stop Mr. Avery from marching through it."

With the smallest of satisfied smiles, Quentin turns back to Colonel Eklund. "Can you describe the events that prompted you to recommend Private Cage for that award?"

Eklund reaches into his inside coat pocket. "I actually brought the nomination letter with me. I just hope I brought my proper glasses."

"You can just tell us in your own words what happened."

"I'd rather read the nomination letter. I wrote it in 1950 while recuperating in Japan. I'm getting on in years, as you can see, and I figure the letter's more accurate than my memory."

"As you wish."

If this is all theater, prearranged by Quentin, it is very effective theater. But something tells me that Colonel Eklund is exactly what he appears to be: a willing witness with an important story to tell. And as he moves the yellowed letter nearer to and farther away from his face, searching for the proper distance, I sense that I am about to learn what my father meant when he said, "Korea wasn't all like what happened in that ambulance."

"Should I just start, Judge?" Eklund asks.

"Go ahead, Colonel."

The man clears his throat once, then begins in a strong baritone that reverberates through the courtroom.

"The nomination reads: '*27 November 1950, Ch'ongch'on River, North Korea. For conspicuous gallantry and intrepidity at the risk of his life above and beyond the call of duty while serving with Company J in action against enemy aggressor forces. At midnight the company, assigned the defense of Hill 403, came under overwhelming fire by two full divisions of Chinese infantry. In the chaos of this night assault, it was impossible to determine how many American foxholes had been overrun. Cries from wounded men came from every side, including false ones made by the enemy in an effort to pinpoint the few holes still held by J Company. With complete disregard for his own safety, Pfc. Cage crawled from foxhole to foxhole, administering aid and encouragement to his fellow soldiers, most of whom were mortally wounded. During this hours-long effort, Pfc. Cage was exposed to constant enemy fire, as Communist troops continued to pour through the American lines. When a second company medic was shot on open ground, Pfc. Cage braved a gauntlet of machine-gun fire to carry his fellow aid man to shelter. Approximately ten minutes later, an enemy grenade dropped into the command hole, and Company J's lieutenant received disabling shrapnel wounds to the face, chest, and legs.*'"

Colonel Eklund gives Judge Elder a crooked smile and says, "That's me, Your Honor, as you can see from my scarred-up kisser."

Soft chuckles come from the balcony.

I turn in my seat, looking for Walt Garrity, wondering if he was the second aid man whom Dad carried to safety. After a few seconds, I spot him, on the ground floor this time, about five rows back, in the gallery. Walt catches my eye, shakes his head, then returns his gaze to his former commanding officer.

"Please, go on," says Judge Elder.

"'Pfc. Cage stabilized his commanding officer, then remained at his CO's side and helped to direct the remainder of the company by serving as a runner, even as the position was overrun by the enemy. When a Chinese soldier leaped into the command foxhole, Pfc. Cage picked up an entrenching tool and killed him by striking him in the neck. After the main body of Chinese had passed through the American lines, Pfc. Cage made a circuit of the foxholes to determine how many members of his company remained alive. During this effort he was wounded in the shoulder by shrapnel. Pfc. Cage treated himself with morphine, then returned to the command hole to report. Of the original eighty-two men on Hill 403, only fourteen remained alive. Eleven were gravely wounded. With his CO disabled, Pfc. Cage rounded up the survivors for evacuation, formed stretcher parties of wounded men, then led them down the hill and took shelter in a ravine, where they came under sniper and strafing fire. While sheltering in the ravine, eight defenders succumbed to their wounds or to enemy fire.'"

Colonel Eklund pauses for a moment and looks at the ceiling. After blinking a few times, he wipes his face with his sleeve, then pushes on.

"'Using an M2 carbine borrowed from a fallen comrade, Pfc. Cage fought vigorously to repel a Chinese charge. During this attack, he received additional shrapnel wounds caused by fragmentation grenades, yet he continued to resist. Just before dawn, Pfc. Cage led the six survivors of Company J out of the ravine and eventually joined elements of two shattered Second Division companies moving toward Kunu-ri.'" The colonel clears his throat again, then finishes in a quavering voice. *"'By his unwavering fortitude, sustained personal bravery, and indomitable fighting spirit against overwhelming odds, Pfc. Cage reflects the highest glory upon himself, and upholds the finest traditions of the U.S. Army Medical Corps.'"*

When Colonel Eklund stops speaking, no sound can be heard in the court.

"Thank you, Colonel," Quentin says softly. "I don't imagine that's an easy night to recall."

"No, sir. It was one of the worst days in the history of the U.S. Army. But I'm proud of how my men fought, regardless of the outcome."

"Your Honor," Shad says irritably, "this is descending into melodrama."

Colonel Eklund continues speaking to Quentin and Judge Elder as though Shad did not object. "I'd like to add that those colored—excuse me, African-American boys from Love Company fought just as hard as mine did. Nearly to the last man. You fellows ought to be proud of them."

"Your Honor!" Shad cries. "It is no longer 1950!"

Despite the colonel's politically incorrect language, Judge Elder seems inclined to be gentle with him. "Mr. Johnson, you made this bed. Don't whine about lying in it."

While Shad gapes at the judge, Joe Elder says, "Mr. Avery, have you finished with this witness?"

"Not quite yet, Your Honor." Quentin turns back to the witness box. "Colonel Eklund, did Private Cage receive the medal you recommended him for?"

"No, sir."

"Why not?"

"The Medal of Honor requires three witnesses to the act of valor, and a lot of other things besides. We had the witnesses, though for a while it looked like none of us would make it out alive. And there was no question that Tom had earned it. In fact, a few weeks after I put him up for the award, I heard that President Truman was going to give it to Tom along with another boy from that same few days of fighting. I knew because they pull a man out of the line when he's going to get the big one. In the old days, too many boys had gotten killed right after winning the Medal of Honor, and that was embarrassing to the service."

"Was Private Cage in fact pulled out of the line?"

"No, sir."

"Why not?"

"Well, I didn't find out why right away. I just got word he was to stay on the line while we waited for replacements. But later on, my commanding general told me that the medal had been quashed for political reasons."

"Political reasons?" Quentin echoes, emphasizing the word *political* enough to remind the jury of Major Powers's story of the murder charges he'd brought against Dad and Walt. "Did he specify those reasons?"

"The general himself told me that an air force pilot had made accusations of murder against Private Cage and Private Garrity from our company. He claimed they'd killed some of our wounded during the retreat from the reservoir. Well, by that time the defeat at Chosin Reservoir had become a huge embarrassment for General MacArthur. The marines came out looking okay, but the army looked terrible. The last thing MacArthur wanted was accusations flying between the services about medics killing our own men. He wasn't about to let something like that become a scandal, so Tom's Medal of Honor vanished into the Big Nowhere along with the pilot's accusations."

Quentin seems content to let the jury chew on this for a while. After he figures they've digested the information, he says, "Colonel, have you heard about the charges Major Powers made again in this courtroom against Dr. Cage? About what happened that night in the wrecked ambulance?"

"I read it in the newspaper a few minutes ago, on my way to the courtroom."

"What's your opinion of those charges?"

"Objection," Shad says with barely contained anger. "On multiple grounds. Opinion rule, for one. The witness has not been qualified as a military expert."

"Your Honor," says Quentin, "I submit that after thirty years of military service, in three wars, the colonel is qualified to give an opinion characterizing Private Cage's actions in combat on that night or any other."

"I'll allow it."

"I wasn't in that ambulance," Colonel Eklund says. "But a dozen factors play into every combat situation, especially in an emergency like that. How severely injured are your wounded? How has the enemy been treating your prisoners? Is there any reasonable expectation of aid? Are you obligated to stay with your wounded in the face of certain capture? That's probably not even half of what went through those two medics' heads during the first hour inside that ambulance, and they weren't even twenty years old. I figure they were in shock, being wounded themselves. And there was no doubt about what would have happened if they were captured. I personally saw an American ambulance that the North Koreans had torched with living wounded inside it. Every man in the theater had heard those stories, I guarantee it."

"So, knowing all those factors as you do, do you believe that Private Cage and Private Garrity committed murder on that night?"

"I guess I believe that what they did falls outside the boundaries of rules and regulations. All I can tell you is that I never saw Tom Cage act out of fear or selfishness. Not even when his life was at stake. At eighteen years old, the man did his job in all circumstances, regardless of the risk to himself. Whatever he did in that ambulance that night, he did for the welfare of the men under his care. I'd stake my life on that."

"Thank you, Colonel. One last question. In your experience, did American pilots receive special treatment as compared to other prisoners taken by the North Koreans and Chinese?"

"Absolutely. That was common knowledge. The Chinese wanted to learn all they could about our fighter and bomber capabilities, so all enemy combatants and civilians knew to pass pilots up the chain for interrogation. I'm sure they suffered plenty in captivity—and a few got murdered with bamboo spears in one incident I know about—but unlike GIs and grunts, they weren't shot out of hand, burned, starved, or left to die in the snow. Not as a rule, anyway."

"Thank you, Colonel. No further questions."

"This is when you find out how good a lawyer is," I whisper to Rusty.

Rusty leans over to me. "If I were Shad, I'd cut my losses and get General Patton there off the stand as fast as possible."

But Shad has no intention of retiring from the field. He stands and approaches Colonel Eklund without the slightest trepidation. "Colonel, how long had you known Private Cage before the Chinese hit you on the night of the twenty-fifth?"

"About four months."

"Did you ever see him again after the morning of November twenty-sixth, 1950?"

"No."

"Did you recognize him when you came into court today?"

Colonel Eklund smiles sadly. "No, I didn't, I'm sorry to say. He looks a lot older than the gangly kid who served under me, but then we all do. I'm glad to see him, though, no matter how he looks."

"Of course. But isn't it fair to say that you never really knew him intimately?"

"Beg your pardon?"

"You only knew him for four months, you said."

"Mr. Johnson, after the night of November twenty-fifth, I knew Private Cage better than most people ever get to know anybody."

Shad steeples his fingers as he walks. "Because you served in combat together?"

"That's right."

"So one night of combat brings men closer than, say, a man and wife who live together for fifty years?"

"Have you ever served in combat?"

"No."

"Well. If you had, you'd know that you can get closer to someone in fifteen hours of fighting for your life than you could in fifteen years of living in the same house with them."

"A common belief. But there's no way to prove that statement, is there?"

"I beg to differ. In combat, soldiers are asked to prove their love for their fellow men in ways that people in civilian life never are."

This answer throws Shad off his rhythm.

"Ask any Vietnam wife," Colonel Eklund says. "Who knows her husband better? Her? Or the men who spent a year in the mud and the blood with him in Southeast Asia?"

Shad seems to honestly weigh the implications of this. He's breaking a cardinal rule of jurisprudence, asking questions to which he does not know the answers. For a few moments I am confused, but then it hits me: *Shad actually believes that Dad murdered Viola.* And because he does, he believes that even in this story of heroism, he will find some hint of the moral decay that led to Viola's murder five decades later.

"I listened closely to the nomination you made for the Medal of Honor. Let me ask you this, Colonel. Couldn't it be said that on that night Private Cage—rather than going above and beyond the call of duty—performed his duties exactly as required?"

"How do you mean?"

"I'm suggesting that Private Cage performed the standard duties of an army medic, performed them well, and then, after your position was overrun, did whatever was required to save himself and the other survivors from certain death."

"That's what he did, all right."

"Is that in itself remarkable?"

Colonel Eklund takes his time with this one. "It is. You might think that performing one's duty under fire is standard procedure. But after serving in three wars, I can tell you it's not. I've seen muscle-bound hero types cower in trenches, while skinny runts held together with spit and whipcord charged machine-gun nests, howling like the hounds of hell. What's remarkable about the night the Chinese overran us is that Private Cage survived at all. He had more burp gun rounds sprayed at him than what you see in these silly shoot-'em-up movies they make nowadays. But somebody upstairs was looking out for him that night. As for duty . . . the men who served with Tom Cage knew that if they went down, he would do everything in his power to save them. They *knew* it, you hear me? And because of that, they fought hard. And when they fell, he kept his end of the bargain. He crawled out into a dark so full of Chinese soldiers you couldn't move without one trying to bayonet you. You can't ask more of a man than that. And you can't teach it in boot camp. A man's either raised up to do his duty or he's not."

"A stirring speech, Colonel. I have to admit, you've convinced me. Tom Cage acted heroically on the night of the twenty-fifth. But let me ask you this: Have you heard of cases where men who acted heroically in war committed crimes later in life?"

The colonel's face clouds with unpleasant recollection. "Ah—"

"Objection," says Quentin.

"On what grounds?" asks Judge Elder.

I can see from the colonel's face that Shad struck vital tissue with his thrust. Dad's going to take a hit here; Quentin senses it, too. Colonel Eklund remembers something, and he isn't about to lie on the stand. But Quentin himself already argued that Eklund qualifies as an expert on military matters, and by Quentin's own strategy, trying to suppress any part of the truth—even an unpleasant part—would be a mistake.

"Withdrawn," Quentin says softly.

"Colonel?" Shad prompts, smelling blood.

"I knew a sergeant in Vietnam who killed his wife after he got out of the service. Killed his wife and then himself. He suffered from battle fatigue. Or PTSD, they call it now."

"Is that the only such case you remember?"

Colonel Eklund hesitates, then says, "No. A guy I served with went to jail for robbing a bank in Illinois."

"After he'd won an award for bravery?"

"The Bronze Star."

"Any other cases?"

"I don't think so. You hear things, you know. But those are the only instances in my personal experience."

Shad nods as though he and the colonel share some difficult knowledge about life. "I personally know that one veteran of the Mogadishu raid dramatized in *Black Hawk Down* was convicted of child molestation. They left his character out of the movie because of that."

"Move to strike," says Quentin.

"So ordered," says the judge. "You've made your point, Mr. Johnson, and the jury will disregard that last statement."

Shad lifts one hand in acknowledgment. "War changes men, doesn't it, Colonel?"

"Yes and no," Colonel Eklund says after reflection. "Depends on how much action they see, and where they see it. Tempo is the thing. In the Pacific, you could endure a year's worth of hell in five days of combat. Two days could break a man. In Vietnam, you had lighter contact, but it never let up. Two or three hundred days of exposure in the field, to land mines and trench foot and booby traps and sniper fire. It's like a Chinese water torture."

"Did you return to combat in Korea after receiving your wounds?"

"Yes."

"Did you ever serve with Private Cage again?"

"No."

"So, you have no idea what kind of operational tempo he experienced in the months that he remained in the Korean theater?"

"That's true."

"Is your opinion of him based entirely on his actions on the night of November twenty-fifth, 1950?"

"And four months of operations leading up to that night," Eklund clarifies. "We saw a fair amount of action prior to that."

"But nothing comparable to that night?"

"Naktong was pretty hairy, but not like after the Chinese came in. That's true."

"Thank you, Colonel. Most enlightening."

Colonel Eklund nods warily, not quite trusting Shad's solicitous tone.

"And thank you for the information about Love Company—the 'colored boys,' as you called them. I thought the army had been desegregated by that time."

The colonel shifts on his seat as though to get the blood flowing in order to stand. "On paper it had been. But there were still all-black units in the early months of the war. The army doesn't like change."

"Nor does society at large, Colonel. Thank you. No further questions."

"Shad just earned his paycheck," Rusty says in my ear.

Judge Elder looks at Quentin and raises his eyebrows. "Redirect?"

"Nothing further, Your Honor."

"You're free to go, Colonel," Judge Elder says.

Colonel Eklund looks up at the judge and nods with obvious respect for the office. Then, with a last look around the courtroom, he rises, steps out of the witness box, and walks to the center aisle. As he passes the defense table, he stops and looks my father full in the face. Then he straightens up, raises a wrinkled right hand, and snaps out a salute that would make a West Point officer proud. This act, a superior officer initiating a salute to a man of lower rank, is a courtesy reserved for winners of the Medal of Honor.

A flush of surprise and humility comes into my father's cheeks. With a grating screech, he pushes his chair away from the table, comes slowly to his feet, and raises two rigid fingers to his brow with a faint echo of military precision. I feel my mother squeeze my right arm with her shaking hand.

As with the spitting incident, no one seems sure how to react. Shad stifles an objection as Colonel Eklund gives Dad an encouraging smile, then marches down the aisle. As he passes through the crowd, Walt Garrity stands and snaps out a salute. Colonel Eklund returns it, then marches on, to the big doors at the back of the room.

"I wish the jury had to vote right now," Rusty whispers in my left ear. "Twelve to zero for acquittal, I guarantee."

"Don't be too sure," I whisper back. "Pundits thought Bush *père* was untouchable after winning the Gulf War in '91, and Clinton beat him."

"A year later."

Rusty is probably exaggerating the colonel's impact, but one thing is sure: if anything can erase the memory of Major Powers spitting on Dad's chest, Colonel Eklund's salute comes closest.

For a moment I wonder if Quentin stage-managed that whole scene, but then I dismiss the idea. Neither my father nor Colonel Eklund would taint the memory of their service by trying to sway a jury in that way. Not even with the stakes as high as they are.

"Mr. Avery?" prompts Judge Elder. "You may call your next witness."

"Your Honor, I'd like to recall Cora Revels, the victim's sister, to the stand."

Shad Johnson looks as surprised as I am by this move, but when I turn, I realize that our reaction is nothing compared to that of Viola's sister.

Cora Revels looks terrified.

CHAPTER 50

SNAKE KNOX WAS looking out over a field of kudzu in Rodney, Mississippi, when his burner phone rang for the first time that morning. He had no idea who the caller might be, and he was surprised when Toons Teufel identified himself in the exultant voice of a man happy to be delivering news.

"What the hell do you want?" Snake asked warily.

"We got back to surveilling your old Klan buddies, and just in time, too. Because one of them just flew the coop."

"What are you talking about?"

"Will Devine and his family disappeared sometime between last night and sunrise. Cleaned their place out."

Snake processed this news in silence. As his mind worked, he noticed the way the kudzu vines threw runners into the open air, searching for purchase like starving serpents, climbing and eventually strangling even the tallest trees.

"You there, Grandpa?"

"What do you mean, 'cleaned the place out'?"

"Clothes, money, files, family albums . . . they left the place a wreck. We talked to the neighbors, but nobody heard nothing."

"Devine has kids. Grown kids."

"They're gone too, baby. It's a clean sweep."

Snake felt the ground shift beneath his feet. "Then I don't guess you got back on the job in time, did you?"

"Hey," Toons said, his voice hard. "You still want those shooters today or not?"

"Everything stays the same. Eleven A.M. at the ruins."

Snake ended the call and ran back toward the house. Alois was walking down the concrete porch step, and the second he looked up he read the anger and worry in Snake's face.

"What is it?" he asked.

"Get the boat key," Snake ordered.

"What's happened?"

"The FBI flipped Will Devine."

Alois blanched. "Mother*fucker.* Where we going? Are we bailing?"

"Hell, no," Snake barked, slapping his son's shoulder as he passed him. "We're going to Natchez."

Alois let out a rebel yell and ran toward the International Harvester pickup that held the key to the boat.

Snake watched his son for a few seconds, thinking about how in the end, everything came down to blood. There was your family, and then there was the rest of the world. Snake would have given a lot to have Frank at his side for what was coming, but Alois would have to do. He would be enough.

Alois was blood.

CHAPTER 51

WHEN CORA REVELS took the stand two days ago, she looked like a grieving church matron reluctantly testifying about her family scandal in the hope of getting justice for her sister. Today she's equally well dressed, but her eyes are those of a frightened woman with something to hide.

When Quentin speaks, his words are courteous, but his tone isn't as solicitous as it was the last time he questioned the victim's sister. "Ms. Revels, I'm sorry to bring you back up here. I only have a few questions for you."

"All right."

"Did your sister leave an estate behind when she died?"

"Estate? All we had was Mama's house, and that weren't no *estate*. It doesn't even have central air."

Muffled laughter comes from the rows of lawyers.

"I don't mean the house only, Ms. Revels. I mean whatever property your sister might have had left in her name when she died, after the medical bills were paid. It could be a checking account, a savings bond, stocks or bonds."

"Oh. Yes, Vee did have a little bit of money put back."

"Approximately how much did she have?"

"Objection," Shad says, later than I would have expected him to. "I fail to see the relevance of this line of questioning."

Quentin looks at Judge Elder without the slightest hint that he might back away from this. "We will all see the relevance very soon, Your Honor, I assure you."

"Overruled," Elder declares.

"Exception."

"Noted."

"May I approach the bench, Your Honor?" Quentin asks.

Judge Elder nods.

Shad practically scrambles out of his seat to reach the bench at the same time Quentin does. After Judge Elder covers his mike, an indistinct hum of discussion follows, lasting about thirty seconds. Then Shad returns to his seat with a grim look, and Quentin wheels himself back over to the podium.

"Now that *that's* settled," he says, "would the witness answer the question?"

Cora is looking at someone in the spectators' seats, I realize. Someone to my left. She was focused on the same spot throughout the sidebar. It's *Lincoln*. He's sitting one row behind the prosecution table. Cora is searching for guidance, and so clumsily that Quentin turns and stares at Lincoln himself, so that the jury will see what's happening. Under this scrutiny, Lincoln cannot risk coaching her with the slightest signal. He sits with his jaw clenched tight, staring straight ahead.

"Ms. Revels?" Quentin repeats.

"Um . . . Vee had about seventy-two thousand dollars in an account up in Chicago."

Quite a few spectators gasp at this figure, and I sense that most of them are black.

"Seventy-two thousand dollars," Quentin echoes. "And the house?"

"The house was mine."

"Was it always yours?"

"No, that was Mama's house. But she deeded it over to me after I got hurt at work."

"Where did you work?"

"At the tire plant. I fell and hurt my back, and since then I can't do no work. All I got is my disability check. Mama gave me the house so I'd always have somewhere to stay."

"Did she give Viola anything at that time?"

"No. She knew Vee could take care of herself. Vee always knew how to do that."

For the first time, I hear resentment in Cora's voice when she speaks of her sister. I can't remember whether she or Viola was the younger sister, but I think it was Viola.

"Back to the seventy-two thousand dollars," Quentin says with the persistence of a dripping faucet. "What happened to that money?"

Again Cora looks at Lincoln, but she finds no help there. He's pretending to look out one of the tall courtroom windows. "It was divided up according to the will," she says. "Viola's will."

"I see. And how was it divided?"

"Objection!" Shad says. "We're far afield from the death of Viola Turner, Judge."

"Are we?" Quentin asks, looking straight at Shad. "Judge, my client has been charged with murder. He is entitled to explore the possibility that someone else committed the crime."

In that sentence, the entire dynamic of the courtroom changes. It's as though Quentin has suddenly taken a croaker sack from his briefcase and released a rattlesnake under the chairs.

"*Holy fuck,*" whispers Rusty. "This is where Quentin was headed all along."

"Let's see."

"I'll allow it," Judge Elder says. "But we'd better see how this fits pretty quickly, Mr. Avery."

"Understood, Your Honor. So, how was the money divided, Ms. Revels?"

"Just like the will said. I got thirty thousand, six hundred dollars, Lincoln got the same, and the rest went to Junius Jelks."

"Viola's husband?"

"Yes, sir."

"And where does Mr. Jelks reside now?"

"In prison, in Illinois."

"That's right," Quentin muses, as though he had forgotten. "Tell me, who drew up your sister's will?"

"Mr. Alvin Dupuis. A Chicago attorney who had grown up in Natchez."

I once met Alvin Dupuis, when he was in town for a reunion of some kind. He was old then, and a black police detective told me that Dupuis had worked in the gray margins of the legal profession for many decades.

"When was this?" asks Quentin.

"A long time back," Cora answers. "Soon after Lincoln got out of law school, I think it was, him and Vee went down to Mr. Dupuis's office and drew up the will. But he be dead now. Mr. Dupuis, I mean."

"I see. Ms. Revels, when the will was probated, did anyone contest it?"

"What do you mean?"

"Did anyone come forward with any *other* will that they claimed was your sister's? Or did anyone claim that the will you're talking about was invalid?"

Again Cora glances at Lincoln, who by now is looking everywhere but at his aunt.

"Well," Cora says uncomfortably, "one lady did try to say that Viola had promised to give some money to that reporter, Mr. Sexton. But she didn't have no proof, so the judge threw her out."

"I see. Who was this woman you're referring to?"

"I don't remember her name. She was Mr. Sexton's mama, I believe."

"I see. How much did Mrs. Sexton claim that your sister had promised to give her son?"

"Fifty thousand dollars."

More expressions of shock from the gallery.

"That's more than sixty percent of your sister's total estate. Why would she give that kind of money to Mr. Sexton?"

"She wouldn't!" Cora blurts. Then she leans back as though embarrassed by her passion.

"What did Mrs. Sexton claim was the reason?"

"She said Viola had promised Mr. Henry that money to help finish some movie he was making."

"What was this movie about?"

"I don't know."

Quentin's skepticism is obvious to everyone in the room. "And Viola never spoke to you about willing Mr. Sexton some money?"

"No, sir."

"Not even a small amount?"

"No."

"Did Viola ever tell you that she was going to change the will that Mr. Dupuis had made long ago, and write a new one prior to her death?"

"No, sir. She never done that."

"Never wrote a new will? Or never spoke about it?"

"Neither one!"

Quentin rolls his chair a little closer to the witness stand. "You seem upset, Miss Cora."

"'Cause you trying to pull some kind of lawyer trick on me! Take my rightful inheritance."

"I'm not trying to do any such thing, I assure you."

"That's all the money I got in the world!"

"Objection!" Shad breaks in. "Counsel is badgering the witness, and for no reason I can understand."

"Mr. Avery?" Judge Elder asks.

"No further questions, Your Honor. I tender the witness."

Shad seems to be of two minds about questioning Cora Revels. But after about twenty seconds, he rises and walks close to the witness box.

"Ms. Revels, your sister's will was probated in Cook County, Illinois, was it not?"

"Yes, sir."

"You filed that will with the clerk of court there?"

"My nephew did."

"I see. And no one brought forward any other will to challenge the one that was probated, did they?"

"No, sir. That's right."

"Thank you. No further questions."

Judge Elder gives Quentin a curious glance. "Redirect, Mr. Avery?"

"None, Your Honor."

"The witness may step down."

In all my years as a lawyer, I've rarely seen a witness more eager to leave the stand than Cora Revels. As she hurries back to her seat by Lincoln, Rusty whispers, "What you wanna bet the love child is up next?"

Just as Cora reaches her chair, Quentin says, "The defense recalls Lincoln Turner to the stand."

Lincoln rises slowly, then walks up to the witness box with the same relaxed stride he did yesterday. But this self-possession must be a pose. Quentin would not be walking him down this road unless there was trouble at the end of it.

Easing out of my chair, I lean up toward Quentin's table and whisper, "What's all this stuff about the will?"

Quentin stuns me by actually leaning back and answering me. "Viola wrote a new will only a few days before she died."

"Do you have a copy of it?"

"No."

"Then what good can this do you?"

"Maybe none. But you can't be choosy about what vine you grab when you're sliding down a cliff. Get back in your seat."

Quentin rolls forward to his place beside the podium. "Mr. Turner, did you write the will that was probated after your mother died?"

"I did not. An attorney may not draw up a will from which he benefits. I may not have gone to Harvard, but I know that much."

"You and I share that distinction, Mr. Turner. Only Lawyer Johnson there graduated from Harvard Law School."

Shad makes a sour face.

"But back to the will," Quentin continues. "Were the bequests specified as your aunt named them?"

"No. Mama didn't know how much money she would have when she died, so she used percentages to divide whatever she might have left."

"I see. Were you surprised that she had that much money left when she died?"

Lincoln shrugs.

"The witness will give a verbal response," Judge Elder says.

"Not really."

Quentin nods, but he looks troubled. "According to the testimony of both you and your aunt, money was pretty scarce in your household. I'm trying to understand how your mother could have saved seventy-two thousand dollars when her husband was spending everything she made, and she was putting you through college and law school."

"Once Daddy went to prison, and I was out of school, her bills weren't so bad. And Mama was always resourceful."

"I see. So you assume the money came from her salary as a nurse?"

"Where else?"

"Exactly. But let's leave that for now. Mr. Turner, what did you think of the challenge of your mother's will by Mr. Sexton's mother?"

"I thought it was bullshit."

"Mr. Turner," the judge snaps. "You know better than that."

"I'm sorry, Judge. But Judge Carroll in Chicago didn't think any more of that claim than what I just said."

"Just watch your language."

"So the challenge was denied," Quentin says, "and the original will was affirmed. Tell me, do you know what Mr. Sexton's movie-in-progress was about?"

"It was a documentary, I think. About the civil rights movement."

"Don't you think that's a cause your mother might have sympathized with?"

"The cause, yes. A homemade film by some white reporter from Ferriday, no."

"I see. Did your mother ever speak to you about changing her will before she died?"

"Absolutely not."

"Objection, Your Honor," Shad says with obvious irritation. "If the defense has a copy of some other will, they should produce it. If they have a reputable attorney who can testify that he drew up such a will, they should call him as a witness. Otherwise, this is all just a waste of the court's time."

"We talked about this subject during the sidebar, Mr. Johnson. I will decide what is worthy of the court's time. Your objections are overruled. Mr. Avery, continue."

Quentin looks back at Lincoln. "Did your mother ever ask you about how a person might make a holographic will?"

"No. Never."

"Can you explain to the jury what a holographic will is?"

"I can."

"Will you, please?"

Lincoln looks at Judge Elder, who nods.

"A holographic will is a handwritten will," Lincoln says testily. "Handwritten, dated, and signed. All you need to make one is a pen and a piece of paper."

"Just so," says Quentin. "Did you ever see any such will written by your mother? Either before or after she died?"

I'm looking for fear in Lincoln's eyes, but all I see is sullen anger. Yet this time there's a second of awkward hesitation before his answer.

"No," he says. "Absolutely not."

Quentin seems pleased by this answer. "Were you surprised that your mother would leave money to her husband, a man who treated her rather poorly?"

"It was her money. He was her husband. That makes it her business."

"I see. And were you happy with your share of the seventy-two thousand dollars?"

"I've got no complaints."

"No. Clearly not. Thank you, Mr. Turner. I tender the witness."

This time, as Quentin rolls back to the defense table, Shad gazes at Lincoln on the stand. The district attorney looks like a man in a poker game with people he thought he knew, but who have turned out to be imposters.

"Mr. Johnson?" prompts the judge.

"No questions, Your Honor."

"The witness may step down."

As Lincoln returns to his seat, he glances at Quentin only a moment, but held in that moment is rage sufficient to drive a knife into Quentin's chest. Quentin responds with a knowing smile.

"Call your next witness, Mr. Avery."

"The defense calls Mrs. Virginia Sexton."

A few moments later, a deputy escorts Henry Sexton's mother through the back doors. She looks like my maternal grandmother once did: an elderly country wife dressed for church, in a white blouse and a skirt that falls well below her knees. After she seats herself and is sworn in—in a shaky voice, I notice—Quentin rolls up to the witness box and smiles.

"Thank you for coming, Mrs. Sexton."

The old woman nods once, her expression grave.

"Were you related to Henry Sexton, the newspaper reporter?"

"He was my son."

"Did your son ever talk to you about interviewing Viola Turner?"

"Yes, he did. He talked to me about most of his cases."

"What did he tell you?"

"He believed Viola Turner was the source he had been looking for since he'd begun his work. Henry called her his 'dream' source."

"What did he mean by that?"

"Objection," says Shad. "Opinion rule. Irrelevant."

"Overruled on both counts," says Judge Elder.

"Henry worked on a lot of cases from the civil rights period, but the three major ones were the murder of Albert Norris, the kidnap-murder of Joe Louis Lewis, and the kidnap-murders of Jimmy Revels and Luther Davis. He told me that—"

"Objection," Shad says irritably. "Hearsay. Irrelevant."

"Overruled."

"Exception."

"Noted."

Quentin says, "Did he talk to you about these cases on the day Viola died, Mrs. Sexton?"

"Yes. Henry believed the Double Eagle group was responsible for all those crimes, and he said that Viola was one of the rarest things around here."

"What was that?"

"A Double Eagle victim who had survived. He believed she knew a lot about the group, but that fear had kept her quiet for decades. He thought Viola was getting close to telling him what she knew. That's why he left that video camera at her house. He left an audio recorder, too, early on, but that's never been found."

Mrs. Sexton's last sentence sends a strong echo back to my internal radar. This is the first I've heard of any audio recorder left with Viola. Henry never mentioned it to me.

"Tell us why you contested Viola Turner's will," Quentin says.

Mrs. Sexton's face goes red and splotchy before she speaks. "Henry told me that Viola Turner was very interested in his work. So far as she knew, Henry was the only person who had been working almost continuously on her brother's case. She'd tried to contact the FBI several times, but they would never tell her anything. Viola was amazed at the things Henry had uncovered, and she wanted to help him any way she could. After her second long interview with Henry, she told him she was going to leave him a bequest in her will to help fund his work, for the film he was working on."

"Tell us more about that."

"Henry was making a documentary. A joint venture with an award-winning filmmaker from Syracuse University. That's up in New York.

They were more than half finished, but they were having trouble getting funding to complete the project. The man from Syracuse had talked to Morgan Freeman's people about narrating the film, and he wanted to do it. But Morgan couldn't take it on for several months yet. A couple of backers pulled their support after they heard that. When Viola found out about this, that was when she offered her support to Henry. It moved him so much. Henry cried when he told me about their conversation. And he hardly ever did that."

As Quentin prepares to ask his next question, Judge Elder's secretary comes out of his chambers, climbs to the bench, and hands him a note. This kind of thing happens all the time in court, but as soon as Elder looks at the sheet of paper, I know this is different.

"Court is recessed for one hour," he says sharply. "The witness is released. The jury will retire to the jury room, and the defendant will be returned to custody. I need to see counsel in chambers immediately."

While the audience breaks into a hum of surprised speculation, the judge gets up and heads straight for the private door to his chambers. Shad and Quentin share a glance; then Shad follows the judge. As Quentin goes after him, I leave my seat and follow.

As we bunch around the judge's door, Quentin looks over his shoulder at me. "What are you doing?"

"I'm listed as part of the defense team, and I'm coming with you. Don't even try to stop me. Elder looks scared."

"Christ. All right."

By the time we reach the judge's inner sanctum, Joe Elder has already pulled off his robe and is holding a cell phone to his ear. He covers the mobile's microphone with his finger and looks over at us.

"There's been a bomb threat at my home. One of my children was there with the housekeeper. They've evacuated the house, the bomb squad is on its way. Both the ATF and FBI have been called. I suspect this is a hoax meant to disrupt the trial, but until I know that for sure, we're in recess."

While Shad gapes at the judge, Elder says, "I'm on my way" into the phone, then grabs his keys off the desk and heads for his receptionist's office.

"Are you sure it was for your house?" Quentin asks, "and not the court?"

"The caller gave my address, but the ATF will search and scan the courtroom as well."

"Did the caller say anything else?" Shad asks.

Joe Elder pauses in the doorway and looks back at us. "He said he wasn't going to let a nigger judge jail a white man for killing a nigger without paying a price."

"Shouldn't we just adjourn for the day?" Shad asks.

Joe Elder cuts his eyes at Shad, not quite believing that the DA is trying to run tactics on him even now. "No, Mr. Johnson. I'm not letting anybody intimidate me into derailing this trial, no matter which side he's on. Whatever it is you want to do, you've got one hour to do it."

Then the door closes behind the judge.

Shad, Quentin, and I regard each other in silence. This turn of events has left our heads spinning, but all good trial lawyers know how to recover quickly from the unexpected, and even turn it to their advantage, as Shad just tried to do.

"What's all this crap about another will?" he asks.

"Why don't you ask your witnesses?" Quentin suggests.

"You obviously don't have a copy of it. If you did, you'd already have entered it into evidence."

"Like that adrenaline ampoule nobody could find?"

I'm glad to hear this retort, because until I did, I didn't know Quentin had paid any attention to the forensic case.

Shad dismisses his comment with a wave of his hand. "I'll bet we're done for the day."

"You hope we are." Quentin gives him a strange smile. "You didn't have somebody call in that bomb threat, did you? I think you feel the ground shifting, Shadrach."

Shad jabs his middle finger at Quentin, then turns and marches out of the room without a word.

"What do you make of this?" I ask.

Quentin shrugs. "I'm past being surprised by anything. I don't see that it affects our case at all."

"Our case?"

The old lawyer makes a clucking sound with his tongue. "Come on, Penn. Aren't you starting to see a little method in my madness?"

"Too little, too late. That's what I see. You haven't even dented Shad's forensic case."

"Everything in time."

"Do you think there could really be a bomb?"

"I'll know when they tell me."

"The Double Eagles were big fans of plastic explosive. And they used a bomb as a diversion at the Concordia Courthouse when—"

"When they killed Sonny Thornfield in the jail," Quentin finishes. *"Shit."*

His preternatural calm has finally evaporated, and my pulse is pounding in my neck.

"Dad could be back in his cell by now."

Quentin digs out his phone, but I figure I can be across the street and inside the sheriff's office by the time Quentin gets the dispatcher to do anything.

He hasn't even gotten an answer by the time I hit the door.

CHAPTER 52

DAD WAS ALIVE when I reached the visiting room, and a call from Quentin to Judge Elder had ensured a double guard on him—men who understood that they were there to protect their charge, not merely to keep him from escaping. The deputies would not let me stay with him, though. The bomb threat had put everyone on edge.

As I left the sheriff's department, I looked up and saw the trial spectators exiting the courthouse doors across the street. On both sides of the broad marble steps, two men wearing business suits photographed everyone who passed down to the sidewalk beneath the spreading oaks. *FBI agents,* I surmised. *Kaiser's men.* As soon as Kaiser got word of the bomb threat, he must have figured the caller might have someone inside the courtroom giving him progress reports. Since nobody is required to sign his or her name as they enter the courtroom, the photographs will ensure that the Bureau can eventually trace everyone who was there this morning.

I'm still watching the mass exodus when a familiar white pickup truck stops on the street in front of me, and the passenger window drops into the door, revealing Lincoln Turner behind the wheel. My half brother's big face and shoulders lean into the open space, his eyes bright with a strange energy.

"You look like a man who needs a ride, Mayor. Where's your wingman?"

I left the courthouse so fast—and by such an unexpected route—that I lost my protection on the way. "I'm good," I say, a little nervously.

"No," says Lincoln, "you only think you are. I want to make you a proposition, *brah*. It won't take more than five minutes."

"I'm listening."

Lincoln tilts back his head, indicating two cars that have stopped behind him. "Get in the truck. I'm not gonna hurt you."

"Just pull to the curb."

The second car behind his truck gives a long blast on its horn. Fifty people from the crowd look our way.

"You want to keep Big Daddy out of Parchman or not?"

"You're the one who made this whole trial happen."

A taunting smile touches his wide lips. "Yeah. But a trial is a fluid thing, like a war. The tides change fast. Every lawyer knows that. You want to hear what I've got to say."

Translation: Quentin got onto something with that last line of questioning. Both drivers honk angrily now, drawing the attention of a deputy beyond the big glass door behind me, but I still don't get into the truck. "You're talking like this is a civil suit and you want to cut a deal."

Lincoln shrugs. "There's different kinds of settlements. I'm driving away in five seconds. The deal leaves with me."

I hate to be manipulated, but before five seconds pass, I climb into the truck's passenger seat, wishing I had my pistol. But I never take a gun into court.

Lincoln drives around the block, then heads down to Canal Street and turns toward the twin bridges over the Mississippi. He looks at me a couple of times as he drives, but he doesn't say anything.

"What's across the river?" I ask as the bluff drops away and a hundred feet of space yawns beneath us.

"Rednecks. All the way to New Mexico."

"Lots of brothers, too."

"Yeah. But outside the cities, they're an endangered species."

"This recess may not last long. Let's hear your offer."

Lincoln laughs heartily, turning south at the foot of the bridge. After passing between a few houses and a one-story school, he drives over the top of the levee to the Vidalia, Louisiana, riverfront. Compared to the Natchez shore, where growth has been stymied for years by a multimillionaire, the Vidalia shore has seen the construction of hotels, restaurants, an outpatient surgical center, and a public amphitheater. Lincoln drives slowly past the train of new buildings, then pulls onto a white shell road that leads to the steep boat ramp beneath the bridge. My stomach flips as we tilt nose-first toward the vast river. Stopping the truck within a few feet of the water, Lincoln switches off the motor but leaves on the battery.

"You planning to shoot me and drop me in the river?"

He grins gamely. "That is kind of a tradition on this side of the river, isn't it? Only it's my tribe that gets dumped."

I roll down my window and listen to the deceptively faint trickle of water moving over and through the gray riprap rock placed here by the Corps of Engineers to retard erosion. Beneath that sound I hear the nearly subsonic drone of tugboat engines pushing a quarter-mile-long string of barges upriver. If this truck rolled five feet farther down the ramp, the river would snatch us and send us tumbling toward Baton Rouge like a child's toy.

"Look over there," Lincoln says, pointing across a mile of open water at Natchez Under-the-Hill, and the great bluff above it. "Looks like a storybook, doesn't it? The big antebellum mansions on the hill and the bars below, the lumber mill south of town and the Victorian palaces to the north. The cemetery and the Devil's Punchbowl beyond them. But just a few streets back from all that, there are houses with holes as big as car tires in the floor. Shotgun shacks that look like they're in some third-world country. And you're the mayor of all that. How does that make you feel?"

"Tired. What's your proposition, Lincoln? What are you selling?"

"I'll let my product speak for itself."

He reaches out one big hand and presses a button near the center of the dash. The truck's cab fills with hissing static. Then I hear an old woman's voice, cracked and reedy.

"I ain't scared of you two," Viola says. *"You want to do what you done before, go ahead. I'll bet you can't do it anymore, anyway. You're too old, like me."*

"You don't want to test us," says a strangely familiar male voice. *"I promise you that."*

"I ain't scared of you, Snake Knox. Or you either, Mr. Sonny Thornfield. That's right, I recognize the both of you. I can call you by name. And I will, any time I feel like it. Your kind don't rule this world anymore, not even down here in Mississippi."

"You keep talking to that reporter," growls Sonny, *"you'll find out what we can do around here."*

"Any damn thing we want," says Snake. *"Same as it always was."*

"I talk to who I please," Viola says bravely, but then she coughs herself into a fit that lasts half a minute. Lincoln's eyes probe mine as I wait for the voices to resume, but I give him nothing. *"You'll have to kill me to stop me from telling what I know,"* Viola goes on, *"and you can't do worse to me than God's doing already. I'm getting my punishment. I only wish I'd live to see you get yours. There's a fearsome reckoning coming for you two. Yes, Lord."*

"Listen here, nigger," says Snake. *"You can die easy or you can die hard, like your brother."*

"Don't call me that, scum. That's not even a word. You show me where it says 'nigger' in the Bible."

Viola starts to wheeze, and both men laugh. *"What if I just come over there and pinch that oxygen hose shut?"* Snake asks. *"Probably wouldn't take more'n a minute to shut off the lights, shape you're in. Your days of jawin' with liberal reporters would be over."*

"Go on, if you want another stain on your soul. Do it. That's the only way you're going to shut me up."

"Just keep on," Sonny says, sounding like a nervous grade-school bully, *"and one of these nights, we will."*

I don't realize how hypnotized I am until Lincoln ejects the tape with a mechanical click and whir. I grab for the tape, but by the time my fingers jam against the empty slot, Lincoln is holding the old-style cassette outside his open window, smiling with confidence.

"I'm waiting," he says.

"For what?"

"Your offer."

Acid has flooded my stomach. "That's evidence, goddamn it. You're obligated to give that to the police."

Lincoln belly laughs at this. "Is that your considered legal opinion, Mr. Mayor? That redneck sheriff you got over in Natchez might just misplace something like this. He'd love to see your daddy go down for killing my mother."

"He's your father, too."

As the words leave my lips, Lincoln's face lightens a shade—his blood is draining from it.

"Where did you get that tape?" I ask. "Who made it?"

"You heard Henry Sexton's mother. Henry left Mama an audio recorder a week before he set up that video camera. He wanted her to put down her memories of the 1960s, and especially anything she remembered about her brother, Jimmy. She had it in the bed with her when them two come in. She just hit the button and taped what they said."

This I can believe. "Okay. What do you want for it?"

"Look in the glove box."

I do. Lying atop the truck's owner's manual is a white notecard. Typed on the card is a series of numbers and the name of a bank: *Cayman West Holdings, Limited.*

"I'm going to check the balance of that account in one hour," Lincoln says, looking out over the river. "And if I feel happy after the call, the tape you just heard will turn up in time to be used as evidence in the trial. If I'm *not* happy—"

Lincoln flicks his wrist, and the cassette goes sailing out over the brown water of the Mississippi. It stays afloat, swirling gently, but it's moving south fast. "Just a copy, of course. What you're paying for is the original."

"Goddamn it," I mutter. "If you've had that tape all along, why are you pushing to have your own father convicted?"

"Is that a trick question?"

When I don't reply, Lincoln sighs and looks into his lap. "That tape doesn't prove he's innocent. Not by a long shot. Not to me, and probably not to a lot of jurors. But does it sound like reasonable doubt? I'd say so. You need to decide what that's worth, and you don't have much time."

Staring through the windshield, I can no longer discern the tape on the water rolling southward. Without further discussion, Lincoln cranks the truck, backs carefully up the boat ramp, then executes a three-point turn and drives over the levee. Soon we're on the westbound bridge, and as we follow its arc over the river, I finally ask the question he wants to hear.

"What's the magic number?"

He lets the truck roll all the way down to the Mississippi shore before answering. The tires thunk onto asphalt with good dirt under it, and Lincoln switches the heater on full blast, fogging the lower half of the windshield. While I watch in confusion, he reaches out and writes some numbers in the moisture on the glass. Leaning sideways to change the angle of the light, I see a one followed by six zeros.

A million dollars? For that tape?

The empty feeling in the pit of my belly tells me how serious he is. I already put fifty thousand dollars into the grubby little hands of Nita Devine this morning—or the hands of her sister—through my friend Kirk Boisseau. Lincoln's request proves just how bush league the Devines are when it comes to larceny.

"One hour," Lincoln says, driving past the Natchez Welcome Center and pulling into the turn lane for Canal Street.

"That's impossible," I tell him, switching off the heater. "Even if the answer was yes."

"Don't insult me. I know you've got the money."

He turns left, heading back into the heart of downtown.

"Did you have someone call in that bomb threat so you could make this offer?"

He chuckles softly. "Don't get paranoid, man."

"You're the one who's scared. Quentin Avery is about to crawl right up your ass, isn't he? You can feel him warming up the proctoscope, and you don't like it. That's why you're going to plan B. You want to split town with a sackful of money. What's he got on you? Did you really destroy a second will?"

"That's got nothing to do with the price of freedom in Mississippi, brother." Lincoln rolls right past the turn for the jail and the courthouse, but he speaks before I can question his driving. "Look at it this way, Mayor. If *Daddy* was lying in an intensive care unit, about to die—"

"Last October, he was."

"Okay, so think about that. If he was lying in the ICU, and a doctor told you he could save his life for one million dollars, would you pay it?" Lincoln turns to me with his eyebrows raised.

I don't answer.

"'Course you would. Even if he only had another few months to live, you'd pay it. What's six months with your father worth? His last six months on earth? But that's not even the bottom question. The bottom question is, what would those months be like with him *behind bars*? And how many months would he lose by being there? I watched

Junius Jelks get old in jail, and it happens *fast*. He was in and out several times, but he aged three years for every year he spent inside."

"I know what prison does to people. I've put enough people there."

"I guess you have, at that."

"Do you have any other tapes?"

"I told you that was a copy."

"No, I'm talking about videotapes."

Lincoln looks puzzled. "Ain't no other tapes, man. Big Daddy had the one Mama made Sexton in that Texas Ranger's van. He erased it. And he fried the other one in that MRI machine. The one they found in the Dumpster." Lincoln laughs softly. "I never said he was stupid."

The truck suddenly veers right and stops beside the curb on Main Street.

"Why are you dropping me here? I need to get back to City Hall."

Lincoln smiles. "This is your bank, isn't it?"

"Jesus. I need to talk to Quentin first. And to Dad."

"You don't have time for that. This is one of those decisions you make yourself. Don't call my cell, because I won't answer. Don't try to discuss this in person or via any type of media. There won't be any sting operation. This conversation never happened, and we're never discussing it again. Either the money is there in an hour, or it's not. After that, I destroy the original and we all take our chances with the jury."

I look at my watch. "A million dollars in an hour? That's impossible."

"For you, maybe. Not for you and your mama. Tell her to crack open that retirement account."

You son of a bitch, I curse silently.

I open the door and slide one foot down to the concrete. "If you get your money, how soon will that audiotape be miraculously discovered?"

"Immediately. I'll take it to Shad myself and tell him I just found it hidden in Mama's house." Lincoln's eyes glint with a con man's infectious excitement. "Reasonable doubt on a silver platter, my brother."

"Shad won't thank you for it."

Lincoln's expression goes sour. "Fuck that negro. Now get out of my truck."

As soon as I close the door, he leans over and raps on the window.

Then he lowers it and says, "If court resumes before the money's been transferred, old Quentin better steer well clear of the track he's been on."

This is his confession: Quentin has him by the balls, and he senses a knife is being sharpened.

"You know, I've actually felt sorry for you during this whole process. But I see now that you've got no honor at all."

"You don't see shit," Lincoln grumbles. "And you don't know shit. Especially about me. And you never will."

"I know you'd tell any lie in the world to get money and revenge. I don't care what the DNA test said . . . you're not my father's son."

His white teeth slowly disappear, and his eyes take on a lethal cast. "That's where you're dead wrong. I'm his *true* son—not you. You're what he wishes he could have been. That's one thing you'll learn for sure before I leave this town." Lincoln laughs with harsh pleasure, then yanks the gearshift. "Nice doing business with you, Mayor."

As his truck rumbles away, I enter the bank, count to ten, then exit onto Commerce Street and sprint toward City Hall.

CHAPTER 53

BY THE TIME I reach City Hall, I've learned from Doris Avery that she and Quentin are back down at Edelweiss. With the traffic around the courthouse still snarled from TV trucks, I decide to run the five blocks to the river. I draw a lot of looks from people on the street; they're not used to seeing their mayor pound the pavement in a sport coat and tie. But then most of them remember that my father is on trial for murder and figure it must make sense at some level.

I'm soaked with sweat when I near the back of the chalet, approaching it from Washington Street, just as I did two days ago. Once again I trot through my neighbor's backyard and steal through the rear gate of the fence that borders my property.

Looking up, I cry out in surprise and nearly collide with a man trying to exit through the same gate. At first I assume it's a trespassing reporter, but then I see that it's John Kaiser. Kaiser looks at me rather sheepishly, an expression I've never seen on his face.

"John? What the hell are you doing here?"

"I needed to talk to Avery."

Kaiser talking to Quentin? "What about? Will Devine?"

"I can't tell you. And you know I don't say that easily."

I take hold of his upper arm. "You're kidding, right? This case means my father's life. What would you hold back from me?"

The pain in his eyes is clear, but so is his commitment to silence. "I'm sorry, Penn. All I can tell you is talk to Quentin."

"He's not going to tell me anything. Look, the Devines promised me they would testify for Dad. Are they going to come through on that?"

His face tightens again. "I'm working to make that happen."

"Have you got the plea deal signed or not? Is the U.S. attorney cooperating?"

Kaiser closes his eyes as though wrestling with a desire to come clean. When he opens them, though, I still see his professional shield in place. "Penn, I want your father to be acquitted. But in the end, I'm here representing the Bureau. That's all I can tell you right now. I know it sucks, but a lot of things about this job suck. Same as being a prosecutor or a mayor. Now, I need to go. Court's going to start back up soon."

"What about the bomb at Judge Elder's house?"

"A hoax, apparently."

Again I wonder if Lincoln Turner called in the threat to empty the courtroom and get access to me.

"What are *you* doing here?" Kaiser asks, suddenly realizing that my being here makes little sense.

For an instant I'm tempted to tell him about Lincoln and the tape, but the impulse passes. "Doris is having a problem with the security system. I promised her I'd come down and fix it."

After a couple of seconds' steady gaze, Kaiser grips my shoulder. "Keep the faith, man."

"Faith? Do we still believe in the same things?"

After a single nod, the FBI agent turns and disappears through the back gate.

"WE DON'T NEED his damned tape," Quentin says with finality. "And certainly not for no *million bucks*. Jesus. Do you even have that kind of money?"

His wheelchair sits just inside the back door to the kitchen of Edelweiss. A cup of coffee stands on the creamy marble counter behind him, an insulin syringe lying beside it. Doris is upstairs, supposedly taking a shower, though it's midday.

"Don't you think you should talk to Dad before you make that decision?" I ask.

"I don't need to. I know what his answer would be. We're damn sure not going to break the law to buy anything Lincoln Turner is selling. Under other circumstances, a sting operation might be appealing, but I'm not going to play those games with that boy."

"You'd better be sure, Quentin. I heard the tape, and I recognized both Sonny Thornfield's and Snake Knox's voices. They threatened to kill Viola, and they did it between the time Viola returned to Natchez to die and the day of her death. You should have heard her, man. She *taunted* those bastards. She practically dared them to kill her. That tape is reasonable doubt on a silver platter, just like Lincoln said."

"For one million dollars, paid in advance," Quentin says skeptically.

"The money's not the point. When you cross-examined Cora Revels, you asked her if any Klansmen or Double Eagles threatened Viola in those last weeks. I'm telling you now that there's *proof*. Hard evidence. And you're blowing me off?"

Quentin at last gives me his full attention. "What guarantee do you have that as soon as Lincoln gets the money, the original tape won't go into the river, just like the copy did?"

"None."

"But you're still willing to pay?"

"I don't know. A sting operation is probably the way to go, but we'd have to put it together fast."

"They can't do it in an hour. And Lincoln told you he wouldn't talk to you anymore. Hell, that tape you saw go into the water was probably the original."

"No. A guy like that isn't going to dump his ace in the hole."

"You have no idea what kind of guy he is. What you do know is that he just made his play. Now he's at risk, so long as he has that tape."

"Wrong. If the cops stopped him right now, he could claim he just found the tape. Only when he exchanges it for the money does he commit a crime, and even then, he could say he was just bringing it to me out of a sense of obligation."

Quentin ponders what I've told him.

"We don't need it," he says finally. "Lincoln's already hung himself."

"How? You scared him, all right, but what's the other shoe?"

"You'll find out soon. You just have to trust me until then."

"How am I supposed to do that? You've been giving me the mushroom treatment from the beginning."

"I'm sorry. You know that wasn't my choice. Let me just say this: if Lincoln Turner knew what I have, he'd fill that big truck of his with gas and hightail it back to Chicago."

"Are you talking about Will Devine? I saw Kaiser leaving here."

The owlish eyes flash. "You talked to him?"

"Mm-hm."

"Kaiser didn't tell you anything."

"No. But you should."

"I'll tell you this: you'd be crazy to pay Lincoln Turner a dime. If you want to pay somebody a million dollars for an acquittal, pay *me*. I'll guarantee it—even if I have to confess to killing Viola myself."

Quentin's grin does nothing to ease my anxiety.

"Seriously, Penn. Stay away from Lincoln. When you get twisted the way that boy was growing up . . . there's just no hope. Let's leave it at that."

"He's no boy anymore. He's a grown man. A lawyer. And regardless of what happens in this case, he's going to file a federal suit against Dad for violation of his mother's civil rights. He'll probably file a medical malpractice case as well. You know I'm right. That audiotape has value beyond this case. A million dollars might sound cheap before this mess is finished."

Quentin reaches out and lays his hand on my forearm. "Listen to me. If I was worried, I'd be trying to buy that tape myself. But I'm not. When a crook like Lincoln Turner starts trying to work the system for revenge, he always screws up. Lincoln's mistake is greed. Don't play into it. Let him twist in the breeze. By the time I'm done with him, he won't be filing shit against your father or anybody else. He'll never get his license back."

"And Will Devine? Do you have him now or not?"

Quentin taps the tip of his nose with his long forefinger. "Put it this way: If I get him, I'll be happy to squeeze him like a rotten lemon. But if I don't, I'm happy to proceed without him." Quentin gives me a wink. "Remember . . . the Lord helps those that helps themselves."

CHAPTER 54

WHEN THE TRIAL resumed at 1:35 P.M.—after exhaustive searches of the judge's home and the courthouse—I couldn't keep my mind on the testimony of Virginia Sexton. For one thing, I was stunned to find that my mother had finally agreed to let Annie attend the court proceedings. This morning's recitation of Dad's war heroism must have tipped the balance. Annie sits at Mom's right shoulder, Mia beside her, then Jenny. Annie looks fascinated by the whole spectacle, while Mia takes in everything with her usual cool thoroughness.

I can't stop silently replaying the tape recording I heard in Lincoln's car. That recording alone would inject reasonable doubt into the collective mind of this jury. And Lincoln was right in his assessment of my character: if someone had told me on day one of this trial that one million dollars would buy my father an acquittal, I would have found a way to pay the money.

Now it's no longer an option.

Despite his bravado back at Edelweiss, Quentin is still painstakingly following the thread of Viola's supposed alternate will, which, despite the remainder of Henry's mother's testimony, remains theoretical. Shad releases the tearful Mrs. Sexton after getting her to admit that she never saw any will even purportedly written by Viola Turner.

Next, Quentin calls to the stand a history professor from Syracuse University, a pale, soft-spoken man whose voice carries great conviction. The professor has brought with him an e-mail written by Henry Sexton ten days before his death. In this e-mail, which the professor reads aloud, Henry informs him that Viola told Henry she had changed her will, and in the new will stipulated that Henry would receive fifty thousand dollars to be used to finance the continued investigation of Viola's brother's death, and also to complete his documentary film about that investigation, among others. The problem, despite the professor's passionate sincerity, is that no one will come forward and swear they ever saw such a will, much less produce it for the court.

When I glance at Rusty on my left, he looks half-asleep, but when he sees me looking at him, he covertly makes a masturbatory gesture with his right hand. Clearly, his reassessment of Quentin as a genius has taken a beating in the past hour. After Shad gets the professor to admit that he never saw a copy of the supposed new will, the district attorney faces the jury and turns up his hands, as though to say, *Why are we wasting our time with this nonsense?*

I am inclined to agree with him until Quentin, in a revitalized voice, says, "Your Honor, the defense calls Mr. Junius Jelks to the stand."

Shad whips his head toward the back door so fast that he might require a visit to a chiropractor, and only with obvious difficulty does he squelch the compulsion to bark "Objection!" But he has no grounds for objection. Shad is merely stunned that Viola Turner's husband—a man who until ten seconds ago Shad believed was safely behind bars in Joliet, Illinois—is about to take the stand and say God knows what. Trying a case without the benefit of discovery is proving to be a devilish ordeal for the district attorney. I can only thank my stars that this was never an option for defense attorneys in Texas.

When the big back doors open, I don't see the witness, but two federal marshals. One holds open the door while the second stands a few feet inside it, awaiting their charge. With a jangling clink of metal on metal, a black man of medium height enters the courtroom with a graceful walk and a twinkle in his eye. Junius Jelks's hair is gray, but he still looks virile, and he seems to draw keen pleasure from the hundreds of eyes now riveted upon him. As he walks down the aisle, an audible hiss rises from the gallery. The sibilant rush is soft, snakelike, but when it continues without break I realize it must be coming from many mouths at once. This crowd clearly remembers Lincoln's testimony about how cruel this man was when he acted as Lincoln's pretend-father. And if the crowd remembers that description, the jury does, too.

When Jelks passes me, I note the handcuffs on his wrists; they look odd on a man wearing what looks like a funeral suit. In my mind's eye, I see the old con man selling "preordered" Bibles to recently bereaved widows, à la Ryan O'Neal in *Paper Moon*. He probably dragged Lincoln to every door with him, like the little girl in the movie.

While the clerk swears Jelks in, Rusty leans to my ear and says, "Vondie Curtis-Hall."

"What?"

"That's who Jelks looks like, Vondie Curtis-Hall, but old."

"Rusty, I don't know these actors."

"Shit, Vondie's been in everything from *Crooklyn* to the *Sopranos,* but you probably remember him in the movie they made of that James Lee Burke novel. The one with Alec Baldwin as Dave Robicheaux, not Tommy Lee Jones. He played Minos Dautrieve."

"I guess I need to get out more."

"He looks just like Cora Revels made him sound. A born con man."

"What the hell's he doing here? That's my question."

Rusty chuckles and whispers, "Quentin wouldn't have brought him down from Joliet if he wasn't going to set off some fireworks."

"Fireworks are dangerous, Rusty, especially in court."

Quentin rolls up to his spot beside the lectern and regards his witness sternly. "Mr. Jelks, I see you've brought a few people with you today. What is the reason for that?"

Jelks gives a rueful smile. "They're federal marshals. Apparently they consider me a flight risk."

"Where did you travel from to be with us today?"

"The Illinois State Prison."

"What are you presently serving time for?"

"Uhh, they said I tried to bribe a judge, but that's an oversimplification. A man of your legal experience would see it in a minute. They—"

"I'm going to lead this discussion, Mr. Jelks, if you don't mind. What was your relation to the victim, Viola Turner?"

"I'm her husband. I was, anyway."

"How long were you married?"

"Oh . . . 'bout thirtysomething years. Thirty-five or -six."

"And how did you meet your wife?"

Jelks chuckles softly. "I was preaching a sermon in the Abundant Life Church in Chicago, and she happened to be there."

"Are you an ordained minister?"

"Not exactly. I'm more of a lay preacher."

"I see. And Viola had a son at the time you married her?"

"Yes, sir."

"Were you the father of that child?"

"No."

"Did you know who was?"

Jelks takes his time with this. "Well . . . I knew what she told me. But that wasn't the truth. Took me a long time to find that out. I doubt Viola told ten lies in all her life, but every one she told was about that child."

"Who did she tell you the father was?"

"Her first husband, James Turner. The war hero."

"And when did you learn different?"

"Thirty-two years later."

"How did that come about?"

"Somebody sent me a picture of James Turner's death notice in the Natchez paper. That's when I realized he'd got killed in Vietnam nine months before Lincoln was even conceived."

"Do you know who sent you that picture?"

"Yes, sir."

"Who?"

"Cora Revels."

"Like I said," Rusty whispers in the stunned silence. "Fireworks."

"The defendant's sister?" Quentin asks.

"That's right."

"How do you know that?"

"She admitted it to me, two days later."

"Cora Revels testified in this court that someone had sent you such a picture, but she didn't know who."

Jelks chuckles knowingly. "I'll bet she did."

"What did you do when you got the picture?"

"I questioned my wife."

"Did you beat her?"

"I may have slapped her a time or two. I was pretty upset, as you might imagine."

"What did she tell you?"

"First, some BS story about a one-night stand. I knew that was a lie. Viola never had a one-night stand in her life. Then she told me the Ku Klux Klan had raped her back in Mississippi. That I could believe. When I called down to Natchez to check, some people told me that rumor had gone around back in '68. The numbers added up, so I bought that story."

"When did you learn that Tom Cage was in fact Lincoln's father?"

"Three months ago, when the story hit the national papers. After Viola died."

Glancing to my right, I see my mother sitting as pale and motionless as a marble in the British Museum. Only her right hand, clenching Annie's, gives any indication of life.

"Did you ever tell Lincoln that his birth had resulted from a Klan rape in Mississippi?" Quentin asks.

"Yes, sir. Seven months ago."

"Why did you do that?"

"The boy disappointed me. I was upset. I wish I hadn't done it now, but wishin's no use. Wasn't his fault, however he got born."

Quentin rotates his chair toward the jury box but continues to address Jelks. "Let's go back to Cora Revels for a moment. Please characterize the relationship between Cora and her sister, as you came to understand it after you joined the family."

"Well . . . it wasn't good."

"How do you mean?"

"Cora was always jealous of Viola. Viola was the pretty one, the smart one, she could sing and dance like somebody on TV. Like Martha and the Vandellas. The Supremes. Cora was like Mary Wells to Viola's Diana Ross. Only Viola was like Diana Ross with Mary Wells's voice. She had it *all,* brother."

Suddenly Jelks catches sight of Cora sitting in the row behind the prosecution table. She looks as though she's trying to shrink beneath her seat.

"There you is, Cee. Ha. Don't crouch down, baby. You still looking good!"

Judge Elder says, "Mr. Jelks, don't speak unless you are first asked a question."

"Yes, sir, Judge."

Quentin says, "How well did you come to know Cora during the thirty-five years you were married to her sister?"

"Well . . . about as good as a man can come to know a woman, if you know what I mean."

A shocked murmur ripples through the crowd. Everyone is staring at Cora Revels.

"When Mae Ola was dying," Jelks goes on, "—that's Viola's mama, Mrs. Mae Ola—Cora and me got a little closer than we should have. I ain't proud of it. Just stating a fact. But a man's got needs, and all Viola could think about during those weeks was taking care of her mama. She was bone tired every day. But Cora didn't strain herself like that. Viola always did most of the work, 'cause she was a nurse, I reckon. But those two women were just different. Always was. And having this jealousy thing between them, Cora wanted to try me out, I guess. So I let her. I didn't care what her reason was."

So this is what Lincoln was referring to on the stand when he said his mother had lost a lot of sympathy for Junius Jelks after her mother died . . .

"You're saying Cora slept with you out of a desire to hurt her sister?"

"Objection," says Shad. "Is this soap opera leading to anything relevant?"

Judge Elder looks curiously at Shad. "When you were directing the soap opera, Mr. Johnson, you seemed quite content to hear this kind of lurid detail. Overruled."

"Like I said," Jelks intones, "being with me was one way of getting back at Viola for all those years of feeling second class. If Cora could take Viola's man, then she could feel superior for just a little while."

"Did Viola ever learn about this extramarital affair?"

"Uhh, I'm afraid so. The night before we were due to go back to Chicago, she caught us messin' a little in the kitchen, and she saw the way it was. Then out of nowhere Cora busts out and says I'm leaving Viola for her, which was complete bullsh— *non*sense. I wasn't that kind of fool. But the upshot was, Cora and Viola didn't speak to each other for a long time after that."

"How long, Mr. Jelks?"

"Years."

"How many years?"

"Eight or nine, I guess. Until Viola got the cancer."

"And it was during this period that Cora sent you James Turner's death notice?"

"That's right. For a long time Cora felt real guilty about me, and Viola wouldn't ever ease up on her. So eventually Cee got mad. She wanted to prove to me—and to Viola—that Viola wasn't any better than she was. Hell, I knew Viola wasn't perfect. But she was as perfect as any mortal woman I ever met, and better than I deserved."

"Mr. Jelks, two days ago, right there in that chair you're sitting in, Cora Revels painted a verbal picture of the time when her mother was dying. She described it as a period of special closeness between her and her sister. She said it was then that Viola had confided the secret of Lincoln's paternity to her."

"I don't know about Viola telling Cee that. But I know that time wasn't any 'period of closeness.' Cora spent every minute trying to find excuses to get away from the house to have sex with me."

A hum of conversation rises, then dies. A rustle of cloth to my right makes me turn, and I can see that my mother deeply regrets allowing Annie to attend these proceedings. But if I know Annie, she won't be leaving until court has adjourned for the day. Not without making a scene, anyway.

"The day we left town," Jelks adds, "it would have taken an ice pick for Cora to get one word out of Viola."

Quentin nods as though he expected this answer all along. "I see. Well, why didn't Viola divorce you over this incident?"

"I've thought about that a lot. She said it was because she wanted Lincoln to have a stable family. But looking back, I think the real reason was she was afraid I'd get mad and tell Lincoln I wasn't his father. That was her greatest fear, that he would find out the truth about himself."

"But you yourself didn't know who Lincoln's real father was at that time, did you?"

"No. That's right. But she knew I'd tip to it eventually."

Quentin rolls his chair closer to the witness box, testing the invisible boundary that exists in the judge's mind. "Mr. Jelks, did your wife ever talk to you about any crime that she might have committed back in Natchez, Mississippi?"

This question obviously strikes Junius Jelks as absurd. "A crime?

Viola? She was the most proper woman you ever met, except for her drinking. And she always drank at home. Butter wouldn't melt on that woman's tongue, brother. Not unless she wanted it to."

"So, your answer is no?"

"My answer is *hell* no. She never mentioned committing any crime." Jelks smiles crookedly. "I was the criminal in our marriage."

"In your earlier testimony, you said you told Lincoln Turner just last year that he'd been fathered by Ku Klux Klan rapists. Is that correct?"

"Yes."

"Did you and he have any contact after that?"

"Not really. I was in prison, and he stopped coming to see me."

"What about phone calls?"

"Coupla angry ones the first couple of weeks, but then nothing."

"How did Viola react to you telling Lincoln the Klan rape story?"

"She told Lincoln that as far as she was concerned, I was dead. She never wanted to hear my name again. He told me that during one of those calls."

"Did you ever again hear from your wife prior to her death?"

"Just once."

"What was the nature of the contact? A prison visit? A call?"

"She sent me a letter."

"To the prison?"

"That's right."

"What did the letter say?"

"Well . . . I brought it with—"

"Objection!" Shad barks. "We've had no notice of this letter. Contents of writings, recordings, and photographs."

"Your Honor," says Quentin, "we enter this letter as Defense Exhibit Five subject to verification of Viola Turner's handwriting by the State's expert, which our own expert has already done to our satisfaction."

"Your Honor," Shad goes on, "this witness is a known confidence man and convicted felon. How can the court give any weight to anything he might bring before us?"

"That's up to the jury to decide," Judge Elder says calmly. "Denied. I'll allow it, subject to authentication. Please continue, Mr. Avery."

"Exception," Shad says testily.

"Noted."

"Please read the letter, Mr. Jelks," Quentin says.

"Junius. I am writing to inform you that I am cutting you out of my will."

A sharp babble of conversation erupts in the gallery.

"Order," demands Judge Elder.

"You will probably think I am doing this because your actions got Lincoln disbarred, and possibly ruined his career, but that is not the reason. I would have divorced you for that, but since I am dying, there's not much point in going through all that. I don't have the strength for it, anyway. You may also recall that I didn't cut Cora out of my will, not even after she committed adultery with you.

"I am disinheriting you because I have finally found a cause for which I would give anything, even my life. There is a reporter down here working on Jimmy's and Luther's disappearance, still working after all these years. A white man named Henry Sexton. He and a producer are trying to make a movie about the case, and they need money to finish it. I have looked into this man's eyes, and I trust him in a way I have never trusted anyone but my brother. So I am taking what little money I've managed to save and giving it to Mr. Sexton, in the hope that Jimmy's killers will finally be brought to justice, and the truth brought to light at last. I am still giving Cora and Lincoln small bequests, but less than half of what they were going to get before. You, on the other hand, have no need of money since you are in prison and may well die there. Bribing judges and buying drugs do not count as legitimate needs.

"Cora and I have finally reconciled after all the years of silence since what happened around Mama's death. I have secured a new will, and I am trusting Cora to make sure my wishes are followed. I believe she'll do it, but just in case, I have taken one further step to be sure you can't twist her to your own ends once more. But that's my business. It's already done, so don't try to talk me out of it. My mind is made up. Jimmy was the only one who stayed true to me, and to Mama and Daddy.

"As for us, I thought you broke my son's heart when you told him that story about the rape, but I understand now that you broke him long before that. I only wish I'd known then, so I could have left you in time to help him. You have so much charm, but there's something in you that brings out the worst in people. You tempted my sister into adultery, and you even turned my own son against me. I know Cora was at fault also, but she was weak, and you took advantage. That's what you do, Junius, you exploit human weakness. I know better than to hope that prison will change you any more than it did

before, but I pray that you will someday find faith, or at least peace, behind those walls.

"I know I am not without blame in what happened to us. My heart was broken before you and I ever met, and that may be what doomed us. I don't know. When you think of me, try not to be angry. We shared some joy in those early years. I still remember my first winter of snow, how magical it was to a Mississippi girl. I only learned to dread it later, much as I did with you. I suppose everything has both good and bad qualities. In spite of all, I thank you for the comfort you gave to me and my boy during the hard times in the beginning, and I forgive you for your weakness.

"May you find peace before you go to where I am going soon.

"Vee."

"I don't suppose that was a very easy letter to read," Quentin says softly.

"No, sir."

"And why *did* he read it?" Shad cries. "No man would read that without getting something in return. Especially a convicted con man!"

"I didn't hear an objection, Your Honor," Quentin says gently.

"Nor did I," says Judge Elder. "Take your seat, Mr. Johnson."

As I watch Shad sit, I realize that Lincoln, rather than trying to disappear into his seat, like Cora, is sitting ramrod straight and staring at Junius Jelks as though he means to kill him with his eyes. The ramifications of Jelks's testimony—and Viola's letter, if authentic—are just beginning to sink into my brain. Before I can reflect upon them further, Quentin drives the knife home.

"Mr. Jelks, did you inherit any money from your wife upon her death?"

A small, strange smile lights the old con man's face. "I did."

"How much?"

"Ten thousand, eight hundred dollars."

"Did that surprise you?"

"You could say that."

"Did you inquire of anyone why this apparent mistake had been made?"

Jelks's only response is a low laugh.

"Answer the question," orders Judge Elder.

"No, I did not."

"Given what your wife's letter had said about disinheriting you, what did you think had happened? Did you think she'd had a change of heart?"

"Objection," says Shad. "Leading."

"Sustained."

"What did you think had happened, Mr. Jelks?"

"Objection!" Shad shouts. "Vague."

"Overruled."

"I figured Lincoln had learned something from me after all."

"What do you mean by that?" Quentin asks, with the soft implacability of an ocean swell that will soon build into a tidal wave that could sweep all before it.

"That boy had been working cons even before he knew what he was doing. By the time he was six, he was as good as anybody I ever saw. He could run up to a lady crying he was lost and come back with her pocketbook and her watch, and her not miss them till five blocks later."

Jelks actually has pride in his voice, but the image he conjured only serves to tell me how radically different my childhood was from that of my half brother.

"I figured he'd found a way to lose Viola's new will," Jelks continues, "so the old one would stay in effect."

"Objection, Judge!" Shad presses. "Witness is speculating and has no knowledge of any such event."

"Sustained."

Jelks chuckles low. "I know it probably killed Lincoln to give me that eleven grand. But there wasn't no way around it, see? He still got twice as much for himself than if he'd let Vee give the lion's share to that white reporter."

"I've warned you about speaking out of turn, Mr. Jelks," Judge Elder snaps. "The jury will disregard the witness's last comments."

"*Right,*" Rusty says in my ear. "Quentin was planning this all along, Penn. He let them spend two days hanging themselves."

"Mr. Jelks," Quentin says, "when your wife's will was probated, why didn't you come forward with the letter you read today?"

Jelks shakes his head, but then he goes through the steps for the sake of form. "I wasn't going to look a gift horse in the mouth. And Vee was doing me wrong, changing her will like that. Illinois is one of the only states in the whole country where you can stop a spouse from inheriting. Anyhow, I sure didn't blame Lincoln any."

Quentin's sigh is freighted with a lifetime's weariness of dealing with self-serving convicts. "You were still Viola's spouse at the time she changed that will, Mr. Jelks. But in any case . . . is there anything you want to say before I hand you over to the district attorney?"

Junius Jelks looks down at the letter in his lap, then out over the crowd. "Only this. Viola was right about me. I wasn't no saint, as you can see from these guards I got with me. But then, I couldn't afford to be. Lord, was it hard to look her in the face knowing how far you'd fallen short of what she expected—and deserved. But Vee was wrong about her brother, Jimmy. By dying young, that boy stayed a kind of saint to Viola. But it was him and Luther that got her in trouble with the Klan, got her raped and such. Not me. Ain't that something?"

Quentin turns to Shad and gives him the first completely unshrouded look he has given anyone since the beginning of the trial. It's as though a man wearing a cloak has suddenly thrown it back to reveal a gleaming sword. Shad actually slides a couple of inches back in his chair.

But Junius Jelks isn't finished. Just as Quentin opens his mouth to tender the witness, Jelks looks down at my father and says, "Doc, I don't know if you injected that poison or not, but you damn sure killed Viola. I drug on her my whole life, but you broke her heart before I ever laid eyes on her. It was you who killed her. At least my conscience is clean on that."

Quentin gapes at Junius Jelks, probably reflecting, as most trial lawyers have, that even a good witness can be a double-edged sword. "Your witness," he says finally.

Shad sits blinking in confusion, like a young boxer after catching a surprise hook from an aging champion.

As Quentin rolls back toward the defense table, Rusty catches his eye and gives him a covert thumbs-up. Quentin doesn't deign to acknowledge the signal. Even in the wheelchair, his regal bearing makes it clear that he exists above both the criticism and praise of men like Rusty Duncan.

Shad stands and approaches the witness box, walking right past the lectern and taking a combative stance that makes clear he feels only disdain, even disgust, for Junius Jelks.

"Why are you telling us all this now, Mr. Jelks?" he asks.

"What do you mean?"

"I mean, sir, that a man like you doesn't do anything for free. What have you been promised in exchange for your testimony?"

Jelks smiles in tacit agreement. "I see. Well, nobody paid me, if that's what you mean."

"Did anyone make you promises of any kind?"

"Well, sure. Mr. Avery there promised to look into my case and see if he might be able to get my sentence reduced, on account of what that judge done. How he went to jail for taking bribes, and such. But that's all."

"That's *all*?" Shad asks with theatrical verve, looking at the jury.

"Is that illegal?" Jelks asks, with perfectly acted sincerity, and only then does Shad realize that he has stepped on a spring-loaded land mine.

Judge Elder is staring at Shad as though waiting for the answer, but Shad isn't about to give one unless ordered to from the bench.

"Mr. Johnson?" he prompts.

"Yes, Judge?"

"The witness asked a question. I think the jury would probably like to know the answer."

Shad looks at the floor and swallows what must have been an acid retort, but when he raises his head, he says, "No, that's not strictly illegal. However, it certainly raises the probability that this witness would never have come forward without such an inducement."

"And the jury will be instructed to consider that," says Judge Elder, "in due course. Please continue."

"Mr. Jelks," Shad muses, "what if your testimony today results in you losing your inheritance? How will you feel about that?"

Jelks shrugs philosophically, the gesture of a pragmatic man who can calculate the odds of any proposition before most people even understand the question. "Mr. Johnson, money don't mean much to a man facing thirteen more years behind bars. Not a man my age. Even a small chance of freedom is worth fifty times the paper I've got rotting in the bank."

"Obviously. And given your feeling about this, is there anything you would not do to hasten your release from prison?"

"Probably not."

"You would lie on the witness stand?"

"Of course. I might even kill somebody, if he was the only thing standing between me and freedom."

Loud murmurs come from the crowd behind me. Shad faces the jury and again turns his palms up, as if to say, *What are we to do with such a man?*

"But my wife wouldn't lie for any reason," Jelks says with conviction. "Except maybe to protect her child. She wrote that letter, sir. Nobody can prove different."

"I didn't ask you a question, Mr. Jelks."

"I don't care, *Mister* Johnson. But I sure thank you and all these good people for getting me a day outside that stink-hole of a prison. I almost feel alive again."

Judge Elder looks as though he's endured all he intends to from Junius Jelks, but what can he do? The man's headed back to prison anyway, and it's better for Mississippi taxpayers if his room and board are paid by the State of Illinois. "Any further questions, Mr. Johnson?" Elder asks.

"No, Your Honor."

"No redirect, Mr. Avery?"

"None."

"The witness is released. Will a marshal please get this man out of my courtroom?"

As two marshals walk to the witness box to escort Junius Jelks from the court, I hear a commotion behind me, and I turn. Behind the prosecution table, Lincoln Turner has risen from his seat and is staring at the man he once believed was his father. He looks as though he might bull-rush Jelks at any moment.

I'm about to suggest that a bailiff get between the two when Lincoln says in a clear voice: "Judge, I want to speak."

Even the marshals escorting Jelks pause as Judge Elder looks down at Lincoln.

"You had your time on the stand, Mr. Turner. Though I suspect you may find yourself back in court before too long. Please sit down."

But Lincoln doesn't sit down. In fact, it looks like it might take a squad of cops to make him sit. I have seen that look on faces in court before—more than once on the faces of men who opened fire on defendants.

"Judge?" I say, coming to my feet, but Elder has finally picked up on the escalation. He motions for me to sit even as he speaks to the bailiff.

"Bailiff, if that man does not sit down, you will remove him from the court. And if he attempts to follow the witness out of this room, stop him."

The armed bailiff seems flummoxed by the turn this trial has taken, but he steps away from the wall with his right hand on the butt of the pistol at his belt.

As I take my seat, I realize that Quentin is staring at Lincoln with an uncertain look on his face. With an electric shock I realize what he's thinking. As calmly as I can, I move out of my chair and lean over the rail toward Quentin.

"Rest your case, Q. It's over. You just destroyed the State's witnesses."

"No, I didn't," he says, still looking at Lincoln. "I only wounded them."

"Quentin—"

"If I rest now, Shad can call Lincoln up on rebuttal and let him say whatever he wants."

"I doubt he'll risk that."

"Then you're a fool."

Quentin is right: Shad has the technical right to recall Lincoln to the stand. It would be unusual in a Mississippi trial, but if Shad thinks Lincoln can rehabilitate himself to any degree, he might give it a shot. And knowing Quentin's penchant for control, he will not cede to his enemy the power to choreograph Lincoln Turner's final appearance before the jury.

"Your Honor," Quentin says after only a few seconds' reflection, "the defense recalls Lincoln Turner."

Judge Elder's long face whips around to Quentin as though the old lawyer had suddenly started barking like a dog. I can almost hear him asking, *Are you sure?* But of course he doesn't.

"Please take the stand, Mr. Turner," Judge Elder commands.

Rusty grabs my left forearm and squeezes tight. "What the fuck is Quentin doing?"

"Playing chess. Very risky chess."

"Chess, my ass. Trial lawyers are like painters. Every one of 'em needs a guy with a hammer standing behind him to hit him on the head when the painting's finished."

"I agree, buddy. Be my guest."

But Rusty, despite his passion, knows there's nothing we can do to save Quentin from himself—or my father from Quentin—if indeed they need saving.

As Lincoln Turner walks to the witness stand, the bright-eyed man who during lunch tried to sell me a tape that could free my father looks as remote as the convict the marshals are escorting through the back door. His eyes now see nothing immediately before him; they're focused on the vanished past and a provisional future.

They're the eyes of a man with nothing left to lose.

CHAPTER 55

"MR. TURNER," QUENTIN SAYS from his place by the defense table, "I can see—indeed we all can see—that you are very anxious to speak. I can understand that, after the testimony of your . . . your former stepfather. I have recalled you because I don't want to silence anyone who can contribute to our understanding of the full truth in this case. I only ask one thing from you, and I ask it with the gravest possible concern. Please . . . remember that you are still under oath."

"I know that," Lincoln says with unalloyed bitterness.

"I don't say that to insult you, but to remind you that in passion men often say things they later wish to take back."

As if Lincoln has not already said a dozen such things . . .

"I know what I want to say, old man."

"Mr. Turner!" Judge Elder says sharply. "Watch your tone, or you'll pay a price."

Quentin looks at Lincoln a few more seconds, then nods once and rolls his chair toward the witness box.

"Mr. Turner, did you destroy that second will?"

"I did."

The collective gasp at this frank admission is like a wind at my back. I'm stunned enough, because I'm pretty sure that act could buy Lincoln two years in the county jail, and maybe longer, since his mother would have been considered elderly and vulnerable at the time.

"I'll tell you about that in a minute," Lincoln says. "But first I want to tell you about Junius Jelks."

Shad looks like he might have a heart attack any second, but he knows there's nothing he can do to stop this—only delay it.

"Mr. Turner," Quentin says for form's sake, "would you describe your familial relationship with Junius Jelks?"

"That man," Lincoln says, shaking his head, "for most of my life, I thought he was my father. But he wasn't. He pretended to be, when it suited him. And he taught me a lot, the way a father's supposed to teach his son. He taught me that a lie was better than the truth, that stealing was better than working, that winning meant nothing if you hadn't cheated to do it. Winning without cheating was just luck, he said, and any dumb sucker can get lucky.

"That term, 'con man,' it doesn't sound bad, does it? Makes you think of some slick Hollywood actor. But that's the biggest lie of all. Like Mama's letter said, Junius Jelks preyed on the weak his whole life, like a jackal in the desert. He cheated old people and the sick. He steered runaway kids to pimps for a cut of the take. He used me to help him do that, even before I knew what I was doing. He fleeced every immigrant and minority class there is—used their ignorance like a gun against them. I've seen him talk thirteen-year-old girls right out of their clothes. He can fake his way through five languages and doesn't know a one of them. *'Caveat emptor!'* he used to yell after he'd taken somebody. 'Let the buyer beware!'"

"Mr. Turner," Quentin says gently. "I think we get the point. Your stepfather was no saint, as he said himself."

Lincoln nods intently, as though trying to focus through the furnace glow of his anger on some wavering point beyond it.

"What about your mother's will, Mr. Turner?"

After several seconds, Lincoln looks up, and this time it's Quentin who rolls back about a foot in the face of his withering stare. "Mama made a new will, just like her letter said. And I burned it. I burned it as soon as I got to Natchez that morning." Lincoln looks over Quentin at the spectators. "Who in this room wants to condemn me for that? All my life, Mama told me she was going to take care of me. She often talked about her will and said she was going to do all she could for Cora and me. And she meant to, right up until a couple of weeks before she died. Right up until that white reporter got her alone and filled her head with crazy dreams about Jimmy. My mama was *sick,* man. She was on drugs! She was *dying,* and that Henry Sexton took advantage of her just like Junius Jelks used to cheat them old folks in the nursing homes in Chicago. I *deserved* that money, people. Cora did, too. Mama wanted us to have it, and then a smooth-talking white man came along and cheated her out of her life savings on her deathbed. Do you think I should have stood by and let that crook walk away with my mama's life savings? When my auntie can't hardly pay her electric bill?" Lincoln looks down at Quentin. "Do you really believe that?"

Quentin sits silent in his wheelchair, seemingly cowed by the intensity of Lincoln's indignation. This is exactly what I was afraid of, though I didn't know Lincoln would go quite so far in expressing his righteous anger. But Jelks's testimony so enraged him that he seems unconcerned by the prospect of being charged with fraud, or whatever the charge will be for destroying his mother's valid will.

I want Quentin to put an end to this, but there's really no way to do it. If he tries to shut Lincoln up, Shad can simply walk up on redirect and let him finish whatever he wants to say. Quentin knows this, of course. That's why he let Lincoln get up in the first place. My mother has leaned across Annie to speak urgently to Mia, and I can guess what she's telling her, but Annie's having none of it. If Mom wants Annie out of this court, she's going to have to miss the proceedings herself, which she's unwilling to do.

Lincoln turns to the jury, his eyes glinting with tears. It's unexpectedly moving to see such a large and muscular man reduced to this.

"Listen to me, folks," he implores. "Please listen to this, if nothing else. What Tom Cage and his lawyer are doing is just what Junius Jelks taught me to do. What every good con man and magician does. They're getting you to look at one thing—one hand—so you don't see what the other hand is doing. But it's that other hand that's dipping into your pocket, or pulling the fifth ace from a sleeve. That other hand does the real business, see? Don't let yourselves be taken in! Don't be *suckers*."

Lincoln blinks at the twelve bovine faces like a prophet trying to get through to a crowd of tired peasants. "People have been talking about Tom Cage like he's some kind of saint. The patron saint of downtrodden black folks. Don't you know why? Who's going to convict a saint of murder? Nobody. But have you ever asked yourself *why* he's spent his life doing things for black people? Did you ever wonder if what drives him might be *guilt,* and not Christian charity?"

Lincoln jabs his forefinger toward the audience. "I've talked to people in this town! Everybody from Natchez talks about the light in my mama's eyes. They say she could light up a whole room. But by the time I knew her, that light was all but gone. She was just a husk of a woman sitting in front of the TV after work, drinking cheap wine and crying over stupid movies. I saw that light flicker up a few times, when I'd bring home a good report card or something. But that was all. Mama hardly left that apartment after I was ten years old, except to go to work or the liquor store. Always sent me out to get her cigarettes. I've seen pictures of her taken down here . . . she looked like a movie star. But by the time she was thirty-five, she looked fifty years old. Ten years after that, she looked like a bag lady. You think that's easy for me to say?" Lincoln closes his big hand into a fist and hammers it against his heart. "It's not. But I say it to let you know what Tom Cage did to her. He filled her full of hope for something she could never have, and then he snatched it away! He made her lie to protect his reputation, and his white family. He made her lie to keep me invisible. He stole the life out of her, the same way Jelks stole people's last dollar!"

Hearing a shuffle to my right, I turn. Mom is actually holding her hands over Annie's ears. For a moment I consider getting up and leading Annie out. But she's already heard this much, and I'm not about to miss the remainder of Lincoln's soliloquy. As he continues, though, my mind sticks on the things he said last, and I realize that I'm no longer picturing Viola Turner as the nurse I knew so long ago, but as Serenity Butler. What would it take to completely break down a woman with Serenity's strength, beauty, and intelligence? By all accounts, Viola had possessed each of those gifts.

"Take the word of a man raised by a con man and educated to be a lawyer," Lincoln goes on. "And what is a lawyer but a con man with a degree?"

Several jury members nod at this.

"Quentin Avery has spent all this time getting you focused on Mama's will so that you won't focus on the one thing that really matters—the crime that brought us here—my mama's *murder.* And not one thing he's said has disproved a single fact about what happened on the night Mama died."

"It was you who brought us here," Quentin says, just loud enough to be heard by the jury. "And I think we're all beginning to understand why. You're a very angry man. And while that may not be the main issue before the bar, perhaps it should be. The courts, Mr. Turner, do not exist to be used for personal revenge."

"Objection," says Shad. "Judge, we've gotten far afield of the central issue. Mr. Turner is right, his mother's will is a matter for the chancery court, not this venue."

"You may be wrong about that," Judge Elder says ominously. "But this has gone far enough. Mr. Avery, bring this to a close."

Quentin rolls his chair to within three feet of the witness box. I'm put in mind of a veteran lion tamer getting dangerously close to the beast he wants to manipulate.

"Are there any other lies you wish to confess, Mr. Turner? If so, now's your chance."

"I've said what I had to say."

"All right, then. No further questions, Judge."

"Mr. Johnson?" says Judge Elder.

"Nothing further, Your Honor."

Elder turns to Lincoln. "You may step down."

As Lincoln walks back to his seat, where his aunt Cora waits like a woman who has suffered a mild stroke, the silence in the room reminds me of some public venue where someone has done something shocking and no one is quite sure whether they did it because they're uncouth or because they're mentally ill. By any conventional assessment, Junius Jelks proved that two of the State's main witnesses lied on the stand for the basest of reasons. That alone has introduced sufficient reasonable doubt into the case to trigger an acquittal. But somehow Lincoln's impassioned plea to the jury—uttered so obviously against his own interest—has raised the specter that despite his and Cora's venal lies, my father might still be guilty of murder.

"Tell him to rest his case," Rusty says in my ear. "Hurry! Quentin looks like he's going to call another witness!"

A horrifying prospect causes me to rise from my seat and risk Judge

Elder's wrath by moving through the rail to kneel beside Quentin's wheelchair. "You're not still thinking of calling Dad to the stand?"

"Calm down," Quentin says irritably. "And get back to your seat. I have things well in hand."

"So quit while you're ahead!"

"Go back to your seat, Penn."

"You've *won,* damn it."

"If you think that, you've misjudged the issues in this trial." Quentin glances toward the judge. "The defense calls Mr. Vivek Patel to the stand."

"Who the hell is that?" I hiss.

"You're about to find out." With a shove off my shoulder, Quentin rolls away from me.

As I take my seat, a dark-skinned Indian man sits in the witness box and takes the oath, though as a Hindu he does not put his hand on the Bible, and he "affirms" rather than "swears" that he will tell the truth. He seems eerily calm compared to the jurors and spectators, who just witnessed Lincoln's spectacular tirade. His dark eyes gleam with intelligence, and he waits for the first question like he has all day to spend in court.

"Mr. Patel, would you tell us your occupation?"

"Yes, sir. I own a motel in Jefferson County, on Highway 61. Between Fayette and Port Gibson."

"How far away is that from Natchez?"

"Twenty-eight miles."

"What's the name of your motel?"

"The Belle Meade Inn."

"Mr. Patel, have you been sitting in court during the past fifteen minutes?"

"Yes, sir."

"Did you see the man testifying before I called you up here?"

"Yes, sir."

"Have you ever seen that man before today?"

"Yes, sir."

"Where?"

"He was a guest at my motel."

"When was this?"

Mr. Patel removes a folded piece of paper from his pocket.

"What is that you're looking at, Mr. Patel?"

"It's a photocopy of my guest register."

"I see. Please go on."

"Yes . . . the man who testified before me stayed at my motel just over three months ago. Last December."

"Do you have the exact dates?"

"Yes." The man checks the paper in his hand. "He checked in on December ninth, and he checked out on December thirteenth."

Quentin pauses to let the jury grasp the significance of these dates. "Are you aware that this is a murder trial, Mr. Patel?"

"Yes, sir."

"Are you aware of the date on which the victim in this case was killed?"

"Yes, sir. December twelfth of last year."

"Precisely. And at that time, the man you identified had been staying at your motel for four days?"

"Exactly so."

Rusty's hand closes on my arm again, this time with painful force. Like me, he has sensed that the ocean swell that began during Junius Jelks's testimony is now about to smash into Lincoln Turner—and Shad Johnson's case—with shattering force. "What name did he register under?"

Patel consults the register again. "Keith Mosley."

"Keith Mosley? Are you sure?"

"Yes, sir."

"*Holy fuck,*" Rusty breathes. "*Lincoln killed his mother.*"

"Bullshit," I say under my breath, but we both turn to look at Lincoln, who is sitting with the mute stillness of a mahogany carving.

"Did you ask for ID when he registered?" Quentin goes on.

"Of course."

"What did he show?"

"A driver's license."

"Then what was he doing here all that time?" Rusty whispers.

"Waiting for his mother to die," I think aloud. "Waiting for Dad to kill her. So he could bring us here."

"No, man. I think he killed her. For the money."

"From what state?" asks Quentin.

"Illinois."

"In the name of Keith Mosley?"

"Yes, sir."

"And how did he pay you? With a credit card?"

"No, sir. Cash."

"Cash. Did you find that suspicious?"

"No, sir. Many of my guests prefer to pay in cash."

"I see. Are you positive that the man you have pointed out is the same man who registered as Keith Mosley?"

"Absolutely."

"And how is it that you came to be here today?" Quentin asks.

"Well . . . at the beginning of the week, or Tuesday rather, my wife called me over to where she was reading the newspaper—"

"Excuse me, what paper was that?"

"The Natchez paper. The *Examiner.*"

"Thank you. Please continue."

"There was a picture of this man in the paper. And my wife said, 'Vivek, this looks like the man who stayed with us last December.' When I looked at the photo, I instantly agreed. But then I noticed that he was called by another name in the caption, and in the story."

"What name was that?"

"Mr. Lincoln Turner. This puzzled me, and I tried to convince myself that we were mistaken. But then my wife began to read every detail of the story, and the trial. She went on the Internet and studied back issues of the newspaper. She found another picture of the man, and I showed both pictures to one of our housekeepers at the motel. She identified Mr. Turner immediately as Keith Mosley."

"What did you do then?"

"I telephoned the authorities."

"The city police, or the sheriff's office?"

"The municipal police, but they referred me to the sheriff's office."

"And what did the sheriff's office tell you?"

"They told me I was mistaken."

Quentin pauses again to let this sink in, and he cuts his eyes at Sheriff Byrd as he does so. "How could they be so sure?"

"I do not know, sir."

"You told them everything you told us here today?"

"Most assuredly, sir."

"But they wouldn't listen."

"Objection," Shad says. "Leading."

"I'll rephrase," Quentin says smoothly. "What action did the sheriff's office take, if any?"

"None, to my knowledge, sir."

Judge Elder is glaring at Billy Byrd.

"What did you do then?" Quentin asks.

"I tried to forget about it."

"And could you?"

"No, sir."

"Why not?"

"My wife would not let me. My wife . . . once she gets hold of something, there's no stopping her. It was she who told me I should contact the attorney for the defense of Dr. Cage."

"And why would she suggest that?"

"As I said, she had been following the trial. And she understood that Mr. Mosley—or Mr. Turner, rather—had claimed that he only arrived in Natchez on the morning his mother died. That in itself was not technically false, since my motel is in an adjacent county. However, he also claimed to have just arrived from Chicago on that morning, which I knew to be false."

Quentin is nodding slowly. "It surprises me a little that you took the action you did, Mr. Patel. Not many Americans are so eager to come forward with information that might put them in the middle of a criminal trial."

Patel gives a very formal nod. "I understand, sir. Indeed, our housekeeper said she wanted no part of this, once she learned why I had asked her about the photograph."

"But that didn't deter you?"

"No, sir. This is a most serious matter. If a man gives false witness under oath, it is the duty of every citizen to point this out. The law cannot work impartially otherwise."

Quentin smiles with something like wistful admiration. "You're right, Mr. Patel. In the way that converts make the most scrupulous religious practitioners, I often find that immigrants make the most dutiful American citizens."

Mr. Patel sits a little straighter. "Thank you, sir."

Quentin nods at the Indian man, then looks up at Judge Elder and says, "I tender the witness."

I do not envy Shadrach Johnson.

Shad rises with slow deliberation and crosses from the prosecution table to the lectern, his expression projecting an air of accusation.

"Mr. Patel, were you offered anything in exchange for your testimony today?"

The innkeeper looks perplexed. "Exchange, sir?"

"Shad's not going to get anywhere with that," Rusty whispers. "Not with this guy."

"He's just stalling for time."

"Do you have a relative who might be incarcerated, for example? Someone Mr. Avery might be able to help you with, on a pro bono basis?"

As the thrust of the question comes to him, Patel's face darkens. "I have no relations in prison, sir!"

"What about your housekeepers? I'll bet at least some of them have legal trouble. Or their husbands?"

"Regrettably, yes. I help where I can. But Mr. Avery has offered me no assistance of any kind."

"I see." Shad paces out the space between the witness stand and the lectern, apparently intent on some line of thought. Suddenly he stops and looks at the motel owner. "Mr. Patel, do you have security cameras in your motel?"

"Only at the check-in desk."

If I were Shad, I would not ask the next question, but he's seen one level deeper than I on this issue. "Have you gone back and checked your tapes for Mr. Turner's face?"

"I have."

"And what did you find?"

"The time we are speaking of was three months ago. We recycle our tapes every sixty days, to save money. Regrettably, we do not have a recording of Mr. Turner checking in. We do have his receipts and the register, though."

"You mean you have Keith Mosley's receipts and signature."

The helpful look vanishes from Mr. Patel's face, replaced by one of consternation. "I stand by my testimony, sir. It is the same man."

"He's *lying*," Lincoln says from his seat behind Shad's table. "He made a mistake."

"Silence, Mr. Turner," Judge Elder says.

"I recognize his voice as well," Mr. Patel says with almost feminine snippiness.

"You're a liar," Lincoln asserts.

Joe Elder gives Lincoln a burning glare. "One more word, Mr. Turner, and you're going to jail. Mr. Johnson, do you have any further questions?"

"Nothing further, Your Honor."

Judge Elder nods at Mr. Patel. "You may step down, sir."

"Shad did all right," Rusty murmurs.

"Call your next witness, Mr. Avery."

Before Quentin speaks, I scoot up to the table and speak in his ear once more. "Okay, *now* you've destroyed Lincoln. Don't call any other witnesses. It's time to rest your case."

"Your Honor," Quentin says testily, "may I have a moment to confer with my co-counsel?"

"A brief moment."

Quentin turns to me with his last reserve of patience. "Go ahead, if you must."

"The jury believed that guy. If not all of them, then three-quarters, surely enough to get an acquittal."

Quentin lays his wrinkled brown hand on my forearm and fixes me with eyes that look ancient. "One more witness. That's all."

"You're both wrong," says my father, leaning over from his chair beside Quentin. "I'm still going up there."

"To take the stand?" I ask in disbelief. "That would be insane at this point. We're way past reasonable doubt. Quentin just planted the possibility that Lincoln himself killed Viola. For God's sake, it's time to declare victory and go home."

Dad shakes his head slowly, and white hair falls over his wrinkled forehead. "Snake Knox is still out there, son. Have you forgotten that?"

"Snake's another problem for another day!"

"No. He's always been at the heart of this case. Penn, you've got to trust that we know what we're doing."

I look back at Quentin. "Are you really going to put him on the stand?"

"Let's see how the next witness does."

For the first time in the trial my father's face darkens in anger. "We talked about this. We have an agreement."

Quentin cuts his eyes at Dad. "I know."

"You promised the jury I would testify."

"Mr. Avery," prompts Judge Elder, "we're not getting any younger."

"You've got a lot more cushion than I do, Joe," Quentin says under his breath.

"I beg your pardon?"

"I was just clearing my throat," Quentin says. "The defense calls Will Devine."

CHAPTER 56

THIS TIME WHEN the back door opens, the courtroom doesn't fill with federal marshals but with FBI agents. I can tell from their suits. Kaiser gets up from a seat about halfway back in the gallery and confers with the lead agent, then four men surround and escort Will Devine into the courtroom. Contrary to how he's looked when I've seen him—brandishing a shotgun in my face—Devine now appears as a mild, balding man with an oxygen mask on his face. One of the FBI agents rolls a trolley behind him with a green metal tank on it. But what draws the eyes of everyone in the courtroom is the bulletproof vest Devine is wearing.

"Quentin?" I murmur, turning and searching the court for Devine's family. I see no sign of Deke, Nita, or Will Junior.

"He's having some health issues," Quentin says. "But he's here."

"Where's his family?"

"Already in protective custody. Now sit down and pray that we're lucky."

A Double Eagle is about to testify in court. I guess fifty thousand dollars buys more than I thought it did. "Lucky how?"

"That he'll testify against Snake Knox. Thinking about it is one thing. Doing it is another. Now, *go sit down.*"

As I crab-walk back to my seat, an FBI agent commandeers a seat next to an older man who looks like he might be one of the more obscure Double Eagles. The young man being displaced argues in a muted voice, but the agent makes it clear that the guy is leaving his chair, one way or another. The old man beside the agent watches this like an airline passenger watching a stranger being thrown off a plane.

"Who the hell is the guy with the oxygen mask?" Rusty whispers. "Jesse James's long-lost grandson?"

"Close. He's a Double Eagle. One of the first bunch."

Rusty suddenly realizes that I must have had something to do with this. "Jesus, Penn. Quentin's about to make history."

"Let's just hope he gets Dad off. I'll settle for that."

"Look at this shit, buddy."

Four very tense FBI agents have taken up stations along the walls of the courtroom, one at the back door, and another beside the witness stand. Their weapons aren't showing, but no one has any doubt that they're armed.

Glancing up and behind me to the balcony, I see Serenity leaning forward, against the rail. When she sees me looking up at her, she makes a fist and gives it a subtle pump of triumph.

As I turn back toward the bar, Quentin rolls up to the lectern and says, "Mr. Devine, are you able to remove your mask for a few minutes?"

Devine looks reluctant, but after taking two deep breaths, he slides the clear mask to one side.

"Thank you, sir. I'll try to be brief."

Devine blinks his watery blue eyes but says nothing.

"Where do you live, Mr. Devine?"

"Concordia Parish. Across the river. All my life."

"Did you know a man named Frank Knox?"

"Yessir. Grew up with him."

"How old are you, Mr. Devine?"

"Seventy-nine years old. One year younger than Frank would be if he was alive today. I was just behind him in grade school, when we wasn't in the cotton fields."

"Are you aware that Frank Knox was once a member of the Ku Klux Klan?"

"He was for a little while. I was in there with him. The White Knights, not the UKA. That's United Klans of America."

"Did Frank Knox leave the Klan?

"Yes."

"Why?"

"Just a second." Devine slides the mask back over his face and takes a couple of greedy breaths.

Lord, is he milking this act . . .

"Frank thought the Klan was too soft," he continues. "Both the White Knights and the UKA was et' up with federal informants, and they was shying away from using violence. Frank believed in direct action."

"What did he do about that?"

"He formed his own group."

"Did that group have a name?"

"Yes, sir. The Double Eagle group, he called it."

"And were you a member of that group, Mr. Devine?"

"Yessir, I was."

The silence in the courtroom is absolute. Most natives of the surrounding counties know that a confession like this can still bring swift death to the man who makes it.

"For how long?"

"Well, technically, I'm still a member. It's a 'once in, never out' kind of deal."

"I see. And why have you come here today?"

"Because of Dr. Cage. I know he's being tried for murder, and I couldn't sit by and watch him go to jail without telling some things I know. I don't want to betray my brothers, 'specially the ones I fought with during the war. But I've lived long enough to see that we were wrong about some things. I don't have much time left till I stand before the Lord, so I want to do right by a man that I know did good while he could, even if it costs me dear."

"What might it cost you, Mr. Devine?"

The old man swallows hard, then speaks softly. "Well . . . according to the bylaws, by revealing anything about what we done back then, I forfeit my life. My family's, too. That's why we're going into the witness protection program, at least until certain folks who are still active aren't a threat no more."

This time the hum of voices rises until Judge Elder warns the crowd.

"Still active," Quentin echoes, glancing at the jury box. "I see. Are any of those folks in this room with us?"

"Could be," Devine says cryptically.

"But you won't say?"

"Not just yet, if you don't mind. I'm not right in my heart about that yet."

Quentin looks out over the audience, and like him I see people sitting next to elderly men wondering if they might be shoulder to shoulder with members of the Double Eagle group.

"Mr. Devine," Quentin says, turning back to his witness, "before we get into the specifics of what you came to say, do you have any proof that you actually belonged to this notorious group, the Double Eagles?"

The watery eyes blink several times. "Yes, sir, I do."

"What do you have?"

"Got my gold piece."

"Will you explain what you mean by that?"

Once again Devine goes through the breathing ritual with the mask. His breaths seem to be getting shallower.

At length, he says, "Frank wanted us all to carry some sign of membership. For us original guys it was a twenty-dollar gold piece, minted in the year of our birth. For the younger men, it was the 1964 JFK half-dollar, which the government minted after Kennedy was assassinated. They'd stopped making the gold pieces in the 1930s, but that's where Frank took the name, the Double Eagles. I didn't know why he wanted us to carry them, since we all knew each other, and since it might put us at risk from the FBI. But after a while, I understood. If you showed that coin around to a white man—even a cop—he'd do damned near anything you told him to. And if you showed it to a black man, he'd wet his pants or run for the woods. As for the FBI, I think Frank halfway wanted them to know who we were. In his mind, we was at war with the Bureau."

Quentin nods slowly, giving the jury time to process the details. "I see. Well, Mr. Devine, would you show us your gold piece? I don't doubt your word, but I think the jury might benefit by seeing something so historic firsthand."

Will Devine takes a couple more theatrically labored breaths, then fishes in his shirt pocket and tugs out a dark leather cord with a dull flash of gold at the end of it. He stretches the cord between his fingers and holds it out so that the heavy gold coin is suspended between them. The gold piece gleams under the courtroom lights, and to me it exudes a palpable malice, as though someone had taken an SS badge from his pocket and admitted to wearing it in action.

As the old man's hands start to shake, Quentin says, "You can put it away, Mr. Devine."

As Devine does this, Quentin says, "Let's talk about Viola Turner. Did you know her before she left Natchez in 1968?"

After closing his shirt, Devine reaches for his oxygen mask, then jerks sideways on his chair, as though a disc in his back suddenly caught painfully. After a moment, he leans to one side and slides his right hand beneath his buttocks. Then his left hand rips the oxygen mask from his face, and he heaves himself to his feet.

For a couple of seconds I think he must have sat on a bee, or maybe a spider. But then he starts to jerk spasmodically, his movements clearly uncoordinated. Several people in the audience cry out, but I only stare at Devine the way you stare at an audience volunteer during a Las Vegas magic show, trying to ascertain the nature of the profound change in him.

"Is he having a heart attack?" Rusty cries. "A seizure?"

Devine's eyes are wide open, and there's only panic in them. As my father rises from his chair, Devine doubles over and falls to the floor with a heavy thud. Dad hurries toward him.

"Everyone back in your seats!" Judge Elder commands, his voice booming through the courtroom like the voice of the law itself.

The bailiff has drawn his gun and is scanning the crowd with fear in his eyes. A stunned FBI agent restrains my father, but Judge Elder orders the agent to stand aside. The agent hesitates until Kaiser appears and pushes him out of the way. Dad slowly gets to his knees beside the fallen Double Eagle, but I don't know what he can do. From where I stand, Will Devine looks as dead as a veal calf after the bang stick has been put to its skull. As I stare at his motionless body, Tim and Joe and two more of our bodyguards sprint into the space between the audience and the bench to cover Annie, Mia, Mom, and Jenny.

"Sit down!" Judge Elder shouts into his microphone. "The officers in the room will lead an orderly evacuation of the court."

For a second it strikes me as strange that Judge Elder is talking about evacuation. After all, if a witness has a heart attack in a crowded courtroom, the best course is to keep everyone in place so that paramedics can quickly evacuate the patient. But Joe Elder senses malevolence behind this act. I suppose the closest parallel would be a Mafia trial. When a star witness against a Mafia don drops dead in the witness box, you don't assume natural causes.

As Dad works over Devine, I notice Kaiser examining the chair in the witness box. Taking out a penknife, he carefully runs it over the blue upholstery, then stops about eight inches from the chair back.

Looking left, I see that Devine, if he's not dead, soon will be. Dad is leaning over his mouth, where a white foam now covers the old Double Eagle's lips.

"What was it, Dad?"

"Cyanide, I think. Notice the cherry color of his lips?"

Now I do . . .

"There's still a heartbeat, but it's faint."

"Get me an evidence bag!" Kaiser cries above the general clamor.

Turning again, I see that the FBI man has cut open the chair seat, exposing springs, and from within removed a small metal cube, which he places on the rail of the witness box.

"What is that?" I ask, moving closer.

"Careful, Penn," he warns. "There's a needle sticking out of it."

He's right. I see a sliver-thin hypodermic protruding from the dull metal cube.

"We do need to clear the courtroom," Kaiser says, "but I don't want anybody in here to get out and away without being questioned."

Before I can respond, someone yells, "They shot him! They used a silencer! *They're still shooting!*"

For one pregnant moment, everyone in the room goes still. In this surreal slice of time, a face seems to zoom out of the crowd toward me. I don't know it well—as I do so many in this crowd—but something in its eyes triggers a primal reaction in my central nervous system.

What do I see? Every other set of eyes within my field of vision radiates fear and confusion. These eyes radiate . . . *triumph.*

"That's Snake Knox," I whisper.

Then a woman shrieks and pandemonium erupts, starting a general stampede for the single accessible exit. I feel like I'm standing at the edge of a hurricane. A few clever souls run for the door to the judge's chambers, but the bailiff blocks it with his drawn pistol. At this point, Tim and his men have begun physically covering the Cage women and Mia with their bodies.

"Goddamn it!" Kaiser curses, furiously scanning the mob. "Somebody triggered that device! Somebody in this room! It could be Knox himself."

"It *was,*" I confirm, catching Kaiser's arm. "I just saw him. I saw Snake."

"What?"

But already the man I believed to be Snake Knox has been swallowed by the panicked mob.

"Dr. Cage!" Kaiser calls. "What's Devine's condition?"

"Heart just stopped."

"Can you believe it?" says a resigned voice from below and behind me.

Quentin has rolled his wheelchair up to me. He's staring down at Will Devine's body, and my father is looking back at him.

"Believe what?" Kaiser asks, motioning for his agents to break through the crowd and come to him.

Quentin slowly bobs his head at the corpse on the floor. "Snake Knox just silenced another Double Eagle. He cut it fine this time, but he pulled it off."

"John," I say, reaching out for Kaiser's arm again.

"Are you okay, Penn?" he asks, looking at me strangely.

"He's here, John."

"What?"

"Snake Knox was here. Twenty feet away from us."

The FBI agent goes still. "Are you sure?"

"Ninety percent. Nothing else about him looked like Snake. But the eyes were his."

"What was he wearing?"

"I don't know." I close my eyes, trying to let go of everything but that hypercharged moment of eye contact. "Dark suit, maybe. Expensive. And dyed-black hair. Really black. He looked like . . . like Ronald Reagan."

CHAPTER 57

TWENTY MINUTES AFTER the death of Will Devine, our defense team gathered in my office at City Hall, which is adjacent to the courthouse. Quentin's pleas to the judge have resulted in my father being allowed to remain with us until after the jail has been searched for any similar devices, and also for explosives. Two deputies stand guard outside my door, in my secretary's office—probably trying to hear anything they can, at the order of Sheriff Billy Byrd—but the real security is provided by Tim Weathers and four of his associates. Annie and Mia are waiting down the hall in our lounge, where there's a refrigerator, a microwave, and plenty of snacks—though I doubt either of them feels like eating. Walt Garrity brought my mother and sister up here before even we arrived, which for the first time puts all the principals of our side in one room.

Mom and Jenny keep asking Dad whether he feels all right—translation, isn't about to suffer a heart attack—after the shock of Will Devine's murder. They seem to have forgotten that he survived suicidal Chinese charges at the Ch'ongch'on River. As Mom stands behind Dad's chair, rubbing his shoulders, Jenny insists that *surely* the judge is bound to stop the trial now. Quentin and I don't bother to argue; we've both tried cases in which witnesses were murdered—outside of court, it's true—but that does little to alter this case. The death of Will Devine has not wiped away the murder charge against my father or nullified the criminal proceeding against him. Quentin could ask for a mistrial, of course, but he's unlikely to get one from Joe Elder.

To my surprise, even Jenny has worked out that the poisoned needle device concealed in the witness chair was probably planted before the trial ever began and was waiting for whatever witness looked to be the most damaging to the Double Eagles.

"How long have you had that Mr. Devine waiting in the wings?" she asks Quentin. "From the beginning?"

"No," Quentin admits. "I knew nothing about him until last night, and we didn't know he would testify until this morning."

"That needle was waiting for Tom," Mom declares in a flat voice. "That's who they're most afraid of, Snake Knox and his gang." She comes around the chair and looks down at Dad. "That could have been you, Tom. It was *supposed* to be you."

Dad sighs and takes her hand. "But it wasn't."

This gives Mom no comfort, but she allows the conversation to be steered away from imminent danger. Jenny is the slowest to calm down, and as I watch her, I realize my older sister is one of those children who seem to take after neither parent. After another couple of minutes of decompression, Quentin tells Mom he needs some time alone with Dad, and together Mom and Walt shepherd Jenny toward the door. As I walk them out, Jenny takes my hand and whispers, "Will you please talk some sense into them? I can't understand what they're trying to do."

"It's going to be all right," I tell her, though I'm far from sure of this.

Mom motions for Walt to escort Jenny down the hall, then looks back at me and whispers, "Don't let your father take the stand."

The idea strikes me as absurd. "Dad's not going to testify now. No way."

She closes her eyes for a moment. "Don't be so sure. He's going to want to. You and Quentin have to talk him out of it."

"But we've won the case."

Mom's eyes narrow as though she's trying to see whether I'm lying. "Have we?"

"By any normal standard we have."

"Well, they're not acting like it. Quentin looks anything but triumphant, and Tom has sunk inside himself. I know how he is when he gets that look. There are things driving him that we know nothing about." Mom reaches out and squeezes my hand; her skin is startlingly cold. "Don't let him sway you, Penn."

I consider questioning her further, but there's no time or privacy to do it. "I won't. Go catch up with Walt. And please do whatever Tim tells you to do. That's your only job now."

"I will. Penn, did you really see Snake Knox out there?"

"I think I did."

She sighs and bows her head, then turns and hurries down the hall to catch up with Jenny. I give Tim a pointed glance, and he gives me a firm thumbs-up.

As Mom's heels click down the steps, I hear her speak to someone, and then Rusty Duncan appears at the head of the staircase. He raises his eyebrows, asking permission to join the group in my office. I beckon him on and lead him into the suite.

"What's he doing here?" Quentin asks as we enter.

"Two against two is a fairer fight," I reply, taking my chair behind my desk and motioning for Rusty to sit down before Quentin can argue.

Rusty sits in a club chair facing the sofa where Dad has stretched out, while Quentin holds court from his wheelchair in the space between.

"Will the judge stop the trial?" Dad asks. "Or postpone it?"

"Doubtful," says Quentin. "Since they had that bomb threat on Joe's house, there are probably BATF techs in town who can screen the courthouse overnight. And I know Joe Elder. He'll take this as a personal insult. It would take an act of Congress to stop this trial now."

"What do you think, Penn?" Dad asks.

"I've seen witnesses murdered before. It didn't stop the trials."

"Ever seen one murdered *on the stand*?" Rusty asks.

"I saw a defendant shot on the stand. Died instantly."

"That's different," says Quentin. "You can't have a trial without a defendant."

"You should move for a mistrial," Rusty advises.

"Yeah!" Quentin says with mock enthusiasm. "I don't know why I didn't think of that. It's a good thing you showed up, Rust Bucket. Hmm . . ."

"Let's assume the trial will go forward," I say, signaling for Quentin to get off Rusty's ass. "It's over anyway, right?"

Dad and Quentin share a look that I can't read but makes me nervous.

"Mom's worried you're still going to put Dad on the stand," I say slowly, watching Quentin, who seems to be studying a print on the wall. "She's crazy, right?"

With painful effort, Dad gets his elbows under him and sits up straight on the couch. Before he can speak, my phone pings. The text message is from John Kaiser.

Judge Elder wants to see all counsel in the conference room at the DA's office in 30 minutes. I'll be there. Your father should remain in your office under guard until the ATF guys have signed off on the jail being secure. I'm coming over to update you in 15. No sign of Snake, but we've got every LE officer in the city on the streets. What a nightmare.

"We have to meet the judge in Shad's conference room in half an hour," I tell them. "Kaiser is coming over here in fifteen minutes to update us."

"Joe's going to either postpone the trial or tell us to finish up tomorrow," says Quentin. "I've got a thousand bucks that says the latter."

Nobody takes him up on it.

"Back to Dad taking the stand," I say. "Does any lawyer in this room not agree with my assessment that, at this point, that would be insane?"

Quentin doesn't speak, or even meet my eye.

Rusty clears his throat and says, "In my humble opinion, after what the jury just witnessed—and after Junius Jelks and Mr. Patel gutted Lincoln Turner on the stand—I'd say giving Shad Johnson a shot at Tom would pretty much qualify as malpractice."

"Quentin, you're not saying anything," I observe. "That worries me."

At last the old lawyer looks over at me, and in his eyes I see a weariness I didn't see in the courtroom. "You need to talk to your father, not me."

All eyes turn to Dad, who's scratching one of the psoriatic lesions beneath his shirtsleeve. Pinpoints of blood appear on the light blue cotton.

"There are four reasons that I have to take the stand," he says with deliberation, as though about to go through a differential diagnosis for a medical student.

I groan, but that doesn't stop him.

"One, the jury wants to hear me say I didn't do it."

"*Will* you say that?" I ask him. "That's not what you told me at the Pollock prison."

His eyes look almost steely. "I'll say it."

But will you mean it? I ask silently.

"Two," he goes on, "Quentin promised in his opening statement that I would testify."

I glare at Quentin, who gives Dad a look that says, *Promises are made to be broken.* "You don't have to do that, Tom, given what's happened."

"Forget what just happened. You told the jury I would get up there, and if I don't, they're going to think I'm hiding something. You've based your whole defense on my character and forthrightness. And a man with good character isn't afraid to take the stand in his own defense."

"A valid point," Rusty concedes.

"So relieved you think so," I mutter.

"Third, the truths that lie behind my relationship with Viola impact a lot of people, and they've been buried for too long. Remember my eulogy for Henry Sexton? I called on people to break their silence, no matter the cost. It's like Reverend Baldwin coming forward with Albert's ledgers after forty years. That's what we need."

This kind of thinking is what Mom is afraid of. "Reverend Baldwin didn't publish the contents of those ledgers in the paper. He gave us copies of a couple of pages. A courtroom is no place to confess your sins, Dad. Not under oath. Write a book, if you want to wash your soul clean."

He looks at the floor and shakes his head with mulish resolve. "I can't do that. I owe it to Viola—and to Jimmy and Luther and all the others—to tell what I know. I owe it to Henry, and I owe it to Caitlin, too."

I get up and walk over to the sofa, crouching before him. "Caitlin wouldn't want you to risk going to jail out of some misguided sense of duty to reveal the past."

His eyes meet mine with unsettling fervor. "Caitlin *died* trying to uncover the past. Not to save me, or to win glory for herself. She wanted to know what happened to Jimmy Revels. And she was right to want to know. This poison has been tainting this area for too long. It's time to lance the abscess once and for all."

"Fine, I agree. But you don't have to do it from the witness stand.

Not with your life on the line. You can work side by side with Kaiser and me to make sure every last Double Eagle goes to jail or to the grave. But don't destroy your own life in the process."

"I've come damn close to destroying it already. What more harm can I do?"

"Things can always get worse. Quentin?"

The wheelchair creaks as Quentin leans forward. "He's right, Tom. Have we established reasonable doubt? Absolutely. But there are two things you never know in life: who your daughter's going to marry, and what a jury's going to do. The forensic case against you is still strong. You and Walt destroying that videotape looks bad, if they believed that."

"That's another reason I need to testify. I need to deny erasing that second videotape from the hospital Dumpster."

For the first time since we arrived here, my office goes quiet. No one, it seems, wants to touch the matter of the DV tape blanked by the MRI machine.

"I didn't finish what I was saying," Quentin says. "Despite Lincoln's little scheme with the will, he got to the jury when he talked about you hurting his mother."

"Junius Jelks landed a blow, too," Rusty says with reluctant admiration.

"That no-'count bastard," Quentin says. "I'll be damned if I'll ever take a look at his case. He can rot in Joliet till he's lost his last tooth."

"We don't have a lot of time, guys," I remind them. "As far as alternate suspects for sympathetic jurors to pin the murder on, I see two candidates. First, Lincoln. Could the jury believe that Lincoln might have killed his mother?"

After a brief silence, Quentin says, "No."

"Then why did he come to Natchez early and lie about it?"

"He was waiting for your father to fulfill the assisted-suicide pact. And he wanted to be close by to orchestrate the destruction of the will and the reporting of the crime."

"Is the jury smart enough to figure all that out?"

Quentin nods. "Twelve people can see through a brick wall if you give them enough time."

"Rusty?" I prompt.

"That jury won't think Lincoln killed his mother."

"Why not?"

"You want it straight?"

"Yeah."

"Black folks don't kill Mama."

Dad looks up at this. "Why do you say that, Rusty?"

Rusty gives my father his lopsided smile. "That's conventional wisdom with prosecutors, Doc. When you get a perp who killed his father or mother, it's almost always a white male. Now and then a white girl will do it, to stop sexual abuse, something like that. But as a general rule, blacks don't kill their mothers."

"To my everlasting amazement," Quentin says, "Rust Bucket is right. Maybe it's because we're a matriarchal society, I don't know. But it's true. The jury won't buy that theory."

"Wait a second," Rusty says, "Lincoln Turner is only *half* black."

An awkward silence fills the air, but then Quentin scoffs and says, "Next question, Penn."

"Second candidate: Snake and the Double Eagles. Will the jury believe—without Will Devine's testimony—that the Double Eagles murdered Viola?"

"I don't think so," says Dad. "Not without hard evidence proving that they wanted to kill her. Or threatened to kill her. In this century."

The audiotape Lincoln tried to sell me flashes into my mind, and I glare at Quentin, but he silences me with a slight shake of his head.

"Won't the fact that someone just murdered a Double Eagle witness for the defense make the jury think that witness was about to implicate the killer?" I ask. "And that the killer was a Double Eagle? Quentin?"

Quentin looks far from certain. "They might just think an old Klansman was about to break his blood oath, and he got killed for it. That doesn't necessarily have anything to do with Tom."

Rusty looks incredulous. "Come on! They triggered that needle just when you asked Devine about Viola. Penn, help me out here."

"The question," I say, drilling into Quentin with my eyes, "is did the Double Eagles represent a *present-day threat* to Viola? Had they threatened her within weeks or even days of her death?"

"Will Devine was about to verify that," says Quentin.

"Well, he'll never tell anybody about it now," Dad says.

"Damn it," I mutter, still thinking of Lincoln's audiotape. Unable to contain my frustration, I turn to Quentin. "I'll bet you wish you'd let me buy that tape from Lincoln now."

He dismisses me with a wave of his hand.

"What tape?" Rusty asks.

"Forget it," says Quentin. "Some scam from Lincoln."

"Maybe it's worth exploring after all," Dad says, looking preoccupied.

"What the hell are you guys talking about?" Rusty demands.

"Fairy tales," snaps Quentin.

Before Rusty can push harder, there's a knock at the door.

"Got to be Kaiser," I tell them. "Rusty, ask him to give us a second."

Rusty jumps up with surprising speed, considering his bulk, and I move closer to my father. "I think it's worth trying to get that tape from Lincoln. I heard it. It would definitely push at least some of the jurors to believe Snake killed Viola."

"Trust that boy and it'll bite you on the ass," Quentin says.

"Uh, Penn," Rusty calls. "We've got deputies out here to pick up your dad."

As I look up at the door, two ACSO deputies enter my office, their jaws set tight. "Mayor, the jail has just been declared secure. The sheriff ordered us to take your father back to his cell."

Dad's heavy sigh makes it plain how much he's enjoyed sitting here strategizing with us, free from manacles and the stink of the jailhouse.

"I'll see you all in the courtroom," he says, getting to his feet with a loud creaking. "Goddamn knees."

"Be glad you got 'em," Quentin says with a wink.

"Yeah, yeah."

Dad squeezes my shoulder, then leans down between Quentin and me and says, "Ya'll make the call about Lincoln's tape. But either way, I'm going to testify."

As he walks into the custody of the deputies, Quentin and I share a look of perfectly attuned awareness. We may disagree about most issues in this case, but on one point we are as one: *Dad does not need to take the stand.*

"Penn, it's John," Kaiser calls from my secretary's office. "Judge Elder wants you over in Shad's conference room, and he's in no mood to wait. I need two minutes with you guys before we go."

"Come in."

Kaiser waits for the deputies to escort Dad through the door, then hurries into my office. "We've got about a minute before we have to start walking."

I can tell by the FBI agent's face and posture that he has bad news for us. "Are our families okay?"

"Yes. It's not that."

"Then it can't be that bad."

"You be the judge." Kaiser looks at Rusty. "Mr. Duncan, I need you to leave the room."

"Whaaaat?" Rusty almost whines.

"Go, Rusty," I snap, sensing more gravitas than usual in Kaiser's manner.

After Rusty closes the door behind him, Kaiser begins speaking quickly.

"Since 9/11 the U.S. intel community has poured hundreds of millions of dollars into digital forensics. Maybe billions. When your only looks at Osama bin Laden come from videotapes or discs, that's where you put your money. Every major tech university in the country has a classified program working on new methods to recover, restore, or rebuild captured digital material, whether deleted, erased, shredded, or burned."

"Shit." I sense where this is going. "And?"

"The Bureau has the best restoration technology extant today. Better than the NSA, better than the CIA. And a *lot* better than Sony."

"What did you do, John?" I ask, trying to keep the frustration out of my voice.

"I'll tell you what I did," he says defensively. "I held off asking Shad Johnson for those tapes for a lot longer than I should have. But when Devine was murdered on the stand, I got a call from an assistant director in D.C. And he told me we need to know what's on those tapes."

"Wait a minute," Quentin says. "An assistant director called you out of the blue about a state murder case?"

"This is no normal murder case, Mr. Avery. I invoked the Patriot Act three months ago when I started investigating the Double Eagles. When Snake Knox knocked down our plane in December, we lost new evidence in the JFK assassination. That's as big as it gets. And after all the deaths we had—Glenn Morehouse, Sleepy Johnston, Henry Sexton, Brody Royal—I've had some serious Bureau oversight on me. They almost pulled me out of here when we lost that plane. So you can imagine what keeping your client under protective custody cost me in political capital. Now, I'm sorry it's come to this, but we are here now."

The tension in Kaiser's voice brings back a flood of memories from three months ago. The heated conversations with Kaiser and Dwight Stone about the Working Group and their assassination theory about mobster Carlos Marcello. It's been weeks since I've thought of what was lost in that FBI plane crash: a handwritten letter from Lee Harvey Oswald to his wife, Marina; rifles taken from Brody Royal's trophy gun cabinet, one of which was supposedly the weapon Frank Knox used to shoot John Kennedy from the Dal-Tex building—

"I understand all that," Quentin says with some gratitude in his voice. "But has this tape restoration technique ever been used in a civilian trial on American soil? Criminal or civil?"

"I doubt it. The whole technology is classified."

"Then what the hell are we talking about it for? We might as well be discussing using a laser defense system."

"You're wrong," I tell Quentin. "At this point, the bureaucrats in D.C. will do just about anything to atone for the mess they've made of the Double Eagle investigation. Forty years of chasing somebody is too long. If the FBI can't nail Snake Knox, how the hell can anyone believe they'll ever apprehend top foreign terrorists?"

Kaiser nods grimly. "As per instructions, I went to Shad and told him we'd like to take a look at those tapes in our crime lab."

"Nothing more?" I ask. "No hint that the Bureau might succeed where Sony failed?"

"Shad wouldn't need anything more," Quentin says dejectedly.

Kaiser looks down at his hands, then wipes them as though trying to remove some invisible residue. "I was prepared to wait until Dr. Cage's trial was over to request the tapes. But it's out of my hands now. Shad called one of his Harvard Law classmates, who happens to work for the attorney general. Those tapes are going to D.C. today on an FBI plane."

"God*damn* it!" Quentin bellows. "I thought those tapes were behind us."

"You can't outrun the past," I mutter.

"It's far from certain that the lab can restore those tapes," Kaiser says, trying to offer us hope. "They might get only a partial restoration, or even none at all."

"How long does the process take?" Quentin asks.

"That can vary. We're talking about supercomputer time, plus bleeding-edge chemical and mechanical processes. It could take five hours, five days, or five months. There's no way to know until they start."

Turning away from Kaiser, I kneel in front of Quentin's chair. "How bad is this? I mean, if they succeed in restoring the tapes. I need to know."

Quentin shakes his head. Even if he knows, he's not about to answer in Kaiser's presence.

"We're already late," Kaiser says. "I told Judge Elder I'd get you there on time. Let's move."

After a last look into Quentin's unreadable eyes, I stand, move behind his chair, and follow as he rolls quickly toward the door, which Kaiser holds open for him.

CHAPTER 58

SHAD AND JUDGE Elder are waiting when we arrive in Shad's conference room. As we take our seats around the table, I find myself thinking about Joe Elder being the son of Claude Devereux, and how impossible that seems. It must seem even stranger to him. Does he hate Devereux the way Lincoln hates my father? If Quentin's assessment can be trusted, he does.

"Gentlemen," the judge begins, "what happened today was not only a violation of the sanctity of my courtroom, but of the American judicial system. Agent Kaiser has determined that this poisoned needle contraption was triggered by someone in the courtroom using a radio detonator. I'm hopeful that the FBI and ATF will identify the killer in a very short time, and that you, Mr. Johnson, will seek the death penalty for him." Elder nods at Kaiser. "I'm sure there will be federal charges as well, but I want whoever killed that witness to spend his last living hours in Mississippi."

"Absolutely, Your Honor," Shad says unctuously.

Our DA has periodically made noises about being against the death penalty, but never with much conviction, and whatever principle he may have believed he had, he throws to the wind before the judge's anger.

"What about *this* trial, Your Honor?" Quentin asks.

Joe Elder gives Quentin a penetrating stare. "Are you hoping for a mistrial, Mr. Avery?"

"Never entered my mind, Your Honor."

Shad looks at Quentin with ill-concealed shock.

"I'm surprised, Mr. Avery," Judge Elder says in his bass voice. "And gratified. For it is my intention to continue this trial."

"When?" Shad interjects.

"Tomorrow, if possible, Mr. Johnson."

"What about security?" Quentin asks.

"We have ATF bomb techs searching the courthouse now, and more on the way. They'll have the building secured well before midnight. Federal agents will search and clear City Hall as well. The jail has just been designated a secure area, so Dr. Cage can be returned there."

"Judge," I cut in, "I'm still concerned about my father's safety."

"Your father will still be held in his own private cell," Judge Elder assures me. "I'm well aware of the danger, Mayor Cage. I've also made the sheriff aware that I am aware."

"Thank you, Judge."

"What about the death of my star witness?" Quentin asks.

Judge Elder's lips draw tight before he speaks. "That was a regrettable tragedy, Mr. Avery. I suspect Mr. Devine's murder dealt a serious blow to your case. However, unless you can bring Mr. Devine back from the grave, there's nothing to be done. Not unless you want to move for a mistrial."

"I've resurrected a few dead cases in my time," Quentin says, "but never a dead man."

The hint of a smile touches Judge Elder's lips. "You're being modest. I know of two men, at least, who were within hours of execution when you saved them from the gas chamber."

"In my prime," Quentin says wearily, but not without pride. "But I'm willing to continue in this case, in spite of Mr. Devine's murder. As I've told the mayor several times during this trial: I don't want a mistrial, I want a fair trial."

Judge Elder sits up straight and smiles with relief. "Excellent. And I'm going to do everything within my power to ensure that your client gets that."

A little late, isn't it? I want to say, but I stifle myself.

"Now," Judge Elder says, "let's discuss the matter of these videotapes."

Quentin settles into watchful stillness in his wheelchair.

"This opportunity to restore this type of media is unprecedented in my experience, and I want us all to be on the same page. Mr. Kaiser?"

"It's unprecedented in my experience as well, Judge. We're talking about highly classified technology."

Joe Elder cocks his head to the side. "That certainly begs the question of why the FBI is willing to rush a forensic process on a tape for a state murder case."

Kaiser clears his throat. "I think it's because this case has connections to civil rights murders involving the Double Eagle group, both past and present. Depending on what those erased tapes contain, they could have direct bearing on major federal cases. Obviously, we were involved in the plea negotiations that allowed Will Devine to testify today—or to attempt to. After his murder, my superiors instructed me to speak to the district attorney about getting those tapes to our crime lab for special processing. When I did, Mr. Johnson made a good guess about my intentions. Then he made some calls to an old Harvard classmate, and now we find ourselves here."

"That's interesting," says Judge Elder. "But we're pretty late in these proceedings. Is it remotely possible that these tapes could be processed and restored in a reasonable time frame?"

"Your Honor, I'm told that it might be," Shad answers.

Elder's eyes move from Shad to Kaiser. "Agent Kaiser?"

"I've been informed that we can transport the tapes on a Bureau plane. My agents can maintain an airtight chain of custody."

A sort of hiccup escapes Quentin's throat, but to his credit he's wise enough not to object to the proposed restoration of the tapes.

"Mr. Avery?" says Judge Elder, turning to Quentin. "What's your feeling about this?"

"We're open to anything that can shed more light on the events in Mrs. Turner's house on the night of her death."

The judge's gaze lingers on Quentin's face. "Well, then. Agent Kaiser, make it so."

"Yes, Your Honor."

Shad freezes for a second, then tries to look natural. "Judge, we may have a small problem with that arrangement."

"What problem could that be, Mr. Johnson? Do you not trust the FBI?"

"It's not me, Your Honor," Shad says quickly. "I have the highest respect for the Bureau. But I suspect that Sheriff Byrd might be reluctant to simply hand over the tapes to Agent Kaiser."

"Why would that be?"

"He feels that Agent Kaiser has been shielding Dr. Cage from the beginning. Also Mr. Garrity, to a certain extent. The sheriff raised the question of why Agent Kaiser didn't offer to restore the tapes when we learned that the manufacturer couldn't do it."

"Is that so?" Judge Elder appears amused by this. "Well, I'll sign a judicial order compelling the sheriff to turn over the tapes to Mr. Kaiser, so that he can sleep tonight without that dilemma weighing on him."

Shad takes his medicine with humility. "Thank you, Your Honor. I'm sure that won't be necessary."

Elder gives him a wry smile. "Outstanding. If there's nothing else, I'll see you all at nine A.M. With a little luck, we can give this case to the jury tomorrow."

"Ah, one more thing, Your Honor," Shad says quickly, emboldened by his success with the tape restoration gambit. "During his opening remarks, Mr. Avery promised the jury that Dr. Cage would take the stand. Should we look forward to seeing that happen tomorrow?"

Joe Elder looks as curious about this prospect as Shad. He inclines his head toward Quentin and raises one eyebrow.

"Given today's events, Your Honor," Quentin says, "we haven't made a final decision on that yet."

Elder's eyes twinkle. "A little suspense, Mr. Johnson. I guess we'll both find out tomorrow."

Shad nods slowly. "Your Honor, with all due respect, I have some concerns about scheduling going forward."

Joe Elder doesn't like the sound of this. "Elaborate."

"First, I'm concerned that Mr. Avery will try to rush forward and close his case before the restored tapes can be delivered."

"Mr. Johnson, we're not going to hold up this trial for a week waiting for tapes that might never come."

"Of course not, Your Honor. But if it's a matter of one day or even two—"

"We'll cross that bridge when we come to it, Counselor."

"Yes, Your Honor. But that coin has another side. If Mr. Avery's next witness is Dr. Cage, and the courtroom is ready tomorrow, I assume you will expect Mr. Avery to proceed with direct examination?"

Judge Elder looks irritated for a moment, but then his eyes narrow in anger. "Mr. Johnson, don't piss on my leg and tell me it's raining. You want Dr. Cage to have to testify before he has any idea whether those restored tapes will be played in the courtroom."

"That seems like the fairest thing all around, Your Honor."

"Except you want it both ways! You want him to testify first thing in the morning, but you don't want Mr. Avery to be able to rest his case and give it to the jury if your precious tapes aren't ready. Correct?"

Shad gives the judge a wide-eyed look of innocence.

"Mr. Avery hasn't begged me for a recess until we know the outcome of the FBI's efforts. He's behaving like a professional."

"It's a difficult situation, Judge."

Joe Elder nods slowly, the scowl still on his face. "I'll reflect on all this tonight, but I'll tell you one thing now. I'm inclined to move forward at our usual pace. If the Bureau can get those tapes here in time for them to play a part in this trial, so be it. But if they can't, we will give the case to the jury."

Shad gulps audibly, then looks at Kaiser.

"The ball's in your court, Agent Kaiser," Joe Elder says, getting to his feet. The former basketball player towers above us. "Please keep me apprised of any developments regarding today's murder."

"Of course, Your Honor."

Elder makes his way to the door, then slips out.

As soon as he disappears, Shad looks down at Quentin with triumph in his eyes. Quentin rolls himself to the door without looking back, like a tribal chief on a chariot, certain that I'll follow like a loyal spear carrier.

As I pass Shad, he catches my arm and whispers, "It's over, Penn. Quentin had it won, but he's lost it now. You should have defended your father. You know that."

"I guess that depends on what's on those tapes, doesn't it?"

I don't look left as I jerk my arm free, but I can feel Shad's smile on my skin like a coat of oil.

ON THE GROUND floor I find Quentin waiting with two of my bodyguards. I don't think I've ever seen the old lawyer look as adrift as he does in this moment.

"Guys, can we have a little space?" I ask.

The guards turn their backs and move twenty feet away.

"Quentin, you've got to ask Elder for a recess until we know whether those tapes are coming in. You should have asked him as soon as he made it clear he would allow the tapes in if they can be restored."

"He's not going to look favorably on that."

"I know. But you can't put Dad on the stand when there's a chance the tapes could come in. If he denies knowing about either one, and then the content proves him a liar . . . that's it. He's going to Parchman."

"You heard your father earlier. He's not going to do what I tell him to do."

"Would he actually get up there while that chance exists?"

"He might."

"I want to see his face when you tell him about this. If he panics, then we'll know something we didn't know before. At least I will."

"Tom won't panic. I've never seen him panic. But you're not going to be there for that conversation."

"Why not?"

"Penn . . . I'm too tired to have this argument again."

Anger rises in me with frightening force, but there's nothing to be gained from yelling at Quentin. "Just tell me this, then. That tape they found in the hospital Dumpster. Did Dad put it there or not?"

Quentin looks up at me with a far more convincing portrayal of ignorance than Shad Johnson could ever muster. "I don't know."

I hear myself sigh. "That hospital serves a lot of doctors. Plenty of them probably have mini-DV cameras. I'm sure some even use them in their practices."

"Maybe," Quentin allows, but his eyes tell me what he really believes.

"If Dad did take both tapes . . . why would he erase one tape one way, and another a different way?" The question spins through my head for a few seconds. "And why would he ditch one immediately but hang on to the other for a week?"

Quentin only shrugs, but the answer comes to me. "Oh, no."

"What?"

"Dad felt like he owed it to Viola to hang on to the tape she made for Henry. He only erased it when he felt he had no choice. But the other—the one that was in the camera while the murder was committed—

that one he erased the morning of the murder, by putting it through an MRI machine."

Quentin is shaking his head. "You don't know that."

"No?"

Before we can go any farther, John Kaiser steps out of the stairwell and into the lobby. "I'm sorry," he says. "Shad pulled an end run, and I've got no way to stop him."

I wave him on.

Kaiser ignores my gesture and walks up to us. "Look, there's another angle to this that could help you guys out. There'll be some powerful factions in the Bureau who'll fight letting this capability become public in this way. Even if the tapes are successfully restored, the director, the attorney general, or even the president might refuse to authorize their release for use in a public trial. The precedent could have a lot of unintended consequences."

I consider the politics for a few seconds, then go with my instinct. "John . . . I have a feeling we've passed the tipping point. Those tapes are coming back to us, like a karmic punishment."

Kaiser looks like he's genuinely torn between his duty and his personal desires. "I have to be frank with you. I want Tom to be acquitted. But if those tapes are restored and authorized for release tomorrow, there's no way I can slow them down. Too many people involved."

"We know that." My voice is tight with frustration. "If you get any kind of progress report tonight, please give me a call."

He gives me an empathetic nod.

"Thank you," Quentin says. "Now you'd better get moving. I have a feeling your own people are watching you."

"I'm afraid you're right. Thanks to Shadrach Johnson."

Kaiser pushes through the door and trots across the street to the brick monolith that houses the sheriff's department and jail.

"Quentin," I say, watching Kaiser enter the ACSO building, "when I was eighteen, Dad was sued for malpractice. The case dragged on forever. He was finally exonerated, but the months of tension almost killed him. It was the cross-examination that did it."

"I know about that." Quentin reaches out and squeezes my wrist. "Go home, Penn. Take care of Peggy and Annie. They shouldn't have seen what they did today."

As I go through the door, I look back and focus on the white shock of hair, the shelled-pecan skin, the owl's eyes. "Quentin, do you know what really happened in that house that night?"

This time, when he looks back at me, I know that he doesn't. Not any more than Walt Garrity did when he called his wife one lonely night three months ago.

"My God, you're flying blind. You can't let Shad get at him, Quentin, no matter what. Shad will tear him to pieces."

Quentin nods with something near to anguish. "Tell me this, brother. How am I supposed to stop him?"

CHAPTER 59

THE IRREVOCABLE EVENTS of our lives happen in seconds, sometimes fractions of seconds. A teenager leaps from the wrong rock and breaks his neck in shallow water. A single cell mutates, evades immune surveillance, races down the road to cancer. You pull distractedly into an intersection and wind up paralyzed. A young girl forgets to text a bodyguard and gets acid thrown in her face. A man settles into a witness chair . . .

As a prosecutor, I dealt with countless people who suffered from split-second breaks of fate, and most never stopped wondering: *What could I have done to avoid that? If only I'd locked my car doors, if only I'd turned left instead of right, if only I'd skipped that last drink, if only I'd listened to my instinct and given that guy a fake phone number, if only I'd remembered my pepper spray or bought that gun I looked at in the sporting goods store . . .*

Hindsight is always 20/20, foresight rarely better than a blur.

The shock of Will Devine's death was very much with us as I rejoined my family in City Hall after the conference in Judge Elder's chambers. As it turned out, one of Tim's guys had rounded up Serenity from the general melee after the courtroom stampede, and we found her with Mia, Annie, and my mother in the lounge down the hall from my office. Serenity wanted to be on the street covering the aftermath of the murder, but Tim persuaded her that she should stick with us for the time being. Although she and I are still playing the role of platonic friends in Annie's presence, Serenity seems to sense that something has seriously rattled me—something beyond the murder of Will Devine. Her eyes cut to mine repeatedly, silently asking questions, so often that I motion for her to wait until we get home.

On the ground floor of City Hall, we divide into two groups. While Annie, Mia, Serenity, and I take the Yukon back to my Washington Street house, Mom and Jenny will be escorted to my parents' house to get "some things" my mother forgot to pack when she first got back to town for the trial. (My gut tells me these "things" probably fall into the benzodiazepine category.)

Emulating our courthouse procedure, we make a fast transfer from the side door of City Hall to the vehicle, and breathe sighs of relief only when the armored doors slam shut with reassuring thuds. Tim Weathers sits in the second row with Annie and me, while his second-in-command, Joe Russell, covers the third seat with Mia and Serenity. The air-conditioning raises the hair on my arms. As Annie leans close to get warm, the driver hands my .38 over the front seat, and I slip it back into my ankle holster.

"Ease off on the air," Tim says as acceleration presses us back into the leather seats.

"Thanks," I say, slipping my arm around Annie's shoulders. "You guys did a great job back there, covering everybody."

Tim winces; I'm sure he's second-guessing every move he made, and even wondering if he could have taken out Snake Knox if he'd somehow been a little better, a little faster.

"At least our crew's okay," he concedes, but his eyes add a postscript: *We're up against some dangerous motherfuckers, my friend . . .*

Thankfully, we don't have far to go: two and a half blocks southeast, one block southwest, and half a block northwest. I'd like to say something to reassure Annie and Mia, but after watching a man murdered before their eyes—while supposedly in an iron ring of security—there's not much I can say. I'm only glad they know nothing about the videotapes John Kaiser just dropped on us like grenades tossed back into a foxhole after being flung out once before. The possible implications of the tape erased in the MRI machine are so grave that Will Devine's murder already seems like a circus sideshow by comparison. No matter how I try to rationalize it, I can't escape the conclusion that the "Dumpster tape" was inside Henry Sexton's camcorder while Viola was being murdered, and that's why my father tried to destroy it.

A lot of people are on the streets as we make our way home—standing outside businesses and residences as we roar up State Street, then veer right on Union. Obviously word of the courthouse attack has spread quickly.

The driver turns hard right again on Washington.

"Almost home," I murmur, squeezing Annie.

"I'm okay," she says, obviously trying to comfort me.

The armored Yukon pulls up in front of my house like an airliner with its thrust-reversers engaged—momentum keeps the heavy body moving forward even as the brakes stop the chassis and drivetrain. Then the body settles backward on the reinforced shocks.

"Everybody ready?" Tim asks, scanning 360 degrees around the vehicle for people and oncoming vehicles.

"Ready," Serenity answers from the backseat.

"We're all getting out at the same time. My group on my side, Joe's group on the other. Understood?"

I look around to be sure everybody gets it. Mia and Serenity nod. I scoot Annie toward Tim so that Joe can push my seat forward in preparation for the quick exit. When the seat comes up, Tim says, "Three count. Ready? And . . . three, two, one—"

He shoves open the door and exits the vehicle, taking a combat stance outside as Annie and I leave the Yukon. Joe is first out on the other side, with Mia and Serenity following.

"Take Annie into the house," Tim tells me, scanning the roofs of the nearby houses.

I'm pulling Annie onto the sidewalk when a thundering report reverberates between the houses. *Shotgun,* says a voice in my head as I snatch Annie into my arms.

One glance over my shoulder shows me Tim Weathers lying facedown on the pavement. Fear and anguish blast through me, but I force my feet to move, aiming for the house. While my eyes search for Mia and Serenity, a sledgehammer smashes into my right shoulder blade, driving the air from my lungs and numbing my whole right side. I try to cling to Annie, but all I can manage is to twist as I fall, so that my weight doesn't crush her when we hit the sidewalk.

"Daddy, watch out!" Annie yells, but another blast booms between the houses, or maybe even two. Annie screams, but Mia's scream overrides hers, and then I hear Serenity shouting something that sounds like orders until another blast silences her.

The frantic whine of an overdriven engine cuts through the din, then the screech of brakes punctuates the whine. I'm trying to move, but whatever hit me scrambled my nervous system. I try to tell Annie to get into the house, but nothing comes from my throat. She's on her knees beside me, looking down into my eyes with utter terror on her face. I want to comfort her, but the pain arcing through my back has paralyzed my vocal cords.

"There she is!" shouts a male voice. *"Get her! Grab the kid!"*

The predatory eyes of Snake Knox fill my mind, and I pray that voice did not come from his throat.

"Annie, get back in the Yukon!" yells a man who sounds like our driver. *"Get inside NOW!"*

He's right, I realize. *The Yukon's armored. It's the closest safe place—*

But it might as well be the moon. Annie has hardly turned toward the vehicle when a man clad in black leather grabs her beneath the arms and snatches her bodily into the air. Filled with rage and terror, I try to roll over, but I can't do it.

The man carrying my daughter runs toward the open door of a gold minivan parked in the middle of Washington Street. Annie is screaming *"Daddy!"* at the top of her lungs, but I can't even get to my knees, much less my feet.

A man in a black business suit suddenly materializes at the rear of the Yukon—our driver. He's pointing a pistol at the man carrying Annie.

"PUT THE GIRL DOWN!" he yells.

Confident that Annie will serve as a human shield, her kidnapper ignores the order.

Shoot him! I yell silently. *Shoot now or she's lost forever!*

Then the familiar *pop-pop* of a handgun echoes between the houses, and our driver falls facedown in the road, blood pouring from his head.

Like the conclusion of a slow-motion nightmare, the man in black leather pushes Annie through the broad side door of the minivan, her eyes bulging white with panic. Some feeling has returned to my legs, but I still can't get them under me. Before I can stand, my daughter will be a mile away, disappearing into oblivion. The space between our locked eyes arcs with the pain of knowing we will never see each other again.

Then Mia Burke sprints from the Yukon to the van and grabs hold of Annie like a young mother possessed. The kidnapper slugs the side of Mia's head, but Mia doesn't even slack off pulling.

"Get her off me!" yells the guy. "Get her off me! Crazy *bitch*!"

From nowhere a second man in black motorcycle leathers appears, but as he reaches for Annie, two quick shots erupt from the far side of the Yukon, and he drops like a deer shot through the spine. Then Serenity Butler appears in the space Mia crossed seconds ago—only Tee has a pistol in her hand. My heart leaps, but another blast rattles the windows of the houses, and Serenity spins and falls beside the van. Her open eyes stare blankly at the sky.

"Get that kid in here, damn it!" shouts a voice from inside the van. *"We ain't got all fuckin' day!"*

"Get this hellcat off me, Axel! Somebody shoot her!"

They have guys on the rooftops, I realize. *That's who shot Tim and me. And Joe. And the driver . . . And Tee—*

The leather-clad biker finally hammers an elbow into Mia's ribs, which gives him enough separation to yank Annie through the van's door. But even as he does, Mia jumps in after her. The biker kicks Mia with his boots, but the van lurches forward, throwing him off balance, and then screeches to a stop again. The boots go back to pounding Mia, kicking hard as she clings to the door frame. Again the tires squeal, and the engine roars as the van accelerates up Washington Street, slowly gathering speed.

A bolt of panic drives me up onto all fours. As I struggle to get my feet under me, I hear Serenity groan in pain. Looking up, I see her on her feet, shaking her right arm as if to get it working again. Then she roars a curse and takes off after the van. Only then do I realize there's no longer a pistol in her hand.

Nothing can stop that van now.

A horror movie unspools behind my eyes, torture-porn written and directed by Snake Knox: Annie and Mia tormented in front of each other, and for a camera, so that my father and I will have to watch every moment of—

The Yukon, I remember.

But by the time I reach my feet, the minivan is just twenty yards from the end of the block, Serenity trailing far behind it. If they make that turn, Annie will disappear off the face of the earth. As my eyes follow the van, an image beyond my capacity for understanding appears. At the end of the block, a man wearing a white cowboy hat has stepped from behind the Episcopal Church and dropped to one knee. The mysterious cowboy raises a pistol with one hand and takes careful aim at the windshield of the van.

Don't! I think. *Don't risk it!*

But something about the stance of the man in the white hat resonates within me. *That's Walt Garrity.* The old Texas Ranger has been with us all along, and now the future has coalesced into a single moment . . .

One shot—

Walt's muzzle flash reaches me before the sound of the blast, and I know instantly that Walt missed, because the van doesn't even falter.

Walt fires again.

This time the van bucks like a tripping horse. Then its motor revs wildly, and the vehicle careens over the curb and up onto the sidewalk, plowing over Walt before he can roll away. The grille crashes through a crape myrtle trunk, rams the great concrete steps of the Episcopal Church, and stops dead, steam pouring from its radiator.

Far ahead of me, Serenity swiftly closes the distance to the van and wrenches open the door without hesitation. As she leaps inside, I finally regain enough muscular control to draw my pistol and start staggering toward the church.

There's a struggle going on in the van, but I can't tell who's winning. As I close the distance, I hear screaming that sounds like Annie, which is good, because you have to be alive to scream. Then a door opens on the far side and a man in black leather bolts from the vehicle and sprints down South Commerce, toward Homochitto Street. Though it kills me to do it, in my desperation to reach Annie, I run past Walt's bloody body to the open door of the van.

The first thing I see is the driver, his skull blown apart by a hollow-point slug. There's blood on every surface, including the people, but what confuses me is what the people are doing. Serenity is naked above the waist, and she's frantically rubbing her left breast and arm while Annie and Mia watch with wide eyes.

"What happened?" I shout.

"He threw acid on Tee!" Annie cries. "She was fighting him. And she was winning! He decided to run, but as he got out, he grabbed a plastic thing and hit Tee with it. It was acid!"

"I had the tube Drew gave me in my pocket," Mia says. "The gluconate stuff. She's rubbing it on now."

Most people in Serenity's situation would be paralyzed by panic, but the former soldier is methodically rubbing calcium gluconate over every exposed part of her skin. *My God, this woman has guts.*

"What about you guys?" I ask. "Were either of you hit?"

"We're good," Mia assures me. "I already called 911 on my cell."

Sure enough, I hear sirens from the direction of the sheriff's department. I only hope Billy Byrd isn't in one of those cars.

"I need to check on Walt," I tell them. "Take care of Serenity."

"We've got her," Mia assures me, but her eyes tell me I shouldn't hold out any hope for Walt Garrity.

ONE LOOK AT my father's old friend tells me he hasn't long to live. Walt's got open limb fractures and a severe crush injury to his skull above his left ear. The full weight of the van slammed into him, face-on, and both axles rolled over him after that. I can't even begin to guess at his internal injuries. Remarkably, Walt's eyes are open, and when I kneel beside him and move into his field of vision, I see a flicker of recognition.

"Walt?" I say softly. "Can you hear me, buddy?"

He groans but does not speak.

"That was something you just did, Cap'n Garrity."

The old Ranger licks his lips, then works his mouth around for a few seconds. "Annie," he finally croaks out. "Is our little gal okay?"

In an instant my throat closes, and hot tears suffuse my eyes. I can't speak, so I simply nod, leaning forward to be sure Walt can see me.

"She's okay," I finally manage to say. "You saved her. Mia, too."

Something like a smile animates Walt's weathered face. Then he says, "Not bad shooting . . . for an old man with cataracts. Huh?"

"Olympic class, I'd say."

"The windshield deflected my first shot . . . but I drilled him with the second."

"Stop trying to talk."

The faintest of smiles again. "Hell, boy . . . if I don't say it now, I never will."

"The ambulance is on its way."

At this Walt actually croaks a laugh. "Tell those boys to turn back to the barn. I'm an old medic, remember? I know when a ticket's been punched."

Kneeling over this old man, I realize that if he hadn't shown up at the Valhalla hunting camp and killed Alphonse Ozan after I killed Forrest Knox, I'd have died in Forrest's office back in December.

"Walt . . . I owe you so much, man."

"That's right . . . you do." He winks, which sends a rivulet of blood into his eye socket. As carefully as I can, I wipe it away with my shirtsleeve.

"Walt, what were you doing by that church? You were at the right place at exactly the right time. Was that just luck?"

"Luck, hell." His eyes strain to move and find mine. "I've been with you every day. Every night. Just like your daddy told me to. No luck involved."

A strange feeling goes through me, almost déjà vu. "Every night? What are you taking about?"

"You saw me . . . you just don't remember. The old man walking his dog?"

As I stare in disbelief, Walt's lips crack into something between a grin and a grimace. "Wasn't even my dog. Just a damn mutt I tied some string to . . . looked less suspicious. He dragged me all over downtown."

"Walt, what the hell?"

"No time now . . . Here's how you're gonna pay your debt to me. Swallow your pain . . . and your pride. And take care of your daddy. You hear me?"

Unbelievable. At the end of his life, this man isn't giving me a message for his wife or his children. He's trying to break down the wall between me and my father.

"I hear you, Walt."

"Bullshit." His eyes look fearful, desperate. "We all make mistakes, son. Tom made some big ones. I made some bad ones in my day, too.

And you're making one now. If you don't wake up soon, by the time you realize it, it'll be too late to do anything about it."

I gently squeeze his hand.

"I'm done preachin'," he groans. "The damn pain's breakin' through. And civilian paramedics don't carry morphine."

"Well . . . I'm not shooting you."

That's probably the only thing I could have said that would make Walt laugh. But laugh he does, a rough chuckle. And before he's done, the light in his eyes winks out. The last air in his lungs passes over my face as it leaves him. I don't know whether his heart gave out or his brain stem swelled too much or an embolus hit his pulmonary artery, and I don't care. I'm just glad I didn't have to watch him die in agony.

The sirens have built to a mind-numbing wail, but somehow I'm only just hearing them. As Annie and Mia pull me to my feet, I see a paramedic checking Serenity, who's now sitting in the van doorway with her feet on the pavement. Her naked breasts hang in plain sight, and she plainly doesn't give a damn.

As the second paramedic kneels to check Walt, I slip my pistol back into my holster and say, "He's gone."

"I gotta check his vitals, regardless."

A sheriff's cruiser squeals to a stop, and two sheriff's deputies run over to us and ask me what happened. I just point up Washington Street.

"That's where all the shooting was. You've got multiple victims down."

Both deputies run back to their cruiser, which peels around the block, headed for my house.

Taking Annie and Mia by the hand, I walk over to Serenity, who looks up and gives us a strained smile. She's obviously in a great deal of pain.

"How much acid did he get on you?" I ask.

She shrugs. "He splashed my right upper arm pretty good. Got a little on my titty."

Annie actually giggles at this.

"Does it burn?" I ask.

"Oh, it burns. But it beats the hell out of being dead in the street."

I shake my head at her bravado.

"I got that gel on there pretty fast," Tee says. She gives Mia a tight but grateful smile. "You saved my ass with that, girl."

Mia's face goes pink. "I'm just glad I had it."

"Maybe that'll spare me the complications Keisha had," Tee adds softly.

I nod, praying she's right.

"Have you heard anything about Tim and his guys?" Tee asks.

I shake my head, recalling our bodyguards lying motionless on the street.

"I'm still not sure what happened," she says. "Sounded like shotguns at first contact. But I didn't see any blood."

"I thought you were hit."

"I was. They must have been using some kind of nonlethal rounds. Beanbags or rubber bullets. So maybe the guys aren't hurt too bad."

"I don't think I'm bleeding either," I realize, twisting to examine my shirt. "But I couldn't move at all. How the hell did you manage to get up?"

"Army reflexes, baby. I hit the deck at that first bang, when they shot Tim. They only caught my arm with that next shot."

"I think they killed our driver, though."

Serenity nods, her expression bleak. "Yeah, the sound was different. And I . . ." She trails off, but I remember the second biker dropping like a dead deer after her shots. The one who was trying to help snatch Annie.

That's who they were after, say Serenity's eyes. *You know that, right?*

I nod again, then pull Annie close.

"Hey?" Tee says.

"Yeah?"

"Who was that guy in the white hat? Was it Walt Garrity?"

"You better believe it," I tell her, my eyes stinging.

"I thought so. That was old school, man." Tee flinches from the paramedic's gloved hand. "Is he gone?"

"Yep."

She shakes her head.

"You were pretty old school yourself back there," I tell her.

"No more than Mia. She grabbed hold of Annie like a mama tiger."

This time Mia blushes full red. "I had to do something."

"And you did," Tee says. "I'll hang with you anytime, girl."

I give Mia's shoulder a squeeze, then ask Serenity, "Why the hell did you run after the van instead of chasing it with the Yukon?"

"Our driver had already taken out the keys. My choice was to hunt for them or start running. I figured here in town, the van might have to stop pretty quick. So I hoofed it."

"We need to get going," says the paramedic.

I raise my hand and salute Tee in my clumsy civilian fashion. "We'll see you at the hospital."

"Bring me a shot of vodka. Good vodka. Make that a bottle."

The paramedic laughs out loud, but Tee only glares at him. "I'm serious as a ruptured hemorrhoid, mister."

The paramedic blinks in surprise. "I believe you."

Before we walk away, I hear the hum and chatter of voices in the street. The neighbors have come out to see what all the noise was about.

"Do you have an extra sheet in that ambulance?" I ask.

The paramedic nods.

Trudging over to the open door, I rip a white sheet off a collapsed gurney and carry it to where Walt's body lies on the sidewalk. A few residents have edged up to within twenty feet of him. Whipping the sheet open with a loud pop, I drape it gently over Walt's upper body and head. To my surprise, Mia catches the other end and pulls it over his legs and feet.

"Thanks," I tell her, looking back for Annie.

She's standing beside Serenity, her eyes filled with awe. Mia starts to say something, but the screech of rubber drowns her voice. Two dark sedans have stopped twenty yards away, and the first man out of the lead car is John Kaiser. He runs toward us with his pistol out, and behind him come four more FBI agents, two brandishing what look like MP5 submachine guns.

"Who's under the sheet?" he asks.

"Walt Garrity. The VK just tried to snatch Annie outside my house. It was an ambush. They took out our bodyguards. Walt stopped them."

"They shot him?"

"No. Their van ran him over."

Kaiser grimaces. "Christ. He was a rough old cob. This is going to be tough on your father."

The words hit me like a hammer.

"John, can you watch the girls?"

"Sure, but—"

"I can't let my dad hear this from somebody else." I break into a run, heading down Washington Street. The jail is probably four hundred yards away, close enough for Dad to have heard the gunfight from his cell.

"Penn, let me drive you!" Kaiser shouts, but I can't stop. The last thing I hear is the FBI man yelling, "Go after him! Keep him covered!"

CHAPTER 60

WHEN I REACH the jail, I find Quentin facing Dad through the scarred wire mesh of the visiting cubicle. I squeeze in behind Quentin's wheelchair and brace my hands on its seat back, my right shoulder blade pounding with pain.

"What's happened?" Dad asks, his face partly obscured by the wire. "We heard shooting from the cellblock. Then some kind of alert. Don't tell me it's Annie."

He's leaning forward in anticipation of terrible news, the fingers of one hand threaded into the mesh. If I had to tell him Annie had been kidnapped, I don't think he could survive it. Walt's death will be bad enough—

"It almost was Annie," I say. "They tried to kidnap her, Dad. The VK guys, I think. The bikers."

"Oh, no. Oh . . . Lord."

"They didn't get her. Walt stopped them."

Dad's eyes widen. "Walt?"

"They knocked down our bodyguards with gunfire, and they got Annie partway into a van. Mia jumped in and fought them, but they were getting away. Then Walt stepped out of nowhere and shot the driver."

Dad hasn't blinked. "And?"

"Walt stopped the van. But . . . not before it ran him over."

My father looks down and swallows. "How bad?"

I hesitate, as we always do in these situations, but waiting only prolongs the torture. "He's gone, Dad. His injuries were catastrophic."

At first he does not react, unless perhaps his eyes squint a little more tightly. But then he leans forward until the crown of his head touches the screen, and a moan escapes his lips.

"Dad . . . are you okay?"

Reaching out, I touch my fingers to his. "I'm sorry. I didn't want you to hear it from somebody else."

Dad keeps his head down.

"Who else was hurt?" Quentin asks from below me.

"Tim Weathers was hit; I don't know his condition. I'm pretty sure our driver was killed. Serenity and I were hit with some kind of nonlethal rounds, and then she had acid thrown on her—"

"Nonlethal rounds?" Quentin interrupts.

I nod, realizing that my right shoulder blade and arm are still mostly numb. "Most of the attackers used some kind of nonlethal round."

"They must have been trying to avoid murder charges."

"I guess so. But I'm pretty sure our driver was hit with a lead bullet."

"What about the attackers?" Dad asks.

"I think two VK were killed. One by Walt, the other by Serenity."

"This is out of control," Quentin mutters. "Why would they do that? Why go after your daughter?"

"Leverage," Dad says, looking up at last. "Snake's a survivor. He's always going to try to neutralize the greatest threat to him. This morning that was Will Devine. Who is it now?"

"You?" Quentin suggests, nodding at Dad.

"Maybe," he allows. "But having Annie also gives them leverage over Penn." Dad's eyes delve into mine. "Do you have it in your power right now to hurt Snake, or to remove some urgent threat against him?"

I shake my head, but my mind is churning through scenarios.

"Who's in a position to send him to jail?" Dad presses.

"Dolores St. Denis," I say softly.

"Who's that?"

"The woman you told me about whose husband got killed in the Lusahatcha Swamp back in the sixties. Her name was Booker then. Dolores Booker. She was raped, and her husband killed. She can testify against Snake over those crimes."

Dad blinks in confusion. "But . . . I thought she killed herself."

"Her family told that story to make the Double Eagles forget about her."

Quentin says, "Where is she now?"

"She was living in New Orleans. I found her and brought her up here. But she's under FBI protection now. I don't know where she is."

"Snake thinks you do," Dad says. "He needs to silence that woman—to kill her—and he doesn't know where to find her. He figures you can find out for him. And threatening Annie is the only conceivable way he could make you do that."

This explanation closes a circuit in my brain, and I collapse against the wall of the cubicle, one hand on the left handle of Quentin's wheelchair.

"You all right?" Quentin asks.

"Penn, listen," Dad says, his eyes filled with urgency. "You've got to get Annie away from Natchez. *Far* away. Peggy, too, if she'll go."

"You know she won't. But I'll get Annie and Mia to some kind of safe house. Kaiser will help me."

"Good, good."

"Dad . . . why was Walt following us? Did you tell him to do that?"

He doesn't answer immediately. Then he says, "Do you remember when you visited me at the Pollock prison?"

I nod.

"I told you then that so long as Snake Knox walked the earth, my acquittal would accomplish nothing. You saw that proved a few minutes ago."

"Did you ask Walt to kill Snake? To hunt him down?"

My father focuses on some indeterminate point between himself and Quentin. "The morning of Henry Sexton's funeral, I told Walt that Snake needed to die. That was the only way to stop the killing. Walt agreed, but he wasn't willing to take the risk. He was happy with his wife, and he didn't want to make her a widow."

And now she is. Quentin and I share a look. Dad is talking like he's in some kind of trance, and perhaps he is. A trance of grief.

"What changed?" I ask him.

Dad bites his bottom lip, trying to work it out himself. "Not too long after Forrest's death, Walt came to me at Pollock and told me he'd realized that the Knoxes were our cross to bear. Our generation's evil, our blight to remove from the world. He'd decided to kill Snake."

Quentin cradles his forehead in his left palm.

"The problem," Dad goes on, "was finding him."

"Is that why you put me on the trail of Will Devine and the other Eagles? You were using me as bait?"

"Snake was always going to come after you, Penn. You killed his nephew. And I killed Frank—his brother. I don't know how much Snake knows about Frank's death, but he knew who'd killed Forrest. In Snake's eyes, that's a blood debt. Until he's dead, you're living on borrowed time. That's why Walt shadowed you for so long. He was waiting for Snake to raise his head."

"Tom," Quentin says quietly, "don't ever speak of this again. And pray to God that Billy Byrd hasn't bugged this cubicle."

"But back at the prison," I murmur, unable to get past the idea that Dad used me to bait Snake Knox, "you—"

"I told you what you needed to hear." Dad's eyes flash with emotion. "And you actually turned Will Devine, by God. Today we almost broke the Double Eagles for good. From the inside out. That's always been the only way to get them in court."

I grimace and look away, unsure of what I'm feeling. "This trial isn't really about getting you acquitted, is it? It never was."

Dad holds up his hands. "Let's not talk about the trial."

"Quentin," I ask, "could I see you outside for a minute?"

I step outside, and thirty seconds later, Quentin carefully backs his chair out of the cubicle. The sheriff's department seems eerily empty, but I know why. Nearly every available man is combing the county, searching for VK members. Not even a wingnut like Billy Byrd can allow biker gangs to shoot up his town and hope to get reelected.

"Did you tell him about the tapes?" I ask Quentin.

He nods. "Right before you got here."

"And?"

"Tom claims he knows nothing about that second tape."

"The Dumpster tape?"

Quentin nods.

This takes me aback. "Do you believe him?"

The old lawyer closes his eyes as though in prayer. "No. His lips denied it, but in his eyes . . . I saw the ledge, Penn. And Tom's damned close to it."

A wave of nausea rolls through my gut. "What's below the ledge?"

"Hell, I think."

"Then we have to go back in there and break him down. We can't go back into court tomorrow not knowing what might be on that tape. And he absolutely cannot take the stand."

"You can't change his mind, Penn. People have died on this road already, and he hasn't given an inch."

"You're right. And that's not rational."

"Or it's supremely rational." Quentin tilts his head, pondering the possibility. "Inhumanly rational."

"That makes no sense. Quentin, Dad has spent months refusing to tell me anything about the night Viola died. Now he wants to get up in front of the whole town and tell *everything*?"

Quentin groans deep in his chest. "Stop trying to reason it out. You heard Colonel Eklund's testimony. A man who did what Tom did in Korea doesn't think like the rest of us. Not when it comes to the big things. In any case, there's no point in you pushing him. Say good-bye and go back to your mother. I'll try to find a way to get him to open up about the tape."

"And if he doesn't?"

"Then tomorrow should be a mighty interesting day in court."

"Do you think Judge Elder will proceed after what's happened to Walt?"

"It's a murder trial, Penn. We still have a defendant, and we still have a jury."

With that Quentin spins his chair and reenters the cubicle.

When I step in after him, I see that my father has been crying. The white, cracked skin of his face has turned an unhealthy pink, and there's moisture in the white whiskers on his cheeks.

"I need a phone," he says. "I need to call Carmelita."

Carmelita Cruz, the jewel of Walt Garrity's later life. "We can't pass a phone through the wire."

"I'll hold mine up to the screen," Quentin says, "after Penn says good night."

He really is showing me the door.

Dad looks small and vulnerable sitting there, his hands folded on the little metal shelf before him. "Walt thought he owed me something for Korea," he murmurs. "But he didn't. We were always even."

"Tell his wife that," I suggest.

"I will."

Quentin tosses his head to send me on my way, but I hang back long enough to take hold of the wire mesh and shake it. "Dad, what's going to happen in court tomorrow?"

This time his eyes find mine, and they are free of dissimulation. "The truth's going to come out. One way or another. Once and for all."

IT'S HALF PAST ten, and the house seems emptier than it has in a long time. After strident arguments and tearful partings, Annie and Mia have been transported by the FBI to private dorm rooms at the minimum-security facility at Pollock, the same place where Annie used to visit my father while he was in protective custody. After hearing about the street battle, Mia's mother was elated that her daughter would be entering federal protection until the conclusion of the trial. My only consolation is that Annie and Mia will remain together, and this should carry them through their separation from the rest of us.

Serenity has been gone even longer than Annie. Despite her quick use of Mia's calcium gluconate, Drew Elliott immediately had her transported to University Medical Center in Jackson. He didn't want to risk the complications that still have Keisha Harvin in critical condition. I never even got to say good-bye to Tee. The ambulance carrying her had already departed Natchez by the time I left Dad and Quentin at the jail.

We've had some turnover in our security detail as well. While the VK attackers used nonlethal rounds against most of us, Tim Weathers took an impact to the back of his head, and he's recovering from a severe hematoma in St. Catherine's Hospital. Our driver wasn't killed outright, but he too had to be flown to UMC in Jackson for surgery, where he remains in critical condition. Our security detail is now led by Tim's deputy, Joe Russell, who is a very solid guy, but he doesn't inspire quite the confidence or sense of intimacy that Tim did.

One hour ago, my mother went upstairs with a migraine, and I went down to my basement office for the tense wait until dawn. To my surprise, when I went up to the kitchen to scrounge for food, Jenny came in to talk about tomorrow's prospects.

I didn't tell her much. I've spoken to Kaiser three times, but all he could tell me was that both tapes have been checked into a special forensic intelligence lab at FBI headquarters, and a team is working on them.

While Jenny nibbles at a bowl of ice cream, my phone pings, and a text from John Kaiser appears. I assume it will be about the videotapes, but it's not.

Snake Knox bought gas in Sulphur, Louisiana, earlier this evening. Paid cash. We got a security cam photo of him and Alois Engel at the payment window. They bought four quarts of beer.

I texted back: *So they're headed to Texas?*

Unless they double back into the Atchafalaya Swamp to hide out. We'll find them. Leave ur cell on tonite.

I text, *Will do,* then click END and set my phone back on the granite countertop.

Jenny seems to be staring at a point on my chin, her expression lethargic.

"Are you thinking?" I ask. "Or having a seizure?"

She starts like a sleepwalker coming awake somewhere unfamiliar. "I'm sorry. Sometimes I get that way when I'm thinking. Slack-jawed."

"What are you thinking about?"

"Dad. Last October, when he had his heart attack, that was the first time I began to truly understand that he will die someday. Probably soon. Whether he's acquitted in this trial or not . . . he'll be gone. Despite all his health problems, I've always seen him as invulnerable. Invincible."

Jenny taps her fist against her chin, and it's obvious that she's dealing with some painful emotions. At last she drops her hand and pats the kitchen counter with both palms. "During the conference at your office today, I could hear some of your discussion from the lounge."

This makes me sit up straight. "And?"

"I thought I heard some mention of a videotape. Is that the tape that Viola left for Henry Sexton? The tape Daddy and Walt tried to get rid of?"

Shit. "There was some discussion of whether it might be possible to restore that."

"And is it?"

"It might be, apparently. We won't know until tomorrow."

"And would that be a good thing?"

How do I answer this? I'm not about to make Jenny lie awake all night in terror.

"I honestly don't know. Let's not borrow trouble, huh? I'd just as soon give the case to the jury first thing in the morning."

"So you don't think Daddy should take the stand tomorrow?"

I think back to my visit in the jail, to the broken look in his eyes. "No. His chances are far better if he keeps his mouth shut."

"I agree. I really worry what Shad Johnson would do to him on cross."

"You're right to. Shad can wield a question like a scalpel. I think Quentin underestimates him."

The swish of slippers on the floor makes us both turn. Mom stands in the kitchen door, sleepy-eyed but alert for any hint of danger.

"Did I hear you talking about the case?"

Whoever said all humans lose hearing ability as they age never examined my mother.

"We were just discussing the possibility of Dad taking the stand tomorrow."

Very calmly, Mom reaches out and steadies herself by grasping the door frame. "Would that be the mistake I think it would, Penn? I'm asking you as a former prosecutor."

"Most lawyers would say yes. Most lawyers would have rested after Junius Jelks testified, or after Lincoln was destroyed. Certainly after Vivek Patel."

My mother nods slowly. "Your father never would listen to anyone else. Not about the big things. And Quentin's following his wishes."

"Mom, I think there's only one person in the world who could stop Dad from taking the stand tomorrow."

To my surprise, she laughs. In that laugh is fifty years of shared living, half a century of knowing another human being as they truly are and sticking with them anyway.

"I've tried," she says. "Oh, how I've tried. But it's no use."

She walks between Jenny and me, then puts an arm around each of us. A shock of pain flashes through my right side, but Mom doesn't seem to notice. This tells me she's definitely been into the pharmaceuticals.

"My two babies," she says, "still with me. We'll just have to hope for the best tomorrow."

A thousand memories flood my mind, but before I can voice a single one, Mom plants a kiss on each of our cheeks and glides from the room.

Jenny looks at me and shakes her head. "All this going on, and you know the last thing Mom told me she was worried about?"

"What?"

"You falling for Serenity."

"God. She started in on me last night with that. And then she walked in on us."

Jenny raises her eyebrows. "In flagrante delicto, I heard?"

"She told you?"

"Mm-hm. Today, when we went to her house to pick up her 'things.'"

"Xanax?" I ask.

"Among other goodies. Can you blame her? Living in a motel beside a federal prison for months? That's not what she signed on for."

"No. But . . . it still disappoints me a little. I'm not being judgmental. I've just never seen a crisis she couldn't handle sober. You know?"

Jenny shrugs. "We all have a breaking point." She stands and rinses her ice cream bowl in the sink. "So . . . ?"

"So what?" I ask.

"You and Serenity?"

"Oh, hell. That's temporary. We just clicked. I hadn't touched a woman since Caitlin, and— I don't know."

"Sure you do."

"Well . . . she seemed to need me as well. And she doesn't play games, you know? She's straightforward, and I needed that. I don't think it'll last beyond this week. She's not going to move here and become Annie's stepmother. And I'm sure as hell not moving to Atlanta."

"Mom will be relieved to hear it."

"Oh, I know. She was practically pushing me into Mia's arms as an alternative."

For the first time in a long while, Jenny laughs.

"I'll tell you something, though," I say seriously. "When Mom walked in on us doing it, she looked like she'd seen death itself."

Jenny stares back at me, her eyes troubled. "The ghost of Christmas past, maybe?"

"I imagine so. I hate that I hurt her in any way."

"You get to live your own life, Penn. But deep down, I think you want Ward and June Cleaver back. I probably do, too."

I look at my watch. "Enough of this. Let's get to bed."

After Jenny and I part, I speed-dial Doris Avery on my way back to the basement.

"Hello, Penn," she says in a sleepy voice, but then I hear her exhale what is almost certainly cigarette smoke. "Do you need Quentin?"

"I do."

"He's right here."

"Last call," Quentin says. "I've got to get some sleep."

"Yeah, good luck with that."

"Speak for yourself. Doris just rubbed my neck, and I'm nearly out. You hear anything more from Kaiser?"

"The FBI supercomputers are churning away. I feel like I'm being forced to lie still while termites devour the walls of our house."

"Let me save you some oxygen. Don't ask me about Tom testifying tomorrow. It's not my decision, and it never has been. If Joe Elder tells us to proceed, Tom's going into that witness box."

"Did you press him about the Dumpster tape?"

Quentin's labored breathing comes over the connection for a while. Then at last he says, "I didn't get anywhere."

"Fuck."

"I'm sorry, Penn. Keep the faith. I'll see you in court."

"Wait! I'm worried about Dad staying in the jail tonight. After getting the news about Walt, you know? What if he gets angina?"

"They'll get him his medicine. Stop worrying. I've done what I can to be sure Tom's all right in there, and we can't get him out tonight anyway."

"What do you mean? What have you done?"

"All I can, like I said. But Christ, Penn. Have you ever considered that Tom dying in his sleep in that jail might be better than what's waiting for him after this trial?"

"*What?* Hell, no! Have you?"

"Not until tonight, I confess. But if Tom did kill Viola, and it wasn't euthanasia—if they had some conversation beforehand—an argument, let's say, and the world sees that on tape—then Tom's going to wish he'd died tonight."

CHAPTER 61

ALOIS ENGEL STOOD on the wet sand west of Rodney and watched a pushboat driving a string of barges up the dark river. Only the moon cast a faint wash of light over the water, and every couple of minutes a blue-rimmed black cloud would scud across its face.

A couple of yards away, his father crouched on the sand, peering out over the water. Snake had asked for silence, but Alois could not contain his frustration any longer.

"Why the *hell* did they use beanbag rounds?" he muttered. "I thought you said those VK guys were supposed to be stone killers."

Snake raised a hand and signaled for Alois to shut up.

"We won't get within a mile of that little girl now. And she was our only damn leverage!"

"For fuck's sake," Snake muttered. "Let me think. It's that old nigger woman we gotta find, and Penn Cage is the only one I figure knows where the FBI's taken her."

"I'm sorry, Daddy," Alois said, "but I've got to speak my piece. We need to cut loose of those VK bastards. Those no-'count pussies ain't done us a bit of good. They're *scared* of the damn FBI! That's why they used that toy ammo."

"The FBI came down hard on them over the past week," Snake said. "Damned hard. Lars don't want to make the top of the most-wanted list on our account. But his boys killed that driver when it went sideways—or as good as, anyway—and he lost two more of his own men."

"Men, my *ass*," Alois grumbled. "That driver got himself shot by a rickety old gomer from Texas. I say to hell with those bikers. We don't need 'em. Didn't you tell me Uncle Frank always said, 'If you want something done right, do it yourself'?"

Snake took out a pack of cigarettes, shook one out, and lit it with a Zippo. "Shut up, boy. You never knew Frank."

"That's not my fault, is it?"

Snake grunted and blew out a long plume of smoke. "I guess it ain't."

"Well?" Alois pressed. "Did Frank say that or not?"

Snake straightened up and rubbed his forehead with his palm as he watched the pushboat pass. Alois felt the ground beneath him vibrating from the torque of those big engines.

"Frank said a lot of things. And he did some big-time shit, back in his prime. But in the end, he drank himself into a stupor, walked under a load of batteries, and let a nigger woman kill him like a damn hog."

Alois felt his throat knot up with a boy's anger. He'd always been told that Frank Knox was the toughest and smartest damn soldier ever to come out of Louisiana, which was saying something. Frank was the alpha dog in any group of men who ever got close to him.

"Where were you when he died?" Alois asked, voice quavering with anger and fear.

At last his father turned to him, and what Alois saw in those eyes was something utterly removed from anything he'd seen in them before. Snake's eyes reminded him of a demonstration he'd seen in his junior college lab. A reckless professor had used a vacuum pump to put cyclohexane into a state where it flirted with the triple point: simultaneously boiling and freezing, cycling through the solid, liquid, and gaseous states. Snake's eyes told his son that a similar reaction was occurring behind them now. Rage and guilt were bleeding into one another, threatening to explode, and Alois knew that the resulting detonation, when it came, would kill anyone close to it.

"I had just got to Dr. Cage's office. I'd been holding Jimmy Revels and Luther Davis at the machine shop when Sonny called me. I hauled ass back to town quick as I could, but I was too late. Dr. almighty Cage had told Sonny and Glenn to stay in the waiting room," Snake said in a guttural voice. "Said there wasn't room for them in his surgery room."

Alois nodded, knowing he'd found the proper lever with which to trigger his father. "And now you know why."

The corner of Snake's mouth twitched, something Alois had never seen it do before. "Doc come out and told us Frank had expired in spite of his best efforts. Expired. Like a fucking magazine subscription."

"So what are we going do about it? I don't see the point of waiting for no fucking jury."

Snake looked back out over the dark water.

"We've got to do something," Alois said.

Snake smoked his cigarette in self-absorbed silence. After a while, he said, "Tom Cage is beyond being threatened, or blackmailed. I've seen it before. He's shaking hands with Death. That's what a guy in my unit used to say."

Helpless fury was building in Alois's chest. "So what are you saying, Pop? Huh? Do nothing?"

Snake tossed the glowing butt into the fast-flowing current and said, "Don't worry about it. I'm gonna take care of the doc before he does something against all reason."

Alois's arteries expanded with excitement. "What are we going to do?"

"I've already done it," Snake said, turning back to the sandy road that led to the house. "Wilma ought to have that venison about ready now. Let's get back inside. I gotta figure a way to trace that woman from Athens Point. I spent twenty minutes fuckin' her in the swamp, and I doubt she's forgot a second of it. She can put my white ass in Angola."

"To hell with *that,*" Alois said, desperate to know what his father had planned. "What have you got going?"

As Snake passed Alois, he let his eyes fall on those of his son. "That trial's over," he said. "Tom Cage will never see the light of morning."

NOT LONG AFTER midnight, Deputy Larry McQuarters opened the cellblock door and strode between the cells to check the prisoners. Several were still awake, and a couple begged him to bring treats or let them borrow his cell phone. Larry ignored them. He'd come to check on Dr. Cage, who was a special friend of one of Larry's favorite people. On Quentin's advice, Larry had varied the intervals between his checks, but even so, he hadn't discovered anything that troubled him about Dr. Cage's treatment. Everybody knew Sheriff Byrd didn't care for Tom Cage, but more than a few deputies didn't care much for Sheriff Byrd, either—

Larry stood before Dr. Cage's cell with his mouth open.

The cell door was closed, but the cell was empty.

"Where Dr. Cage at?" Larry called. "Hey! Where Dr. Cage gone?"

"He said he needed some medicine," answered a drug dealer from a bunk in the adjacent cell. "His chest was hurtin' him."

Alarms rang in Larry's big head. "Who come got him?"

"Dunwoody."

Dunwoody? Sheriff Byrd's pet rat . . .

Larry turned and ran for the door, which required considerable effort since he weighed nearly three hundred pounds. His first stop, once he got through the cellblock door, was the monitor station, where one of several computer screens would display whatever was going on in the infirmary, one floor below.

The monitor that ought to be showing the infirmary was black.

Dead? Larry thought.

Monitors frequently malfunctioned in the jail, due to a lack of funds and qualified maintenance techs, but something in Larry's belly told him this was no accident.

He bolted for the stairs, wrenched himself sideways to fit through the door, then pounded down to the second floor, where he crashed through the door and veered left, toward the little infirmary room. With every step he saw Dr. Cage lying motionless on the infirmary floor, his lips and fingernails blue. Or worse, hanging from a belt like so many inmates Larry had seen in his life.

When he pushed open the infirmary door, Larry saw Dr. Cage sitting in the blood-drawing chair, his open hand held out before him. Deputy Gilbert Dunwoody was passing him one of the little white cups they used to dispense pills.

Three strides carried Larry across the room.

Dr. Cage didn't even look his way, so lethargic did he seem, but Dunwoody backpedaled immediately, like a man with a guilty conscience. Larry closed his hand around Dunwoody's wrist, which he could easily break.

"What you got in that cup, Woody?"

"Nothing!" cried Dunwoody. "Lemme go!"

Larry looked back over his shoulder. Dr. Cage appeared only marginally alert. "Did you axe for medicine, Doc?"

"I was having chest pain. I need a nitro pill."

"Well . . . let's see what kind of pill Dunwoody got in his cup here. Come over here, Doc."

As Tom Cage leaned forward, Dunwoody dropped the little cup from his pinned hand, then stomped on the cup and the floor around it with his boot.

"Dr. Cage already took his pill!" Dunwoody said. "Let's see you prove different."

Larry closed his hand tighter around Dunwoody's wrist and looked hard at the floor. He saw a fine white powder around the crushed cup.

"Ahghh! You lemme go, goddamn it! You're gonna have to explain this to the sheriff!"

"Fuck the sheriff," Larry growled. "I'm gonna go down to one of them TV trucks and tell 'em you just tried to kill Dr. Cage. How 'bout that?"

Dunwoody's eyes went wide.

Larry squeezed tighter, tight enough for Dunwoody to know how badly he could hurt him if he wanted to. Then Larry released the bony wrist.

Dunwoody cried out in relief, then scrambled for the door. After it banged shut, Larry turned to Dr. Cage, who was looking dazedly at him.

"What you think that powder is, Doc? Some kind of poison, you reckon?"

Tom Cage followed Larry's pointing finger with his eyes, then shrugged as though the matter didn't interest him.

"You want me to call Quentin? Or the FBI maybe?"

Dr. Cage shook his head.

"It's okay, Doc," Larry said gently. "I'll get you some more medicine. The right kind this time. And I'll sit by your cell till morning."

FRIDAY

CHAPTER 62

I AWAKEN THIS morning with a sense that Walt Garrity is alive and Serenity Butler sleeping peacefully two floors above me. Three seconds later, reality collapses upon me with crushing finality.

Walt is dead.

Serenity lies suffering in a hospital a hundred miles away.

Annie and Mia are hiding in FBI custody at Pollock FCI.

I remember this cruel trick of the brain from when my wife died, and from Caitlin's death, too, of course. I suppose it's akin to phantom-limb pain. Unable to accept such profound loss, the mind tries vainly to reset itself each night, in the hope that it can reset reality as well.

But nothing can.

I shower quickly, then hurry down to the kitchen to make some breakfast and try to think of a way to bolster my mother for today's ordeal. My primary anxiety is whether the FBI has been able to restore the two erased videotapes, or will in time for them to be entered as evidence in the trial. But under that anxiety, like incipient panic bubbling beneath a surface of manageable fear, is the prospect that my father might, against all logic and advice, take the stand to testify in his own defense. A less cynical man than I might hope that his father wants to testify because he knows he has nothing to fear from whatever information those tapes contain. But I know better. You don't blast a videotape with a high-intensity magnetic field because you have nothing to fear from it.

As I sit down with my coffee, I find a copy of the *Natchez Examiner* on the table. One of our guards probably left it for me. I skim the article about the gunfight and chase that ended Walt's life, then turn to the opinion page. Instead of the expected piece by Miriam Masters, I find a long editorial by none other than Serenity Butler. Above the headline is a head shot cropped from the book jacket photo. Seeing those eyes that I now know so well, I feel a jolt of something I can't put a name to.

Then I begin to read.

American history is punctuated by watershed moments, fulcrum points that separate one sense of ourselves (as a nation) from another. We study the classic ones in school, the American canon, mostly those from the eighteenth and nineteenth centuries: America's declaration of independence from England; the Gettysburg Address, and John Wilkes Booth's assassination of the president who gave it; the Scopes trial. For some reason, these transformations of the prevailing zeitgeist tend to involve wars, crimes, or trials of some kind. All too rarely, they involve signal human achievements, like the discovery of a polio cure, or the moon landing in 1969.

Because of the proliferation of mass media, the twentieth century seems filled with such cultural dividing lines: the assassinations of John F. Kennedy and Martin Luther King Jr.; Woodstock and Altamont; Nixon's resignation; the L.A. riots; the O.J. verdict. Such historic markers might be fundamentally different from one another, but they share one trait: they unite millions of people by revealing some hidden truth about the nation. Woodstock crystallized a powerful urge toward love and peace within American youth culture. Only a few months later, Altamont and the Manson murders shattered that dream with chaotic violence.

Nations are not alone in experiencing such revelatory moments. Cities do, too. Only the scale is different. For Natchez, Mississippi, the trial of Dr. Tom Cage has become such a moment. Though it's now the twenty-first century, Natchez has always seemed to me a city in search of its century. The trial of Tom Cage might finally place Natchez in time. During Quentin

Avery's opening statement, he promised the jury that before the trial concluded, Dr. Cage would take the stand and tell the whole truth behind the crime of which he has been accused. Mr. Avery also promised that when that happened, men in the courtroom would tremble.

Over the past four days, Judge Elder's courtroom has been standing room only, with hundreds of would-be spectators turned away every morning. I suspect that today, likely the final day of the trial, throngs will surround the courthouse as Natchezians await Dr. Cage's testimony and the verdict that will follow.

But why does such an air of expectation pervade the city? Is it only the lurid aspects of the case that have made Natchez ground zero for the entire state this week? I think not. I have come to believe that something far deeper is at work among the people. Natchez is a divided city, as Mississippi is a divided state and America a divided nation. And despite the protests of those who would deny this tragic truth, the root of that division is race—the unfinished business of chattel slavery.

When Tom Cage and Viola Turner reached for each other in 1968, they crossed an invisible boundary, a gulf between two races. They were not the first to do so. The children of such relationships walk the streets of Natchez every day. Their names are written in the pages of dusty Bibles kept out of sight, but kept all the same. In the silent shadows of this town, deep ties exist between black and white, and have for three hundred years. They are ties not only of friendship and love, but of blood. Rarely acknowledged, they're like roots that spread beneath the soil, out of sight but as strong as any plant growing in the light of the sun. And in this racially fraught era of American history, it may be those roots that offer the best and only chance of bridging the gulf that divides us.

If Tom Cage takes the stand today, he will do so not only as himself, but as a symbol of the secret life of his hometown. And whatever his testimony reveals, Dr. Cage will be telling the city something about itself, perhaps something profound, certainly something necessary. Did Tom Cage kill Viola Turner? If so, did he do it out of fear, to silence her and to protect himself? Or did he do it out of love, to spare her an agonizing death? And if Dr. Cage did not kill Viola Turner, then who did? A violent splinter cell of the Ku Klux Klan? Or could it have been the tortured son born from the illicit relationship between Dr. Cage and his nurse?

Any of those answers, once made real, will become a lens through which the city will view itself, and through which it will be viewed by those outside. My hope is that the truth that emerges from this trial will inspire hope rather than bitterness.

I set down the paper and stare into my coffee, wondering how in hell Serenity managed to get an editorial into the paper from her hospital bed in Jackson. But a deeper question troubles me more. How did Serenity, an outsider, spend only a couple of days in Natchez with my family and perceive truths that I'd not seen myself? Was it precisely because she is an outsider? Whatever the case, Tee has answered the question I posed to Quentin last night at the jail: Why must Dad, after telling me nothing for months, now enter the witness box and tell the town everything?

"Penn, are you all right?"

My mother is standing in the kitchen doorway, worry etched in every line of her face.

"Have you gotten bad news?" she asks. "Has Serenity's condition worsened?"

"I don't think so. I . . . was just reading the paper. You should probably skip it."

"I read it an hour ago."

"Serenity's editorial, too?"

Mom gives me a taut smile. "I never said she wasn't sharp."

"Everybody decent?" calls Joe Russell, now the leader of our security detail. "We need to leave in ten minutes."

I hear his footsteps coming up the hall. Reaching out, I take hold of my mother's cold hand.

"Can you stand one more day of trial?"

Her smile gets a little tighter. "I can stand anything, darling."

IT TAKES US forty minutes to travel the few blocks from my front door to the courtroom. After yesterday's gun battle, the streets have become nearly impassable, from both vehicular and pedestrian traffic. Uniformed cops are conspicuous on the sidewalks, and I'm certain that John Kaiser has plainclothes FBI agents moving through the crowds. During our crawl to the courthouse, I receive a text from Kaiser informing me that the FBI forensic team in Washington has succeeded in restoring "Tape S-15"—the tape Viola made for Henry—to a "readable" condition. The only remaining obstacle to using it in the trial is authorization, which will be granted or denied after a conference between the FBI director, the U.S. attorney general, the director of Homeland Security, and (Kaiser suspects) the White House. If such use is authorized, a digitally encrypted video file will be transmitted to the FBI field office in Jackson—where Kaiser is waiting—and a hard copy will be driven to Natchez or flown here via helicopter.

While I try to hide my growing anxiety from my mother, Kaiser sends a more encouraging message. "Tape S-16"—the one discovered in the St. Catherine's Hospital Dumpster—is apparently giving the Bureau's digital wizards more trouble. However, they are still working on it. My heart tells me that Kaiser hopes his colleagues fail in their task, but I was a trial lawyer for too many years to put much faith in miracles.

When we arrive at the courthouse, which appears to be under siege, I learn from the circuit clerk that court has been delayed for an hour by agents of the BATF, who want to make a final sweep of the courtroom prior to allowing people inside. When I announce my intention to take my mother to City Hall to wait out the delay, the clerk offers to bring us to his private office in the courthouse, where Quentin is preparing for the morning's proceedings.

Quentin and Doris greet my mother warmly, but when Doris tries to take her into another room "to get some coffee," Mom demands to know what to expect once court is in session. In a somber voice, Quentin tells us that Judge Elder has decided the trial should move forward regardless of the FBI's efforts to restore the videotapes. Before I can feel relief at the prospect that Quentin might be able to rest his case before the Dumpster tape is restored, he adds that Dad will be taking the stand as his first and only witness of the day.

I expect Mom to faint or stroke out at this news, but she hardly reacts at all, other than to go to the window and look out at the mass of people hoping to be admitted to the courthouse today.

"Look at this," says Doris, turning up the sound on a small TV in the corner of the office.

I naively assumed that only the attorneys would be aware of the side drama of the videotapes, but Shad Johnson has taken advantage of the delay to address the reporters gathered at the foot of the courthouse steps. The first thing I hear when the sound comes up is Shad opining that the "St. Catherine's Hospital Dumpster tape" might break the case wide open.

"That won't endear Shadrach to Judge Elder," I mutter.

"He doesn't care," Quentin says. "He's decided that the potential upside of this is worth any sanction Joe might impose on him."

Shad looks positively ebullient on camera, and if he knew for sure that Quentin is about to call my father to the stand, he might pop open some Dom Perignon on the courthouse lawn.

By the time the BATF gives the all clear and everyone reaches their assigned places in the courtroom, the spectators in the gallery have somehow intuited that Dad means to take the stand. After all, didn't Quentin Avery promise that he would?

Dad certainly looks ready for his turn in the spotlight. He's wearing a charcoal suit, and thanks to my mother's relentless insistence, his white hair and beard have been carefully trimmed. He looks about as distinguished as it's possible to look after three months in jail, yet the signs of his failing health can't be missed.

His skin is as pale as that of an Arctic researcher after long months of night, and a fine sprinkling of dandruff already powders the shoulders of his jacket, as though he's just come in from a snowfall. Hollow cheeks make his weight loss obvious, while crooked fingers and pitted, spooned nails reveal the extent of his psoriatic arthritis. If he were wearing shorts, the edema in his legs would betray the severity of his heart failure, but thankfully his legs are covered. Even his wise eyes appear dull today, their luster gone, and when he finally enters the witness box to be sworn in, the powerful baritone that always reassured his patients is barely a whisper.

The circuit clerk holds an old Bible beneath his hand, then says without the slightest drama, "Do you, Thomas Jefferson Cage, swear to tell the truth, the whole truth, and nothing but the truth, under penalty of law, so help you God?"

"I so swear."

A religious oath is rarely used in American courts nowadays, but this is Mississippi. We have the highest per-capita number of churches and the lowest literacy rate (as Caitlin never tired of reminding me), and such traditions die hard. My father long ago abandoned the simplistic religious beliefs of his childhood, and after forty years of practicing medicine has found no real comfort in any of the world's faiths. Yet today he gave the prudent answer when the Bible was held beneath his hand.

Was that, I wonder uncomfortably, *his first lie?*

As Quentin rolls slowly forward, I hear no electrical whir, and I realize with a shock that he's in a manual wheelchair, not his motorized one. *Did he have an electrical problem?* I wonder, surprised that I didn't notice the change back in the clerk's office. But then instinct tells me that Quentin must be making a subtle play to elicit sympathy or respect from the jury. When the legless old lawyer's still-powerful shoulders grip those big wheels and turn them, you can't help but feel you're in the presence of a man of great fortitude.

Quentin elects to begin his questioning from his customary spot by the lectern, but I have no doubt he will have rolled a half mile or more before he finishes this afternoon.

When he clears his throat, the whispers of the standing-room-only crowd behind me fall silent. Just before he speaks, Quentin glances my way, and I give the smallest shake of my head, letting him know I've heard nothing more from Kaiser about the Dumpster tape.

"Dr. Cage," he says, "did you treat Viola Turner during the last weeks of her life?"

"I did."

"Were you her only doctor?"

"I was."

"What was her chief illness?"

"Metastatic carcinoma of the lung."

Quentin pauses for this to sink in; even for a lay audience, "metastatic" carries the awful weight of mortality. "And what was the prognosis?"

"Terminal."

"So you were not trying to cure her?"

"No. I was providing palliative care. Trying to ease her suffering as much as possible."

"Until her death?"

"Yes."

"Did Mrs. Turner clearly understand this?"

"Yes. She'd been a nurse all her life. She knew her prognosis as well as any doctor would."

"I see. Did she come to your office for treatment?"

"No. I generally saw her at her sister's residence, where the front room had been converted to a sickroom."

"I see. How often did you make house calls on Mrs. Turner?"

"Almost every day."

"That's uncommon these days, isn't it?"

"Yes. I did that because Viola had once been my employee, and also because we had once had an intimate relationship."

A collective intake of breath from the crowd charges the atmosphere in the courtroom.

"An extramarital affair?" Quentin asks, as though asking for clarification of some dull point of cost accounting.

"That's correct," Dad replies, just as clinically.

"I see. Dr. Cage, it has been said in the courtroom that you had a pact of sorts with Mrs. Turner, that you would help her to commit suicide before the pain from her cancer became too bad. Is that true?"

"Yes."

A hundred people shift on their chairs at the same moment.

"Could you elaborate on that?"

"Yes. The issue wasn't just pain for Viola. It was personal dignity. Viola Turner was a proud woman, and as a nurse she had watched countless patients die over the years. There were certain indignities to which she did not want to subject herself—or others." Dad pauses, inwardly reflecting. "Viola also had religious qualms about committing suicide. She was a devout Catholic. She didn't simply want me to provide a lethal dose of drugs. She wanted me to perform the injection."

My pulse has begun to race. I can't believe Quentin is letting Dad wrap a rope around his own neck.

"And were you willing to do that?" Quentin asks.

"I thought I was. I didn't *want* to do it. But because of our personal history, and a feeling that I had let Viola down badly back when she worked for me, I felt I owed it to her."

Quentin nods thoughtfully. "So . . . when you entered Cora Revels's house in the early hours of December twelfth, you intended to accede to Viola Turner's wishes and inject a lethal dose of a drug into her body?"

"Yes."

The crowd reacts with sharply cut-off breaths.

"Had Mrs. Turner requested a particular drug?" Quentin asks.

"She asked for morphine sulfate, a narcotic pain reliever."

"Dr. Cage, did you in fact administer the fatal dose of morphine that Viola Turner had requested?"

"No. I did not."

Stunned silence envelops the courtroom.

"Why not?"

Dad takes his time with this. "For several reasons. One, when I arrived, Viola and I had a conversation. During that talk, she told me several things that disturbed me. One was about a videotape she had made for a reporter, Henry Sexton. She wanted Sexton to have the tape after her death, to assist him with his investigations into the crimes of the Double Eagle group, who had murdered her brother. But the most important revelation was that I was the father of Viola's grown son, Lincoln Turner."

"You did not know that information prior to that night?"

"I did not."

"But Mrs. Turner's sister testified that you'd known this for many years."

"She lied about that."

Turning to my left, I realize that while Lincoln is in court today, Cora Revels is not. Not unless she's sitting back in the more anonymous rows.

"But Dr. Cage," Quentin continues, "the district attorney has established that you sent Mrs. Turner money every month from 1968 until she moved back to Natchez to die. What man would do that if he had not fathered an illegitimate child by that woman?"

"I would. And I did."

"But why? Why did you do that?"

"Because I loved her."

The truth embodied in these words—and in my father's voice—is absolute. No one can doubt it. I don't want to look at my mother, but I can't help myself. Dad's answer must have struck her like an arrow through the heart, yet she shows no more emotion than an effigy filled with sand.

"When and why did you first begin sending money to Viola?" Quentin asks.

"A few weeks after she left Natchez, a letter from Viola arrived at my clinic. It wasn't addressed to me, but to the other female employees. I copied down the return address. It was a P.O. box in Chicago. I knew Viola probably needed money to make a new start, so I sent her a check. She didn't cash it right away, but about a month later she did. That told me she needed the funds, so I just kept sending the checks. And she kept cashing them."

"For thirty-seven years?"

"That's right."

"Dr. Cage, why would you send money for that long, if you did not know that Viola had borne a child by you?"

"I knew she wouldn't have cashed those checks unless she needed the money badly. Viola had too much pride to take charity. I also felt responsible for the fact that she'd had to leave town. I felt guilty. Giving her financial help was the very least I could do."

"I see. All right. Let's return to the night of Viola's death. After she told you that you had fathered her son, what happened?"

"The discussion became very emotional, as you might imagine. I couldn't believe she had withheld that from me all those years. But I soon realized she'd done it to protect me and my family. She felt responsible for our affair, and while she knew I shared that guilt, Viola didn't believe my wife and children should suffer because of our sin. Those are her words."

Again Quentin pauses to let this sink into the minds of the jury. "What happened next?"

"Viola asked me to make her a promise."

"What promise?"

"That after her death, I would make sure that our son was provided for in the future. At first I thought she meant that I should give him a large sum of money, but she didn't want that."

"Why not?"

"Viola believed that Lincoln had been twisted in a moral sense by his stepfather. Also by her negligence, due to her drinking. She felt he wasn't yet mature enough to handle a large amount of money. She suggested that I might establish a trust of some sort for him."

"Did you agree to do that?"

"Yes. But I was hardly rational at the time. All I could think about was that this woman I had loved so long ago had asked me to end her life, and now she was telling me that we had a child together. It was simply too much to handle."

"How did you react?"

"I wanted time to think, to consider what she'd told me. But I knew that if I told Viola I couldn't go through with the pact, two things were likely to happen. One, she'd get very angry, even distraught. She appeared calm, but some people near death—if they're not sedated or unconscious—often experience a great deal of stress, especially over unresolved family issues. Second, I suspected that if I simply left her there, Viola might find a way to inject herself and end her own life, regardless of my wishes."

"So what did you do?"

Dad takes a deep breath, and his eyes glaze with the effort of recollection. "I decided to pretend that I was going through with the pact. I remained calm and agreed to everything Viola said. I kissed her once, as she asked me to. I bowed my head while she prayed."

"What prayer did she pray?"

"I believe she said, 'Holy Mary, Mother of God, pray for us sinners, now and at the hour of our death.'"

"All right. Then what happened?"

"I injected her with morphine."

Several sharp expulsions of breath break the silence of the courtroom, and some spectators begin whispering. A glare from Judge Elder quickly puts an end to the rushing sound.

"But, Doctor, you earlier said you didn't inject a lethal dose of morphine."

"I did and I didn't. You have to remember something about Viola.

She was an experienced nurse. She wasn't going to let me draw up a syringe of saline and inject her. She watched me draw a lethal dose of morphine and tie the tourniquet around her upper arm. Then she watched the needle go into her antecubital vein. I knew she would do that. Her veins were in terrible shape because her PICC line was clogged and she'd been getting needle sticks directly in the veins. Hitting her antecubital required great skill. It was a lot like bluffing in a card game. I injected the drug very slowly, all the while trying not to give away my plan. After about ten seconds, Viola finally lay back on her pillow, certain that the morphine was going into her. Two seconds after that, I pushed the needle completely through her vein and injected the remainder of the dose into the tissue beneath the vessel, essentially rendering the drug harmless."

"Harmless? A lethal dose of morphine?"

"Yes. Cancer patients like Viola build up huge tolerances for narcotics. To kill her with morphine, I would have had to inject the full dose directly into the vein, and in a reasonably short time. Otherwise, she wouldn't absorb the drug rapidly enough to send her into respiratory failure. The rate of absorption is everything in that equation."

"How could you be positive you had pushed through the vein before completing the injection?"

"I've been practicing medicine more than forty years. My judgment's pretty accurate about such things. And the final proof is that Viola did not in fact die from a morphine overdose. The autopsy showed just what I described, a seemingly botched IV morphine injection, and a subsequent death by adrenaline overdose."

Shad is furiously taking notes at the prosecution table.

"Did you at any time that night inject Viola Turner with adrenaline?"

"No. Absolutely not."

"All right. What did you do after Viola fell unconscious?"

"I looked around the house for an audiotape she had told me about, one she had made for Henry Sexton."

So Dad knew all along about the audiotape Lincoln tried to sell me—

"Did you find this tape?"

"No."

"What did you find?"

"I found the videotape she had made for Henry Sexton. It was in the bedside table, where she had said it would be. I decided to take that with me when I left."

Another rush of whispers passes through the gallery.

"With what intention?" Quentin asks.

"I wanted to watch it before I passed it to Henry. I was worried it contained information I'd prefer not to be made public. Things I wouldn't want my family to see."

"Such as mention of your paternity of Lincoln Turner?"

"Yes."

"All right." Quentin steeples his fingers and tilts his face upward, as though pondering abstract matters of great import. "While you were doing all this, did you feel under any time constraint?"

"No."

"But Cora Revels testified that on the night her sister died, she told you that Lincoln Turner was on his way to Natchez from Chicago."

"She never told me that. And besides, we now know Mr. Turner was in Natchez four days prior to his mother's death. All I knew about Lincoln Turner was that he hadn't visited his mother in all the weeks she'd been back in Natchez, despite the fact that she was dying."

A quick glance at Lincoln shows me rage in his face.

"What was the last thing Cora Revels told you on that night?" Quentin asks.

"That she was walking over to a neighbor's house to watch television and get some rest, if she could."

"So you'd found the tape intended for Mr. Sexton. What did you do then?"

"I left the house."

"Where did you go?"

"To my office. I wanted to think about everything Viola had told me. I didn't want to go home to do that. I also had a camcorder at my office that I could use to watch the videotape. When I got there, I watched the recording in its entirety, which was only a few minutes of footage."

"And what did it contain?"

"About what I expected. Some information relating to her brother's murder, to her own rapes, and also information about my history with Viola."

"Did you erase the tape at that time?"

"No. I wanted to. But I didn't feel I had the right. I wanted to discuss it with Viola later, to be sure she understood what could happen if she gave that information to a reporter. At that point I thought Viola would have several more days, perhaps even weeks, to make another tape, one that might be less damaging to me personally but still accomplish what she wanted to with Henry Sexton."

"She never got to make another tape, did she?"

Dad bites his lip and winces. "No."

"But you ultimately did erase that tape?"

"Yes. After a murder charge was filed against me, I decided it would be foolish to keep something like that around."

"How do you feel about erasing that tape now?"

"I've wished a thousand times that I never did it. So much pain would have been saved had I not."

Quentin nods slowly. "How long did you stay at your office, Doctor?"

"Till about five thirty A.M."

"Cora Revels testified that you called her about five twenty, which we now know was eighteen minutes before her sister's death."

"That's true. I called her cell and asked how Viola was doing. Cora told me she'd fallen asleep at the neighbor's house, but that she would go home to check on Viola. I asked her to call me back if there were any problems."

"Do you recall anything else about that conversation?"

"I had a feeling that Cora was worried Viola might have ended her life, with or without my help. I think Cora knew what Viola had been planning, up to a point. But she never raised the issue with me."

"Did Cora call you back?"

"No. I assumed that Viola was still sedated when Cora got home, so I went home and slept for about two hours, then showered and went to work as usual."

"How did you learn Viola had died?"

"My son called me about nine A.M. and informed me. He told me that the district attorney had telephoned him and was considering charges of assisted suicide."

"How did you feel about that?"

"I was stunned to hear that Viola had died, and more shocked that I hadn't been called about it."

"Did you know the cause of death at that point?"

"No. At that point, I assumed she had found a way to commit suicide, possibly with help, but I didn't know."

"You didn't worry that she had died from the morphine injection you gave her?"

Dad shakes his head. "I didn't consider that a serious possibility."

"And when did you learn she had died from an adrenaline overdose?"

"The next day. Again, from my son."

"What did you think about that news?"

"It made no sense whatever to me."

Here Quentin pauses, then rolls his chair to within a few feet of the jury and looks back at my father.

"Dr. Cage, who do you believe killed Viola Turner?"

Dad takes a deep breath, then answers with a cold edge of anger in his voice. "Snake Knox. I believe that Sonny Thornfield was also present, and possibly other people as well."

"Who are Snake Knox and Sonny Thornfield?"

"Members of a violent racist group called the Double Eagles, and the investigative targets of Henry Sexton, as well as the FBI."

"What reason would they have to kill Viola Turner?"

Shad looks like he's gearing up to start objecting, but so far he's held his fire.

"Viola had a long and tragic history with the Double Eagle group. Because of that history, both Knox and Thornfield had come to Viola's house just days before her death and threatened to kill her if she continued to talk to Henry Sexton. This exchange is what Viola had recorded on the audiotape I had looked for after injecting her with the morphine."

"Objection," Shad breaks in. "No such tape has been entered into evidence."

"Your Honor, the witness is testifying to what the decedent told him—"

"Hearsay, Your Honor," Shad objects.

Quentin is prepared for this objection. He smiles and says, "Your Honor, the testimony clearly falls under 803(24). All the criteria are met."

Judge Elder opens a small softbound book, licks his finger, and quickly pages through it. After a few seconds, he says, "Present sense impression . . . I'll allow it."

"Please continue, Dr. Cage," Quentin says with satisfaction.

"The Double Eagles had traced Viola to Chicago only a year after she left Natchez, and they told her that they would kill her if she ever returned here. Will Devine actually visited her in Chicago and made the threat."

"Objection, Your Honor," Shad says again. "Hearsay. That allegedly happened thirty-seven years ago, and neither Viola Turner nor Mr. Devine can substantiate any such threat."

Joe Elder reaches for his book again, but this time does not open it. "I'm going to sustain that."

Quentin could argue another exception to the hearsay rule, but he doesn't. As he and Dad continue, I'm surprised Shad doesn't object more often. Perhaps he knows that if he does, Quentin will argue that everything Viola said to Dad that night could be considered some sort of exception, as there are so many and Quentin undoubtedly knows them all. But more likely, Shad well knows that he induced his witnesses to break the hearsay rules almost continuously, making discretion the better part of valor now.

"Despite the Double Eagle threat," Dad says, "the recent one, Viola told Snake Knox and Sonny Thornfield that she would not stop talking to Mr. Sexton, and that they would have to kill her to shut her up."

Quentin's voice conveys surprise and more than a little skepticism. "Did Mrs. Turner call the police about this incident?"

"No."

"Why not?"

"Because she wanted those men to kill her."

CHAPTER 63

IT TAKES JUDGE Elder half a minute to silence the gallery after Dad's assertion that Viola had wanted the Double Eagles to kill her.

"I beg your pardon, Doctor?" Quentin says. "Are you suggesting that Viola Turner *wanted* to be murdered?"

"Yes, sir. She discussed it with me."

"Why would she want to be murdered?"

"So that the men who had destroyed her family would finally be punished."

"I think we're going to need you to explain that, Doctor."

Dad folds his hands together and speaks directly to the jury. For the first time, his voice begins to rise in volume, taking on some of its old power and persuasiveness.

"As has been testified already, Viola was gang-raped in 1968 by five members of the Double Eagle group. They were Frank Knox, Frank's teenage son Forrest, Frank's brother Snake, Sonny Thornfield, and Glenn Morehouse. Those men brutalized Viola for hours in her home. The trauma of this experience scarred her forever. Viola was never the same afterwards. She ended our relationship because of that crime, although she must have been pregnant by then. It's a miracle that the child survived at all, considering what they did to her."

Quentin appears to be as shocked as the audience by these statements. "And you're telling us that, for this reason, Viola was willing to be murdered? To punish the men who had raped her?"

"It's not that simple. Viola had suffered much more than rape at their hands. At the time Viola was assaulted, her brother, Jimmy, and another civil rights activist named Luther Davis were in hiding. The Double Eagles raped Viola in an effort to lure them into the open. And their plan worked. Jimmy and Luther did leave their refuge—a place called Freewoods—shortly after the rape, and then they disappeared. Of course, Viola also broke off her relationship with me shortly after the rape."

"How long had your affair been going on?"

"About seven weeks, in the physical sense. Emotionally, for much longer."

"How did she end the relationship?"

"Painfully." Dad closes his eyes briefly, like a man calling on deep reserves of fortitude. "Completely by chance, one of the men who had raped Viola was brought into our clinic for treatment. He had been seriously injured on the job."

I feel my pulse start to pick up again.

"Who was that?" Quentin asks.

"Frank Knox. He was hurt while working at the Triton Battery plant. I was the contract physician for that company. Knox should have been taken to the hospital, but his coworkers brought him to me. In those days we did a lot more aggressive trauma treatment in the office."

"What happened when Knox was brought in?"

"Viola initially refused to treat him. But she had always assisted me with trauma cases, so I insisted that she prep him. When I arrived in the surgery, however, I found Knox on the floor. His skin was blue and he was gasping for air."

Every person in the courtroom is on the edge of his seat.

"What was Viola doing?" Quentin asks.

"Standing by the table, watching him die."

"She wasn't trying to treat him?"

"No."

"What did you do?"

"I knelt and checked Knox's airway, then tried to find the source of his difficulty. He'd suffered terrible trauma. A pallet of car batteries had fallen on him, rupturing his chest wall. But I sensed that wasn't the source of his acute problem. I tried to get Viola to help me, but she refused. I actually got up and slapped her, but it did no good. When I asked why she wouldn't help, she told me that Frank Knox and several other men had raped her two days prior."

"Was that the first you'd heard of this rape?"

Dad's face remains stonelike, except for a brief movement of his lips. "Yes."

"What did you do then?"

"I asked why Knox was on the floor and in such bad shape. Viola told me she had injected air into a major vein. I could see the syringe she had used lying on the floor. A very large syringe."

"Air. In a vein. What would be the result of such an act?"

"A bubble of air in a blood vessel won't actually hurt you—not generally. But after questioning Viola, I learned that she'd injected Knox a total of three times. Probably two hundred cc's of air, maybe more. An air embolus of that size would kill the patient when it reached his heart. Knox probably couldn't have been saved even if he'd been in an urban trauma center."

"Nevertheless, did you do what you could to try to save him?"

Dad looks directly at the jury. "No."

This time the spectators make no sound at all. In fact, they are so silent that I can hear my heart pounding in my ears. My father has just admitted malpractice on the stand. And I am certain he is about to make it worse.

"No?" Quentin asks, as though shocked. "What *did* you do?"

"Nothing. Her answer had stunned me, but I was also enraged by what I'd heard about the gang rape. I couldn't bring myself to try to save the man who had done that. I heard a siren. An ambulance my staff had called arrived outside. After a moment's hesitation, I picked up the syringe Viola had used and hid it in a drawer."

Dad falls silent, as though replaying the incident in his mind is all that he can handle.

"And then . . . ?" Quentin prompts him.

"Then I watched Frank Knox die."

"Dear God," someone whispers behind me.

"Stop the trial," I whisper. "You can't let this go on." But of course Quentin's too far away to hear me.

"It didn't take very long," Dad says. "Maybe fifteen seconds."

"Why did you do that, Dr. Cage?"

"Because I didn't think he deserved to live."

I glance to my right. Shad Johnson's mouth is hanging almost slack with awe.

"What about your Hippocratic oath?" Quentin asks.

"I broke it," Dad says flatly.

"Do you regret that?"

"I can't say that I do. If I could live that situation over again, I'd probably do the same thing."

Quentin draws in a deep breath, then expels it in a long sigh. "So," he says in a conclusive tone, "Viola Turner murdered Frank Knox in your office?"

"Yes."

"Out of a desire for revenge?"

"I suppose so. I tend to think of it as a sort of delayed self-defense. Also an effort to prevent what had happened to her from happening to others."

"That sounds like a rationalization, Dr. Cage."

"It may be."

"Frank Knox was defenseless when Viola killed him, was he not?"

"As defenseless as she was when five men raped her."

"Just answer the questions, Doctor," Quentin says irritably. "And you stood by while he died. And then helped to conceal her crime?"

"Yes."

Oh, Jesus, I think, my heart threatening to go to full-blown tachycardia.

Quentin lets the awestruck silence stretch for a long time. The only sound I hear is Shad's pen scratching away on a legal pad.

"Was Frank Knox's death ever recognized as a murder?" Quentin asks.

"Not by the medical examiner. Some of Mr. Knox's confederates had suspicions, but nothing ever came of them."

"Why do you think they suspected that?"

"Because they kidnapped Viola the next day."

And with that Dad has the crowd again. The spectators behind me wouldn't give up their seats now if BATF agents came in yelling about another bomb threat.

"How did you learn that?" Quentin asks.

"Viola didn't show up for work. And she never missed work."

"Did you report your suspicion that she had been kidnapped to the police?"

"No."

"Why not?"

"I was the police physician. I knew that several local police officers were members of the Ku Klux Klan."

"I see. What *did* you do?

"I hired a patient of mine, a former policeman named Ray Presley, to find Viola."

An excited murmur runs through the crowd. The name Ray Presley is well known to many in the room.

"And did he? Find her, I mean?"

"Yes. Ray found Viola in a machine shop. She was being held prisoner by members of the Double Eagle group. Her brother and Luther Davis were also being held there."

"Did Presley ever tell you which Double Eagles were there?"

"No. But Viola named them on the videotape that I erased."

"Did she also describe the murder of Frank Knox on that tape?"

"She did. That's one of the reasons I erased it."

Several spectators croon with satisfaction as the pieces of the puzzle begin falling into place.

"Who did she name on the tape?" Quentin asks.

"The same men who had raped her before, plus some others. But dozens of men witnessed or took part in that crime. It was a nightmare. Frank Knox, Forrest Knox, Sonny Thornfield, and Morehouse are dead, but Snake Knox was attending these proceedings when Will Devine was murdered in this witness box."

"Objection," Shad snaps. "Assuming facts not in evidence."

"Sustained."

Joe Elder can sustain all he wants, but the jury's memory of Will Devine six feet from where Dad is sitting must make the malevolence of Snake Knox almost tangible in this room.

"What did Ray Presley do when he found Viola?" Quentin asks.

"He broke into the machine shop and freed her at gunpoint. She was being sexually abused at the time, by that much larger group of men."

Hisses of revulsion fill the courtroom, and I see Judge Elder's arm moving toward his gavel.

"What about Jimmy Revels and Luther Davis?"

"Ray left them behind."

The spectators can hardly contain themselves now. Dad's testimony about such events in their hometown beats any movie they will ever see.

"He abandoned those boys to the mercy of known killers?" Quentin asks. "Why?"

"Ray didn't believe he would get out alive if he tried to take them, too. Or if he did, he wouldn't escape retribution later. Presley worked on both sides of the law, and he had complex loyalties."

"But he was loyal enough to you to rescue Viola from the Double Eagles?"

"He owed me a favor. More than one, actually."

"How did Viola react to the fact that her brother had been left behind?"

"It was too much for her. She snapped. Her brother and Davis had been tortured in front of her, and she was certain they would be murdered by the Double Eagles. As we know now, they were."

"Why didn't you contact the FBI at that point?"

"Because I was afraid that what had happened to Frank Knox in my office would be uncovered."

"Did Viola share your concern about being charged with murder?"

Dad reflects on this. "Not at that time. She was hysterical. She would have sacrificed her life to free her brother."

"But you wouldn't?"

"I couldn't take that risk. I had young children. Viola didn't. Her husband had been killed in Vietnam. She was pretty much alone. I see now that her urge to protect her brother was as strong as my urge to protect my children. But . . ."

"Go on, Doctor."

"I was fairly certain that her brother and Mr. Davis were already dead by the time I got the story out of her and Ray."

"And were they?"

"I don't think anybody knows for sure."

"What happened after Viola was rescued, Doctor?"

"I hid her for several days. The Double Eagles were scouring the county for her."

"Where did you hide her?"

"I enlisted the help of Nellie Jackson, a black madam who was a patient of mine. Nellie first hid Viola at her place of business, then at a rental house she owned."

The very mention of Nellie Jackson is titillating to the Natchezians in the crowd. A soft buzz of conversation rises, then dies under Judge Elder's glare.

"What was your intention at this time?"

"Just to keep Viola alive. I had to sedate her several times. She was going out of her mind. She said many times that she wished I'd left her to die with her brother."

Quentin shakes his head as though he can hardly believe this tragic tale. "How was this situation finally resolved, Doctor?"

"I had about decided to take Viola to the FBI when she disappeared."

"Disappeared? What did you think had happened to her? Did you think the Klan had found her?"

"For a couple of hours I did. But then I found out she'd given Nellie a note for me. Viola wrote that she was certain her brother was dead, and she couldn't bear to stay in Natchez anymore. She said she loved me, but that there was no future for us and never had been. She told me not to look for her. That was all. Nellie told me one of her men had driven Viola up to the train station in Memphis, but beyond that, she wouldn't tell me anything."

"And the next you heard of Viola was the letter that came to your office, from a P.O. box in Chicago?"

"That's correct."

"When was the next personal contact between you and Viola Turner?"

"Ten weeks before she died, when she called my office and told me that she was dying, and that she intended to come home to do it."

Quentin gives the jury time to digest this. "You're saying that thirty-seven years passed without any direct contact between the two of you?"

"That's right. Just the checks. A couple of times I put a note in with my check, asking if she was well, that kind of thing. But Viola never responded."

"I see." Quentin rotates his wheelchair to face the jury. "So in the eyes of Snake Knox, Viola had not only returned to Natchez—an act for which the Double Eagles had vowed to kill her—but was also talking to Henry Sexton, a reporter actively investigating unsolved murders committed by the Double Eagle group."

"That's correct."

"And you believe Snake Knox had some suspicion that Mrs. Turner had killed his brother Frank back in 1968?"

"I can't be sure of that. I believe he did."

Quentin nods slowly. "Dr. Cage, after you left Cora Revels's house, did you see or hear anything that led you to believe that the Double Eagles might have been involved in Viola's death?"

"Yes. As I drove away that night, down Pine Ridge Road, I saw a pickup truck parked on the shoulder near the turn to Cora's house. In the trees, the way you see trucks parked when people are hunting deer. But I didn't see any people inside it."

"Was there anything remarkable about this truck?"

"There was a sticker on the back windshield. A big yellow 'D.'"

"And what does that sticker stand for?"

Almost everyone in this room knows that sticker is the emblem of Darlington Academy, a predominantly white school founded the year that the federal courts began enforcing desegregation in our area.

"Darlington Academy," Dad says. "Later on, after I'd been charged with Viola's murder, Walt Garrity and I tracked down that truck. I hoped the owner would turn out to be Snake Knox, but it belonged to Will Devine."

"The Double Eagle murdered in this court yesterday."

"Yes. Devine lived less than a mile away from Knox, and I believe Knox took his truck that night to threaten or kill Viola."

Shad doesn't bother to object. Dad has already convicted himself of murder—or accessory after the fact, in any case. Which makes me wonder what in God's name Quentin thinks he's doing. I half expected Dad to destroy himself on the stand, but not this. *Quentin is helping him do it.*

Quentin rolls closer to the witness box. "You've given us a lot to process, Doctor. But let's return to the rather astonishing statement you made a few minutes ago. That Viola Turner wanted Knox and Thornfield to murder her."

"All right."

"Did you mean that literally?"

Dad bites his lip and stares at the floor for several seconds. "Yes and no," he says finally. "Nobody wants to be murdered. But Viola had flagrantly defied a credible death threat in order to come home and die under my care. Once here, the threat against her was renewed, and by the very men who had raped her and murdered her brother. They had escaped punishment for four decades. Viola knew she was going to die in any case. If, by her death, she could ensure that those men would meet justice . . . I think she would have made that bargain."

"But how could that have been arranged?"

"I don't know exactly. But maybe that had something to do with Henry's camera setup and the tapes he left there. Maybe Viola hoped to catch them in the act. Record her own murder. I think the only two people who could have answered that question are dead."

Quentin appears to be analyzing this theory. As he does, the genius of it hits me with bracing force. *Dad has just justified the existence of another videotape in a way that doesn't implicate him.* So long as the Dumpster tape cannot be restored, he's dodged the only damage it can do in its erased state. The sheer audacity of this move is stunning. He's bet everything on black—a fifty-fifty shot that the Bureau won't be able to restore that tape. But why? We already know that they've managed to restore Henry's tape. Why should Dad be more confident about the Dumpster tape? Is it possible that he's telling the truth about his theory of Viola planning to provoke Snake to kill her?

"Mr. Avery?" Judge Elder prompts. "Have you completed your examination?"

"Ah . . . I beg your pardon, Judge. I was having a senior moment." Quentin turns back to Dad. "So, Doctor, when you left the Revels house, you believed that Viola was mildly sedated and would wake up no worse off than she had been before the morphine injection?"

"Exactly."

"Thank you." Quentin rolls back to his table as though finished, but then, as though just remembering something, he says, "Dr. Cage, did you honor the promise that Viola Turner asked you to make?"

"Which promise?"

"The promise to take care of her son in the future?"

"Yes. I set up a trust that will begin releasing funds to him when he's fifty years old."

"Objection!" Shad cries with surprising force. "Whatever scheme

Dr. Cage may have set up, he obviously did it to try to mend fences with the man who was pushing the murder charges against him."

"Not true, Your Honor," Quentin says, lifting an inch-thick sheaf of legal-size paper off his table. "Nine days after Viola Turner's death, Dr. Cage established an irrevocable trust for Lincoln Turner. My wife, a licensed attorney, is the trustee. That trust contains three hundred thousand dollars, and even if Dr. Cage is found guilty, it cannot be revoked. I can also assure you that Mr. Turner knew nothing about it until this moment. I ask that this trust be entered into evidence as Defense Exhibit Six."

Glancing back at Lincoln, I see that he's more surprised than anyone by this revelation.

Judge Elder looks put out by the radical turn this trial has taken. "Do you have any further questions, Mr. Avery?"

"Not at this time, Your Honor."

Judge Elder regards Quentin in stern silence, his eyes filled with reproof. Then he turns to the prosecution table. "Your witness, Mr. Johnson."

For the first time since this trial began, Shadrach Johnson appears to be at a loss for words.

CHAPTER 64

"I DON'T THINK I've ever seen a witness get on the stand and confess to murder without being forced or tricked into it," Shad Johnson begins.

My father regards Shad without much interest. "Is that a question?"

"The question, Dr. Cage, is why? Why did you confess to that crime? Why, after thirty-eight years of silence, did you admit to being an accessory to murder in court, and open yourself to further charges by the State?"

Dad takes a long breath. "I want people to understand the depth of hatred that existed between the Double Eagle group and Viola Turner. And more than that, I want them to know the truth."

Hallelujah, says a voice in my head. *And the truth shall set you in Parchman Farm.*

"I don't think that's the reason," Shad says, half turning toward the jury. "I've been sitting there asking myself why you did that. It took me a minute, but now I know. You're being very subtle, you and your attorney. You're doing something that Lincoln Turner described yesterday in his moment of greatest anger, only he didn't know then how prescient his assessment would prove to be."

Shad faces the jury. "Lincoln warned us that Dr. Cage and his lawyer were doing exactly what his stepfather had trained him to do—what all con men and magicians do. They get us to focus on one hand while the other dips into our pockets and does the real business. Well, ladies and gentlemen, that's what is happening before our eyes."

Every eye in the jury box is on Shad, waiting for him to tell them how they're being tricked. Shad looks back at Dad.

"You admitted to helping Viola kill Frank Knox because in hindsight that killing looks justified—even heroic. Remember the so-called DA's test that Mr. Avery told us about in his opening statement? His famous two questions? One: *Did the victim need killing?* And two: *Did the right person do the killing?* Well, in Frank Knox's case, the answer to both questions would be a resounding *yes,* at least in our hearts. Admitting to helping kill a gang rapist and murderer might technically carry a penalty, but it buys you an enormous amount of sympathy from the jury. By forthrightly confessing to one killing, you hope to buy our faith that you're telling the truth when you deny a different one. You draw our attention to Frank Knox with one hand, while the other injects Viola Turner with deadly adrenaline. But *we will not be taken in*. Killing Viola Turner was a vile, shameful act—"

"Your Honor," Quentin says in a weary voice, "did I fall asleep and wake up for the district attorney's closing argument? I thought this was supposed be a cross-examination."

Several lawyers titter in the rows behind me, but Joe Elder silences them with his dark eyes.

Shad turns back to my father. "There's another reason you spoke so openly about that murder. It's because you're afraid that very soon we will be viewing the tape that Viola Turner made for Henry Sexton. And when that happens, we will find out about that crime in any case."

Dad says nothing to this, and his face betrays no more.

"Isn't that why you confessed to helping to commit and conceal that crime, Dr. Cage?"

"I'm not that devious, Mr. Johnson."

"Don't sell yourself short, Doctor. You were devious enough to carry on a secret affair with your employee while you were married. Devious enough to send her money for thirty-seven years without your family's knowledge. Devious enough to conceal your part in a murder for the same amount of time. You've admitted all this under oath."

Devious my father may be, but I'm betting his reckless honesty and conviction moved at least one or two jury members.

"Mr. Johnson," Dad replies, "the only thing you just listed that felt wrong to me was having the affair. Hiding it from my wife. A few minutes ago, I swore to tell the whole truth and nothing but. I intend to do that, come hell or high water. What happened back then has been secret for too long. That's why I admitted my part in Frank Knox's murder. That son of a bitch deserved to die, and whoever killed Viola deserves the same treatment."

Shad starts to protest, but in the end he settles for shaking his head in amazement.

"Do you know what strikes me most about your testimony, Doctor? That so little of it can be substantiated. Oh, it's a known fact that Snake Knox was a member of the Double Eagle group. But there's no proof whatever that he or anyone else threatened to kill Viola Turner. No one has come forward with any audiotape, and the police found nothing like that at the crime scene."

When I glance back at Lincoln, I find him staring a hole through me. He knows that such a tape exists—or did—yet he says nothing. Would he sell me that tape for a million dollars now? Or would he rather watch his father twist in the wind? *Or has he taken the choice out of his own hands by destroying it, as he threatened to do?*

"The things you attribute to Will Devine cannot be substantiated," Shad goes on, "for the man himself is dead."

"Murdered before our eyes," Dad responds. "After coming forward voluntarily to testify against his former comrades in arms. Don't you find that a little suspicious?"

Shad's temper shows in his taut smile. "Dr. Cage, I can't account for the private feuds of former Ku Klux Klansmen. If Mr. Devine corroborated any of your statements on the record before he died, I'd certainly welcome seeing the evidence. But my understanding is that Mr. Devine refused to tell the FBI anything about what he was going to say on the stand."

Dad shrugs. "I believe Mr. Devine meant to unburden his soul before he died. I can relate to that sentiment."

"Can you really? As for all you claim that Viola Turner said on the night she died, we have only your word for it—you, the man accused of killing her. And that brings us to the only evidence we may actually be able to use to test you. The erased videotapes."

Again Dad shows no reaction.

"Dr. Cage, you admitted that you erased one tape after Mrs. Turner's death because it contained information you couldn't bear to have made public."

"I didn't say I couldn't bear it. I said I would prefer my wife and children not have to deal with it."

"Hair-splitting, Doctor. But what I wonder is, what else did that tape contain? Did it show you killing Viola Turner?"

"No."

"You're under oath, sir."

"It couldn't have shown that. Because I didn't kill Viola."

I shake my head, knowing that Shad's sole objective is to elicit statements from my father that the tapes will prove were lies.

"Did it show you injecting her with morphine?"

"No."

"Do you appear on that tape at all?"

"No. Viola finished making that tape before I ever arrived at the house that night. She talked about me on it, but that's all."

God, I hope he's telling the truth. Surely he knows he must—

"Let's talk about the tape that *was* in the video camera when you arrived."

"I didn't know there was a tape in that camera."

"Goddamn it," I mutter under my breath. "That tears it." *If Shad ever proves he knew about that tape, much less erased it in an MRI machine, Dad will be convicted of murder.*

Shad says, "I would find it very difficult to believe that someone would begin the process of euthanasia with a live camera pointed at the sickbed."

"I'd have to agree with you there," Dad replies, and several people in the audience chuckle.

"What I'm suggesting is that you must have checked that camera to make sure it wasn't recording. At least made sure the red light wasn't on."

Dad shrugs. "I don't recall seeing any red light."

"So you deny, under oath, any knowledge of a videotape that might have recorded Viola Turner's murder or events shortly before it?"

"Yes."

As Dad awaits the next question, I realize that even if the Dumpster tape is restored and shows Dad inside Cora's house, that doesn't mean he knew anything about it. Nor does it prove that he erased it in an MRI machine.

"Listen to me carefully, Doctor. Did you remove one or two tapes from the Revels house that night?"

"One."

"Did you erase a Sony mini-DV tape in the MRI machine at St. Catherine's Hospital?"

This time Dad hesitates before answering. But after a few seconds, he says, "I did not."

What will he do if John Kaiser walks in here with a fully restored Dumpster tape . . . ?

"I only know of one tape," Dad continues. "The one Viola made for Henry Sexton."

As my father falls silent, I am filled with a horrific conviction that he is lying. He's making a brazen gamble, betting his life on his belief that the FBI won't be able to bring that Dumpster tape back from the dead. And that is exactly what Shad wanted him to do. The whole cross up to this point was designed to take Dad to this assertion.

"Well, Doctor," Shad says, "I think we're going to be able to judge that for ourselves in due course. Now, I'd like to—"

The door at the back of the courtroom stops Shad in midsentence. Sheriff Billy Byrd steps inside. Catching Shad's eye, he raises one finger to his right cheek. Shad goes still. Then he holds up two fingers and raises a single eyebrow. Billy Byrd turns up his palms.

"Your Honor," says Quentin, "the district attorney and the sheriff appear to be practicing baseball signals."

"I see that, Mr. Avery. Mr. Johnson?"

My cell phone vibrates in my pocket. With a sickening sense of dread, I pull out the device, already certain of what it will say.

"Your Honor," Shad says, "I believe we're about to find out just how truthful the defendant has been with us today."

"Is that so? Please explain."

John Kaiser's newest text message flashes onto my phone screen with the impact of a prison sentence.

The Attorney General just signed off on permission for restored Tape S-15 (tape from Roadtrek) to be used in the trial. Faxing copy of the signed order to Judge Elder's office. I'm 15 minutes from Natchez on a

Bureau chopper. Will land at Fort Rosalie. I will personally deliver the disk to the courtroom. No luck with S-16 (Dumpster tape) yet. Cannot predict success or failure.

A shudder runs through my body. Like voices from the grave, the restored videotapes could damn my father as a facile liar and a murderer. While I try to regain my composure, Shad announces that the FBI will shortly deliver a restored copy of the tape Viola made for Henry Sexton and may soon provide a usable version of the tape Sheriff Byrd's men found in the hospital Dumpster. Then Judge Elder grants a one-hour recess to await the tape and view it before presenting it to the jury.

CHAPTER 65

AFTER KAISER DELIVERED the restored videotape, Judge Elder asked the attorneys back to his chambers to view it. I tried to accompany Quentin, of course, but he told me that Dad didn't want me in the room. I absorbed this blow as I had all the others, with little grace and less charity, and spent the recess with my mother, trying to keep up her spirits while two men set up a large screen against the wall opposite the jury box.

When counsel finally returns from their private premiere and court is called to order, Quentin's face and manner tell me nothing. I try to catch his eye, but he remains focused on the defense table as he drives his wheelchair to it. Judge Elder makes a few remarks about the chain of custody, and the restored tape is entered into evidence as State's Exhibit 18.

Then the lights go down.

At first we see nothing. Then several bright flashes hit the screen. I hear Judge Elder grumbling. When the FBI agent tasked with projecting the restored video file finally succeeds in opening an image on the screen, I don't see what I expected. The whole image is rendered in shades of blue, which by itself would not be too bad, but the resolution is very grainy. Besides that, the whole visual field is obscured by hundreds of flickering artifacts, some—bizarrely enough—bright pinks and greens. But the longer the tape runs, the more my mind adapts to what it's seeing. What at first seemed only a hazy outline of the sickroom I saw so clearly on Henry's accidental hard-drive recording soon becomes a familiar scene, like that same sickroom illuminated by a dim blue nightlight. And in the middle of the frame, a little left of center, is the woman at the heart of this case.

In America, we don't often see people in their final days prior to death, not even in photographs. For those unused to the sight, it can be a significant shock. The emaciation in particular triggers a natural revulsion in healthy people. I saw this when my first wife died of cancer, and I never really got used to it. The faces of the jury members tell me that despite having seen the hard drive recording of Viola in her death throes, most were unprepared for the sight of the wraithlike figure propped motionless in the hospital bed, staring into the camera lens. Only Viola's eyes, like wet stones, project any sense of life from the screen. But when she begins to speak, the hoarse but articulate voice lifts me erect in my seat.

"*Hello, Henry,*" Viola begins. "*I can't speak too well. I can't catch my breath.*

"*You asked me to talk about Jimmy, and what I might know about what happened to him. You asked me to talk about my life as well. I don't have the strength for much of that. But some of what I went through is tied up with what happened to Jimmy. I took a shot of cortisone this morning, and some morphine a few minutes ago. I drank some sweet tea for the sugar, too, so I might have the energy to talk three or four minutes.*

"*After my husband was killed in Vietnam, I was very lonely. That was 1967. About a year went by when it was all I could do to put one foot in front of the other, and get my work done. I was empty. Hollowed out. The only thing I could feel was worry—about Jimmy, who was working with the NAACP, and doing other things to help the Movement. But then, somehow, I fell in love with my boss, Dr. Tom Cage. I knew it was wrong, him being married, but I couldn't turn away from that feeling he gave me. It was . . . the only thing that made me feel alive.*

"*But as good as that was, things started going bad very quickly. It was hard times for black folks, as you know. The Klan was everywhere, killing people on both sides of the river. What brought Tom and me together finally was that Jimmy and his friend Luther got into a scrape with some Klansmen. Part of that group you're investigating now. But back then I just knew them as Klan. Most worked at Triton Battery, or out at the paper mill. One time I woke Dr. Cage at midnight to come patch up Jimmy, and he came, God bless him. Then the Klan who'd been in the fight showed up at the office, too. We hid in a treatment room till Tom got rid of them. Then he patched up Luther and Jimmy. That was when I first knew something was going to happen be-*

tween Tom and me. That sooner or later we'd consummate whatever we'd been feeling.

"After that night, the Klan started hunting all over for Jimmy. Finally he went to hide out in Freewoods, which you know about from your work. Jimmy stayed there a few weeks, and it was during this time that Tom and I had our affair. It was like a dream, looking back. But you can't commit a mortal sin and expect to get off easy. As soon as I missed my time that month, I knew I was pregnant. I didn't tell Tom about it, for fear he might do something crazy, like leave his family, even though the selfish part of me wanted that very thing.

"Then the nightmare began. I came home from work one day and found five men waiting for me. I recognized them from the office. It was Frank Knox, his brother Snake, Sonny Thornfield, and a big fat boy named Glenn Morehouse. There was a boy with them, too. Now I know that was Forrest Knox, the state police man. They held me down and forced themselves on me. They stuffed a dishrag in my mouth to stop me screaming. Then they all took turns. They sodomized me, like it says in the Bible. I'm speaking as a nurse now, but they tore me up pretty bad inside. One of them used a Coke bottle. The whole time, they told me they were going to kill my brother when he came to get revenge for what they were doing. I knew I'd never breathe a word of what they'd done, but it didn't matter. They spread the word themselves, and Jimmy did just what they knew he would.

"I got word that Jimmy and Luther had left Freewoods, and nobody had seen him or Luther since. I was going out of my mind. Then God smiled on me. Or maybe it was Satan, tempting me, I don't know. But I went in to work, and those same men brought in Frank Knox, half-dead from a bunch of batteries falling on him. As soon as I got into the room alone with him, I knew I was going to make sure he went the rest of the way. His side was split open, and there was a good-size vein showing. I took the biggest syringe we had, filled it up with air, and shot it into that vein. I did that twice, then once in the antecubital. It took longer than I expected, but that air hit that man's heart like Daddy's twelve-pound maul, and that was the end of Frank Knox.

"When Tom came in to treat him, Frank was about gone. Tom asked why I wasn't trying to save him. That's when I told Tom what they'd done to me. He stopped what he was doing then and tried to comfort me. When we heard a siren, he hid the syringe and made things look like they should have looked. Once the ambulance men got there, Tom told them Knox had expired from his wounds.

"Lord, I'm losing my breath." Viola takes a drink of water. *"I told Tom*

our affair was over that day. But that didn't spare us any pain. The next night Knox's gang grabbed me out of my house about two in the morning. They took me to a machine shop out in the county. A place they used to question people. They had special equipment out there, for hurting people. You could see old blood on it. They had knives and chains and iron bars and torches. I . . . don't want to talk about that.

"Anyway, that's where Jimmy and Luther were being held. They were both in bad shape by the time I got there, but the Klansmen never let up on them. Thornfield kept at them about them running guns, and something about Black Muslims, but I don't think Jimmy or Luther knew anything about that. If they had, they would have talked, bad as those men were hurting them. Snake Knox skinned off Jimmy's navy tattoo with a knife. The others raped me some more, right in front of Jimmy. It was like the old nuns used to describe hell in my grade school. Like those forbidden paintings from the Middle Ages. I don't even know how long I was in that place. Maybe that's why they say hell is eternal.

"But then a man sneaked in there with a big pistol and took me out. He was Ray Presley, a man so mean that even the Klan was scared of him. He'd been a dirty cop down in New Orleans, and he knew everybody on both sides of the law. Presley had something he held over Dr. Cage, but he liked him, too. Presley saved me as a favor to Tom."

With a quivering hand, Viola takes another tiny sip of water. *"But Presley didn't save Jimmy. Luther, neither. Something broke inside me that night, when Presley dragged me out of there screaming. I knew those men were going to kill my brother. Presley knew it, too. He told me nothing could change that, not even President Johnson. It was just the way things were. And I guess he was right.*

"There's not much to tell after that. I don't have any firsthand knowledge of how Jimmy died or where they hid his body. I didn't see those men kill Jimmy or Luther, though they shot Luther in the arm with a pistol while I was there. The bullet broke the bone. They were both still alive when Presley took me out of there, but my opinion as a nurse is that without medical attention, they would have died from their wounds, or from shock.

"After that . . . it's all a blur. Tom tried to hide me, and Miss Nellie Jackson helped him do it. She was a good woman, though she'd been a prostitute and ran girls down on Rankin Street. They saved my life by doing that, but the fact is, I didn't care anymore whether I lived or died. I knew I was carrying a child, but not even that mattered to me. I don't think I expected to live the

nine months till it was born. About a week later, I went north to Chicago. And that's where I stayed, until I got lung cancer."

At this point, Viola ceases speaking. She pants softly for about forty seconds, her eyes half-closed. Just when I think she's falling asleep, she starts awake, focuses on the camera, and begins speaking again.

"Things didn't go too well for me up north. But how could they, when you think about what had brought me there? I did what I could to protect Tom. He sent money every month, and I never asked more of him. There were times I thought of telling him we had a child together, but I knew if he knew that, his life would be torture, the way mine was. I couldn't do that to him. I had walked willingly into sin, and it was up to me to live with it. I may be flattering myself—and you may not believe it, seeing the way I look now—but I think Tom suffered enough all those years just from giving me up. He loved me, and he'd wanted to be with me. I was the one who ended it. So he lived with his pain, and I lived with mine.

"Henry . . . I'm about out of breath. I don't have much strength left, and I don't intend to hang around this earth until my sister has to wipe my backside. I can take the pain, but I can't give up my pride. I've tended too many people to the bitter end. After tonight, or maybe tomorrow, I'll be gone. So I want to say some last things.

"I've done what I told you about my will. I wrote it myself, and Cora witnessed it. Some hard things passed between us over the years, but we made up in the end, the way sisters should. Still . . . if there's any problem about the money, you'll have this tape to back you up. I also told Tom to make sure there was no trouble about you getting your money, just in case Cora gets weak, or Lincoln turns her head. As for your part, you promised you'd do all in your power to bring Jimmy's killers to justice, and tell the world what happened to him. What happened to me, I'd just as soon keep private, but I'll leave that to you. I want you to keep Tom's part in Frank Knox's death secret until after he's dead. I don't expect that'll be too long. Tom's heart is in bad shape, and he's got other health problems. He'll be following me pretty soon. Maybe we'll be together after all, somewhere. Lord knows we earned it, even if we're together in the bad place. I could have lied to protect him on here, but I'm done lying now. Even for him."

Viola is silent for several seconds. Then she says, *"Lord, I almost forgot. A few other men came and went during the questioning at the machine shop. Some came just to look at me naked, I think. Others came to see the boys naked. They made a big fuss over Luther's private parts. But I didn't know those men. They were familiar, like I'd seen them on the street or at the Woolco, but I couldn't name them. They were bad men, though. One of them got the idea that Luther and Jimmy should take a turn with me."* Viola shakes her head at the memory. *"That's when they shot Luther. But he still wouldn't do it. I hope that with God's help you can bring those men to justice someday. I fear they've caused a lot of suffering in the years they've trod this earth. For wives and children mostly, I imagine.*

"That's really all I have the strength for, Henry. It seems strange to me that it's a white man coming after all these years to dig up the truth. I wish it was a black man, I won't lie. But maybe that says something about the future. I don't really understand the world anymore. But maybe there's some faint hope that the good people on both sides can come together. I appreciate all you've done. When things get hard for you, try to be strong, as I have, and don't be afraid to lean on the Lord. I believe He sent you here for a purpose, Henry. You've done good work coming this far, but it won't mean a thing if you don't go the rest of the way. I wish I could walk it with you. God bless you and keep you."

Viola holds up the remote, and then the screen goes black.

When the courtroom lights come up, with a harsh glare, the hush is like that in a cathedral during the funeral of a martyr. When Rusty pokes me in the side, I want to slap him. A smart-ass comment from the eternal cynic is the last thing I want to hear. But when his moist breath touches my ear, Rusty says, "If Shad stands up and says a word against that woman, the jury will rise as one and beat him to the floor."

"Mr. Johnson," says Judge Elder, "do you have any questions or points to make?"

"Your Honor, is there any word from the FBI on whether the Dumpster tape has been similarly restored?"

"Agent Kaiser?" Judge Elder prompts.

"Not yet, Your Honor. As the Sony engineers reported, Exhibit S-16 appears to have been much more thoroughly erased than the first. But if they make a breakthrough, clearance has been given to transmit an encrypted version of the tape to me, and I will be able to play it for the court."

"Thank you. Mr. Johnson?"

"Your Honor, I would like to recall Dr. Cage to continue my cross-examination."

Joe Elder glances at his watch. "Very well."

CHAPTER 66

"LET'S GO BACK to the night Viola Turner died," Shad says, rising from his table and looking hard at my father. "Not your fantasies, just provable facts. We know that you were at Cora Revels's house that night. We know you were alone with the victim. You have admitted injecting morphine into her. We know that you always carry adrenaline in your 'black bag,' as you call it. We also know that when Cora Revels returned to her house, she found her sister dead. We have no evidence indicating that anyone else was in that house between the time you left and the time Cora Revels arrived. No witnesses to intruders, no forensic evidence that arouses suspicion of anyone else. Just the dead body of a woman whom you admit you went to that house to kill."

"Another soliloquy, Your Honor?" Quentin asks in a seemingly bored voice.

"Get to your question, Counselor," Judge Elder admonishes.

Shad's jaw tightens, but he focuses his anger on Dad. "On the hard-drive recording of the victim's death, she cried out your name. Can you explain that?"

"I was her physician. I had been coming to the house almost every night for weeks. I was her former lover. I think it's natural that she would call out to me in a moment of terror and pain. Her mother was dead. Her son was far away, at least in her mind—"

"Don't try to change the subject, Doctor. Did you always take your medical bag with you when you visited Cora Revels's house?"

"Not always. I kept some supplies at her house."

"But you took it with you on that night."

"Yes. Obviously that night was different from any other."

"Because you intended to kill your patient."

"To help her commit suicide," Dad clarifies.

"Was there any adrenaline in Cora Revels's house?"

"Not that I knew of. Viola had signed a Do Not Resuscitate order, so I didn't keep any there."

"Have you ever given any patient a lethal injection of drugs, Dr. Cage? I'm talking about during the usual practice of medicine, not in wartime."

There are only two acceptable answers to this question: "No" and "I decline to answer on the grounds that it may incriminate me." But my father says, "On very rare occasions, I have."

This unexpected gift stuns Shad speechless for a moment. "What occasions would those be?"

Dad takes his time with this, and he addresses the jury, not Shad, when he speaks. "When the line between agony and consciousness disappeared. When pain and terror could no longer be controlled. That doesn't often happen, but when it does . . . it's an awful thing to witness. I have hastened the death of a few patients in those dire circumstances, usually only by a few hours. A day or two, at most."

"Are you aware that is a crime, Doctor?"

Dad returns Shad's indignant glare with a physician's disdain for mincing lawyers. "What do you think, Counselor?"

"Your Honor?" Shad prompts.

"Answer the question, Doctor."

"Yes, I know that's against the law."

I cringe at my father's words, but after four days of trial, his frank answers are like cold, refreshing water thrown in the faces of the jury. It's plain to everyone that Dad could easily have denied assisting patients to die, just as he could have denied having adrenaline with him on the night Viola died. He is making statements against his own interest, and this ultimately bolsters his claim that he's telling the truth regardless of the risk to himself. *And that, of course, is the behavior of only two kinds of people: the insane and the innocent.*

"But despite having euthanized patients before," Shad presses, "you did not attempt to euthanize Mrs. Turner on the night in question?"

"That's correct. I pushed the needle through her vein to be sure I did not inject a lethal dose. My goal was simply to buy time, for myself and for Viola."

It's all about that Dumpster tape, I think. Shad is waiting for that recording to appear like God from a machine, literally, to do his work for him.

Shad pauses, head cocked and eyes on my father, as he decides which interrogatory path to take next. He might be a surgeon choosing a scalpel. As he stands there, all eyes upon him, my phone vibrates in my pocket. As covertly as possible I take it out and read the text, which is from John Kaiser.

Classified Tech Division of the Crime Lab reports they are unable to restore tape S-16 to usable form. Particles too scrambled for any coherent reconstruction. I'm about to give Johnson the news.

The sensation of watching John Kaiser walk up to the assistant DA seated behind Shad's table, and then that ADA walk to his boss and whisper in his ear, is one of the more delicious experiences I've had in a long time. Shad's mouth goes slack, then he whips his head to the side in search of Kaiser, who is kneeling by the prosecution table. Leaving his assistant, Shad hurries to his table and engages Kaiser in a frenzied exchange of whispers.

"Mr. Johnson?" asks the judge. "Would you share with us what is going on? Are we about to see another tape?"

"I'm not sure, Your Honor. There's some confusion about that. Would the court grant me sixty seconds to verify something with the FBI by telephone?"

"Is Agent Kaiser unable to give you the information you need?"

Shad grimaces, his eyes burning. "The State requests sixty seconds, Your Honor."

Joe Elder sighs with resentment. "If you must."

While everyone in the courtroom stares, Shad texts someone, then makes a call. A moment later, he's speaking in angry whispers once more. His voice is punctuated by brief silences, but his volume increases after each one. With five seconds remaining of his allotted minute, he hangs up and stands to face the judge.

"Mr. Johnson?"

"Your Honor, the FBI reports that the crime lab will be unable to restore the tape found in the St. Catherine's Hospital Dumpster. The magnetic information was too scrambled to repair."

Judge Elder listens with interest, then purses his lips in thought. "Would more time increase the odds of a successful outcome?"

Shad looks like a schoolboy about to either break into tears or punch somebody in the mouth. "I'm told it would not, Judge. That information is gone. The magnets in that MRI machine basically obliterated it."

I shift my focus to my father, who once again is wearing a mask of sober reflection. But in his posture I sense a change that I can only describe as relaxation. He appears not to have changed position, but I've known him so long that I see things in him others can't. Thirty seconds ago, there was a profound tension in him, an electric current holding his muscles rigid, his face immobile. He was like a gambler with all his holdings sitting on the table, waiting for the turn of a single card. Now he looks like that gambler after the card turned his way.

My God, I think, watching Shad try to adapt to this new reality. Shad was the gambler on the other side of that bet, and he must feel he has lost everything. He stands there with every eye upon him, making a silent inventory of his remaining assets. I can't see that he has many.

"Mr. Johnson, please proceed," says Judge Elder.

"Yes, Your Honor."

Shad said the words, but it takes him a few seconds to get his feet moving. Once he does, he walks to within about eight feet of the witness box and addresses my father again.

"Dr. Cage, what's the purpose of the adrenaline you carry in your black bag?"

"I carry a one ten-thousandth dilution, for IV administration, and also a one one-thousandth dilution for intramuscular injection. Adrenaline has many uses in emergencies. Treating anaphylactic shock, for example. Allergies to things like bee stings or peanut oil. And of course, treating cardiac emergencies. I've always kept an ampoule of adrenaline nearby because of my own cardiovascular disease. Sort of my own personal crash cart. A lot of older doctors do that."

"And did you have adrenaline with you on the night Viola Turner died?"

"I did. As Melba Price testified was likely, I believe."

"Did you inject that adrenaline into Viola Turner on the night she died?"

"I did not."

Shad breaks his rhythm here, and I realize he's not sure where to go from here. He looks into the gallery, then up to the balcony. In the end he seems to settle on the face of Lincoln Turner, who's watching him with desperate hope in his face. Almost imperceptibly, Shad nods, then turns back to my father.

"Dr. Cage, I believe a lot of what you've told us is true. The most effective deceptions are always based on truth, after all. But let me suggest an alternate scenario to you. After a lifetime of keeping secrets, Viola Turner wanted to unburden herself. She'd left a brief record of certain events for Henry Sexton, a reporter, that included her romance with you, your paternity of her son, and the murder of Frank Knox. And she told you she had done this. Why? Because like a lot of people in this room, Viola believed you were a better man than you are. And you played right along, didn't you? Because all you had to do was carry out your side of the pact. She would be dead in a few minutes, and you'd have that tape, and once you erased it, no one would ever be able to prove what was on it. What could be more perfect? She'd asked you to kill her yourself, after all. The irony is almost unbearable."

Dad seems to be focused on a spot on the floor, not his questioner.

"But something happened that you didn't expect. Something made you panic. And I think it was the moment you realized there was a tape in Henry's video camera, recording everything."

Dad looks up slowly, like a tired old bear noticing some distant figure that might be either predator or prey.

"Who put that tape there, I don't know," Shad admits. "Maybe Viola's sister, as Cora Revels testified. Maybe even Lincoln Turner. But once you realized that tape was there, you knew you weren't as alone as you'd believed. Someone was watching you, setting a trap for you. How did you respond? Maybe you shut the camera off, or maybe you tried to brazen things out with Viola, thinking you could take the tape when you left. However it happened, suddenly time was your enemy. You wanted to run, but you couldn't risk leaving Viola alive. Maybe she was fighting you by that time . . . but probably not. My guess is that she believed in you right up until the final seconds."

Quentin looks as though he wants to interrupt this hypothetical, but something holds him back. I only hope his instincts are as good as they once were.

"You started to inject the morphine," Shad says, moving closer to the witness box, "the morphine Viola wanted. But as you depressed the plunger, she saw something alien in your eyes. Something only an old lover would see. You meant to kill her, all right, but not out of mercy. You meant to silence her forever, so that the sins she wanted to get off her chest would never see the light of day. And *that's* when you botched the injection. Maybe she struggled, or maybe you just lost your nerve. Either way, most of the lethal dose went astray, into her muscle tissue."

Shad pushes on breathlessly, unable to do anything but play out the scenario running so vividly through his mind. The terrifying thing is, something tells me he might not be far from the truth.

"Now, you're in trouble," he postulates. "Viola's sedated, but not for long. Her sister's only fifty yards away, at a neighbor's house. Your illegitimate son is at a motel in town—"

"I didn't know that," Dad protests, but Shad plows on like a fever-blind horse.

"You open your black bag in the hope of finding some answer to your problem . . . and that's when you see the adrenaline."

Shad steps even closer to my father, who has gone very still. The image hurls me back to my eighteenth year, when Dad was being sued for malpractice. The lawyer who cross-examined him after months of depositions moved in just as Shad is doing, and on the night of that cross, my father had his first heart attack.

"You know a large dose will overload her weak heart," Shad pushes on, "and if anyone raises questions"—he flips up his fingers like a magician after making something disappear—"you can say you made a failed attempt to resuscitate her. Under normal circumstances, of course, no one would raise any questions. After all . . . you're Tom Cage. You've 'helped' patients into the hereafter before, and no one ever questioned you."

Dad now refuses to look Shad in the face. Disgust is written deeply in his features, in the very angle of his head.

"You cross over to the camcorder and take out the tape," Shad continues, "to make absolutely sure there's no record of your final injection. Only you missed something. There's a hard drive attached to that video camera, set to take over when the tape runs out. Unaware of this, you go back to the sickbed and inject Viola with an overdose of adrenaline. Then you step back into the shadows.

"Seconds later, the woman you claim you loved is jolted from sedated sleep in terror—terror powered by a drug that bursts blood vessels throughout her disease-ridden body. In her struggles, Viola rolls over the remote control lying in her bed, switching on that hard drive and creating the record that will ultimately lead us all to this courtroom. In her final death throes, she calls out your name, but you remain in the shadows, waiting for her to fall silent forever. Once she does, you leave the house, two videotapes tucked safely in your bag."

Shad is breathing hard when he finally stops speaking. He looks as if he's forgotten there's anyone else in the room but himself and the man he hopes to break.

"Isn't that what happened, Dr. Cage?" he asks with surprising conviction.

Shad's tale has gained some traction in the jury box. Several faces show clear signs of emotional upset: flushed skin, pale lips, sweat on the forehead.

When Dad answers, it's in a voice I recognize from my youth—the one he used to chide me with when I let my imagination run a little too wild.

"You should have been a screenwriter, Mr. Johnson. That's a dramatic story you just told. But like a lot of movies, from a medical perspective, it's absurd."

Shad seems taken aback by Dad's matter-of-fact tone. "Absurd? How is it absurd?"

"Had I botched an injection of morphine, as you suggested, and I still wanted to kill Viola, I could have used the fentanyl I had ready to hand."

"Fentanyl?" Shad echoes, rifling his memory for every possible association with that word.

"It's a potent narcotic analgesic," Dad informs him. "A painkiller—only it's one hundred times more powerful than morphine. If I'd needed to finish off Viola in a hurry, as you suggested, I could have given her a little fentanyl, and that would have been the end of her. No pain, no muss, no fuss. That's what a *devious* doctor would have done."

After a few seconds of processing, Shad turns and walks to the prosecution table, where he picks up a sheet of paper, then starts back toward the witness box.

"Doctor, the evidence report introduced by the sheriff's department does not include fentanyl as one of the drugs listed as confiscated from the house."

"That's because it was in my bag."

Shad halts in midstride, then makes a course correction back to his table, where he scans some more papers. His assistant jumps up from his chair and tries to help Shad find what he's looking for, but Shad brushes him aside. Right now he's remembering that, while he induced Melba Price to testify about Dad routinely keeping adrenaline in his black bag, he never asked her to list the full contents of that bag. *God help me, I almost feel sorry for him.* As a prosecutor I had some moments like that—rare, thank God, but it only takes one to scar you for life.

"How would you have explained an overdose of fentanyl," Shad asks, "which would have been detected on autopsy?"

Dad purses his lips like a physics teacher asked to consider some improbable problem. "I would have said Viola was having breakthrough pain. In general, morphine would raise fewer questions postmortem, if for any reason an autopsy was done. Viola knew that. That's why she chose morphine. But she did tell me that if the morphine proved ineffectual, I should use the fentanyl to be sure."

Shad's posture has gone rigid. "You can't prove a bit of that."

"I can prove I had the fentanyl in my bag."

The DA blinks in surprise. "How?"

My ears are roaring. Once again, Shadrach Johnson has stepped off the edge of the map of known answers. It's the prosecutor's equivalent of *Beyond This Point Lie Dragons.*

"When Viola and I first discussed her desire to die peacefully, I prescribed fentanyl, so that we could have it on hand if she actually chose to go through with her plan."

As Shad shuffles through his papers, his assistant pulls a single sheet from a different pile and hands it to him.

"Doctor, I reviewed the records of Leo Watts, Mrs. Turner's pharmacist. He had no record of Viola Turner being prescribed fentanyl."

"I didn't prescribe it through Mr. Watts's pharmacy," Dad says equably. "Leo's a friend, and a churchgoer, and since I knew how the drug might be used, I didn't want him troubled by that kind of issue."

"Or by the police?" Shad says sharply.

Dad inclines his head. "That too, I suppose."

"Where did you get this fentanyl, Dr. Cage?"

"From a compounding pharmacy. But that isn't the point, is it? The point is that I had the drug, and I had it with me that night."

"How can we possibly know that?"

Dad shrugs. "Recall Melba Price, my nurse. She was well aware of the contents of my bag, since she checked its inventory regularly and maintained my drug stocks."

Shad looks like a man who has awakened from a deep sleep with no idea where he is.

"I'd like to remind the court," Dad says, taking advantage of Shad's distress, "that Henry Sexton's hard-drive recording doesn't show me at all. It only shows Viola dying, and in a way I wouldn't wish on my worst enemy. I can promise you this: if I *had* meant to kill Viola, whether out of anger or mercy, I'd have done a hell of a lot better job of it."

Shad should sit down. When a witness gets away from you like this, you have to cut your losses and try to make it up elsewhere. In this case, Shad has only his closing argument left, but that's better than pushing further into uncharted regions. And yet . . . I see almost limitless anger in Shad's face as he grasps the magnitude of his error, and anger makes some lawyers reckless. He walks around the table with a pugnacious stride and stops just short of the witness box.

"Dr. Cage, before any legal action was taken against you, I called your son, the mayor, and asked him to find out what had happened at Cora Revels's house that night. Yet you refused to tell your own son anything. Isn't that true?"

"Yes. I had just learned that Lincoln Turner was my son. Penn hadn't the first idea that I'd had an affair with Viola Turner, much less that he had a half brother. How was I supposed to tell him that, especially with the DA making noises about charging me with a crime?"

"An innocent man would have confided in someone."

"Well . . . I didn't."

"Once you were arrested, why did you jump bail? Is that the act of an innocent man?"

Dad takes a deep breath and looks past Shad to the jury. "I didn't believe the sheriff was interested in learning who had really killed Viola. He'd decided I was guilty on the first day, and he stopped looking for any other solution after that."

"All the evidence pointed to you, Doctor."

"There was other evidence," Dad says doggedly. "But Sheriff Byrd didn't care about that. He'd been looking to get even with me for twenty years, and with Viola's death, he finally got his chance."

"Why would the sheriff want to 'get even' with you, as you say?"

"Because I knew things about him."

"What things?"

"Things he wouldn't want to be made public. I can't be more specific without breaking doctor-patient confidentiality."

"You've been quite cavalier about breaking rules thus far. Why stick at a little talking out of school?"

"Subpoena the sheriff's ex-wife. She'll tell you what his problem was."

"Did you have an affair with her as well?"

"*Ob*-jection," Quentin says in lazy tone. "We're getting mighty far afield of the issue before the bar, Your Honor."

"Sustained. Mr. Johnson, you seem to be taking shots without aiming at this point."

In that moment, reality breaks through to Shad. I doubt he has ever felt more exposed or impotent than he does now. Strangely, I take no pleasure in his torment. If Billy Byrd were standing there like that, I surely would. But Shad, I can tell, believes he is on the side of right. The problem with the law as a profession is that belief, personal conviction, and even knowledge buy you nothing in a courtroom. If you can't prove that something occurred . . . it never happened.

"No further questions, Your Honor," Shad says.

"Thank you, Counselor. Redirect?"

"None."

Judge Elder turns his head to the defense table. "Mr. Avery, do you have any further witnesses?"

"I do not, Your Honor. The defense rests."

A deep silence follows Quentin's declaration, like the silence after a storm has blasted all the birds and insects out of a field. No one can quite believe that the old wizard has emptied his bag of tricks. Shad looks like he's hardly aware of what's transpiring around him.

"Does the State call rebuttal witnesses?" Judge Elder asks.

"None," Shad says dully.

"Very well." Elder leans down to his mike. "At this time, I am going to instruct the jury. Then we'll adjourn for lunch, and return at noon for closing arguments."

"Thank you, Your Honor," Quentin says, his white shock of hair now looking like the flag on an anchored ship.

As Joe Elder begins the tedious process of reading his jury instructions, my gaze wanders to the jury box. If I were trying this case, I'd have been stealing glances at those twelve anointed citizens every chance I got, and having associates watch them for signs of which way they were leaning. But during this trial I've mostly watched the lawyers, and if not them, then the witnesses or the judge. It was Tuesday—an eternity ago—that I advised my mother to do exactly this, and wondered whether I could take my own advice. As it turned out, I have. I've coined no nicknames for these jurors, as was once my habit, and even now I find little of interest in their studiously severe faces.

But when Judge Elder begins instructing them about reasonable doubt, I see some eyes flicker, and I realize that, if nothing else, Quentin Avery has summoned doubt into this courtroom as a living, breathing spirit. This jury is not going to convict Tom Cage of murder. They might go for physician-assisted suicide, but that's not on the menu. So, unless something happens that I cannot foresee, unless Shadrach Johnson performs actual magic during his closing argument, my father is going to walk out of this courtroom a free man.

CHAPTER 67

WE EAT LUNCH at my house on Washington Street, Mom and Jenny and me. Rusty hinted about coming with us, but I worried that his presence during this break might raise our sense of relief to mild euphoria, and I didn't want to risk that. Dad has been taken back to his cell, which for me conjures images of Billy Byrd or even Snake Knox sending someone in there to dispatch him on the verge of acquittal. Quentin and Doris have repaired to Edelweiss, and as they departed the courtroom, Quentin looked back at me and gave me a thin smile. I returned a respectful salute.

A mood of cautious optimism prevails during our meal of salad and grocery-store-made lasagna from the Natchez Market. We get through most of it by avoiding any mention of the day's events in the courtroom. As the clock ticks into the final quarter of the hour, a strange silence descends on the table. Then Mom says, "I miss Walt. Has anybody heard how his wife is doing?"

"A little better," I tell her, though I actually have no idea.

Just as I think we're going to get through lunch without any drama, Jenny says in a brittle voice: "I don't want to jinx anything, but—do you think it went as well as I do this morning? From a legal perspective, I mean. Please don't sugarcoat it."

Mom sighs irritably, but Jenny has made up her mind to push forward. I have a feeling that despite her words, she's scared to death Dad will be convicted.

After a few seconds' thought, I say, "Today was a good day. A great one, actually. But Shad won't lose any time taking the jury back to day one in his close—the forensic case."

Mom's face pinches with concern. "Didn't Tom dispense with that when he explained about the fentanyl?"

"Let's hope some jurors agree."

"I saw several perk up when he explained that point."

"Shad made a huge mistake missing the fentanyl being in Dad's bag. Maybe fatal. But he painted a compelling picture of how Dad might have gone from intending to euthanize Viola for the wrong reasons, to finishing the job with adrenaline. I can't see twelve people buying it, but that scenario would be easy to understand for a layman."

"Daddy never argued that he tried to resuscitate Viola with adrenaline," Jenny points out.

"You're right. That's one of the few virtues of his self-destructive honesty."

Mom's jaw has tightened, and her face lost some color. "Isn't Quentin at his best in things like closing argument? Isn't that how he got the nickname 'Preacher'?"

"Yes. And I expect him to do well. But we'd be foolish to underestimate Shad, and I think Quentin has done that throughout the trial."

Jenny looks more worried than before. "But hasn't Quentin done a wonderful job in the end? He destroyed two of Shad's main witnesses."

"Absolutely. He proved that they both perjured themselves."

"Well, then," Mom says. "That's reasonable doubt right there."

"I think you're right."

"Well, what's about to happen?" Jenny asks. "I tried to pay attention during the judge's instructions, but I kept drifting off. Give me the last act for dummies."

"Closing arguments," I tell her. "Shad Johnson and Quentin each get one hour to summarize their cases for the jury. Typically, the prosecutor will take thirty minutes of his hour, then sit down. The defense is required to give all his remarks in one go, the full hour, if he wants to speak that long. Then the prosecutor has thirty minutes left to finish."

"So Shad gets to hear Quentin's whole pitch before he finishes."

"Right. And that's a real advantage. It helped me win a lot of cases back in Houston."

Mom kicks me under the table, and I feel my face go red.

"I think we're about to see Quentin Avery's finest hour," she announces.

She stands up and flattens her skirt. "I'm going to run upstairs to the ladies' room. I'll see you all in a minute. Jenny, we should get back to the courthouse as soon as possible."

After Mom leaves the room, Jenny swallows her last bite of lasagna. "What's wrong? Were you holding something back in front of Mom? Did we miss something important?"

"No, not really."

"Then what is it?" she presses.

"Everybody seems to be forgetting the fact that when Viola made that tape for Henry, she was doing it in the expectation that Dad was going to euthanize her. The things she said in the recording did a lot to puncture Shad's theories about Dad's motive to silence her, but even if he injected her out of a desire to give her a dignified death, that's murder. Not assisted suicide. I expect Shad to make that clear in his closing. Trying this case on motive may have bitten Shad in the ass, but that doesn't change the facts. Motive doesn't really have anything to do with whether Dad committed murder or not. It comes down to what the jury believes happened in that room. What physically happened. If they think he injected her with that adrenaline as well as the morphine, they could convict him."

"But if they think Daddy injected her out of a sense of mercy, don't you think they'll acquit him in the end?"

The base of my skull has begun to throb. Leaning forward, I squeeze my neck as tightly as I can with my right hand. "Imagine twelve people, most of whom have about a fourth of your scientific knowledge. A lot can depend on who takes control of that jury once they begin deliberations."

Seeing worry in my sister's eyes, I reach out and squeeze her shoulder. "I'm just playing devil's advocate. It's an old defense against getting overconfident. Most people are going to believe Dad did just what he said: pushed that needle through her vein and walked out of there with her alive."

Jenny gets up and walks around the table, then looks down into my eyes. "You're still not telling me everything. Something's worrying you."

She knows me better than I thought. "Only this. If Dad didn't inject that adrenaline, who did? You see? That jury would have a lot easier time if there was a big fat suspect sitting up there for them to pin it on in their minds."

"What about Snake Knox?"

"You're right, I'm sure."

Mom flushing the toilet upstairs sends water rushing through the pipes in the kitchen wall.

"Tell me something, Penn, before Mom gets down."

"What?"

"Did you believe Daddy's story?"

I hesitate, but then to my surprise I speak my mind. "Not a hundred percent, no."

Jenny's eyes flash. "Why not?"

"I just . . . I don't think he's lied much in his life. But when he talked about the injection, his tone reminded me of something."

"What?"

"Something from my childhood."

"A time he lied to you?" she asks.

"I think so."

Jenny closes her eyes, then reaches out and threads her fingers into mine. For a few seconds, I sense she's going to confide something to me. But then she says, "I'm praying it's going to come out all right."

I have no response to this.

"I'm going to run to the restroom myself," she says. "I'll see you in a sec."

After finishing off the remainder of my lasagna, I walk to the half bath at the back of the house to piss, but the door opens and Jenny walks out with her hands in her hair, trying to pin it up. She's got a bobby pin in her mouth, and for a moment I'm thrown back to my childhood, when she was the cool teenager in our house and I the goofy little brother. Smiling, I reach out to pat her arm as I pass, but instead she grabs my hand and pulls me to a stop, her eyes deeply troubled.

"What is it?" I ask.

"Penn, I saw something."

"When? What are you talking about?"

"A long time ago. When I was fifteen. I was riding a bicycle downtown with one of my friends, Tracy Moon. Do you remember Tracy?"

"What did you see, Jenny?"

"Something bad. I was telling Tracy about how, when we were little kids, we used to make milkshakes using the barium mixing machine in the lab at Daddy's office. I thought it would be fun to do that again, if we could. So we rode over to his office on High Street. We went to the lab door like we used to, but nobody answered. I told Tracy to wait while I checked around front. I didn't go to the front door, though. I rode around to the garage to see if Daddy's car was there. But the garage door was closed. I leaned my bike against the wrought-iron fence and walked up to the side door. I heard voices. One was Daddy's. I almost called out, but something stopped me. Instead, I got up on tiptoe and peeked through the glass."

"Jenny, come on. We don't have much time."

She nods quickly, her face red with shame and doubt. "Daddy and Viola were standing in the corner of the garage. At first I thought they were arguing, because he was holding her arms and shaking them. But then he kissed her, and she kissed him back. I don't know how long I stood there, but . . . they were making out the whole time. There was no doubt about what I was looking at. When she started taking off her top, I ran."

"Jenny. I'm sorry. Did you ever tell Dad or Mom what you saw?"

"No, God, no. But I can't tell you how bad it freaked me out. From that moment forward, I was sure Daddy loved Viola more than Mom. And I guess I was right, in a way. But the worst thing was, I knew he was lying to us. I don't think I ever trusted him after that."

Though Jenny's not a big hugger, I put my arms around her and squeeze her tight. "I wish you'd told me about it."

"I couldn't," she says, her voice a sob into my chest. "You were so young, and you worshipped him. I couldn't shatter your respect for him."

"You shouldn't have carried that alone, though."

Her wide eyes are bright with tears. "I had to. I would have died before I ever let Mom find out what I'd seen."

"I know you would."

"But look what's happened. Now Mom knows everything anyway. She had to suffer through it in spite of my silence."

I nod slowly. "These things usually get found out in the end."

Jenny draws back a little. Her mascara has run and made raccoon eyes on her face. "You don't think Mom knew back then, do you? She didn't suffer all that time in silence, the way I have?"

"No. The house would have shaken to its foundations if Mom had found out Dad was sleeping with Viola."

Jenny laughs through her tears, but then her expression turns even more serious than before. "Penn, did you ever cheat on Sarah?"

"*What?* Where did that come from?"

"You heard me."

This is the last thing I want to talk about, but I know Jenny will have no peace until I answer. "I did once, before we were married."

She flinches as though I've caused her physical pain. "But not after?"

"No."

"Never?"

"Never."

"Penn?" calls my mother from the kitchen. "Jenny? What's taking so long?"

"We're coming!" I shout up the hallway.

When I turn back to Jenny, she's staring into space with glassy eyes. "What is it?" I ask. "Jen?"

She seems not to hear me. I guess that despite the decades that have passed since the event, she's still seeing her father kissing his nurse in the office garage.

"Jenny, is there something else going on? Are you afraid Jack's cheating on you?"

Jack is her husband, whom I can't imagine committing adultery if his life depended on it.

"No," she says, still looking dazed.

"Then what is it?"

"Nothing."

"Are you positive?"

She shakes her head once like someone trying to wake up from a nightmare, and then her eyes come clear. "Let me wash my face again. Tell Mom something to buy me a minute."

"I will."

She stands on tiptoe and kisses my cheek, then hurries back into the bathroom.

"Where's Jenny?" Mom asks from the kitchen door. "Is she sick?"

"Just a little, I think. Her stomach. Nerves, I'm sure."

"Well, we can't wait all day. I'm not going to miss those summations."

"We won't, Mom. I promise."

She frowns, then speaks under her breath. "That girl has had nerves ever since she was a child. You'd think that by fifty-three she'd outgrow them."

"High-strung," I answer, walking back to the kitchen with a forced smile. "Isn't that what you always said?"

Mom pats my arm, but I'm not sure whether she's doing it to comfort me or herself. "I'm just glad Jenny didn't have to grow up on a cotton farm," she says. "She wouldn't have made it."

"She might have surprised you."

CHAPTER 68

"LADIES AND GENTLEMEN," Shad Johnson begins, nodding to the twelve jurors, then turning to acknowledge the audience, which has somehow swelled even larger than in past sessions. "Good afternoon."

We're bound to be in violation of the fire codes at this point, but Judge Elder has allowed it, so nothing will be done to thin the crowd. Shad gives a respectful nod to the gallery, then turns back to the jury box.

"I've learned a lot during this case, and what I've learned has tried my spirit. I've learned that no matter how hard I might bend my mind and will to the task of understanding the intimate relations between the black and white races, I can't do it. I can't fathom the pain and guilt and fear that led a beautiful soul like Viola Turner to welcome death from the hand of a man who had once claimed to love her. I cannot plumb the depths of despair in a son who never knew his real father, who sank so low that he felt he had no option but to steal back the inheritance he believed was his birthright. Though it hurts my heart, I must accept that I will never understand these things. I don't think the law is equal to that task. But the law was not written for that purpose. It was written to judge the acts of men, not their motives. Not their hearts. And under the law, Tom Cage is guilty of murder."

And with that, Shad begins as masterful and concise a summation of a forensic case as I've ever heard. He does not merely parrot what he laid out in his opening remarks or his case in chief. He culls what did not work for him and incorporates the elements of Quentin's case that worked against him before this hour. As I feared, he tailors his theory of Dad using the adrenaline to kill Viola while fentanyl was ready to hand by suggesting—as Drew Elliott did to me on the first day of the trial—that Dad had intended to claim that Viola had suffered a heart attack and he'd tried in vain to resuscitate her. He doesn't bother to mention that Dad never made that claim, but instead counts on the details and emotion of his presentation to sweep all doubt before them. Shad speaks with authority and precision, but he manages never to talk down to the jury—something he's been guilty of in the past. Nor does he put them to sleep by delving too deeply into the science of the case. He chooses to conclude the first act of his closing argument with the weakest point of his case: Viola's videotape.

"Ladies and gentlemen, watching that videotape was difficult for me. One reason is that judging by what Mrs. Turner said on that tape, I turned out to be wrong about some of the things I'd guessed about Dr. Cage's motivations. But if I was wrong in part about his motive, I was *not* wrong about his actions. You must remember that all the while Viola Turner was speaking to that camera, she was doing so in the firm belief that only hours later, Tom Cage was going to inject her with a lethal dose of morphine. Nothing she said on the tape disputes that. In fact, Mrs. Turner specifically refers to her imminent death. And so, I will remind you of something I told you in my opening remarks: in the last analysis, motive is not a key element of the crime of murder. Under the law, the question is this: Did Tom Cage, on December twelfth, *intend* to enter that house and end the life of Viola Turner? If he did, he is guilty of murder. And all of the evidence we have indicates that he did."

For a moment I think Shad is about to sit down, but he appears to think better of it. "Ladies and gentlemen, I believe I should address a couple of points before Mr. Avery gives his summation.

"First, we live in a time when public perception of the justice system has been greatly influenced, even distorted, by television shows like *CSI*. Juries sometimes feel that if the State's case is anything less than a parade of high-tech tests and recordings, then they cannot judge someone to be guilty of a crime. In *this* case, purely by chance, video recordings were made of the time surrounding the crime, and of the victim's death. We saw some of that footage. And there's nothing I would have liked more than for us to see the contents of the tape found in the Dumpster of St. Catherine's Hospital. I am almost certain that it showed the actual commission of the murder. However, as you know, the killer's efforts to wipe out this record of his crime ultimately proved successful. Our hopes of seeing Mrs. Turner's murder presented as an objective reality were thwarted.

"But that does not mean that her murder was not real. You saw the terror and pain in Viola's eyes when she died. You heard her cry out the defendant's name. And it falls to you twelve jurors to determine the events that immediately preceded that final recording. You are the finders of fact. You were not summoned here to sit passively and watch a film of a crime. You were summoned to sift through the sum total of evidence brought before you, to listen to the witnesses, and then to the best of your ability judge the innocence or guilt of the accused."

Shad's eyes were on my father as he said the last sentence, but now he shifts his gaze to Quentin.

"Ladies and gentlemen, when my learned opponent gave his opening remarks, he spoke to you about something called the Unwritten Law. He described it as what happens when a jury, for some compelling reason, decides to set aside the rules—the law—and vote what it feels in its collective gut. As you all know now, Mr. Avery has a silver tongue, and he made this phenomenon—known as jury nullification—sound downright noble. Like a vote for conscience, if you will. Like a jury being brave, instead of kowtowing to whatever rules some lazy, cigar-chomping legislators wrote over in Jackson. But I'm afraid that's not the case.

"When Mr. Avery characterized jury nullification as something noble, he was cleverly trying to provide justification for you to set aside the law, and the judge's instructions, and vote in defiance of the evidence. What Mr. Avery was really telling you was, 'If you think Dr. Cage is a fine old fellow, no matter how incriminating the evidence against him might be, just vote your heart. You can get a good night's sleep afterward, because there's plenty of precedent for it. Why, you're showing moral courage by doing it.'"

Shad raises his hands, palms outward, like a man showing he has no aggressive intent, but also no choice about what he is about to do. "But there's a simple corrective for that. Let me give you a little legal history."

Walking slowly between the jury box and the bar, he speaks, gathering power. "Do you know the most common situation in which juries fell back on the so-called Unwritten Law? When a man came home and found his wife in bed with another man and killed one or both of them. In those cases, no matter what the law said, a jury would sometimes acquit the husband. But let me tell you the type of case in which juries historically resorted to the Unwritten Law in *our* state. You might be surprised, after how fine a practice Mr. Avery made it sound. It wasn't cases of assisted suicide. No, it was cases like the Neshoba County trial of the Klansmen who murdered Michael Schwerner, James Chaney, and Andrew Goodman in 1964. It was cases like the one in which the killers of Emmett Till were set free in Money, Mississippi, after one of the most gruesome murders in our state's history. When white juries set aside the law and ignored overwhelming evidence in order to free white men who had lynched African-Americans, they were falling back on the Unwritten Law that Mr. Avery spoke reverently about."

This time when Shad falls silent, a vapor trail of righteous indignation hangs in the room. Each name he mentioned is a talisman, with positive and negative power depending on the race and politics of the listener.

"Well, ladies and gentlemen, these proceedings are not a popularity contest. This is a criminal trial. A *murder* trial. And you are bound by oath to follow the law and the instructions of the judge to the best of your ability. Your duty is clear. Do not let a warm voice and a fine turn of phrase distract you from the cruel facts of this case."

When Shad retakes his seat at the prosecution table, exactly twenty-nine minutes have elapsed, yet not once did I ever see him look at his watch or the clock mounted high on the courtroom wall. The jury looks appropriately impressed by his performance. After he sits, they turn as one to study the district attorney's wheelchair-bound opponent, who suddenly does not seem quite as formidable as he did this morning.

As Quentin rolls his chair forward, I suddenly realize how badly he would like to rise from that chair and walk to the lectern. Like Judge Elder, he would tower over Shadrach Johnson. But Quentin Avery will never walk again, and he must do what he can with what he has.

CHAPTER 69

"MANY LAWYERS AND members of the media refer to me as Preacher Avery," Quentin begins, speaking clearly and calmly from his wheelchair near the lectern. "They do this because I supposedly have a flair for emotional argument, and because I often quote scripture during my discourse. But today I will not preach to you. I never invoke the Good Book lightly, and today I have no need of it.

"Nor do we have need of the Unwritten Law, which Mr. Johnson just made quite a thing of, as I'm sure you noted. Today I'm telling you to forget the Unwritten Law. Because the law on the books is quite sufficient to dispose of the matter before you, a grave matter that was rushed to prosecution, and for all the wrong reasons. Why is the written law sufficient today? Because the law in a murder trial comes down to one thing—the presumption of innocence. In this case, the State—in the person of Shadrach Johnson—had the insurmountable burden of proving beyond any reasonable doubt that Dr. Tom Cage murdered Viola Turner, a woman he loved and respected for decades.

"And the question for you today is not whether a reasonable person might have a solid basis to doubt the State's case. The question is whether any reasonable person could stretch his imagination to believe that the State has done anything more than *accuse* Dr. Cage of murder."

Quentin rolls his chair back a foot and scans the faces of the jury. "For what has the State proved? One, that Dr. Cage was Viola Turner's physician. Two, that he prescribed her medications consistent with those normally prescribed for terminally ill patients. Three, that he administered at least one of those medications, morphine, at various times for therapeutic reasons. Four, that Dr. Cage was in her home on the night she died, as he was on almost every other night for the preceding six weeks. Well . . . Dr. Cage admitted all those things himself on the stand. And why shouldn't he? All of those actions are the actions of an innocent man.

"Just a few moments ago, the district attorney implored you to focus on the facts. Did any of you happen to notice that is the opposite of what he told you to do during his opening statement? Remember? What did Mr. Johnson tell you this case was about? *Motive.* And what was the motive, according to him? Race. *Were it not for the fact of race . . . Viola Turner would not have been murdered.* Do you remember those words? I do. Well, now, after three and a half days of inflammatory accusations by the district attorney and the witnesses for the State, we have finally heard from the victim herself. And I think she surprised the district attorney quite a bit."

Quentin grips the big wheels and rolls a couple of feet toward the rapt jury. "Mr. Johnson and Sheriff Byrd told you that Dr. Cage did all in his power to destroy the videotape that Viola Turner made just before she died. He told you himself why he did that. But here today, thanks to the miracle of modern technology, you have heard Viola Turner speak from beyond the grave. And what did she tell you about Tom Cage?

"First, that Dr. Cage did not know he had a son by her until the night of her death—just as he told you. Second, that Tom Cage helped her to conceal the fact that she had killed a racist who had helped to gang-rape her as an act of terrorism—just as Dr. Cage told you himself. Third, that two known killers had threatened to murder her if she continued to talk to a reporter about unsolved civil rights murders in the past—just as Dr. Cage told you. Fourth, that she intended to give fifty thousand dollars to Henry Sexton, in the hope that it would help him to solve her martyred brother's murder. This testimony directly refutes what two of Mr. Johnson's star witnesses told you.

"Now, let's ask ourselves another question: What did the State try but *fail* to prove?

"They tried to prove that an assisted-suicide pact existed between Viola Turner and Dr. Cage. Their source for that information was Cora Revels, a proven liar. Cora Revels did not know that such a pact existed. Only because Dr. Cage took the stand and freely admitted entering into this pact do we know that it, in fact, existed.

"Mr. Johnson spent many hours of testimony trying to prove that a motive existed for Tom Cage to murder Viola, to ensure her silence. And yet, after all the lies of his witnesses had been drawn out like poison, what did Mr. Johnson prove? That the State's witnesses themselves had profited by the victim's death and sought to cover their crime by getting Tom Cage charged with murder."

Quentin rotates his wheelchair slowly in place, allowing him to make eye contact with not only the jury, but also every spectator in the courtroom.

"And while we're on the subject of motive, let me pose a very simple question, one so simple that I don't believe our ingenious prosecutor even thought of it. *How could killing Viola Turner protect Dr. Cage's reputation from what most threatened it?* Killing Viola Turner would not erase Lincoln Turner from the earth. Lincoln Turner is a living fact. A simple DNA test would prove that Dr. Cage is Lincoln's father, as it did three months ago. So . . . what could Dr. Cage gain by killing the mother of his child? If he meant to cover his sin with Viola and hide the existence of his illegitimate son, he would have had to kill Lincoln Turner as well. But if that was his plan, why did he not wait for Lincoln to 'arrive from Chicago'? Dr. Cage had drugs ready to hand that would have killed Lincoln stone dead. A few drops of fentanyl in a cup of coffee . . . But wait"—Quentin slaps his forehead like a cartoon character—"Lincoln Turner wasn't on his way from Chicago, was he? He was on his way from Mr. Patel's motel, thirty miles from his mother's sickbed! He'd been hiding out by the county line for several days, under an alias, waiting to put his schemes for theft and revenge into motion."

I glance over at the prosecution table. Shad looks as though he might be on the verge of vomiting. What must it feel like to sit mute under a barrage like this? To be made to look foolish by one of the masters of your profession? As a prosecutor in Houston, I experienced some bad days in court, but I never faced an attorney of Quentin Avery's caliber with a case like this one. If Shad is going to get a conviction today, he's going to have to turn iron into gold during his final close.

Quentin presses on relentlessly. "Anyone who watched Lincoln

Turner on the stand saw that he also harbored a deep desire to revenge himself upon Dr. Cage. And the circumstances of his mother's illness and death offered him a perfect chance to do that."

Quentin takes a deep breath, then releases a long, sad exhalation. "Lincoln Turner," he says in the tone of a sorrowful pastor. "It's been a while since I heard anything as tragic as that boy's childhood. Born from an unwanted pregnancy, with a mother who did what she thought was best to get by, but who chose deceit as her tool, and ultimately caused more pain than she averted. That poor boy didn't even know who he was growing up, and he was taken under the spell of an amoral criminal before he had the wits to know right from wrong.

"There can be no doubt that, had Lincoln been raised in the loving home of Tom Cage, with all the advantages of our mayor, his life would have turned out much differently. That is a tragedy. But we all know now that this was not the fault of Tom Cage. For no man can offer to raise a son that he does not know exists.

"Ladies and gentlemen, Dr. Cage took the stand this morning and told you the unvarnished truth, as I promised you that he would. He didn't shy away from the truth to make himself look better than he is. He told you *hard* truths. He said things that could put his very freedom in jeopardy, apart from this proceeding. But he did that because he is a truthful man. The few lies Tom Cage told in his life, he told to prevent pain, and they have haunted him ever since. Today he tried to make them right.

"This trial has proved two things about Dr. Cage. First, as he told you himself—with his wife here to hear it, God help her—that he loved Viola Turner. And second, had he known that he had a son by Viola, he would have done everything in his power to help that boy get raised right. As it was, he sent Viola money for thirty-seven years. What more would he have done had he known the truth? We can only guess.

"But all this is speculation. Lincoln Turner was raised where he was, and he grew into the man who testified before you. A man who admitted that he lied on the stand in an effort to steal his own mother's life savings. But far more disturbing is that, even when given an opportunity to come clean before you, he chose to hide his deepest lie. Despite telling you a heartbreaking story about a prodigal son racing from Chicago to Natchez to reach his dying mother in time to forgive her—

and failing because of the alleged crime of the defendant—Mr. Turner was actually in Natchez *four days prior to his mother's death.* Yet he deliberately chose not to speak to her at all. What reason Lincoln Turner might have for lying about his presence here, I leave to you good ladies and gentlemen, and to the law enforcement authorities of this county."

Up come Quentin's hands with their long and graceful fingers, and he begins enumerating points upon them. When he speaks this way, every assertion he makes takes on a tone of unassailability.

"Did someone murder Viola Turner? Yes, indeed. Cruelly and without mercy, as we all saw on the grisly recording accidentally captured on the camera belonging to the late Henry Sexton. Do we know who inflicted that terrible suffering and death on Viola Turner? *We do not.* Can we guess who might have done it? I submit to you that we all have a pretty good idea.

"Ironically, though, our ideas may be different. Some of you may think Lincoln himself did it. From the testimony in this trial, it's manifestly clear that he possessed the motive, the means, and the opportunity to kill his mother. We know he was in Cora Revels's house on the morning of her death. He claimed to have arrived at the house after she died, but he made similar claims about his arrival in Natchez, did he not? Who is to say when he really got there? Cora Revels?"

Quentin shakes his head with sadness and contempt. "What did I tell you my daddy used to tell me? 'Half the truth is a whole lie.' Well, forget *half* the truth. Cora Revels and Lincoln Turner convicted themselves as liars out of their own mouths. What weight should a reasonable person give to the words of proven deceivers? I know what my mama used to say: 'Fool me once, shame on you. Fool me twice, shame on *me.*'

"We also know that, like his aunt Cora, Lincoln wanted his mother's money—money that Viola had decided to spend in the quest to find justice for her martyred brother, Jimmy Revels.

"We *don't* know where the adrenaline that killed Viola Turner came from. Nurse Melba Price testified that Dr. Cage had adrenaline in his office, and also in his black bag. But that could be said of many doctors in Natchez. The State did not find any adrenaline ampoule at the crime scene, or anywhere else.

"Might the adrenaline have come from Chicago? Possibly. Or could Lincoln Turner have broken into Tom Cage's office sometime during those days he was secretly here, and used that very dose to kill his mother? I tend to doubt this, because Lincoln would have left the incriminating vial for us to find. So . . . there's no certainty in the end. Not for us. Perhaps months or years hence, some guilty soul will cry out for release, and the truth will come to light at last. Whose soul might that be? We don't know."

Quentin pauses long enough for people to get nervous, then changes tack once more. "Did anyone but Lincoln and Cora have a motive to kill Viola Turner? We all know the answer to that. Viola was hated by one of the most racist and violent organizations ever formed in the United States. She was threatened by them forty years ago, before she left Natchez, and she was threatened only a week or so before she was murdered. Members of that group raped Viola in 1968 and most likely murdered her brother as well. Viola had seen them torture Jimmy Revels and Luther Davis on the night she was rescued from captivity by Tom Cage's emissary, Ray Presley.

"For these reasons, those vicious men warned Viola that if she ever returned to Natchez, they would silence her forever. Well, Viola stayed away as long as she could. But like a lot of black folks who left Mississippi decades ago, she wanted to return home to die. But on her own terms, ladies and gentlemen. This poor woman had led a life of biblical suffering, and she wanted to have her final agony ended by a man she knew had loved her all her life. And what did she find? Dr. Cage offered her exactly what she sought—comfort in the face of pain and death. But the demons of Viola's past had not been idle in her absence. Not by a long shot. And they lived in fear of being exposed.

"When Viola began talking to a crusading reporter, they came to her bedside and told her once again that she would die if she tried to tell the truth. But did she remain silent? No. She made the tape you saw this morning, and she changed her will to fund Henry Sexton's investigations into her brother's murder. Even from her sickbed, Viola Turner was a formidable adversary.

"Who among you believes that the monsters who killed Henry Sexton, Caitlin Masters, Sleepy Johnston, and others—who murdered one of their own, Will Devine, before your very eyes yesterday—would hesitate to snuff out the life of Viola Turner?"

Quentin suddenly goes quiet, like a wind falling deceptively as it gathers before a storm.

"Finally," he says softly, "I ask you to consider the district attorney, the man who brought us all to this room and asked us to listen to the *deceivers* he paraded before us. It was Shadrach Johnson who reached back fifty years into the past to try to slander Dr. Cage over his military service to his country. I only thank God that Dr. Cage's commanding officer survived to tell you of his courage under fire on the night the Chinese broke through the American lines back in 1950. And that Captain Walt Garrity could tell you the truth of how he and Tom Cage were forced to make the toughest choice a medic ever could make in the face of certain torture and death for the hopelessly wounded boys under their care.

"And that, ladies and gentlemen of the jury, is what I want to leave you with. This man, this simple small-town doctor, has spent his life in the gray areas that most of us pretend don't exist. As a young man, he was thrown into the crucible of war and asked to do the impossible. He acquitted himself with honor. For the past forty years, he has worked every day to heal the sick and afflicted of our community. He has never sought fortune or fame; on the contrary, he has done countless acts of kindness and mercy without anyone ever learning of them.

"There's an old saying: 'Fools rush in where angels fear to tread.' By that standard, Tom Cage is a fool. A prudent physician would have run a mile when Viola Turner asked him to help her die with dignity. Because the law doesn't do much to help terminally ill people in this country. It doesn't do much to help the doctors asked to care for them, either. The law is mighty quick to condemn a doctor trying to help someone in pain, and mighty slow to help those poor patients find peace. A smart doctor's first thought upon hearing what Viola wanted would have been the potential lawsuit and the possibility of losing his license. But not Tom Cage. Tom did the same thing he did in Korea. He shoved his fear deep down inside, waded in, and did the best he could in the time he had with the resources at hand."

Quentin raises both hands, palms upturned. "But I'm talking like Dr. Cage helped Viola Turner to die! The fact is, he didn't. This man who had the guts to help young soldiers die rather than face torture could not bring himself to kill a woman he had loved, and who had borne him a child. Not even out of mercy. But he *did* bring himself to come here today, take the stand, and tell you the truth, no matter what it might cost him. And as for the assertions of the district attorney, who claims that Tom Cage is playing some sort of con game on us all . . . I ask Mr. Johnson what I asked him at the conclusion of my opening remarks."

With the slow but inexorable motion of a gun traversing in its mount, Quentin turns to Shadrach Johnson and says: "Have you no *shame,* brother?"

The ringing silence that follows this question is like the vacuum after an artillery round blasts open the earth. Several jurors sit open-mouthed as they stare at Shad, awaiting his response, and even Judge Elder appears struck dumb by the force of Quentin's question. A low hum begins to grow in the audience behind me, and within seconds it becomes the wild buzz of a junior-high-school auditorium before the teachers take charge.

Judge Elder's bass voice booms out to the back wall and reverberates through the room. *"Be silent, or I will clear this court!"*

Turning back toward the crowd, I see the first few rows of spectators blinking in disbelief at the volume the judge summoned without the benefit of his microphone. When I face forward again, I see Quentin rolling to his place behind the defense table, his face looking peaceful in repose.

Can he really be that cool? I wonder.

"Mr. Johnson," Judge Elder says softly into the ensuing vacuum, "you may conclude your closing argument."

As Shad stands behind the prosecution table, Rusty's elbow digs into the ribs on my left side.

"Shad's got more balls than I do," he whispers. "You couldn't pay me to get up after what Quentin just did to him. He looks like Dan Quayle after Lloyd Bentsen gutted him on national television."

I nod slightly, but as Shad walks to the lectern, I see something in his eyes that sends a wave of sickness through my belly. *He still believes Dad is guilty.*

"What is it, Penn?" Mom whispers in my right ear. "You just turned pale."

For a moment I try to suppress my anxiety, but at this point there's nothing to be gained by shielding my mother. One way or another, the verdict will come soon.

"Shad truly believes Dad killed her," I murmur. "He believes it in his bones."

In the span of three seconds, I feel my mother's hand go cold.

CHAPTER 70

SHADRACH JOHNSON FACES the jury with the self-possession of a gifted young choir member asked to sing a solo for a strange congregation. With solemn gravity, he says, "Mr. Avery just asked me if I have no shame. That's a hell of a thing to say, ladies and gentlemen. And while I don't believe that he deserves an answer, I believe you do. Let me tell you why I brought this case to trial.

"To help make things clear, I'm going to take a page out of my learned opponent's book. From the very beginning of this ordeal, when I first learned about the relations between Tom Cage and Viola Turner, I was reminded of the biblical parables I'd heard in my youth. And I'll be frank with you: when the pastor told those stories, I often didn't fully grasp their meaning."

Several jurors nod in empathy at this.

"But," Shad goes on, "even when I was confused, I sensed that an important truth was buried in there somewhere. So today I'm going to tell you a parable." Shad steps away from the lectern and begins walking slowly and apparently without destination, with one hand folded into the other at the height of his first jacket button. "I want you to think back to ancient times, to biblical times, to a land known as the Caucasian Empire. That empire was a kingdom of white people. But within it lived many black folks, people who had begun life as slaves but who had shed their chains and lived and worked among the Caucasians, trying to earn a meager living.

"In that hot and ancient land, a young black man and woman were walking down a road. They were brother and sister. And on that road they met five ignorant, cruel soldiers of the empire. Why do I say soldiers? Because what were the members of the Double Eagle group other than the soldiers of an invisible empire? So . . . the soldiers challenged the brother and sister, saying, 'You have broken our law and refused to remain in your place.' When the brother argued, the soldiers beat and killed him. Then they raped his sister, to punish her, and because they had always coveted her. Then they told the girl, 'Leave this land and never return. If you do, you shall suffer the same fate as your brother.'

"That poor girl hobbled down the road, wounded and bleeding. After a while, she came to the house of a learned physician. She knocked on the door and asked for help. The physician took her in, tended her wounds, and asked what had befallen her. When she told him, the physician said, 'I can tend your wounds and nurse you back to health, but we cannot tell the sheriff what happened on the road, because the emperor will not punish his own soldiers for hurting you.'

"The girl stayed in that house and began to heal. But late one night, as he tended her wounds, the learned physician seduced the girl and lay with her in secret. She fell in love with him and believed all he told her. Then one day, a knock came at the door. When the girl answered, she found one of the soldiers who had raped her on the road, bleeding from wounds. 'Call the physician,' he begged. 'I am dying.' The girl let the soldier inside, but there, remembering her pain, she picked up a hammer and smashed the soldier's skull. When the learned physician came down the stairs, he cried, 'What have you done?' The girl said, 'I have killed the man who raped me, and who murdered my brother. Nothing more.' 'Go back to your room and say nothing of it,' said the physician. 'I will make it so that no one asks questions.'

"As the physician predicted, all was well for a few days. But then the girl discovered she had got with child. Confronted by this evidence of their sin, the physician said, 'You cannot stay in this house. I have a wife and children. They cannot discover what has passed between us.' Handing her a few coins, he pushed her out into the road and locked his door. Stripped of her job, her virtue, and carrying his child, she fled the land of her birth. She eventually settled in a far country, where her life grew worse each year.

"And so, ladies and gentlemen, I ask you a simple question. Who did the more terrible deed? The ignorant soldiers on the road, who simply took what they wanted and went on their way? Or the learned physician who knew better? The man who took what he wanted, not with a club or a spear, but with honeyed lies and empty promises?"

Without waiting for an answer, Shad lowers his head, walks toward the bench, then turns toward the spectators, continuing to pace as he speaks.

"Half a century passed, and the beautiful girl became old, frail, and sick. She was dying. Fearing the pain of her illness more than the old threats of the soldiers, she returned to the empire where she was born, to the house of the learned physician. 'I know you hoped never to see me again,' she said, 'but I have one boon to ask of you. Please help me pass to the other world without further pain. Surely you owe this to me.' 'Yea, I will do this thing,' said the physician, 'for I treated you badly in your youth.' The physician made preparations to fulfill her request. But as he did, the woman said, 'Wait—one more favor I must ask before I die. All these years I have been haunted by the sin of murder we committed upon the soldier. I must confess this to the community. But most important, you must acknowledge the child you begat upon me, for his life has been hard and filled with sorrow.'

"Exactly what happened after that, we cannot know. But in the morning, the old woman was found dead from a dose of poison, and the learned physician refused to speak of what had passed between them. It was left to the people of the city to decide what had transpired during the night."

Shad looks at the jury and speaks with quiet conviction. "Ladies and gentlemen, who, upon hearing this tale, would not bring the learned physician before the bar of justice to answer for what happened during that night? *That* is why I brought this case to trial. For these past few days, the physician's lawyer has told you what a kind and wonderful man he is. He has not challenged the physical evidence of what transpired during that fateful night. He has rested his defense upon the physician's character. This physician, he says, has filled all the long years between abandoning his lover and watching her die with good works, and these works should outweigh all else. But take away those things—which I believe were done in penance—and remember the parable as I told it to you. It may be that because of Dr. Cage's kind face and comforting bedside manner, you cannot imagine the man behind that face committing sinful, selfish acts. But we are all sinners, ladies and gentlemen. We all act to protect ourselves and our families.

"Pondering the parable I've told today, I realized that perhaps the learned physician himself did not realize how much closer in spirit he was to the ignorant soldiers than to the woman he seduced and cast into the street. It is not for me to judge him, though. That burden—that duty—lies with you. When you go back into that jury room, think not of Tom Cage and his years of small kindnesses, but rather of the young black girl who met the brutal soldiers on the road, and who came to the learned physician for help. Consider what she received from his hands, both then and on that final night forty years later, when she died. The facts of what happened in that house have not been challenged. The law is clear. And the judgment of the learned physician's character . . . I leave to you.

"Thank you."

As Shad Johnson walks to his seat, the sheer brilliance of his closing argument takes my breath away. What has this trial been but a battle of competing narratives? A *Rashomon*-like drama in which different characters have recounted different versions of the same event and its attendant history? Faulkner did the same thing in *Absalom, Absalom,* demonstrating that no two people ever experience the same event, and that history is doomed to be only a version of events. In his radically unorthodox closing argument, Shad seized control of the narrative. By stripping away all the distracting particulars of the relationship between Viola and my father, he lifted the story into the realm of the mythic and made it universal. And in that symbolic realm, the tragic truth that underlay their relationship was laid bare.

My father, however pure his motives might have seemed to him while living out that episode of his life, was part of the dominant, oppressive class. Viola was only a few generations out of slavery. The power differential between them was almost incalculable, a gulf that could not be bridged in the context of the era in which they lived. As Viola knew—probably long before my father—no positive outcome for them had ever been possible.

As I feared he would all along, Quentin underestimated Shadrach Johnson. Shad did not make the same mistake. Tactically outmaneuvered by his legendary foe, Shad adapted accordingly. By creating a parable with biblical resonance, and tailoring it to the case before the bar, he beat "Preacher" Avery at his own game. Were my father's freedom not at stake, I would be filled with admiration for Shad's accomplishment. But right now my throat burns with the caustic taste of ashes. The cases have been presented, the last argument has been made, and the reality of the present cannot be denied: Quentin Avery miscalculated badly.

And yet . . . despite the genius Shad displayed in his close, no rational jury that followed the law could convict my father of murder. And certainly not this jury, which must contain at least a few people who have loved and admired him for decades.

A few feet ahead of me, my father and Quentin are engaged in muffled argument. Dad is speaking with low intensity, while Quentin seems to be trying to quiet him. Quentin's white hair bobs up and down as Dad's voice gains in urgency. The first coherent phrase I catch is "I won't let you do it." I'm not sure which of them said that, and before I can figure it out, Judge Elder has turned from the jury and focused on the argument.

"Mr. Avery?" he says. "Is there a problem?"

"No, Your Honor."

"Yes, Your Honor," my father says, pushing Quentin away from him. "I want to change my plea."

The shock produced by this statement is so profound that for a couple of seconds no one even breathes. In this brief vacuum, my father turns in his chair and looks back at my mother, his eyes filled with apology. The sorrow and guilt I see there shake me to the core.

Then Judge Elder says, "You want to change your plea?"

Dad faces forward again. "Yes, Your Honor. I want to plead guilty."

"Your Honor," Quentin interjects, "my client doesn't know what he's saying. He's overcome by grief over the death of Mr. Garrity last night, and—"

"No," Dad says with undeniable force. "I know what I'm doing, Judge."

Joe Elder's face darkens as the full import of the situation penetrates his shock. "All right, now. We're going to excuse the jury, and I'm going to have the lawyers approach the bench to discuss this. Bailiff?"

As the bailiff moves to herd the stunned jury from the court, the gallery explodes into conversation. Only then do I regain my faculties sufficiently to realize my mother is in severe distress beside me. She looks like she did on the night I found her in the upstairs hall, thinking she'd had a stroke. The only difference is that she's still sitting erect.

"Mom?" I say, gripping her arm. "Can you hear me?"

She turns her head then, and in her eyes I see despair and desperation. "Go with them," she whispers. "Don't let him do it. Hurry!"

Jumping to my feet, I scan the gallery for a doctor. Every face out there stares at me like a driver gaping at the carnage of a highway traffic accident. I haven't been on my feet for three seconds when Drew Elliott steps away from the back wall and waves to me.

"Drew! Mom needs you!"

My old friend hurries forward.

When I turn back to the bar, I see Quentin, Dad, and Shad following Judge Elder through the door to his chambers, with Doris Avery scurrying to catch them. Without Judge Elder to enforce decorum, the courtroom dissolves into chaos. The deputies on the left wall look like witnesses to some one-in-a-million sports phenomenon, while the circuit clerk and court reporter stand together, shaking their heads, their faces red.

"Penn, go after them!" my sister says from my shoulder. "Drew and I will take care of Mom!"

I cross the well at a run and reach the door just as a deputy moves to take up a post in front of it.

"I'm co-counsel for the defense!" I tell him. "Let me through."

The deputy hesitates, then opens the door and lets me pass.

Ten steps take me to Judge Elder's office, and by the time I get there, Quentin is begging his old clerk to call a recess and have Dad examined by a psychiatrist. But the instant he falls silent, Dad speaks in the voice of a man completely in charge of his faculties.

"Judge Elder, I understand my attorney's distress. But I am of sound mind, and I want to change my plea to guilty. I fully understand the consequences of such a change."

Shad is staring at my father like he might at someone who has done something completely contrary to human nature—which he has.

"Dad, you can't do this," I tell him. "Judge, you can't let him do it. He's distraught over the deaths of Walt Garrity and my fiancée. He's been deeply depressed ever since Caitlin's death, and Walt's death pushed him over the edge."

Joe Elder listens very carefully to me. Then he says, "Your father sounded perfectly in control when he testified this morning. And not particularly depressed."

"Judge, come on. Nobody does this. *Nobody.*"

"Mr. Cage, I have seen criminal defendants change their pleas while the jury is in deliberation."

"Sure, when they know the jury is about to hammer them with life in prison. *This jury's about to acquit.* We all know it. Dad's just had an attack of Catholic guilt."

"I'm not Catholic," Dad says in a matter-of-fact voice.

"It's a suicidal gesture," I insist. "A cry for punishment, because he blames himself for the deaths of his friends."

"I do," Dad says calmly. "But I'm also responsible for Viola's death. I'm sure of that."

In the corner of the room, Doris Avery shakes her head, as though grieving over a death occurring before her eyes.

"Are you sure?" I ask. "Because to plead guilty, you'll have to sign something saying you injected Viola with adrenaline with the intent of killing her. Will you do that? *Can* you do that?"

Dad looks momentarily confused, but before he can answer, Shad says, "Actually, he wouldn't have to do that. He could make an Alford plea."

"What's an Alford plea?" Dad asks.

"Shut up, Shad! Try to rise above your nature, for once."

"Mr. Mayor, you forget yourself," Judge Elder says in a taut voice.

"With an Alford plea," Shad explains, "you can simply say that there's enough evidence that a reasonable person might conclude that you're guilty of the crime, and therefore you've chosen to plead guilty."

Dad nods slowly. "That's what I want to do."

"That's usually done in exchange for a reduced sentence," Quentin says.

"Doesn't matter," Dad mumbles.

"*Listen* to him," I almost yell at Judge Elder. "Is that the statement of a sane man?"

"Penn," Dad says, looking up at me with an expression I've never seen on his face, "I know you don't understand, but I know what I'm doing. You have to let me do this."

I've got it. He looks like a martyr about to walk into the flames. "I can't," I tell him. "No son would let his father do this."

Dad nods slowly, his eyes filled with regret. "Penn . . . I hope you never do the things you'd have to do to be able to understand what I'm doing now."

As I try to parse his words, he says, "Son, you're fired." He turns to Joe Elder. "Judge, I only want Quentin Avery representing me in this room."

Judge Elder stares at Dad for a few more seconds, then he nods and turns to me. "Penn, I'd like you to excuse yourself. I know you don't want to go, but . . . please don't make me call a deputy."

Quentin looks at me with pain-filled eyes, then reaches out and squeezes my arm. "I'll take care of him. You'd better go."

For a moment I wonder if everything that's happened during this trial was leading here all along. But the agony in Quentin's face tells me I'm wrong.

"Mr. Mayor?" Judge Elder says again. "Please leave us to it."

I want to argue, but I feel as though someone has injected me with a powerful anesthetic. As I look from Quentin to my father, and then to Doris, who has tears on her face, someone takes my left hand from behind and gently turns me. It's the deputy from outside. He must have been listening at the door. By the time he leads me through the outer door, my face is wet and numb.

CHAPTER 71

THE COURTROOM IS still a hurricane of activity when the bailiff leads me back into it. But almost immediately deputies begin clearing the room, herding the flustered spectators out without any semblance of courtesy. As I stand wiping my face, Rusty Duncan hurries across the well, his face flushed with effort or emotion.

"What happened back there, Penn? Is Elder going to let him do it?"

"They're not done. Rusty . . . Dad fired me."

"What? Jesus."

"Is my mom okay?"

"I think so, but Drew's taking her to the hospital. He's worried she may be having a stroke. A real one this time. I think she was just overwhelmed. To have that happen after days of sitting there . . . it was more than she could take. More than any wife could take."

"Rusty, what do I do?"

He shakes his head, as much at a loss as I am. "I think it's up to the judge now. The judge and Quentin and Shad. But for God's sake, if your dad's going to plead guilty, it should be to a lesser charge. Shad would have to go for it. That jury was about to set Tom free, no question."

"I don't think Dad cares about the sentence. He's trying to punish himself. And his health is so bad, anything over a year is a death sentence."

Rusty takes hold of my shoulders and squeezes hard, like he once did after high school football games, and I flinch from pain on my right side.

"Sorry," he says. "Let's sit down over here in front of the jury box. We'll wait and talk it out. Quentin won't let your dad do anything stupid."

"But my mother—"

"Drew's taking care of Peggy. Come sit down, buddy. You look like you might faint yourself."

FIVE MINUTES LATER, the door to Judge Elder's chambers opens and Quentin's wheelchair emerges, followed by Doris Avery. When Quentin sees me sitting with Rusty, he doesn't try to avoid us but steers directly toward me. I lean forward, my heart pounding heavily.

"What happened?" I ask as he rolls to within a couple of feet of me.

Quentin takes a deep breath and says, "This is hard, Penn. Please don't interrupt until I've explained the whole thing."

"Come on, Quentin!"

"Your father was going to plead guilty no matter what I did. There was nothing I could do to stop him. And Judge Elder was inclined to allow it."

"You can't be serious—"

"Let me finish, goddamn it. Tom was trying to plead guilty to murder, but I told Joe Elder I'd quit on the spot if he allowed that. Then I told Shad Tom would only plead guilty to a lesser charge. Shad asked what charge I had in mind. I said physician-assisted suicide. The penalty would be loss of Tom's medical license and time served."

"Oh, Quentin . . . thank God."

"You are the *man*," Rusty exults.

Quentin grimaces and holds up his right hand. "Shad wouldn't agree to that, I'm sorry to say. He said manslaughter was as low as he could go."

"Same penalty, though, right? Or a suspended sentence?"

Quentin shakes his head. "He said Tom had to serve some time."

"Oh . . . oh, no. How much—"

"Three years, Penn. That was the best I could do."

His words hit me like a gut punch. Sweat breaks out on my face.

"This can't be happening. This can*not* be happening."

"I'm afraid it is. Now tell me about Peggy. A deputy came in and said she collapsed."

"We don't know," Rusty says. "Drew Elliott's taking her to the hospital."

"Did Dad hear that she collapsed?" I ask.

"No. They'd taken him out by then."

"Back to jail?"

Quentin nods solemnly.

"Quentin . . . this is *wrong*. You know it is."

The old man looks back at me, his face bereft. "I don't know what I know anymore. Except I'm tired. Too tired for this."

"But—"

"Go check on your mother, Penn. You're the head of the family now. It's time to start acting like it."

While I stare in disbelief, Quentin tilts back his head and looks up at his wife. "Let's go home, Doris."

Doris Avery looks at me with infinite sadness. Then she lays her hands on her husband's shoulders and nods twice.

"Let's go, bubba," Rusty says, gently pulling me to my feet. "Let's find out how mama's doin'."

THE WAITING ROOM of the Natchez ER is mostly empty at midday, even on a Friday. The only people there when we arrived looked like they were using the place for routine illnesses. When Rusty and I gave our names to the reception nurse, she asked us to wait by the door, then came out and escorted us to an empty treatment room. For a couple of minutes, I was sure Drew was going to walk in and tell us Mom had died, but Rusty kept insisting that was impossible, that my mother might well outlive us both.

When Drew finally did come in, Jenny was with him. He told us then that he was fairly certain Mom had suffered some sort of cerebral vascular event. He'd hoped it was a repeat of her silent migraine episode, but instinct told him there was something more serious going on. "I've ordered quite a few tests, and we've started them. But Peggy wants to see you before we take her down for her MRI and other scans."

"Okay," I say dully, trying to wrap my mind around everything.

Jenny says, "She's scared to death, Penn. For Daddy mostly, but I think she's actually afraid she might die for once. That's why she wants to talk to you."

"I'll go talk to her."

"Wait about ten minutes," Drew says. "There's a med tech in with her now."

"Just let me know when I can go in. And thanks, Drew. Thanks for being there and moving so fast."

"I'm just glad I was." He starts to go, then from the door says, "I'll be here all day, okay? We'll get to the bottom of this."

I nod thanks, then turn to Jenny, who has begun shivering. When Rusty puts his arms around her to warm her up, she starts to cry.

"Come on, now," I say, trying to calm her down. "Mom's going to be all right."

"It's not Mom I'm thinking about. I mean . . . not the stroke, if that's what it is."

As I look into my sister's eyes, I see a well of fear that appears to have no bottom. "Rusty, can you give us a minute?" I ask, not taking my eyes off hers.

"Sure thing. I'll be right outside. Holler if you need anything."

Rusty doesn't wait for an answer, and soon Jenny and I are alone.

"Talk to me," I tell her, taking hold of her hands, which are limp and clammy.

"Why did he do that, Penn? You don't believe . . . Daddy really killed her?"

"No. I think he's distraught over Caitlin and Walt. Viola, too, of course. He changed his plea out of an overwhelming sense of guilt. Survivor's guilt, you know? Like the Holocaust, or wartime. He wants punishment."

Jenny nods, but I can see she doesn't fully accept this explanation.

"What is it?" I press. "What are you thinking about?"

"Penn, I need to tell you something else."

"I'm listening."

"The night Viola died, I was in England, of course. But I called the house, and Mom didn't answer."

"So?"

"I was worried, because it was early morning in Natchez."

"How early?"

"Before dawn."

I start to say "So?" again, but suddenly I understand why Jenny is upset. My mother is not merely a light sleeper; she has lived her nocturnal married life awaiting the late-night phone call heralding family tragedy. She's always been haunted by dreams of Dad falling asleep and hitting a tree on the way to some distant house during a night call; and once Jenny and I could drive, Mom's Pavlovian response to the telephone during those hours was forever imprinted in her brain.

"Can you be any more precise about what time you called?"

"That's the thing," Jenny says, her brow knitted with anxiety. "Because of the time zone difference, I didn't think about it much in the beginning. But I called her during my noon break at school. With a seven-hour difference, that means it was—"

"Five A.M., or thereabouts," I finish. "Viola died at five thirty-eight."

Jenny shakes her head like a child trying to deny some dreaded reality.

"Did you just call once?"

"No. I thought she might have been in the bathroom, so I kept calling back." Jenny flattens one hand against her chest as though to slow her heart. "When I finally reached her, much later, Mom told me she'd been sleeping and hadn't heard the phone. God, my chest hurts."

"Stop talking for a minute. Stop thinking, too."

"I can't. Penn, I think Mom was lying. She *never* doesn't answer the phone in the early morning like that. I don't think she was home. Dad, either."

I blow out a rush of air, trying to force myself to think rationally. "Jesus. I don't know what that means. When did you remember this?"

"It was on the plane ride over that it really started to bother me. I didn't know what Daddy was trying to do by keeping quiet, and I was afraid to ask him. That's why I only went to see him in jail that one time. I knew he would sense that I suspected something. I've been obsessing about it ever since the trial started, but I couldn't bear to mention it to you. I was trying to trust in Daddy. For the first couple of days I was terrified, but starting yesterday it seemed like everything was going to turn out all right. But now *this*—"

"What about Mom, Jenny? Have you asked her about it since you got here?"

My sister nods again. "She totally blew me off again. Said she never heard the phone."

"Maybe Dad left the TV on when he went out," I suggest, "and that covered up the phone."

Jenny dismisses this by closing her eyes. "You know that's wrong. He has it blaring all the time in bed, and she still wakes up for the telephone. She's like a mama bear sleeping through a storm, but waking up at the slightest peep from one of her cubs." Jenny twists her neck with apparent pain, then shakes her head as though to rid herself of her thoughts.

"They're going to call me in to see Mom in a second," I remind her.

"I know." Her bloodshot eyes find mine. "Was I right to tell you?"

"You had to tell me," I assure her. "I don't know where we're going from here, but it's long past time we knew the truth."

The door opens and the reception nurse leans in. "Mayor Cage? Your mother's waiting to see you."

I hug Jenny, then hurry through the door.

Before it closes I hear the nurse say, "Your brother's the mayor and your daddy's Dr. Cage? Isn't that something. Can I get you a Coke or some coffee, hon?"

"No, thank you."

CHAPTER 72

"SHE'S SLEEPING AGAIN," says the white-clad duty nurse who leads me into Mom's treatment room. "She'll come around again any minute, though."

My mother is lying on her back beneath a thin sheet. She has an IV in her arm and monitor cables hanging off various parts of her body. The soundtrack of beeps, hums, and clicks is my least favorite in the world. She looks so small and vulnerable on the treatment table, it's as though she is here to serve the machines lining the wall and not vice versa.

"I'm fine waiting," I say, taking a seat in the plastic chair someone has provided for me. "Thanks."

"Anything you need, just let me know. I'm Verbena Jackson. Dr. Cage is my favorite doctor. Has been ever since the old days."

"Thanks, Verbena. I'll tell him you said that."

"Yes, indeed." She lowers her voice. "And all this mess in the papers lately, that's just a *shame*. Gettin' up in people's business. Lord, I'm gonna miss that cigar of his, the way he'd leave it at the nurses' station while he made rounds in the rooms, then pick it up on his way out. They don't make 'em like Doc anymore." Nurse Jackson checks Mom's monitor screens, then nods and walks to the door. "Like I said, you let me know if you need something."

"I will."

After she closes the door, I sit and watch my mother's chest rise and fall in shallow breaths, like those of a restless child. After a couple of minutes, I reach out and lay my hand on her leg, which feels cold and still beneath the sheet. As the beeps and clicks mark the feeble workings of her body, I remember something Lincoln said on the witness stand the first time he was called up by Shad. Lincoln was talking about his mother lying to him about who his real father was, and how he had known she was lying. He said that because of his experience as a con man, he could always tell when people were trying to deceive him. When Shad pointed out that Viola had been successfully lying to him about his paternity since he was a child, Lincoln said: *When a woman who never lies tells her first lie . . . nobody questions it. Nobody catches on, because they can't even imagine that person trying to deceive them. It's the Big Lie. But inside a family. And that's why I never caught on . . .*

Mom's leg jerks under my hand, and her eyes flutter, but they remain closed. Getting to my feet, I lean down to her ear and murmur, "Mom, you're in the hospital, but you're fine."

At the sound of my voice, her eyes open, and after some effort she focuses on me. I don't see recognition in her eyes, though, only confusion.

"You recognize me, right?"

"Where's Annie? Where's Mia?"

"They're safe, Mom. They're still in Louisiana, with the FBI watching over them."

"Oh . . . oh, yes. That's right."

I see pain rush in like a dark tide as her short-term memory returns to her. "Oh, Penn," she says, her voice freighted with grief. "Why did he do it? After all that . . . why did Tom plead guilty?"

I take a deep breath before answering, and then I find that words fail me.

"Is it too late to change the plea?" she asks.

"Yes. Quentin bargained it down to a lesser charge, but—"

"But Tom still has to go to prison."

I nod. "Three years."

"Oh, God." She pulls the sheet up to her neck with one hand clenched like a claw. "He's going to die there."

"I'm going to do everything humanly possible to get him out. But right now we need to focus on you."

"Oh, that doesn't matter."

"It matters, Mom. It matters to Annie. It matters to Jenny. It matters to me. And most of all, it matters to Dad."

This time she doesn't respond. She just lies there with tears leaking from her eyes, and she makes no effort to wipe them away. *How hard do we work to blind ourselves to things we don't want to see?* I wonder. *Even if they're right in front of us?*

Mom lied to me the day after Dad jumped bail—about not being in contact with him—but when she admitted it to me, I wrote off the anomaly as loyalty to her husband. *How many lies have the two of them told to protect each other? Or to protect us, their children?*

"Mom," I say, reaching out and gently squeezing her shoulder, "I need to ask you something. Did you go to Cora Revels's house the night Viola died?"

She doesn't answer, but her eyes focus on me, and the muscles in her face almost shiver in their struggle to convey incredulity, denial, indignation, anger, and finally . . . relief.

"How did you find out?" she whispers.

"Jenny told me she called your house several times that morning, and you never answered."

"Well, that's not—"

"Mom, don't."

She takes a deep breath, then wipes her eyes and exhales very slowly.

"Dad lied on the stand, didn't he? To protect you."

"What is it you want to know, Penn?"

"What happened in Cora's house that night."

My mother's mouth tightens into a line, and her eyes flick around the room. "What's the use? Viola's gone, and your father's going to Parchman. Nothing's going to change that, is it?"

"I need to know the truth. It's time. Ya'll kept it from me till now, and look how things have turned out. If I'm going to help Dad, I have to know what happened to Viola."

She reaches up and takes hold of my arm, like someone clinging to a ship's rail in heavy weather. "Those last weeks before she died," she says, "I knew something strange was going on. It had been a long time since Tom had gone on so many house calls, or stayed out that late. So, one night I followed him. As soon as he turned onto that little road, the road to Cora's house, I knew where he was going. It was the same house Viola's parents had lived in back in . . . before."

"You knew about the affair back when it happened, didn't you? In 1968."

Mom hesitates, then nods.

"Nothing ever got by you, did it?"

"Not much. In this case, I wish it had. Today, in court, I realized that I hadn't known about the affair until after it ended. After Viola was raped, she stopped sleeping with Tom. He was acting like himself up to that time. But when she ended it, he changed. Overnight. He couldn't sleep, he got short with me, with everyone."

"Did you have any idea what Viola had done to Frank Knox?"

"No. I didn't know about the rapes at all. Not then."

"What did you know?"

"Only that something was wrong with my husband. So I followed Tom one day, just like I would forty years later. And he drove to a little house on the colored side of town. Nellie Jackson owned it, as Tom said today. Viola was hiding there."

A prickle of apprehension raises the hair on my neck. "What did you do, Mom?"

She shakes her head slowly, her eyes focused on a scene from the deep past. "I waited for Tom to leave. As he did, I saw Viola through a crack in the door. Just a glimpse, but in that instant I understood everything. Wives are very sensitive to that kind of threat. I was sure he was in love with her—which he was. I didn't go inside then. I drove around for a while, scared to death. I was terrified that Tom would leave us to be with her."

"You should have known better than that."

"Don't be so sure. He came closer to leaving than he'll admit. And if Viola had wanted him to leave us, he might have. She was a good person. Remarkable, really. In most ways . . . I couldn't compete with her."

"Mom, that's—"

"There's no use lying now, son. Anyway, the next morning, I went back to that house while Tom was at work, and I knocked on the door. Viola let me in. She was a mess, Penn. Suicidal. Nellie had a man staying with her. I think she would have killed herself if he hadn't been there. Viola was frantic. She was certain her brother was dead. She didn't know what to do."

"What *did* she do?"

"Begged me to forgive her for harming our family, first. She said the affair had been a terrible mistake. But all she could really think about was her brother, Jimmy. She knew the Ku Klux Klan was trying to find her and kill her, but she still had to be restrained from leaving that house to hunt for her brother. I don't think she cared what Tom thought or felt by that point. Nellie Jackson was trying to convince her to leave town. Nellie had connections in Chicago, and she wanted Viola to go there."

"Did Nellie get her out of town?"

"Not right away. The problem was money. Viola didn't have any. While I was there, Nellie drove up in her big Cadillac. Her man had called her. Nellie and I spoke in another room while the man watched Viola. Nellie told me Viola would need money to take care of herself until she could get a job in Chicago. Nellie's contacts were . . . in her business. Or the gambling business. She realized that Viola needed a legitimate job. Tom would have given Viola any amount of money, of course, but not to leave town." Mom closes her eyes, and tears fall from their outer corners. "He didn't want her to go."

"Mom . . . you don't have to—"

"Yes, I do. I've kept it in all this time, and now . . . I need to be free of it. Nellie Jackson told me something else, Penn. She told me Viola was pregnant."

"Had Viola told her that?"

"No. But I suppose in Nellie's business, she'd developed a sixth sense about pregnancy. Like the old midwives, I guess." My mother shudders under the sheet. "I was sure the baby was Tom's. I was terrified. I told Nellie that if she could arrange to get Viola to Chicago, I would supply the money.

"That afternoon, I went down to the Building and Loan and withdrew four thousand dollars from my personal savings account—all the money I had saved from teaching. That was frightening enough, since I was worried your father might leave us. But I had to take the risk. I drove back to the house with the money and gave it to Nellie's man. I spoke to Viola before I left, as well."

"What did you say?'

"I asked for her promise that she would never come back to Natchez. At least not for Tom. Also that she would never try to get him to come to wherever she settled. And she promised me." Mom shakes her head, and more tears come. "She loved him, I could tell. But she'd been shattered by something. I assumed it was because no one could find her brother, but now I know it was the rapes, and . . . everything else."

"The trial was the first time you heard about the rapes?"

"No. Tom eventually told me about the first one, the one in Viola's house, not the machine shop. You see, he knew nothing about my contact with Viola, so I had to play the charade of asking why she no longer worked at his office. At first he tried to act like her leaving was routine, but then his voice cracked, and he broke down. I didn't want to press him, but if I hadn't, he would have sensed that I knew more than I should."

"Did he tell you about their affair?"

"No, no. Only the rape. He told me the Klan had probably murdered her brother, too. In his mind, that explained his tears, you see? He could pretend to be upset over what she'd suffered at the hands of the Klan, and not their affair. And as terrible as it sounds, I was filled with hope. Hope that Viola had gotten pregnant by one of those Klansmen, and not Tom. I feel so awful for saying that . . . but that's what I felt." Mom closes her eyes. "My God, that girl suffered torments."

I start as the door opens to my left, but it's only Verbena Jackson again. "See, I told you she'd wake up. Everything okay?"

"We're good, thanks."

"She's due for another scan in about five minutes. I can stretch it to ten, if you need it."

"We'll try to finish up."

The nurse nods and softly closes the door.

"What about the night Viola died, Mom? Three months ago?"

Mom stares at the ceiling as she tells me the story, as though it's playing out above her in the muted colors of an old Super 8 movie and she's only describing what she sees.

"The first night I followed Tom to Cora's place, I walked down to the house and peered through a window. When I saw the woman in the sickbed, I didn't recognize her at first. But I knew who she had to be. A few nights later, Tom went out again and stayed gone for a very long time. And he'd been upset earlier in the evening, I could tell. So I waited awhile, and then I went after him. Sure enough, his car was parked at Cora's. I parked off the road and waited for him to leave. He eventually did, around four thirty in the morning."

A half hour before Jenny called you. "You went inside?"

"Not right away. I was very upset. I'm not sure how long I waited to go down there, but it was still dark. When I knocked, no one answered. The doorknob turned when I tried it, so I went in. I heard soft moaning. I called out to see if anyone was home, but Viola seemed to be alone in that sickroom. I couldn't understand why she was alone. Now, of course, I know her sister had fallen asleep at the neighbor's house."

"What did you do, Mom?"

A shadow passes through my mother's eyes. She works her mouth around, then licks her lips. "I wet a dishrag and wiped Viola's face with it, and she woke up. She was groggy but lucid enough. I guess she'd built up a very high tolerance for morphine."

"Did she recognize you?"

"Oh, yes. She said I'd hardly changed, which was a lie, of course. But she did know me. But Penn . . . *she* had changed beyond recognition. When she left Natchez, she was one of the most beautiful women I'd ever seen, just as her son said on the stand. But when I talked to her that night, she looked ninety years old. She was *sixty-five*. But only her eyes held any trace of the woman I remembered."

I push out all thoughts of the terrible life Viola endured in Chicago. "What else passed between you?"

"She asked where Tom was. I told her I'd seen him leave. She told me then that he'd tricked her. That she'd expected to die, but that Tom must not have had the heart to go through with it."

"And? What happened then?"

"She cried a little. She asked about our family. Whether I'd been happy. She told me a little about her life in Chicago. She was terribly sad when she talked about her son."

"Did you know Dad was Lincoln's father at that point?"

"No. No one had ever told me that. But I'd always feared it, of course, down deep. That's why . . ."

"What?"

"Tom wasn't the only one who sent Viola money all those years."

"Tell me, Mom."

"Didn't you wonder where all that money they kept talking about came from? The money in Viola's will? If you listened early on, you know that Junius Jelks spent everything she earned. But then all of a sudden she had seventy-two thousand dollars to leave to Henry Sexton and her family?"

"*You* sent that?"

Mom nods on the pillow. "Over the past thirty-seven years. And Viola never spent a dime of it. She cashed the checks, all right, but she put the money in a secret account to save for her son. Tom was right when he talked about Viola's dignity. She was too proud to ever use that money for herself. She saved it for Lincoln, praying the day would come when she could trust him with it, or trust Jelks not to steal it from him some way."

"Dad never knew you were sending that?"

"Lord, no. I took it out of the money he gave me to run the house. You and Jenny and I had to do without some things, but that was a small price to pay to keep Viola and her baby in Chicago."

The thought that for more than three decades my mother operated in this dual reality is hard to fathom. "Good God, Mom."

She shrugs under the sheet. "We do what we have to do. Anyway . . . Viola was well aware that my money hadn't paid the debt I owed her. Because that night, she called in her marker."

"What do you mean?"

"She told me that she'd stayed away all those years, even though she was miserable a lot of the time, and now she needed my help."

My heart flutters. "What did she want?"

Mom's eyes harden. "She wanted me to do what your father couldn't."

"You didn't inject her with adrenaline—"

"No. Morphine. There was a nearly full bottle there, just out of her reach. Tom had given her enough to sedate her, but he'd diluted it with saline."

"On the stand he said Viola would have caught him if he tried that."

Mom shakes her head. "He was just trying to protect me when he said that. He injected her in a deep vein, in the inner thigh. She couldn't see down there. Her muscular control was very poor by then. That's why she couldn't inject herself."

"I thought it was because she was a devout Catholic."

"Well . . . that, too, I suppose. Are you ashamed of me? For doing that?"

"I'm just surprised. I don't know why, though."

"Penn, if you had been there . . ." With great effort, Mom lifts her left hand and touches my cheek. "Do you remember when Sarah was suffering like that?"

If I truly open myself to that period of my life, horror and pain flood in like a black tide. "I remember."

"Viola's physical pain wasn't as bad as Sarah's, but her emotional state was worse. Far worse. Sarah was taken from a happy life, a beautiful family. But Viola died believing she had failed her only child. That's almost unendurable for a mother."

Mom is in the grip of confession now, willing herself forward. "That's why I agreed to do it. Your father loved her too much, but I could put myself in her place. I realized how lucky I'd been to have the life I'd had with you and Jenny, and I owed all that to Viola's sacrifice. We all owed her, Penn." My mother's eyes shine with unshakable conviction. "Because she could have taken your father from us, if she'd wanted to."

"Mom, you're wrong."

She forces a smile and nods, making a show of believing me, but the truth is in her eyes.

"So, it was you who botched the morphine at her antecubital vein?"

"Of course it was. Viola's veins were in terrible shape, especially the big one at the elbow, which was the only one I had any chance of hitting. I pushed straight through the vessel. But I didn't know that at the time. I have no medical experience. I left that house believing I had euthanized her."

"Was that the only injection you gave her?"

"Yes."

"And you drew the morphine out of the bottle yourself?"

"Yes."

"How long after that did you leave the house?"

"As soon as Viola fell unconscious. I felt I should stay with her, but she'd told me I should leave. And once she was asleep, I felt so alone. Alone and afraid. I didn't think there was *any* chance she would wake up."

"And you never realized there was a tape in the camera?"

"God, no. I never even considered that."

I blink in disbelief as the sequence of events comes clear in my mind. "So you couldn't have killed her."

My mother swallows audibly. "No. Sometimes I wake up wondering if the pharmacy somehow mislabeled the bottle, but Tom assured me they didn't. The murder investigation would have uncovered that."

"He's right. Plus, if you'd injected that adrenaline, you would have known instantly. It would have hit Viola's system before you got out of the room. She'd never have passed out. No, someone injected that adrenaline after you left."

Relief fills her eyes, lessens some of the tightness in her face.

"The question is, who?"

"You don't think it was Cora, do you?" she asks. "Or Lincoln? After all that business about the will? My God, it's too horrible to think about."

"I don't think Cora could do that. Lincoln . . . I don't know. I don't think so."

"I don't believe he did it," she says. "It had to be Snake Knox. And he's still out there somewhere. That's the hell of all this. The absurdity. Tom is in jail, and that monster is walking free, still killing people—"

"Take it easy, now." I suddenly have the feeling she's trying to distract me from something. "Mom, look at me. And answer one question. Did Dad go back to Cora's house after you left?"

Her eyes widen, but her mouth remains still.

My pulse is picking up, and my face feels hot. "Did Dad do it, Mom? Did he inject that adrenaline?"

"No, Penn. He told me he didn't."

"What did he say happened?"

My mother looks like a trapped animal; I've seen thousands of witnesses and defendants look that way.

"Did you and Dad talk on the morning Viola died?"

"Penn, I don't want to keep anything from you. But if you want to know more, you're going to have to speak to your father. I don't want to say or do the wrong thing. And I don't ever want to put you in a position where you'd have to lie. During this whole trial, I've been terrified that Shad Johnson would call me to the stand. Spousal privilege isn't absolute, you know. I didn't know that until I started researching it, but it's true. I've been close to breaking every day of this accursed business."

"Mom, Dad's not going to tell me any of this. I doubt he'll even admit what you've already told me. And to stand even a chance of getting that plea revoked, I need the whole truth."

She refuses to meet my eyes. "I don't know what to do. You need to go see your father. All I can tell you now is this: I wanted to tell the truth from the beginning. It wasn't to protect myself that I let Tom take the risk. It was for Annie, and for Jenny's children."

"What do you mean?"

"Your father nearly *died* five months ago. We'll be lucky if he lives another year. And given that . . . I've had to face the fact that Tom is right. I have a duty to stay free, in case anything should happen to you. After all, you don't live the safest life in the world. Annie's only eleven. Somebody has to be there for her. Jenny's kids, too. They're older than Annie, but they're no more independent than your sister was at their age."

"Mom, come on—"

"What have I always told you?" she asks, gripping my arm with surprising force and shaking it. "*Family.* Family is all that matters in this world."

Verbena is going to open the door again any second. As I try to think of a way to persuade Mom to tell me more, another thought strikes me, one I can scarcely credit. "Did Quentin know about this? About your part in what happened?"

"Not as far as I know. When your father said no one could know about something, he meant no one."

Like his war years, I think bitterly. When my dad shuts the door on something, it stays shut.

"Are you going to tell Jenny this?" Mom asks, the worry in her voice making her sound more like her old self than anything she's said since I came in. "There's really nothing to be gained by making her think about any of it."

In my mind I see my sister shivering in the waiting room. I don't know whether Mom is right or wrong, but I don't want her to worry about it now. "I'm going to tell Jenny you slept through her calls. That you took a Lorcet Plus."

Mom nods slowly, her eyes filled with gratitude. At least in Jenny's eyes, she thinks, her image as a perfect mother will remain intact. "I'm sorry you had to go through this in the dark," she says. "But you always were the strong one."

"My mother's son, right?"

A faint, proud smile touches her lips. She never was very quick at picking up irony. "Where are you going now?" she asks. "Are you going to see your father?"

"I don't see that I have a choice."

"Good." A bell dings out in the hall. "Remember what I said. *Family.* It's all that matters."

I kiss her forehead, then leave her bedside. But at the door I turn back. "Mom, you asked me why Dad changed his plea. Now I'm asking you. Is he still trying to protect you? Because I think you're safe now."

She looks at me over the little hump of her sheet-covered feet. "None of us is safe so long as Snake Knox is free. But that's not why Tom pleaded guilty."

"Then why did he do it? Guilt over Caitlin? Walt? Henry?"

"Tom did it because he chose us over Viola. He lived up to his vows and fulfilled his duty. He did what good men do. Good fathers. But Viola paid the price for his honor. A terrible price. And . . . he couldn't live with that anymore. That's why he put himself in prison."

I can't look long at the pain now revealed in my mother's eyes.

"I'll be back to see you later," I tell her. "Try to get some sleep. There'll be a guard covering you at all times."

"Don't be too hard on your father, Penn."

"I'll see you later. Try to sleep."

And then I go.

CHAPTER 73

AFTER LEAVING MY mother's room, I told some white lies to Jenny, then texted Rusty and asked him to pick me up at the old west entrance to the hospital in fifteen minutes. I wanted some time to gather my thoughts before heading to the jail to see Dad, and I didn't want a bodyguard dogging my every step. After a tense conversation with Joe Russell, I managed to free myself from my own shadow.

I'm standing inside the old doctors' entrance of St. Catherine's Hospital, which after decades of neglect is undergoing a massive remodel. This entrance is the site of one of my clearest childhood memories, the first occasion that I realized my father was "important." Here, just inside the big green double doors, a panel was mounted that held a hundred rectangular push buttons. Each button had a white label affixed to it, and most of the labels had names typed on them. After every name were the letters M.D. Whenever a doctor entered the hospital, he would press his personal button, and a yellow light would go on behind it, like a light in a fighter plane or a Gemini spacecraft. And somewhere upstairs, a central operator would know that specific doctor was in the hospital and available to handle patients.

I was only five years old the first time Dad took me to this hospital with him, the first time I saw that light go on at the end of his straight, strong forefinger. And my little chest filled with a pride I've hardly experienced since. I knew then that people needed my dad—depended on him—and because of that, he mattered. And if he mattered, then *I* mattered.

When I grew up, I wanted to matter just as much as he did.

That old panel is still set in the wall, but most of the labels peeled off the buttons long ago, and a harness of loose wires hangs beneath the aluminum frame. Even with all the millions spent on renovations over the years, no one ever removed this device. Since the public never sees this entrance, the bean counters probably figured the expense wasn't justified. Now the quaint relic sits lifelessly in the wall, as outdated as an orphaned pay phone.

When that panel blinked with light, the building wasn't called St. Catherine's, but the Jefferson Davis Memorial Hospital, after the president of the Confederacy. Back then, there were eighty doctors in Natchez, and the city thrummed with life. But as times changed, the name of the hospital changed, too. Sometime in the 1980s, when I was practicing law in Houston, it became St. Catherine's, named for the nearby creek that the Natchez Indians lived along before they were slaughtered by the French who settled here. Today there are less than forty doctors in Natchez, thanks to bad tort laws, medical turf wars, and a moribund oil industry. And I am the mayor of what remains.

Bending at the waist, I squint at the faded letters on the few labels that remain. To my amazement, near the bottom left corner, I see *Thomas Cage, M.D.*

As I made my journey from the ER to this exit door, every few steps carried me past a portrait of a chief of staff gone by. The most recent twenty or so hang in the lobby, but my father was chief back in 1972, so his portrait resides in this forgotten corridor. I wonder if the other visages I passed concealed secrets like my father's behind their dignified masks. Some did, perhaps. But most of those faces probably hid the usual small-town sins shared by men across America, regardless of race, religion, or section of the country.

My father was different. He couldn't live blindly amid the ruins of a gilded empire where the lost children of Africa worked with false smiles among their former masters. So he thrust himself into the troubled borderland between black and white, and in his passion to do good, he did also what other passionate men had done who trod this deep soil made rich by sweat and blood. He strayed from his own kind, mingled his blood with the blood of Africa. That was common on this dark bend of the river, as it was across the South before Thomas Jefferson ever became a founding father. But *my* father's offense was that he cared for the woman he bedded, and for her people, and in this atavistic corner of the New World he learned that the fearful, clannish Anglo-Saxons who'd settled it always exacted a price for such betrayal.

And blood and death followed.

I'M STILL STARING at the old call panel when my phone pings with a text message. Rusty is waiting for me outside in his car. As I raise my arm to press the wide steel bar on the exit door, time slips, and I see my father walking through ahead of me, leaning into the steel to keep his frail body erect while he forces it open. When I was five years old, he could throw out one hand and swat this door open as though it were made of cardboard. Now . . .

Of course, Dad will never open this door again. At this moment, he is sitting in a jail cell, waiting to be transferred to a state prison in the Mississippi Delta that I'm told is close to hell on earth.

And he's chosen to go there.

THE VISITING CUBICLE of the Adams County jail is no luxury accommodation, and I've occupied it as both visitor and prisoner. But never did I imagine that I would enter it to speak to a man who put himself here on purpose. Dad is supposedly being escorted to this depressing box, but I've been waiting ten minutes already.

I'd hoped to make my way here without crossing Sheriff Billy Byrd's path, but word quickly spread of my arrival at the ACSO, and he made sure he was standing at the duty desk when I logged myself in. Byrd tried as hard as he could to bait me, but I refused to be goaded, and I left his gloating face behind me with the laughter of his deputies.

"Don't pay 'em no mind, Mayor," said the big black deputy who escorted me to the visiting room. "They don't know nothin' 'bout nothin'."

"Thank you, Deputy . . . ?"

"McQuarters. Larry McQuarters. I been looking out for your daddy for Mr. Quentin."

"I appreciate it, Larry. My whole family does."

"I'll have Doc in there soon as I can."

THE DOOR BEYOND the metal screen opens, and my father edges into the cubicle with Larry McQuarters behind him. His hands are cuffed, his wrists bright red, but after he sits, his knees creaking in protest, Larry bends and unlocks the cuffs.

"You be good now, Doc. Sheriff Byrd be on my ass if he finds out I took these off."

"Don't worry, Larry," Dad says with gratitude. "Thank you."

The crappy fluorescent lights in this place don't do the complexion any favors, and Dad's prison pallor, which was masked by good clothes and light in the courtroom, is painfully obvious here. He looks through the metal screen without any obvious emotion I can read, except perhaps a dread of being asked things he would prefer not to speak about. If I'm going to get him to tell me about the night Viola died, I need to establish some kind of rapport with him.

"I've just come from the hospital."

"How's your mother doing?"

"Drew's still evaluating her. He thinks she's had a stroke."

Dad must have heard this already, but he bows his head and murmurs something I can't make out. Then he says, "Ask Drew to let me know as soon as he knows for sure."

"You know he will. But I'll remind him."

"Thank you."

Before the silence can swell into a suffocating blanket, I say, "When I left the hospital, I passed through that wing they're redoing. They still have the old call panel on the wall. Disconnected, of course."

He looks surprised by my choice of topic. "Is my name still on it? I can't lean down there to read it anymore."

"It's still there. Do you remember your call number?"

"I was sixty-two for a long time. Not anymore, of course."

He waves a hand like this doesn't matter, and I notice the once-straight finger now curled with arthritis, its nail pitted and opaque.

"I still think of that place as 'the Jeff,'" he says, a wistful look in his eyes. "You know? It's a good thing they changed the name, of course. Though a lot of my patients don't even know who Jefferson Davis was."

This makes me think of our maid, who died in St. Catherine's Hospital seven years ago. "Ruby didn't know who Colin Powell was, the year he considered running for president."

"Christ. I can't bear to think of that."

This time the silence stretches out, and Dad looks as though he's afraid I'm going to start berating him about his plea decision.

"I'm not here to talk about your plea."

Once more his eyes register surprise. "Thank you."

"I'm here as your lawyer, to give you legal counsel."

My formal tone takes him aback, but I need to establish that fact before mentioning anything that could be used against either of us.

"I'm here because I know Mom was in Cora's house on the night Viola died. I know she injected her with morphine."

His face loses what little color it had. "Jesus, Penn." He looks around as though someone is listening. "Can this room be bugged?"

"In theory? Yes. In practice, no. Now they couldn't use what they recorded anyway. Because I'm your attorney, this is a privileged conversation."

"I see."

I wait for him to continue. When he does, his voice barely registers above a whisper.

"Did Peggy tell you she was there?"

"Who else could have told me that?"

"I'm not sure."

"Jenny suspected it first, but she doesn't really know. She just started chattering about calling the house the night Viola died, and Mom not answering the phone. When I pressed Mom about it, she finally cracked."

"Was anybody in the room with you and Jenny? A nurse? Drew, even?"

"No. Now, come on. The trial is over. I've got to know what happened."

Dad leans back in the plastic chair, then brings his hands together in front of him. "Things happened exactly the way I described on the stand, only I left out everything to do with your mother."

"Obviously. So?"

"Just the facts, ma'am?"

"Please."

He nods again, and flecks of dandruff fall onto the metal tray below the screen. "I'd gone there to fulfill the pact Viola and I made. But once I was there, and she told me about Lincoln, I knew I couldn't go through with it. Not without thinking about it a lot more first. So I diluted some morphine to look like a big dose and injected her in the inguinal vein. She went to sleep, and I left."

"What about the tape she made for Henry?"

"I took that with me. She'd told me what was on it. I went to my office and watched it anyway, all the while thinking about the enormous secret she had kept from me all those years. Lincoln."

"Okay. Go on."

"I left the tape at my office and drove back to Cora's house. Viola was the only one there, and she was sleeping soundly. I was surprised, given the relative mildness of the dose I'd given her. I stood there and watched her breathing and tried to see the young woman I'd fallen in love with all those years ago. But I couldn't. Anyway, as I waited for her to stir, I heard a sound. A whirring. It seemed to be coming from the camera Henry had left there, but there was no red light on. Still, I walked over to the tripod to check, and that's when I realized the camera was on. On and recording."

The Dumpster tape, I think with a chill. *You flat-out lied about that.*

"And the lack of red light told you someone had set it up that way? To secretly record what happened while you were there that night?"

He nods. "Exactly. And I panicked. As quickly as I could, I unloaded that tape and hurried back to my car."

"Viola was still alive?"

"Absolutely."

"And then?"

"I went back to my office and watched that second tape. It had started recording about ten minutes before I got to the house."

"You think Cora started it?"

"That was my guess. Now I wonder if it was Lincoln."

"It could have been."

Dad closes his eyes, thinking back to that night. "The tape was set on slow speed, so it could record six hours. My whole first visit with Viola was there, but that wasn't what shocked me. Five minutes after I left the first time, your mother walked into that sickroom like Donna Reed in a goddamn movie. I saw everything she did, heard everything she and Viola said. That was when I learned that Peggy had known about Viola back in 1968. That she'd even helped her to leave town, sent her money all those years."

"So what did you do then?"

"I went home and pretended I knew nothing."

"*What?* What about the tape?"

"I kept it with me—both of them, actually. Peggy was home, pretending to be asleep. I couldn't bear to go through all that pain with her right then. Think about it. As far as I knew, Viola was going to live for another week or ten days. There was time to manage things. If someone had been trying to trap me with that second tape, they had no evidence of anything."

"But you erased it anyway, didn't you? In the MRI machine?"

"Of course I did. I took it with me on morning rounds and taped it under the tray inside the MRI unit. For an hour that tech blasted it to hell without even knowing it. Then I retrieved the tape and took it back to my office. I thought everything was fine. I didn't even throw that erased tape into the hospital Dumpster until the next day, on my way out to Walt's van."

"When did you talk to Mom about what had happened at Viola's?"

"The previous morning. When you called me about Shad Johnson and the potential murder charge . . . I knew I had to talk to Peggy."

"What did she say?"

"She wanted to tell the truth from the start. You know your mother. But I wouldn't hear of it."

"Why not?"

"Penn, once the facts about my affair with Viola came out—and they were going to come out—no one would have believed Peggy did what she did out of empathy, or mercy. They'd have said it was jealousy, or a cover-up, or murder for revenge, pure and simple. You know I'm right."

I do. When I was an assistant DA, I saw plenty of cases where people in their seventies and even their eighties shot or stabbed each other over romantic triangles, or even past infidelities that only came to light years later.

"Then why the hell didn't you confide in me? The very first day?"

"Because I knew your instinct would be to tell the truth and take our chances with the system. You'd have thought you could make people see the truth. And in a perfect world, you probably could have. But with Shad Johnson so hungry for revenge against you, and

Billy Byrd aching to give me some payback, they'd have railroaded your mother to get *their* revenge."

Dad brings his hands to his face and pulls his cheeks down like a man at his wit's end. "For the last three months I've lived in dread that Peggy would snap and go to the police. Especially while I was in jail. But she turned out to be even stronger than I knew."

"Not that strong. She broke today."

At this he closes his eyes and bows his head again.

"So, Dad . . . I have to ask you. And I need an answer. Who really killed Viola?"

He opens his eyes and looks at me as if the answer to this question is self-evident. "Snake Knox, of course. Him and Sonny, and maybe one more with them."

"Did they arrive during your second visit?"

"Hell, no. They were there when Peggy was. They saw her leave."

"What? How do you know that?"

"Remember the message Snake sent me through the VK guy you shot? The message you brought me at the Pollock prison?"

"Sure. 'Wives and children have no immunity.'"

"That was Snake telling me to remember that Peggy's freedom was on the line. He masked it just enough that it seemed like a simple threat. But that was code, and I knew what he meant. Either I took the fall for Viola's death, or he would put Peggy in my place in that trial."

"How could he do that? How much did he know?"

"At first? Probably nothing. Snake and Sonny were probably parked in the trees on the road when Peggy left, waiting to kill Viola. Peggy being there wouldn't have told them anything, of course. They probably assumed she was just sitting with Viola, or doing female chores. Cleaning bedpans, like that. They probably figured Viola was a friend of the family. But once I was accused of the crime—thanks to Lincoln—they saw me acting guilty. That must have puzzled them for a while. But Snake figured it out soon enough. Because either I believed I *had* killed Viola—which no doctor would, after seeing the tape of her death—or I was afraid of something else. And once he heard the details of the affair . . . he knew he had me set up to take the fall for him."

"And he knew you well enough to know you'd sacrifice yourself to save your wife."

"He was certain of it. Because he knew how far I'd gone to save Viola from the Double Eagles back in '68."

"You got in bed with Carlos Marcello."

He shakes his head. "I don't like thinking about that."

"I imagine not."

This time Dad doesn't shrink from my gaze. In his face I see the resolve of a man who did what he had to do to protect a woman he loved.

"So how much of all this did Quentin know?"

Dad sticks out his bottom lip and sighs. "Very little. Quentin was as exasperated with me as you were."

I mull this over for a while. "And Walt?"

"Walt knew even less."

"Goddamn, Dad. You sure ask a lot of your friends."

This time he looks down at the tray below the window and says nothing.

Faced with the yawning void of his deepest motives, I grasp at a niggling detail that's bothered me for two days. "What about that hair-and-fiber evidence tampering? When Jewel told me Billy Byrd's deputies were messing with that evidence, you had Quentin shut me down quick."

"Of course I did. Because I knew exactly what was going on. That's another irony of this screwed-up case. Byrd's deputies probably destroyed or replaced Caucasian hairs that might have turned out to match Snake or Sonny, but by doing so, they inadvertently protected Peggy. I wasn't about to let you open that can of worms. The FBI might have gone in there and found a dozen more gray hairs from your mother's head."

For the first time in a while, I feel like laughing, at the thought of my father exploiting Billy Byrd's corruption to protect my mother. But Dad isn't smiling.

"Of course, I couldn't be sure that Snake hadn't told Byrd everything," he goes on. "That was one more thing I had to sweat. Did Billy Byrd have Peggy's hair sitting over there in an envelope, ready to drop into the case file on command from Snake if it looked like I was going to be acquitted?"

"Christ. But they didn't do that. They thought they had you. And once things began turning your way, it was too late to drag Mom into it."

Dad's eyes settle on me with disturbing intensity. "Was it?"

"What are you saying?"

"If I'd been acquitted, couldn't someone else have been charged with Viola's murder?"

I feel as though my father just sucked the gravity from the entire building and I might float up off the chair. "Are you saying you changed your plea because they threatened to charge Mom with Viola's death?"

He looks back at me without answering for several seconds. Then he says, "No. I was afraid of that, sure, but that wasn't my reason."

Again we've come to the question of why he changed his plea to guilty. This time I don't steer away from it. "Shad got to you with that parable of his, didn't he? That's what triggered your change of plea."

Dad acknowledges this with a single nod. Then he says, "What do you think about Shad's theory that everything I did for black people over the years was motivated by guilt?"

"I don't think it matters. They needed help, and you helped them. Few others did."

He doesn't look convinced.

"Didn't you start all that long before you knew Viola?"

"A couple of years before, I guess. It's hard to remember now."

"So forget it."

He doesn't look like he's going to stop second-guessing himself anytime soon, and in prison there's not much else for a man to do.

"Dad, I need to ask you two questions. And I need you to answer them. No matter how much you think it might hurt me."

"All right. You're entitled, after the hell I put you through these past months."

"Did you know Lincoln was your son all along? Is that why you sent the money all those years?"

His eyes narrow, and then he hooks the fingers of his right hand in the wire screen and shakes his head without a trace of deception. "No. I told the truth about that. I never even suspected Lincoln was mine. And Viola confirmed that on the tape, remember?"

"Yeah."

"Then what . . . ?"

"Back in October, when you had your last heart attack, Caitlin and I were out on the river in a boat. When Mom called us, she told me you kept saying there was something you needed to tell me. Something you could only tell me. After you recovered, you denied ever saying that. I've been thinking that might have been about Lincoln. That you were going to tell me I had a brother."

Dad's eyes fill with pain and something else, maybe shame. "No, Penn. That was about Viola, though. I was going to tell you to make sure she didn't want for anything during her last years. See, at that time I didn't know Peggy knew about her, so I couldn't put anything in my will. That kind of thing needs to stay between father and son. But after I got better, I thought I could procrastinate a little longer. I guess one of these days I'm going to have to face the fact that I'm not going to live forever."

Before I lose my nerve, I say, "If Viola had wanted you to leave us, would you have gone to Chicago with her?"

My father's eyes widen like those of man slapped without warning. He swallows, then drops his hands and looks away from me, pondering the question. I'm not sure I want to hear the answer. Maybe his delay is the answer.

"I think your mother worries about that a lot," he says softly.

"She does."

He sighs with infinite regret. "The answer is . . . she did."

"Wait a second. Who did what? I don't understand."

Dad looks straight into my eyes. "Viola broke her promise to Peggy. She *did* ask me to come to Chicago. I lied on the witness stand, Penn. About the notes I sent with my checks."

"I'm confused. What do you mean?"

"About four years after she got to Chicago, Viola sent one of my notes back to the clinic. She sent it in an envelope marked 'personal.'"

My heartbeat is accelerating. "Was there a letter in it?"

"No. Just two words, written above my note asking whether she was all right."

"What were the words?"

Dad looks down and takes a deep breath, as though summoning the strength to answer. Then he looks up with wet, bloodshot eyes.

"Save me."

CHAPTER 74

I STARTED DRINKING gin as soon as I got home from the jail. I had no limes, but it didn't matter. I had tonic. I ran out a half hour ago, having spent the hours until sundown padding through my Washington Street house wondering exactly when everything started going off the tracks for our family. Until three months ago, the Cages had a pretty blessed run. Excluding the death of Annie's mother, of course. But on balance, we'd been far more lucky than not.

Now it's all gone to hell. Caitlin dead. Dad in prison. Mom in the hospital. Annie in protective custody a hundred miles away. Friends dead—some because of what they did to try to help us. Henry Sexton, Walt Garrity, even Viola. Lincoln Turner poisoned by lies and hatred. And yet, as my mother pointed out . . . Snake Knox still roams free.

As I drank away the afternoon, a single line spoken by my father in Judge Elder's chambers kept repeating in my head: *I hope you never do the things you'd have to do to be able to understand what I'm doing now.* When I wasn't pondering this, I was sifting through the information my parents had given me about the night Viola died. Once I knew my mother's role, of course, all that had followed seemed simple enough to understand, and maybe even inevitable.

But no matter how much gin I consumed, I couldn't rid myself of the image of my father's face behind the wire screen, revealing that Viola had asked him to leave us after all, her heartrending plea carried in two desperate words: *Save me.* Given Viola's pride, Dad would have known what it cost his old lover to beg him for deliverance. What had it cost him to hear her plea and then ignore it? To give up Viola for my mother, Jenny, and me? By the old standards of honor and loyalty, he did the right thing. But for himself, and for Viola . . .

Lincoln was right when he said that in some ways what our father had done to his mother was worse than killing her. Dad gave Viola a glimpse of another world, a better world in almost every way, and then took it away, condemning her to a half-life in exile from her home, with a man who did not love her. It was Viola who ended the affair, but only because she realized first how impossible any future together had been. Dad had the luxury of self-delusion; she didn't.

In the end only one thing matters: he chose to stay with us.

I tried to leave the jail without berating him about his guilty plea, but in the end I couldn't. All I said was, "You know, if you were religious, I might be able to understand this self-flagellation, at least a little. But you're not. Not at all." He smiled then—to himself, not me—and said, "I don't believe in God, it's true. But I guess I do believe in atonement."

Atonement.

I told him I thought there were less dangerous ways to pay for transgressions than locking himself up with a bunch of killers and gangbangers.

"Maybe," he allowed. "But I don't think so. When Judge Elder turned to that jury to send them back to deliberate, I knew they were going to set me free. Four jurors looked right at me and told me that with their eyes. And I was terrified. I knew then that if I let that happen, I would never pay for what I had done. Never balance the scales. So I took away that option."

"Oh, you left human nature behind today. You got on the Jesus train, whether you intended to or not."

"No, Penn. I followed my conscience, that's all."

"And you do realize where it's led you? What will you do in Parchman when Snake Knox sends some skinhead with a shank to kill you?"

Dad considered this, then shrugged. "Maybe I'll get lucky. Maybe one of the black gangs will look out for me."

"Get real."

He looked at me the way missionaries look at nonbelievers. "Who knows what I'll find in there? Maybe I can use my medical skills to help some people. People who really need help. Whatever happens . . . I'm resigned to it. Ready for it, even."

When he said that, I dropped all pretense of normalcy. "You don't have to do this. I know why you're doing it. Because of Caitlin, and Walt, and Henry, and all the others. You feel responsible for their deaths. And you *are,* at least in part." At that point I stuck my fingers through the screen and touched the papery skin of his hand. "But not one of them would want you to do this. It would *break their hearts* to see this."

Dad had no answer for that, at least not one he would share with me.

When I left him, I told him nothing about my plans to try to get his plea bargain revoked. The odds of success are low, and the process could take a long time. But if Dad actually goes to the penitentiary, my mother will go mad. My cold assessment is that he will be transferred to Parchman, and that my best—and probably only—hope of getting him released before he dies there is to prove that someone else murdered Viola. And I don't know how I can do that when the full resources of the FBI have proved insufficient to find and capture Snake Knox.

It took switching from gin to scotch to have my epiphany. After this additional chemical assault on my normal thought processes . . . I saw to the bottom of my father's soul. Was alcohol the lantern that allowed me to see what I had failed to while I listened to Dad through the wire mesh screen of Billy Byrd's jail? Maybe whisky was only the catalyst that shoved me out of my own way. In any case, I now understand something I did not before, and like anyone else who's had his last illusion torn away . . . I want it back.

Dad didn't condemn himself to prison because he chose us over Viola—to remain with his wife and children rather than leave them for a mistress who loved him. If that had been his only crime, he would have put it behind him decades ago. Viola's desperate plea to be saved had carried more within it than a desire to spend the rest of her life with Dad—a lot more. Back at the jail, as my father talked to me about God and atonement, there was a deeper knowledge in his eyes—a knowledge of himself with all self-delusion stripped away. What remained was the truth, and the burden of it was terrible. Dad was trying to tell me what he'd realized about himself while Shad told his parable in court, but he couldn't find the words to carry the awful weight of his discovery. Here in my house, though, alone with my whisky in the rubble of my father's decision, I have finally plumbed the well inside him.

Dad didn't choose to stay with us out of honor and duty. That was part of it, sure—but not all. If he had acted out of loyalty, he wouldn't feel the need to punish himself as he has. The truth is, *there never was a real choice for him.* Because he never had it in him to leave his own culture and go through the hell he'd have had to endure to share a life with Viola. What would that have been like in 1968? In Mississippi, it might have meant being murdered. But even up north, it meant being ostracized. Shunned. Constant stares . . . harsh words . . . getting kicked out of restaurants and hotels. He'd have been cut off from all the comfort of his former life, maybe even from his own parents and siblings.

Dad had wanted Viola, but he hadn't wanted everything that came with her. He did a lot to help black people over the years, but he wasn't willing to join their ranks. Not in that way. So he took the best that Viola had to offer and refused the worst. In the end, he let things unravel in the way that they do when you don't stop them. For Dad, that meant a little guilt over the years. But for Viola . . . it meant a lifetime of suffering and regret.

Before I left the visiting room, Dad made a general sort of statement, something I took as guilty rambling. Now, drunk as I am, I remember it nearly word for word. He said: *Our country's messed up, son. Mortally wounded. And I can't for the life of me see how we're going to heal it. Your generation can't do it. Even you're too old. The new ones coming along . . . that's where the hope lies, if there is any. We've got to acknowledge what we did to those people. But I don't think we ever will. People hate admitting guilt, but we can't blame it all on the Knoxes of the world. We're all guilty. Blacks are messed up, too . . . but how could they not be? White people fight this so hard because they know the truth in their bones. You know? You don't get that angry unless you know you're wrong.*

"Is that why you're going to prison?" I asked him. "You're taking on the sins of your race?"

"No," he said. "I'm not that ambitious. I'm only doing penance for my own."

THE RATTLE OF hailstones hitting glass brings me out of a sound sleep or a drunken stupor. I must have passed out after remembering Dad's jailhouse rant. Getting to my feet, I realize I'm on one of the basement cots the guards have been sleeping on, and that the "hailstones" are actually the sound of someone banging on one of the tall windows of my basement office. I figure some pushy reporter has slipped past my guards and dropped down into the light well that surrounds the house. But when I look around the corner, I see the dark face and intense eyes of Lincoln Turner willing me over to the glass. After cautiously moving to the window, I crouch and raise the sash, and he bends and clambers into the room where a week ago I had my first real conversation with Serenity Butler.

"What do you want?" I ask him.

Lincoln looks around the room, cocks his head at the bottle of Hendrick's on my desk. "There's something we've got to do."

"We? What's that?"

His smoldering eyes find me again. "You know."

I try to think through the fog of gin, but I can't identify any areas of mutual benefit. "Sorry. I don't."

"Think about it."

This time, the obvious comes clear with a flash of memory of wild eyes in a face that reminds me of Ronald Reagan. "Snake Knox?"

"You get the prize, brother man."

"Nobody knows where Snake is."

Lincoln smiles strangely. "I know."

"So it's pointless to talk about."

"That's not what I meant. I mean *I* know. I know where Mr. Snake is at. I found his hidey-hole."

This revelation blows away some of the gin fog. "How?"

"Don't matter. We can talk about it on the way."

"On the way where?"

Lincoln looks around my office again. "I said we can talk about it on the way. Get your shit."

"What shit would that be, exactly?"

"Whatever you want to bring. Just make sure you bring a gun."

Okay. I see where this is going. "Where is he, Lincoln?"

"Sorry. Not taking any chances on you playing Boy Scout and calling your FBI buddy. We're past that now. *Way* past."

Only now do I realize that my half brother is wearing black jeans and a black polo shirt. He smells like he's drunk at least half as much alcohol as I have, and also like he's been sweating for a while. Or maybe that's the stink of homicidal anger.

"Look, what the fuck else you gonna do?" he growls. "Sit here and drink yourself into a stupor?"

"How far are you talking about going? Five miles? Fifty? Five hundred?"

"I'll tell you on the way, goddamn it. We don't have a lot of time. So *get your shit.*"

Maybe it's the gin in my system, but his argument seems persuasive. "How many people does Snake have with him?"

"Two, to the best of my knowledge. But if we keep talking, he could be gone. Or we could have a dozen of those skinhead motorcycle freaks burning a cross for kicks."

"What makes you say that?"

"Two guys on Harleys showed up while I was there. Not right at his place, but not far from it. I didn't get the feeling they're on the best of terms."

"What kind of place is he hiding in?"

"A dump. Little two-room shack behind a house. Sitting in some poplar trees."

I think about this for a while. "So maybe we let the VK guys take him out."

"Can't rely on that. They haven't killed him so far. And it might go the other way. We can't take a chance on him disappearing again."

"Why are you so sure Snake's about to rabbit?"

"FBI's turned up the heat. Big time."

"Then it might make more sense for him to sit tight where he is."

"No. Snake's fixing to blow this country."

I walk to my desk, where my pistol lies at the moment, and mull over Lincoln's suggestion. "I think Snake had some fantasy that he was going to be able to stay here. But not now. Kaiser's got a witness who can finger him for a murder back in the sixties. A woman."

"Then I'm right. We gotta move."

"What's your plan, Lincoln? You sound like you just want to execute the guy."

"Sure I do. Did you not hear what he did to my mother? They tied her to a table in a machine shop and took turns raping her. They sodomized her with a goddamn Coke bottle. They tortured my uncle and his best friend, and then they killed them. And they would have killed Mama if that Presley guy hadn't busted her out."

"That's a hell of an irony, you know? Because Ray Presley was a very bad guy. Take my word for that."

Lincoln shrugs. "I got no problem with that. Most guys I grew up with were bad by any technical definition. Bad guys do good things sometimes. But you're missing the point, man. I want to kill Snake, but you've got no choice. You *have* to kill him."

Something in his voice chills me. "Why's that?"

"Because once your father—and mine, as strange as that sounds—passes through the gates of Parchman, he's a dead man walkin'. I doubt he'll live a week. Snake will reach out to whatever Nazi gang is on top in there, and Tom Cage will die. And take my word for it—he'll die rough. Is that what you want?"

I warned Dad of this very threat only hours ago. "I get that. But what I told you before is true. This woman Kaiser has, Dolores St. Denis, she can put Snake on death row."

Lincoln isn't impressed. "How long will that take? A year? Two? You think if Kaiser arrested Snake *tonight,* he couldn't reach out from whatever jail he's in and kill the doc? Man, what world do you live in? I thought you'd been a prosecutor in Texas."

This guy is starting to piss me off. "Okay, let's say Snake dies tonight. A certain threat to Dad may be reduced, but he's still going to spend three years in jail."

"So?"

"He won't live to serve that time. He's in heart failure now. Anything over a year was a death sentence."

Lincoln turns up his palms. "We can't change the sentence. What are you suggesting?"

"I need to get him out. *Free.* Snake can do that. Because he killed your mother. Him and Sonny Thornfield. And I need to get him to admit that on tape."

Lincoln snorts, then laughs in derision. "You can forget that shit. The only way Snake would do that is if he was about to kill you. Taunting you. And we're not trying that kind of sting."

"Tell me where he is, Lincoln. Can't we bug the place?"

"No way. And he won't be there long enough for us to set up something fancy and wait. This is an in-and-out thing."

"Lincoln . . . you remember I've got a daughter, right?"

"Yeah. So?"

"So if I were to get killed on this little trip with you, she'd be an orphan."

"Is that what you were thinking when you went out to that hunting camp to see Forrest Knox three months ago?"

Touché. "I wasn't thinking then. That's my point. And you're not thinking now."

"You're wrong. I've thought it through. I'm here because something told me that, given the chance, you'd go with me. So either tell me to get the hell out, or pack your shit and let's go."

"I'm bringing a tape recorder."

"You can bring a box of Havana cigars if you want, just bring your fucking piece. And some extra ammo, if you got it."

"Handgun?"

"That'll work. But if you've got a long gun, bring that, too. It's a fluid situation we're going into."

The process of decision is a funny thing. One minute you're explaining all the perfectly rational reasons why you can't do something insane; the next you're opening a drawer and taking out a nine-millimeter pistol, then going into the next room to fetch a Remington .308 hunting rifle from your father's old gun cabinet.

While Lincoln watches me with satisfaction, I hand him the rifle, then sit at my desk and grab a legal pad and a pen.

"What the hell you doing now?" he asks, checking the bolt action on the Remington.

"Writing a holographic will."

"Christ. A lawyer to the end, huh?"

"Let's hope not. But let's not pretend this isn't a high-risk play."

He shrugs. "Can't lie about that."

As I start to write, I have difficulty making the letters clear. I'm not *that* drunk. Then I realize that adrenaline is flooding my system, making fine motor tasks difficult. I try to breathe deeply and regularly as I finish the note.

March 17, 2006

To Whom It May Concern,

I, Penn Cage, being of sound mind and body, do here attest that I wish to add a codicil to my existing will, which should remain in force but with these additional bequests added. To Mia Burke, in appreciation for her generous aid in taking care of my daughter during a painful time (and for her critical work during the trial of Drew Elliott two years ago), I leave $150,000. To Keisha Harvin, who worked bravely to complete Caitlin's work to bring the Double Eagles to justice, and who suffered disability at their hands, I leave $100,000. The remainder of my assets and copyrights I leave and/or assign to my daughter, Annie, less the smaller bequests listed in my existing will.

Penn Cage

Lincoln watches me scrawl my name, then lets out a long whistle.

"You're really handing out the candy, aren't you?"

"Both those girls need money. I'd leave you something, but Dad fixed up that trust for you. Besides, your chances of making it through the next few hours aren't any better than mine."

He chuckles with appreciation. "My truck's parked one block over. Can you take care of your security guys?"

"Yeah," I say, getting out my phone.

"Oh, I'm gonna need that when you're done."

"Need what?"

"Your phone. In about twenty-five minutes you're going to figure out where we're going. And you're not going to be texting anybody our route."

CHAPTER 75

THE MAIN ROAD north out of Natchez is U.S. 61, the blues highway. If you stay on 61, it'll carry you up to Vicksburg, then to Yazoo City and the Mississippi Delta. But there's a far older road that runs north from my hometown—the Natchez Trace—and Lincoln takes it once we leave the lights of Natchez and its outlying settlements behind.

The two-lane blacktop follows an ancient Indian path, winding north through Adams County, past Jefferson College, Emerald Mound, Loess Bluff, and a hundred other landmarks before it leaves the state following the old flatboatmen's route back to Nashville, Tennessee. The northwest corner of Adams County is mostly old plantation land, thickly wooded, nearly impenetrable in some places, and it's there that Lincoln leaves the Trace and steers his big pickup deeper into the forest.

For the first few miles, lights are sparse, cars few. Then both disappear altogether. Somewhere out to the west of us, the Mississippi River is flowing. To the north lie Alcorn State University, the river city of Bienville, and the Grand Gulf Nuclear Station. But from where we are, you'd never know it. I feel like we're following a narrow stream through a primeval forest. The hills get steeper, the gullies off the shoulders deeper, but the trees never relent.

"You guessed where we're going yet?" Lincoln asks.

The only settlement that I know about up this way is Church Hill, to the west, but I'm pretty sure we've already passed it. As I ponder what I remember of this region, a vision of dark Corinthian columns against a night sky comes to me, the only survivors of a once-great plantation house that burned in the 1800s—and one of Caitlin's favorite places.

"Windsor Ruins?" I ask.

Lincoln laughs softly. "Close, but no. That's in the next county up."

"Aren't we almost out of Adams County by now?"

"No."

"What's left? Who lives up here?"

"Nobody, baby. We're going to a dead place."

"What does that mean? A cemetery?"

"Might as well be."

"What the hell are you talking about?"

"Those Double Eagle bastards, the few that are left . . . what are they, really? Devils who outlived their time. They're ghosts. You know what I'm saying?"

"Sure. But I still don't get it."

"Where do ghosts feel safe?"

"I don't know. A church?"

"Close again."

"For God's sake, Lincoln."

"A ghost town!"

It takes a couple of seconds, but then I get it. Just south of the Claiborne County line lie the remnants of Rodney, a once-prosperous town abandoned by the Mississippi River in the 1800s. My father took me there when I was a boy, because the place had been the site of a small but famous Civil War action. All I remember of Rodney is a two-story brick church with a Yankee cannonball embedded high in its front wall, and a lot of sand and dust.

"You got it now?" Lincoln asks.

"What the hell is Snake doing in Rodney?"

"You just answered your own question."

"Does anybody still live up there? The river left it high and dry a hundred years ago."

"There's probably forty people spread through the woods up there. Maybe fifty. There's a big hunting camp, though. Sound familiar?"

A chill runs up my back at the memory of the Valhalla hunting camp. "Is that where Snake is?"

"No, I told you back at your house, he's in a two-room shack behind a bigger place owned by somebody he knows. It's a good hiding spot. There's a couple of ways in and out on land. There's also a road through some swamp bottom that will take him to the river. He's got a speedboat tied up down there. His hole card, I imagine. I figure that's how he got to Natchez without being caught by the FBI."

"How the hell did you find Knox?"

Lincoln takes his time with this. "Old Mr. Snake's been in contact with Sheriff Billy Byrd."

"How on earth could you know that?"

"I've been talking to a black deputy who works for Byrd. Been paying him for information."

"How long?"

"Ever since I got to town. I've even got a phone number for a burn phone Knox is using, and this morning I got the GPS coordinates on the Rodney place. I drove down right after the trial and checked it out. He's there."

"How did you keep from being seen?"

Another low chuckle fills the truck cab. "Ran a little con, of course. I borrowed a piece-of-shit truck with a lawnmower in back, threw in some cane fishing poles, then rode up here wearing some old yardman shit. Told the only two people I talked to I was looking for work up this way. Gave 'em the idea I needed to get out of Natchez in a hurry. They didn't think anything about it."

"I'll be damned."

"After tonight, you may be, if you're not already."

Thanks for that. "I need to ask you something. Did you put the videotape in Henry's camera on the night your mother died? The tape Sheriff Byrd's men found in the Dumpster?"

Fresh bitterness comes into Lincoln's face, but then a faint smile shows in profile. "Cora loaded that tape in there, like she testified. But it was me who told her to do it. And I told her how to set it so the red light wouldn't come on. The tally lamp, they call that, in case you're interested."

"I figured that was you."

"Didn't do me no good though, did it? Daddy Tom found the tape and nuked it in that MRI machine. Pretty smart, really."

To this I say nothing.

After staring into the darkness for a while, I say, "You said there are three people where we're going?"

"Last I checked."

"Do you know who they are?"

"Snake. That blond kid. And a woman, about sixty-five. Looks like a bitchy old redneck."

"Wilma Deen, probably. Glenn Morehouse was her brother. The kid is Snake's son. Illegitimate."

"Lot of that going around, seems like." Lincoln grunts and scoots forward on his seat like a man feeling drowsy.

"Sorry. The FBI thinks Wilma Deen threw the acid in that reporter's face. Keisha Harvin."

"Blinded her, didn't it?"

"She's got about ten percent of her vision left."

"Well, then. No need to worry about collateral damage with those motherfuckers."

In the silence after this assertion, I realize that I haven't seen a light for several miles, other than the moon. We have to be getting close to our destination. Though I've seen no visual sign, I sense that the Mississippi River lies just to the west of us, a great tide of mud and water that alters the very atmosphere for miles on either side of it.

"Do you have any sort of plan?" I ask in a neutral tone. "Or do you just plan to bust into this little shack with guns blazing?"

"I can come up with something better than that. But don't kid yourself. We don't have any options here. You think of that house as a nest of snakes, if it helps you. But don't start looking for some other way. There isn't one."

"There's got to be. I want to see the layout. How far do we have to go?"

Lincoln taps the brakes and points through the windshield as he eases onto the dark shoulder. "Not far. We're here, brother."

A quarter mile ahead, a single light flickers through the trees like a distant star. Lincoln kills the headlights and stops the truck with a crunch of gravel. The high thrumming whine of night insects is so loud it penetrates the window glass.

"Rodney, Mississippi," he says. "Get your guns. And get your game face on, Mayor."

THE TRIP FROM the truck through the nearly lightless skeleton of the old town is like walking back through history. I feel that we are the ghosts who earned the town its name. We walk past the place where the pavement gives out on the east-west access road coming in from the highway, then down the single lane that was the only real street Rodney ever had. The rifle in my hands sends energy vibrating along both arms, and my heart flutters at the realization that I cannot hear our footsteps. There's enough humidity in the air to keep the dust settled around our shoes, so maybe that's deadening the sound.

Lincoln keeps to the center of the dirt street, staying well clear of the broken string of buildings that line it, as though they hold sickness. Several appear to be abandoned, including a gutted old Baptist church of brittle wood. The brick church I remember stands across the road from the wooden wreck, and it perfectly matches the image in my mind. I can even see the cannonball in the moonlight, set high in its face. Out front a Confederate battle flag flies from a short pole, and a sign on the pole reads THESE COLORS NEVER RUN.

"Time to get off the main drag," Lincoln whispers, grabbing my arm and pulling me under some trees where a tiny gravel road runs behind a large, dark house.

As soon as I feel grass beneath my feet, he drops down and begins belly-crawling through it. Slinging the rifle over my left shoulder to avoid aggravating my bruise, I do the same. The pale soil feels sandy beneath the grass, and even here it smells to me of the river.

"There," Lincoln whispers.

Fifty yards ahead, two windows in a small frame house glow yellow with what looks like lantern light.

"No electricity?" I ask, pausing to adjust the strap of the .308 across my back.

"Listen," Lincoln says, stopping beside me. "Isn't that a generator?"

He's right. A hollow, rattletrap rumble like a car engine from the 1920s fills the bass spectrum of the wild hum of night insects in these deep woods. All I see beside the house is an ancient pickup truck parked near a big poplar tree.

"The generator must be in its own shack or something," I think aloud. "Not to be any louder than that."

"Good cover for us."

"How far behind that house is the river?" I whisper.

"Couple of miles. Straight shot through the swamp on a dirt road."

The little house before us appears to be a dependency of the larger house nearer the road. We saw no lights in it as we slipped past, but that doesn't mean it's empty.

"What are you planning to do?" I whisper.

"Wait a little, see if they're moving at all."

I grunt but say nothing. I'm not a hunter. Never have been—at least not since I shot my first deer at eleven, on a trip with a friend. My dad never liked it, either. I have hunted men, by necessity, with Daniel Kelly. But this doesn't feel like that. Lying in the humid dark with gnats buzzing my face and mosquitoes draining my arms of blood feels like hunching in a hide waiting for a deer to walk by, one preoccupied enough or oblivious enough to let me shoot it from thirty feet away. But it's not deer sitting in the yellow light beyond the windows of that little house, I remind myself. It's people. Armed people. And we don't even know how many.

"You ready?" Lincoln says suddenly.

"Fuck, no! Listen, I know where you are, believe me. But you're crazy if you want to just bust into that house. We don't know shit yet about what we're facing. You're better off setting it on fire and shooting them as they run out."

He turns to me, his eyes glinting in the moonlight. "Like the old cowboy movies, right? I bet there's a can of gas back at one of those houses we passed."

"There'll be dogs, too."

He grimaces.

"This is the country, Lincoln. You can't assume nobody saw us walking in here."

"All the more reason to move now."

I grab his arm. "Wait—"

The door to the house has opened. First through is a wiry figure that even from this distance I recognize as Snake Knox. The mere sight of him starts my heart pounding. Next through is another male figure, probably Alois, and then a woman.

"*They're leaving,*" Lincoln hisses, panic in his voice.

I grip his arm tighter. "Stay still, goddamn it. Let's see."

I breathe a little easier when the trio walks past the truck and heads across the grass, on a line that will take them about forty yards to our left. A faint but steady flicker tells me Snake is using his cell phone. Behind him, the woman lights a cigarette and starts puffing away. The orange eye bumps up and down as they walk.

"Must be going to the main house," Lincoln whispers. "We could take them right now."

"Would you please calm the fuck down? You don't want a shootout on open ground, without cover."

"I'll be smoking that bitch's cigarettes in two minutes."

"You charge them now, you'll do it alone."

"We don't have to charge them. Use your rifle to take out the blond kid. Keep firing as they scramble. I'll go get Snake. Kill the woman if she turns to fight. If not, let her go till we've got Snake under control."

"You're not going to kill him?"

"I'm going to have a word with him first."

I'm hearing Lincoln's tone more than his words, and he doesn't sound like a man using objective judgment. "I'm no sniper, okay? Especially not at night. And you're not, either."

His jaw flexes angrily as the three figures recede, then disappear into the main house nearer the road.

"So what's your plan, genius?" he growls.

The best course of action seems obvious to me. "They just made it easy, actually. Let's just go into the dependency and wait for them. They're bound to come back."

Lincoln watched the trio vanish like a hunter being forced to let prize game walk in and out of his sights. But he says, "Okay. Let's go."

"Crawl or run?"

"Let's run it. I'm tired of crawling."

Unslinging the rifle, I work the bolt and chamber a round. Then, with a last glance at the main house, I start running.

Eight seconds of sprinting carries us to the door of the dependency.

Snake didn't bother to lock the door; it opens almost soundlessly. The interior barely qualifies as spartan. Moth-eaten sofa, a Formica table, a couple of chairs. One sink with rusting fittings. The stink of mildew permeates the air, and I'd bet my last dollar termites have eaten 80 percent of the wood in the walls. The back room contains two cots and a scarred end table. There's no toilet I can see. Probably an outhouse in the back.

"How you want to play it?" I ask, gripping the rifle tight.

Lincoln looks around. "Stand to each side of the door, so we're behind them as they come in. Put 'em together on that sofa, too low to jump up and make a move."

"You're not planning to shoot them as they come in?"

Lincoln shrugs. "That's fine with me. I thought you wanted to talk to them. I saw you put your tape recorder in your pocket."

"I'd prefer it."

"I'll give you two minutes. But if they even think about shooting, they're dead."

I nod.

"If we have to open up," he says, "I'll shoot Snake, and you take whichever one of the others looks likely to fire first. That way we don't throw away our lives shooting the same person."

"Maybe you are thinking after all."

Lincoln starts to move toward a window, but I hiss at him, and he freezes.

"You hear something?" he asks.

"No. But don't go near a window. Your night vision will suck, being in this light, and they'll see you long before you see them. Let's sit with our backs against the front wall. They shouldn't see us as they come in, and we'll be behind them. They'll also be walking in out of the dark, which should give us a slight edge."

Lincoln nods slowly. "Thinking about it like that . . . it seems best to shoot right away. At least take out the woman and the blond kid."

"Alois."

"Whatever. If we shoot them outright, Snake will realize it's suicide to keep fighting."

"Been in a lot of gunfights, have you?"

Lincoln glares at me. "More than you."

"Not as many as Snake, though. Whatever that old bastard does, the one thing he *won't* do is lose his nerve. Don't think of him as an old man. He's a wily old crop duster who never refused a dare in his life. He's walked away from two plane crashes that I know about, and he was a sniper in Korea. He's killed a lot of people, both legally and otherwise. So don't count on being able to predict what he'll do."

"Then let's shoot him in the back of the head and take away his options."

I breathe deeply, then sigh. "I'd rather talk to him, if we can manage it. All of them. If not . . . we'll do what we have to do."

After a few moments of reflection, Lincoln kneels on the floor, then turns and sets his broad back against the front wall. I crouch and move to the other side of the door, then sit and press my back against the mildewed wallpaper. Leaning my rifle against the wall, I take my Springfield nine millimeter from my pocket and jack the slide, then lay my arm across my knees.

Maybe a minute passes. Then Lincoln says, "What you think they're doing in the main house?"

"Eating. No stove or fridge out here."

"Yeah. No shitter, either."

"You saw Snake was on his phone?"

"Uh-huh."

"Let's hope he's not calling reinforcements."

Lincoln says nothing at first. Then he laughs with bitter humor. "I'd hate to be surrounded by a trigger-happy motorcycle gang in this place. These walls wouldn't keep us safe from a BB gun."

Looking around the shack, it strikes me how odd it is that Snake passed up a chance to live out his days with his son Billy in the luxury of Andorra in order to try to rebuild his former criminal enterprise—without the benefit of his nephew's political connections or army of dirty cops. Did Snake realize when he made that choice that his life would likely end in a mildewed shack near the Mississippi River? Probably not. But even if he had, he might have made the same choice. Snake Knox is a southerner through and through, and dying on soft sheets in a tax haven between France and Spain would almost certainly feel to him like a coward's way out.

"What's the point of this place, anyway?" Lincoln asks.

"Keep your voice down."

"This town, I mean. You know anything about it?"

"A little. This two-bit place was almost the capital of the Mississippi Territory. During the Civil War, a Yankee gunboat was stationed down in the river, and the sailors on board broke regulations to come ashore. With some regularity, apparently. Enough to make time with the local belles. Some local Confederates got word of it and busted into the church one Sunday, captured most of the crew. One of the Yankees actually hid beneath the hoopskirt of his girlfriend. The whole thing made national news in 1863."

"You a history buff or something?"

"Not really. My dad brought me—our dad, I mean—he brought me up here when I was about eight, I guess. Maybe ten."

Lincoln nods, his expression hard to read. "Old Junius Jelks didn't waste time with that kind of field trip when I was growing up. If he took me anywhere, it was to work a con."

"I'm sorry, man."

"Yeah . . . fuck it. That's life, ain't it?"

I let some time pass. "What did you think about Dad changing his plea?"

Lincoln shakes his head and doesn't say anything for a while. "I guess he came out a lot better than he could have. Three years in jail, when he could've got life. Pretty smart, in the end."

"That jury was going to acquit him, Lincoln."

"I think you're probably right. And when he yelled out like that . . . I swear, I thought he meant to plead guilty to the full charge. To first-degree murder."

"He did mean to. He tried to. Quentin got it pled down."

Lincoln nods. "I been thinking about that."

"And?"

"I don't think Doc killed Mama."

"He didn't."

"But I think he knew that, in a way, he done worse than killing her. You know? And he wanted to be punished for it."

"That's exactly it. But he didn't have to go to prison."

Lincoln shrugs. "Maybe he did. For himself. But tell me this. You know for a fact he didn't kill her?"

"Mm-hm."

"Who did?"

"The man who's about to walk into this house. And Sonny Thornfield."

Lincoln takes a long, deep breath and looks down at the semiautomatic pistol in his hand. "There's not really anything else to say, is there?"

"I guess not. You all right?"

This time he says nothing.

CHAPTER 76

I FEEL THE footsteps through the floor before I hear voices. When you're listening so hard you can hear your pulse in your ears and watch your belly jump with each heartbeat, the impact of three people walking comes through your butt and your feet like the vibrations of a timpani drum.

I look across the ten feet that separate me from my half brother, knowing that in ten seconds one or both of us could be dead.

What if only one walks in while another stays outside to finish a cigarette? Or two walk in but one stays out? If Wilma stays out, Lincoln will probably open up on the guys—

The door swings open and Alois Engel comes through, two feet to my left, wearing Levi's and a red T-shirt and a shoulder holster. My hand tightens on my pistol to the point of pain. *If he turns before the others come in—*

The second body through belongs to someone I don't recognize, but he's bigger than Alois. He's young, and there's a pistol in the holster on his belt. My Springfield comes up with a will of its own, lining up on the stranger's back as the smell of cigarette smoke floats through the door. He starts to turn as someone else comes through behind him. I'm expecting Wilma, but it's Snake, thank God, because the last thing I want is a gunfight with Snake Knox outside.

Somebody laughs, but I don't know who because Wilma is right on Snake's ass, and before I can think the stranger turns, sees Lincoln, and grabs for his gun. I pull my trigger, but Lincoln shoots him first, right under the breastbone, probably in the heart because the stranger drops like a steel girder hit him in the chest.

When the others spin, they're staring straight into our raised weapons. My heart is pounding so hard my vision blurs, but my brain can't fix my gaze on any object for more than a fraction of a second anyway. All it registers is eyes: panic in Wilma's, rage in Alois's, and Snake's ravenous eyes vacuuming up details, devouring everything—

"Hands up or die!" Lincoln yells. *"You've got two seconds!"*

Alois goes for his gun.

Lincoln swings his aim onto the kid, but before he fires Snake drives his elbow into his son's arm, ensuring he can't get to his gun.

"Stand down, goddamn it!" Snake yells. "They've got us!"

For a couple of seconds Alois looks like he might still go for his gun, but the urgency in his father's eyes—and the hate in Lincoln's—finally tips the balance.

The acrid stink of powder fired in anger hurls me back to nights when I was the one who did the killing, and my stomach threatens to betray me. The man on the floor is already dead, thank God. I don't know if I could stand here watching a stranger gurgle out his last living breaths.

"People heard those shots," Lincoln says. "You want to talk to him, get to it."

It takes a few seconds for me to regain control, but then I motion toward the sofa with my pistol. "I want to talk to all of you. Get over on the couch."

"*Fuck* you," snarls Alois, his blue eyes filled with contempt.

"Shut him up," Lincoln growls at Snake. "Or I'll blow his fucking spine out."

"Alois," Snake intones.

The kid's eyes drip disdain.

I can't get over Snake's appearance. Someone has transformed him from a wild-haired hell-raiser into a dyed-black, Brylcreemed church deacon. But even this new incarnation is tied to death in my mind, to the writhing body of Will Devine dying on the floor of the Adams County courthouse—

"Throw your guns in that sink," Lincoln orders. "Right now."

Alois starts to say something, but Snake says, "Do it, Junior. This ain't the time."

The guns ring dully as they go into the sink: Snake's first, then Alois's. Wilma Deen's hands are floating about head high, and her eyes look like those of a panicked hostage, but she must be carrying something. When Lincoln jerks his gun toward her, she points to her pants pocket, then pulls out a small black automatic—it looks like a .25—and drops it into the sink with a clang.

While Lincoln herds them onto the broken-backed sofa, I reach into my pocket with a shaking left hand and take out the Sony tape recorder I use for memos during the day. I prop it on the back of the sink and face the three on the couch. Snake sits on the left, Wilma Deen in the middle, Alois on the right.

"Go," Lincoln tells me, obviously frustrated.

A premonitory shiver runs through my body, a feeling that by doing this I might be sentencing Lincoln or myself to death. If we simply killed them now, we could walk away. Every passing second probably brings someone else closer. The owner of the main house . . . one of the living ghosts of Rodney . . . VK gang members . . . We don't have to kill these three to stay safe, of course. We could call the FBI, and Kaiser would have a tactical team here in less than an hour. Maybe half that, if he has a chopper on call. The proper call would be to Sheriff Byrd, of course, but Byrd already knows Snake is here—

"You had two minutes," Lincoln says, "and you're burning the second one right now."

"The tape recorder's not on yet," I tell my captive audience. "When I hit *Record*, I want somebody to tell me who killed Viola Turner. If you do that, I'll have some evidence, and you'll get to live a while longer. If you don't, I'm going to walk outside and let this man do what he came here to do. Do you understand?"

Snake's eyes look like those of a professional gambler calculating odds in Las Vegas.

Alois says, "Nothing we say here could be used as evidence in court. It would be under duress."

"That's bad news for you, Junior," Lincoln says. "Real bad."

"Keep your fuckin' mouth shut," Wilma snaps at Alois, but her eyes are on Snake. She's looking for a magic escape card from her fearless leader.

"You ready, Snake?" I ask, reaching for the RECORD button.

"That nigger's gonna kill us no matter what," Snake says. "I see it in his face."

"You got good eyes for an old man," Lincoln says, and I hear a wild edge in his voice.

"Not if you tell the truth," I say evenly.

Snake laughs. "Bullshit. I can see it, even if you can't."

"He's already called the FBI," Wilma Deen says in a shaky voice. "Don't say nothin'. This is a trick. He's trying to get us to talk."

"No, darlin'," Snake says, his eyes on Lincoln. "Kunta Kinte there is gonna shoot us."

Wilma Deen's eyes are wide with fear. I figured her for a stone-cold bitch, but this obviously isn't her kind of situation. Maybe the dead guy on the floor has given her a premonition of her future.

"Will you talk?" I ask.

Snake's eyes move from Lincoln's to mine. "You killed my nephew, Cage. Hard to believe, really. I guess he figured you didn't have it in you."

"You raped my mama," Lincoln intones. "You tortured my uncle. And you either killed him or ordered it done."

"Your mama killed my brother, Mr. Turner." Snake turns up his hands. "But hey . . . what's done is done. Right?"

"Except we ain't done, cracker."

"Do you know how an air bubble kills a person?" Alois asks in a strange voice.

"Shut up," Snake says softly.

"It moves through your veins until it reaches your heart. Then, if there's enough air, it creates a vapor lock, the way air will do to any pump. The heart muscle is fighting for all it's worth to pump blood, but there's nothing there. No blood to prime it, see? So you lie there with a sledgehammer slamming the inside of your breastbone, and then your heart starts squirming, and then finally your whole inner works just seize up, and *then*"—the blond kid snaps his fingers with a startling report in the little room—"your brain burns out like a light."

Snake Knox has maintained a placid expression through his son's description of his brother's murder, but I'm pretty sure he's gritting his teeth. After a long, slow breath, he says, "My son's clearly got a lot to learn about forgiveness. He wasn't raised on the Good Book."

I feel I've just heard Satan preach the gospel. Knox's words trigger a memory of Dolores St. Denis describing Snake howling scripture as he raped her in the Lusahatcha Swamp, and that brings to mind the preacher father who raped both Snake and Forrest when they were boys.

"They're playin' us!" Wilma cries, her eyes frantic. "They got the FBI outside listening!"

While Snake disabuses her of this notion once and for all, I press RECORD on the little Sony.

"You blinded a young woman," I say to Wilma. "Didn't you? Threw acid in her face."

Wilma Deen shakes her head violently. "I didn't do no such thing."

"Oh, for fuck's sake," Alois mutters. "Own it, why don't you? Sure, she did. That little nigger bitch asked for it."

Lincoln says: "I'm gonna enjoy straightening you out—" but I cut him off and say, "We're on tape, everybody. Let's say what needs saying."

Lincoln cuts his eyes at me, but he doesn't finish his sentence.

"Keep your mouth shut, Junior," Snake says. Then he looks at me again. "Your father pleaded guilty to killing Viola. That's the end of it, so far as the law's concerned."

"We're not concerned with the law right now. We're concerned with the truth. I know when my father walked out of Cora Revels's house, Viola was alive. Somebody went in and injected her with enough adrenaline to blow up her heart. I think it was you. All I need is a yes or no."

Snake's eyes move from me to Lincoln, then back again. Despite the dire straits in which he finds himself, the glint of humor never leaves his eyes. I can almost feel Lincoln's hunger to snuff out that light.

"So that's what this is about," Snake muses. "What do I get, if I tell you? You're gonna let me walk out of here?"

"No. But I'll call the FBI."

"Why haven't you called them already?"

"He's stalling," Lincoln says, glancing at one of the windows.

"No, he's talking for the tape. He's making sure that anything he says will be inadmissible in court."

"So what's the point in going on?"

I never had much chance of using my tape as evidence. But looking into Snake's eyes—eyes that watched Jimmy Revels bleed as he cut the navy tattoo from the boy's arm, that watched Viola scream as Klansman after Klansman climbed on top of her and raped her, that watched Glenn Morehouse and Sonny Thornfield and countless others choke out their last breath—I realize that I am truly not concerned with the law. All I want is the certainty that only Snake can give me—that he, and not my father, murdered Viola Turner.

"You were in Viola's sickroom that night," I say softly. "Tell me what happened."

"I was there, all right," Snake says, and I feel Lincoln go absolutely still beside me. "But I don't think you want to know what happened."

"Are you talking to me or him?" I ask.

"Both. But you more than him, Cage. You think you want the truth, but you don't. It's like Jack Nicholson says in that movie. You can't handle the truth. My daddy was a preacher, did you know that?"

"You know I do."

"He used to quote scripture all the time. You know what scripture says about the truth?"

"What?"

"It's a terrible thing to fall into the grace of God." Snake smiles strangely, and I remember all the depraved acts this preacher's son has committed in his life. "That's it, right there. Are you sure you're ready for that?"

"You're the one ought to be worried about meeting God," Lincoln says.

"Let's hear it," I say, gesturing with my gun.

Snake clucks his tongue a couple of times, then looks at the floor. "Me and Sonny had been out there a couple weeks before Viola died. Just to remind her of the deal she made back in '68. We told her to stop talking to Henry Sexton, and if she didn't, well . . . we'd have to shut her up for good.

"I could see right off she wasn't going to stop. I wanted to go ahead and finish her, but Forrest didn't want any trouble that might get in the papers. Forrest was always more worried about the dollar than anything else. So, me and Sonny would ride out that way every day or so, see who was out there. We saw Doc Cage's car quite a few times, sometimes his nurse. But then we saw Henry's car again. I decided we had to finish it, no matter what Forrest said."

Maybe Snake really is crazy. I can't believe he's about to confess to killing Viola in front of her son.

"So that night, we parked in the trees up above the house, where Doc testified he saw our truck—Devine's truck, really, but we were in it. Anyway, Doc was already there when we got there that night. I figured we'd wait for him to leave, then go in and do it. Well, after about fifteen minutes, Doc comes out and drives off. But just as we was walking down there, here comes another car." Snake looks up at me, his eyes shining brighter. "And who's in it . . . but *your mama*? Mrs. Peggy Cage, mistress of the plantation."

My face feels hot. I start to glance at Lincoln, but I can feel his gaze on me like a lamp. He wants to know if Snake is making this up.

"She was in there a while, then she come out in a hurry. Once she drove out, me and Sonny went in."

I want to say *This is bullshit,* but Lincoln would hear the lie in my voice.

Snake looks at Lincoln and shrugs. "When we got in there, your mama was gone. She looked just like she did in the picture I saw from that video. There was no tape in that camera, either."

"You're lying," Lincoln says. "He's lying, right?"

"He's lying," I affirm.

"You wish I was," Snake says. "You had no idea, did you?" His eyes watch mine with almost sexual pleasure. "Thought you wanted the truth, huh? The truth is, your mama killed the woman your daddy used to screw back in the day. Maybe out of anger, maybe out of trying to keep things secret. Or maybe just out of shame."

"Tell me he's lying," Lincoln says.

"He is. My mother was there that night, all right, but he's only telling part of the story."

"She *what*?" Lincoln asks, unbelieving.

"I just found out today. Dad didn't want to go through with the suicide pact. To fool your mother, he injected a diluted solution of morphine into a deep vein, to give himself time to process everything she'd told him. About you, especially. But Mom had followed him there that night. She'd followed him a few nights earlier, too, and discovered he was seeing your mother again. That second time, Mom went into the house after he left, to find out exactly what was going on. Viola woke up while she was in there. They talked, and your mother begged mine to do what Dad had been unable to do."

"Bull*shit*," Snake says.

Hot anger rises in my gullet. "It's the truth! Mom tried to do what Viola wanted, but she screwed up. She was the one who botched that morphine injection. She didn't have the skill to hit in the vein."

"So she injected adrenaline instead," Snake says. "However you slice it, she killed the nurse." The wily old bastard fixes Lincoln in his gaze. "You see? I didn't kill your mama, boy."

"Yes, you did," I insist, wondering if there could be any truth to what he's saying. "My mother left thinking she'd succeeded. But Dad came back, just as he'd planned to do when he left. He found Viola still sedated, and he found the tape in the camera. He saw on the tape that Mom had been there, what she'd tried to do, and that ended up being the thing that drove everything that happened afterward—his desire to protect his wife from a potential murder charge."

"Who told you that fairy tale?" Snake asks in a taunting voice. "Your daddy, I'll bet."

"They both told me—separately."

"Because they finally got their story straight. They had months to work on it before that trial, didn't they? How many people died to protect your mama, Mayor? The mistress of the plantation couldn't go to jail for killin' an old used-up slave, could she? Even if that slave kept the master's bed warm all those years ago—"

"Shut up," Lincoln mutters.

Black glee fills Snake's laugh. Our suffering is like liquor to him. "I never killed your mama, boy. And now you know it."

I hear Lincoln take a long breath, and when it passes out, I feel him shifting into another state of consciousness, like a truck downshifting to climb a hill.

"You did worse than kill her," he says, his bass voice nearly inaudible. "You broke her. You wounded her soul."

At last I turn and meet my brother's eyes. All I see there is pain. He will call me to account for keeping what I knew from him, but not until this business is done. As I stare, I see a question in his face: *Do you want to stay in here, or do you want to go outside while I do it?*

"Wait, now," Wilma Deen says, as though talking to herself. "Hold up, mister. Don't do this. I can't die like this. This ain't fair."

"Fair?" echoes Alois, mocking her. *"Fair?* I am so goddamn sick of your shit—"

Wilma Deen slaps Alois so hard that the sound reverberates through the little shack. For maybe two seconds, the kid gapes at her; then he slugs her in the temple. He looks like he's gearing up to do it again when Lincoln fires a bullet into the couch an inch from his shoulder. I don't know if Lincoln meant to miss or not, and I sense that the next bullet is going into someone's head.

"I didn't kill nobody," Wilma says, first softly, then with escalating fear. "I didn't kill nobody. I threw the acid on that girl, but that's it, I swear to God."

She looks up at me, then Lincoln, her eyes imploring us. "I didn't kill your mama, sir. I never even met her. Snake and Sonny done it—just like they killed my brother Glenn. You hear me? He bragged about it all during that trial!"

Alois's face is so pale that I know he'd kill her if he had a weapon ready to hand.

"All my life Snake used me," Wilma goes on, "used me and threw me away, over and over again. I ain't dyin' for *him*!"

Snake hasn't said anything. He's calmly watching his minion turn on him, and probably gauging whether anything she's said could be used against him if he somehow survives this night.

"That tape won't help you," Wilma says breathlessly. "I know that much law. But *I* can help you. I can testify, like Will Devine was gonna do. But you have to protect me, okay? You gotta put me somewhere *he can't reach*."

"There's nowhere I can't reach," Snake says softly. "You know that, baby girl."

Wilma shivers at this sound of what must be a pet name between them. Lincoln and I share another glance. I know what he's thinking: *Right now she's dying to confess, but let her get out of this shack and lawyer up, and we'll never get another word out of her—*

Wilma's truncated scream brings both our gazes back to her, but too late.

True to his namesake, Snake has pulled a knife from somewhere and he has the blade to her throat, with most of his body concealed behind hers.

"All right, now," he says, getting his legs under him and lifting Wilma to her feet.

The guy's survival instincts are breathtaking. Even before Wilma finished speaking, Snake realized that she had taken on value to us—and in that instant she became his ticket out of here.

As Snake moves laterally toward the door, Alois's eyes flick from Lincoln to me and back again, alert for any chance to make a move to help his father.

"You're not going out that door," Lincoln says to Snake. "I'll shoot right through her to kill you."

"No, you won't," Snake says, edging sideways. "The mayor's not gonna let you. He wants this dried-up hag on the witness stand, saying what she just said. He'll do everything he can to keep telling himself that his old man's innocent. But now you know the truth."

"Don't kill her," I tell Lincoln. "And don't listen to that bastard. He's poison."

"I'm the only truth teller in here," Snake says, nearly to the door now. In one sinuous motion, the old man shifts the knife into the hand of the arm locked around her throat, while his free hand searches blindly for the doorknob.

"Don't let him take me!" Wilma screeches. "Now that I said what I did, he'll kill me for sure!"

As my eyes dart from Snake's hand to the knob, Alois lunges off the sofa onto his dead comrade, grabbing for the pistol that the dead man never reached.

"Shoot him!" Lincoln shouts, but I can't bring myself to do it while the kid is vainly scrabbling beneath his friend's corpse.

Fixing my aim on Alois's back, I yell for Alois to stop, but he doesn't.

Lincoln's pistol bucks with a deafening blast, and a bullet punches into the corpse only inches from Alois's head.

"Goddamn it!" Lincoln bellows, and a split-second shift of focus tells me Snake and Wilma have vanished through the door.

Lincoln fires two rounds after them, then charges outside, leaving me to deal with Alois, who has finally got his hands on the butt of his friend's pistol.

"Don't do it!" I scream, but he doesn't listen.

As the long-barreled revolver appears from beneath the corpse, I shoot Alois Engel high in the back. The impact drives him into the body beneath him, but after a couple of seconds, he thrusts himself up once more and tries to lift the gun. His eyes slowly track around to me, and the gun follows—

I close my eyes and fire again, this time into the center of his chest, where I know his heart is pumping violently. My second bullet slams him to the floor and keeps him there, while a pool of blood spreads quickly from beneath him.

With a curse of fury and guilt, I turn, grab my rifle, and crash through the door after Lincoln.

CHAPTER 77

OUTSIDE, I SEE Lincoln walking slowly after Snake, who has one arm tight under Wilma's chin while his other holds the long-bladed knife to her throat, beneath his forearm. Snake has nearly reached a pickup truck parked about twenty feet from the house.

"Help me!" Wilma cries. "Don't let him take me!"

"You're not going anywhere," Lincoln says, keeping pace with Snake.

"I'm here!" I shout.

"Get around to the side of him!" Lincoln orders. "Flank him. Don't let him in the truck."

"Easy now," Snake says, his voice surprisingly steady. He sounds like he's trying to calm a spooked horse.

"Is the blond kid dead?" Lincoln asks me.

"Yeah."

Snake winces, but he doesn't utter a word in anger or regret. "Cage just killed my son," he says in the tone of a man laying casino chips on a green baize cloth. "He already killed my nephew. Let my son be enough."

"It ain't the same," Lincoln says, cutting his eyes at me. "Get around him!"

As I try to do that, a low rumble reaches my ears. In five seconds the sound doubles in volume.

"You hear that?" I ask sharply.

"Motorcycles," Lincoln says. "Goddamn it."

Triumph dances in Snake's eyes. "You boys are in the shit now. Things turn quick, don't they? You better haul ass."

Lincoln's going to kill them both—

The rumble has become a thundering bellow, reverberating off the abandoned buildings on Rodney's main street. Headlight beams spear the darkness a hundred yards behind us, growing brighter by the second.

"We've got to go!" I yell, darting to the truck, which looks like an old International Harvester.

"You can't leave me!" Wilma cries. "He'll kill me for sure."

"Those bikers don't know which house it is," Lincoln says.

If I open the door to the truck, its interior light will go on, pinpointing our location. From the passenger side, I squint into the dark and see there's no key in the ignition.

"Snake's got the keys!" I call to Lincoln. "Or one of those kids."

"Not for long."

"No!" Wilma screams. *"Don't shoot!"*

Lincoln has taken two steps forward and steadied his aim.

"Don't do it!" I shout. "A gunshot will bring those bikers right to us!"

I'm moving toward Lincoln when Wilma Deen snaps. She drives her elbow into Snake's ribs, but not hard enough, because his knife rakes over her throat and a rush of black blood runs down into her blouse. Wilma's hands fly to her throat. She staggers a couple of steps, then holds her bloody hands in front of her face and shrieks like a madwoman.

Deprived of his human shield, Snake turns to flee into the dark, but Lincoln closes the distance in three seconds. At the limit of my sight, Lincoln swats Snake's knife hand away, grips him by the throat, lifts him off his feet, and slams him against a poplar tree. Snake's feet kick wildly, like those of a man being hanged, and the eyes that always looked either cool or crazy bulge as though they'll burst from their sockets. Without knowing how or why, I find myself yanking on Lincoln's arm, trying to tear it free from Snake's neck.

"Quit!" Lincoln bellows. *"This has to happen!"*

I might as well try to rip an arm-thick limb from a tree with my bare hands. If Lincoln were strangling Snake in open space, I might be able to break his grip, but with his feet planted and all his weight wedging Knox against the tree, I don't have a prayer. Snake's face has gone purple, his eyes dim, and not even a choked gasp passes his throat.

"Don't kill him!" I plead hopelessly, my hands on the iron muscles of Lincoln's forearm. "We'll never be sure what happened."

This gives Lincoln pause. His arm stays rigid, but his eyes cut toward me. "I thought you were sure."

"I don't know, man! What's the difference between killing him now and five minutes from now? If we don't get out of here, we're dead."

"You want to *bring* him?"

"Her, too. Throw him in the truck."

Lincoln looks back at the headlights, which have grown from a set of cones into an ambient glow that silhouettes the buildings on our side of the main street. "Our only chance is the river."

Shoving my pistol into my waistband, I grab at Snake's pockets. A key ring jangles in his left front one. When I dig it out, I find not only a GM key for the truck, but a small key with an orange float wired to it.

"We're golden! Let's move."

Lincoln's big forearm relaxes, and Snake slides just far enough down the tree for his feet to touch the ground. The old man coughs, then desperately sucks for air. When the oxygen hits his bloodstream, his eyes open, and I see life in them, awareness even. An instant after Lincoln sees the same thing, he pulls Snake away from the tree, then slams him back against it. The light in the old eyes goes dark, and Snake's body slides down the tree as if it has no bones in it.

"Get the woman," Lincoln says.

While Lincoln whips off his belt and ties Snake's hands, I go to Wilma Deen, who's lying on the ground, gripping her throat and staring at the sky with horror in her eyes. She's still breathing, but she's lost a good bit of blood. In this light it's not worth pulling her hands away to try to gauge the severity of the wound. We're twenty-five miles from Natchez by boat, but at least she stands a chance with us.

The truck door opens, and when I turn, I see Lincoln stuffing Snake onto the floor of the backseat.

"Dome light!" I hiss. "Goddamn it, they'll see it!"

"Get your ass in here!"

Taking Wilma by the feet, I drag her to the Harvester, where Lincoln helps me lift her into the passenger seat.

"Why not the backseat?" I ask, my eyes on the headlights back on the town road.

"Somebody's gonna have to keep pressure on that neck if she passes out. And somebody's gonna have to shoot to keep them off us. You want to drive or shoot?"

"I'd better drive."

"You know where the river is?"

"It's a straight shot west, right? Two miles?"

"Yeah. But it ain't much of a road."

"I'll find it. Let's go."

We close the doors with a creak of rusty hinges, but my heart sinks when I crank the truck. There's nothing to be done about the noise.

"It's a standard shift," I think aloud, stepping on the clutch and throwing the truck into first gear.

"The river road's about a hundred yards that way," Lincoln says, pointing out to my left with his gun hand. "If you go out to the main road, they'll see us. You've got to drive through these trees."

There's a moon out, but not enough to drive through trees at any speed. As we roll forward, man-thick trunks loom out of the darkness every few yards, sometimes in pairs. About seven miles an hour is all I can risk. Glancing to my right, I see that Wilma has braced herself against the passenger door. She's got both hands clenched to her neck, and her face is the color of skim milk.

"Looks like two Harleys pulling up to the main house," Lincoln says, peering back through the windshield. "Three now. Shit, four. Can't you go any faster?"

"Not without hitting a tree."

"Christ. If they shut off their engines, they'll hear us from there."

Progress is maddeningly slow, and I'm afraid of missing the river road in the dark. From curiosity, I risk one glance over the backseat. Snake is laid out on the floor like a sack of sticks, dead to the world.

"You've got to keep separation between us and them," Lincoln says, "or we'll never make it into the boat, even if we reach the river."

"Is Snake alive?" I ask, my right hand riding the vibrating gearshift.

"Who gives a fuck? Watch where you're going."

"I think I see the road!"

"Good, because they've seen us—or heard us. Get ready. They'll be coming fast on those bikes."

I press harder on the gas pedal, and black tree trunks flash out of the night like darkness incarnate.

"Turn the headlights on!" Lincoln cries. "If you hit a tree now, we're dead."

A pale line of earth stretches westward through the trees to my left. As soon as I'm sure it's the river road, I gun the Harvester, fishtail onto sandy mud, and hit the headlights. We pick up speed fast, at least by the standard of the previous two minutes, but the instant I feel encouraged, Lincoln smashes out part of the rear windshield with the butt of his pistol in preparation for a gun battle.

"They're coming," he says, his voiced edged with fear and anticipation. "Don't stop for anything. Not even if you're hit or blinded. Just keep your foot on the gas."

Once I get the Harvester in fourth gear, I focus on keeping the big truck on the narrow dirt road. But at the edge of my vision I see that Wilma Deen has slid down the door with her hands limp in her lap.

"Goddamn it," I mutter, reaching out and pressing hard against the laceration on her bloody throat. Her skin is so slick, it's hard to keep my hand in place.

Lincoln's first rifle shot hammers my eardrums so hard that I swerve on the road.

"That slowed 'em down!" he roars. "Gun this old bitch! *Go! Go! Go!*"

At sixty miles per hour, the truck begins launching itself into the air when we top random humps in the road. Every time we crash back to earth, the bone-rattling impact makes it seem the truck is about to fall to pieces.

"Here they come again! Gonna give 'em a few this time—"

Lincoln empties four rounds from my rifle, the noise shattering in the cab of the truck.

"You hit anything?" I ask, watching for sinkholes in the rutted dirt.

"I hit one guy dead in the chest," he says, sounding dazed. "If those freaks catch us now, they'll skin us alive."

"They still coming?" I ask, trying in vain to see behind us in the jouncing rearview mirror. All I see is distant lights.

"Oh, yeah. Faster now. There must be ten bikes back there."

A bolus of fear blasts through me, raising every hair on my skin. As

I struggle to coax some more speed from the old truck, a drumroll of lead slams into the tailgate.

"They're shooting back," Lincoln says. "That sounded like a goddamn machine gun."

"What can I do?"

"Can you kill the lights?"

"Sure. It's staying on the road that's the problem."

The trees that lined our escape route to this point have vanished. Now water stretches away from both edges of the road. My margin for error is gone. With a pang of guilt, I release Wilma Deen's neck and clench both hands on the wheel. If we go off into swamp water with those bikes behind us, we're going to die, one way or another. Drowning in slime, or getting shot trying to crawl out of it.

Another staccato burst of lead slams into the truck. With a silent prayer, I kill the lights.

"Only two rounds left in the rifle," Lincoln says. "I'm going to let them get closer, make these count."

In my mind I see a God's-eye view of our predicament: a lumbering beast being pursued by hunters on steel horses down a narrow causeway, the hunters rapidly closing the gap—

"Come on, come on," Lincoln murmurs.

As I brace for his next shot, something slams into my seat back, then cracks against my head. Jerking forward, I risk a look behind me. Two booted feet are flailing around the cab. It's Snake, kicking wildly from the floor of the truck. Now he's trying to hook a foot around my head.

"Make him stop!" I yell. "I'm gonna wreck!"

"What?" Lincoln asks, still aiming the rifle through the back windshield.

He doesn't even know Snake is conscious. While I try to keep the old man's feet off my head, his boot glances off the seat and connects with the dome light, which flashes on again, illuminating Lincoln as he aims his pistol down at Snake's thrashing body. I'm not going to stop him this time, but before Lincoln can fire, another fusillade rips out of the dark behind us, and he flies forward with an explosive grunt.

"Lincoln!"

Panic hits me with a force that makes fear seem trivial. Twisting in my seat, I scrabble in vain at the dome light with my right hand, then hammer it with my fist until it breaks. Blessed darkness envelops the cab once more.

Lincoln's breath is a shallow wheeze in my ear.

"Talk to me, man! Where are you hit?"

"Shoulder blade," he croaks. "Smashed it, I think."

"Right or left?"

"Left . . ."

Before I can think of anything to tell him, the Harvester's left rear door flies open and a rushing wind fills the cab. At first I'm certain that a biker somehow managed to dive into the bed of the truck, then work his way around to the door. Then I realize Snake must have done it—

"He jumped!" Lincoln yells, pushing himself off my seat back with a roar of pain. "Snake's out of here! Stop!"

"Are you crazy?"

"The bikers slowed down . . . they don't know what happened, or who he is. Let me shoot him. Stop!"

With a supreme act of will, I pump the brakes until we manage to stop without sliding off into the swamp.

Cursing in pain, Lincoln somehow gets my rifle up on his right shoulder and braces it on the frame of the shattered windshield.

"Can you see him?" I ask, looking down at Wilma once more. Her entire chest and abdomen are covered in blood, and her eyes are closed.

"I've got him. He's silhouetted in their headlights. You see him?"

Twisting in the seat, I'm startled to see a triangular shadow against living arcs of light. Snake must be on his knees, about forty yards behind us, well within the point-blank range of the .308.

"Say a prayer, Penn. I'm sending him to hell."

I don't think Lincoln has ever used my first name, and I don't have time to reflect on it because my thoughts are blasted into oblivion by another burst of gunfire from behind us, which tears into the metal and glass of the Harvester.

Lincoln jerks backward, clawing at his face with both hands. *"I can't see! There's glass in my eyes!"*

Behind us, the triangular silhouette wavers against the light, then a taller shadow joins it. The pack will be after us again in seconds. With a violent yank on the gear lever, I manhandle the transmission into reverse.

"Get down," I yell, "they're going to shoot again."

"What are you doing?" Lincoln cries. "Get to the river!"

"We won't make it. *Get down!*"

When I jam the gas pedal to the floor, Lincoln covers his head with both hands and rolls onto the floor. Heeding my own warning, I slide as far down as I can without losing sight of my target. The Harvester gains speed, and the air rushing through the side door builds to a buffeting wind inside the cab.

The bikers don't realize what's happening until it's too late to get out of the road, but Snake hears us. The silhouette stutters against the lights, doubles in height as Snake struggles to his feet, but before he takes two steps our rear bumper plows him over at fifty miles per hour. The heavy metal Harvester doesn't even slow down until it smashes into the first Harley. The momentum of the old truck carries implacable force, and three motorcycles crumple in the face of it. After the fourth collision, the Harvester finally judders to a stop.

Screams of rage and pain reach my ears, but before anyone has time to react, I shift back into first and floor the accelerator again.

"What happened?" Lincoln croaks from the backseat.

"Snake's dead."

"You saw him go down?"

"He's gone. Obliterated. How bad are you hit? Can you get to the boat?"

"I think something clipped my lung . . . can't breathe right. How close are we to the river?"

"Close."

"Don't go too fast. The last thirty yards top a little berm, and there's nothing but river after that."

It takes inhuman restraint to slow the Harvester, but as I battle the fear coursing through my body, I remember Colonel Eklund describing my father's actions in Korea. If Dad could do what he did in the face of almost certain death, then I can ignore what's behind us and slow down to keep from launching us into the river.

"See any lights behind us?" Lincoln asks in a hoarse voice.

"Not yet. Do they know Snake has a boat out here?"

"I don't know. Let's pray that boat was Snake's ace in the hole. Maybe they think they have us penned against the river."

Without warning the truck tops a rise and the Mississippi River appears like the dark edge of an ocean. I kick the brake pedal, then ease back enough so as not to skid, and finally the old truck shudders to a stop.

"Where's the boat?" I ask.

"It was tied to a tree this afternoon. Look to your left."

Sure enough, about thirty yards downstream, I see gleaming chrome rails bobbing in the powerful current.

"Can you make it if I bring the woman?" I ask.

"I'll make it. Is she alive?"

"I don't know. Yell out if you need help."

As I go around to the passenger door, I remember that Wilma Deen is the woman who blinded Keisha Harvin. But it's not her I'm rescuing. It's the testimony about Snake Knox killing Viola that Wilma began back in the stinking shack. *Will she ever repeat those words?* I wonder as I catch her under the arms and drag her from the truck. *Or is all this for nothing?*

It takes me nearly two minutes to drag her limp body down to the tree where the boat is moored. By the time I get there, Lincoln has pulled the ski boat over to the bank.

"I can't help you lift her," he says.

"Just hold the boat."

As I did with Sleepy Johnston three months ago in the basement of Brody Royal's house, I get down and work myself under the woman until I'm in position to get her into a fireman's carry, then heave her into the air by main strength. My knees nearly buckle from the strain as I struggle erect, and before I make it, the familiar rumble of engines makes my heart stutter.

"Throw her in!" Lincoln shouts. "In thirty seconds we die."

"You get in! Use the ladder in the back."

As four headlights top the rise, I roll Wilma over the gunwale, then climb into the boat like a kid rolling over a fence.

The key on Snake's ring fits the ignition. One glance into the stern shows me Lincoln dropping to the deck and waving for me to go. As the boat drifts away from the riverbank, I lower the motor's trim, hoping to get some separation from the shore without having to crank the motor and pinpoint our location.

The headlights on the bikes cut through the mist over the water like spotlights in an old war movie. *What are those guys thinking? That we rode into the river and drowned?*

Just as I think we're going to slip away clean, one of the bikers sweeps his headlight right to left along the surface of the river. There's nothing to do now but run. With a turn of the key and a little choke added, the inboard roars to blessed life, and when I shove the throttle forward, the boat throws me back against the seat with reassuring power.

But light travels faster than matter, and the headlight picks us out before we make much headway. Another burst of gunfire kicks my heart into overdrive, this time accompanied by blinding muzzle flashes from the bank receding behind us. Shoving the throttle to the wall, I crouch low and pray for deliverance.

The next shots come from Lincoln, who's kneeling in the stern with his right arm outstretched, emptying the clip of his pistol at the shore. *Get down,* I urge silently, afraid he'll be killed by the last stray bullet fired in anger, like some soldier who dies an hour after a peace treaty is signed. The bikers' return fire chops up our growing wake, and then a bullet punches through the hull. If they hit the engine, we're screwed.

"Get down, you crazy bastard!"

After a few more reckless seconds, Lincoln drops to his knees and crawls slowly up to the captain's chair to my left. Blood streaks the deck beneath him. Looking back, I see that we've cleared the range of anything but a rifle, and not even one-percenters carry rifles on their bikes. Sawed-off shotguns, maybe, but not long guns.

With heroic effort, Lincoln struggles into the captain's chair and faces forward. His breathing is alarmingly ragged.

"How long, you figure?" he asks, coughing.

Natchez lies roughly twenty-five miles south: one river bend, then a long, straight shot down to the big bluff and the landing at Under-the-Hill. "Forty minutes, max. Thirty if we're lucky."

Lincoln nods, then grimaces.

"Can you make it?"

"Somebody needs to live through this shit. Might as well be me."

Snake's speedboat is making fifty-three knots now. The broad river runs silver-black under the moon tonight, the Mississippi shore looming high on our left, the Louisiana Delta fading away on our right.

Clouds of stars fill the sky over this dark stretch of water. A mile ahead, the lights of a pushboat and its barges are rounding the bend. At long last, I realize, we are headed downstream. Even if our engine fails, the river will carry us home.

"Hey," I say. "Where's home for you? Chicago?"

Lincoln considers the question. Then he shrugs. "Ain't got one, really. Not anymore. Guess I need to find me a new one."

"Or an old one."

"What's that mean? Mama's dead now. Nothing here for me."

"Maybe. But at least you've got a start here."

"What you mean?"

I laugh quietly, thinking of Serenity. "You've got Mississippi blood, man."

"Mississippi blood? Shit. What's that mean?"

I recall reading Serenity's galley in my basement, and with that memory comes the taste of her skin and the scent of her hair. "Just something that writer put in one of her books. Something her uncle used to say. An old pulpwood cutter named Catfish."

"Yeah? What was that?"

"He said, '*Mississippi blood is different. It's got some river in it. Delta soil, turpentine, asbestos, cotton poison. But there's strength in it, too. Strength that's been beat but not broke.*'"

Lincoln grunts. Then, after a period of reflection: "I reckon that describes Mama pretty well. If she hadn't had that, she'd have died a long time ago."

"I think you're right."

I can tell from his breathing that he's turned the chair to face me.

"What is it?" I ask, a little anxiously.

"What you think about what Snake said? About your mama being the one?"

I turn to him and shake my head. "No way. She tried to do what your mother wanted, and she failed. The Double Eagles murdered Viola. Just like they killed Henry, and Caitlin, and Walt, and Sleepy Johnston, and all those black boys so long ago. And now they're dead themselves. The ones who did the worst of it, anyway."

Lincoln nods slowly, weighing my words. "Are you sure you killed Snake back there?"

"Brother . . . that Harvester crushed three Harleys *after* it hit him. He's nothing but a pile of meat on that road. The possums and coons are already eating him. Don't give it another thought. It's over."

I turn my gaze back to the dark water, and to the faint dome of light over the horizon that marks the presence of Natchez and Vidalia. Already fewer stars are visible overhead.

"Mississippi blood, huh?" Lincoln murmurs.

I nod and smile into the wind. "You got it on both sides."

EPILOGUE

AGAINST ALL ODDS, Wilma Deen survived her throat wound. I hoped she might feel some gratitude to me for saving her life, but I should have known better. Thus far she has shown no inclination to repeat the accusation that Snake Knox and Sonny Thornfield murdered Viola Turner. John Kaiser told me she's hired a tough lawyer, one who's trying to negotiate the most generous plea bargain he can get for his client. And because the U.S. attorney is disinclined to bargain with the woman who blinded Keisha Harvin with acid, I have no idea yet whether Wilma might possibly help me get Dad released early from prison.

Cleotha Booker came out of her coma after dawn on Saturday morning, only a few hours after Snake Knox died. Her condition is guarded, her prognosis fair. According to Kaiser, Dolores St. Denis has refused to leave the Baton Rouge hospital where the Cat Lady is being treated. Kaiser had hoped that Dolores would send Snake Knox to death row at Parchman, but I'm glad she won't be put to the test. I'm not sure she could have faced Snake in a courtroom and recounted the terrible events that had bound them together for so long.

Lincoln survived his gunshot wound, but he required a lengthy surgery, plus an additional procedure on one cornea, which had been lacerated by splintered glass from the truck's rear windshield. Three nights ago, not long after I brought him into the hospital covered with blood, Sheriff Byrd showed up and started trying to arrest us both. Rodney does lie within his county, after all. But I had phoned Kaiser for help as Lincoln and I approached the boat ramp at Natchez Under-the-Hill, and while the FBI agent was furious at me over our "freelance" expedition to Rodney, my revelation that Billy Byrd had been in contact with Snake Knox all along refocused Kaiser's anger entirely. Within fifteen minutes of Sheriff Byrd's arrival at the hospital, Lincoln and I became the least of the corrupt lawman's concerns. This morning the sheriff was relieved of duty by the governor of Mississippi, and he departed office with federal charges pending against him.

Lincoln remains in St. Catherine's Hospital in guarded condition, both eyes covered with gauze pads. The two times I've been to see him, he'd been given some serious painkillers, so we couldn't say much.

I plan to go back as soon as I can.

FOUR DAYS AFTER Walt Garrity died, he was buried in a flag-draped coffin in Navasota, Texas. He would have been surprised by the turnout—not only the size of the crowd, but by who showed up.

There was an Honor Guard from the U.S. Army, their M-16s and polished hardware gleaming in the pale sun. There was a formidable cohort of Texas Rangers, some so old their faces looked like tack leather beneath their white Stetsons, others young enough to have been Walt's grandchildren.

The district attorneys of several counties showed up, including my former boss, Joe Cantor, from my old stomping ground of Houston. Most DAs brought their top investigators with them. You couldn't count the cops from various jurisdictions, but I recognized many by the way their eyes took in the scene. Once a cop, always a cop.

Walt's wife, Carmelita, was a little short with us at the church, but in my view we were lucky she didn't curse us out of the building. All she'd wanted from life was to spend Walt's last years with him, and we had denied her that. Him, too.

We had quite a contingent at the funeral. My mother, of course. Annie and Mia, too. Joe Russell and a couple of our bodyguards drove a slowly recovering Tim Weathers over from Dallas. Even Serenity flew from Atlanta to Houston and rented a car to reach the church shortly before the service started. She told me she was writing an article about Walt's life for the *Journal-Constitution*.

Jamie Lewis, Miriam Masters, and Caitlin's father were there representing the *Natchez Examiner.* I was surprised John Masters had taken time out of his day for something like that, but a private jet can get you anywhere in the country pretty fast. When I first spied him outside the church, the media baron saw the surprise in my face and said, "Walt Garrity died saving my step-grandbaby. Or near enough, anyway. I think they ought to put up a goddamn statue of him."

The eulogy was given by Karl Eklund, the colonel who had commanded Walt and my father during the Korean War. Colonel Eklund told a few stories about Walt, some funny, others poignant. But he brought tears to the eyes of some very hard men when he said:

"Corporal Garrity lived by a hard code. He always did his duty—in all weathers, no matter the odds—and he did it to the end. Like the Good Book says: 'Greater love hath no man than this; that a man lay down his life for his friends.' Amen."

When the seven rifles cracked over the Texas plain, cops and soldiers alike looked like stone figures carved in the act of saluting. But by the time the echoes faded, some were coughing into their fists or wiping their eyes on their sleeves. My mother moved in unconscious synchrony with them, softly dabbing her eyes with a lace handkerchief.

Annie tugged at my hand, and I leaned down for her to whisper in my ear: "I want to do something for Mrs. Garrity."

I thought about it. "There's really nothing you can do for her. But you can do something for Walt. Don't ever forget what he did for us. Thirty years from now, when you're grown up with children of your own, and you look down at them and feel lucky . . . think about Walt for just a minute. That would make him the happiest, if he knew."

Annie looked up at me with confusion. "He *will* know, Dad."

I wish I believed that, I thought, looking over the heads before me at the faded funeral tent, and in its precious shade the coffin on its bier. The head of the Honor Guard handed Carmelita Garrity the folded American flag.

"What happens now?" Annie asked softly.

"Usually the people leave at this point."

"Who finishes burying him?"

"The cemetery has men that do that. Gravediggers."

"With shovels?"

"In the old days, yes. Now they use a backhoe for most of it."

Annie looked concerned about this. Rising on tiptoe, she peered between the bodies of the slowly dispersing crowd.

"I don't think they're going to get to use their backhoe today," she said.

Looking toward the grave, I saw Colonel Eklund and three other men picking up shovels lying near the tent. One man took hold of the chemical-green Astroturf covering the dirt pile and tossed it to the side. Then Colonel Eklund gave a quiet order, and the old soldiers spaded their shovels into the Texas earth and began to fill the open grave. I started when I realized that one white-haired man was missing. If Dad were here, he would have said to hell with his failing heart and picked up a shovel himself, and not even my mother would have asked him to stop.

"Tom should be here," Mom whispered in my ear. "Those are his men."

I squeezed Annie's hand, then walked forward and stood behind the oldest man laboring to fill Walt's grave. After two more shovelfuls, he turned unsteadily, met my eyes with a questioning gaze.

"Tom Cage's son," I said quietly.

He put the shovel in my hand.

This is how it should always be, I thought, spading the metal edge into the dirt.

It meant something to be with those men—a quiet band who had bled for their country and for their brothers. During those sweaty minutes, I had the feeling that everything I'd believed as a child was true: that right meant more than might; that being faithful and good meant more than being rich; that honor superseded all.

If only that feeling could last.

While the crowd dispersed, our group clumped together near the grave. As we spoke in hushed tones, I saw Serenity hovering at the periphery, her gaze on me. When the chance presented itself, I slipped through the black-clad bodies, took her hand, and led her under a tree about twenty yards away.

"It's good to see you," I told her. "Away from everyone else."

She smiled at that and squeezed my hand. "I've missed you. That was an intense few days."

I nodded but said nothing. What could I possibly say that would convey my true feelings in that moment? I very much wanted to kiss her, but how would Tee react to that? Or Annie? Or my mother? I knew that if I looked back toward the grave, I would see Mom peering at us from between the mourners.

"How are your burns?" I asked as we pulled apart.

Tee waved her hand to dismiss my concern. "Coupla more scars to show in bars, that's all. How's Lincoln doing?"

"I think he's going to be okay. I'm going to see him tonight. We're flying back after the funeral."

She absorbed this news with a forced smile. "Good. Maybe you guys can find a little common ground now."

"Maybe."

A gust of wind kicked up, sending a blast of Texas grit flying against us. We turned our backs to it and huddled shoulder to shoulder.

"Penn," Tee said softly, looking past me to my mother, "something's been bothering me. I've tried to forget it, but I can't get it out of my head."

"My head's full of things like that."

She hesitated, then plunged ahead. "Remember that last night we were together? The night your mother walked in on us in bed?"

"Of course."

"You spoke to Quentin on the phone that night. And he basically ordered you not to pursue the report that the sheriff's deputies were tampering with the hair-and-fiber evidence."

I tried to keep my face impassive as I looked back at Serenity, and perhaps I succeeded, because she went on without noticing my discomfort.

"The thing is, that made absolutely no sense. The cops already had a match on your father's hair, so why tell you not to pursue the tampering? Who could Quentin possibly have been trying to protect?"

My breathing slowed to almost nothing. Serenity's dark eyes probed mine, not with intrusiveness, but with genuine puzzlement. "Am I crazy?" she asked. "Have you ever figured that out?"

Without quite meaning to, I raised my hands to her upper arms and took hold of her, my eyes never leaving hers.

"You're not crazy. But I can't go any further than that. Okay?"

She looked back at me, still lost, but then her eyes widened and she swallowed hard. Just when I thought she was going to ask another question, she laid her face against my chest and hugged me tight.

"I miss this," she said in a fierce whisper.

"I do, too. More than you know."

"If you're ever passing through Atlanta—"

"I know. I will."

But as we broke apart and went our separate ways, we both knew that I wouldn't. For if I passed through Atlanta, Annie would almost certainly be with me. Even if she wasn't, she would still be waiting at home. And that worry didn't begin to address the realities of Serenity's personal life, which were undoubtedly complicated. As I rejoined my group, my mind and heart remained with Tee, walking alone through the tombstones, back to her rental car for the long drive back to the airport. I felt the tidal pull of sexual gravity from her receding body, and keen regret that I hadn't lowered my face to hers for a kiss. I saw relief in my mother's face as I laid my hand on Annie's shoulder, but for my part, I felt none.

WE GOT BACK to Natchez a lot faster than we'd expected to. John Masters offered us a ride in his plane, which was a first for Annie. The nearest commercial airport to Natchez is ninety miles away, so having the Masters Media jet drop us only ten miles from our house was a real treat. As soon as I got Annie settled at home, I climbed into my Audi and headed through the night toward St. Catherine's Hospital.

When I asked the duty nurse if Lincoln Turner was still in the same room, she frowned and told me he'd checked out against the advice of his physician, about four hours earlier. I stood there blinking, trying to divine what impulse would have compelled Lincoln to do that.

"He left you a note, Mayor," the nurse said, and then she retrieved a sealed envelope from a drawer.

My name was scrawled across the front. I ripped the end off the envelope, pulled out the folded paper, and read the brief letter with a dazed feeling.

I'm going back to Chicago. I need to think. I'm sorry for all the trouble. I'm glad we did what we did, and that the right people got killed, for the most part. Don't try to find me. You don't owe me anything. Maybe we'll cross paths again someday. L

I stared at the note for a long time, a missive from a man without a living mother or a father he will accept. I studied the words so long that I was stunned when the elevator dinged behind me. When the door opened, an older doctor I recognized smiled and said hello. I nodded and walked past him, then took the stairs down to the silent lobby and into the parking lot.

THE NIGHT AIR is cool, the parking lot mostly empty. Instead of going to my car, I walk out toward the Highway 61 bypass. Not far from the tar-stinking frontage road stands the same little flower bed and the light pole where I waited for my father when I was a boy of eight. The night he left me alone for hours while he made love with Viola on the colored side of town. The flower bed is now filled with pea gravel and ornamental rocks, as though this were New Mexico, but the relentless weeds of Mississippi are already sprouting through this façade. I stand under the humming streetlight and watch the cars go by, just as I did almost forty years ago, fighting the tears of a little boy abandoned. Now, though, I realize that I endured only a few hours of the sadness and anxiety that ran through Lincoln's life like an undertow, always pulling him away from the light, into darkness.

My father had two sons, and one of us was doomed to be an orphan. Looking back over our lives, I'm glad it was Lincoln. But now I understand something I did not before: that the happiness of my childhood was bought with the pain of a black boy who had hurt no one. Tonight that grown-up boy is driving northward, following the twisting river and the dark old vein of Highway 61 as far as Cairo, Illinois; there he'll shoot straight up Interstate 55 to Chicago, where so many of his ancestors fled before him.

We are brothers, Lincoln and I—half brothers, anyway—and long after my father passes from this earth, his blood will flow through both our veins. The genes of Northern Europe are my legacy, and my destiny, but Lincoln carries the genes of both Europe and Africa within him. I hope that someday he can free himself from the lies that shrouded his youth and become what Viola must have dreamed he could when she carried him down the streets of that cold and unfamiliar city: a man who embodies the best of both his parents. With a father who chose the cruel path of duty and a mother who chose martyrdom, who deserves it more?

I'M SITTING IN a rocking chair on the gallery of Edelweiss, waiting for Annie to come home from school. After deciding she was ready to rejoin her classmates at St. Stephen's, my daughter also declared that from now on we should live in the house that Caitlin had intended to share with us. I wasn't so sure, but I'm willing to try anything that gives Annie a sense of control over her life. With my father in prison in the Mississippi Delta and my mother traveling there every week, Caitlin's ghost is a welcome force in our lives—at least for the time being.

Annie brought a few of Caitlin's things to the new house: a favorite coat that's a little too big for her, Caitlin's laptop, mementos of vacations we took together. Mounted above the fireplace in Annie's room is Caitlin's Pulitzer Prize, the award she won for her coverage of the Delano Payton case. John Masters sent it to Annie the week after Caitlin's funeral, with a written note expressing the hope that she would work as hard as Caitlin had to reach her dreams. I hope the same thing; I only pray that Annie doesn't have to pay as high a price to attain them.

Surrounded by these artifacts, I remember how happy Caitlin was that I'd bought this house, and that we would finally begin our own family, as well as make her status as Annie's new mother official. On one mantel inside sits a photo of the three of us, taken by my father only weeks before Caitlin died. In it, Caitlin and I are swinging Annie between us: me gripping her ankles while Caitlin holds Annie's wrists with the surprising strength in her lithe frame. The photographer captured us at the point of tossing Annie into a pile of autumn leaves. We're all laughing, the girls' hair flying, the moment frozen forever in the stream of time. Sometimes I look at that picture and see joy made eternal; other times I see a brutally truncated history, an amputated life.

"Hey, Penn! You'd better fill out that change-of-address form soon, or you won't see me for a while."

My mailman is walking up the sidewalk from the direction of State Street. Theo Driscoll is about my age; he went to the public school when I was at St. Stephen's.

"I can't keep giving you this special treatment," he says with a smile, "even if you are the mayor. You need to un-ass that rocking chair, man. The main post office is only four blocks down Broadway!"

"I'll go do it as soon as Annie gets home," I promise.

Ignoring the copper box mounted on a brick pillar on the ground floor, Theo climbs the right-hand staircase with a sheaf of mail in his hand.

"Got another letter from Europe," he announces. "I still can't believe they publish your books in all those languages. How many now?"

"Twenty-six."

"What would Mrs. Holland say about that? Too bad she didn't live to see it."

Mrs. Holland was a legendary English teacher who taught at both the public and private schools during her long career. "She lived to see my first one published. That's good enough."

I reach out for the mail, but he doesn't hand it to me yet. Like a lot of people I went to school with, Theo likes to talk.

"Went to the clinic two days ago. Had a damn boil on my leg. Drew Elliott had to lance it. It's so damn different without your daddy there. The nurses feel the same way. Melba said they might not even keep her on much longer."

"Oh, I don't believe that. Drew will probably take her over."

Theo looks skeptical. "I don't know. She's old school, like Doc Cage."

"I'll check into it."

"Are you making any headway on getting him out? I swear, not one person in this town thinks he was guilty."

I'm not so sure this is true, but Theo means well. "It's complicated, Theo. But I'm not going to quit. There's still reason to hope."

The mailman's face falls as he picks up the truth in my tone. "That Parchman's a wicked place, Penn. My cousin's boy had to do a stretch in there on a dope charge. His parents couldn't hardly stand to visit him."

"All penitentiaries are grim, Theo."

"I guess. Well, you keep at it. I know things'll turn out right in the end. Everything happens for a reason."

For half a second I want to smack Theo Driscoll in the face. His throwaway assertion carries such a muddle of childish faith, fatalism, and predestination that it would take me an hour to properly respond.

"That is technically true," I say in a restrained voice, but in my mind I hear Inigo Montoya saying, *I do not think that means what you think it means.*

Looking confused and a little put out, Theo hands me the mail.

"Thanks," I tell him. "I'll see you soon."

"If you fill out that change-of-address form, you will. Otherwise I'm sending everything back to Washington Street."

As he descends the opposite staircase and heads toward the Parsonage, I flip through the mail. A couple of bills go through my fingers; then I see the letter Theo mentioned. The one from Europe. April is a royalty month, and the envelope is made of the ultrathin paper I associate with foreign communications. Whatever's inside feels heavy, though, and padded. The postmark looks unfamiliar, which is surprising after years of receiving letters from readers around the world. The postmark is smeared, too, so I can't even read the name of the country. The stamps show a coat of arms in yellow and orange, but the words beneath are printed in French. There's no return address, either. Just my name and our old Washington Street address, above U.S.A. printed in block letters, as though by a child.

Opening my eyes wide, I hold the letter farther from my face and look down my nose at the smeared postmark. Finally the name of the country of origin comes clear: *Andorre.*

"Andorra," I whisper, a chill racing along my arms. "Billy Knox?"

After a moment of paranoia, when I visualize opening the letter in a little cloud of toxic powder, I rip the end off the envelope and pull out the paper inside.

The thrice-folded sheet appears to be blank. As I start to unfold it, what I felt through the envelope falls out into my palm. It's a coin. Dull silver, about the size of an American half-dollar, with a leather cord tied through a hole near the edge of it. *It* is *a half-dollar,* I realize.

When I turn the disk over, my hands go cold. The eagle I was looking at has been replaced by an image of President John F. Kennedy in profile. Below the line of his neck is the date *1964*. And right about where his ear should be, another hole has been punched through the